ELECTION DAY

A PROSECUTION FORCE THRILLER

LOGAN RYLES

SEVERN ⚓ RIVER
PUBLISHING

Severn River Publishing
SevernRiverBooks.com

This is a work of fiction. Names, characters, businesses, places, events and incidents are either the products of the author's imagination or used in a fictitious manner. Any resemblance to actual persons, living or dead, or actual events is purely coincidental.

ISBN: 978-1-64875-475-3 (Paperback)

ALSO BY LOGAN RYLES

The Prosecution Force Series

Brink of War

First Strike

Election Day

Failed State

Firestorm

White Alert

The Reed Montgomery Series

Overwatch

Hunt to Kill

Total War

Smoke and Mirrors

Survivor

Death Cycle

Sundown

To find out more about Logan Ryles and his books, visit

severnriverbooks.com

For The Fumble

1
_____

They came at dawn. Maybe a hundred. Maybe a thousand. It was impossible to tell because they didn't storm the war-torn city in a wave. They infiltrated slowly, over hours of darkness, sneaking past Russian army checkpoints and using their unmatched knowledge of the winding Chechen streets they called home to obtain strategic positions around the twelve thousand invaders holding the city hostage.

And then hell commenced.

Fedor Volkov had spent fourteen months of his twenty-month military career engaged in Chechnya. Shortly after being conscripted by Moscow for use in suppressing the separatists, Volkov's talents as a shooter were found to far exceed those of any average Russian knuckle-dragger. Kill-shots at three hundred meters with rudimentary Kalashnikov rifles were child's play for the Saint Petersburg native. He earned an involuntary ticket to sniper training school, where an SVD Dragunov was shoved into his eighteen-year-old hands, and he was directed to extend his talents to farther ranges.

Much farther ranges.

Volkov had never been good at anything—not like he was with the sniper rifle. He was a poor kid from a poor neighborhood, skinny and often hungry, another victim of the economic devastation left in the wake of the crumbling Soviet Union.

The Dragunov changed everything. In another time, in another place, he might've shot for Russia's Olympic team or spent years training for special forces operations. He might've had a long and profitable career, knocking off targets at a thousand meters. He might've been a star.

But with the unrest in Chechnya and Moscow's relentless desire to bring the separatists back under Russian control, the Dragunov held a different fate. Volkov was shipped directly from training camp into the Caucasus, where he was thrust into the heart of pure horror.

President Yeltsin expected the offensive to last a few weeks, at most. Overwhelming Russian force, coupled with vastly superior weapons technology, should subdue the Chechens quickly, bringing them back into the fold.

Eighteen months later, thousands of Russians were dead, Grozny was a burning desolation, and the war raged on in the mountains to the south. The Chechens proved themselves to be relentless, brutal guerrilla fighters, often beheading prisoners of war and placing their skulls on spikes along the roadways into Grozny. Alternatively, they left the heads on and hung the bodies on the outside of buildings while they sheltered inside, forcing the Russians to shoot at their comrades' corpses in order to engage the enemy.

And then there were the snipers. Hundreds of them. Chechens armed with the same Dragunov rifles issued to Volkov, dug in throughout the shattered city, often shooting to wound instead of kill. Gut and groin shots would fester for days before merciful death finally claimed another victim.

No place was safe. No hole was deep enough to hide in. War had come for everyone.

By the time the Russians finally drove the rebels out of Grozny and into the hills, there was little left of the city. Volkov and twelve thousand other Russians were left to hold the Chechen capital while the war raged in the mountains. It was easy to hear the continued thunder of distant artillery and smell blood in the air. But at least the city was secure. Or it had been, anyway, until 5:50 a.m., on the morning of August sixth, when the Chechens returned to take Grozny.

Volkov's first warning came as the voice of two dozen AK-74s opened fire on the sleeping Russians nestled around the base of a ten-story hotel on the outskirts of downtown. He kicked out of his sleeping bag on the seventh floor and scrambled over shattered glass to reach the Dragunov.

The window was already blown out, as was most of the sill. Lying on his stomach six feet inside the building, he had a clear field of fire over the avenue stretching northward toward the gunfire. In the square below, the two dozen Russians left to guard the roadway were still fumbling for their weapons, disoriented and half awake. Volkov saw one of them fall under a storm of lead, his face blown apart while two more writhed on the concrete.

The wind carried screams and the taste of gunpowder. An artillery shell detonated half a block away, shaking Volkov's position. He ignored it all, ratcheting a fresh round of 7.62 ammunition into the rifle and settling his cheek against the stock. In a millisecond, the chaos was gone, blocked from his mind by an innate ability to ignore the world outside his scope. It was part of what made him so good. When he put his eye to the PSO-1 optic and focused on the illuminated reticle, his own existence ceased to matter.

There was only the rifle, the target, and the moment he blew that target out of existence.

Sweat ran down Volkov's nose. He swept his crosshairs across a field of muzzle flash, three hundred meters distant, and didn't even pause as he squeezed off a shot.

Bullet to the head. Target down. Child's play.

The next Chechen who fell under the reticle was dug in at four hundred meters, nestled behind a crumbling block wall. He knelt to change the mag on his AK-74, and the moment the top of his head rose into view, Volkov squeezed the trigger. Blood sprayed across the concrete, and Volkov swept back to the left.

Shots three, four, and five all resulted in bodies rolling into the rubble. Volkov fired without pausing . . . without thinking. He measured his breaths and kept his finger on the trigger, casings piling up next to him like copper-colored confetti.

But the Chechens kept coming. Dozens turned to hundreds as the small-arms fire intensified. Volkov was conscious of his comrades falling back from the base of the hotel, leaving the dead and wounded as he slammed a fresh mag into the Dragunov and felt the first tinge of panic tighten his chest.

This wasn't a random raid. The Chechens wanted Grozny back.

A bullet kissed his elbow, pinging off concrete and zipping into the darkness. Volkov rolled to the right, his heart breaking into panicked thunder as the next shot whizzed only inches over his head. Volkov scrambled behind what remained of the wall, cradling the rifle and breathing hard. He looked into the ashen streets far below and saw his fellow Russians beating a retreat, clawing their way over crumbled buildings and blindly returning fire into the oncoming storm.

Volkov saw a flash of orange out of the corner of his eye, and then one of them went down, shot through the chest. He twisted his head around the edge of the wall just in time to catch the next muzzle flash from the top of a shattered apartment block, maybe twelve hundred meters away.

Chechen sniper—a damn good one, wreaking havoc on the Russian retreat.

Volkov turned for the door, preparing to run. An AK-74 waited next to his bedroll, ready to shield his retreat in close quarters. Taking a pre-planned escape route between the shattered buildings, he could be kilometers away within the hour.

Then he heard another scream and looked down to see a Russian infantryman lying in the street, clutching a bleeding leg. Except it wasn't a man. The kid looked barely old enough to serve—a year or two younger than Volkov—one of Yeltsin's conscripts, torn from his home to destroy somebody else's. The kid wasn't dead, but fully exposed to the sniper, he was about to be.

Volkov dropped back behind the Dragunov, resting the piping hot barrel against a section of block wall. At twelve hundred meters, the 7.62 bullet was far out of recommended range. The Dragunov platform itself was only good to eight or nine hundred meters, in theory. The PSO-1 optic was good for a lot less, in Volkov's experience.

But the Chechen was finding a way.

Volkov blocked out the storm of gunfire and ignored the fear fighting to explode into his mind. He twisted the elevation adjustment knob on the PSO-1, focused on the reticle, and relaxed his shoulders. He wiped sweat from his forehead and leaned into the scope. Twelve hundred meters. A distance clouded by smoke and haze and an endless din.

An impossible shot.

The sniper fired again, and Volkov zeroed in on his muzzle flash. He thought he heard the kid in the street scream, or maybe his strained mind only imagined it. It didn't matter.

He made another adjustment of the elevation—a tilt of the crosshairs to the left to compensate for a gentle eastward breeze and the spin drift it would exacerbate. Volkov didn't know the complex math required to make a hit happen. He didn't have the advanced tools to calculate the shot properly. He only knew what his instincts told him and what the right moment felt like. Volkov held his breath, focused on that spot, and saw muzzle flash light the early morning grey once more.

Then he fired.

The Dragunov slammed into his shoulder, and the gunshot split the stillness. The world descended into slow motion as Volkov ratcheted the optic back on target. No second shot was required. A long black rifle fell from the apartment window, twelve hundred meters away, then blood ran down the exterior wall. Volkov crouched dumfounded for a moment, the residual strain he had blocked out of his mind now tumbling in and overwhelming his body.

Then the roar of gunfire blasting his floor resumed, and concrete dust exploded in his face. He ran, abandoning the Dragunov and reaching for the AK. Someplace below him, voices shouted, and the hotel shook as another artillery shell made direct impact on the roof.

Volkov barreled into the stairwell, choking on the dust that rained from the ceiling. He made it two floors down before hearing boots thunder on the metal stairs from directly below, then an AK blared.

Volkov slammed against the wall as hot lead whistled past his knees and slammed into the ceiling. Something seared into his face, and he clutched his right cheek as blood gushed out. Volkov tripped and hit the floor, the AK spinning out of his hands. He scrambled to grab it, then rolled onto his back and clamped down on the trigger.

The first two Chechens fell under a hail of steel-core bullets. Volkov's hands shook, all his practiced calm now long gone as he kicked through a doorway and into a burned-out hotel room. The Chechens followed, their gunfire riddling the walls. Volkov kept shooting until the AK clicked over an empty chamber, then he dropped the rifle and clawed for the Makarov pistol in his belt.

It was too late. The Chechens stormed the room. Volkov rolled to his knees and clawed his way to the blown-out wall. Beyond it, sheer emptiness waited for him, along with a four-story drop to the cratered streets blow.

A rifle barked, and enormous pain erupted below his right knee. Volkov grabbed the edge of the concrete floor, his hands tearing on exposed rebar as the rifle fired again. Then he jerked forward, and without pausing to think, rolled over the edge and into the emptiness beyond.

2

"Ladies and gentlemen, the president of the United States . . . Margaret Trousdale!"

Cheers thundered through the arena as Maggie stepped out of the shadows, standing tall with one hand raised toward the darkened rows of seats. She stopped halfway to the podium and smiled—not only because it looked good on camera, but because it felt good to be standing there, even after months of grueling campaigning and over four dozen rallies across the nation.

It felt amazing to be only a week from Election Day—and a breath away from winning it all.

"Hello, Boise!" Maggie shouted into the mic.

The arena resounded—packed with twelve thousand attendees, all rabid to see her. It didn't sound like a political rally. It didn't sound like a rally at all. It sounded like a rock concert the moment the band takes the stage. It sounded like a basketball game with ten seconds left on the clock, the home team down by one, their best shooter ripping down the court

with the ball in hand. It sounded like history in the making. A fully independent presidential candidate about to steal the show.

"Boise, I hear you!" Maggie called. "And you know something?" She
jabbed her finger in the general direction of DC. "So do they!"

The arena shook. Maggie felt it in her soul. She didn't bother trying to
calm the crowd. This late in her campaign, everybody knew her talking
points, agendas, and policies. Everybody knew what another four years of
Trousdale–Stratton promised to bring. The twelve thousand people gathered in the arena hadn't come to be won over. They'd come to be super-
charged to help her take Idaho and the four electoral college votes it
promised.

Because in a race this close, every vote mattered.

The cheers died slowly, and Maggie gently swept dirty-blonde hair
behind one ear. She ducked her head in faux bashfulness and allowed
herself to blush. "Damn, y'all. That was one hell of a welcome. You know, if
it weren't so freaking cold up here, I could get used to that."

There were laughs and cheers. Maggie knew how to get them going.
She knew they craved the simple backwoods girl from New Orleans, the
muddy Cajun who had stared down Russia, defied the Chinese advance
into North Korea, and held a nation together, even as it toppled on the
brink of chaos.

They wanted their small-town hero.

"I was in Seattle last night," Maggie said. "Portland the night before. We
had people in the streets, just like we do tonight! Packed seats and fully
booked hotels. People who drove for *miles* to be here. From rural towns and
big cities, I'm talking about everyday Americans. Cops and teachers, engi-
neers and doctors, sanitation workers and business owners. I'm talking
about tens of thousands of voices in this corner of the nation alone, all
giving up family time and sleep to say one thing—they don't want more of
the same. They're *sick* of an America torn apart by petty two-party politics,
ping-ponging from one side of the aisle to the other, and getting worse all
the time."

Maggie pulled the mic from the podium and began to pace, jabbing one
finger toward the crowd. "They told me what *you're* telling me! That

Governor Jeffreys and Senator Cuthbert better not quit their jobs because they're still gonna need them next Wednesday."

Her face flushed at the chants and claps, and she tilted her head back to flash the girl-next-door smile at the nosebleeds. She couldn't see them with the lights pointed in her face, but she knew what they wanted because it hadn't been that long since she was in their shoes. Just another Louisianan fed up with corrupt politicians and bureaucratic bullshit.

Hungry for change. Inflamed by passion.

It was the single most powerful thing on the planet. The kind of thing that toppled empires and built new ones. It was dangerous, but she was learning how to harness it.

Maggie returned to her podium. "I know how excited we all are for next Tuesday. Somebody asked me last night if I was nervous." Maggie laughed. "I was like, 'Hell yeah, I'm nervous!'"

The crowd laughed back.

"But you know, I'm not really thinking about Tuesday. I'm not even thinking about the next four years, to tell you the truth. Or the next eight. I'm thinking about the next fifty because we've got *serious* problems in this country."

She allowed her words to hang—building tension, sharpening focus. And not only for the arena, but also for the hundreds of thousands watching on TV.

"I don't have to tell anyone here about the painful divides ripping through the soul of our nation. It feels like every day one party or the other is handing us something new to hate each other over. And you know the worst part? Those petty party punchlines are just a smoke screen. They tell you we have a two-party system in America, but neither of those parties begin with a D or an R. They're the parties of money and power, and they're consuming this country like a plague."

Maggie smacked the podium, and angry cries radiated from the stands. She gave them only a moment to indulge, and then she pressed on.

"I'm talking about the backroom deals made by members of both parties. Oh, you think these people actually hate each other? Only when you're watching. The moment you turn your back, they can't *wait* to get busy selling your children's future to the highest bidder. You want details?

Okay, how about the gulf shore leases? Hundreds of miles of oil-rich drilling zones, right off our beaches, leased to Russian and Chinese companies linked directly to power players in Beijing and Moscow. While we're busy scraping nickels out of the cupholder to afford skyrocketing gas prices, our nation's biggest rivals are growing rich off *our* oil."

Boos radiated from the crowd.

"And it's not only foreign interests poaching our natural resources and sucking wealth from our economy. It's domestic business, also. Mega corporations nominally headquartered in our biggest cities, investing billions of dollars in international conglomerations scattered around the globe, shipping away jobs and industries by the *millions* with Washington's blessing. They can't be bothered to pay their frontline workers a living wage, so instead, they'll ship that business overseas, where profits are used to build missiles aimed right back at us."

Maggie punched her finger toward the crowd again. "It's not 'just business' anymore. Our economy is throttled, our future is mortgaged, and our national security is jeopardized by corrupt businesses and manipulative politicians working behind closed doors to exploit this nation, one dollar at a time."

Twelve thousand people rose to their feet, and Maggie knew she wasn't the only angry one.

Air Force One rose over the Rocky Mountains and pointed east, toward Billings. The Montana city wasn't much bigger than a large town, but it was the largest city in the state, and Maggie couldn't afford to miss a stop.

The race was extremely close. Pollsters argued endlessly about whether Tennessee governor Rick Jeffreys or Connecticut Senator Diane Cuthbert was in the lead. But they all agreed that regardless of which party held an advantage in the race, they both had a Trousdale problem. A big one. Because Maggie's relentless anti-corruption message was striking a chord with the heartland of America. She'd spent a majority of her campaign working smaller states and smaller towns, fighting to initiate grassroots momentum that would spill into bigger cities.

The strategy was bold, and it was working. After Billings and Bismarck, Maggie would appear in Chicago, which would mark only her fifth rally in a major American city since the campaign began. The amphitheater she would speak from had been sold out for weeks, and tens of thousands were expected to gather in the park outside. The brutal grind was paying off in spades, but it was also wearing her out.

Maggie cradled a glass of water in one hand. A pounding headache began sometime about three months before, only breaking at times when medication or a few hours' sleep subdued it. So many of her speeches were delivered in small arenas and convention centers that the contained noise must have damaged her hearing. She was looking forward to an open-air venue in Chicago.

The door opened, and Maggie looked up. Jordan Stratton, the sitting vice president and her running mate, stepped in. He was tall and fit, dressed in an impeccable black suit and maroon tie—his customary look—with an American flag pin stuck to his lapel as if he were born that way.

Stratton was a Republican by name, but an Illinois Republican in reality, which made him closer to a moderate Democrat. He was the only member of her campaign to associate with either primary party, but after months of campaigning alongside Maggie on a largely anti-establishment message, Stratton's association with party leadership was nominal at best. They had largely put him out to pasture—a punishment for rocking the boat.

"Great speech," Stratton said.

Maggie laughed. "Boise, Seattle, or Portland?"

He grinned. "Yes."

Stratton stepped across the conference room to a small wet bar and poured himself a bourbon, taking a moment to sniff the rich liquor before draining the glass. Maggie noted more lines in his face and streaks of grey above his ears. His hair was so perfectly black when she first met him that she thought he must dye it.

Stratton possessed better-than-average genes in a mix of English, German, and Native American heritage, but the nature of the job was that of a meat grinder. Another four years, and he might not have a black hair left.

Again, the door opened, this time admitting Jennifer Holmes, Maggie's campaign manager. She bustled to the end of the table and laid down a computer.

Holmes looked every bit as exhausted as Maggie felt, with makeup crinkling on her cheeks and her shoulders sagging, but when she spoke, she sounded upbeat. "Fantastic speech, ma'am. We're making real progress in these rural districts. I think Idaho is close to a lock."

Stratton snorted. "No such thing as a lock in this race."

Holmes shrugged. "Okay. So, it's leaning our way, then. As are Montana, both Dakotas, and Wisconsin. Twenty-four electoral votes, in total."

"What about Illinois?" Stratton asked, frustration creeping into his voice.

Maggie couldn't blame his irritation. Despite Illinois being her running mate's home state, they were struggling to lock it down. Cuthbert had invested millions of dollars and a lot of rally time into capturing the traditionally Democratic state, and even Jeffreys had slung some money into the mix, probably hoping to simply muddy the water. Maggie had expected the Prairie State to be decided by now, and she couldn't help feeling nervous.

"Still a toss-up," Holmes said. "It might've been a miscalculation not to invest more time in Chicago. We really need to nail the rally this weekend."

Nobody said anything, and Maggie sipped her water. She wondered if Holmes and Stratton were thinking what she was thinking about the nuclear option held in their back pocket the entire race. An extreme step, but maybe the advantage they needed in Illinois.

"Should I renounce?" Stratton asked.

Maggie looked to Holmes.

The campaign manager slid her glasses off, rubbing her face. "Honestly . . . I don't know. If you leave the Republican Party, you stand a chance of drawing in some swing voters in Chicago. People who can't get past the R next to your name. But you also risk alienating Republican voters we're poaching from Jeffreys in the southeast and Texas. Particularly Texas. We're this close to taking the state, and if we do, that's forty electoral votes in the bag. Jeffreys can't survive that."

"But if I declare myself an independent," Stratton said, "we might have a shot at California. Fifty-four votes."

Holmes shook her head. "Not now. Maybe two months ago. Cuthbert has it locked at this point. She's done a good job of painting your campaign as right of center."

Maggie rolled her eyes. "I was a registered Democrat in college."

"Sure. But nobody cares about that. Since you've taken office, you've been a hardliner on international policy, big on domestic production, and tough on crime. Those are Republican talking points."

"Oh, kiss my ass. We're not taking talking points from anyone. That's the *point*, Jen. This is an à la carte agenda. We evaluate issues independently and select the best policy for each problem."

Holmes folded her arms. "You don't have to sell me, ma'am. I'm on board. I'm just telling you what perception says."

Maggie looked to Stratton, and he rubbed the stubble on his cheeks.

"You want my honest opinion?" Holmes asked.

"Always."

"Hold off on anything drastic. We're six days from the finish line. It's too late in the game to make big moves. Drive home the message. Trust the voters."

Maggie fingered her water glass, watching ripples on the surface as the big plane passed through a patch of turbulence.

Holmes stood, closing the computer and circling the table. She stopped next to Maggie's chair. "I wouldn't worry much, ma'am. You've got a real shot at this."

Holmes ducked out, and Maggie looked back to Stratton.

"You think she's right?"

Stratton let out a dry laugh. "I hope so, because two or three more of those speeches, and we won't have a friend left in Washington."

Maggie smirked. "One can hope."

3

It was warm enough in late October to leave the sliding glass door of the condo open, allowing salty sea breeze to drift in from the beach. The gentle wash of waves over white sand filtered through the screen.

Reed lay awake, and he could still see the faces. They were fading quickly, but the remnants of the nightmare were still clear enough in his memory to make out every detail. The kid with the backpack moving down a crowded street. Crosshairs dancing over Reed's blurred vision. Somebody screaming at him over his headset. The crack of his rifle slamming into his shoulder.

It all blended together into a mental salad, built of every stimulation, every horrific detail, all woven together into one moment.

Take the shot.

Reed twisted out of the bed and placed both feet on the floor. His hands shook, and he stared at them, dumbfounded. He'd never dreamed like this before. Never woken up in cold sweats like this. For well over a decade, in one capacity or another, Reed had been a soldier. First as a rifleman with the Marine Corps, and then as a Force Recon sniper.

Then came the court-martial and prison, Oliver Enfield, and the underground criminal organization that freed Reed in exchange for a blood contract. He became an assassin, killing bad people for bad people, making his living in carnage, and finding a way to survive, until that too blew up. His next war was waged against the criminal empire he helped to build.

Next came the running, the hiding from the FBI, the shielding of his family, the offer of a lifeline from the president herself. The missions in Turkey and North Korea—more horror, but no dreams, cold sweats, or sleeplessness.

This was new.

Reed walked to the door, stepping into a wash of sea breeze. Banks, his beautiful wife of almost two years, slept quietly on the bed behind him. Next to her, their eight-month-old son, Davy, snored like only babies do—softly, with irregular rhythm.

The fan squeaked, and the wind whispered through the screen, but the sounds Reed heard weren't those of the condo on the fifteenth floor of the resort. He heard gunfire and screams. He saw the kid running, the backpack bouncing on his shoulders. He heard that voice in his headset, shouting again and again.

Take the shot. Take the shot.

Reed looked at the clock. It was just past midnight. They went to bed sometime around ten, after a full day on the beach. He should be exhausted.

Walking to the bedside table, he scooped the SIG P365 off the nightstand and tucked it into his pants, then pulled on a T-shirt. Tennis shoes and a hotel key joined him on the way to the door, and then he took the elevator to the lobby.

A few late-night drinkers laughed at the hotel bar, and a desk clerk greeted him on his way to the pool deck. Reed took the steps down to the white sand beach stretching out on either side, as far as he could see. He looked up at the condo tower, half expecting to see Banks leaning against the railing of their balcony, looking for him.

There was no one.

He walked through the loose sand to the spot where the surf had washed the shore smooth and hard. The tide was receding now, leaving a wide patch of firm ground for him to walk on as he turned east, the ocean to his right.

He flinched as the voice resumed in his head, the buildings around him faded, and he saw the dream again. The kid rushing down a narrow street. The sun blazing over Reed's face. The pressure of the trigger resting beneath his finger.

Reed began to run, crashing down the coast with damp sand flung up in his wake. Someplace far ahead, the sky was dimly lit by more condo towers and late-night bars. He focused on that glow, using it to block out the memories of the desert sun and panicked screams—the moment the trigger clicked and the rifle bucked.

He blocked it all out.

And he ran.

4

The man they called The Ghost slipped off the yacht just before it turned north for Manhattan. Diving under a clouded sky, he barely made a ripple as he descended beneath the surface. Water closed over his face but didn't penetrate the dry suit he wore. He sank ten feet, then treaded water awkwardly, one leg stiff and aching. The massive yacht passed overhead, churning toward the harbor, and he gave it time.

There was no rush.

He breathed easily through a full-face scuba mask and checked his watch. The numerals glowed underwater, reflecting local time. A quarter after midnight. Right on schedule.

The Ghost twisted in the water, wincing as the cold ignited further stiffness in his leg, but he blocked the pain from his mind as he flicked the start switch on his DPV, or underwater scooter. The electric pod hummed, and the propeller on its rear spun to life, towing him through the salt water at a smooth four miles per hour.

It took him less than twenty minutes to reach the Jersey shore. He could taste the pollution as he surfaced, lifting the mask and quickly scanning the horizon. Waves crashed against a narrow beach, and the lights of Keans-burg illuminated the horizon.

But there were no people. Not this late, while it was this cold. The Ghost crept easily onto the sand and quickly stripped off the face mask, air tank, and harness, carrying them all up the beach to a public bathhouse, where he deposited them on a bench.

None of the gear would be there the next morning. It might be too cold for tourists, but this was still Jersey. The diving equipment would be long gone by lunchtime, probably dispersed across a half dozen pawn shops in the region.

Perfect.

The man stripped out of the black dry suit, exposing blue jeans and a flannel button-down, then combed the water out of his short hair. His right leg still ached, and it hurt to stretch. His face stung—the mess of scars surrounding a small hole in his right cheek inflamed by the icy wind. Getting old sucked, but he was used to the pain. He'd been used to it for a long time.

Pulling a jacket out of his dry bag, he checked for his wallet, then left everything else on the bench and started up the boardwalk toward the street. The suburban homes lining the coast west of the beach were quiet and dark. He didn't recognize most of the street names he passed, but he didn't need to. Counting blocks instead, he turned north at seven and walked three more before turning west again.

The house on the corner was being renovated. Stacks of construction materials lined the front yard, and white plastic clung to the exterior walls. The owners—Russian expats, only recently relocated to the States and not yet moved in—had scheduled the repairs while they spent the winter in Florida. That left the property relatively unguarded, with nobody to notice as he traversed the curved driveway to the garage in back and reached into his pocket for the remote.

The door rumbled open, exposing a black Ford Edge parked inside with Illinois plates, no bumper stickers, and no parking permits pasted to the glass—nothing to make it remarkable in any way.

The man stepped inside and closed the garage door, then reached under the driver's side rear wheel. The key was right where it should've been, housed in a magnetic box. He unlocked the doors and circled to the back, lifting the tailgate. The rear cargo compartment was loaded with three items—a grocery sack full of nonperishable foods and water bottles, a small suitcase packed with two changes of clothes and spare shoes in his size, and a rectangular Pelican case about four feet long and eighteen inches wide.

Only the Pelican case interested him. He slid it to the back of the car and clicked open the latches, then swung the lid back. A rifle inside was disassembled into two parts—a rear receiver, complete with an adjustable stock, and a twenty-eight-inch bull barrel free-floated inside an aluminum handguard. A large scope was affixed to the top of the receiver, and at the bottom of the box was a foam compartment stacked with polished brass rifle cartridges.

The Ghost ran his finger along the row of ammunition, stopping at the last round and lifting it into the light for a closer inspection. The cartridge wasn't marked with any sort of manufacturer or caliber, but he knew both. The round was handmade in Saint Petersburg—the bullet custom-cast and hand-shaped. The caliber was .338 Lapua Magnum, and the load was hot enough to sling a 300-grain bullet well over a mile and still wreak havoc when it arrived on target.

The Ghost pressed the cartridge back into the foam, then snapped the case closed and shut the Ford's tailgate. He found his place behind the wheel and opened the garage door again, backing into the street.

Ten minutes later, he was west of Keansburg, taking the Garden State Parkway north across the Raritan River before turning west for Pennsylvania. The GPS on his dash had already marked his route, making navigation easy, even in an unfamiliar environment. The ETA read twelve hours, or about one p.m. the next afternoon. Plenty of time. Right on schedule.

He settled into the seat and set the cruise.

5

"How would you characterize the Trousdale approach to foreign relations?"

Maggie sat upright on a stool, across a glass table from a man in an expensive suit. Bright lights blazed down on them, and a row of TV cameras lined the shadows to her right.

She ignored it all, keeping her hands folded in her lap and a confident smile plastered on her face. She hadn't slept since the rally in Bismarck, late the night before. But with Ben Fisher—one of America's leading political talk show hosts—sitting across from her, she couldn't afford to indulge the exhaustion.

This quiet room exposed her to far more potential voters than any arena could hold.

"In a word?" Maggie said. "Proactive. American foreign policy has been reactionary for much of my life, and we routinely pay the price for allowing our rivals to set the tempo of diplomacy and trade. While serving the duration of President Brandt's term, we've worked hard to restore confidence in American leadership, and that won't change after reelection."

Fisher cocked his head. "You're not an isolationist?"

Maggie laughed. "No, I'm afraid not. I wish I could be. But we don't live in that world anymore. What happens in Turkey or North Korea carries very real consequences for American national security and the stability of a global economy. We can't afford to bury our heads in the sand and allow Russia, China, and militant factions of smaller nations to control that narrative. That's why I use the word *proactive*. As president, it's my job to establish strong working relationships with other nations. And, when necessary, confront the bullies in the room."

"You mean Russia."

Maggie made a noncommittal tilt of her head. "The Russian Federation is a different fish than the Soviet Union. Less bombastic and overtly hostile, certainly, but I would argue still dangerous. You often hear me use the term *rival* when referring to Russia and China. Obviously, our economic interests often conflict. That doesn't mean I settle for confrontation. Diplomacy is always my preference."

"Is that what happened in the Persian Gulf? Diplomacy?" Fisher blinked behind oversized round glasses.

The question caught Maggie off guard. It wasn't on the list of discussion points she'd reviewed before stepping into the interview. But she should've known it was coming.

Everybody wanted to know what really happened in the Middle East following the crash of *Air Force One*. The official narrative was that Russia engaged in unrelated military exercises.

The truth was something darker.

"The Persian Gulf is a great example of a dangerous situation de-escalated," Maggie said. "During a crisis, it's easy to get tunnel-visioned on one thing and forget to watch your peripheral. That's why I tasked the National Security Council with monitoring international activities, even while we were still reeling over the loss of President Brandt. When Russia's military exercises began, we were ready to engage with diplomacy and avoid a potentially catastrophic misunderstanding."

Fisher grunted softly, and for a while, he just stared. Maggie felt uncomfortable, suddenly getting the feeling he didn't believe her, and wondering if that moment of mistrust radiated through the cameras.

At last, Fisher set his notes down. "Madam President, may I be frank?"

"Of course."

"Many Americans view Russia's extensive show of force following the *Air Force One* crash as an overt threat. You've campaigned extensively on issues of national security and the defense of the free market against corrupt multinational corporations. On no less than thirty-four occasions, you've directly referenced Russian-backed companies as threats to the future of safe and equitable global trade. My question for you is, just what exactly *is* your opinion of the Russian Federation and the Nikitin regime?"

Maggie's smile faded as the question sank in. Fisher waited patiently, and for a moment, she felt as though she could see the millions of Americans waiting for an answer from the other side of the cameras.

"You want to know what I think of the regime in Moscow?" Maggie held her chin up. "Well, let me be blunt. President Nikitin is an imperialist, a Soviet dreamer, and a man of violence. We've seen prior Russian leaders leverage military might against Chechnya, Georgia, Afghanistan, Syria, and Ukraine. Nikitin came to power with transparent intentions to perpetuate that trend, and we kid ourselves if we think his hunger for exploitation will ever end. The only answer to the problem of global security is for a strong, united West to make a stand against authoritarianism. I'm not a war hawk, but I'm realistic about global realities. The Trousdale administration will speak softly and carry a damn big stick."

She ended the spiel, and Fisher rewarded her with a subdued nod. He stood and circled the table, offering his hand, and she met him halfway.

"President Trousdale, thank you for joining me this evening. I hate that we missed Vice President Stratton."

Maggie's high-wattage campaign smile returned. "He wanted to be here. Thank you for having me. We'll catch you again soon."

She waved to the cameras, then somebody yelled, "Cut!" In a millisecond, the mood changed. Fisher unclipped his mic, the cameras dropped, and Maggie turned for the door.

Her personal bodyguard, James O'Dell, met her immediately outside. O'Dell was tall and exclusively wore black suits, razor stubble turning grey over a bold chin. Not officially Secret Service but operating immediately alongside them, O'Dell had served at Maggie's side since her days as Louisiana's governor, and he was hands down the most loyal member of her staff. He was more like a friend than a bodyguard, even though he refused to address her as anything other than "Madam President."

Maggie waved to the news media staff and stopped to shake a few hands. O'Dell hung right beside her, flanked by two Secret Service agents. Then they were outside, walking down a short flight of stairs to her waiting limousine. O'Dell opened the door, and Maggie slid in, her smile melting the moment she was encased behind bulletproof glass.

"Where the *hell* is Jordan?" Maggie demanded, addressing the question to the only other person in the car.

Jennifer Holmes looked up from a computer, dark crow's feet encroaching on her eyes. "Ma'am, I've been trying all night. I can't get him on the phone."

"What do you *mean* you can't get him on the phone? He's the vice president of the United States. He doesn't just disappear!"

"The Secret Service says he never left his hotel."

Maggie made a fist over one knee. The car pulled off, and blue lights flashed as their Chicago PD escorts guided the motorcade through downtown.

"That was the last big TV appearance before Election Day," Maggie snapped. "They were expecting him."

"I'll call again," Holmes said. "I'm sure there's an explanation."

Maggie leaned back in the plush leather seat and closed her eyes. The headache had returned, consuming her skull and radiating down her spine.

Five days. One way or another, it would all be over in five days.

6

The Guthrie Hotel
Chicago, Illinois

Stratton made it a point to avoid the Windy City at all costs, but whenever fate doomed him for a visit, he stayed exclusively at the Guthrie. Located on Superior Street, the five-star, thirty-story hotel offered more than a luxury suite and fine dining delivered as room service.

It offered discretion. Stratton's extensive family empire found value in discretion—so much so that they purchased a majority share of the property and hand-selected a hotel manager who would cater to their needs and safeguard their privacy.

That sort of exclusive leverage was useful now and then, when you were the fifth-richest family in Illinois and neck-deep in politics. The Strattons might carry Rs next to their names, but they kept a finger in every corporate and political pie Chicago boasted.

It was that sort of obsessive involvement that made Jordan Stratton hate Chicago. It felt more like a prison than an empire, but that didn't keep him from leveraging it. When he won the Republican nomination for Illinois's Class 3 senate seat, he celebrated at the Guthrie ballroom. When he upset the Democratic incumbent to become the first Republican senator for the state in twenty-five years, he packed out the entire penthouse with old friends and drowned them in Dom Pérignon.

And when Maggie Trousdale tapped him to be her new VP, they turned that penthouse into a dance club on the Las Vegas strip. The hotel manager cleaned it all up, accepting a four-figure tip and saying nothing of the scattered cocaine on the floor or the questionable women in skimpy dresses who joined the party. That was the kind of discretion money could buy, and it was why Stratton chose the Guthrie when he needed to disappear.

Seated in the outdoor dining section of the rooftop restaurant, America's vice president sipped a cocktail and cradled an unlit cigar. He didn't really feel like smoking. In fact, the rooftop was technically a smoke-free venue. But he'd also learned, long ago, that the image of a powerful man dressed in a five-thousand-dollar suit, sipping a twenty-dollar drink, and puffing on a thirty-dollar Cuban cigar could be really intimidating.

And he wanted to intimidate tonight.

His phone rang again, and Stratton flipped it to mute without checking the caller ID. It was Holmes. Or maybe Maggie. Either could wait.

Stratton had called the hotel manager and blocked out the rear corner of the restaurant, then directed his Secret Service team to cordon off a subtle perimeter, ensuring privacy. There were plenty of other patrons on the rooftop, and a line of some billionaire's kids drunk at the bar, posing for selfies. Stratton blocked out the irritated knots in his stomach and checked his watch. She was late.

He drained the glass and lifted it toward the waiter as he felt the burn of the alcohol in his empty stomach and thought about ordering something. But he couldn't eat. He'd be lucky to sleep. This wasn't like running for senate. All the stakes were much higher now. A successful term as vice president could lay a platform for future ambitions. Executive ambitions.

And what cash-flushed, red-blooded American hadn't dreamed of that?

Glass doors flashed in the city lights, and a woman appeared on the roof. She was tall and curvy, dressed in a red cocktail dress, with brown hair swept over one shoulder. She strutted more than walked, her hips swaying just enough to suck the dress tight against her ass. Probably late twenties, with a sly, commanding look about her.

She saw him seated in the corner, and slinking like a fox, she started straight toward him.

He lit the cigar, blowing a cloud of smoke through the side of his mouth as she cleared the line of Secret Service agents, then sat across from him. He saw goosebumps on her skin—probably from the chill of the endless Chicago wind. But she didn't shiver. She was too proud for that.

The waiter set Stratton's drink down and asked for her order. She requested a dirty martini, her voice carrying the commanding edge of a woman who was used to having her way.

"How's the campaign, Jordy?" she asked, folding her hands with a coy smile.

Stratton puffed on the cigar, holding her gaze. He reached beneath his jacket and withdrew a bubble mailer. It was yellow and unmarked, unsealed, and packed thick. Without a word, he slid it across the table.

She raised an eyebrow. "No foreplay?"

"Count it," Stratton said.

She lifted the mailer, exposing the ends of banded stacks of cash— hundred-dollar bills, ten grand to a stack. Forty thousand in total.

"Just like that?" the woman said.

"Just like that."

She cocked her head, the sly smile returning. "You really are one stone-hearted SOB, aren't you?"

Stratton held the cigar near his cheek, staring her down. "Is it done?"

She sealed the envelope, then laid it in her lap. The waiter returned, and she took a long sip of the martini, then ran a seductive tongue across her lips. "It will be."

"And I'm supposed to believe that?"

She rolled her eyes, twisting the martini glass. "Relax, Jordy. Have I ever let you down?"

He lowered the cigar and leaned across the table. "This is the last I hear from you. The last *anyone* hears from you. Am I clear?"

"Are you threatening me?"

For the first time, Stratton indulged in a smile. "Don't forget who you're dealing with. My family doesn't make threats. We make business deals and headstones. Your choice."

The sly confidence plastered across the woman's face flickered, and she glanced away.

Stratton relaxed into the chair again, drawing deeply on the cigar. It wasn't half bad, he thought. It tasted like power. "Don't spend it all in one place."

The woman smoothed the mailer in her lap, rolling her shoulder just enough for one strap of her dress to slide carelessly over her arm. "You have a suite?"

Stratton snorted. "Don't patronize me."

She took a long sip of the martini. "What if I'm not? You never had trouble mixing business and pleasure before."

He drew once more on the cigar, his gaze gliding down her body, then he stubbed the smoke out on a dinner plate. "Watch your step. If this comes back on me, I won't go down alone."

The woman tilted her head, allowing the shoulder strap to drop another inch. She flicked her hair and slid it back in place with a quick pass of one nail-polished hand. "You were always so stiff, Jordan. It's really too bad. But I guess that's how Carolyn likes it, huh?"

Stratton stiffened, and she laughed. Then she stood, taking the mailer with her. With a wink, she started back across the roof, the dress sucking close to her hips.

He watched, but he wasn't thinking about the curves or her solicitation. He was thinking about the forty grand in the envelope and what it bought him.

One step closer.

7

Destin, Florida

The sun sank slowly, and Reed enjoyed every minute of it. He and Banks sat out on the beach with Davy, smiling as their son belly-laughed at a scurrying crab dancing ten feet away.

The breeze was warm, the sky clear. The last day of a near-perfect vacation. The first family vacation Reed had enjoyed in almost twenty years.

They took Davy back to the room for a bath, then the three of them settled into a table at the resort restaurant, and he and Banks ordered steaks with red wine and cheesecake for dessert. The food was delicious— just as it had been all week. They had barely left the property, and Reed didn't mind. It was moments like these, sitting across from his beautiful wife, feeding baby food to his son, that he felt the closest he ever had to family.

To peace.

"Did you sleep last night?"

Reed looked up from his plate, blinking twice before Banks came into focus. She sat with cheesecake globbed onto her fork, her head tilted. She hadn't worn makeup all week, and her face was flushed with sun that was already fading into a gentle tan. She looked amazing, he thought.

"Reed. Are you hearing me?"

He shook his head to clear it. "Yeah . . . sorry. Just drifting off."

"You didn't sleep, did you?"

"What do you mean?"

Banks set the fork down and shot him a glare.

He poked at the cheesecake, suddenly feeling very full and very tired. Because he hadn't slept. Not all week. "I think it's the mattress. No place like home, right? Which reminds me . . . We should really get a king size. Little dude is taking up more than his fair share."

He wiped mashed peas off Davy's face, not blaming his son for spitting them out, and Banks didn't comment. She probably knew he was lying. It was only a matter of whether she would press him about it.

"Are you dreaming again?" she asked.

He fixated on cleaning Davy's face, then scooped a baby spoon full of carrots and tried to shovel them in. Davy stuck his tongue out and turned his head away.

"What do you mean?"

Banks pushed her plate away. "Dammit, Reed. Why do you lie about this stuff? I know you're not sleeping. I hear you when you try."

He glanced her way. "Hear me? What does that mean?"

She looked away, brushing hair behind one ear and gazing across the darkened beach. He saw the strain in her face, and not for the first time, he felt leaden guilt in his gut. He'd seen that look before—many times, for many different reasons. But it was almost always his fault.

"You . . . say things," she whispered. "Fragments of things."

He set the spoon down. "What things?"

"Military stuff, mostly. Ranges. Radio codes. Names, sometimes. Other Marines."

Reed didn't try to deny it. He didn't know he talked in his sleep, but he didn't doubt it, either. He heard his own voice in his dreams—always in the same sequence. Hitting the dirt behind a sniper rifle. Shouting for Turk to spot the targets as he slammed a fresh cartridge into the chamber. Rushing to take out the suicide bombers before they blew up another marketplace or school.

It wasn't always a specific memory. Usually, it was a collage of things, all jumbled up and loud as though they were replaying over stadium speakers. But lately, it *had* been specific. That time in the desert sun . . . with the kid.

"I have dreams," he admitted. "But . . . it's not a big deal. I'm probably just drinking too much." He winked and took a pull at his beer, but Banks didn't look amused. He reached across the table and traced her hand, smiling gently. "Hey . . . You know what I was thinking about?"

"What?" she mumbled, fiddling with her fork again.

"Tuesday night."

"What about it?"

"You know," he said, winking again.

She blushed but played it coy. "Oh yeah?"

"Been thinking about it all week."

"What are we gonna do about it?"

"Well, I was thinking. Last night of vacation and all . . ."

"Encore?"

"You bet."

She dropped the fork and reached for Davy. "I'll put him in bed."

Reed drained the beer. "I'll get the check."

8

Banks took Davy upstairs, and Reed waited for the check. After five minutes, the server hadn't come by, so he waded through the tables to the bar to track it down himself.

He saw the woman sitting in the back corner, but it took him a second glance before he recognized her. She sat alone, nestled in shadows, dressed in loose black pants and a blouse, auburn hair tied into a ponytail. She was petite, with frail shoulders and hollow eyes.

It was the eyes that threw him off. At first, he thought he imagined the face, and he blinked, wondering how many beers he'd knocked back. Thoughts of Banks and the little red number she wore to bed Tuesday night faded as he stared at the woman.

She stared back, then lifted one hand and waved softly, but she didn't get up. Reed looked away, feeling suddenly on edge. He surveyed the restaurant quickly, looking for other familiar faces, scoping out threats. Panic crept into his mind, and he felt for the SIG where it rested beneath his shirt.

Then he stopped and caught himself. The woman was alone, and she wasn't trying to sneak up on him. The corner she occupied was shadowy, but not concealed. She wasn't trying to hide. She *wanted* him to see her.

"Sir?" The bartender said the word with annoyance, as though he were repeating himself.

Reed tilted his head toward the table. "I was coming for my check."

The guy opened his mouth to object, probably irritated to be pulling server duty. Then he sighed and turned to the computer.

Reed didn't wait for the total. He peeled a hundred-dollar bill out of his pocket and laid it on the bar, then started toward the darkened corner without asking for change.

The woman said nothing as Reed settled into the chair across from her. Light bruising on her neck was joined by pallid skin and chapped lips. She wore no makeup, and her skin was greasy and unwashed looking.

He noticed the tremble in her hands, too. Very faint but persistent.

"Lucy?" he asked.

The woman smiled. It was a humorless expression—dry and haunted. "Hello, Reed."

Her voice sounded nothing like the spunky, vibrant young woman he knew eighteen months before. She *looked* nothing like that woman, either.

Reed first met Lucy Byrne when they both worked as assassins for a criminal empire, two or three years prior. During his war against that empire, Reed had recruited Lucy to help him investigate a certain criminal operation, which eventually became the Resilient Pharmaceutical scam. Lucy, alongside Wolfgang Pierce, Rufus Turkman, Maggie Trousdale, and Banks herself, was instrumental in the successful destruction of that empire. But Reed hadn't seen her since his wedding. Since Venezuela. Since Lucy embarked on a one-woman quest to run down child traffickers in Southeast Asia.

And now this.

"What are you doing here?" Reed asked. It probably would've been kinder to ask how she was doing, or skip that step and find out what the hell happened to the once lithe—and deadly—killer. But part of him didn't want to know, because he could already guess. And he knew it wasn't an accident that Lucy turned up in the same beachside resort he'd been staying at all week.

She was there on purpose.

"Straight to the point, as always," Lucy said.

Reed shrugged apologetically but didn't comment.

A waiter came by and deposited water glasses. Reed waved him off when he asked for an order.

"I went to Thailand," Lucy said, sipping water. "Laos. Vietnam. Southeast China."

"Did you find them?"

During the Resilient Investigation, Reed and his cohorts had uncovered a child trafficking ring outside of New Orleans with roots in Southeast Asia. Following the conclusion of that investigation, Lucy was the only member of the team in a position to do anything about it. She flew to Bangkok on her own, leaving Reed to wonder about her sometimes, but with no way to contact her, though he wasn't sure if he would have had he been able. He wasn't sure he wanted to know what she found.

"Oh, yes," Lucy whispered. "I found them."

"And?" Reed pressed.

She met his gaze. "And I dealt with them . . . and dealt with them . . . and kept dealing with them."

"That bad?"

She laughed. "It's like . . . killing ants. There's no way to win. You bust one ring and cut their throats, then uncover another ring. And another. It just . . . keeps going. There's no end."

She trailed off, looking away.

Reed saw tears, and her fingers trembled as she held the water glass. "What happened?" he asked.

She licked her lips and looked down. "What always happens, I guess."

"You got caught."

She nodded. "Not by the gangs, thank God. They would've killed me."

"Police?"

"Dirty cops. Which is kind of repeating myself down there. I was in prison for a couple months. Managed an escape but lost everything. All my money, my ID. Everything I needed to get out. And then I was jumped by some street thugs in Hanoi. They . . . well, you know."

She faced him again. He saw death in her gaze. It was a look that might have chilled a normal man, but Reed had seen it before. In her day, Lucy Byrne was one of the deadliest assassins he knew. Completely ruthless, with a penchant for blades and poison. A stone-cold killer. But clearly, those days had passed.

"Why are you shaking?" Reed asked.

Lucy almost spoke, then hesitated.

Reed lowered his tone. "What are you taking?"

"Opioids."

"How long?"

She shrugged. "Long enough, I guess."

"Why?"

She slid her left foot out from under the table and lifted her pants leg. The flesh she exposed was twisted and scarred, white and red, swollen in places and recessed in others. Burn marks.

"How?" Reed asked.

Lucy dropped the pants leg. "After they raped me, they tied me to a fence and lit me on fire. I guess it was their thing. Some kind of trademark. Gasoline on my legs, then a match."

"They didn't try to kill you?"

"I expect they meant to. Patrol cops turned up and put the fire out, but not before . . ."

Reed felt his stomach twist, and he gave her time. She deserved that much.

"In the hospital, they cleaned the wounds and gave me painkillers. Opioids. But after a few days, they wanted payment, and I couldn't pay. So they kicked me out. The pain was still crazy, and it's easy to find pills down there. So, I just—"

"Kept taking them."

She shrugged.

Reed crossed his arms, his internal urge to sympathize colliding with a more personal reality. The battle scars he saw in Lucy's eyes were remnants of a war he'd put behind him. There was a reason he didn't follow her into Bangkok. He knew what she would find. An endless, mired web, with layer after layer of increasing evil—just as she said.

Banks had endured enough. She deserved a quiet life for her family and a loving husband who was steady and strong, who cut loose of the ugly side of life because he knew he could never defeat it.

Whatever had happened to Lucy, she couldn't bring it here. Not to his family.

"Why are you here?" Reed said.

Lucy looked up, visibly concentrating her confidence into a ball—a final push to ask for something. "I need help."

"I think you do," Reed said. "Do you need money?"

"No . . . well, yes. But I'm not asking for that. I need a job. Something stable."

"You're in no condition to work."

"I know. But I can be. I just . . . I need to get back on my feet. And I know you've found work."

Reed grew very still. "Who told you that?"

"Trousdale is president now. She's hiring you, isn't she?"

"Why would you think that?"

"Because you're *here*, driving a brand-new SUV, and vacationing in a resort in broad daylight. When I left you in Venezuela, you were running for your life with the FBI on your heels. There's only one person on the planet who could've washed that away, and she wouldn't have done it for free."

Reed watched the pleading look in her face, then slowly stood up and reached into his pocket. Scooping out what remained of his vacation cash, he peeled off a thousand dollars and dropped the bills on the table, then replaced the remainder into his pocket. "Get help," he said. "And don't show up around my family again."

Lucy looked at the money, then started to stand. Her knees shook. "Reed, please . . . I'm not trying to rock your boat. But I need this. I need something steady. Maybe you'll hear of something? I bought a burner phone. I put the number on that forum we used to—"

"I put that life behind me," Reed said. "So should you. Find a regular job."

"A regular job? I'm a killer, Reed. I cut throats. I don't flip burgers."

Reed lowered his voice. "I *told* you not to go, LB. I told you what you'd find. I hate to see you this way, but I can't change it. What I can do is protect my family . . . and I will. From anyone."

He withdrew the remaining hundred bucks from his pocket and dropped it on the table. "Get help. And don't come near my family again."

9

The Ghost made it to Chicago right on schedule, only stopping once to refuel the Ford. He parked on the street two blocks from his destination and left the bags in the trunk before starting down the sidewalk.

It was eight p.m.—later than he hoped to arrive, but the young woman he texted assured him it was all right. She was leaving later that night, catching a red-eye flight to Nashville for a girls' weekend. Her apartment on the eighteenth floor of the Lake View Apartments building would be vacant for three nights. She was only too happy to rent it out for the weekend—illegally, of course, via an off-the-books version of Airbnb designed to offset the burden of excessive rents in big cities around the world.

It was a hip thing. A millennial thing. The same kind of mindset that led people to rent out their cars and boats to complete strangers. Apartment management would throw a fit, of course, but they wouldn't know. Not until it was too late, anyway.

He reached the Lake View building after fifteen minutes of steady walking. His right leg ached, much as it always did, now further inflamed by the cold wind drifting off the lake. Before long, that wind would be a problem for a different reason, but The Ghost wasn't intimidated. He knew how to overcome it.

He passed through the polished doors on the ground floor and approached the security desk, asking for the woman by name and saying he was expected. The guard lifted a phone and made a call, then unlocked a second row of doors and directed him to the elevator.

It was a short ride to the eighteenth floor, and he used the reflection of the polished stainless-steel doors to inspect his appearance. He was a little road weary, but that was to be expected. He was a traveling music producer, after all. From a big label in Stockholm, there to seek out local American talent. The hard rock scene was big in Europe at the time, and he knew the young woman knew that. She loved metal music. A quick sweep of her social media confirmed that.

She was only too eager to select a short-term tenant in such an occupation. The scars on his cheek might alarm her at first, but he'd headed off that problem by warning her that he'd been involved in a car accident some years ago and looked a little scary. He made a joke out of it, and she replied with laughing emojis in the chat box. He took that as a good sign—an open-minded young American, eager not to discriminate. Eager to be agreeable.

The elevator dinged, and the doors rolled open. The building was old but well maintained and updated, with smooth carpet and off-white walls. He found her door easily enough on the north face of the building—apartment 1809.

The Ghost knocked. The woman answered. She was maybe twenty-five, not gorgeous, but plenty cute. Dressed in torn jeans and a tank top, with dyed blonde and green hair, and a nose piercing. Not a rabid metal head, but certainly a stylish goth wannabe.

She opened the door with energy and a grin, but that grin flickered when she saw the scars on his face. The pencil-sized hole in his right cheek where the bullet had torn through, and botched battlefield surgery had failed to repair it.

He saw her eyes lock on the spot and uncertainty pass through them. But not for long.

She looked away, flashed him the "rock on" gesture, then extended a fist. "Paul?"

"Leslie?" He muted his accent the best he could. He didn't expect an average American to understand the difference between a Swedish accent and a faint Russian one, but all the better to keep it subdued.

"Yeah! Come on in. Glad you made it."

He followed her inside, smelling coffee and cat litter on the air. The apartment was painfully small—a studio, maybe six hundred square feet—but reasonably clean and neat. Her suitcases were already packed near the door. The floor was freshly vacuumed, and she had lit a candle near the stove.

"Well . . . this is it! Yours for the weekend. You don't smoke, do you?"

The Ghost shook his head, playing shy. She showed him the bathroom and the TV, then pointed out the Wi-Fi password on a napkin near the refrigerator. He admired the view out her north-facing windows—expansive, with the lake on his right and the city spilling out ahead of him.

"Beautiful, isn't it? I probably overpay, but I love the view."

He nodded, hands in his pockets. "It's perfect."

She hesitated as if she was ready to go but wasn't sure if she should.

He smiled. "Thank you for your hospitality. I always enjoy visiting Chicago."

"Right on. You'll have to let me know if you sign any local bands."

He glanced up at the ceiling. "Are there cameras?"

Leslie frowned. "Cameras?"

"Security cameras."

"Oh . . . um . . ."

He shrugged innocently. "I want to make sure you're not watching while I shower."

She laughed. "Oh, right. No, no cameras. Just a normal apartment."

"That's perfect."

She shifted on her feet, a little nervous now, twisting her cell phone in one hand. "Well, I guess that's everything."

He nodded, and she turned for her bags, but she never reached the kitchen. He swept his arm beneath her chin, lifting and grabbing her face with his free hand. She didn't scream. She didn't have the chance. Her neck snapped like a twig, and her body fell limp. In a moment, she was stretched across the couch, staring at the ceiling, her black lipstick smeared across one cheek.

He stood over her, breathing easily, then stooped to retrieve her fallen phone. It was locked, but he held it over her blank face, and it unlocked automatically.

It wasn't hard to locate the girls' group chat in her messaging app. It was full of emojis, abbreviated messages, and GIFs. He wondered absently if the girl pronounced the word with a hard or soft G, then tapped out a quick message complaining about food poisoning. The replies were quick and contained a lot of crying emojis.

He turned the phone off and tossed it onto the couch, then returned to the window. Chicago was dark, but if he concentrated, he could see between the buildings to a spot in the distance—a park with an amphitheater. Not really visible this far away, but he knew it was there, over two thousand meters away. An impossible distance for almost anyone.

But not for The Ghost.

10

Maggie slept barely six hours before she was up at dawn, showering and scrubbing her face for a fresh application of makeup. It was Saturday, October thirtieth. Three days to the biggest day of her life, and the pressure was setting in.

She dreamed about Election Day. Saw herself waving at cheering onlookers on her way to the ballot box, there to perform the most symbolic and useless act of her entire campaign: voting for herself. The media loved her, and the votes were pouring in. Jeffreys and Cuthbert were slipping across the board. Maggie slowly tightened a chokehold across one state after another.

And then the unthinkable happened—every night, the dream was the same. Stratton or Holmes or Maggie's chief of staff, Jill Easterling, took a call. Their faces went pale, they mumbled incoherent objections, and then they turned to her and said, "We lost Louisiana."

Maggie usually woke at that point, cold and clammy.

I lost my home state.

The ultimate shame. The unthinkable humiliation. And the hallmark of a doomed campaign.

As she twisted her hair into a towel and stared in the mirror, Maggie tried not to relive the nightmare. She knew it was completely irrational. She led Louisiana by double digits, even deep in the heart of New Orleans, where progressive voters leaned toward Cuthbert. She would land the Pelican State, and probably most of the southeast along with it. Early polls in Texas following the previous night's talk show appearance were also promising, and moderate voters across the Midwest were leaning her way.

But she wouldn't sleep until it was over. The feelings of crushing failure brought on by the dreams were too visceral. Two years before, she couldn't have imagined ever running for president, let alone being this close to winning it all. Now she couldn't imagine anything else. It was everything to her. It was the meaning of existence.

Maggie applied makeup carefully, monitoring the clock on the counter and absently checking her phone for messages from Stratton. She still hadn't heard from her absent VP, but Holmes texted to let her know he was still at the Guthrie Hotel. According to his security detail, he had never left.

If he were with her now, she would've slapped him in the face. Blowing off the last major TV appearance prior to the election was more than irresponsible—it could be fatal. Nothing could be left to chance this late in the game. There was no time to recover if they stumbled.

But she'd deal with Stratton later. Right now, her mind was already sliding into her next appearance—the cards-on-the-table, all-in appeal to lock down Illinois. At noon, she would step on stage at the amphitheater in Millennium Park, and in front of an estimated forty thousand people, make her pitch for the Prairie State's nineteen electoral college votes.

The polls said she was close. It was time to nail it shut.

She chose a black dress first, then discarded it in favor of a deep blue. An American flag pin, subdued heels, and minimal jewelry completed her look. She fiddled with her hair for twenty minutes, putting it up, then taking it down—styling it in different ways. Frustrated with everything.

There were makeup artists and a stylist to help her with this, of course, but Maggie didn't like using them. They made her feel like an art piece, tweaked and toyed with to please the cameras. She only indulged them on occasion, when the moment demanded it. But not today. If Illinois was going to vote for her, they would vote for the real Trousdale.

Maggie gave up on her hair, settling for a loose style falling around her shoulders, then retrieved her purse and checked her phone. Still no word from Stratton, and it was nearing ten thirty.

That SOB is playing with fire. And why?

There was a soft knock on the door. Maggie called for the visitor to come in, and she immediately recognized O'Dell's firm footfalls. Her bodyguard was dressed in his customary black suit, but to her surprise, he had forgone the black tie in favor of a subdued blue one. It almost matched her dress.

The big Cajun stopped just inside her suite. His mouth opened as though he were about to speak, but he didn't.

Maggie looked up from her phone. "James?"

He blinked, seeming to snap out of something. "I'm sorry, ma'am. We're ready when you are."

"Great. I'm almost done."

She sat on the end of the bed and peeled her heels off, now convinced they were too subdued. O'Dell turned to go.

"You can stay," she said.

He paused by the door, shifting awkwardly on his feet.

"Did you get any sleep?" she asked, suddenly hungry for conversation. Of all the staffers, aides, security, and politicians who surrounded her on a day-to-day basis, O'Dell was the only one who remembered her as governor. He was the only one she felt truly comfortable around.

Maybe it was their shared swamp heritage. Maybe it was his gentle mannerisms or relentless loyalty. The world felt more stable with O'Dell in the room. Maggie felt more herself.

"Not too much, ma'am," O'Dell said. "They keep us hopping."

"I wish you wouldn't call me that," Maggie said, slipping her feet into a fresh set of shiny, three-inch heels. Too much.

"Ma'am?"

She looked up, flashing him a friendly smile. "Exactly."

He hesitated. "The Secret Service—"

"You're not Secret Service, James."

He flushed, and she regretted the words. It was true, despite the governmental ID in his pocket and the gun on his hip, O'Dell wasn't technically a

Secret Service agent. He'd been a Louisiana State policeman when she was governor, and she insisted he be brought along as her personal bodyguard when she became vice president.

The Secret Service hadn't appreciated that, but she liked to think they valued his contribution at that point. Even so, they wouldn't grant him an official title, and that burned O'Dell.

Maggie said, "I just mean . . . You know. You're one of the inner circle."

He ducked his head, and she stood.

"How do I look?"

She'd switched back to her original subdued heels. They just felt like her. And anyway, who would be looking at her feet?

O'Dell surveyed her ensemble, stopping at her face, but he didn't answer. She cocked her head, and he swallowed.

"Amazing," he said.

Something in his face was different than before—softer and more sincere. The room felt suddenly still and warm.

O'Dell must have noticed it, too, because he quickly looked away and stepped back, holding his hand toward the door. "After you, ma'am."

They met Stratton on the ground floor. He stepped in, flanked by Secret Service agents, dressed in his customary overpriced suit with an Illinois flag pin alongside the American. His hair was slicked back—the picture of confidence, like a freaking cologne model.

Maggie sipped coffee and offered him a warm smile, conscious of the cameras snapping from one corner of the room. She put her arm around his back and turned for the cameras, speaking out of the side of her mouth. "Where the *hell* have you been?"

Stratton shook a hotel worker's hand and thanked her for the hospitality, regardless of the fact that he hadn't slept there.

"Just buttoning up some local stuff," he said. "I'll explain later."

Maggie's blood boiled, but she kept calm, following him toward the door. "You don't freaking *disappear* on me. I swear, you ever pull a stunt like that again, you'll be on your ass." She stopped at the brass doors, tilting her head up to make eye contact. He maintained an easy smile but looked distant and a little cold as they pushed into the crisp Chicago morning.

A light breeze whispered down Michigan Avenue, pulling at her hair as a storm of cheers erupted from the street. She peered into the sunrise, surprised to see two or three hundred people crowded behind a steel fence, waving little American flags on sticks and calling her name. Poster board signs glinted in the sunshine, decorated with colorful letters and bold exclamation points.

We love you, Maggie!

Give 'em hell, swamp girl.

Chicago for Trousdale!

Maggie stopped, dumbfounded, then she glanced up at Stratton.

He grinned and lifted his hands like a quarterback calling for the crowd to cheer. The voices rose, and he spoke just loud enough to overcome them. "You hear that? That's local stuff. Buttoned up."

11

The Ghost sat at the dead girl's table, the rifle resting in front of him. It took under thirty seconds to assemble, but he stretched the process into ten minutes, carefully inspecting each part before locking it in place.

The weapon was nearly five feet in length, with a heavy bolt, a bulky bipod, and a scope that, by itself, weighed nearly six pounds. It was made by Leupold and cost twice as much as the rifle.

Good glass, good shot. That was his motto. He'd take an average rifle with a premium optic over a premium rifle with a discount scope any day of the week. The rifle could be managed. A gritty trigger could be overcome. But a lying scope was a lying scope. He had to know those crosshairs were dead on—and the Leupold was. One hundred percent.

Leaving the rifle, he moved to the kitchen, where four rounds of hand-loaded .338 Lapua Magnum waited on a dish towel under a heat lamp. Using a laser thermometer, he checked the temperature of each round, both at the base and the bullet's tip. Every bullet was within half a degree of the other three, but The Ghost was a perfectionist. He'd spent years of his life and tens of thousands of rounds learning the minute performance impacts caused by the slightest variations in shooting conditions.

Temperature was a big one. His custom handloads were scientifically refined to produce the most extreme consistency, but he could dial that performance in even further by heating the rounds to a designated temperature prior to firing. With the apartment thermostat set at 72 degrees, he was comfortable with the temperature of the rifle itself. It would be a cold-bore shot, of course, but he'd trained for that.

He'd trained for everything.

The Ghost walked past the couch, where the dead girl lay, still staring up at the ceiling. He ignored her and lifted the curtain just enough to inspect the thermometer he'd pinned to the outside of the window. Forty-one degrees. A cold day, with a steady wind blowing west off the lake at eleven miles per hour.

They didn't call Chicago the Windy City for nothing, and wind was a sniper's worst enemy. But the lake effect at least produced a relatively consistent speed and direction. At over two kilometers, his problems extended far beyond the wind, anyway.

With a flight time of nearly nine seconds, there was humidity to think about. Gravity. Even the rotation and curvature of the earth came into effect. Known as the Coriolis effect, it meant he would need to compensate for as much as six inches of deflection to the right—or the north.

Then there was spin drift, a phenomenon that causes a bullet to drift in the direction of the weapon's rifling. Not a problem inside a thousand meters, but at over two thousand, the spiraling path of the projectile would further drag it to the right. All these factors, along with the most relentless of all—gravity itself—had to be calculated together and merged to form a perfect shot. It was a lot of math, and if any factor changed while aligning the crosshairs, those mental calculations would need to be made all over again. And quickly.

It was the kind of thing maybe half a dozen people on the planet were capable of, and five of them were probably astrophysicists or math freaks at Ivy League universities. But one of them was a shooter, and those mathematics, coupled with years of refined marksmanship, made him absolutely lethal.

When The Ghost settled behind a rifle, physics and distance be damned.

Someone was about to die.

12

The limo ride from the Four Seasons to Millennium Park lasted half an hour. The Secret Service took their time, rolling along wide avenues lined by thousands of cheering onlookers standing behind barricades, waving signs and screaming at Maggie's car. The energy was unprecedented. Not even when she campaigned at Louisiana State University, her alma mater, did she experience so much enthusiasm. Chicago was alive, and Holmes texted to let her know the park was packed to capacity with fifty thousand people.

Maggie couldn't believe it. She felt stunned and a little disconnected, as if she were floating on a cloud, watching herself riding in the oversized Cadillac. She saw the people and the signs, but she simply couldn't register that they were all there for *her*.

She shot Stratton a look, and he returned it with a semi-smug smirk, but he didn't say anything. She thought back to his excuse at the hotel—that comment about buttoning up last-minute business.

There was no way he could be responsible for this turnout, Maggie thought. He won the senatorial race by the skin of his teeth. He wasn't *this* popular. Was she?

The Cadillac turned onto Randolf Street, and the crowds disappeared as the Secret Service barricaded them back. Chicago PD lined the sidewalk, joined by Secret Service agents with dogs and submachine guns, while a helicopter rushed by overhead. Everything felt electric, as though the concrete itself were alive. Maggie never remembered a rally like this. She could hear the chants of the gathered crowd in the park, even through the limo's bulletproof glass.

They were ready for her.

The Cadillac rolled to a stop twenty yards behind the amphitheater, and agents circled her door. Two dogs passed by, sniffing the path ahead of her as one final security check, and then O'Dell appeared outside her window. The big man put his hand on the door and turned to make contact with Agent Jenkins, the head of Maggie's detail. The agent nodded, and then the door swung open.

Cold air filled her lungs as Maggie stepped out, her bare arms turning to goosebumps. Stratton followed her, waving at the crowd gathered at the end of the street, his perfect white teeth gleaming like a billboard.

"This way, ma'am!" O'Dell said. Maggie followed him dumbly, stopping at the rear entrance of the amphitheater. Stratton took the lead, bounding up the stairs, through the darkened entrance, and then on stage to a thunder of applause.

Stratton's voice boomed over immense speakers. "Chicago! Damn, it's so good being home!"

The ground shook, and cheers turned to chants. Maggie heard her name repeated over and over, breaking through the trees that lined the park. Stratton laughed, and she imagined him switching to his bashful smile—a calculated expression that won people over in droves.

"You know what?" he said. "I'm a pretty big fan myself!"

Another round of cheers. She knew Stratton had a short speech planned—an intro to warm up the crowd before she took the stage. But the crowd didn't need to be primed. They were ready, and Stratton took the hint.

"You guys ready to see her?" he called. "Ladies and gentlemen, the current and *next* president of the United States . . . The leader of the Free World . . . The only independent to ever ascend to the Oval Office since George Washington. My running mate, my boss, and my friend . . . Give it up for Muddy Maggie Trousdale!"

Maggie's heart thundered, but the nervousness was gone. Rushing up the steps toward the amphitheater floor, she felt O'Dell at her heels. She broke through the door and saw Stratton standing fifty feet away, holding his hand toward her.

"Ma'am?"

The crowd was so loud, her head exploded into another headache. But this was her moment.

"Ma'am!"

Maggie stepped out of the shadows, only inches from crossing into daylight. She heard the voice behind her but didn't really register it.

"Maggie!" O'Dell's shout broke through the chaos ahead of her, and she looked over her shoulder to see him pointing to her hand. It was only then that she remembered her cell phone still clamped between her fingers. She'd left her purse in the Cadillac, but in the rising excitement, she'd held on to the phone.

Maggie glanced self-consciously at her pocketless dress, then saw O'Dell still holding out his hand. She tossed him the phone, and he caught it with a shy smile.

"Give 'em hell," he mouthed.

She grinned, then faced the stage and lifted her arm.

13

With the apartment window two feet off the floor, a prone shot was impossible. But that was okay because The Ghost had trained for this.

Setting the kitchen table three feet inside the window, he rested the rifle on its surface like a shooting bench, then positioned a kitchen chair behind it. The furniture was solid. He noted that while reviewing the rental listing. It was one of the reasons he chose this spot. The table wouldn't move as he aligned his crosshairs. One more variable checked off a list of possible problems.

He adjusted the scope for distance and elevation, consulting a notebook filled with shooting data spread on the table next to him. That notebook— or *dope book*, in sniper vernacular—contained nearly ten thousand rounds of carefully collected and evaluated shooting results with this very rifle, fit with this very scope—data that told him how to adjust for temperature, wind, and even humidity. A handbook of customized cheat sheets. His secret weapon for making an impossible shot on the first round through a cold barrel.

The Ghost reached for the cartridge next, selecting the best of the four by temperature and carrying it with a gloved hand to avoid depositing finger oil on the bullet. That kind of thing was extremely unlikely to make a difference, but why take the risk? Drawing the rifle's bolt, he placed the cartridge into the chamber, then gently closed it with a sliding of metal on metal. The satisfying thump of the bolt locking over a loaded chamber sent a thrill up his spine—a wave of anticipation. He would never get over the flood of power he felt while ramming a new bullet into a rifle.

It was more than satisfaction. It was like being a god, carrying life and death in his hands.

Settling behind the weapon, he checked the optic for any dust or smudges and fit his hand around the grip. It was cool and familiar, like a worn pair of shoes. A precision weapon capable of taking life at over two kilometers.

He twisted his foot, pulling the string attached to the curtains, and they slid back four inches. He'd already cut a hole in the glass, just five inches square but plenty large enough to allow passage of the projectile.

He settled behind the scope and breathed in deeply. Slowly. He could see across Chicago, straight down Indiana Avenue, between NEMA Chicago on the left and The Grant Luxury Condos on the right—two skyscrapers barely fifty meters apart. Across Grant State Park, Ida B. Wells and East Jackson Drives, over the top of the Art Institute of Chicago . . . and straight into the mouth of the amphitheater.

14

James O'Dell never dreamed of working for the president. In fact, if he'd had his way, he never would've worked for anyone. After washing out of Basic Underwater Demolition School, the U.S. Navy's training camp for SEALs, O'Dell swore he'd never fail himself again, and he set his sights on building his own version of the Teams.

Ambitions of being the owner of a private security firm staffed by veterans and serving the world's premier corporations were sidelined when his wife left him. Their daughter was only eight at the time. Vickie took off on a Tuesday night, little Holly in tow, and ran all the way to Austin before O'Dell even knew she was gone.

Suddenly the appeal of operating a travel-intensive business was squelched, and O'Dell was determined instead to do whatever it took to get Holly back. He attended Law Enforcement Academy, was hired by the Louisiana State Police, and became a patrolman. Seeking further stability, he transferred to the executive protection division and worked his way up through the Louisiana Senate, the Attorney General's Office, and then the Office of the Governor.

That was where he met Maggie, and right away, he knew she was something special. More than special, Muddy Maggie Trousdale was electric.

She took the state by storm and went straight to work, tearing through the ingrained corruption she swore to destroy.

The first time they met, he was serving as her driver, and she asked him if he knew how to use his weapon. After he affirmed, she said, "Excellent. You just might have to." And he did. Several times. Maggie Trousdale's rise from unknown governor of a state nobody cared about to the highest office in the land was as meteoric as everything else about her crazed life, but O'Dell clung on and embraced the chaos.

Why shouldn't he? Holly wouldn't talk to him and hadn't spoken a word to him since her twelfth birthday, two years before. Vickie had effectively poisoned his daughter's mind against him, leaving him with nothing other than his work. Work . . . and Muddy Maggie. The swamp girl turned president of the United States.

He stood in the shadows at the perimeter of the amphitheater and watched as she took the stage, walking gracefully, but without any of the pretentious poise of a polished politician. She looked like an average American, who, by mistake or fate, had landed on that stage. She looked that way because she *was* that way. He watched her grin and shoot the peace sign at a group of college kids waving Trousdale–Stratton campaign signs, then lift her face toward the far reaches of the park and raise her arm in an open wave.

She was so relaxed. So perfectly herself. And radiant at the same time. Like a falling star, consuming this moment in the galaxy.

O'Dell looked down at the cell phone still clamped in his hand. One of the Secret Service agents posted nearby gave him the side-eye, and he self-consciously dropped the phone into an interior pocket of his jacket, then straightened his back and adjusted his sunglasses. All business. Protecting the president. The only thing that got him out of bed in the morning was keeping Maggie safe.

He'd seen her life threatened before—twice—both as governor and president. He'd be damned if she was ever so much as scratched on his watch.

"Hello, Chicago!" Maggie took her place behind the podium, still beaming. O'Dell shifted his position to the left, giving him a better view of the packed amphitheater. Across the park beyond it, another twenty thousand onlookers crowded in, waving more signs and cheering. They felt the same authenticity O'Dell felt. The same special something that had propelled Maggie all the way to the top and would keep her there.

Because if there was one thing he knew, it was that Wednesday morning, Maggie Trousdale would wake up president-elect of the United States. It was as sure a thing as the sun rising.

"Wow! You guys really know how to make a girl feel welcome."

O'Dell swept the crowd, looking for somebody who stuck out or didn't belong. It was cold, so hoodies and jackets were the norm. That made it difficult to search for weapons, but these people had already been searched and passed through metal detectors. He focused on their faces instead, looking for anger instead of joy. Angst instead of excitement. Anyone who might break ranks and catch a bullet.

The Glock 19 strapped beneath O'Dell's jacket was clean and oiled, and as he had told Maggie all the way back in Louisiana, he very much knew how to use it.

The noise died down as Maggie began her speech. She started with a few words about Chicago and Stratton. The crowd cheered at his name, albeit with a lot less enthusiasm, then she dove into policy—foreign and domestic. Economy and education. Global trade and national security.

O'Dell had heard it all before, but he had to admit—she was on fire today. Every word flowed with balance and ease, with no need for a teleprompter. Her passion carried her from point to point, propelling the crowd along with her—an unstoppable wave of change sweeping through the Windy City on its way to Washington.

O'Dell scanned the rear ranks of the crowd, working his way up the hill where twenty or thirty thousand additional onlookers were camped out. The faces began to blur, but with the sun directly overhead, there was nothing to obscure his vision. He watched dogs pacing on leashes in front of agents dressed in body armor and wielding AR-15s. They sniffed the rows of onlookers but didn't bark. There was nothing to worry about. Not there.

He repeated his inspection to the perimeters, along the south side of the park, then he moved to the back and turned toward the river. That was when he saw it—a brief orange flash, barely visible between two skyscrapers, more than a mile distant and gone in an instant. He shielded his eyes to aid the sunglasses, noting the spot and puzzling for a second.

Glass flashing in the sun? No, it was high noon. The sun was pointed directly down, which meant . . .

O'Dell broke ranks with the agents and hurled himself toward Maggie. The stage descended into slow motion as he cleared twenty feet in four quick strides, already reaching for her. Already screaming. Maggie's head pivoted toward him, confusion clouding her face. Somebody shouted into his earpiece, and O'Dell's hand collided with her arm, shoving her back.

Then the bullet struck—a hiss and a snap. Blood drained onto Maggie's dress, and the confusion in her face flashed to pain. His shoulder collided with her sternum like a charging linebacker, and they both hit the floor.

15

Stratton saw O'Dell move first. Maggie's bodyguard hurled himself out of right stage, screaming her name only a moment before he collided with her arm. The two of them collapsed, and then the Secret Service descended on the VP.

Cold hands grabbed his arms and yanked him back away from the stage, even as an army of agents closed over O'Dell and the president like ants swarming a crumb. Somebody forced his head down, and Stratton ran, barely keeping his feet as agents shoved him through the back door and down a row of steps. He didn't have time to think or question anything. The back door of the second presidential limousine was hurled open, and he was thrown inside. The motor roared, and somebody shouted from the back, "Haul ass!"

Tires screamed. Stratton tried to get up, but they held him down. His heart thundered, and his hands shook. The limousine hurtled around a corner with surprising agility, and blue lights flashed through the heavily tinted windows. They were already blocks from the park, racing toward the heliport where *Marine One* waited, ready to carry Maggie and her vice president back to the airport.

Then Stratton heard a voice barking in the earpiece of the agent sitting next to him—so loud he could easily make out the words from a few feet away.

"Saint is down! Repeat! Saint is down."

16

The Secret Service kept an ambulance on standby. It reached the amphitheater less than sixty seconds after O'Dell hit the floor, one shoulder slamming into the hard plywood while his right hand was clamped around Maggie's stomach.

There was blood everywhere. He felt it surging between his fingers and saturating her dress. Maggie's head rolled back, and her eyes closed.

O'Dell didn't know if she was unconscious or dead. He pressed against the wound as agents with submachine guns stormed the stage and blocked out the crowd. A stretcher appeared, and O'Dell felt Maggie being pulled from his hands. He struggled to hold on.

"Let go!" somebody shouted.

O'Dell saw Jenkins's stern face breaking through a haze of stress, and then Maggie left his arms. She hit the stretcher and was rocketed toward the rear of the amphitheater.

O'Dell found his feet. He ran, shoving through the mass of agents and keeping pace with the stretcher. The floor shook as the helicopter swept low overhead, snipers riding the open doors, their weapons sweeping the crowd.

Too little, too late.

The stretcher slid into the ambulance, and Jenkins jumped inside. The doors began to close, and O'Dell saw her slipping away as he hurled himself forward, blocking the door.

"Get in, or get out!" Jenkins shouted.

O'Dell got in. The door slammed, and the motor roared. His earpiece was flooded with communication—crisp orders laced with tension.

And one message echoing in his mind.

Saint is down.

Sirens screamed. The ambulance hurtled down the street, flanked by police cars and surging black Tahoes. O'Dell scrambled to his feet and pressed in next to Maggie.

Two paramedics and Jenkins huddled around her motionless form. They had already cut her dress, slitting it from the bottom hem up to her sternum, and Jenkins was holding pressure over the wound. The bullet had entered the left side of her stomach, a few inches below the ribcage. Maggie's face was washed white, and O'Dell thought he saw her eyelids flicker.

He shoved in next to Jenkins and grabbed her hand, squeezing tight and calling over the roar of sirens. "Hold on!"

The paramedics shoved Jenkins out of the way, and the head of Maggie's detail stepped back, lifting his wrist to his mouth. "Saber One to all channels. Saint en route to Lakeside Memorial. Condition uncertain. Establish a security perimeter, and block all access routes."

Confirmation orders crackled through O'Dell's earpiece, and he heard the chopper roar directly overhead. He looked to Jenkins and saw something he'd never before seen in the stone-faced agent—fear.

Lakeside Memorial Hospital lay less than two miles from the amphitheater. It was predesignated by the Secret Service as the medical center of choice in the event of an emergency, and medical staff were already on standby—standard operating procedure for any presidential travel. But as O'Dell watched Maggie's blood dripping onto the floor, he wondered if it was already too late.

"All channels, be advised. Rook is secure. Repeat, Rook is secure."

Stratton.

The vice president's detail would've separated from Maggie's immediately following the shot, rushing him first to *Marine One* and then to the airport. Just like 9/11, the safest place for Stratton would be high in the clouds, secluded within *Air Force One*.

Or, it should be, anyway. O'Dell's mind flashed back to the previous year when Brandt went down in flames. His stomach twisted, and for the first time, he gave momentary thought to what the hell was happening. But it didn't matter. Not now. Only Maggie mattered.

The ambulance hurtled under the emergency pavilion, and O'Dell shoved the doors open before they even stopped. Tahoes screamed into place behind them to block off the parking lot, then Maggie's stretcher was on the move again, down onto the concrete, wheels clicking into place. Through the sliding glass doors, a wall of Secret Service agents with guns drawn cordoned off a passageway straight into triage.

O'Dell ran, one hand on the stretcher, one hand clutching Maggie's. Her fingers were limp, but her eyelids fluttered over an oxygen mask. A mess of bandages and wound sealant covered her stomach as blood continued to drip off the stretcher. When the doors opened, somebody shouted for the on-call surgeon.

Maggie was raced into surgery, and a big guy dressed in scrubs put his hand on O'Dell's chest and pushed back. O'Dell tried to fight, but the stretcher rushed on. Maggie's hand tore free of his. He slipped and caught himself against the wall as the doors clapped shut.

And then she was gone.

17

The interior of the yacht's main salon was dark, but the man sitting in the corner liked it that way. He leaned back in a luxurious leather chair and dragged slowly on a cigar, the orange tip the only thing illuminating the room. All the windows were shut, covered with automatic blinds, but he could hear the ocean outside. The waves were high that day, rocking the three-hundred-fifty-foot boat.

But the room was quiet, as was the rest of the yacht. The fifteen-person crew knew to leave him alone, and they were only too happy to oblige.

He sucked on the cigar, listening to the crinkle of burning tobacco, and blew smoke out between his teeth. The flavor was rich and exotic, a premium stick from Nicaragua—a daily luxury for the man in the shadows. A spark in a life otherwise dull and oppressive. Like eating filet mignon in jail.

The yacht might be worth half a billion dollars, and he might've been one of the wealthiest men on the planet, but that didn't make him any less a prisoner of circumstance. Even the wealthiest, most powerful men could be ostracized.

A blue glow flashed from the table next to him, and the man clamped the cigar between his teeth, punching a button on his armrest.

"Is it done?" he growled.

"I don't know."

The man on the phone spoke with a muted Russian accent—easily confusable for any manner of Slavic dialect. But the man with the cigar knew better. He knew all about the limping sniper—the man they called The Ghost. And he liked to keep him at a distance. A *long* distance.

"What do you mean? Did you shoot her or not?"

"I shot, but before she was struck, one of her bodyguards pushed her. The bullet hit low. They took her to the hospital."

The man with the cigar chewed the end of the tobacco and twisted the stick in his mouth, contemplating. Evaluating. Bottling his frustration and calculating his next move. "What do you think?"

The Ghost took his time answering. "It's a large bullet. Even a gutshot could be devastating."

"But you don't know?"

"No. The best thing is to watch the media. Let them tell us."

He continued chewing on the cigar. "Where are you?"

"Laying low," The Ghost said. "I left the city."

"No trouble?"

"No trouble. Not yet."

The man in the yacht spat bits of tobacco across the floor. "Stay where you are. Call me when you hear something. If she's still alive, we'll have to try again."

"That may not be possible. They'll increase security."

The man in the yacht jabbed his cigar toward the shadows. "When I hired you, they told me you are the best. Is it true or not?"

"I'll call you when I know," The Ghost said.

18

Reed stood in the driveway, blasting the front bumper of the family SUV with a garden hose to wash away the biological fallout of an obliterated opossum. Bits of hair and rodent flesh broke free of the bright red paint, and he felt a twinge of regret for the hapless critter.

It was his fault, really. Banks had been asleep, and Reed drifted off along with her. His eyes never closed, but his mind sort of shut down. He saw the opossum on the shoulder and knew he was drifting. He just didn't think to do anything about it. Not until bone met bumper and Banks sat up with a frightened shriek.

Reed dropped his hand into the water and ran it over his face, shaking his head to clear it. Then he blasted the gore off the driveway and began to wind up the hose.

Their car was a Volkswagen Tiguan—some small SUV that Banks liked. She drove a VW Beetle when they met, and even though the Tiguan had about as much in common with that antique as Reed had in common with the deceased opossum, she loved it.

Reed wrote a check for the SUV, brand-new off the lot. Thirty-four thousand of his payout from the North Korean mission six months earlier.

Then they bought a car seat for Davy and a seat cover for Baxter, the family bulldog. Grocery trips merged into a Costco membership, and they used the new Volkswagen to haul home a barbecue grill.

Reed had never felt so suburban. But he liked it.

He cut the water off and stood over the spigot, his mind unoccupied. He felt like something should be in there, though—like there was something he was thinking about or should be thinking about. All he saw was damp brick and the wound-up hose with a little green lizard crawling up it.

He blinked, and the lizard vanished. Had it been there at all?

I need to sleep.

He wiped his face and turned for the door, then he heard a scream.

"Reed!"

It was Banks. Reed broke for the door, rushing inside and already reaching for SIG in his belt. He didn't know why. It wasn't a conscious thought—just an automatic response fueled by a decade of muscle memory.

He cleared the kitchen and made it to the living room, finding Banks standing frozen over the carpet. She held Davy, and he slept peacefully despite her shout. Reed swept the room, looking to the sliding glass door and then to Baxter.

All was calm. Nothing was wrong.

"What is it?" he said, his hand still resting on the SIG.

Banks stared blankly at the TV. The sound was off, but colors flashed from a news broadcast. Reed pivoted toward the screen, watching as the picture switched from news anchors to a replay. It was some manner of amphitheater. Reed saw a crowd waving signs, and then the camera panned to Maggie Trousdale standing behind a podium, one arm raised. As Reed watched, a black-suited man blazed out of the shadows. He hit her in the shoulder, and red sprayed across the podium before they both went down. The screen froze, and a tape ran across the bottom half.

President Trousdale Shot — Condition Unknown.

Reed released the pistol, his hand slumping at his side. The anchors talked while a split screen played the clip again. It was all a blur. There was confusion on Maggie's face . . . and then pain.

"Reed . . ." Banks whispered.

He watched the clip a third time, and then his phone buzzed in his pocket. He didn't need to check the caller ID to know who it was.

"You watching?" Turk said.

"Yeah."

"Heard from O'Dell?"

"No. Nothing."

Banks wrapped her arms around Reed's shoulder and pressed her mouth against his arm.

Turk said, "I think we will be."

19

O'Dell wouldn't leave the hospital. From triage, Maggie was rushed immediately into surgery, but almost five hours had passed, and still, he'd heard nothing.

They marooned him in a waiting room, where he paced the floor, checking his phone every couple minutes for word from Jenkins or one of the other Secret Service agents. Stratton, maybe. Anyone.

But nobody called. The entire floor of the hospital had been cleared, leaving only an army of agents and medical staff that were necessary for Maggie's care. Outside, the streets around the hospital were swarmed by cops and unmarked SUVs, and the helicopter snipers from before were now joined by three military choppers, all churning in endless circles around North Chicago.

Barricading. Protecting.

But it was already too late. Saint was already down.

O'Dell collapsed into a chair and dropped his face into his hands. He saw the flash on the horizon again and relived those precious moments where he stood like a fool and wondered what he'd seen. Of *course* it was a gunshot. From a long way away, beyond the Secret Service's protective radius, apparently. So far away, it took seconds for the bullet to make impact.

Precious seconds O'Dell wasted, gawking at the skyline like a moron.

He punched himself in the leg. His knuckles made impact with an explosion of pain, and he saw Maggie stumble again. He could feel the impact of the slug radiating through her body and into his. He could see the shock and fear in her eyes. And then they hit the floor.

Why hadn't he been quicker? Not a second. Half a second. Enough to place himself in front of her and block the shooter's path with his own body.

The shooter.

The edges of O'Dell's vision turned red. He thought about the impossible distance and that glimmer of fire far to the south. Who had pulled that trigger?

And why?

O'Dell clawed the phone from his pocket, dialing Jenkins first. He wasn't surprised to be bumped to voicemail, so he moved down his contact list to Jenkins's boss—Samuel French, director of the entire Agency.

O'Dell wasn't supposed to have his number. He stole it from Jenkins's desk when the agent wasn't looking, just in case there was ever a moment when he needed to skip straight to the top. A moment like this.

"Hello?" French was all business.

"Mr. Director, it's James O'Dell."

French growled. "How did you get this number?"

"Is she alive?" O'Dell barked.

French didn't answer.

O'Dell clutched the phone to the side of his head. "Mr. Director . . . please."

"I don't know. She's still in surgery. Where are you?"

"At the hospital," O'Dell said. "They locked me out. They—"

"Are you hurt?" French demanded.

"No, sir. I—"

"Go back to your hotel. Wait for Jenkins. And don't call me again." French hung up.

O'Dell cursed and slammed his phone against his side. He ran a hand through his hair and paced, his heart beginning to race. He saw the flash again. Saw Maggie fall. Heard the breath leave her lungs as he collapsed on top of her.

O'Dell flung the phone, screaming at the wall. It shattered against the drywall, and he fell back into a chair. He should've died. He should've taken that bullet.

Urgent footsteps tapped in the hallway. O'Dell looked up to see a doctor in a surgical apron rushing by, his face hidden behind a surgical mask.

O'Dell bolted, reaching the door and wheeling around the corner as the doctor peeled the mask off and turned for a restroom.

"Wait!" O'Dell called.

The door clapped shut, but O'Dell followed. He barreled through just as the guy was lining up with a urinal, peeling his pants open.

"Doctor!"

The surgeon jumped, one hand rising defensively, then he saw the government ID badge clipped to O'Dell's belt, and he caught his breath. "What the hell?"

"Is she alive?" O'Dell demanded.

The surgeon wiped sweat from his forehead with the back of one hand. "Who are you?"

"I'm her bodyguard!"

The surgeon zipped his pants and turned for the door, apparently uninterested in urinating. "You should go before I call security."

"I *am* security!"

The surgeon reached for the door, but O'Dell caught him by the arm. "Please . . . I need to know. Is she alive?"

The surgeon stopped. For a moment, he swept O'Dell up and down, pausing over the bloodstains and dirt. "You pushed her?"

O'Dell nodded.

The surgeon peeled his glasses off and pulled his arm free of O'Dell's grasp.

"She's alive," he said softly. "The bullet broke apart on impact. Fragments splintered through her intestines and stomach. One kidney is completely gone, but the liver is the worst of it. The core of the bullet tore right through the top. We've stabilized her for the moment, but it will take hours to remove all the shrapnel. Maybe all day. And if her liver can't be saved—"

"Does she need a transplant? Take mine."

The surgeon replaced his glasses slowly. "Breathe, son. You did your job. We'll do ours."

The surgeon left the room, abandoning O'Dell in the smell of harsh cleaners and cold tile. He stood dumbfounded, imagining the shattering bullet. Like a shotgun blast, right to the gut.

O'Dell pushed through the bathroom and back down to the hall to the waiting room. He found his phone on the floor, busted from the impact with the wall. He frantically fought with the power button, but it wouldn't turn on. The screen flashed pixilated red, green, and blue, and he slung it into the trash.

He reached impulsively into his pocket for a cigarette, but his fingers hit something harder instead. Maggie's cell phone.

20

Air Force Two took off the moment Stratton was safely inside, and within minutes, he was gliding thirty thousand feet over Illinois, turning west. Because the pilots had to fly somewhere, and west was as good a direction as any. Just so long as he wasn't on the ground being shot at.

They put him in the conference room, his team of Secret Service agents operating like a battalion of trained Marines. They didn't wait or ask for orders. They rushed him into that room and asked him to buckle in, and then the door shut.

Stratton might have objected, but no sooner had the seatbelt sign clicked off than the phone on his desk rang. It was Jill Easterling, Maggie's chief of staff. Then it was Nick West, director of National Security, followed by the secretary of defense, Steve Kline.

They all barked through the phone with a mixture of panic and reassurance, as if they couldn't decide whether Stratton worked for them or they worked for him. For his part, his brain was consumed by such a fog of shock and disorientation, he wasn't sure if he could decide, either.

He ordered the SecDef to assemble an emergency meeting of the National Security Council, then ended the call and dialed French.

The director of the Secret Service answered on the first ring.

"Sir?"

"What happened?" Stratton said.

French responded with smooth proficiency, sticking to the facts.

"She was shot, Mr. Vice President. Condition is critical. I just got off the phone with the surgeon, and he said her intestines and stomach are shredded but should be repairable. She'll lose a kidney. The worst of it is her liver. They've sedated her, and she's undergoing surgery to remove the projectiles."

"Projectiles? More than one?"

"The bullet fragmented on impact, sir. Not unusual at that range."

"At *what* range?"

This time French hesitated. "We're still gathering intelligence. We don't know where the shooter fired from yet, but our security perimeter wasn't breached, and it extends fifteen hundred yards in every direction. We maintain surveillance beyond that distance, also. So, for the shooter to have evaded us . . . At least two thousand yards. Probably farther."

"Two thousand yards? Is that even possible?"

"I don't know, sir. We're investigating now. I'll keep you posted."

Stratton wiped his forehead. He was sweating, despite the chill of the conference room. "See that you do. I want all updates for the entire investigation routed through my office. Nothing hits the press without my approval. Am I clear? Nothing."

"Yes, sir."

Stratton moved to hang up, but French caught him. "Sir?"

"What?"

"I take full responsibility. You'll have my resignation the moment our investigation concludes."

"I don't want your apology, Mr. Director. I want results. Call me."

He hung up, flexing the fingers of his left hand between his right and popping the knuckles one at a time. The conference room felt very quiet and still. It had been only two days since he met there with Maggie and Jennifer Holmes, planning the resolution of the campaign.

That felt like a lifetime ago.

Something buzzed in his pocket, and Stratton sat up. He dug his cell phone out, expecting to see his father's name plastered across the screen.

Barrett Stratton II was sixty-four, up to his neck in the political power circles of the Midwest, and a constant presence just outside the limelight of Stratton's vice presidency. Even with details of the shooting closely guarded, it was a guarantee that Barrett already knew more about the event than any journalist in the state, and he would be calling to press his own agenda.

But it wasn't Barrett Stratton whose name illuminated the screen. It was Maggie Trousdale.

Stratton's gut lurched, and his palms began to sweat. He hit the answer button without thinking, blurting out a question. "Maggie?"

"Mr. Vice President, it's O'Dell."

The voice was so unexpected, it took Stratton a moment to reset. Before he could respond, O'Dell plowed on.

"They say the president needs a liver. I'm ready to donate mine. But she needs more medical staff. Better doctors. The surgeon here is worn out—"

"Stop!" Stratton cut him off. "How the hell are you calling me?"

"I have the president's phone, sir."

"It wasn't locked?"

"I used Siri."

Stratton bit back a curse. "That's illegal use of government property. I don't have time for this. Don't call—"

"Sir." O'Dell's voice popped like a bullwhip. "The president is *dying*. I won't let that happen. I need you to call somebody. We have to find a liver."

"You want to find something? You find the shooter. You do your job for a change. And don't call me again!"

Stratton hung up and threw his phone across the room. He gulped down water from a glass on the table and hit the intercom key on the desk phone.

"Yes, sir?"

"Turn the air down," he snapped.

"Yes, sir."

Stripping off his tie, Stratton tossed it next to his phone. He thought about O'Dell and the moment he watched the big Cajun hurtling across the stage floor, ramming Maggie aside. Shifting her away from the bullet. Was it enough to save her? Maybe. But they wouldn't know for hours. Maybe days.

And in the meantime . . . he was president.

21

O'Dell clenched his fingers around the phone. He almost called back, but he knew the vice president wouldn't answer. It was a one-time trick, and Stratton wouldn't help him, anyway. He thought about what it would take to give Maggie his liver. He knew a person couldn't live without a liver, and the doctor couldn't carve his body apart while he was still breathing. He'd need to eat a bullet first.

But before he could do that, he needed to sign something and make sure she got what she needed. He needed to make sure red tape didn't get in the way. He began to pace again, frustration and panic filling his body until his fingers shook. He wanted to punch something. He wanted to punch *somebody.*

But there was no one to blame other than himself. He'd been on watch when Maggie was shot. He'd seen the muzzle flash and failed to move in time. If she died, her blood was on his hands.

He placed one palm against the cold glass of a window.

Think.

Maggie wasn't dead yet, and neither was he. What did she need from him right now?

The doctors wouldn't discuss the liver issue until they finished removing the shrapnel and assessing the damage. If she could speak, what would Maggie ask him to do?

Find the shooter. Do your job.

Stratton's harsh words cut through him like a scalpel, and O'Dell's face snapped up. He pocketed Maggie's cell phone and turned for the hallway, taking the elevator to the ground floor and stripping his tie and coat off. The last thing he was worried about was official dress code.

In the lobby, he was greeted by a storm of government personnel and medical staff, all working in a chaotic soup as the hospital struggled to accommodate the Secret Service's sudden and demanding intrusion. Patients were rushed by in wheelchairs and rolling beds, an ambulance flashed outside, and news media lined the sidewalk beyond an improvised barricade.

O'Dell hurried right through it, clearing the front doors and flashing his badge at an agent who accosted him. "I need a vehicle!"

"Huh?" The guy looked at him like he was crazy, then hurried to push back a reporter who was moving to breach the barrier.

O'Dell scanned the street, past the rows of Chicago police cars and three ambulances, to the end of the line, where a Secret Service Tahoe idled by itself. The door was open, and the driver was busy working with his partner to open a lane for another ambulance.

O'Dell ran, breaking through the agents and past the reporters and then sliding into the Tahoe without bothering for permission. He slammed the door and shifted into gear, laying on the horn as he busted free of the perimeter. In his rearview, he saw the agent running after him, shouting and waving a fist.

Within moments, he was back in the crush of Chicago traffic, hopping a curb to move around a line of stopped vehicles before steering south, back to Millennium Park.

He made it half an hour later. It took time to fight his way through the swarm of curious citizens and busybodies who had descended on North Chicago, heedless of personal safety or legal ramifications as they fought for a glimpse of the place where the president was shot.

The crowd of fifty thousand from hours earlier had long since departed, and the park was completely cordoned off. Yellow FBI tape circled every entrance, and more Chicago PD blocked the street ahead.

O'Dell hit the brakes, rolling his window down and flashing his government ID at the nearest cop. "I'm with the Secret Service." It was kind of true. "Who's in charge here?"

The guy pointed to a black semi-truck parked a hundred yards away, an FBI command trailer resting on stabilizer arms behind it. O'Dell hit the gas without waiting for directions, plowing past a sawhorse barrier and not stopping until he cut the engine off next to the semi.

A stream of FBI agents in black and yellow windbreakers moved in and out of pop-up tents surrounding one side of the trailer, while some guy in a cheap suit shouted orders. Radios crackled. Cell phones rang. But despite the apparent chaos, everybody appeared busy.

O'Dell left the Tahoe and barged right in, bloody shirt and all. He approached the guy in the cheap suit and cut him off in the middle of another shouted order. "Are you in charge?"

"That's right. Who are you?"

"James O'Dell, presidential security detail."

Something flashed across the guy's face, and O'Dell imagined what he was thinking.

Your fault.

It was true, but O'Dell didn't have time to bellyache. He had work to do. For Maggie.

"I saw the shooter," O'Dell said.

The guy's countenance changed immediately. He motioned O'Dell to a quiet corner of what appeared to be the command tent and then lowered his voice.

"You *saw* the shooter? As in, his face?"

O'Dell hesitated. "No, not his face. I was standing on the stage when the shot was fired. I saw the muzzle flash. I was the one who tackled the president."

Momentary frustration at O'Dell's initial statement faded to respect, and possibly sympathy, when he mentioned tackling Maggie. The guy watched him without comment, and O'Dell gestured to the south toward the high-rise where he'd seen that momentary blast of orange.

"I think I know where he fired from. I can show you."

The guy didn't break eye contact or seem impressed by the information. "You brought her down?"

O'Dell nodded, feeling suddenly ashamed, remembering again those costly seconds he had wasted wondering. Doubting.

"Come with me," the agent said. He left the tent, and O'Dell trailed him past the semi-truck to another government Tahoe. The FBI agent got behind the wheel and motioned for him to ride shotgun, then he hit the emergency lights and turned south toward the high-rise.

"I'm Baker," the guy said at last. "Special agent in charge . . . at least until the director arrives."

"The director of the FBI?"

Baker shot him a sideways look. "Isn't *your* director on the way?"

O'Dell didn't answer, but he figured it was probably true. There couldn't be a more critical investigation than this. The politics alone were over-whelming.

"I think it was an apartment building," O'Dell said. "Maybe a business tower. It was hard to see."

"Lake View Apartments, eighteenth floor," Baker said. "We already found it."

The street leading south alongside Millennium Park was already mostly clear, having been cordoned off by Chicago PD. What cars remained moved quickly out of the way as Baker drove hard, not stopping until he pulled into a parking lot across from a tower rising out of downtown Chicago and blocking out the lake only half a mile away.

Baker cut the motor but didn't reach for the door handle. Instead, he drew a toothpick from a container in his pocket, placing it absently between his lips and staring up at the building.

O'Dell traced his line of sight to the eighteenth floor. He couldn't see anything from that angle—no open window, no yellow crime scene tape. But a knot of FBI vehicles was clustered around the building's entrance, and a steady stream of men and women in blue and yellow windbreakers moved in and out like ants.

"He fired from a kitchen table," Baker said, rolling the toothpick between his lips. "The rifle is gone, and there are no shell casings. But of course, it was high-caliber. He cut a corresponding hole in the window. I'm surprised you saw the flash."

"I saw it," O'Dell said.

Baker looked back to the tower and twisted the toothpick between a forefinger and thumb. "There's a body."

"Huh?"

"Some kid. The registered occupant of the apartment. We don't know how he connected with her, but there were no signs of forced entry. She let him in willingly. Then he broke her neck."

O'Dell winced. "A kid?"

"Well. Twenty-something." Baker withdrew the toothpick. "You know how far it is from here to the stage?"

"No."

"Two thousand four hundred twenty-seven yards. One point three nine miles."

The numbers hung in the air like random digits. O'Dell tried to visualize the distance, but without a landmark, the number was simply arbitrary, like trying to picture a million dollars in cash.

"I want to see," O'Dell said. He reached for the door, but Baker shook his head.

"Consider what I've told you a professional courtesy. I don't envy your position—especially if what you told me is true. If you saw the muzzle flash . . . and waited."

O'Dell glared at Baker. "Excuse me?"

Baker shifted into gear. "This is an FBI investigation now. You want to help? Stay out of the way."

22

Reed sat at the family dinner table, Banks's laptop laid out in front of him, the TV running on mute in the background. CNN kept replaying the same video—Maggie on stage, passionately delivering a campaign speech only moments before a man in black tackled her and everybody screamed.

There was no footage of the gunshot, but the implication was obvious, and it was confirmed by the online research Reed had conducted over the past half hour. Margaret Trousdale, president of the United States, had been shot. Most media outlets confirmed that her condition was critical, but as of yet, nobody had reported her passing.

All anyone knew was that she was barricaded inside a Chicago hospital, and Vice President Jordan Stratton had yet to make a statement.

A board in the hallway creaked, signaling Banks's approach. Reed looked up from the computer as she entered the kitchen, hugging herself and still looking flushed from the Florida sunshine.

"Davy's asleep," she said.

Reed grunted but didn't answer. She walked to the fridge and brought him a beer, running a gentle hand across his back and reading over his shoulder.

Reed leaned back with a tired sigh and chugged the beer.

"Are you okay?" Banks asked.

"Sure. Why wouldn't I be?"

Banks sat down next to him. "I mean . . . you've known her awhile."

"Who? Trousdale? You run for office, you put a target on your back. I'm more curious about *how* it happened than why."

"I thought the Secret Service protected against snipers."

"They do. Very well." He sipped more beer, still staring at the screen, then he pointed to the TV at another slow-motion replay of the man in black tackling Maggie.

"That's O'Dell."

Banks nodded. "Yeah, I thought so."

Reed shut the laptop and twisted the bottle in one hand. Condensation ran over his fingers, and he focused on Maggie's face. The frown of shock quickly replaced by a twist of pain. The moment she was hit. But *how*?

Reed had spent a good portion of his life killing people. Not politicians. Not people like Maggie. Usually, they were crime bosses and mobsters. But weirdly, crime bosses and presidents had a lot in common. They were both incredibly well protected, sheltered behind a legion of professional body-guards, confined to armored vehicles and defensible buildings, and monitored day and night against attacks.

On more than one occasion, Reed had knocked off a VIP under similar protective circumstances. Once or twice he'd even done it with a precision, long-range shot.

But none of that compared to killing POTUS. Maggie Trousdale was easily one of the most protected people in the world, surrounded by a literal *army* of specialists who lived and breathed her security. The Secret Service knew more about keeping a person safe than any organization on the planet. Which meant, if she was shot, there were only two possible ways it could have happened: either it was an inside job, or the shooter was a long, *long* way away. Much farther than anybody expected or accounted for.

Reed picked up the remote and switched the TV off. He cupped Banks's hand in his and offered her a gentle smile.

"You know something? You look amazing with a tan."

Banks rolled her eyes and looked away. He could see the stress in her

face, and it made him sick to his stomach. Far too much of their relationship had been consumed by that strain. It had aged them both, and not in a
good way. He wouldn't let that poison back in, especially after investing a
week at the beach to wash it away.

"I'm starving," Reed said. "Pizza?"

"Only if we watch *Grey's Anatomy*."

Reed feigned an abused groan. "You're killing me, woman."

She giggled and went for the phone. Reed finished his beer, still
watching the black TV screen and thinking about Trousdale.

It's not my problem.

Banks dialed up the pizza place. He heard the guy on the other end
rambling through specials, then his cell phone buzzed in his pocket.

Reed stiffened, pretending for a moment that he'd imagined it—
wishing that he'd imagined it. The phone rang again, and he almost hit the
power button and tossed it into the trash. But instead, he looked at the
screen and recognized the contact.

James O'Dell.

Reed stepped onto the back patio before he hit the answer button.

O'Dell spoke in an endless stream of barely coherent gibberish. He
sounded like a shell-shocked Marine. "Reed? It's O'Dell. Where are you? I
need you on a plane."

Reed slid the glass door shut. "What happened?"

Reed heard a muted curse followed by the blare of a car horn. O'Dell
was driving.

"She was shot," O'Dell said. "She's in surgery. I need your help."

"I *know* she was shot. The whole world knows. I'm asking *how*."

"A sniper, obviously! Are you listening to me?"

Reed settled into a patio chair, taking his time to respond. He'd known
O'Dell about as long as he'd known Maggie, and there was little love lost
between them. Reed accepted some responsibility for that—he'd
kidnapped Maggie during the early days of the Resilient investigation,
leaving O'Dell looking like a fool. It was a complex time full of conflicting
priorities. But now, O'Dell was calling him, wanting *his* help.

"How far?" Reed asked.

"Twenty-four hundred yards. Give or take."

Reed did a double-take, processing the number but still struggling to grasp it. "Are you sure?"

"That's what the FBI said. They found the place he shot from. It was outside our security perimeter. Look, I don't have time to talk about this. I'm headed back to the hospital now, and I need you headed this way. You and Turk both. I need you up here investigating. We have to find this guy."

"What you need is to calm down. Is the president alive?"

"She's alive, but she may need a liver. The bullet fragmented on impact. If it *was* a bullet. I mean, that's an impossible shot, right? The FBI has to be wrong. It's over a mile."

Reed rubbed his chin, focusing on a rotting fence plank in the backyard and traveling back in time to his years with the Marine Corps as a Force Recon sniper. He'd made a lot of long shots in his day—eleven, twelve, and even thirteen hundred yards on steel targets. He'd made a kill shot once at just over a thousand. A long shot, even for the best military shooters. Not an average day, by any means. He'd never met anyone who claimed a kill shot beyond twelve hundred. Let alone twice that.

And yet . . .

"It's possible," Reed said.

"At over a mile?"

"Back in Afghanistan, some Canadian guy made a kill at about that range. The Australian commandos claim to have made kills at over three thousand yards. It's definitely possible, but the range isn't the issue."

"What do you mean?"

"I mean that Canadian guy took a few shots before he made a hit. I would assume the Australians did, also. But your shooter made contact on the first shot. Cold bore. In one of the windiest cities in America."

"What are you saying?"

"I'm saying he's a *freak*," Reed said, "or else you're reading this all wrong. I'm saying there are maybe six people on the planet who could make a shot like that, cold bore, without a spotter. And I'm sure as hell not one of them, which leads me to ask why you think I can help."

"The FBI cut me out of the investigation. They won't even let me see the shooting position."

"I don't blame them. You're not an investigator. Let them do their job."

"But they're taking too long. You know what to look for. You were a sniper, right? You might see something they don't."

"The FBI keeps hundreds of subject matter experts on speed dial. There's nothing I can add they won't already know. You should let them work."

Reed heard a gearshift grind, then a motor died. O'Dell's strained breaths quieted for a change, and Reed almost thought he'd hung up.

"Reed, I'm asking you."

"Asking me for *what*?"

"I . . . I saw the shot. I mean, not the shot. The muzzle flash. I thought it was the sun, but by the time I put it together . . ."

Reed connected the dots but said nothing.

"It's my fault," O'Dell said. "I should've moved quicker. But I can't change that now. All I can do is find the shooter. And *you* owe me a favor."

"How do you figure?"

"If it weren't for me, you'd still be sweltering away down in Honduras, raising a kid on the run. I'm the one who put my neck on the line to go down there and find you."

Reed snorted. "Trousdale wrote the pardon, not you."

"So, you owe it to her, then. The point is you *owe*."

Reed chewed his lip.

"I've never asked you for anything," O'Dell said. "And I'll never ask again. But I need this."

The glass door grumbled on its track, and Banks stepped out. Reed didn't look up. He ended the call, not bothering to give O'Dell an answer.

Banks settled into the chair next to him. "O'Dell?"

Reed nodded.

"What does he want?"

"Help investigating, I guess. He's desperate."

Banks brushed dirty-blonde hair behind one ear and turned bright blue eyes on him. "You going?"

He took her hand, running his thumb over smooth skin, losing himself in those wide pools of blue, just as he had a thousand times before.

But he didn't answer. He didn't have to.

23

Los Angeles, California

The past seven months had been a whirlwind for Turk. After returning from a gritty undercover op in North Korea, he'd been only too glad to set foot on American soil again. A battered body and ears that still rang from the gunfire in Pyongyang begged him to return to his quiet East Tennessee home and sleep for a month.

But then there was Sinju, the daughter of the North Korean defector Reed and Turk had infiltrated the Hermit Kingdom to recover. Sinju was an unexpected—and at first, unwelcome—addition to their extraction plan.

That was until he first looked into her hazel brown eyes and felt something click deep inside of him. Gok Sinju was four years his junior, spoke only passing English, and was about as traumatized by her North Korean upbringing as anybody had a right to be. But beyond the fear, the bruises left on her face by concentration camp prison guards, and her shaken faith in humanity, there was something special about her that defied logic.

More than logic. It defied reality itself. Despite what the young Korean had endured, her hope for a brighter world on the far side of the ocean was unquenchable. Sinju was curious. She was passionate. She was more American in her devotion to freedom than most natural-born citizens.

And Turk was desperately in love with her.

He'd been in love before—or thought he had. But those feelings of temporary infatuation, affection, or simple lust paled in comparison to being with her. The CIA hadn't expected any of Gok Chin-ho's family to request asylum alongside him in the States, so when Sinju arrived in California, they put her up in a small apartment on the poor side of Los Angeles and pretty much ignored her.

She might have found herself on the street, or else deported if it hadn't been for Turk. He booked a hotel and spent the first month with her, guiding her through the city, helping her with immigration, and ensuring that she would never again live outside the land of the free. And then, when it was time for him to return to Tennessee, she asked him to stay.

Reed warned him that she was hot for a fiancée visa, and he might've been right. But Turk didn't really care. The long days and longer nights he spent alongside Sinju were the best of his life. It was the only time he felt whole since leaving the Marine Corps almost four years prior. And all he wanted was to make that feeling last forever.

Turk sat behind the wheel of his rental car and watched Sinju wave from her apartment door, her cheeks red and puffy. He waved back with a soft smile, feeling something dry in his throat and hot in his stomach. For a moment, he almost reached for the keys. He almost switched the car off, abandoned his flight, and rushed up the steps to sweep her off her feet again.

But he'd already rescheduled his trip back to Tennessee twice, and he was fifteen minutes late. He hadn't been home for more than two or three nights at a time in nearly six months, and his cousin was growing impatient with looking after Turk's four-year-old golden retriever. He had to go home, at least for a while. Long enough to think about what the next steps could look like. Long enough to list the house and find an apartment of his own in SoCal.

He never thought he'd leave Tennessee, and he still didn't want to. But the days when he watched Sinju fade in his rearview mirror were growing short. He was thinking about diamonds. He was thinking about forever.

Turk pulled away from the curb, settling back into his seat as the knot in his stomach tightened. He drove slowly, boarding time be damned, and cranked up the radio to kill the awful silence in the car.

Sinju talked constantly. Her English had improved a lot since reaching the States, and she loved to exercise it. At times, it grew tiresome. But the moment she was gone, the world felt so empty Turk would've given anything to listen to her ramble about supermarkets overflowing with produce and restaurants with menus four pages long.

No, he didn't mind the rambling. He'd listen to her ramble all day about anything. Just so long as he was with her.

Turk's phone buzzed, and his heart lurched. He looked at the screen, hoping to see Sinju's goofy grin smeared with soft serve ice cream, Disney Land rising in the background. She hated the picture. He adored it.

Instead, he saw a plain black screen with the name "Montgomery, R." plastered across the face.

Turk answered without hesitation, switching to speaker mode. "Hey, dude."

"Where you at?" Reed asked.

"Uh . . . Los Angeles. About to head home."

"Go ahead and switch that flight for Chicago. O'Dell called."

The knots in Turk's stomach heated into a hot weight, and he sat up. "What happened?"

"Sniper. Twenty-four hundred yards."

"Are you serious?"

"Yeah, I think so."

"What are we supposed to do about it?"

"O'Dell is in meltdown mode. I've never seen him like this. I think he's grasping at straws, but . . ."

"But?"

"Twenty-four hundred yards, Turk."

Turk accelerated on the freeway, following giant green signs for LAX. He licked his lips and thought back to his years in the Marine Corps serving as a Force Recon spotter. As Reed's spotter.

Turk wasn't a sniper—not even close. He could nail a deer at five or six hundred yards with the right rifle—a lot better than your average redneck, but nothing like Reed.

Still, it didn't take an expert shooter to know how impossible a distance twenty-four hundred yards was.

It was superhuman.

"You wanna have a look?" Turk asked.

"Yeah," Reed said. "I think I do."

"Okay. Meet me at O'Hare."

He hung up, then checked his watch. Thoughts of Sinju faded as he pictured himself behind a spotting scope, calculating the distance and reading off the wind as Reed lay behind his rifle, ready to kill. And then he thought about doubling their longest shot. Doubling, and then some.

Yeah. He understood why Reed wanted a look. And Turk thought he did, also.

24

An hour southeast of the Illinois State Capitol, the Stratton family had built a manor. Situated on a hundred acres of rolling farmland with a ten-acre fishpond, enough forest to attract whitetail deer during hunting season, and an oversized pool deck built behind the seven-thousand-square-foot mansion, it was truly the headquarters of a powerhouse family.

And it wasn't an accident that it lay so close to the capital city. The Strattons had been neck-deep in Illinois politics since Illinois was shipping soldiers to suppress the rebellion in the cotton states, and even though they had switched parties a few times, cozying up to the establishment or the revolutionaries as it suited them, they always seemed to land on top.

The sprawling, two-story home was a testament to Stratton's success and heritage alike, filled with photographs of prominent patriarchs shaking hands with governors and presidents. There was even a bust in the foyer, crafted after the likeness of Anthony Stratton, the first Stratton to ever set foot in Illinois and—supposedly—lay claim to this very plot of land.

Jordan Stratton knew it was all contrived nonsense—the heritage, the celebrated pedigree, and the transparent loyalty that each member of his extensive family claimed to all the others. The Strattons were savages, plain and simple. Pirates. Barbarians. Pillagers of cumulative opportunities, centuries in the making, which had eventually landed him in Washington. When he campaigned as a Republican for the United States Senate, the choice was strategic. It won him the lower half of the state.

And those liberals in Chicago? They might not be big on Republicans, but this wasn't just *any* Republican. This was a *Stratton*.

More BS. But even if he saw through the cracks in the century-old foundations of the family home, it was still the first place he thought to go when the world exploded around him, and the Secret Service was only too happy to oblige. They'd already familiarized themselves with the property during his frequent visits while serving as Trousdale's vice president. They were comfortable with the landscape and confident America's acting president could be better protected in rural Illinois than almost anywhere short of NORAD.

So, they landed *Air Force Two* at Scott Air Force Base outside of St. Louis, then flew him eighty-odd miles aboard *Marine Two* to the family home. By the time he landed, the place was crawling with Secret Service, from the property perimeters to the house itself. Everywhere he turned, he almost ran over a heavily armed agent, and the director of the Secret Service called to ask Stratton to remain on the property.

Now the manor felt more like a prison than a home, but that was nothing new. All things considered, Stratton was grateful to simply not be stuffed in some underground doomsday bunker across the country.

He stood on the balcony of the second floor, overlooking the rolling fields of the front fifty acres, the fishpond planted squarely in the middle of them. Night had fallen some two hours before, and he was confident that two or three dozen commandos equipped with automatic rifles and night vision monitored him from the deep shadows of the forest beyond the pond, but the simple fact that he couldn't see them gave him more peace than he'd felt in days.

Even if it was an illusion, it was good to feel alone.

Stratton dug into his suit jacket and liberated a cigar, tearing away the plastic and cupping his hand to light the tip. It was another Cuban, rich with the complex flavors of communism, authoritarian tyranny, and black-market capitalism.

A perfect cocktail.

Stratton tugged hard, allowing some of the smoke to slip past his throat and into his lungs before he blew out slowly. His body felt rigid, like a stretched rubber band only fractions of an inch from snapping, but he knew he was a long way from breaking. He couldn't afford to break. He was the vice president of the United States, and at any moment, he could take a call that promised an immediate promotion. Maggie's life hung in the balance. Stratton stood only one heartbeat away from the presidency.

A door creaked open behind him, and Stratton involuntarily closed his eyes. He heard a lighter spark at his elbow long before the visitor spoke, but the faint smell of expensive cologne was a dead giveaway. Barrett Stratton II never left bed without coating himself in the stuff—it was as much his trademark as the jet-black Bentley he drove or the way he always wore a suit but never a tie.

Barrett believed in making an impression his friends and foes alike would never forget. He believed in being a thermostat, not a thermometer, and he'd never been afraid to use brute force to make that happen.

"Any word?" Barrett asked.

Stratton shook his head, cradling the Cuban and accepting the glass of Kentucky bourbon Barrett passed him. It was as pungent and overbearing a drink as Barrett himself, but Stratton enjoyed the burn. He needed it to ease the strain on his mind.

Barrett snorted. "Leave it to a redneck to take a bullet and not have the courtesy to die."

Stratton sipped the whiskey, ignoring the comment. Barrett's feelings about Trousdale were both bullish and transparent. He held little respect for anyone from the South, but particularly disdained Cajuns. In Barrett's mind, Maggie was an interloper, an outsider who somehow found her way into the inner circles of American power and was now busy making waves she had no business making.

But for all his dedication to the establishment, Barrett was also an opportunist. Which was why, when Maggie tapped his oldest son for the job of vice president, Barrett was all over it. Be she an interloper or not, Maggie was a star. And the closer you drew to a star, the more that radioactive quality rubbed off on you.

Stratton himself didn't see it that way. Sure, he had his political differences with Maggie, and there were things she didn't know about—things she *couldn't* know about. But there was a momentum to her movement that was undeniable. It was lightning flashing across the sky, and he was intent on bottling it.

"Did you draw forty grand from the general fund last week?" Barrett asked, abruptly changing the subject.

Stratton flinched, caught off guard, but he didn't bother to lie. "Yes."

"Why?"

"Don't worry about it."

Barrett guzzled bourbon. "It's my money. Pardon me if I *do* worry about it."

Stratton sucked on his cigar, slow and methodical. He'd learned years before that the only way to manage his father was to challenge the tempo of his aggression. It was a ballsy move, but hell, he was vice president of the United States. Barrett could get in line. "I'm liquidating some stocks next week. I'll pay you back then."

Barrett snorted. "You think I care about a lousy forty grand? It's not the money, Jordan. It's the *why*."

Stratton faced him, cradling the bourbon. "And again, I say, don't worry about it."

Barrett's sly eyes glimmered in the dull balcony light. He had rodent eyes, Stratton thought. Not small, but calculating, reflecting a sharp and exceedingly shrewd mind.

"You got something you need to tell me, boy?"

Stratton snorted and drained his glass. "Better you didn't know."

"Watch yourself, Jordan," Barrett said. "If there's something that needs doing, you call me. Or call your brothers. You can't afford to leave fingerprints anymore. You're too valuable."

Jordan flicked ash off his cigar.

Barrett leaned in, tilting his head back. He was four inches shorter than his son, but no less muscular. Barrett Stratton took pride in extensive workouts, fancying himself a man's man, even if he'd never done a physical day's work in his life. "Are you using again?"

Stratton bristled, slamming the glass down. Barrett didn't blink. He crammed his cigar between his teeth and turned for the door.

"Don't forget where you came from, Jordan. I built your empire. I can tear it down, too." He reached for the door. "Goodnight, son."

Stratton watched him go, then flung the butt of his cigar off the porch and into the pool, fifteen feet below. He could play it cool in Barrett's presence. Keep calm and hold his head up. But nobody on Earth could get under his skin the way his old man could, and Barrett knew it.

Stratton reached for the bottle. Part of him wished he *was* using again. It would be a simpler problem to fix. Sweat ran down his scalp, and he thought about Maggie crumpling over on stage and O'Dell rushing in. He thought about the forty thousand dollars, quite possibly wasted.

Stratton reached for his phone. He never liked James O'Dell. The man was much more an interloper than their mutual boss, but without any of the benefits. He was arrogant and secretive, but maybe what irritated Stratton most was how Maggie held the Cajun in her confidence more than her own VP.

And yet, left alone, O'Dell was a liability. A loose cannon. Stratton couldn't afford either. If O'Dell was going to dig, Stratton would control where.

25

O'Dell was half-asleep, stretched out across multiple waiting room chairs, when Maggie's phone rang. He almost fell to the floor, scrabbling to dig it out of his pocket and recognizing the vice president's name across the screen.

The waiting room was dark, and as before, this floor of the hospital was dead quiet. But through the windows, he saw the steady flash of blue police lights against a black sky and remembered where he was. He remembered Maggie.

The phone buzzed again, and O'Dell sat up, answering quickly. "Hello?"

"James, it's Jordan. I hope I didn't wake you."

The vice president's words sounded soft, as though he were relaxed. Drunk, maybe?

"Of course not, sir. What can I do for you?"

"Actually . . . I was calling to apologize for my outburst earlier. You didn't deserve that. And I want to let you know how much I appreciate what you did for the president."

O'Dell wasn't sure what to say. He hadn't expected an apology or a call at all. He'd known Stratton for only a few months, but in O'Dell's experience, the man was aloof and austere, detached, and always seeming to hold something back. O'Dell didn't trust him. But he didn't really trust anyone.

"Thank you, sir," O'Dell said. "Is there any update? They still won't talk to me."

"None so far. You should really go home. There's nothing more you can do for her."

O'Dell stood, approaching the window. Outside, the army of Secret Service agents knotted around the main entrance worked slowly to process each and every person who filtered through the hospital. Everyone was searched. Everyone was questioned. No exceptions.

"Actually, sir, I'm glad you called. I need your help with something."

"What's up?"

"I called in some help for the investigation. People the president knows and trusts. They'll be here tomorrow, but we may need some authorizations. Access to the crime scene."

The phone went dead silent, but O'Dell waited it out.

"Who did you call?"

O'Dell rubbed his mouth. He didn't know where to start or how much the VP already knew. Stratton hadn't been around for the Turkey operation when Maggie became president, but he was there for the North Korean standoff seven months earlier.

O'Dell wasn't sure he knew about the Prosecution Force—the CIA's code name for the off-the-books strike team spearheaded by Reed Montgomery. He wasn't sure he wanted to tell him, either. But if he didn't, Stratton might not help. And in the unfathomable event that Maggie didn't survive, Stratton would need to know. He'd need Reed on hand.

"Are you alone, sir?" O'Dell said.

"Yes . . ."

O'Dell settled into his seat. "Mr. Vice President, there's something you should know."

26

Reed landed at eight a.m. and found Turk sleeping in the corner of a waiting area, slumped against a duffel bag. He toed him in the shin, and Turk sat bolt upright, making a fist and cocking it back.

His sleepy eyes met Reed's. "Damn you, Montgomery. You keep me waiting all night, then you shin-kick me?"

"I never said I was taking the red-eye. You want a coffee?"

Turk shouldered his bag, still grumbling, and they navigated to a convenience counter for two cups of cheap black caffeine, then to the rental car line for transportation. Reed carried only a small backpack with a single change of clothes and his toothbrush. Turk looked more heavily loaded, with the duffel, a backpack, and a small suitcase.

"Traveling heavy," Reed commented.

Turk scratched his unshaven face. "Yeah, well, I was headed home."

Reed surveyed the half-open lid of the duffel bag, noting the corner of bright red silk, lined with lace, poking from beneath a dirty T-shirt. He raised one eyebrow, and Turk flushed as he quickly zipped the bag.

"A memento?" Reed asked.

"Screw off."

They rented a compact SUV, and Reed paid. He figured he owed Turk that much for leaving him sleeping in an airport chair all night. They navigated to the garage and dumped Turk's gear in the back before Reed settled in behind the wheel of the VW Tiguan, like Banks's. Just sitting in the familiar seat made Reed miss home.

"How's my nephew?" Turk asked. He hadn't seen Davy since he was born, but he always referred to Reed's son as his nephew, and Reed didn't mind. Turk was the closest thing he had to a brother.

"Fat and happy," Reed said. "Starting to get an attitude."

"Well, that's his mother's fault," Turk said.

"Damn right it is."

They shared a laugh, and Reed sipped his coffee. It was weak, but better than nothing. "How's Sinju?"

Turk grunted and looked immediately away. Reed gave him the side-eye and noticed his cheeks flush again.

"Well?" Reed said.

Turk dug in his pocket, producing a folded piece of paper. He smoothed it open, and Reed glanced across the top.

"Oh, you've got to be kidding me. A fiancée visa?"

Turk shrugged, cramming the paper back into his pocket.

"Dude," Reed said. "Are you *thinking* right now?"

Turk flashed him a grin. "Not really."

"Well, good for you, buddy. Good for you."

Reed hit the brakes as a long line of taillights illuminated in unison. In the near distance, the Chicago skyline rose toward the clouds, stretching out on either side like an unending painting. But as the column of vehicles fighting their way downtown slowed to a crawl, that painting seemed permanently out of reach.

"I don't miss this," Reed said, thinking back to his years living in Atlanta, a city famous for its traffic.

"Try Los Angeles sometime," Turk said. "You're better off walking."

The rental car crept forward, and Reed checked his watch. They were due to rendezvous with O'Dell within the next hour. He couldn't see the obstruction ahead but already guessed they would be late.

"What's the rundown?" Turk asked.

"She was shot in a park. Shooter fired from an apartment building twenty-four hundred yards away. The FBI has the place locked down, but O'Dell said he's got access."

"So, we're just supposed to . . . "

"Consult," Reed said. "We're here to consult."

"I'm sure the FBI will love that."

Reed adjusted his seat, accepting the inevitability of the traffic and resigning himself to the grind. They should've taken the train, but he didn't like being without a car, even in a big city.

"Do you believe it?" Turk asked.

"Which part?"

"The twenty-four hundred yards part."

Reed looked out the window. He picked an office building almost a mile away. He pictured a man standing on the roof, barely a spec through a high-powered scope, all but invisible with the naked eye. And then he pictured him making that shot. Cold bore. First time. With wind ripping off the lake. "I don't know."

It took almost two hours to reach downtown, but O'Dell didn't complain. He was waiting for them three blocks from the hospital Maggie was being treated at, and he looked like absolute hell. His hair was disheveled, and heavy black bags hung beneath his eyes. He smelled of body odor when he piled into the back of the SUV, and his clothes were wrinkled. Reed noticed a dark stain near the bottom of one pant leg and wondered if it was blood.

The president's blood.

O'Dell shut the door and nodded once to each of the men in the front seat. "Turk . . . Montgomery."

Reed watched him in the mirror, barely recognizing the man he saw. He'd known O'Dell in one capacity or another for a couple years now, and the guy never looked particularly great. But he was always clean, always held his chin high, and seemed to take pride in being put together. The man seated behind Turk now looked more like a vagrant than a member of the president's security detail.

"Where to?" Reed asked.

O'Dell pointed the way, and Reed drove, navigating outside the Secret Service's protective perimeter around the hospital, then turning south.

"What's the update?" Reed asked.

"No update," O'Dell said. "I spoke with the vice president last night. He authorized you to see the crime scene. Then he may want to talk to you."

Reed exchanged a glance with Turk. "What did you tell him?"

O'Dell looked out the window, his shoulders slumped. "Only the highlights. What you did in Turkey and Pyongyang. What you're capable of. Nothing about . . . before."

Reed grunted but didn't comment further. He didn't know Stratton—not well enough to have an opinion of him. But in absence of an opinion, Reed's default was to distrust people. He also didn't like the idea of a man in O'Dell's state of distress making decisions about which classified information to disclose.

But that ship had sailed. It was something to worry about later.

"How's Maggie?" Reed asked.

O'Dell's gaze dropped. "Still unconscious. I'm guessing they have her artificially sedated, but they won't update me directly."

Reed surveyed the congested downtown streets behind dark sunglasses. He didn't need to know what had happened there to know that *something* had happened. The tempo of the city was all wrong, and it wasn't just the news vans lining the streets or the numerous jet-black government vehicles at every turn. The very heartbeat of Chicago was off. There was fear in the air.

"Park there." O'Dell pointed to a small lot surrounded by a hastily erected chain-link fence and guarded by a guy dressed in all black, with an M4 assault rifle hung over his chest.

Reed pulled up next to the man, and O'Dell passed him a government ID through the back window.

"Who are you guys?" the guy said, addressing Reed.

"Consultants," O'Dell answered before Reed could. "They're expected."

The guy looked ready to object, but a tall man in an FBI windbreaker appeared between the rows of vehicles, waving one hand and calling to the guard. There was a brief exchange, then Reed was directed to a parking spot.

"I'll do the talking," O'Dell said.

Reed cut the engine and climbed out as the tall guy in the windbreaker confronted O'Dell. "You're a real pain in my ass, you know that?"

O'Dell ignored him, slamming his door and tilting his head toward Reed and Turk.

"This is Mr. Montgomery and Mr. Turkman. I believe the director called ahead?"

The guy glared from Reed to Turk, then demanded ID. They passed him Alabama and Tennessee driver's licenses, and he inspected them as though he were scrutinizing fake IDs at the front door of a bar. Then he looked up. "All right. Cards on the table. I'm Special Agent Baker, and I'm the SAIC of this investigation. I don't know who the hell you guys are, but if it were up to me, you wouldn't be here. So, you'll touch *nothing*. You'll bother *nobody*. You'll see what you need to see, and then you'll get the hell out. Understood?"

Nobody answered.

Special Agent Baker handed his driver's license back. "Great. Let's get this over with."

27

They visited the amphitheater first. It was heavily guarded with a metal barrier erected all the way around it, but the inside itself was relatively bare. SAIC Baker put some minion on them to make sure they didn't break any of his rules, then O'Dell led Reed and Turk up the steps and onto the main stage.

It was bigger on the inside than it looked from the outside. Reed surveyed a wide field of semi-circular terraces designed to provide escalating levels of outdoor seating for onlookers, and he imagined the space packed with rally attendees. Thousands of them, all crowded close to the stage, but sunken into the ground enough not to block a sniper firing from an elevated position. The stage was a big bullseye, he thought. Elevated, like a steak on a platter.

"I was standing here," O'Dell said. He pointed to a place in the shadows, near the back corner of the stage. Then he motioned to the podium. "She was behind the mic."

Reed walked to the podium, stopping where crime scene tape outlined a section about the size of a queen mattress. The floor was black but stained darker in a wide pool to the left of the podium. Reed noted the disturbed patterns on one side of that stain and figured that must be where O'Dell's and Maggie's legs landed. A gruesome, ugly mess.

Reed had seen it before, many times. But not usually from this end. "Got binoculars?"

He held out a hand, and Baker's minion dug in a duffel bag to produce a pair. They were compact and not overly powerful, but better than nothing.

"Show me," Reed said.

O'Dell stood beside him and pointed across the park to the south, far beyond the trees and over multiple streets to a row of buildings glinting in the morning light.

"Between those two towers . . . the brown brick building."

Reed squinted. "Where?"

O'Dell pointed again. "There . . . between the high-rises."

Reed adjusted the focus on the binoculars. Then he saw it. But not as a building—more as a distant, vague smudge. Twenty-four hundred yards away.

He studied the spot, imagining taking a shot at a man-sized target. Except Maggie was slimmer and shorter than a man.

"Twelve to fourteen miles per hour," Turk said.

Reed lowered the binoculars and saw Turk standing at the front of the stage, an anemometer held out in one hand. The little blades of the device spun as a steady lakefront breeze washed through it, carrying consistently south and west.

A steady wind. An impossible distance.

Reed rubbed his thumb across the binoculars, now focused on the building through his sunglasses alone. He imagined a muzzle flash from the top floor, just behind the window. The fact that O'Dell caught it at all was a testament to his above-average attention to detail. It would've been no brighter than a glinting windshield and lasted no longer than a split second.

"I want to see the overwatch," Reed said. "Take me to the apartment."

The drive to the apartment was slow, highlighting how far twenty-four hundred yards was. Once there, Baker's minion had to talk to three separate people before they were allowed past the front door, and even then, they were required to wear gloves and were once again reminded not to touch anything.

The apartment was on the eighteenth floor, one down from the top, and faced directly north. Reed led the way through the front door, picturing the shooter stepping in for the first time. The guy would have surveyed the kitchen first, getting a bearing for everything behind him while he took the shot.

There was a reason the Marine Corps gave their snipers spotters—and it wasn't just about calling distance and windage. While stretched out behind a scope, focused on a target and aligning a perfect shot, Reed was blind to the world around him, and particularly behind him. It was Turk's job to keep his M4 handy to blow somebody away if they tried to sneak up on them.

The sniper would've locked the door, cleared the small apartment, and adjusted the thermostat to a comfortable seventy degrees—warm enough to relax in but not so warm as to sweat.

Reed moved through the kitchen to the main living space, where a heavy wooden table was laid out in front of the window. A hole in the curtain corresponded to a hole in the glass, each about six inches across and two feet from the end of the table. A perfect shooting position. Sheltered, protected, hidden from view with a clear shot. Every advantage the shooter could contrive for himself.

"Did you analyze the GSR on the curtain?" Reed asked Baker's minion.

The guy frowned. "What do you mean?"

"The powder might tell you something. You can bet it was a custom load. It's worth a check."

The guy appeared irritated, and Reed ignored him. He looked to the couch resting three feet to the left of the table and noted evidence tags scattered across it.

"What's this?"

"There was a girl," O'Dell said. "She leased the apartment. The shooter killed her."

Reed asked the minion, "How was she killed?"

The man shot him another irritated frown. "What do you mean?"

"There's no blood. Was she suffocated?"

"No. Neck broken."

"How?"

"How? What do you mean how?"

"How was her neck broken?"

He shrugged. "That's not really my department. I haven't even seen the body."

"Did they X-ray the break?"

"Probably. That would be the autopsy guys."

"I'd like copies, please."

The guy gave him a blank look.

"Of the X-ray . . ."

Baker's minion looked ready to object, but O'Dell closed in to remind him who had sent them. Reed ignored the exchange and moved to the window. He had to squat to align his eyes with the hole without touching the curtain. From that vantage, he couldn't even see the stage. He could barely see the park, and much of his view was obstructed by the two highrises the sniper had fired between. An incredible, almost unthinkable shot.

Turk squatted next to him, keeping his voice low. "Those buildings would create crosswinds."

"Probably," Reed agreed.

"At twenty-four hundred yards, you've got spin drift," Turk continued. "Coriolis effect."

"Both pulling your shot right. But the wind would push it left."

Turk grunted. "That's a lot of trigonometry. Way more than I could do with a calculator, let alone in my head."

"There would've been flags," Reed said. "American flags all around the amphitheater. That's how he identified wind direction. And look . . ." Reed pointed to the top of the righthand high-rise the sniper had fired to the left of. There was a red streamer tied off to the railing of the rooftop, like a remnant of a summer party. "I'd bet money he placed that there to measure crosswind."

"But that still doesn't give him wind *speed*," Turk said.

Reed chewed his lip, placing himself behind the rifle and imagining the moment before the trigger broke. It was an instinctual thing, born and honed by years of practice and thousands of shots. Sure, it was math, but at some point, you trained your brain to perform some of that math subconsciously. You fired again and again, so many times that you *knew* the right moment without having to be told.

But at twenty-four hundred yards, with twelve-mile-per-hour winds and no guaranteed way to measure them, how many shooters could make that shot? There couldn't be more than a few on the globe, and if they could make that shot, they had been shooting for a long time. Long enough for the right people in the right places to know about them.

Reed stood. "Make sure that guy gets the X-rays. I've got a call to make."

28

"How long?" Wolfgang avoided the doctor's gaze. He looked out the misted glass of the hospital's fourth floor instead, staring out over a bleak, meaningless city. It was a place he'd called home for nearly a decade, yet it felt as cold and hostile as it had his first winter.

"Six months," the doctor said. "Eight, at most."

Wolfgang nodded slowly.

The doctor shut his binder, ducking his head as he stood. "Give us half an hour to clean her up. I'm sure she'd like to see you."

The doctor left the room, leaving Wolfgang alone next to the glass, watching early snowflakes drift down from the sky. Late October was a little early for snow to blanket the city. These snowflakes would melt as they hit the pavement, but the dreary sky still seemed a hallmark of the luck this place had brought him . . . and Collins.

Wolfgang lowered his face into his hands, and for a moment, he tried to cry. He hadn't cried in years—not since Megan died. He buried his fiancée in a meadow behind his rural upstate home and poured his life from that point forward into saving Collins. Whatever it took. Whatever it cost.

His little sister was consumed with cystic fibrosis and had been since childhood. The doctors called it incurable. Wolfgang spent years in premium universities and a couple million dollars of blood money trying to prove them wrong. He earned one doctorate degree and was well on his way to a second. He built a private laboratory under his home and investigated any and every lead possible, desperate for a cure—desperate to save the last person he cared about from the clutches of impending death.

But the harder he fought, the more he failed. And the sicker she became. Now in her early twenties, she should still be on track to live another fifteen or twenty years, yet Collins's time was running out. The disease was taking her much more quickly than most. It was sucking her life away, corrupting her lungs, draining the soul right out of her. And leaving Wolfgang alone to face the bitter cold of his own failure.

He sat back in the chair, unable to cry or feel anything, and he focused on clearing his head. No matter how defeated he felt, he couldn't let Collins see it. She had to believe he was fighting for her. She deserved the hope.

Even if that hope was a lie.

Wolfgang's phone rang, and he almost ignored it, but he wanted something else to think about. He answered without even checking the caller ID. "Hello?"

"Wolf, it's Reed."

Reed's voice was short and clipped, much as it always was. Wolfgang had first met him almost three years prior, in North Carolina. It wasn't a pleasant meeting, but neither of them was to blame. Reed was working as a rogue assassin, hunting his former employer after that employer backstabbed him and threatened Banks.

Wolfgang was also an assassin at the time, using the profits of a lucrative killing career to fund his research into a cure for Collins. He was hired on behalf of Reed's former employer to eliminate the man they called the Prosecutor. He and Reed met, clashed, and they both walked away. Several times. And then that employer grew impatient and chose to threaten Collins in an effort to motivate Wolfgang.

Motivation hadn't been Wolfgang's problem, but once Collins was in the picture, he found himself strongly aligned with Reed. The enemy of his enemy and all that.

They'd been frenemies ever since, edging closer to friends after Reed risked his own life to drag Wolfgang out of a hellhole in Colombia. But Wolfgang still didn't really know Reed—not outside the context of perpetual chaos.

"Hey, Reed." Wolfgang cleared his throat subconsciously.

Reed hesitated. "You good?"

Wolfgang almost brushed the question off, but then his throat caught, and the tears he'd attempted to cry minutes before threatened to bubble up.

"How's Collins?" Reed said.

"Six months. Maybe eight."

"I'm sorry, Wolf."

Wolfgang felt like Reed meant those words, as useless as they were.

"What can you do?" Wolfgang said, forcing a humorless laugh. "Can't kill this one, Reed."

"Is she comfortable?" Reed asked.

Wolfgang slouched into his chair. "I guess. They're talking about morphine to relax her."

"Let us know what we can do," Reed said.

Wolfgang knew he was talking about the funeral arrangements, but there wouldn't be a funeral. He would bury Collins like he buried Megan, in his makeshift family cemetery with a simple headstone. Or maybe he would take her back to West Virginia and lay her to rest next to their mother in the coal hills. Just him and her.

"What's up, Reed?" Wolfgang said, eager to change the subject. "I know you didn't call to talk about this."

"You watch the news lately?" Reed said.

"Sure." There was a TV across the room, and he'd gotten his fill of the Trousdale shooting. The "impossible shot," as CNN called it.

"I'm in Chicago," Reed said. "O'Dell called in a favor and wanted me to take a look."

"And?" Wolfgang didn't really care, but it gave him something to focus on.

"Twenty-four hundred yards, give or take. Fired from the eighteenth floor of an apartment complex, sitting at a table. Shot through a five-inch hole."

"Impressive," Wolfgang said. He wasn't a rifle guy—never had been. Wolfgang's favored method of death was a choke wire or a suppressed 10mm automatic to the skull. But anybody passingly familiar with firearms could appreciate a shot that extreme.

"He killed a girl, too," Reed said. "Broke her neck. I'm still waiting on the X-rays, but a neck break . . . a precision shot like that, seated back from the window in concealment . . ."

"Gotta be military," Wolfgang said.

"Yeah. Or ex-military, probably. Maybe half a dozen people on the planet who could make that shot."

"Are you one of them?"

"Hardly," Reed said. "Actually, I was hoping you might know somebody. You ran in different circles than I did. I figure with a guy this good, word gets around."

Wolfgang rested his chin in one hand and thought for a moment. It was true. He ran in vastly different circles than Reed, back when they both worked as contract killers. Reed worked for a wing of organized crime in Atlanta and busied himself with a lot of domestic stuff. Wolfgang was more international, finding work in Europe, Asia, and Africa. He knew a lot of killers, at least by code name. But no extreme shooters came to mind.

"Distance shooting was never my forte," Wolfgang said. "But I can poke around. I'll let you know."

"Thanks," Reed said. "I'll update you if we learn anything else."

Wolfgang grunted but didn't hang up. He fixated on a cheap painting on the wall—one of those dumb things hospitals and hotels buy in a transparent attempt to add style to their lobbies and waiting rooms without actually having to pay for it.

"Hey, Wolf?" Reed said.

"Yeah?"

"I'm . . . I'm thinking about you, man."

Wolfgang sat up, feeling suddenly awkward. "Yeah . . . thanks. I'll call you." Then he hung up, once more consumed by the emptiness around him.

29

The Secret Service had done a good job of locking down the hospital. In fact, they had locked down that entire section of the city, with local PD scattered beyond.

The closest The Ghost could get was two blocks away, at a sandwich shop that managed to stay open under the crush of oppressive security. He ordered a meatball sub and took his time eating it, sitting near the window and watching the vehicles that drove back and forth, in and out of the makeshift checkpoint the Secret Service had erected. Watching and thinking. Evaluating.

Planning his next attempt.

The president wasn't dead. That much was clear. If she had been, it would've been all over the news. There would've been a lot of fanfare over Jordan Stratton taking her place, memorials discussing her life, and talking heads pontificating about the survival of democracy.

The Ghost saw none of those things on the news, and that meant somehow, she survived. At least thus far. He knew he'd hit. He saw the panic amid Trousdale's security as they swarmed in to recover her, and then the ambulance that rushed her away.

Three hundred grains of lead, flying that fast, making an impact anywhere in her torso . . . It should've been enough. Yet she had survived. Which meant the job wasn't done and he had to reevaluate. There would be no chance at a second shot. The Secret Service would keep her bottled up inside that hospital, then move her to the White House until well past Election Day.

The job had to be complete before then. The man on the yacht demanded it.

So, The Ghost would have to think of something else. Something up close and personal, unfortunately, which put him in an excessive amount of personal risk, and also well outside his comfort zone. He was a shooter, not an assassin. But his shot had failed, and that voided his personal guarantee. It was up to him to make that right.

The Ghost wiped his cheek where a trace of marinara sauce had oozed out of the pencil-sized hole, then pushed away the remainder of the sandwich and watched as a medical services vehicle pulled up to the checkpoint. The Secret Service swarmed it, moving in to inspect the drugs and medical equipment loaded in the back, their dogs circling the base and sniffing for bombs.

It would be impossible for him to access the president directly. He'd be lucky to make it to her floor, let alone her room. With so much focus on every item moving past the checkpoint, it seemed impossible to sneak an explosive device into the hospital, either. But what if the weapon didn't *look* like a weapon? What if it looked like something the Secret Service expected to see?

The germ of an idea wriggled in the back of his mind—close, but out of reach. Something about medical equipment . . . Something about a Trojan Horse passing right through that checkpoint without a hint of resistance.

The Ghost dumped his sandwich in the trash and moved for the door. He wasn't confident about the details yet, but he knew where to start.

30

Lakeside Memorial Hospital
Chicago, Illinois

Maggie was alone. She knew it because the White House was deadly silent. Never before had she considered how alive the old mansion felt, but as she listened now, the world itself stopped spinning.

It was black outside—deeper than night. Swirling mist clung to the windows of the Oval Office in long, wispy fingers. She glided past the Resolute Desk, and her feet never touched the floor. It was as though she were weightless. She couldn't feel a thing.

Except the cold.

It radiated out of her very core, and when she looked at her fingers, they were chalk blue and translucent. She could see right through herself, and the sensation made her heart thunder. Maggie screamed. The sound echoed off the walls, and she ran to the window. She passed right through into pure blackness and fell, head over heels, still screaming. She saw faces rushing by, so consumed by darkness that she couldn't recognize them. Indistinct voices called to her, their words muffled. Their demands unclear.

But nobody reached out to stop her fall. The cold black rushed by as though she'd jumped from a skyscraper, feeling like it would never end. Feeling like she'd fall forever.

Then she hit the hard, rough ground. Something wet coated her arms. She looked down to see crimson drenching her dress and hands, gushing from her stomach. She covered the spot, but the blood kept coming. She screamed louder for security. For O'Dell.

Nobody came. A cyclone of fog swirled around her, and gallons of blood spread across the floor until she was swimming in a pond of her own body fluids. She kicked and writhed, still clutching her stomach, but now she was coated in red.

She couldn't see. She couldn't hear.

The blackness was complete.

31

Reed booked a suite, fully intending to demand reimbursement from the White House for whatever service he rendered in the investigation. He and Turk spread computers, maps, and notebooks across the table in the spacious living area, then ordered Chinese food as the clock ground toward midnight.

Implementing Google Earth and what meager notes the FBI had shared, they established the final distance of the sniper's position at 1.31 miles from the amphitheater.

It wasn't an impossible shot—not even an unheard of shot. Reed had seen plenty of shooters employing the .338 Lapua Magnum—or more commonly, the .50 BMG—make hits on man-sized steel at over a mile. Across the nation, there had to be two dozen precision shooting clubs with members on the roster capable of making such a shot.

But not cold bore. Not on the first press of the trigger. And not while fighting a steady wind, caught amid buildings and blowing back and forth two or three times between the shooter and the target. Not while shooting in downtown Chicago.

Reed slumped into a chair and tapped a cigarette out of a half-empty pack. The metal trash can next to him was already littered with a half dozen butts, some of them still hot. The hotel would throw a righteous fit when they found out, but they'd get over it.

Right now, he needed the nicotine, not because he was stressed but because smoking helped him think. Something about the passive activity, keeping his hands busy while his mind shifted into overdrive, served to unlock advanced problems. It had worked for him before. It needed to work now.

Turk slouched against one end of the table, working his way through a tray of General Tso's chicken with a pair of chopsticks. Turk sucked with chopsticks. He always had. He wasn't much on any skill requiring fine motor skills.

But Reed was amused to note that he'd improved significantly since their tour of North Korea earlier that year. Apparently, dating an Asian girl lent itself to learning traditionally Asian skills.

"How would you do it?" Turk asked.

Reed stared at the iPad displaying the Google Earth map with a long yellow line marking the distance—Lake View Apartments to the amphitheater, right along the lakefront.

"I wouldn't," Reed said. "I wasn't capable of a shot like that on my best day, let alone now."

"Okay, but assuming you had to . . . How would you go about it?"

Reed sucked on the cigarette. He thought about the wind, the buildings, and what a target would look like at that distance.

"The problem isn't the distance so much as the variables. Shifting wind, further distorted by the buildings. Blend that with spin drift and Coriolis effect . . . that's some serious math. You'd need an advanced program to calculate on a computer, let alone do it in your head. And you can't forget, he didn't have all the variables. He didn't know exactly how fast the wind was blowing or if it would shift after he pulled the trigger. At that distance, we're talking about eight or ten seconds of flight time. That's a *long* time."

"Long enough for O'Dell to jump," Turk said.

Reed nodded and took another drag. "Long enough for the shooter to reacquire the target. Watch as she was hit. Long enough for the sound waves to disperse, making it almost impossible to locate his position in case he needed to fire again."

"But he didn't."

"No, he didn't."

"Luck or skill?"

Reed thought again about the apartment. About how perfectly every piece was arranged—the shooting table, the hole in the curtain and the window. Even the floor the shooter selected was high enough to offer the perfect vantage point—but not too high. Reed had checked the nineteenth floor. The shooter would've had to draw much closer to the window to make the shot from that angle, exposing himself.

This guy *knew* what he was doing. It wasn't luck.

"Skill," Reed said.

Turk nodded his agreement. "What does that mean?"

Reed knocked ashes into the trash can. "It means he's a shooter, not an assassin."

"What's the difference?"

"Well, they both kill people, but their approach is very different. An assassin might choose any number of methods, depending on the situation. A gun, a knife, poison, or a fake suicide, maybe. It all depends on the circumstances at play. A shooter is always going to shoot because that's what he knows. The shooter is to an assassin what a specialist is to a general practitioner."

Turk fumbled with his chopsticks and spilled fried rice on the floor. He cursed and set the plate down, brushing his shirt off. Reed kept studying the iPad, smoking slowly now, envisioning the shooter as the specialist he described—somebody whose primary objective was placing rounds on target. Thousands and thousands of them. Years of practice and advanced training.

"Maybe he's a competition shooter," Turk said. "One of those guys out west who make those crazy distance shots. I mean, even if you're not used to killing people, at that distance, a person is just a blob in your scope. For enough money, anybody could do it, right?"

"No. The guy's military, one hundred percent. And he's seen action. A lot of it."

Turk cocked his head. "How do you figure?"

"Because of the girl. He killed her with his bare hands, then threw her on the couch right next to him. She still had her eyes open when the FBI found her. He didn't even bother to close them."

Turk sipped the Coke, then spoke softly. "Did you?"

A knot in Reed's stomach tightened. He looked away from the screen for the first time, the cigarette forgotten in his hand, and thought about the people he'd killed. Not as a Marine. Not even as an off-the-books operator working for the White House.

He thought of the people he killed as an assassin. Working for criminals, knocking off criminals. The darkest part of his violent life.

Yes, he'd closed their eyes. When he could.

"Sorry," Turk said.

Reed looked up. The cigarette had burned out, and he dropped it in the trash, already reaching for another.

"The point is, the guy is callous," Reed said. "Callous and highly trained. The training could have been civilian, but the callousness indicates military action, so it makes sense he was involved in some kind of elite sniper detachment."

"One of ours?"

"I doubt it. The FBI will locate and establish alibis for every advanced shooter we have, active or discharged. But I don't think he was an American."

"Why?"

Before Reed could answer, there was a knock at the door, and O'Dell called out from the other side. Turk let him in, and Reed watched through a haze of smoke as the president's bodyguard entered the suite.

The man looked like hell. He'd changed clothes since the shooting but clearly hadn't slept more than a couple hours. Reed could only imagine what it felt like to be charged with the protection of the most important person in the nation and then fail so spectacularly. He didn't look down on O'Dell for that, but he didn't have time to waste sympathizing, either.

"Want something to eat?" Turk asked.

O'Dell shook his head, his gaze falling on Reed's half-empty pack of cigarettes. Reed tossed him the pack without asking, and Turk handed him a lighter. The disheveled man lit up and crumpled into a chair, blowing smoke at the ceiling.

"Get any sleep?" Reed asked.

O'Dell dragged on the smoke again, then looked to the table. "Any progress?"

Reed glanced at Turk, silently evaluating whether he should fill O'Dell in on his train of thought or whether O'Dell would be best left out of the loop. It was no secret the guy was operating well outside of the parameters of whatever Secret Service mandate he was under. Reed had spent most of his life as a loose cannon, and he appreciated the benefits of the approach.

But he also understood the dangers.

"We're still working on it," Reed said. "Any update on Trousdale?"

O'Dell stared at the floor so vacantly Reed thought he might have drifted off with his eyes open. "They've still got her sedated. Working on her liver now."

"What about the FBI?" Turk asked. "Have they found anything?"

"I wouldn't know if they had. They aren't talking to me."

"Who's running the investigation?" Reed asked.

"The director."

"What about Stratton?"

O'Dell shrugged. "He's safe. They've got him secluded somewhere nearby. I don't know specifics."

"Have you spoken to him?"

"Some."

"So, he knows we're here?"

"Yeah."

Reed finished his smoke and dumped it, then reached for a bottle of water. He wasn't sure why he came to Chicago. As a favor to O'Dell, maybe, despite the historical tension between them. But he didn't think he'd be staying long. The FBI would mop this up soon enough. Trousdale would either survive, or she wouldn't. The shooter would either be caught, or he wouldn't.

But there was still something nagging at him. Something in the back of his mind. He thought it concerned the crime scene, but he couldn't put his finger on it.

"Oh," O'Dell sat up. "They sent me those X-rays you asked for. Of the girl's neck."

O'Dell dug his phone out, and Reed instructed him on what email to send them to. It took some time, but when the message finally popped through, Reed was able to use the iPad to load a series of black-and-white images. He glanced across the first and flicked quickly to the second.

On the third, he stopped cold, the water bottle halfway to his lips. He zoomed the image, then set the bottle down as Turk closed in behind him.

"What is it?"

Reed pointed.

Turk's breathing hitched.

O'Dell sat up. "You see something?"

Reed flicked through the next two images, but he didn't really need to. That third X-ray already confirmed what he suspected the moment he stepped into the apartment. And it validated the fear nagging at the back of his mind.

"Can you reach Stratton?" Reed asked.

O'Dell nodded. "I think so."

"Get him on the line. I need to see him tonight. In person."

32

Shelby County, Illinois

Stratton's cell phone woke him after midnight. He had it silenced for all but a few critical numbers—top of the list, Maggie Trousdale.

O'Dell was calling. Stratton left his wife, Carolyn, sleeping in their bed and stepped into the hall, almost bumping the call. But the moment he answered, he heard the urgency in O'Dell's tone, and he listened long enough to catch the gist of his request.

Montgomery wanted to see him. Tonight. Wherever he was. He refused to speak over the phone.

It took time to push the meeting through the Secret Service. Stratton called Director French himself to have his men make arrangements to fly Montgomery, O'Dell, and some guy named Turk out of Chicago. French insisted on extensive security measures while the meeting was underway. The trio would be brought by helicopter to the Stratton family compound, where they would be admitted only after an extensive search. And even then, French wanted two of his agents in the room while Stratton and Montgomery spoke.

It was something in French's voice that cued Stratton off. Maybe the director's reverence for Montgomery's skill set or his mistrust of Montgomery's motives.

"You've met this guy, haven't you?" Stratton demanded.

"Yes, sir."

Momentary frustration flashed inside of Stratton like a gasoline fire. As vice president, he knew there was a lot happening in the White House that he wasn't aware of. He knew national security measures in particular were closely guarded secrets, divulged on a strictly need-to-know basis.

But it still pissed him off that there was, apparently, an entire executive arrangement made with off-the-books operators that he knew absolutely nothing about. It was that frustration that motivated him to allow the Montgomery meeting at all. He needed to get a handle on this guy before something spilled out of control.

That . . . and he was curious. O'Dell said Montgomery found something the FBI may have missed. Something urgent.

It took four hours for a Marine helicopter to collect Montgomery and company from Chicago and return them to the Stratton compound. From there, they were ushered into a modular office trailer where the Secret Service had established a sort of temporary headquarters and subjected to whatever sort of extensive body search French had arranged.

By the time they were finally ushered into the house, Stratton had showered and put on a fresh suit, having given up on sleep for the night. Then he directed his security detail to show Montgomery alone into what Barrett called "the oratory."

Much less a chapel and much more a library, the room was massive, situated at one end of the house, built with floor-to-ceiling bookcases constructed of dark mahogany. The floor was hardwood, covered with an ornate rug, and a gas fireplace burned along one wall while high-backed chairs faced it. Weapons, artifacts, and little trinkets linked to Stratton heritage littered the room, hung on the walls and displayed in glass boxes, all testaments to a familial lineage of savages.

The whole space reminded Stratton of the library printed on a Clue board—old-fashioned and relatively uncomfortable. Barrett called it an oratory because, for him, it served as a sanctuary dedicated to his triad of personal gods: family, legacy, and most importantly, power.

It was all too self-important for the vice president, but the room was quiet and isolated from the rest of the house. A good place to arrange a covert meeting.

Stratton found his way to the minibar situated across from the fireplace and sifted through the bottles for a selection of Woodford Reserve, one of his go-to bourbons. He poured three fingers over ice and looked up as the door opened.

"We're ready, sir," an agent said.

"Show him in."

Stratton sipped whiskey, staring into the crackling gas fire. Fake logs were engulfed in flames, always on fire but never burning away. The metaphor felt a lot like Washington—or American politics in general. The house was always on fire, but it never quite collapsed.

Again, the door opened, and a sequence of footsteps clapped on the hardwood. Stratton looked over his shoulder.

The man escorted in was an impressive figure—taller than himself by two or three inches and broad shouldered. He wore faded jeans, tennis shoes, and a T-shirt tight enough to display a muscled physique. Short brown hair was cropped in a distinctive military style, but the guy didn't carry himself like a soldier. He was more relaxed, almost as though none of the pomp and circumstance of meeting the acting president impressed him.

"Thank you, Jack. That will be all." Stratton motioned the agents out, but the lead man stiffened.

"Sir, we were directed—"

"Out!" Stratton snapped his fingers.

The agent reluctantly backed out, and the door closed.

The tall man remained standing, hands in his pockets, silent.

Stratton scrutinized him, guessing the man to be a few years his junior. Right around thirty, he thought.

"Reed Montgomery, I take it."

The guy nodded. "Mr. Vice President." He spoke the title, but his tone said he wasn't impressed by it.

Stratton turned back to the minibar, flushing with mild irritation. "I'm afraid you have me at a disadvantage, Mr. Montgomery. It seems you know a lot more about the Trousdale administration than I do."

He poured bourbon into a second glass. Montgomery accepted with a grateful nod, and Stratton motioned to a chair.

"I'm not here to make waves," Montgomery said, taking his seat. "If it were up to me, I wouldn't be here at all."

"But you are." Stratton fingered his drink.

O'Dell had said on the phone that Montgomery had something, but Stratton wasn't in a hurry to push. Alarm bells in the back of his mind warned him that he was on dangerous ground. Maybe because of who he was talking to. Maybe because of what they were talking about.

Regardless, the brief research Stratton conducted while waiting for Montgomery to arrive told him enough. He didn't have to dig very deep to find records of the man the FBI had once named a domestic terrorist, but he did have to dig past a presidential pardon, penned by Maggie Trousdale only days after President William Brandt's untimely demise.

A coincidence? Stratton never believed in coincidences. By nature, or by circumstance, the man sitting across from him was dangerous. If Stratton had to guess, Montgomery's involvement in Turkey following that plane crash had been exchanged for the pardon.

"I owe O'Dell a favor," Montgomery said. "That's the only reason I flew to Chicago."

"Have you known him long?"

"A few years."

Stratton set the glass down on an end table and leaned forward. "Okay, Mr. Montgomery. Clearly, you're not a man for formality, so let me cut straight to the chase. I don't know you. I have no idea where you came from or why you seem to be entangled in the heart of this administration. But I don't like it. Were it up to me, you'd be back on a plane to wherever the hell you came from. You're only here because America just got clocked in the face, right before Election Day. I don't have time to screw around. So, if you've got something I need to know about, you better get on with it."

Montgomery swallowed bourbon, then retrieved a cell phone and tossed it to Stratton.

Stratton caught it midair, and when he looked at the screen, he was immediately confronted by a black-and-white image. It was blurry, and Stratton thought it might be out of focus at first. Then he recognized the outlines of bones—vertebrae, specifically, with a harsh crack ripping through the middle, outlined in black ink.

Reed said, "The shooter fired from the eighteenth floor of an apartment building, twenty-four hundred yards from the pavilion. He used a high-powered, precision rifle. I don't know what caliber, but I would guess no lighter than a .338 Lapua Magnum. He fired from a table behind a curtain, with a hole cut in the glass. Classic sniper's technique. Do you play golf, Mr. Vice President?"

Stratton continued to study the image. "Sure."

"Ever hit a hole-in-one?"

"Once."

"What par?"

"Three, I think." Stratton looked up. "What's your point?"

"Imagine hitting a hole-in-one on a par five. At five hundred yards. In a thunderstorm. That's what this shot was like."

Stratton felt an involuntary chill run down his spine, and he tossed the phone back. "What's with the X-ray?"

"That was taken from the woman found in the apartment. The shooter killed her before laying her body across the couch. He shot from right beside her. He didn't even close her eyes."

The chill returned. "He broke her neck?"

"Seems so. She was young, maybe twenty-two. Healthy, strong bones. It's a lot harder than it looks in the movies. To snap the vertebrae like that, he'd need a precise technique. Lift up and twist, hard and fast. Not the kind of thing you learn at the local tae kwon do gym. Your shooter was military."

Stratton resisted a hard swallow. "One of ours?"

Montgomery shook his head. "No. The U.S. military doesn't instruct that kind of hand-to-hand combat. They rely on firearms and knives—basic wrestling moves, sometimes. Not neck breaks."

"Okay, so . . ."

Montgomery set his glass down. He seemed hesitant.

Stratton knew the look of somebody who was thinking something but was unwilling to commit to it in front of a politician. Nobody trusted politicians. Stratton couldn't blame them.

"You didn't fly here on a hunch," Stratton said. "Speak your mind."

"Asian armies train extensively with martial arts," Reed said. "But mostly for incapacitation. I'm only aware of one nation in the world that trains their people how to break necks that way."

Stratton raised his eyebrows. "And that is?"

"Russia."

33

Stratton sat frozen. Montgomery didn't blink, but the comment still felt like a bad joke.

Russia?

"What are you saying?"

Montgomery's voice remained calm. "All I'm saying is that whoever took that shot is one hell of a shooter. Training alone isn't enough. We're talking extreme talent paired with years of extensive practice. But the neck break and setup at the scene are very military, and the fact that he was able to take the shot with a cold body lying next to him says a lot about his state of mind. He's completely callous. Somebody who's seen *a lot* of death."

The mental image Montgomery painted was vivid. Stratton wondered why the FBI hadn't communicated details of the neck break or the shooter's possible military affiliation, and then he wondered if Montgomery was talking out of his ass. Stratton really had no way of knowing, and he suddenly felt the need for another drink.

"How much of this is speculation?"

"Most of it," Montgomery said. "Which is why you haven't heard it from the FBI. But if I'm right about any of it, you don't have time to wait for an investigative conclusion. This guy is going to try again."

"*What?*"

"He pulled the trigger, and he made the hit. But he knows Trousdale is still alive. Whoever hired or sent him to kill her isn't going to accept that. The shooter will try again, very soon. You need to relocate the president."

Stratton stood, a little stunned, a little confused. He'd been on and off the phone with the director of the FBI, the director of the Secret Service, and the entire National Security Council all day long. They'd talked extensively about the efforts underway to catch the shooter, keep the president alive, and stabilize the country.

Nobody had mentioned the possibility of the shooter trying again. Director French had deployed a literal army around the hospital Maggie was encased in, including extensive detachments of the Illinois National Guard to secure that entire section of the city. There were fighter jets deployed over the lake, monitoring all incoming air traffic and prepared to take down a Cessna if it wandered off course. Maggie's hospital, for the moment, was one of the most protected places in North America.

"I appreciate your concern, Mr. Montgomery. You can rest assured the president is secure."

"Like she was on that stage?"

Stratton bristled.

"This guy isn't impressed with the Secret Service, Mr. Vice President. He's already proven his capacity to think outside the box and strike from a blind side. That creativity alone should tell you he's dedicated to the job and won't stop until it's done. You need to get the president out of Chicago immediately. Put her on a plane and find a bunker somewhere."

Stratton breathed a curse. "She can't be moved. She's too unstable. They think . . ." He broke off, suddenly feeling that he'd said too much. There was something about Montgomery—maybe his silent confidence or the fact that Stratton found him at the heart of the Trousdale administration—that made him feel trustworthy. But Stratton couldn't afford to trust anyone. Especially not now.

"They think she may die," Montgomery said.

Stratton nodded. "Her liver is a mess. They've put her in an induced coma while surgery continues."

Montgomery grunted, looking into the fire. He seemed lost in thought, and Stratton wondered if he was personally worried for the president. They'd known each other a long time. Maybe there was a friendship.

"Call CNN," Montgomery said. "Tell them she passed in the night."

"What?"

"It'll buy you time. If the guy thinks she's dead, he might back off long enough for you to regroup and get her stabilized."

"Are you out of your mind? I can't lie to the nation."

Montgomery snorted. "Give me a break. You people lie all the time. It's how you get elected."

"You know what I mean," Stratton growled. "There are dominos in place. When a president dies, procedures kick into play. Protocols. Shifts in power. Things you can't come back from. Either I resist those things and everybody immediately knows she isn't dead, or I go along with the ruse, and we have a constitutional crisis on our hands if she survives. You've got to be out of your mind if—"

Montgomery held up a hand. "Okay, I get it. Bad idea."

Stratton turned away, still shaking his head. He dumped the remainder of his drink down his throat. He'd drunk too much. He was loosening up.

Montgomery said, "If you can't lie, and you can't move her . . ."

Stratton looked over his shoulder and saw him slumped in the chair, the glass in one hand, his face resigned.

"Then you're going to have to hunt him," Montgomery finished. "Go on the offensive before he strikes again."

"No shit. The Secret Service is already—"

"The Secret Service is a defensive mechanism, Mr. Vice President. They prevent problems from happening. They have neither the training nor the resources for proactive manhunting."

"And the FBI?"

"The FBI is effective but slow. They catch shooters after bodies are cold. You need somebody who can think like this guy thinks. Move quickly and use lethal force on demand. You need a kill team."

Stratton turned from the fire.

Montgomery remained relaxed in his chair, the same resigned look on his face and a half-finished whiskey rested in one hand.

"That's what you do, isn't it?" Stratton asked quietly. "That's what you did in North Korea."

Montgomery stood up. "It doesn't matter what I've done. Believe me when I tell you there's a million things I'd rather be doing. But if you don't put me on this case, Trousdale will be dead by Election Day. And probably a lot of innocents along with her. He won't be surgical this time. He'll burn the house down."

Stratton set his glass down and folded his arms. "What do you need?"

"Three things. First, I need resources. Weapons, vehicles, transportation. Probably some running money. Second, you don't work for free, and neither do we. Call Director O'Brien with the CIA. He has standing arrangements for items one and two to be covered off the books."

Stratton's stomach tightened. Someplace deep in his head, a voice warned him that he was wading into the deep end, and he could already feel his feet slipping. At the same time, a louder voice warned him that Reed was right. Twenty-four-hour news was having a field day with the presidential shooting. Panic was sweeping the country again. Only days from Election Day, he couldn't afford another attack, even if it failed. There could be societal repercussions. People might panic like they did after 9/11. They might stay home. They might not vote. And he needed those votes. His entire future depended on it.

"I'll make the call," Stratton said. "What's the third thing?"

Reed walked across the room to a lavish writing desk stacked with a humidor and a decorative fountain pen. He took the pen and removed a sheet of paper from a notebook in the top drawer, then walked back to the firelight and held out both items. "Third, I want your authorization on paper. If this gets messy, there's no way in hell it's blowing back on me."

34

The Ghost caught the man from behind and broke his neck with the same jerk and twist he employed on the girl in the apartment. It required more force, but technique is everything. The vertebrae collapsed, the spinal cord severed, and the guy went limp.

The Ghost took his clothes first, removing the one-piece jumpsuit uniform, the boots, and the utility belt. But most importantly of all, the ID badge. He folded them all into a duffel bag, then heaved the guy into the trunk of the Edge and covered him with a blanket.

His cell phone was locked, but it unlocked easily enough with a press of the dead man's thumb against the home button. The sniper scrolled through his contacts until he found a text message stream that quickly identified itself as a conversation between the corpse and his boss. The sniper read enough of the dead man's messages to identify the cadence and style of his texting, then punched out a new message declaring himself sick and unable to come into work.

It was the same trick he'd used with the girl in the apartment—eloquently simple and brutally effective.

Don't fix what isn't broken.

The drive to the abandoned warehouse took fifteen minutes, and he pulled right through the half-open door. It was dark and dusty inside. Abandoned machinery and tools littered the floor, and light shone down through pinholes in the metal roof.

This entire part of the city was full of places like this, owned by some bank or investment firm and not worth the effort of attempting to sell. That was the way of a big city, and no matter where in the world he was, the sniper could always find a place like this to hide . . . and plan.

He dumped the dead man in a back corner, not bothering to cover him and not worried about the smell. He'd be long gone by the time the body began to decompose.

Then he drove the Edge back to a front corner of the building and parked. There was a workbench there, propped up on a stack of abandoned concrete blocks. He used the Ford's headlights to illuminate the bench and the two tall green oxygen bottles set in front of it.

They were stuck with warning labels and hospital usage guides, but the screw-in valves were removed from their tops. He'd placed both valves on the table next to one of his duffel bags, then fully disassembled them.

The pieces lay scattered across marred wood in no apparent order, but as he picked up the bottom half of one valve and peered inside, he made out a pocket behind the knob. It was about the size of a kidney bean. He'd placed it there with a drill bit—small enough to maintain the structural integrity of the valve under pressure, but large enough to serve his purpose.

Because a bean-sized wad of C-4 nestled on top of two hundred cubic feet of compressed, highly explosive oxygen was one hell of a weapon.

35

Wolfgang's house sat by itself on a hilltop surrounded by trees. A long drive wound up from a county road, leading to a garage where his Mercedes S-Class coupe rested in the shadows.

The property, the house, and the car were all souvenirs of various stages of his tumultuous life. He bought the property when he was young and in love, dreaming of marrying a fellow espionage operative and growing old with her, drenched in the simple life. Then she was killed, and he went dark, spending a number of years alone in a battered camper, parked a hundred yards from her grave.

The house came after a brutal mission in Southeast Asia that nearly killed him but left him flush with cash. He found meaning in life under a new purpose—that of finding a cure for his baby sister. He invested in the home as his personal operations center, building the basement into a state-of-the-art laboratory.

It took two years to construct and cost the better part of a million dollars, but he stuck with it, financing the progress with a newfound skill set—killing people for money.

A few years after finishing the home, he bought the car. Not because it represented any practical value or even because he needed a car, but because the bodies were stacking, and the voices had begun. Voices of guilt whispering in the back of his mind, condemning him for his ugly career.

Wolfgang never questioned his choice to terminate human scum in exchange for the funding he required to pursue a cure for Collins. He only accepted contracts for targets he truly believed deserved to die—even if the people paying him probably also deserved to die. But still, there was only so much bloodshed a person could witness—and be party to—before it seeped into the soul and the questions started.

The Mercedes was a distraction, paired with expensive suits, elaborate hotels, and a growing reputation as The Wolf. A James Bond–style killer who lived in the shadows and struck like a snake. For a while, the whole persona worked, and Wolfgang almost found peace with himself. Then Reed Montgomery happened. Then the Resilient investigations happened. Then Wolfgang lost his leg, his career, and his whole manufactured identity. Now, the land, the house, and the car were just haunting reminders of everything he'd once had.

Wolfgang sat on the back porch under a harvest moon and stared at a laptop screen. Two burner phones and an iPad were arranged around him —hardware from his former life—all programmed and calibrated to shelter his IP address and enable access into the heart of the criminal underworld.

The dark web was aptly named—it was a dark place. Wolfgang was a medical mind by training—not a technical one. But over the years, working alone, he'd acquired a lot of technical skills. He knew his way around a computer better than most IT specialists, and he knew his way through the intricate corridors of the dark web better than the FBI. That was the key to leveraging its capabilities without being caught.

Currently, he was neck-deep in "Killer Central"—a hidden marketplace dedicated to the arrangement of contract kills. Wolfgang knew it well because Killer Central had been his chief source of employment back in the day. He'd learned how to sort good jobs from bad, identify employers willing to pay well and on time, and how to sniff out the occasional FBI setup.

But this was his first time posting a contract for hire. His first time posing as an employer himself.

NEED: PRECISION SHOOTER CAPABLE OF EXTREME DISTANCE, COLD-BORE SHOT. PREMIUM COMPENSATION ON OFFER. DETAILS TO FOLLOW CONTRACT.

It was a simple ad, not overly detailed or unreasonably enticing—the hallmarks of an FBI sting. But after fourteen hours, he'd received only two replies. Both killers immediately balked when he asked about shots exceeding two thousand yards.

Not his man.

Wolfgang checked the listing, then tabbed out of Killer Central and moved into a discussion board. It was a simple black forum with plain text links and little boxes housing each message—a crude sort of thing that reminded him of message boards during the early 2000s. But despite the bare-essentials visual of the place, it had a grimy feel, like a dark back alley on the wrong side of a rough city.

There was a new comment on his post about extreme long-range shooters. This wasn't a job listing like the other post. It was framed as a simple inquiry. Wolfgang posed as "a friend of a friend" who was looking for a specialist to perform an unusually extreme job. A kill shot in excess of two thousand yards.

The distance the sniper had fired from in Chicago was not yet public knowledge—the news media only knew that Trousdale was hit by a rifle bullet from someplace in the city. So, Wolfgang wasn't immediately worried that his inquiry would be painted as an FBI investigative probe. Still, with so much recent attention on the attempted assassination, he knew he was playing with fire.

The new message was from a user named Falkirk1298, a name and date Wolfgang recognized as the site of a major battle during the first Scottish war of independence. An odd username for a presumed criminal, but then again, everybody has their interests.

FALKIRK1298: SOUNDS LIKE YOUR FRIEND NEEDS A GHOST.

Wolfgang hovered over the message, evaluating for a moment whether the message was a legitimate lead or a sarcastic remark. It sounded sarcastic, but Falkirk had capitalized the word *Ghost*. Was that on purpose?

Wolfgang typed a reply and hit post. The message appeared under his handle, LW10mm, an abbreviation of his Lone Wolf nickname coupled with his favorite handgun cartridge. Because everybody has their interests.

LW10MM: CLARIFY?

He stroked his chin, not fully expecting a reply, but Falkirk didn't keep him waiting.

FALKIRK1298: WHO'S ASKING?

LW10MM: SOMEBODY WITH MONEY.

There was a long delay before the next comment. Wolfgang almost wondered if he'd spooked the guy. At last, Falkirk returned.

FALKIRK1298: CONTACT GREYWALL008.

Wolfgang clicked the new name and opened a chat box. He shot out a quick message, inquiring about a long-range shooter. Then he tabbed out of the menu and dug into a third dark web forum, where his generalized request for a talented sniper was being met with a slew of suggestions.

Most shooters didn't fit the bill. When asked about their longest possible shot, they claimed fifteen hundred yards, max. One went as high as eighteen. Nobody mentioned an excess of two thousand, but he cataloged their names anyway. Just in case.

The computer dinged, and Wolfgang switched back to the second forum.

A new message waited from Grey Wall.

GREYWALL008: WHO'S ASKING?

LW10MM: INQUIRING FOR A FRIEND. IN SEARCH OF A PRECISION SHOOTER WITH SKILL SET IN EXCESS OF 2,000 YARDS.

Wolfgang stopped, glancing back to Falkirk's initial message and reevaluating the capitalization of that one word.

An accident? Or something worth investigating?

He returned to the chat box and added another line before smashing send.

HEARD YOU MAY HAVE LEAD ON "GHOST."

Wolfgang rubbed his fingers against the table, ignoring the chilly wind drifting off the trees. Waiting.

GREYWALL008: NEED DETAILS.

Wolfgang hesitated. Part of him wanted to jot down a quick reply. If

Grey Wall was willing to talk, he should keep him talking. This was the best lead he'd had yet.

But another part of him wondered . . .

LW10MM: Need shooter capable of 1.5 mile shot. Prefer non-American. Will pay premium compensation.

The next message popped through.

GREYWALL008: Go to hell, fed.

The screen blinked, and the messages disappeared. Wolfgang's stomach fell, and he hit the refresh key, attempting to reload the chat.

Grey Wall was gone, as was the forum. Then a message popped up across his screen.

ACCESS DENIED.

Wolfgang slapped the laptop closed, running a hand over his tired face. What had given him away? He'd said nothing that should have set off alarm bells. The distance was extreme, but not a special number by any means.

His personal cell phone buzzed, and he found a message waiting from Reed.

Progress?

Wolfgang typed back quickly.

Working on it. Will keep you updated.

Reed's reply bounced right back.

Just spoke with Stratton. We're officially on the case. En route back to Chicago. Pour on the gas. I need a lead.

Wolfgang watched the cursor on his phone blinking, then shut it off and opened the computer again. He hadn't slept in almost eighteen hours, but that wasn't changing anytime soon.

36

The Marine VH-60N flew Reed and Turk back to Chicago through a light rain. It was one of the numerous aircraft operated by HMX-1, the helicopter squadron responsible for the transportation of the president, vice president, visiting diplomats, and various heads of state.

As such, it was technically a Marine helicopter. But even though this specific aircraft wasn't one of several available for use by Trousdale, it was still far quieter and more comfortable than any Marine chopper Reed had ever ridden in. And he'd ridden in more than a few.

After texting Wolfgang for an update, Reed left Turk to snore near the cockpit, and he retreated to the tail to dial Banks. He hadn't spoken with her since leaving the house and knew she deserved an update.

"Hello?"

Banks sounded tired, and Reed checked his watch. It was nearly midnight. He'd completely neglected to take note of the time.

"Hey," he said softly.

"Hey, Cowboy," Banks almost whispered, and Reed turned the volume up on his phone. He figured Davy was probably sleeping. Their son still shared their bed, and now that he was teething, he didn't sleep well. Once awakened, he sometimes took hours to put back to bed.

"Hold on," Banks whispered.

Reed waited until he heard a door click, then Banks's soft footsteps padded down the hall. A chair scraped back, and something popped, then hissed.

Banks swallowed loudly, and Reed sat up.

"Are you . . . drinking my *beer*?"

Banks giggled. It reminded him of two years earlier at that parking garage in Atlanta. The night he fell in love.

"You left it," she said. "Finders keepers."

"Vulture," Reed scoffed. "Let me turn my back, and you swoop right in. Bet you took the car for a spin, too."

"The Camaro? Nah, I put it up for sale. Figured I'd get myself a Miata. I mean, you're never around anyway."

Reed winced. He figured she meant it as a joke, but the comment still stung.

"How's Davy?"

"Fussy. His gums are all messed up. I think they itch."

"Did you give him that chew toy?"

"Teething toy," Banks corrected. "You can't call it a chew toy."

"Why not?"

"Because it makes him sound like a dog."

"Well . . . if the shoe fits."

Banks chuckled and swallowed more beer. It made him thirsty listening to her. It made him imagine her lips on his, the faint taste of alcohol on her tongue, her hand sliding up his shirt . . .

"How's it going up there?" Banks asked. "I've been watching the news."

Reed ran a hand across his face. He knew he was exhausted, but he still couldn't sleep. He hadn't slept more than a couple hours since leaving Birmingham. It was now Sunday night, the day after Maggie was shot. The pressure was setting in.

"I met with Stratton," he said. "He hired Turk and me to look into some things. I'll be a few more days."

"Is she going to live?"

Banks's voice was tentative, and Reed thought he knew why. There was no love lost between Banks and Muddy Maggie Trousdale. If he was honest, that was more Banks's fault than Maggie's. His wife was feisty and unforgiving where her family was concerned, and her perception that Maggie had stabbed Reed in the back at the close of the Resilient investigations had been slow to die.

"Touch and go," Reed said. "She may need a liver transplant." Reed put his feet up in the chair across from him. He settled his head against the leather and closed his eyes. "I wish you were here."

"Where is here?" Banks asked.

"Someplace over Illinois. The Marines are giving me a ride."

"Reckon they can send a plane for me?"

"I presume that would be an abuse of taxpayer funds."

"Oh? So, you're not getting paid? Because I'm kinda serious about that Miata."

Reed smiled. The phone fell silent for a while, and they both just enjoyed being together, even if they were six hundred miles apart and connected only by technology. It was still better than being alone.

"I love you, Banks."

Banks didn't answer. He heard the beer can twisting on the table, and knew she was picking at the label. She always did that when she was tired or stressed. Or lonely.

"Be careful, okay? Promise?"

"I promise," he whispered.

⸻

The VH-60N descended directly to the roof of the Lakeside Memorial Hospital. Stratton was a man of his word—he'd made some calls, and the way was paved for Reed and Turk to hunt a killer.

Tom Jenkins, the head of Maggie's protective detail, was waiting on the roof as the chopper touched down. Despite their failure to protect her during the speech in Millennium Park, none of the Secret Service agents on Maggie's detail had been asked to resign, and none of them were voluntarily stepping down until her recovery was ensured and her killer was caught.

Reed liked that. He appreciated motivated men. But he also knew how dangerous it could be if those men lost sight of the discipline that drove their profession. When things became too personal, a train could leave the rails.

"Reed, Turk." Jenkins held out a hand, locking each of theirs in a powerful grip. His face was windblown and wet from a light thunderstorm still washing over the city, but he looked alert. He looked angry.

"Stratton call you?" Reed asked as they pushed through a metal door into a concrete stairwell.

"Director French did. He said we were to give you every assistance in pursuing the shooter." Jenkins paused halfway down a flight of stairs. "He also said you were concerned about another attempt."

Reed nodded. "It'll happen sooner than later. I'd like to discuss current security protocols in place. If we're able to identify a weakness, it could be an opportunity to lay a trap."

Jenkins's face turned dark. "You want to use the president as bait?"

"She's already bait, Agent. I want to trap her killer before she's dead bait. It's not enough to know who this guy is. We need to know who sent him."

Jenkins didn't look convinced, but he continued down the steps. Two floors later, he pushed through another metal door into a hallway, where bright fluorescent light shone over an army of men and women in black suits. They all bustled in and out of hospital rooms, now cleared of patients and converted into a hasty operations center. Coffee brewed on a nearby table, donuts and sandwiches stood in stacks next to bottled water, and everybody seemed to be talking at once.

Jenkins led them into a room on the right where four men and a woman stood around a table laden with computers and a mess of blueprints. He shut the door. "Guys, this is Reed and Turk. They . . . work for the president. They're here to assist in capturing the shooter."

The looks washing across him weren't friendly, but Reed didn't mind. He was used to the discomfort that radiated from a room when he entered it. He couldn't really blame anyone for it.

"Show me what you have," Reed said.

He advanced to the table, and Jenkins gestured to a map. It outlined the hospital and the surrounding three or four blocks with little marks in red Sharpie.

"Each of these marks is a security point," Jenkins said. "The smaller ones are lone agents or snipers, while the larger represent QRF teams or checkpoints. All these guys are Secret Service."

He gestured with a pen to another round of marks filling the buildings directly adjacent to the hospital complex. "The FBI is assisting us with monitoring the perimeter and filtering any personnel who are entering or exiting the hospital. They have additional security teams, including snipers and detachments of HRT, on standby at command posts within a block of the hospital to respond if needed. Beyond the FBI, we have a five-block radius secured and under control of the Illinois National Guard. The governor authorized two hundred guardsmen to establish a perimeter and assist in checkpoints to manage traffic flow. Most of them are unarmed, of course. But we're maintaining constant centralized communication with everyone and rotating personnel regularly to keep everybody sharp."

"What about hospital staff?" Reed asked.

"The FBI ran background checks on everybody allowed in the building. Anyone with even a minor criminal record was removed, and nobody is allowed on the president's floor without a Secret Service escort. We're subjecting all incoming staff to metal detectors and full pat downs, and all outgoing staff are escorted to the outside of the FBI perimeter."

"And the president's floor?"

"Completely isolated. The hospital shifted all existing patients to other floors, and we're only allowing essential staff near the president. We've got an entire QRF team located in the lobby immediately outside the primary elevator, and all secondary elevators have been reprogrammed to block access to the president's floor. In addition, we've got bomb-sniffing dogs in the main lobby and throughout the building, and we've installed temporary bulletproof shields behind every window on her floor."

Jenkins stopped, tapping the pen against his open hand and nodding a couple times as if he'd forgotten something but couldn't remember what.

"Subfloors?" Reed asked.

"Right." Jenkins held the pen up. "More dogs, another QRF team, and constant patrols throughout the basement and any nearby sewers. Additional security around the main electrical supply and the backup generators. Same with water."

"Good." Reed scratched his cheek, surveying the map and doing something he hadn't done in a long time. Something he hoped to never do again. Putting himself in the shoes of an assassin. Strategizing a plan to circumvent some of the best security in the world and kill somebody.

Because there was always a way, no matter how perfect the protection. No matter how extensive the precautions. No matter how many lethal men armed with automatic weapons were ready to gun down absolutely anyone. There was *always* a way.

"Take me to the president's floor," Reed said. "I need to see her room."

37

None of the agents looked happy about it, but Jenkins didn't argue. He led Reed and Turk out of the command center, through two metal detectors, past half a dozen suspicious dogs and two detachments of the Secret Service's proprietary quick-response force before finally taking an elevator to the seventh floor.

Once there, he was subjected to yet another pat down, then two men wielding FN P90 submachine guns fell into step directly behind him. Impressive security, but the security was the box. The sniper would think outside that box, searching for the crack nobody else saw.

Jenkins led the way beyond the checkpoint, around a nurses' station, and into a long hallway. There was something eerie about the seventh floor that Reed didn't immediately identify. Three nurses sat at the station, all monitoring computers and working quietly on clipboards and iPads. In the hallway, he passed two doctors, both looking exhausted and overworked. Additional Secret Service security patrolled the halls, all wearing body armor, drop holsters, and wielding P90s.

But there were no other people. No crowded waiting rooms. No bustling nurses or rattling carts. The place felt apocalyptic, as though the world had stopped spinning and this was the end.

Jenkins was stopped at the end of a hall by two of his men, each casting suspicious glances at the tall outsiders trailing him. Jenkins made a brief explanation, then asked for the door to be opened.

President Trousdale lay on a bed, alone in an expansive hospital room. Reed stopped at the door, the Secret Service agents behind him tense and on guard, and he looked past a row of medical carts laden with monitoring equipment and medical devices.

Maggie looked like death. He'd seen her many times before, in many different circumstances. He'd seen her stressed and afraid, exhausted and cornered. He'd seen her at the end of her rope and on top of the world.

But he'd never seen her quite like this. Her face was ash white, and her head rolled to one side, an oxygen mask pressed across her face. Wires and hoses ran from the medical carts, beneath the blankets, and out of sight. A computer beeped, monitoring a steady heart rate.

But Maggie didn't look alive. She looked like a corpse, recently passed.

Reed surveyed the scene and felt a sudden flush of anger. The emotion was unexpected and took him a moment to acknowledge, but when he did, the spark of indignation grew into something closer to rage. This wasn't somebody he knew or worked with—and for—on different occasions. This wasn't just somebody on TV or on a ballot. This was the president of the United States of America. *His* president.

And some asshole had the nerve to attack her.

It wasn't about Maggie. It was about everything he ever fought for, believed in, stopped believing in, and was maybe starting to believe in again.

It was his country, kicked in the balls. It made him want to kick back.

Reed scanned the remainder of the room, taking note of the heavy bulletproof shields erected across the windows and the entire exterior wall, bolted in and then covered with a Kevlar shrapnel barrier. The air vents were fit with automatic filters, devices programmed to terminate all flow at the first hint of gas or toxins.

Outside, he knew an army of sharpshooters placed at strategic locations around the block maintained constant surveillance of this side of the building. If a threat was perceived, they'd shoot first and ask questions later. But still, it wasn't enough.

Reed left the room without comment, returning down the hall with the agents trailing him. He stepped into an abandoned waiting room, motioning for only Turk and Jenkins to follow, then shut the door. Jenkins dropped quarters in a vending machine and cracked open a Mountain Dew without comment. Turk followed suit.

Reed stared at the blocked windows, arms crossed, picturing himself with an urgent, obsessive desire to kill the woman in that hospital room, no matter the cost. No matter the difficulties. Then asking himself how he would make that happen.

"Well?" Jenkins sat down, resting the drink on one dirty pant leg. His eyes were bloodshot. His hair disheveled. He looked nothing like the polished agent Reed was accustomed to.

"You're in trouble," Reed said.

Jenkins's lip twitched. "What do you mean? What did you see?"

"It's not what I saw. It's how the board is set. I was right before—you should move her, immediately."

"We *can't* move her. She's barely alive as it is. If they move her now—"

"Do you remember 9/11?"

"Of course." Jenkins seemed irritated.

"Bush was at some PR event when it happened, reading books to kids. You remember what they did with him?"

"They put him on *Air Force One*."

"Exactly. Because when you don't know what's happening, the best you can do is keep moving. It was the same in Iraq. I used to tell rookies all the time: if you want to stay alive, keep moving."

"But we *can't* move her."

"That doesn't change my point. You've built a fortress here. You've got an army. But you're still a sitting duck. This guy knows you can't move. He knows exactly where the president is and where she'll remain for the foreseeable future. He's got time to evaluate your systems and slowly pick them apart. I'd bet money he's already been doing that, pretty much ever since she arrived here."

"We *know* that," Jenkins snapped. "There are five hundred security personnel surrounding this hospital. Another five thousand around the country working overtime to figure this out."

"Yep. And none of that saved you the first time, did it? It's not about how tough you are or how ready you are. It's about blind sides. I spent years exploiting them, hitting people where they least expected it, right when they think they're safest. I realize you guys are the best in the world at this. You've been dealt a crappy hand, and it's not your fault. But I didn't come here to pad your ego. I came here because he's going to try again, and this time we have to catch him."

Jenkins fingered the pull tab on the top of his soda can and stared at the floor. Turk exchanged a glance with Reed. The look on his face said it all. He was thinking exactly what Reed was thinking. The president might die if they moved her.

But she might die if she stayed, too.

Jenkins drained the can. "Okay. What do you need?"

Reed sat down, smoothing the pants over his knees. He focused on a worn spot on the floor and sucked his teeth, thinking slowly, the way the sniper would think. "He'll strike soon. Probably tonight."

"Tonight?"

"The longer he waits, the more gaps you close," Turk said. "Time is in his favor, but not entirely."

"Okay . . ." Jenkins spun the empty can between his fingers. "So, how?"

Reed thought about it, remembering what he'd said to Turk earlier about this guy being a shooter, not an assassin. It was still true, but it was also true that the Secret Service had pretty well encased Maggie inside a bulletproof box, effectively terminating that option.

"He'll know what floor she's on," Reed said. "You tipped your hand by blocking it off. All the patients who were being treated on this floor will have families they've been texting. So, you have to assume the secret has leaked."

Jenkins nodded. "Okay."

"He might know her room number, also. You said you're cycling through medical staff, right?"

"Yeah."

"Any number of them could have told him. All he'd have to do is jump them outside the security perimeter. I assume you're not keeping tabs on all of them?"

Jenkins shook his head, flushing. Reed scratched his chin with one finger, still staring at the worn spot on the linoleum. "It'll be one of two things. Either he hits the hospital from the outside, or he detonates a weapon from the inside. It won't be a shot."

"What do you mean, hits it from the outside?"

"A bomb. A missile. A plane. Something like that."

"A missile?"

Reed shrugged. "It's unlikely, but don't forget, we have no idea who's behind this guy. It could be another nation. Sitting right here on the lake, jammed up against another country, it's not unthinkable for a shoulder-mounted weapon to be snuck into the city. Then all he'd need is to get close enough."

Sweat trickled down Jenkins's forehead, and he brushed it away. "So, what do we do?"

"Position additional lookouts and snipers on the hospital roof. Have them maintain constant surveillance of surrounding rooftops and windows facing the president's room. Communicate with the Air Force, and have them tighten their patrols around the lake. Turk and I will establish our own vantage points and assist your men. Maybe we'll notice something they miss, or vice versa."

"What about the interior threat?"

"Nothing you can do there except tighten your checkpoints. Have them double-check everybody. Sweep all incoming equipment and supplies. Challenge *everything*. And rotate your perimeter agents frequently, at least every two hours. You need these guys fresh."

Jenkins persisted with the subdued nod. Reed could tell he was processing slowly, and he knew why. He recognized the same distant, semi-disoriented look on Jenkins's face that he saw in the mirror. Exhaustion was wearing away at him, one hour at a time.

"One last thing," Reed said.

"Yeah?"

"You have to sleep."

Jenkins glared at him. "Are you kidding me?"

"You're no use to anybody like this. You've got people covering your back. Trust them. Get some sleep, at least for a couple hours. Tell us who your second-in-command is, and we'll make sure the gaps are covered."

Jenkins looked ready to object again.

Reed kept his voice steady. "Don't worry. We're gonna get this guy. You'll be there when we do."

38

The dead man's jumpsuit fit well. It rode a little high in the crotch and pulled up from The Ghost's ankles. But with boots in place, it would suffice. He wore nothing but a white T-shirt beneath it, and put nothing in his pockets except the truck keys and his brand-new ID.

It was a scanned and modified version of the dead guy's ID. The Ghost had exchanged the picture for one of his own, then adjusted the personal details to match the character he had invented: Ricky Peltov. The Russian last name would excuse his subdued accent. The American first name would indicate him as a second-generation immigrant. Somebody who was now a part of the established order. Another piece in the machine, not to be overly suspected of anything nefarious.

After adjusting the jumpsuit and double-checking his face in the mirror of the Ford, he wheeled the oxygen bottles on their cart to the tailgate of the stolen delivery truck—open-backed, equipped with racks for medical gas bottles. He found the truck in a parking lot surrounded by a high chain-link fence, directly adjacent to a medical gas company's distribution center. There were ten other trucks there. He took the one that corresponded to the keys he stole from the lockbox just inside the employee access door.

There was no security system, and the lock itself was easily defeated with a pair of picks. Who needed to protect gas trucks, anyway? Who would bother stealing a vehicle so clearly marked and impossible to sell?

He loaded the truck with a number of pressurized cylinders, all filled with medical-grade oxygen. He used rubber hoses to transfer some of that gas into the two cylinders with the modified valves, then loaded them all onto the truck. Ready for their nine-mile journey into North Chicago.

The Ghost double-checked all the retention straps and ensured the hand truck was chained to the tailgate. Then he moved to the cab and started the engine. The truck was almost new and ran smoothly. He adjusted the climate controls and sat for a minute in the welcome warmth of the heater, thinking about the next two hours. Imagining each step. Each possible problem.

And the eventual solution.

A lot could certainly go wrong, but he knew it was a good plan, both because it was eloquently simple and impossibly obvious. Exactly the sort of thing that a massive security team, fixated on high explosives and poison gasses, would easily overlook. At least, he hoped.

The Ghost shifted into gear and left the warehouse, leaving the Ford and the naked body behind. He turned down an industrial street and found his way to the highway, then navigated south toward the hospital . . . and Muddy Maggie Trousdale.

39

Lakeside Memorial Hospital
Chicago, Illinois

Turk stood on the roof of the hospital's main tower, a pair of binoculars in one hand, a thermos of coffee in the other. It was chilly in Chicago, unlike the warm California breezes he'd recently enjoyed.

Turk never thought he'd like California. He never thought he'd like much of anywhere outside of his East Tennessee hometown. Maybe it was the mild weather or the vibrance of the sprawling cities, but most likely, it was Sinju that brought the charm to the City of Angels.

The first week, he missed his muddy Jeep Gladiator. By the third week, he could barely remember what color it was. All that mattered was Sinju. Long walks on quiet beaches, sleeping in on lazy Sunday mornings, and soon, the days blended together.

The CIA had cut him a healthy paycheck following the North Korean operation the previous April. Enough so that Turk wasn't worried about bills or employment or what day of the week it was. Not for a while, anyway. Not until the custom, two-carat diamond ring arrived from the jeweler in Los Angeles, and he thought of a way to pop the question. He wasn't in a hurry. He might wait until next spring or even early summer. But

Turk knew. He knew where he was headed as sure as he knew Reed was right about the killer.

The guy was coming back.

Turk swept the skyline with the binoculars, cradling the coffee in his free hand and watching his breath mist around his face. Lakeside Memorial was situated in the heart of North Chicago, meaning that many of the buildings surrounding it were tall enough to block any distant view. In a way, that was helpful. It eliminated the risk of another crazy, hyper-long-distance shot from the sniper. But in another way, it left Turk feeling claustrophobic, as if he were nestled in a valley with rising ridges on either side.

A cow in a killing stall.

Turk lowered the binoculars and glanced at the Secret Service sniper stretched across the rooftop next to him. The guy cradled a Knights Armament precision rifle chambered in 7.62 NATO, gently sweeping the optic across the same skyline Turk had been monitoring. His finger was rigid above the trigger guard, and Turk noted that the rifle's safety was already disengaged.

The Secret Service wasn't screwing around. If some schmuck with a water gun pointed it in the wrong direction, he might well get popped.

Turk rubbed his hands together to fight the numbing cold, and he moved down the roofline, passing two more snipers and three guys behind spotting scopes. Nobody acknowledged him, but Turk noted brief glances as he passed. They didn't trust him, and he couldn't blame them. If he were in their shoes, the last thing he'd want was some stranger pacing around in his blind spot.

But the blind spot Turk was most concerned about now had nothing to do with standing behind the snipers. He reached the corner of the roof, overlooking the main entrance of the hospital nearly two hundred feet below, and raised the binoculars again. Somewhere out there, amid the shadows and twinkling lights of America's third largest city, a killer waited.

Watching. Planning. Looking for an opportunity.

Maybe he'd already found one.

Maybe he was already moving to exploit it.

40

Jenkins slept for maybe an hour, then he was back on the seventh floor alongside Reed, reviewing security camera footage and guzzling coffee. Reed didn't bother objecting—both because he knew Jenkins wouldn't listen and because if Reed were in his shoes, he wouldn't have, either.

The Secret Service's array of upgraded surveillance was impressive and far superior to the rudimentary hospital equipment it had replaced. Additional cameras had been installed at every entrance, along every hallway, throughout the parking garage, and along the adjacent streets. They all connected via closed circuit to a centralized surveillance center on the seventh floor, built inside a repurposed nurses' station and staffed by half a dozen attentive agents.

Reed stood behind Jenkins and watched the color screens, noting the rhythmic passage of patrolling agents and the extensive filtering of incoming patients at the main entrance. All non-emergency hospital services had been forcibly relocated to other nearby medical centers, while the bare minimum of public care continued under heavy Secret Service supervision.

Lakeside Memorial had become a fortress, but it was still a fortress with windows, doors, and the leader of the Free World clinging to life in a lonely hospital room. As Reed watched the screens, his initial instinct that the sniper would strike again was only reinforced.

"Prosecutor to Rocky Top. Sitrep, over." Reed spoke quietly into the wrist-mounted microphone the Secret Service had supplied him with. It corresponded to a curly wire and an earpiece, and linked by radio waves to only one other unit—Turk's.

"Rocky Top, cold as balls up here. Nothing to report."

Reed left the bank of screens and reached for more coffee. There was no sugar or cream next to the cheap coffeepot, but that didn't bother him. All he needed right now was caffeine, and a lot of it.

Jenkins joined him, filling his own cup. "Turk see anything?"

Reed shook his head. "All clear so far."

Jenkins glanced toward Maggie's room. A number of doctors and medical staff had checked in and out over the past half hour, but none had stopped to talk.

"Any update?" Reed asked.

Jenkins sipped his coffee. "Director French called an hour ago. He said they think they can save her liver. Apparently, it can regenerate?"

Reed nodded. "Up to ninety percent. The only human organ that can."

"Incredible," Jenkins said.

"They know what they're doing," Reed said. "Have some faith."

Jenkins shot Reed a sideways look. "And you?"

"What about me?"

"Do you know what you're doing?"

Reed drank slowly, wrapping his hands around the warm cup. "Why do you ask?"

Jenkins eyeballed him. "I read your file."

"Okay."

"Or, I should say, what's left of it."

Reed said nothing.

"You were a Marine. A scout sniper, among other things. A few tours in Iraq. And then . . ."

"What?" Reed met his gaze, daring him to continue.

"And then you weren't," Jenkins said. "You dropped off the DOD payroll in early 2015 and didn't reappear until last year when the president wrote you an executive pardon."

Reed still didn't speak.

Jenkins looked away, swallowing coffee. "I'm not asking. It's not hard to guess. You don't vanish from the DOD without a damn good reason, especially with your skill set. You don't fall off the face of the planet without help, either. And you don't resurface needing an executive grant of clemency unless things went sideways. Badly."

Reed grunted. "Your point?"

"My point is, you keep popping up. First, when *Air Force One* went down. Again, when North Korea went off the rails. And now here you are, at the heart of our investigation, with the VP standing behind you."

"Hell of a thing," Reed said.

"Yeah. Hell of a thing . . ."

Reed set his cup down. "All right. I guess if I were in your shoes, I'd have some questions."

Reed knew Jenkins wouldn't ask—maybe because he respected the vice president's authority too much to question it. Maybe because he was afraid of the answer he might receive. But Reed also thought he owed Jenkins a bone. The guy was under enough stress without second-guessing unknown quantities.

"The DOD records were scrubbed," Reed said. "But the reason I left the Marines is because I shot the wrong people."

"Fratricide?" Jenkins asked.

"Fratricide is unintentional. What I did was very intentional."

Jenkins grew still.

Reed lifted his coffee again. "Her name was O'Conner. She was from Georgia. Dreamed of getting an MFA in Atlanta after she finished her deployment. Only, she never made it that far. A gang of contractors jumped her one night. They raped her, strangled her, and dumped her body. I balanced the scales."

Jenkins grew very still. "How many?"

"Five."

"Shit."

"After the court-martial, a lot of things happened. But the summary is that I found employment doing what this guy does." Reed tilted his head toward Maggie's room.

Jenkins's eyes narrowed. "You . . ."

"Killed people for money, yes. Criminals, mostly. Gang bosses and kingpins. Drug lords. Underworld VIPs. Turns out, I was pretty great at it. I knew how to find blind spots and exploit them."

"That's why you needed the pardon?"

Reed shrugged. "The pardon was something Trousdale owed me. But the bottom line is, I'm not in that line of work anymore. I'm just a guy now. A guy with a family to feed. A guy who happens to know a *lot* about how killers think and how to stop them. I don't blame you if you don't trust me. But the vice president chose to, and I promise you that Trousdale does."

Jenkins studied his shoes for a while. They were dirty, much like his pants, stained with sweat and dust. Reed gave him time.

At last, Jenkins reached for the pot again. "How do I know you're not in on it?"

"Because if I was, she'd be dead."

Jenkins froze, the coffeepot hanging in midair. Before he could respond, Reed's earpiece buzzed, and Turk's voice broke through.

"Rocky Top to Prosecutor. I've got something."

41

There were dogs everywhere. The Ghost saw them emerging from the shadows, held on short leashes by men in bulletproof vests as he stopped the truck.

The checkpoint was impressive. He couldn't deny that. An absolute army of Secret Service agents choked off the street, barricading it with a gate and a row of concrete barriers, while bright lights shone down from SkyWatch mobile surveillance towers, nearly blinding him as they gleamed off the truck's dirty windshield.

A half block ahead was the hospital, rising out of North Chicago amid a cluster of taller towers. Most of its windows were now black, and another swarm of Secret Service agents wielding assault rifles gathered near the main entrance. In little more than a day, the Secret Service had converted an average medical center into their own version of Fort Knox.

And yet The Ghost knew he was about to cruise right through. He would make it past the dogs, past the barriers, past the surveillance towers and the rifles, and the hard men in bulletproof vests. Because he wasn't a threat. He was just a guy doing his job.

An agent rapped on the driver's side door. The Ghost rolled the window down and presented his ID. The agent asked him to exit the truck, and he complied without complaint.

Then the search began.

Dogs, mirrors, and bright flashlights were all employed as the cab, the engine bay, the undercarriage, and the cargo box were all examined in detail. Rows of medical gas bottles clinked together as they were each inspected individually, small amounts of gas being leaked into testing devices to confirm their contents.

The inspection was oppressive and required the better part of twenty minutes. The Ghost submitted to a full body search, then stood quietly by and waited, his mind calm.

They wouldn't find the tiny amount of C-4 packed into the valve system of the third green oxygen bottle strapped behind the cab. The explosives were encased in cayenne pepper to mask their scent, but the total volume of C-4 itself was so meager as to make it undetectable anyway.

The lead agent approached The Ghost, handing his ID back. "Where are you headed?"

"Seventh floor. Medical supply room."

"How many bottles?"

"Just three."

"Okay. You can drive around to the loading dock, then we'll escort you from there."

The Ghost pocketed his ID, then climbed back into the truck. It was another five minutes before the dogs finally cleared out, pulled away on their leashes while the agents lifted the gate.

The Ghost drove slowly down the block, following Secret Service directions to the back of the hospital. He didn't look up to the seventh floor where he knew the president lay, clinging to life by a thread.

He'd be there soon enough.

42

Turk watched the medical gas truck as the Secret Service descended on it like ants swarming the crust of a PB&J sandwich. Through his binoculars, he made out the careful sweep of the vehicle, with dogs sniffing around the base and agents sweeping long mirrors beneath the chassis. Then the rear was searched, the hood was lifted, and the cab was turned inside out. A slow, methodical process.

His earpiece crackled, and Reed's voice spilled through. "Prosecutor to Rocky Top. Secret Service has the vehicle on schedule for an oxygen delivery. All clear."

Turk lowered the binoculars. "Copy that, Prosecutor. Will monitor."

The agents began to part, and then the gate lifted. The truck rolled through, then disappeared around a corner as it circled toward the back of the hospital, out of Turk's view. He watched it go and almost jogged to the far side of the roof to keep it in sight.

Then he decided against it. He'd called the truck in because it was a large vehicle approaching a primary checkpoint—always something to be worried about back in Iraq. But if the Secret Service cleared it, he wasn't going to second-guess them. He adjusted the binoculars and resumed his search, sweeping the surrounding buildings and streets alongside the precision shooters stretched out next to him. Still looking for the sniper.

43

The photograph loaded slowly, reminding Wolfgang of years gone by when faulty dial-up internet resulted in grainy images that appeared in blocks, beginning at the top of the screen and moving gradually downward. Like a printer, spitting out the image one half inch at a time.

But the slow connection wasn't the fault of weak internet. He knew it probably had more to do with advanced firewalls, proxy servers, and a network of sheltered IP addresses. Things he didn't really understand but knew enough about to appreciate both their complexity and necessity.

Shaking the FBI was next to impossible. The next best thing for most digital criminals was simply to make the chase too long, too complex, and too aggravating for an agency of limited resources to pursue.

Another inch loaded, and Wolfgang saw cold eyes nestled under a heavy brow. Wolfgang could barely see his pupils, yet he knew the man was angry. A high hairline was marked by twisted and blotched skin, almost as though he'd been subjected to a botched facelift. Or maybe he'd been burned. The image was black-and-white, and it was hard to tell.

Another half inch. Whatever distant server Wolfgang's computer was connected to might have only been fifty miles away, but the IP address he'd already backtracked led to Istanbul, Turkey. Wolfgang figured it was the first of many stops along a network of red herrings and misdirection.

He sat back and sipped hot tea. Phantom pain from his obliterated leg raced up to his hip, but he'd learned to block it out. The tea helped—maybe more because it gave him something to focus on versus any natural, herbal therapy.

The image blinked, and then the last two inches loaded all at once. Wolfgang saw a complete face, and he inhaled involuntarily. The right cheek was twisted, a mess of scars running up to the ear, lifting the lip in a soft sneer and leaving a pencil-sized hole just above the jawline. The anger he'd seen only moments before, Wolfgang now reinterpreted as pain—physical, and maybe something deeper, also.

A mutilated face and a cold sneer aimed directly at the camera, almost as if the guy were posing for a mugshot. He was maybe forty-five or fifty years old, heavily weathered, and totally detached. A soulless man, staring right through whatever he looked at.

Wolfgang hit a key on his keyboard and returned to the chat box, punching in a quick message.

LW10MM: GOT IT. DETAILS?

The identity he was now messaging had voluntarily connected with him after responding to one of his posts on a dark web message board. Wolfgang knew nothing about the faceless persona other than his username: BloodChill458.

It sounded like a twelve-year-old's gamer tag, but looking at the man in the picture, it felt more sinister.

BLOODCHILL458: THEY CALL HIM GHOST. PICTURE IS FROM RUSSIAN SVR FILE. TARGET MARKED KOS.

Wolfgang switched back to the photo, reviewing that death stare again. It was no more or less unnerving than the faces of the three other men he'd collected over the past eight hours—all precision shooters from around the world, rumored to have the capacity for extreme long-range shots.

Most of those rumors were probably just that—rumors. Finding details of these people was like studying Mars through a cheap telescope. Everything felt vague and out of reach, plus most of the informants wanted money, which, in Wolfgang's mind, tainted the reliability of their information. But the images and the names—or pseudonyms—associated with them were something. A lead for the FBI, and for Reed.

BLOODCHILL458: WANT CONTACT INFO? CAN ARRANGE FOR THE RIGHT PRICE.

Wolfgang rattled off a quick reply.

LW10MM: WILL LET YOU KNOW. THANKS.

He closed the page and opened his email, tabbing to a new message and entering Reed's address before dropping in all four images. Wolfgang hit send, then sat back and rubbed his chin, still staring into those dead eyes. Something about them touched him, like a sniper's bullet from twenty-four hundred yards.

A kiss of death.

44

Reed was on his third cup of coffee, and fatigue was setting in. The feeling wasn't unfamiliar. Back in the Marine Corps, he was used to "hurry up and wait," killing long days and longer nights, hoping for something to happen.

Yet, this was different. The deep blackness outside the hospital kept him on edge. He watched an army of doctors descend on Maggie's room, prepping for yet another round of surgery, and he felt the nagging sensation in the back of his mind that he was missing something.

But what?

"Prosecutor to Rocky Top. Sitrep."

"All quiet," Turk said. "Nothing to report."

Reed rubbed his face, his attention arrested by a number of Secret Service agents marching toward the elevator, led by Jenkins. The doors rolled back, and a tall guy in a grey-green jumpsuit appeared, dark and dirty hair pinned down by a matching ball cap. He backed his way out of the elevator, dragging a hand truck behind him laden with a trio of medical gas bottles, each about five feet high. Outside the elevator, he was directed to set the bottles down, then the Secret Service commenced barking questions into their wrist-mounted mics.

Reed tilted his head toward the nearest agent—a skinny guy seated behind the bank of surveillance screens. "What's this?"

"The guy from the oxygen truck," the agent said. "He already passed inspection."

Reed lifted his coffee cup, then stopped halfway to his mouth as the man in the jumpsuit turned, exposing his face for the first time.

Reed's stomach tightened. The entire left side of the guy's face was a mess of ghastly scars, ripping up from his chin to his hairline with a small hole opening right through his cheek and into his mouth, surrounded by swollen and mangled flesh. He made eye contact with Reed, and Reed saw nothing. No uncertainty, no stress, no discomfort with the Secret Service agents clustered around him, inspecting his paperwork and patting him down yet again.

The guy's face was totally empty. Almost dead.

And then he looked away.

Reed's stomach loosened, and he thought he'd imagined the mutilated face and the hole in one cheek. It was all too specific and bizarre to really believe.

I'm wearing out.

Reed gulped the coffee as the Secret Service escorted the guy down the hall toward Maggie's room. A storage closet situated directly next to it was locked and guarded, where vetted bottles of oxygen linked into a proprietary gas line system that fed Maggie's face mask. The agent stationed there was already busy unlocking the door and making room for the fresh supply. A hospital technician was on-site to help make the transition.

A routine switch, apparently.

Jenkins left the small crowd and rejoined Reed. "Anything from Turk?" he asked.

Reed shook his head, slipping his hand into his pocket to retrieve his buzzing phone. There was a single-word text message from Wolfgang.

EMAIL.

Reed tabbed to his email app and waited for the message to load. The Secret Service had cell signal blockers installed all around the floor, completely isolating his signal and forcing him to rely on their highly regulated and very slow Wi-Fi.

A message appeared from Wolfgang with the subject line "Possibles." There was no text inside, only four attachments.

Reed sucked down coffee and watched them load. Down the hall, the new bottles of oxygen were offloaded, and the Secret Service had replaced them with empties. The guy in the jumpsuit was headed back to the elevator, trailed by agents.

The first image loaded. It was a distant black-and-white shot lifted from a security camera. The man featured was tall, olive-skinned, and busy checking into a hotel. His face was obscured and difficult to make out. Reed flipped to the next image, which loaded as slow as the first, one half inch at a time, starting at the top. Tangled black hair, laced with grey. A high forehead.

A spinning "loading" icon filled the middle of the screen. Reed reached for the refresh button, listening as the technician near Trousdale's room gave directions for Jenkins to help him connect the new bottles. The image vanished. The elevator door dinged. The doors rolled back.

Then the picture returned, all at once, and Reed's stomach flipped.

Dead eyes, a scarred face. One small hole in the left cheek.

Reed dropped the phone and looked for the elevator. He saw the guy in the jumpsuit, and again, their gazes met, followed by the hint of a sneer. The doors rolled shut, and Reed whirled for the oxygen bottle.

"No! Don't touch it!"

The technician reached for the valve, and Jenkins's face snapped toward Reed. The technician made half a turn on the knob as Jenkins sprang into action, yanking the bottle away from the wall.

Then a bone-shattering explosion ripped down the hallway, and Reed crashed to the floor.

45

Reed's shoulder slammed into hard tile as fire belched out of the hallway, pouring into the converted nurses' station as glass shattered and screams ripped through the air. The flames passed only inches from his face, and he clawed his way back, bits of ceiling tiles and shards of furniture raining down.

His ears rang. He couldn't hear a thing. The world around him spun, and Reed saw blood. He checked his chest instinctively, rolling onto his back and searching for wounds. Crimson coated his shirt and dripped down his arm, and he rolled to his right over a sea of sooty glass.

He couldn't find his injury. Everything felt numb, and his ears continued to ring, then his hands fell across soft flesh, and he pulled. It was the arm of the guy sitting behind the computer screens only moments before, now completely disconnected. Reed looked for the torso and saw the man flopped across the tile.

Dead.

Reed fought his way to the body. Smoke and dirt clouded his vision. He thought he heard shouting to his right, but when he looked that way there was nobody—just a smoky room littered with debris.

Reed felt the dead man's belt and searched for a pistol. He found the Glock 19 holstered on the guy's hip and yanked it out, completing a press-check without even thinking about it. Then he stopped to stretch his jaw, trying to clear his ears. The shouting continued, but only in his right ear.

Reed felt something lodged there and probed it with numb fingers. He felt curly wire and suddenly remembered the earpiece.

"Reed! Do you copy?"

The shouting was Turk.

Reed lifted his wrist to his lips. His own words sounded distorted and unclear, and he couldn't tell how loud he was speaking.

"Bottle truck!" He coughed. "Stop it!"

Reed clawed his way to his knees, holding onto the desk. Half the monitors were blown out, roasted by the cloud of fire that had roared down the hallway. Reed felt something wet on the desktop, but when he looked down, it wasn't blood. A shower of fire sprinklers kicked on overhead.

"Bottle truck!" Reed shouted again. He stumbled around the desk, not even bothering to look back down the hall as he rushed for the stairs.

The hospital technician was dead. Jenkins was dead. Maggie might well be dead.

But the killer was still alive and in the hospital.

46

Reed's words flooded the earpiece in a garble. Turk covered his ear and shouted into the mic. He smelled smoke, and after looking down from the roof, he saw the source streaming from shattered windows seven floors down.

The president's floor.

"Reed! Do you copy?"

"... truck!"

"What?"

"Bottle truck! Stop it!"

Turk lifted the binoculars, scanning the hospital entrance far below. The agents around him snapped call signs and command confirmations through their headsets, both calm and angry, all at once.

Then Turk saw the truck. It barreled out of the garage, crashing straight for the checkpoint. The front end leapt a speed bump, and the windshield cracked as the wheels slammed back to earth. Then Turk saw the driver leaning low, his head barely visible over the dash.

"Stop that truck!" Turk shouted, pointing towards the truck. The sniper on his right pivoted to align his scope with the street below. He leaned out over the roof parapet, the rifle not so much as twitching as the muzzle gaped toward the truck.

"Blow out a tire!" Turk shouted again.

The sniper didn't respond. Turk heard him speaking quietly into his throat mic, but the rifle remained silent.

The truck crashed onward. It reached the checkpoint and blasted straight through the gate, reaching the street and screaming northward. The agents gathered around the checkpoint scrambled for cover, but nobody opened fire.

"Shoot!" Turk screamed.

"I don't have authorization!" the sniper said. "I don't know who I'm shooting at!"

Turk jerked the binoculars back to his eyes, tracing the truck.

It was already half a mile away, blazing northward along Fairbanks Court. Unhindered.

"Turk!" Reed's voice broke through the earpiece as the truck rolled into a left turn along East Chicago Avenue and disappeared from sight. "Where is he?"

"Just turned west on Chicago Ave. I'm losing him!"

47

Reed took the steps two and three at a time, the Glock held at his side. Turk's voice was clouded by the fog in his brain, but as he reached the fifth floor and broke into a hallway, three words rang clear.

"I'm losing him."

Reed scanned the directory hanging from the ceiling, then he turned right and bolted for the door. He passed a Secret Service agent running in the opposite direction, then heard a nurse scream as her gaze fell on his gun. Emergency lights flashed from the walls, and the fire alarm howled like a demented beast of the underworld.

Reed kept running. He reached the entrance to the parking garage and barreled out into a crowd of fleeing hospital staff and civilians, all scrambling for personal vehicles. More Secret Service agents fought to corral and filter the tsunami of people, but Reed knew it was far too late.

The sniper was loose.

Reed ground to a stop and searched the line of cars parked nearest to the door. A doctor still dressed in scrubs and wearing a surgical hat rushed toward a Porsche 911 Carrera, and Reed made a beeline.

He met the doctor at the driver's door and thrust the Glock into his face. "Keys!"

The guy blanched and tossed Reed a fistful of keys as he stumbled back.

Reed snatched the door open, dumping the Glock in ahead of him and folding himself inside. The seat was much too near the steering wheel, and his legs jammed against the dash. He hit the switch to roll it back and slammed the door, then searched for the ignition.

The starter button was next to the wheel, and his left foot found the clutch. A seven-speed shifter rose from the console, and the car roared to life only a moment before he slammed it into reverse.

Tires screamed against concrete, and a horn blared. Reed didn't bother to look back, cutting the wheel and slamming on the brakes before finding first gear. The three-liter flat-six resting behind him drove power to the wheels, and this time, they didn't break traction.

Reed cut around a corner in the garage, already calling to Turk. "Where is he?"

Turk's words were muffled by wind, but the ringing in Reed's ears had begun to die down. He could make out complete sentences again.

"I lost him on Chicago Ave. He's headed north."

Reed punched the maps icon on the infotainment system and was rewarded by a zoomed image of North Chicago, a blue dot marking his place in the concrete jungle. He hit the brakes as a line of cars gathered at the garage exit. Secret Service agents knotted around the gate were busy sweeping each car, dogs on leashes sniffing their wheels, and horns honking as panicked hospital staff fought to leave.

"Turk! Tell them to clear the garage exit!"

Turk didn't reply, and nothing happened at the gate. Reed saw an SUV pulling in behind him, a sweating nurse talking into a cell phone. Reed shifted into reverse and hit his horn. The nurse saw him but didn't react.

He lifted the clutch and cut the wheel. The Porsche rolled backward and smacked the front bumper of the SUV. Reed applied gas, and the SUV rolled backward a foot as the nurse laid on her horn.

He found first gear again and turned left. The Porsche sped out of line and cut toward the entrance of the garage, where a row of orange cones and a fiberglass gate blocked his path. Reed reached second gear and made contact. The windshield cracked as the gate bucked upward and scraped across the car's roof, then cones rolled over the Porsche's hood. In a moment, he was outside, Secret Service agents yelling for him to stop as he fled northward.

"Where is he?" Reed hit third gear and blazed past a row of black Tahoes. Emergency lights flashed everywhere, and a police helicopter roared overhead.

"They're deploying a chopper," Turk said. "I've lost him."

A row of cars was backed up at a traffic light ahead, and Reed swerved into the oncoming lane. A rushing motorcycle almost took off his rear bumper while screaming pedestrians gathered on the sidewalk. Reed glanced to the infotainment system and cut another left at the next intersection, onto East Chicago Avenue.

"Turk! I need something."

"Hold on. I'm talking to the chopper."

Reed stomped on the brakes as he rushed toward the next stoplight. Another line of cars blocked his path, but this time, oncoming traffic in the left lane prevented him from circling them. The Porsche slid to a stop behind a van.

"Turk!"

"We—" Turk broke in and out, the earpiece crackling.

Reed thought it might be losing signal, and he reached for his phone. He couldn't find it, but his fingers met blood as he touched his stomach. He looked down to inspect the wound, then Turk's voice broke through.

"North on Michigan Avenue!"

The cars rolled forward, and Reed dumped the clutch. He'd already marked the next intersection on the map, and he pulled the Porsche into a harsh turn. The rear wheels broke traction, and the back end swung out. Reed shifted up as the tires caught. Pedestrians lining Michigan Avenue turned into a blur as he swerved around a pickup truck. Far overhead, he saw two more choppers swooping in to join the police bird—both Army National Guard Black Hawks.

Reed couldn't hear Turk anymore. The earpiece died as he left the hospital far behind. But he traced the spotlights streaming down from the helicopters and found their junction directly ahead, maybe a mile away.

Reed speed-shifted to fourth. The twin-turbocharged motor churned out torque, and his head snapped against the seat. The front end lifted, and a city bus flashed by on his right as though it were in reverse. Then came another string of cars parked next to meters along the curb, the last in line parked in reverse with its nose crossing into Reed's lane.

Reed swerved around it, pushing the little car beyond seventy miles per hour.

Up ahead, cars began to pile up. Reed jerked the wheel to the right, sliding to a stop with his window exposed to the point on the street highlighted by the helicopter's spotlights.

The bottle truck rested on its side, hot fire exploding from the cab. Medical gas cylinders rolled across the street, and cops shouted at civilians to stand back as the flames grew taller.

Reed traced the path of the disaster over a smashed sedan before the truck had slammed into the curb and then . . . detonated? Placing himself in the sniper's shoes, Reed thought like a killer—a man on the run. A man who had planned for everything. He shoved the shifter into first and snatched the wheel to the right. The Porsche spun around in a cloud of tire smoke, and he turned south, back in the direction of the hospital.

48

Reed found the line of parked cars right where he left it, but the last car in line—the one parked in reverse, giving it an easy exit away from the wrecked bottle truck—was gone. He pictured the moment he'd swerved around it, trying to remember the make and model. It was silver. A Honda? A Toyota? Something innocuous like that. Something anybody could see and everybody would miss.

No, it was a Ford. Reed remembered the open black grill and the long nose. A Ford Fusion, late model. He stomped the accelerator and swerved to the left, catching a glimpse down the long line of cars gathered in front of him. The oncoming headlights flashed in his face, and another horn blared.

But Reed saw the Fusion turn right at the next intersection, catching Chestnut Street. He gunned the motor, hopping the curb and laying on his horn. Pedestrians screamed and broke in waves as he drove onto the wide sidewalk and hit the gas.

A woman in heels jumped aside and hurled her Starbucks at him. The coffee exploded over the windshield, and he hit the wipers reflexively, still blaring the horn.

The Porsche bounced over the curb again, and he jerked it right onto Chestnut. Ahead he saw the Ford stopped at a traffic light. The Porsche's wipers swept across the windshield again, and for a split second, Reed thought he saw the car's driver look over his shoulder. Then the brake lights died, and the tires screamed. The silver vehicle shot into the intersection, narrowly missing a passing Honda, and raced forward.

Reed dropped into third and hit the gas. The Porsche blazed through the intersection amid a blare of horns. Ahead of him, the Ford reached the next stoplight and hung a hard right. Reed followed only fifty yards behind and closing. The Porsche swung wide into the intersection and grazed another car, then the back wheels caught and launched him forward.

Street signs advertised North Rush Street. It was aptly named. Reed laid the hammer down, and the tachometer bounded to redline as the digital readout next to it flashed through the fifties and back toward seventy miles per hour. The Ford was still a full intersection ahead now, weaving through traffic and outpacing the Porsche by sheer luck. Each time Reed closed ground, another car pulled in front of him, or he was forced to slow as he ran up behind a city bus. At times he closed on the Ford, once so close he saw the guy's head bobbing over the top of his seat. Reed reached for the Glock, now sliding around in the passenger footwell, before being forced to grab the shifter again and pull back into neutral, swerving around an oncoming bread truck.

Reed cut the wheel and slid around the nose of the truck, ignoring the blast of the larger vehicle's horn. Then he caught second gear as the Ford yanked a left at the next intersection—Division Street.

Reed reached the stoplight and raced through on yellow. Division Street was twice as wide as Rush, with a smattering of cars moving in closed ranks, east and west. As Reed found his place in the right-hand lane, he thought he saw the silver sedan three cars ahead.

He upshifted and planted his foot on the gas. The Porsche howled and devoured ground, running up on the minivan ahead of him as Reed laid on the horn. The van swerved to the right, and he surged around it.

The Ford was dead ahead now, sixty or seventy yards. The driver risked a panicked look over his shoulder, then accelerated straight into the back of the sedan ahead of him. Metal met metal with a crunch. The driver of the rear-ended sedan lost control, spinning into the oncoming lane as the sniper rushed forward.

Reed drew nearer, passing the last car left between them as buildings all blurred together. He felt the heartbeat of the Porsche throbbing through the steering wheel—shooting up his arm from the shifter and vibrating through the seat. It was completely different from the raw and loose power of the '69 Camaro he kept back home.

A different language.

But Reed understood the dialect. He pushed the car harder as he saw the Ford hit a bridge thirty yards ahead, crossing the Chicago River onto Goose Island beyond.

Reed pressed his foot into the accelerator, feeling the Ford sucking into his grasp only seconds away, already thinking about ramming the rear bumper and knocking it into the bridge wall.

Then the Ford's taillights blazed red, and the driver yanked the wheel to the right. Reed instinctively turned left, flashing by the sedan's left side as he smashed both the clutch and the brake. The Porsche's tires screamed and broke traction, and he yanked the wheel to the right, embracing the spin as the back end swung wide. In an instant, he was facing the way he'd come, staring down the nose of the Ford fifty yards away.

The Ford didn't move, and the driver was gone. Reed reached for the Glock and hit the gas. His front bumper made contact with the sedan. The cracks already racing across the Porsche's windshield expanded into a spiderweb as it slid to a halt and Reed reached for the door, leading with the G19.

The driver's door of the Ford was half-closed. Reed swept the muzzle of the Glock across the windshield, his finger hovering over the trigger. No driver. No sniper.

No man with one mutilated cheek.

Then Reed heard a soft clink. He snatched the gun up over the roof of the Ford as headlights from oncoming cars blazed across his face. Moving around the driver's side, he traced the noise to a metal superstructure built along the outside of the bridge, blocking the street section from the pedestrian bridge that ran alongside it. The superstructure was built of galvanized metal, rising eight feet high with large diamond-shaped gaps between the bars.

A minivan slid to a stop at the end of the bridge, its headlights diving toward the pavement and flashing across the superstructure. Then Reed saw the sniper standing on the pedestrian bridge beyond a diamond hole, looking over one shoulder, dead at Reed. The emptiness in the sniper's eyes verged on soullessness. A complete vacancy framed by the mutilated cheek.

The guy stood with one arm cradling a backpack by the straps, the other hanging loose and empty at his side. He dropped the bag, turned for the outside railing of the pedestrian bridge, and jumped.

Reed lunged forward, grabbing the superstructure and hurtling through, Glock in hand. He landed feet-first on the pedestrian bridge still semi-illuminated by the headlights pouring over him from the minivan, and shoved the Glock over the water.

The guy was gone. Ripples in the filthy, dark water mixed with brown bubbles, but there was no body. Reed raised the Glock, finger on the trigger, ready to fire.

But he stopped. There was nothing to fire at. The sniper had vanished into thin air, leaving the backpack.

The backpack.

Reed grabbed the railing, throwing himself over without waiting to think. His feet cleared the bridge, and he lurched over empty space.

Then the second bomb detonated, blasting him into the Chicago River.

49

Stratton awoke to the pound of a heavy fist on his bedroom door. He sat upright, Carolyn already rubbing sleep out of her eyes as the pounding was met with a barking voice.

"Mr. Vice President!"

Stratton put his feet on the floor and reached for his shirt.

Carolyn grabbed his arm. "Is . . . is she dead?"

Stratton pulled away, tossing the shirt aside as the pounding on the door continued.

"Mr. Vice President! We need you to come with us."

Is this it?

Another fist struck the door, and Stratton yanked it open. "What?"

Jim Dorsey, the head of his Secret Service detail, stood immediately outside, his fist still raised to pound the door. Dorsey looked strained, his Irish face streaming with sweat. Two more agents stood immediately behind him, and now that the door was open, Stratton could hear the sleepy cries of his twin daughters from down the hall.

"Dorsey, what the hell?" Stratton said.

"We need you to come with us, sir," Dorsey said. "We're evacuating the residence."

"Why?" Stratton was still only half-awake, blurry and disoriented. He glanced over his shoulder and saw Carolyn clutching the blanket to her chest, her face pale.

Carolyn Presley Stratton wasn't a strong woman. Not physically and not emotionally. She spent an excessive amount of time in bed, swallowing sedatives like Tic Tacs to battle perpetual emotional distress. She was, by any social standard, a basket case. But she was also the daughter of Arthur Presley, the second-wealthiest man in Illinois. Who said marriage was about happiness, anyway?

Stratton stepped out of the bedroom and smacked the door shut behind him, cutting Carolyn out before she could descend into a panicked outburst.

"What happened?" Stratton whispered.

"There was another attempt, sir," Dorsey said.

"What?" Stratton's heart skipped, and his palms turned cold.

"It was a bomb at the hospital. We don't have details yet."

"And the president?"

"I don't know, sir. Please, I need you to get Mrs. Stratton and come with us. We're moving you back to the plane."

Stratton looked down the hall. Louise and Lindy, his twin six-year-old daughters, were being ushered by female agents toward the stairs. Pre-packed bags rolled behind them even as the girls cried and looked back for Stratton. He lifted a hand and smiled, ushering them to go along with the agents. Lindy sobbed and reached for him, but an agent swept her up and hurried down the stairs.

"Sir, please. We need you to hurry."

Stratton pushed back into the bedroom. Carolyn was up, her nightgown flowing around her feet, a single tear dripping down one cheek.

"Jordan? What's happening?"

"We're returning to the plane," Stratton said. "Get dressed."

He ducked into the walk-in closet, itself as big as a small room, and swept a sweatshirt off a hanger.

Carolyn went to the window and peered outside, holding a hand over her mouth. "Jordan! Where are the girls?"

"Get dressed," Stratton repeated. He pulled jeans over his boxers, grabbing his phone and watch from the nightstand as he turned for the door. Carolyn hadn't moved from the window.

Stratton snapped his fingers. "Carolyn! Let's go."

She looked over her shoulder, wide eyes staring dumbly at Stratton. The he saw the bottle of heavy sedatives lying open next to the bed, a couple pills spilled over the nightstand. He breathed a curse and barreled through the door, meeting Dorsey outside.

"Have somebody assist the Second Lady," he said.

Dorsey snapped orders into his wrist mic, following Stratton down the spiraling wood staircase and into the main living area below. It was alive with agents, each busy packing up the personal items the Stratton family might need aboard *Air Force Two*.

Or was it now *Air Force One*? The moment Trousdale passed, the designation would change. The thought crossed Stratton's mind, and he felt a chill up his spine.

Stratton scooped his reading glasses and a bottle of water off the counter on his way to the door. Halfway there, Barrett appeared from the shadows, accosting his son next to the coat rack. Stratton was surprised to see him—he thought the old man was back in Chicago—but he should've known better. Barrett Stratton was a shark. He smelled blood in the water.

"Jordan," Barrett snapped. "What happened?"

Stratton glanced back up the stairs. Two female agents were busy escorting Carolyn. She still wore the nightgown, but they had at least wrapped her in a coat.

"We should go, sir," Dorsey pressed, standing at Stratton's elbow.

Stratton tilted his head toward the door, ushering him out.

"*What* happened?" Barrett repeated.

"I don't know," Stratton said.

"Is she dead?"

Stratton saw a distant light in his father's dark eyes and the vaguest hint of a smile lifting the corners of his mouth.

"I don't know," Stratton repeated, turning for the door.

Barrett caught him by the elbow, holding him back. "Remember the family, Jordan. The family comes *first*."

Stratton felt ice creep into his stomach, slow and relentless. He tore his elbow free, then he was rushing across the lawn, the engines of *Marine Two* howling from the helicopter pad fifty yards away, Dorsey at his side. Moving into the dark.

Moving into the unknown.

50

"You did the right thing, Corporal."

The voice echoed and wavered, as though the speaker were trapped on the other side of a cavern. Reed stood at a metal desk, sweat streaming down his face and his fingertips burning. Spread across the desktop were images—dozens of them—all depicting the same thing: a backpack bomb built beneath the kid's lunch box, with enough C-4 to blow a dozen Marines into a thousand pieces.

Reed's head swam, and he fumbled with one photo. The edges cut his fingers, and he saw blood. It ran across the image and mixed with the sweat and grime coating his hands. The Marine colonel sitting across from him was just as sweaty, his words echoing as though he sat a thousand miles away.

"You served your country, son. I'm proud of you."

Reed looked up, but he didn't see the colonel. He didn't see the tent walls. The pictures and the desk faded from his mind and were replaced by an open desert. It stretched for miles in every direction, as hot as an oven, the sun blazing down so bright he could barely see. The desk vanished, and in its place a pit opened, wide and gaping, with giant teeth shooting out from the perimeter like the mouth of a subterranean monster.

Reed scrambled back, watching the blackness below. He couldn't see the bottom and somehow knew there *wasn't* a bottom. The pit went on forever, deeper and deeper, straight to Hell.

Then he saw the kid, a gaping hole in his neck where Reed's thirty-caliber slug tore straight through. He fell backward into the pit, his arms thrashing, reaching for Reed. Screaming for help.

Reed lunged forward and felt his feet slip. He toppled, clawing at loose sand. One of the teeth caught his pants leg and yanked down. Rocks tore at his hands, and still, the boy's scream filled the pit. Pounding. Echoing. Consuming.

Reed grabbed a stone and clung on as the tooth pulled down. He saw red. He saw the crosshairs hovering over the kid's neck. Then his grip broke, and he fell. The pit swallowed him. The teeth faded overhead. The desert sun grew dim.

And he kept falling.

Reed's eyes snapped open, and he gasped for air. Something plastic was pressed against his face, making him feel suffocated. His fingertips still burned, and his lungs felt starved as though he hadn't breathed in days. He gasped on pure oxygen and reached up to claw the mask away when he felt a strong hand on his arm.

"Reed! Calm down, brother."

Reed's head pivoted to the left, and he saw Turk. His friend was red-faced but clean. He wore different clothes than he had the last time Reed had seen him.

Reed's muscles loosened, and he collapsed against a thin pillow. His vision refocused on what he now identified as a hospital ceiling, and he peeled the mask off. Somehow, sour hospital air was easier to breathe. It felt more natural.

"Where?" Reed rasped.

Turk reached for a bottle of water and poked a straw into it before Reed sucked it down.

"Vista Medical Center," Turk said. "You're making the rounds."

"And?" Reed rasped. He didn't need to waste words. Turk would know what he meant.

"And you've got one hell of a concussion, plus a little shrapnel action across your stomach. Nothing life-threatening. They've already removed the metal and stitched you up."

Reed winced, feeling the stitches in his chest and stomach. That explained the stiffness. "Sniper?" he asked, finishing the bottle.

"He got away," a new voice said. "But we know who he is."

Reed ratcheted his head to the right. Wolfgang sat next to him, seated in a cheap hospital chair, his prosthetic leg propped up on Reed's bed. He looked a lot thinner than the last time Reed had seen him, nearly two years previously. His hair was long, reaching down to his shoulders, and looked unwashed. He hadn't shaved, either. Not in a few days.

But for all that, he looked alert. Reed still saw a glimmer of the man he once knew as The Wolf—the only killer who ever came close to bringing him into permanent retirement.

"Wolf," Reed croaked.

Wolfgang grunted, dropping the prosthetic back onto the floor and reaching into a carry-on bag next to him. He retrieved an iPad and flipped it on, then pivoted it to face Reed.

"This guy?" he asked.

Reed saw the face of the bottle truck driver—twisted and mutilated on one side, the hole in one cheek.

The face of a monster.

Reed nodded. "Yeah."

"After the bomb, the Secret Service pulled their surveillance tape," Turk said. "I sent the picture to Wolfgang to help his search. Apparently, he'd already found the guy."

Reed nodded. "I got the email right before the bomb went off. What about Maggie?"

"She's alive," Turk said. "By a miracle. One of the oxygen cylinders was packed with something. A tiny bit of C-4, probably. Not enough to be detected, but coupled with the oxygen, enough to set off one hell of a blast. They had that cylinder hooked up straight into the gas lines feeding the president. Jenkins yanked it loose just before the bomb went off. If he hadn't, the blast would've sent a fireball straight into Trousdale's lungs. Lights out, no question."

Reed again imagined the flash of flame. The floor-shaking blast. "Jenkins?" he asked, facing Turk.

Turk shook his head softly. Reed saw the president's head of security again—his face all haggard, refusing to sleep, far too dedicated to his job to quit.

Reed had challenged his focus in context of his exhaustion. But in the end, it was Jenkins, not Reed, who put the pieces together in time, thinking to yank the bottle free of the president's oxygen line. Jenkins's mind had worked like a steel trap, right to the end.

Meanwhile, Reed had walked up on that backpack, stupidly ignoring it, fixated on the man vanishing into the black.

Fool.

"I turned the photo over to the FBI," Wolfgang said. "They haven't got anything, but they're looking into it."

"What do you have?" Reed asked.

"Not much. I found the image on the dark web. His name is Ghost, apparently. Or The Ghost. No other details, but my contact seemed to think he was capable of an extreme distance shot."

"Nationality?" Reed asked. "Background?"

"Not sure. Possibly Russian."

Russian.

Reed fixated on a stain on the far wall. It was brown and dripped toward the floor—the mark of an old pipe leak, probably. It was something to center his mind on while he unpacked the details shoveled at him. They weren't much to go on, but it was a start.

"He'll go to ground next," Reed said. "Two failed attempts inside of a couple days. Plus, we know what he looks like now. He can't risk a third exposure. He'll go dark for a while to reevaluate. Connect with his employer."

Wolfgang grunted. "I thought so, too."

"So, what's next?" Turk asked.

Reed hit the switch on the side of his hospital bed, lifting the back until he was sitting upright. "It's not enough to find this guy," Reed said. "If he's a pro killer, then he's working for money, and that means there's somebody behind him. Somebody who won't stop trying until the job is done."

"The employer," Turk said.

"Right. We need that name."

The three of them sat quietly, Reed's mouth watering as he suddenly craved a cigarette. He fixated on the water stain and tried to reverse-engineer the problem. Who would want Trousdale dead? There could be a million and one people—political rivals, international adversaries, crackpot conspiracy theorists living in single-wide trailers on the wrong side of nowhere.

But who would have the money and resources to contract a man like Ghost? Who *was* Ghost, anyway?

"I may have a lead," Wolfgang said.

Reed pivoted toward him. "What kind of lead?"

Wolfgang folded his arms. He looked weary, almost broken. Reed suddenly realized he'd failed to check up on Wolfgang since he and Banks were married and then disappeared into South America.

He'd never stopped to think about the one-legged killer or how he was making out. The CIA had cut Wolfgang a sizable check, right alongside Reed and Turk, following the North Korea mission. But money was only one of a slew of personal needs. Clearly, it hadn't assuaged whatever demons were slowly eroding The Wolf.

"I knew somebody . . . from before," Wolfgang said. "A Russian contact."

"When you were an assassin?" Turk asked, suspicion creeping into his tone. Turk didn't know Wolfgang as well as Reed did, and he probably didn't trust him.

Reed held up a hand, but Wolfgang didn't seem to notice the edge in Turk's voice.

"No, from before that. When I worked in espionage."

"Who is he?" Reed asked.

Wolfgang indulged in a dry smile. "Not somebody you'd know."

"Okay," Reed conceded. "So, how can he help?"

Wolfgang rested his elbows on his knees, wincing a little as weight descended on his prosthetic leg. "If Ghost is a Russian, it's reasonable to assume that he may have been Russian military."

"We thought so, too," Reed said.

"Could be spec ops," Wolfgang said. "Or some kind of precision shooter detachment. Regardless, he isn't Russian military any longer. But if they had somebody this good, they'd remember."

"Your contact is Russian military?" Reed asked.

Wolfgang shrugged. "In a way."

"What makes you think he'll talk to us?"

"He won't," Wolfgang said. "But he might talk to me. He owes me a sizable favor."

Reed exchanged a glance with Turk, but Turk only shrugged.

"Well, get him on the phone," Reed said. "We'll take any help we can get."

Wolfgang shook his head. "It doesn't work that way. I'll need to fly over there. Meet in person. He's not a Facebook friend."

"Okay," Reed said. "So, take Turk with you. We'll call the CIA and arrange an SAC jet."

"No. He'll spook if I bring anyone. I should go alone."

Reed sucked his teeth, glancing toward Wolfgang's fake leg before he could stop himself.

Wolfgang noticed and indulged in a self-deprecating smile. "Don't worry. I can always beat him with it if things go sideways." He stood with a soft grunt, pocketing his hands. "I'd tell you to get some rest, but we both know you won't."

Reed lifted his chin in a subdued salute. "Fly safe, Wolf. Keep us posted."

Wolfgang ducked his head, then slipped through the door with a soft tap of the prosthetic leg. Turk watched him go with a semi-suspicious squint, but Reed wasn't worried. Wolfgang's lead was either good or it wasn't. Either way, there was plenty of work to be done in Chicago.

"We should drill down on a possible employer," Reed said. "Wait for Wolf to get back with us."

"I think you should rest, dude. You got pretty banged up."

"I've been resting for nearly six hours," Reed said, glancing at the cheap clock on the wall. "We don't have time to drag ass."

Turk sighed, dusting his hands against his pants before standing. "Okay.

I'll reach out to Director French and find out who will be replacing Jenkins."

"Good." Reed leaned back, his head still pounding like a drum.

"You need anything?" Turk asked.

"Water," Reed said. "And some ibuprofen."

"I'll find the nurse."

Turk moved toward the door, but Reed called after him. "One other thing."

"Yeah?"

"Have French send some people to my house. I want Banks and Davy under protective custody, immediately. Call Stratton if you have to. That guy saw my face."

51

Wolfgang stopped outside the hospital, pulling his peacoat tighter around his shoulders as the bite of Chicago wind whistled in from the lake. It was bitter in Illinois—almost as bitter as upstate New York. It made Wolfgang think of hot, lazy places with white sand beaches.

He dug his phone out and tabbed to his email application, scrolling through a six-inch list of email addresses, each associated with various pseudonyms from his years as a contract killer. Most of those addresses had lain unused for nearly two years now, and most of them never received anything other than random junk mail.

But one of them was known to a certain overseas contact—a man he hadn't spoken to in eight or ten years. A man who, for all Wolfgang knew, could be dead. Or retired. Or chief of his division. Or he could've disappeared, like so many people in his industry. Fallen off the face of the planet as though he never existed.

The last Wolfgang spoke to him was in another part of the world, in a totally different time of his life. A dark time that he wouldn't revisit for anything.

Wolfgang tapped out a quick note, signing off with his initials and hesitating over the send button. It had been a long time. The man he knew nearly a decade ago was violent, unpredictable, and not exactly a friend.

But he also had a heart deep beneath the bluster and bloodshed. And most importantly of all, he knew things.

Wolfgang hit send and pocketed the phone. Stepping to the curb, he held his thumb up to the nearest cab and piled eagerly into the warmed cabin.

"Where to?" the driver asked.

Wolfgang settled into his seat, briefly recalling Reed's mention of a Special Activities Center jet from the CIA. A free means of travel, certainly, but not an altogether invisible one. For a man like his contact, the presence of a CIA plane might send the wrong signals. It was better to fly commercial and remain completely independent of Washington.

"O'Hare," he said. "International terminal."

52

Maggie saw darkness again, but this time, she wasn't in the Oval Office. The cold that had saturated her consciousness now radiated out from her core instead of stabbing into it. She looked down at her hands and saw the same spidery fingers she'd noted before—still coated in blood, now dry and sticky.

Her blood. Was she dead? Was this Hell?

Maggie struggled to breathe. She felt something pressed against her face, like a pillow cutting off airflow, but when she reached for her mouth, there was nothing there. She screamed. Called for help. She tried to walk, but her feet floated over a black void instead, failing to make contact with anything. She kicked, but it was as though she was spinning in outer space.

There was nothing to grab onto. Nothing to touch or feel. Only the cold bursting from her chest and leaking into the darkness forever and ever. Even her own screams failed to echo back—they were sucked into the darkness like oxygen from her lungs, evaporating and leaving her breathless.

Maggie felt tears on her face and grew still, focusing on keeping her mind calm even as it begged her to freak out. She clutched sticky hands over her face and envisioned someplace safe. Someplace she knew well.

It was what her mother taught Maggie to do when she was a small child, when the nightmares came and she couldn't sleep. Maggie clamped her eyes shut and immediately saw the house by the lake. A slouched, sodden thing with a five-foot alligator creeping through the backyard. Moss grew on the shingles, and slime crept up the walls.

But the more Maggie focused, the clearer the image became, and calm began to fight back the cold in her chest. She knew this place. She knew it better than the Governor's Mansion in Baton Rouge or the college bars outside Louisiana State University.

This was her home. The family vacation spot used for frequent weekend getaways with her grandparents. A safe place. A place so very far away from Washington and . . . wherever she was.

Maggie opened her eyes and saw the darkness again. Immediately, she began to gasp as the panic returned. The lake house was long gone, replaced by emptiness. She was alone and so very cold.

"Help!" Maggie called. "Where am I?"

Her body shook as the fear began to overcome her. Maggie thrashed and began to fall. Whatever she'd been floating on only moments before gave way, and she pitched backwards, flailing for something to grab onto and screaming all the way down.

"Madam President! I'm here!"

A strong hand broke through the darkness and grabbed hers. Maggie felt warmth shoot up her arm, and she stopped falling but continued to flail, like a child whose feet slipped free of the pool floor.

The hand squeezed harder. "Ma'am, please. Stay calm. You're okay. You're okay."

The voice sounded distant but familiar. "O'Dell?" she called, tears streaming down her face.

Another squeeze of her hand, and a face broke through the darkness— strong and weathered, much like the cabin by the lake. Deep, soft eyes. A faint smile.

"Maggie," O'Dell whispered. "I'm here."

Sudden calm washed over her like a wave. Her body loosened, and a feeling of peace drove back the panic.

"Hold on," O'Dell said. "Don't let go."

Maggie looked into his soft, kind eyes. She'd never noticed them before and how they made her feel like the only woman in the world.

Maggie's hand loosened, and everything went black.

"Keep your hands away from her chest!" the doctor shouted.

Maggie thrashed on the hospital bed. Her eyes flicked open and closed, and her hands tangled amid the sheets. Nurses crowded in, but nobody attempted to calm her. They simply pressed near the bed to keep Maggie from rolling off.

O'Dell rushed to the door, climbing over soot and the debris of the oxygen bomb. Jenkins's body had only just been removed, and the tile was still stained with his blood. But Maggie couldn't be moved. The moment her oxygen had been disconnected, right before the blast, her vitals began to fade. Now her body shook and thrashed like a fish flipping across a dock, desperate to drop back into the water.

O'Dell shoved past the distracted Secret Service agent standing at the door. Tearing through the heavy Kevlar sheets that had just recently sheltered the president from a storm of shrapnel, he crowded in close to the nurses and reached for Maggie's hand.

"Don't touch her!" the doctor snapped. "She's having a seizure."

O'Dell peered over a nurse's shoulder, right down to Maggie's sweaty face. Her hair lay in a tangled mess around her scalp as her eyelids continued to flicker. An oxygen mask was still pressed to her face, and she kept pawing at it, twisting and almost rolling off the bed.

They caught her and rolled her back, then backed off again.

The doctor shouted orders to the nurses, then his angry gaze passed across O'Dell. "Get out!"

O'Dell ignored him, fixated on Maggie. Maddened panic crossed through his mind like he'd never felt before—not even in the moments he raced to shield her from the incoming bullet.

At least then there was something he could do. Now he was helpless. Completely useless.

"Stand back!" the doctor shouted.

Maggie's lips moved over a dry tongue, and the thrashing continued. O'Dell thought he heard a low grunt escape her mouth, but he couldn't be sure.

Squeezing past a nurse, he knelt next to the bed. "Madam President, I'm here."

The shaking continued. The doctor yelled for help from the agents outside, and the nurse pulled on his shoulder.

O'Dell ignored them all, his hands resting on the bed next to Maggie's, his gaze fixed on her strained face. He took her hand, softly at first, wrapping his fingers around her sweaty palm, and then squeezing. "Ma'am, please," O'Dell whispered, only inches from her face. "Stay calm. You're okay. You're okay."

Maggie's twitching subsided. Her arms rested on the bed, but her body continued to convulse while her head rolled side to side.

Steps pounded on the tile behind him. More agents streamed into the room. Somebody called his name, but O'Dell ignored them.

He squeezed the president's hand a little harder, his own hand shaking, fear thundering against the gates of his mind. "Maggie . . . I'm here."

The president grew very still. The tremors faded from her body, and her hand twitched inside of his. Then her face twisted toward him, eyes closed, sweat running in a waterfall from her cheeks and around the mask, but now calm.

"Hold on," O'Dell whispered, stroking the back of her hand with one thumb. "Don't let go."

Maggie breathed smoothly. Her chest rose and fell, and the heartbeat monitor next to the bed began to slow, beeping more rhythmically as her fingers relaxed.

O'Dell squeezed once, then felt firm hands on his shoulders.

"Step back, O'Dell," somebody said.

O'Dell reluctantly released her hand, standing slowly. Two agents shoved in front of him, and nurses crowded in. O'Dell made eye contact with the doctor, and the guy nodded once.

Then he was back outside the room, back in the bombed-out hallway, as unbelievable exhaustion broke over him.

53

Reed and Turk sat behind a conference table on a quiet floor of the FBI operational center, slouched back in cheap government chairs with cups of cheap government coffee growing cold in front of them. It was one p.m., eight hours after the second attempt on the president's life. The day before Election Day.

Reed was flat-out exhausted, but he wouldn't be sleeping anytime soon.

Across the table, White House Chief of Staff Jillian Easterling was joined by Secret Service Director Samuel French. In the middle of the table, a speakerphone rested, connected to *Air Force Two* and Vice President Stratton.

Reed didn't know where the plane was. He didn't care. After being sucker-punched twice in barely more than two days, the Secret Service wasn't taking any chances. Stratton would remain on the move until the crisis was resolved.

"How did this happen?" Stratton growled. He sounded more angry than alarmed, and a great deal better rested than any of the four people surrounding the table.

"Mr. Vice President," French began, "we believe the perpetrator smuggled a minuscule amount of explosives inside a medical cylinder—"

"You let him *into* the hospital?" Stratton said.

French remained calm as he walked the vice president through every known detail of the incident, including Jenkins's quick thinking and selfless sacrifice. Stratton interrupted multiple times, blasting the director with semi-accusatory questions.

Reed, Turk, and Easterling remained quiet.

"Reed, you saw this guy?" Stratton demanded at last.

"I chased him through North Chicago," Reed said, his torso stinging as he spoke. The headache was gone, thanks to heavy painkillers and a ton of water. But he couldn't deny the impact of being blasted off a bridge and washed a mile downriver before being fished out of the water, unconscious and bleeding.

Somewhere in Chicago, a physician was pissed about his hundred-thousand-dollar Porsche, all but totaled. Reed didn't care. After being knocked unconscious by the blast, he should've drowned. If one of the Illinois National Guard helicopters hadn't tracked him downriver and guided Turk in for the rescue, he probably would have.

"How did he escape?" Stratton demanded.

"He set off another bomb," Reed said. "I lost him in the Chicago River."

Stratton muttered a string of curses, and Reed tuned him out. He was already thinking about where the sniper would go next. He'd have swum downriver, probably. Maybe exited on the west side, away from downtown.

Did he have another car waiting? Possibly. The Ford was certainly positioned ahead of time, as was the backpack of C-4. This guy thought ahead. He *knew* what he was doing.

"You got a look at his face?" Stratton asked.

"We matched him to a photograph an associate of mine pulled from the dark web," Reed said. "The guy goes by the alias Ghost. Probably one of numerous pseudonyms. He's likely Russian."

"You informed the FBI?"

"Of course," Reed said, barely disguising his irritation. "My associate is tracing a lead as we speak. We'll keep you updated, but the guy will go to ground now. He won't try again. Not at the hospital."

"Who's your associate?"

"A friend," Reed said.

"Does he have a *name*?" Stratton asked.

"No, he doesn't."

Silence. French looked to Reed, but Reed couldn't tell what he was thinking.

"Mr. Vice President, we've cleared the entire hospital of non-essential staff and patients and moved the president to a new room," French said. "For the time being, the property is under complete Secret Service control."

"Was she hurt?" Stratton asked.

"Not by the blast, no, sir. We had her room hung with Kevlar sheets to protect her from shrapnel. Her condition is still critical, but no worse than before."

Stratton went back to cursing, and Reed watched as the president's chief of staff referred to a notepad. Easterling was a small woman—one of the smallest women Reed had ever seen. Maybe ninety pounds soaking wet, with bright blonde hair and a mousy face hung with delicate glasses.

She pushed the glasses up the bridge of her nose. "Mr. Vice President, we need to discuss a public appearance. Even if you make a televised statement from an undisclosed location, it's important for you to reassure the nation. The blast is all over the news."

"I'll make a statement when I have something to state," Stratton said. "Reed, what are you doing to catch this guy? You told me you could hunt him."

"Like I said, we're working leads. While my associate speaks with his contact, Turk and I will be unpacking this thing from the back side."

"Meaning?" Stratton said.

"Meaning we're going to look into who could have hired this guy in the first place. Find out who might want the president dead."

The phone went quiet, and Reed exchanged a glance with Turk.

"You don't think he's acting alone?" Stratton asked.

"We have no evidence—" French began, but Reed cut him off.

"Definitely not. A guy like this is a specialist—a killing machine. Somebody has to finance that machine and give him a target. We're looking at a wealthy, powerful player. Probably a political player. Could be foreign. Could be domestic. We won't know until we learn more."

"Learn more about *what*?"

"About the president. About her campaign, her administration, her foreign policy, her list of friends and foes in Congress. About everything."

"The FBI is already covering that," Stratton said. "I thought you were a soldier. I thought you hunt these people."

"I do a lot of things," Reed said. "And they all defend freedom in the end. Let me do my job, Mr. Vice President."

Reed looked to Easterling, who was fixated on the pad again, maybe uncomfortable with the direction of the conversation. She probably hadn't known about Maggie's secret black ops team. Almost nobody had. But now the cat was out of the bag.

"Okay," Stratton said. "Jill, can you facilitate their research, please?"

"Of course, Mr. Vice President," Easterling said without hesitation, but still didn't look up.

"I want this kept off the books," Stratton continued. "Whatever you think, whatever you find, you come to me *first*. No publicity. No rogue action. Am I clear?"

"Of course, Mr. Vice President," Easterling said.

"And Reed," Stratton said. "One more thing."

"Yes, sir?"

"When you find this guy, he doesn't walk away. Period. Am I understood?"

"Don't worry," Reed said. "I'm not in the habit of letting anyone off the hook."

54

Somewhere in Indiana

The hotel room was old and smelled sour. Half the light bulbs in the bedside fixtures were blown, and the bed groaned when The Ghost sat on it. It was the kind of place that reminded him of slums in Eastern Europe and Africa.

Places to be avoided if you cared about remaining healthy. But the attendant at the front desk barely gave him a second glance and didn't ask for ID when The Ghost checked in. He was able to complete the entire transaction with the right side of his face turned away from the attendant, sheltering the scars that so easily identified him.

It hadn't mattered, though. The guy was high as a kite, and besides, The Ghost had monitored the news media on his phone, and his face was nowhere to be seen. Either the Americans hadn't identified him, or they were holding that card close to their chests. There were no wanted posters circulating the media. No alerts to look out for the two-time attempted assassin of the president.

The Ghost peeled his boots off and stretched his jaw. Even after so many years, the mess of scars on his face still felt tight and restrictive—as though that side of his mouth was slowly shrinking. The hole in his cheek whistled with each breath and leaked when he ate or drank. When he looked at himself in the mirror, he didn't recognize his mother's son. That man was long, long dead.

The Ghost dug the phone from his pocket and speed-dialed the lone contact. The man on the yacht didn't leave him hanging. He'd probably been waiting for this call all night.

"Is it done?"

"I'm not sure," Ghost said, running his tongue along the swollen interior of his cheek. "The bomb went off, but one of the president's men called an alarm as I was leaving."

"One of the Secret Service?"

"Maybe. I don't know. He wasn't dressed like the others."

"Did he recognize you?"

"Maybe. It was all very quick. He gave chase, and I had to use another bomb over the river. That's where I lost him."

The line went quiet, but The Ghost didn't mind the silence. He was frustrated by his initial failure, but not angered by it. A twenty-two-hundred-meter shot? There were maybe five people in the world who could find their target at that distance, and he might be the only one who could do it cold bore. The fact that he hit Trousdale at all was a testament to his skill. The fact that she survived was simply bad luck.

If the second attempt had also failed, he would be further frustrated. But again, blowing people up wasn't his specialty. The man in the yacht couldn't blame him.

"There's nothing on the news about the president," the man on the phone said. "Only about the bomb."

"She couldn't have survived," The Ghost said. "Her lungs would've been roasted from the inside."

The man on the phone grunted and remained quiet awhile. The Ghost gave him time.

"We will know soon," the man said at last. "For now, you should go to ground. Make your way to Miami. I'll be there to pick you up."

The Ghost hung up without acknowledging. The man on the yacht knew he would be in Miami on schedule.

Standing, he made his way around the bed to the vanity outside the bathroom. The mirror was smeared and cracked in one corner. It made him think again of war-torn places, battered and broken.

A hotel like this might be the only survivor of a missile strike or of ten days of endless shelling. It could be a shelter from the storm. A place to snort cocaine before the next engagement. A place to sleep with dirty women who were probably infected with HIV. But a recess from Hell, nonetheless.

The Ghost untucked his shirt, then slowly pulled it over his head. It stuck to his sweaty skin, peeling and tugging at tender flesh. He dropped it to the floor and stared into the mirror. His body was a patchwork of red and white scars, ripping up from his stomach and across his chest, down his arms and sides, over his shoulders, and down his back.

Burn marks. Slice marks. The gouged holes of red-hot pokers. The swollen scars of cigarettes extinguished against his neck. The crooked place beneath his right arm where two ribs had been smashed and never healed properly.

Torture scars.

Souvenirs of a war he would never stop fighting.

55

The FBI set Reed and Turk up in another conference room, provided a pair of laptops linked to a secure internet connection, then brought boxes of files and research material to stack on the table. They piled up until there was a mountain that Reed could walk behind and completely disappear—a slew of information about Maggie's history, her campaign, her associates, and everything else the nation's premier criminal investigatory agency had collected about her.

It was an impressive sight, but Reed was less intrigued by the sheer volume of information and more interested in how readily it was surrendered. In his experience, there was a lot of mistrust between one branch of the military and another. The Navy disliked sharing things with the Marines, even when the Marine Corps was technically a division of the Navy Department.

He could only imagine that mistrust and territorialism extended across the three-letter agencies. And yet the FBI was perfectly willing to disclose extensive amounts of internal documents to two complete strangers, only requesting that none of the hard copies leave the building.

Maybe it was Turk's brief history as an FBI agent. Or maybe it was Stratton's direct influence over Victor O'Brien, director of the FBI. Reed didn't know. But it was an observation worth noting.

They ordered a stack of submarine sandwiches from a deli down the street, along with energy drinks to keep them awake, then settled around the table next to Jill Easterling, and went to work.

Almost immediately, Reed liked Maggie's chief of staff. Jill was energetic and focused. She was also enormously intelligent and didn't waste words. But for all the professionalism and dedication, she was strained to her core. Reed could see it in the way she kept pushing her glasses up even when they were firmly seated against her face. Caught in evil limbo, not sure if her boss would live or die, and maybe also fearing for her own life, Easterling had to be questioning everything she ever believed.

It was understandable, but Reed didn't need the noise. He thanked her for her support and promised to call if they had any questions, then suggested Easterling return to her hotel. She didn't argue, and soon after, he was alone in the room with Turk, a half-eaten sandwich at one elbow.

Turk said, "This is all . . . "

"Very strange," Reed finished. He jabbed a thumb at the mountain of paperwork. "Is this typical?"

"What do you mean?"

"Is the FBI usually this accommodating of complete strangers?"

Turk shook his head. "Not at all. I've never worked anywhere so secretive and mistrusting. The FBI would have you questioning your own grandmother."

"I thought so. Which makes me wonder what they're hiding."

"How do you mean?"

"Well, there are basically two ways to conceal something, right? You either put it someplace out of sight or drown it in meaningless noise. Like a needle in a haystack."

Reed looked down at his laptop. It was a list of Maggie's campaign stops over the past four months, complete with hyperlinks to each of her speeches. Most were recorded, but a few were also transcribed. He scanned through them, taking note of the pictures and the people she appeared next to: A smattering of congressional representatives and a couple senators. Stratton, most of the time. Movie or music stars, on occasion.

It all depended on the context—where she was speaking and who she was speaking to.

Reed knew almost nothing about politics, but he knew a little about sales, mostly from buying things over the years. He knew it was all about positioning. A salesperson worked to trace a line between what his customer wanted and what he had to sell.

A politician couldn't be much different. If Maggie was speaking to college students, she would address the rising cost of education and the future of the workforce. If she was speaking at a manufacturing plant, that speech would pivot to address union concerns and healthcare.

It wasn't necessarily dishonest. A president's job was to be concerned with the needs of all Americans, and Reed couldn't draw any direct correlations between Maggie's campaign and her attempted assassination. But still, he knew something had to be there, buried in the noise, hiding in plain sight. A motivation for somebody to take a literal shot at the most powerful person in the Free World.

Reed's vision blurred, and even when he blinked, it was difficult to refocus. He knew he wasn't firing on all cylinders and felt a little disconnected. Almost as though he were watching himself from the outside.

"You okay, man?" Turk asked.

Reed reached for his drink. "Yeah, man. Solid." He swigged coffee, feeling it burn on the way down. It helped a little, bringing the photo back into focus, but his mind still felt mired, like a 4x4 up to its axles in mud.

"You haven't been sleeping, have you?" Turk asked.

Reed looked up. "Huh?"

Turk just watched him.

Again, Reed saw the scope pressed near his face and felt the stock held against his cheek, the trigger under his finger. He saw the backpack. The kid. "You . . ." He hesitated. "You remember that op in Samarra? The one with the kid."

Turk's gaze dropped. "All the time."

Reed stared back at the screen. Maggie filled it, but he didn't see her. He saw the kid pitching forward. The detonator flying out of his hand. The crimson on the ground.

"I never used to have dreams," Reed said. "Not in Iraq. Not when I was a contractor. Not when I was in South America, running from the FBI. But since things got quiet . . ."

"It works that way," Turk said. "Something about focus and distractions. When you get still, all this stuff boils up—stuff you forgot or tried to forget. There's a psychological name for it, but I don't remember what it is."

"You saw somebody?"

Turk grunted. "A few times. Just a general therapist. Nothing mandated or anything. It helped a little. Meds can help, too."

"Meds?"

"Sometimes."

Reed looked down at his hands. His fingertips were trembling again. Another symptom he'd never experienced before. Was he losing it? Was he cracking? Back in the Corps, he used to scoff at soldiers who went to counseling. He refused to depend on anybody known to be taking psychiatric medication. He called them cracked. Busted. Unreliable and used up.

Was he becoming one of those people? Had the quiet finally caught up with him?

"You should see somebody, Reed. It won't get better until you do. Banks and Davy deserve that much."

Reed kept his gaze on his hands, focusing on making his fingers grow still. He did what he always did when he was stressed and worn. He pictured himself behind a rifle, not pointed downrange at a kid but at a faceless military-age male brandishing an assault weapon. A tango.

He felt the rifle against his cheek again and placed his finger over the trigger. He held his breath and squeezed. Another tango down.

Reed sat up, realizing he'd fallen silent for much too long. He finished the coffee and shook his head, pushing the feelings away, bottling them back up while he focused on the moment. He ran a hand over his face and felt dirt and sweat, then his gaze settled back on the image—not on Maggie, but on the man next to her.

"We're ignoring an obvious suspect," Reed said.

"Stratton," Turk answered.

"He stands to win it all if Maggie's taken out."

Turk ran a finger inside one cheek, prying away a chunk of salami. He pondered a moment, then shook his head. "I don't know, man. Trousdale's popular. She's a breath away from winning this thing. That keeps Stratton in the White House. Four, or eight years from now, he could run on his own."

"Assuming she keeps him around that long."

"You think there's tension?"

"Who knows? She's an Independent. He's a Republican. She's an outsider, and he's part of the establishment. I could see it."

"But why do it now? Why not wait until after the election?"

"Sympathy vote, maybe. Enough to push him over the finish line. Especially if he talked Governor Jeffreys into joining his ticket. Consolidate the Republicans."

"No way. A week before the election?"

"They can't change the ballots, but maybe it could happen. I really don't know."

They grew quiet again, each scanning through documents on the computer.

Turk was next to speak. "He didn't seem happy that we were investigating a cause."

"Nope," Reed said. "And he drowned us in this paperwork."

"But if Stratton's behind it, why would he have authorized us at all? Why not tell us to take a hike?"

Reed shrugged. "Keep your friends close. Keep your enemies closer." His phone buzzed from his pocket, and Reed pried it out. It was Banks. He felt a wave of guilt, realizing he'd forgotten her since the helicopter ride back to Chicago. She'd probably seen news of the oxygen bomb and was freaking out. Add to that the Secret Service agent on her doorstep, deployed compliments of Director French, and she had a right to be shaken.

"Let's keep that theory close to our chests," Reed said. "See where the evidence leads."

Turk shot him a two-finger salute, and Reed stepped across the hall to a vacant office. It was quiet and dark. He didn't bother with the light. "Hey, babe," he said softly.

"Reed. Where are you? Why didn't you call?"

"I'm still in Chicago. I'm sorry . . . time got away from me."

"There's some woman here from the Secret Service. She said you sent her?"

"It's just a precaution. I thought you could use some company."

It was a paper-thin lie, and he regretted it as soon as it left his lips. Banks was nobody's fool. It was one thing he loved so much about her.

Reed heard a door close, followed by a whisper of wind. Banks had stepped outside, but the next noise took him off guard—the grind of a cigarette lighter, followed by a deep breath.

"Are you smoking?" Reed asked.

Banks didn't answer immediately. "You left a pack at the house."

"I stopped keeping cigarettes in the house months ago."

"I didn't say when," Banks snorted.

"So, you've been . . ." Reed ran a hand over his face. "That's not healthy."

"Kiss my ass, Reed. You've been chain-smoking as long as I've known you."

It was true. And fair.

"What's happening?" Banks asked. "For real."

Reed slumped against the wall, squatting until he was seated on the carpet. "There was another attempt on Trousdale. We're trying to find the killer."

"Is she alive?"

"For the moment. She's in rough shape. They thought she'd need a liver transplant, but now they're hoping to save it."

Banks sucked on the cigarette, and Reed wished he had one. He wondered what it would be like to smoke with her. They'd never shared a cigarette before. It sounded nice.

"It wasn't supposed to be this way," Banks said at last.

"What way?"

"*This* way. You being gone all the time. Always working for Trousdale. Always dodging bullets. Me waking up late at night to find some woman I don't know with a gun on her belt storming into my house."

"I know," Reed said. Somehow, her words made him feel like a failure. Like this was his fault.

"I'm sorry," he said. "We'll wrap up soon. Then I'll be home."

"Will you?"

"Of course."

"But will you *be* here? Or will you be a thousand miles away, half-awake, never sleeping?"

Reed assumed Banks knew about his sleeplessness, but he hadn't realized how much it had poisoned his daylight hours.

"Banks . . ."

"You need help, Reed. Real help. Some kind of therapy."

The office door opened, and Turk stuck his head out.

"Montgomery?"

Reed looked up. "Babe . . . I need to go."

Banks sucked on the cigarette again. He could hear the ember crackling through the tobacco, then her fingers thumped as she flicked it away.

"Call me," she said. "Please."

"I promise. I love you."

"I love you, too," Banks whispered.

Reed crammed the phone back into his pocket, pushing his fingers through his hair and staring at the carpet.

"All good?"

Reed looked up. He'd already forgotten about Turk standing there.

"Yeah, dude. What's up?"

"You should come see this. I think I may have found something."

56

Somewhere over the Atlantic Ocean

Wolfgang booked a flight from Chicago's O'Hare International Airport to Heathrow, in London. He still hadn't heard back from his Russian contact, but he figured that when he did, his next stop would be someplace in Eastern Europe, meaning he would probably have to connect through London anyway. May as well get a head start.

He paid for coach, taking the middle seat between an overweight businessman and a harried mother cradling a fussy infant. A dull hum of restless intensity filled the cabin, and Wolfgang thought he knew why.

People were strained. Not only because of the president's uncertain condition, but because of *their* uncertain condition. While Trousdale was still vice president, America had brushed against World War III, facing down Russia and Iran as energy prices skyrocketed.

Then came North Korea —a standoff most Americans knew very little about. But it was public knowledge that China had occupied the northern half of the Korean peninsula and never left. Everybody knew that tensions with Beijing were on the rise. They knew oil prices had never returned to pre-Trousdale levels.

And amid it all, the nation was enthralled in a three-way dead heat—

something Wolfgang had never witnessed. It was more than contentious—it was confusing. Clouded. It made the whole nation feel tumultuous. Everywhere he went, on every street corner, at every grocery store, people talked politics. It felt like every home displayed a campaign sign for somebody.

The nation's RPM was edging close to redline long before the sniper pressed the trigger on Trousdale. Twenty-four-hour news was pouring on the heat.

And still . . . Americans didn't know the half of it.

Wolfgang pulled out his phone and connected to the airplane's Wi-Fi before checking his email. An empty mailbox greeted him, and for the third time, he checked to ensure his message had been sent. Now it was a waiting game. His contact would either reach out, or he wouldn't.

Wolfgang switched his notifications on, then turned the phone off and looked across the aisle to the nearest window. Wide blue sky passed far outside—an early morning, bright and hopeful. It made him think of years gone by, back in his younger days, when he caught a red-eye flight from New York to Miami to meet the woman he hoped would become his fiancée.

She didn't know it, but he already had the ring in his pocket. He booked a hotel near the beach and hit a restaurant on the sand for dinner. Then they danced to soft music in the warm wind.

It had been sunny that day, bright and clear like the sky outside of the plane. As the light faded and night resumed, he remembered walking on the beach, taking a turn down a random pier lined with bobbing yachts. He remembered slipping his hand into his pocket and fingering the box with the ring in it. Contemplating the perfect moment.

And then he remembered the gunshots.

Wolfgang looked away from the window. He ran the back of his hand across his nose and saw the woman with the child looking at him sideways. Suddenly, he wondered when he had last showered, and he felt grimy.

His phone vibrated, and Wolfgang snatched it up from his lap. There was a new email message waiting in his burner account.

When the message loaded, his blood pressure spiked.

MINSK. EMAIL WHEN YOU LAND. I WILL SEND A CAR.

Wolfgang looked to his watch, quickly calculating the time. He'd reach Heathrow in the next hour. Without a checked bag, he'd leave the plane and remain inside security, avoiding customs. He lifted the phone again and navigated to a travel website, searching flights.

Heathrow to Minsk.

57

"Look at this."

Turk settled in behind his laptop and unlocked it. The screen was populated with a Twitter feed, a video tweet near the top. Reed squinted at it, only semi-familiar with what he was looking at. He'd never liked social media. He never saw the point.

"After our discussion about Stratton, I decided to look into his association with the campaign to see if there were any visible rifts between him and Trousdale."

"And?"

"And he blew off a joint interview the night before she was shot. It was a big deal—a national spotlight hosted by Ben Fisher."

"Who?"

"Man, you really don't watch TV, do you?"

Reed tilted his head toward the ceiling. "Get to the point."

"Well, I did some more digging, trying to find out where he was that night. I called French, and—"

"You didn't tell French we suspect Stratton?"

"Of course not. I just asked him why Stratton blew off the interview.

French said he never left his hotel—the Guthrie, here in Chicago. So . . . I went to Twitter."

"Why Twitter?"

"Are you on Twitter?"

"What do you think?"

Turk turned back to the screen. "There's a thing people do on Twitter. It's like bird-watching. When they see a celebrity, they'll often post a picture with a hashtag. You know what a hashtag is, right?"

"I know I'm about to put one on your face."

"Screw off. Point is, I searched for Stratton on that night . . . and this is what I found."

Turk hit play on the video. Reed watched carefully. It was filmed from the back corner of a restaurant, with the camera pointed at the opposing corner. Reed recognized Stratton sitting behind a corner table, dressed in a subdued suit, sitting opposite a woman in a seductive red dress. The video only lasted about four seconds. The woman laughed, partially exposing her face, and Stratton remained relaxed. Then it was over.

The caption alongside the video read: "OMG. Is that #VPOTUS???"

"I don't get it," Reed said.

"Watch closely."

Turk played the video again, highlighting a spot on the screen with the cursor. And then Reed saw it. Stratton slid the woman a large envelope— quickly and discreetly. She laughed right after she took it.

Reed settled into his chair, scratching his chin. "It doesn't mean anything."

"He blew off the interview," Turk said. "Then he meets a woman and pays her?"

"Could be a prostitute," Reed said. "Look at the way she's dressed."

"Well, that's the thing. She's not a prostitute."

He twisted the laptop toward Reed, tabbing to another page.

Reed squinted at the screen. "Heidi Cunningham?" A Wikipedia page showed a woman in her early thirties with a brief biography arranged next to the photo. She was the youngest daughter of a billionaire Chicago busi-nessman and currently worked as a reporter for some online media company he'd never heard of.

Turk said, "She's the second daughter of Harold Cunningham. He's the CEO and primary shareholder of Cunningham Enterprises, a multinational energy conglomeration headquartered in Chicago."

"Okay. I still don't see the point."

"Well, I googled Cunningham Enterprises."

Turk tabbed to another page, and Reed scanned the headlines.

"Cunningham in Partnership with Russian Energy Oligarch to Tap New Gulf Oil Wells."

"Cunningham Ent. Strikes Deal with Chinese Corporation for Natural Gas Expansion."

"Cunningham CEO: 'Global energy is the future of energy.'"

Reed scrolled down the list, but the headlines only repeated themselves. Many of them were six or ten months old, published in business journals and financial newspapers, but they all told the same story: Cunningham Enterprises was heavily invested in international energy deals. Hundreds of billions of dollars worth of such deals, primarily with Russia and China.

"Doesn't Trousdale oppose energy trade with Russia and China?" Reed said.

"Staunchly. She's curtailed international gulf oil leases and campaigned for domestic energy independence. It's one of her foreign policy hallmarks."

Reed studied the screen, switching back to the bio about Heidi Cunningham. She was pretty—some might even say hot. A bit overstated for Reed's tastes, but certainly a woman most men would take a second look at.

"Maybe he's screwing her," Reed said.

"If he were screwing her, he wouldn't risk being seen with her in public. He's married."

"So, what's with the envelope?"

"Could be anything. Communication, documents. But there's really only one reason you meet in person to pass an envelope."

"Cash," Reed said. "Off the books."

"Exactly."

"Even if it was cash, that doesn't prove anything. One meeting means nothing."

"I'm already assembling a travel history for Stratton," Turk said. "A lot of it is public record. But if he does have some sort of illicit relationship with the Cunninghams, that won't be on the record."

"Even if it was, it wouldn't nail him to the wall. We need to know who hired the shooter. It's the easiest way to lock this down."

"But that could be impossible to prove. There would be miles of insulation between Stratton and the sniper. Corporate layers . . . maybe some international involvement. The shooter is Russian, after all."

Reed bit his nail, unpacking it all slowly, focusing on one item at a time. This wasn't his area of expertise. He much preferred simply breaking bones until the truth exposed itself.

But there was something here. He could feel it.

"You said Cunningham Enterprises is headquartered in Chicago?"

"Yeah. They lease a tower downtown. Why?"

"Remember what Stratton said? For us to keep everything off the record? To talk to him first?"

"Spoken like a man with something to hide."

"Exactly." Reed pivoted to face Turk. "So, let's rattle the cage."

58

Minsk, Belarus

It took almost six hours to reach Minsk. No Western airlines served the so-called "last dictatorship in Europe," forcing Wolfgang to fly first to Vilnius, Lithuania, before boarding a Belarusian-owned 737 for the thirty-three-minute flight to finish his journey.

Wolfgang was cold and irritable by the time the plane finally landed. Vilnius had been grungy and dismal. Almost no one spoke English, and there had been very little to eat during his four-hour layover.

He expected Minsk to feel much the same, given that both Belarus and Lithuania shared a heritage as members of the old USSR. But he couldn't have been more wrong. Minsk was cold, but it wasn't grungy, and it wasn't dismal. Midday sun broke through the clouds and streamed over a sprawling airport as he stepped out of the terminal. Wide roads and rows of brand-new cars greeted him in the parking lot, and in the distance, he saw the skyline of downtown rising toward a late afternoon sky. The buildings looked clean and fresh—not at all like the imperial Stalinist architecture he'd witnessed in Lithuania.

"Mr. Pierce?"

Wolfgang looked up from his phone as a short guy in a leather jacket approached from a jet-black Mercedes sedan. He'd been checking for an email from his contact, relaxing under the welcome glow of the sun. The sound of his own name being called by a complete stranger melted that moment in an instant, putting him on immediate guard.

"Excuse me?"

"I'm here to collect you," the guy said in perfect English.

Wolfgang thought he detected a Russian accent, but it was either mild or heavily suppressed.

"I'm good," Wolfgang said. "Thanks."

The guy smiled and dug a cigarette out of his pocket, lighting it before taking two steps closer and lifting his jacket. The grip of a Russian-made Grach handgun protruded from his belt. "Please, Mr. Pierce. I insist." A grin crept across grimy teeth. "You *are* the Amerikos, are you not?"

Wolfgang lowered the phone slowly. The stench of tar-heavy Russian cigarette smoke drifted toward him, and he wanted to turn away. But that name—Amerikos—reassured him. There was only one person on the planet who had ever called him that. The same man who promised to send a car.

"Well," Wolfgang said. "If you insist."

The guy led him back to the sedan and opened the rear door. The vehicle was empty, and Wolfgang slid inside, tossing his carry-on ahead of him. The door smacked shut, and Wolfgang noted that the interior door handle had been removed. He felt a constriction in his chest, almost as though a snake were curling around his torso and crushing inward, but he remained calm.

He'd expected something like this. His contact was a suspicious guy. A careful guy. A guy with a messed-up sense of humor.

The driver cracked the window and continued to smoke as he turned toward downtown. Wide, smooth highways led into the city, filled with late-model cars and shiny city busses. Billboards in Belarusian and Russian advertised the arrival of a new Hilton hotel downtown, along with a slew of casinos. Wolfgang couldn't read the Cyrillic, but he recognized the logos and spinning dials of a slot machine.

"First time in Minsk?" the driver asked.

Wolfgang didn't answer.

"You will love it! Is beautiful city. Great food, great casinos . . . beautiful women." He grinned as he finished the sentence, looking into the rearview mirror, smoke clouding around his face.

As they neared the core of the city, the traffic intensified, and among the shiny glass buildings piercing the sky, Wolfgang noted a smattering of older, stone-faced structures. Stars and blocky Cyrillic text adorned many of them, and in one place, he was surprised to actually see a hammer and sickle still imprinted in concrete.

"Eighty percent of Minsk was destroyed in the Second World War," the driver said, the cigarette dancing between his teeth as he spoke. "This means we rebuild! All is new. A European paradise, no?"

"If you say so."

The driver wound deeper into downtown, passing more busses and wide sidewalks populated by pedestrians and bicyclists. Melting snow ran down drainage ditches as the sun washed away the remainder of the previous night's precipitation, and everything looked remarkably clean. Hardly a paradise, in Wolfgang's mind, but a lot brighter than he expected from a Soviet relic still clutched in the grasps of a corrupt government.

The driver pulled to the curb in front of a tall, black-glass building. Belarusian flags flapped from the metal awning overhanging the sidewalk, and valets in black vests and white gloves hurried to greet them.

Wolfgang looked past the tinted glass and saw crimson carpet, golden chandeliers, and the distant flash of bright lights. It was a casino. A big one.

The driver got out, and Wolfgang waited for him to open the door—having no other choice. A valet caught the car keys and moved to take the Mercedes away as Wolfgang shouldered his bag and surveyed the casino. He wasn't sure what he expected in Minsk, but this wasn't it. Maybe a seedy bar on the wrong side of town, or a gambling den beneath a quiet restaurant. Someplace discreet and off the books.

But really, he didn't care. Not as long as his contact showed.

The driver flashed another toothy grin and motioned for Wolfgang to walk ahead. Tall doors opened automatically as they passed into the lobby, and Wolfgang's senses were immediately assaulted by heavy air fresheners and the clicking noises of a casino floor. Across the lobby, down two or three steps, was a field of slot machines, with roulette and blackjack tables beyond.

The driver motioned him past a reception desk to a bank of elevators, directing him to punch the third button on the left once they entered. Wolfgang had no idea what floor number it was. Everything was still written in some variation of Cyrillic.

The elevator hummed upward, and Wolfgang regarded himself in the reflection of polished brass doors. The driver stood behind him, feet spread, one arm of his leather jacket flopping lifelessly downward as his actual arm remained invisible beneath the garment.

Clutching the Grach, Wolfgang figured.

The doors rolled open, and Wolfgang followed the driver's promptings down a hallway laid with more crimson carpet. Gold fixtures and an ornate chair rail ran along one wall. The driver stopped him in front of a door halfway down, then folded his arms and took a step back. Wolfgang raised one eyebrow. The driver nodded to the door, still smiling, an unlit cigarette dangling from his teeth.

Wolfgang glanced suspiciously down the hallway, then placed a hand on the doorknob. It was unlocked.

He looked back to the driver once more and saw the guy's smile spread into a grin. It was a crafty look, but Wolfgang knew he was only playing games.

Wolfgang pushed the door open and stepped inside.

It was cold and dark in the hotel room. None of the lights mounted to the wall or the chandelier overhanging a large breakfast table were lit. The room was some manner of a suite, with a bathroom on one side and a door on the other, probably leading to a bedroom.

Directly ahead lay the table, a couch, and a wide bank of windows all covered in curtains. The only light that entered the room seeped from beneath those curtains, glowing softly like strings of rope lights.

Wolfgang hesitated, his fingers flexing. For the first time since leaving Chicago, he second-guessed his decision to go unarmed. The CIA could've flown him directly into Minsk aboard one of their SAC jets. So long as Stratton was calling the shots, Reed could've made it happen. And then

Wolfgang would be armed. He wouldn't be standing alone in some casino hotel, completely at the mercy of whatever happened next.

Wolfgang dropped his hand into his pocket, clutching over thin air. He almost turned back for the door. Then he heard a footfall in the bedroom. A shadow passed across light leaking beneath the bedroom door, then that light vanished and the door swung open.

The man who stepped out was nothing short of imposing—well over six feet tall, built like an MMA fighter. His hair was shoulder-length, pulled back into a ponytail. His face was iron hard—creased and lined by age and mileage alike. Late fifties, Wolfgang figured. Maybe early sixties.

But in awesome shape, age be damned. He was shirtless, and iron muscles rippled across his chest as he walked. Those muscles continued down taut arms, crisscrossed in places by scars and overlaid in others by tattoos. His nose had been broken, also. Bashed to one side by the lid of a French toilet.

Wolfgang knew it had been a toilet lid, because it was Wolfgang who did the bashing.

"Hello, Amerikos," the Russian said, unsmiling.

"Hello, Ivan."

59

The big Russian stepped forward, cracks of sunlight slicing between the curtains and cutting across his chest. He stopped short of Wolfgang and swept him from head to foot.

Wolfgang remained loose, hands at his sides. "You look good, Ivan."

The Russian's nose twitched, and he grinned. "You don't."

Wolfgang snorted, and Ivan extended a hand. Wolfgang clasped it, expecting a shake. Instead, Ivan pulled him into a bear hug, slamming his back with his free arm.

Wolfgang coughed, his face buried in black and grey chest hair. "Good to see you, Ivan."

The Russian completed the hug with a needlessly aggressive squeeze. "Hell's angels, Amerikos. What happened to you?"

Wolfgang shrugged, stumbling back. "You know how it is. You can't dodge them all."

"This is true." Ivan turned for the minibar. "Have a seat, my friend. What will you have?"

Wolfgang chose a chair at the breakfast table. "I still don't drink, Ivan."

Ivan shot a look over one shoulder. "What? Not even a little?"

"Nope. But I'll take some water."

Ivan joined him with a bottle of water and a bottle of vodka—no glasses.

Wolfgang cracked the water open and sipped.

Ivan guzzled the liquor. It was strong, and Wolfgang's nose tingled, but the big Russian didn't seem bothered.

He wiped his mouth and slouched back in the chair. "Seriously, my friend. How are you?"

"I'm all right. Staying busy. I've had a few careers since we last spoke."

"You became a killer," Ivan said, a smirk playing at the corners of his mouth.

"You kept tabs on me?"

Ivan shook his head. "Only rumors. After Sydney, well . . . I find myself occupied."

"You still with the SVR?" Wolfgang asked, referring to Russia's version of the CIA.

"Was I ever with the SVR?"

Ivan said it with another sly smirk, and Wolfgang ducked his head in surrender.

"How is your sister?" Ivan asked.

"Not good. She's . . . she's dying."

"I am sorry. Only life would be so cruel."

Wolfgang extended his bottle in salute, and they both drank. Already, a third of the vodka was gone.

Ivan didn't look the least bit unsettled. He set the bottle down, then folded his arms. "Okay, Amerikos. Why are you here?"

Wolfgang evaluated the Russian silently, taking his time. To say he was friends with him would be a massive stretch. Ivan was the sort of guy who would cheat at cards, then knife you in the back if you refused to pay up. The Russian's chief redeeming virtue was his patriotism—not so much to Moscow as to Moscow's people. That faithfulness to the greater good had served Wolfgang in the past, but that was a long time ago. He wasn't sure how much had changed or how much he should say. Better to move slowly.

"Why the casino?"

Ivan made a dismissive gesture with one hand. "Gambling is illegal in most of Russia. Many government officials come to Minsk to . . . how do you say? Blow off steam."

"So, nobody knows I emailed you?"

"Nyet. I book travel for Minsk as vacation. No one knows you are here."

Wolfgang scratched one cheek. What Ivan said made sense. He'd hoped the Russian would respond to his email discreetly, turning up in Minsk alone.

But for all he knew, the hotel room was bugged, and this was a setup. If Ivan was still involved with the SVR, he'd probably be a high-ranking member by now. And if he knew Wolfgang had become an assassin following that last meeting in Sydney, he might also know that Wolfgang had recently been involved in helping the Trousdale administration solve difficult problems. This entire meeting could be a sting operation. Or the groundwork for a future sting operation.

Regardless, Wolfgang had reached out. He'd have to play a hand at some point.

"You watch the news?" Wolfgang asked.

"As little as possible."

"Wise man. But you know about Trousdale?"

A shadow passed across Ivan's face, and he sipped vodka. "Is she dead?"

"What would you say if she was?"

Ivan took his time answering, then he grunted. "I would say it is a shame. As a good Russian, I can't help but admire strength. Your president is very strong."

"Maybe not strong enough to take a bullet," Wolfgang said. "She was shot from twenty-two hundred meters. Give or take."

Something in Ivan's face told Wolfgang the Russian already knew this tidbit of information. That said something, because as far as Wolfgang knew, it wasn't yet a publicized fact.

"This is a difficult shot," Ivan said.

"It's an *impossible* shot."

"Apparently not."

Wolfgang reached into his pocket, retrieving his phone. He slid the device across the table, an image plastered across it. "You know him?"

Ivan didn't touch the phone. He merely studied the image.

Wolfgang saw pain in Ivan's expression, like storm clouds laced with lightning. But it was over and gone almost as quickly as it came.

"You work for Washington, now?" Ivan asked.

"Sometimes."

Ivan shook his head and swigged vodka, standing and walking to the window. He stood in a crack of sunlight for a long time, his muscled back turned to Wolfgang, the bottle in one hand. "Damn you, Amerikos. If I knew this, I would not have come. You know what position you put me in?"

"You said nobody knew I was here."

"They don't! But if they find out—"

"Nobody's going to find out, Ivan. Even my own government doesn't know I'm here. I flew commercial. I came on my own."

Ivan looked unconvinced. He stared over one shoulder, his rough lips working in a pucker, then he turned away.

"Who is he?" Wolfgang asked.

Ivan didn't answer.

"We know he shot the president," Wolfgang said. "Now we want to know who he's working for. I'm sure you can see the benefit in helping us before suspicions fall on Moscow."

Ivan merely shook his head. "You are an amateur at this game, Amerikos."

"Maybe. But you're not. So, help me."

Ivan took another long drink. "Do you ever hear of Russia's wars in Chechnya?"

Wolfgang frowned, taken off guard. "Some?"

"In 1991, the Soviet Union fell. I imagine you are too young to remember. At the time, I was a young man, an officer in the Red Army. After the USSR collapse, it was chaos. First, the government fell, and then slowly, the union disintegrated. Moldova, Ukraine, the Baltic states . . ." Ivan snorted and gestured to the window. "Belarus. They all leave. The great Motherland melted, right in front of us."

Ivan returned to the table, scraping a chair back and descending with a tired sigh. "After this, the Russian Federation was born. A man called Boris Yeltsin was president, and it was his job to restore order. Salvage what he could. Now, most of the Soviet nations had already left. Nothing could be done about this. But there was one piece of the old empire that Moscow was unwilling to surrender."

"The Caucasus," Wolfgang said.

Ivan jabbed a finger at him. "You know your history."

"Only pieces. What happened?"

"Chechnya happened. They declared independence, and in December of ninety-four, President Yeltsin sent forty thousand troops to the Caucasus to silence the separatists." Ivan stared into the vodka bottle. "I was one of them."

Wolfgang pointed to the phone. "Was he?"

Ivan took another swig, ignoring the question. "We sweep into Chechnya like American cowboys. We think two, maybe three weeks. Then the rebellion is over, and we all go home for holidays. We take six thousand mechanized troops and attack Grozny—the Chechen capital. Rockets. Artillery. Everything short of nuclear weapons. We pound them day and night, like cheap whore."

"And?"

"And they fight back. Hard. They arm themselves with Soviet small arms, and they ravage our ranks. Snipers, improvised explosive devices, guerrilla warfare . . . What poor fools were captured faced gruesome torture before death." Ivan's lips wrinkled in disgust. "I have seen many ugly things in my life. But the Chechens . . . they were animals.

"After some weeks, we drove them out of Grozny, and they retreated to the mountains. It was much more difficult to fight them there. Many of the Chechens had fought in Afghanistan and knew how to leverage the terrain. We left a few thousand soldiers in Grozny to hold the city, then dug in for a mountain campaign."

Ivan looked at the phone. "His name was Fedor Volkov. I never met him, but before the war was over, we all knew his name. He was a sniper, part of the detachment left to hold Grozny. He was there when the Chechens attacked. There weren't many of them—maybe a couple thousand—but they took us by surprise. Young Volkov's detachment was quickly overrun and slaughtered. He may have taken a few shots before they reached him, but then he made a terrible mistake."

"He was captured," Wolfgang said.

"Da, Amerikos. He was captured. The Chechens had a special hatred for snipers. Maybe because our snipers had learned their tricks. We would aim for the groin—make them suffer the way they made us suffer. Volkov disappeared for two weeks . . . two weeks of absolute hell."

Ivan sucked his teeth and shook his head. "The Chechen counterattack was effective. The war in the mountains was faltering. Eventually, Yeltsin was forced to sign a cease-fire. But not before The Ghost of Grozny was born."

"The Ghost?" Wolfgang asked. He remembered the chat room on the dark web. The name BloodChill458 had assigned to the photograph.

"Somehow, Volkov survived the torture. He escaped. He hid in the city, nursing himself back to health. By the time he was healthy enough to leave hiding, the war was almost over. But not for Volkov. He found a rifle and went to work the way the Chechens did. A one-man war."

"How many?" Wolfgang asked.

Ivan shrugged. "Who can say? Rumors of his campaign leaked across the Caucasus. A ruthless soldier without an army, slaughtering Chechen soldiers around Grozny long after the war had ended. Some he killed by hand. But usually, he used the rifle. Long shots, far from enemy security." Ivan looked up. "Impossible shots."

Wolfgang said nothing.

Ivan pushed the phone back toward him. "I left the army after the war. I found other employment."

"The SVR," Wolfgang said.

"You may say so."

"And Volkov?"

"He returned to Russia, looking for home. But the military would not have him. His girlfriend would not have him. He was lost. A man without a soul. His file came to me at my new job."

"And?"

Ivan shrugged.

"Did he become a government asset?" Wolfgang pressed.

"His skill set was impressive, but his mental state was very unstable. He was useless to us."

"So, what happened to him?"

"Who knows? I heard rumors of Russian mob employing him for a time. Truth be told, Amerikos, this picture is the first I see of him in twenty years. If I had to guess, he is long dead. Probably by his own hand."

"What if I told you he was in Chicago yesterday? What if I told you he tried to bomb the president?"

Ivan cocked his head and pursed his lips. "Well, I would say I find that highly unlikely. But if you say so."

Wolfgang held the big Russian's gaze. "Don't BS me. We both know how dangerous this situation is. If Washington decides a Russian shot the president—"

"That proves nothing," Ivan said, jabbing a finger at Wolfgang. "Your bosses would be wise to think carefully before leveling accusations. President Nikitin does not suffer fools."

Wolfgang narrowed his eyes. "Why do I feel like you're not giving me the full story?"

Ivan finished the vodka. He stood up, his face flushed, his muscles rippling beneath taut skin. "I come here today, and I tell you what I tell you, because of what happened in Sydney. Not only for what you did, but for what you lost. Consider it a kindness. Now, you should leave."

Wolfgang waited a beat longer, testing the iron in Ivan's face. It was obvious the Russian was done talking, whether he'd told the truth or not.

Wolfgang retrieved his bag and offered his hand. "Thank you."

Ivan took the hand with a bone-crushing grip, the iron fading from his face. "Of course, Amerikos. Next time you are in Moscow, let me know. I take you for swim in Moskva River."

The hint of a smirk played at Ivan's lips.

Wolfgang shook his hand once, then turned for the door. As he stepped out into the hallway and the driver fell in behind him, he still wasn't sure which parts of Ivan's story he believed, but it felt like the truth. Or maybe just half of it.

60

Ivan Sidorov watched Wolfgang fade through the door, his hands now loose at his sides. The ache of a long life full of heavy physical activity and not enough sleep was eased by the 375 milliliters of vodka he'd just consumed, but the warmth in his face from the alcohol couldn't melt the ice in his mind brought about by that picture.

The picture of Fedor Volkov. The Ghost of Grozny.

Ivan reached for his cell phone and hit speed dial on a top contact. The man didn't keep him waiting.

"Da?"

"Prepare the plane. We're going back to Moscow."

61

From a park bench situated next to the harbor, Lucy could see her ocean-facing, fortieth-floor condo. Or what *used* to be her ocean-facing, fortieth-floor condo. She rented it back in her days as a contract killer, when money was plentiful and she never worried about the credit card bill. Back before Southeast Asia and the endless hunt through a pandora's box of filth and crime . . . and opioids.

She'd never refuse codeine. Morphine was a reliable standby. But oxycodone . . . that was the shit she couldn't get enough of. Her petite body latched onto it like a barnacle on the bottom of a cruise ship, digging in and refusing to let go. Time itself blurred out of existence. Meals were missed or doubled. She would sleep all day, or not sleep for days.

Worst of all, she couldn't remember herself. When she looked into a mirror, she saw a face that looked familiar but didn't feel like her own. Sunken eyes matched hollow cheeks and stringy hair. Her arms were pock-marked with scars from morphine needles, and she bruised easily.

It was a far cry from the fit, curvy looker she'd been only twelve months prior. Lucy always knew she was hot, and she'd never been above leveraging it. Tight clothes and bold makeup was her style of choice. They made her feel edgy. Confident. Comfortable in her own skin.

Now she couldn't blame the guys who hurried past her park bench without a second glance. She kept the hood of her jacket over her head and poked her arms deeper into the pockets. It wasn't cold in Tampa, but she shivered anyway.

She was hungry, but the money Reed had given her in Destin the previous week was already gone. She'd used some for a bus ticket to Tampa, thinking she might feel more at home in her old city and maybe find a way to get back on her feet. The moment she saw the condo and remembered everything she had now lost, those hopes backfired. She became deeply depressed, impulsively using the rest of Reed's cash to purchase a two-week supply of oxy.

It lasted three days.

Now the high was wearing off and the cravings returned. Her head felt fuzzy, but not so much that she couldn't see the inevitable crashing toward her like a freight train. This couldn't go on. Not for another month, let alone another year. Lucy was still reasonably good-looking, if you could ignore the bruises. She could prostitute herself to get by—a possibility that felt more like an inevitability by the day.

But that would only last so long. When she was too washed up and worn out for a twenty-dollar john to take a second look at, what then? How would it end? A jump from a bridge? A fall in front of a bus? Or would she simply slip into Tampa Bay and sink deep into the dark water?

Just let go.

A tear slipped down one cheek. Lucy felt trapped and alone, but more than anything, she felt defeated, as though the wheels of life had ground over her bones and left her crushed in the mud.

She looked up and watched the lights of downtown reflect over a darkened bay. It was beautiful there. A restaurant was nearby, and she saw a young couple in evening wear wandering back to their hotel. The woman was drunk and stumbled. The guy held her up, a loving smile on his face. Maybe they were just married. Maybe on their honeymoon. Maybe leaving on a week-long cruise the next day.

Happy. Not alone.

She envied that more than she envied their full stomachs or the money in their pockets.

The couple wandered by, and Lucy stood up, fishing for the last three dollars in her pocket. It was enough for a candy bar and some water. She began the one-mile walk to the nearest convenience store, thinking she'd probably sleep on the bench afterward.

She liked to look at the bay. Even as her own world burned to the ground, the stillness of the dark water brought some peace to her mind.

Something buzzed in her pocket, and Lucy stopped. For a moment, she thought it was a hallucination—one of many brutal side effects of opioid withdrawal. But the sensation repeated itself, and she suddenly remembered the burner cell in her pocket she'd purchased after returning to the States. Back when communication felt important, for some reason.

Lucy fished it out and squinted at the caller ID. It was a 205 number. Alabama?

She hit the green button and waited for the caller to speak first.

"LB?"

Lucy didn't try to hide the surprise in her voice. "Reed? How ... how did you get this number?"

"You put it on the forum, remember?"

Lucy had already forgotten about her desperate plea to Reed for a job, and the old forum they and plenty of other "contractors" used to communicate. It all became a blur when she loaded up on oxy.

"Where are you?" Reed asked.

"I ..." Lucy's mind moved slowly, like it always did during the early phases of withdrawal. "Tampa."

"I need your help," Reed said. "Can you get to Chicago?"

Lucy returned to the bench. She rubbed her face again. "Chicago? Why?"

Reed spoke gently. She couldn't imagine the Prosecutor ever being gentle. "I'm working on the Trousdale thing, and I need your expertise. Can you get to the airport?"

"I ... yeah. I guess so."

"Take the first flight to Chicago. I'll be there to pick you up."

Lucy swallowed hard. "I'm ... I'm out of money."

"Can you get to a Western Union? I'll wire you a grand."

"Okay."

"Hurry. It's important."

"Yeah, okay. I'll text you when I know my arrival time."

"Terrific. See you then."

"Reed?"

"Yeah?"

"I . . . I don't think I can help you."

"Sure you can. I'll explain when you get here."

"I'm not like I used to be. I'll need something."

"What?"

Her eyes watered. "Oxycodone."

"Just get to Chicago," Reed said. "I'll take care of it."

62

The Secret Service would have kept Stratton aboard *Air Force Two* until the end of time, but after a full day of aimlessly orbiting North America, he ordered the plane back to Joint Base Andrews and returned to the White House.

It was nearly midnight on the East Coast. Almost Election Day. Thoughts of the most important political race of his life had faded since Maggie collapsed over the stage in Chicago and were further dampened by the second attempt on the president's life.

But the election still mattered. In some ways, it mattered more than ever. America needed to believe in itself right now. Americans needed to know that democracy wouldn't be threatened by a thug with a sniper rifle.

In the morning, Stratton would deliver a final campaign speech, making a last pitch for the Trousdale–Stratton message. Even if, only hours after casting their vote for the swamp girl from Louisiana, Jordan Stratton took the oath of office.

One of the Marine helicopters carried him from Andrews to the White House, where a field of Secret Service agents rushed him inside. He met first with a skeleton of the National Security Council. Half the members were unavailable on short notice and joined via speakerphone.

The discussion was simple. Security procedures for Election Day, progress from the FBI on the investigation, and the inevitable discussion of international tension. America's enemies were only too happy to kick her while she was down, and Secretary of State Lisa Gorman was hard at work communicating with allies and rivals alike to ensure they all knew the Trousdale administration was still firing on all cylinders and wouldn't be cowed.

Following an exhausting ninety-minute meeting, Stratton dismissed the council and remained slouched in the vice presidential chair at the end of the table, staring at the wall as everyone departed the West Wing. Carolyn and the twins were already upstairs in the residence. Being single and overly simple, Maggie used very little of the mansion's residential sections, reserving large swaths of it for executive guests and exhausted staff. There was a room ready for the Stratton family to crash in for the night, but Stratton didn't think he would join them.

He didn't feel like listening to Carolyn whine about being rushed around the country and suffocated by the Secret Service. With luck, she'd pop another heavy sedative and piss off for twelve hours.

Stratton ran a hand over his face and sucked in a deep breath of recycled Situation Room air. He thought about Trousdale, lying in a Chicago hospital room, hooked to half a dozen machines. Only a heartbeat from vacating the most powerful office in the Free World.

And leaving him to claim it.

Stratton stood and shrugged his jacket off, abandoning it on the table as he stepped into the hallway. There were Secret Service agents everywhere, including Dorsey.

"Do you need something, sir?"

"I'm good, Jim. When do you clock out?"

"I don't, sir. Not until this crisis is resolved. But I may catch some shut-eye if you're okay with it."

Stratton patted Dorsey on the shoulder. "Yeah, Jim. Get enough for both of us, okay?"

He found his way to the elevator but took the stairs instead, rising to the first floor of the West Wing. It was quieter than he ever remembered. During his eleven months as Maggie's vice president, he'd spent more time in the West Wing than his own home. Maggie wanted an engaged, involved VP. Somebody who could advise, share leadership duties, and watch her back.

Long days and late nights at the seat of executive power gave Stratton a taste for the future. A prospect of what assuming that office himself could feel like.

And a hunger for it.

Stratton exited the stairwell and turned toward his vice presidential office. Then he stopped, looking over one shoulder. The building was perfectly still. Almost desolate. A couple lights gleamed from beneath occupied rooms, and he heard murmured voices behind two or three doors. But no one was in the corridor. No rushing aides, harried White House correspondents, or other members of the Trousdale cabinet.

Just him.

Stratton rubbed his mouth, then stepped away from his office, deeper into the building. He passed a row of advisory offices on the right and the Roosevelt Room on his left. Then he stopped. The Oval Office lay directly ahead.

Stratton placed a hand on the brass doorknob, glanced over his shoulder again, then pushed inside. Twin couches faced each other over a cream rug, with the Presidential Seal embroidered in the middle. But Stratton's gaze drifted away from the body of the room and to the Resolute Desk.

Maggie's tall leather chair sat squarely behind it, nothing but a pen cup and a telephone arranged on the mahogany desktop. He shut the door and crept across the carpet, placed one hand on the smooth leather of the chair, and pushed it back. The wheels rattled as they moved. He looked once more to the door and sat slowly.

The chair hissed as he settled into it, and he placed both arms on the desk. It was cool to the touch, and he faced the fireplace. A portrait of George Washington overhung it, staring down at him stoically. One president, looking down on the next.

Stratton turned his palms down, touching the smooth wood, and held his head up. He pictured Maggie in that hospital again, hanging on by a thread. Maybe consumed into a vegetative state. Maybe ready to surrender this chair forever.

Stratton looked at the phone. The clock on the digital screen read 12:01.

Just after midnight.

Election Day.

63

It was nearly two a.m. before Lucy landed. Reed took his rental SUV from the FBI headquarters to the airport, leaving Turk to assemble what gear they would need. He'd hoped to initiate his plan earlier in the night, but he didn't mind the prospect of executing it in the dark hours of the morning, right when security guards would be the most bored and disengaged.

He parked in short-term and waited until Lucy texted, then drove to meet her in the pickup lane. The moment he saw her, he reevaluated the rationale that had led him to call her in the first place.

Lucy looked worse than when he'd last seen her. She hunched over in a dirty jacket, huddled into it without any sort of suitcase or carry-on. When he caught her attention, he waved two fingers, and she approached the car with her face down, sliding into the passenger seat without a word.

Reed watched her out of the corner of his eye, steering toward downtown by the light of the rental's built-in navigation system.

Lucy picked at dirty nails. She looked like a shell of herself. As if the body was there, but the person had gone.

"Did you bring it?" she asked, her voice wavering.

"Glovebox."

She opened the compartment a little too desperately, snagging a nail on the latch. The oxycodone she'd requested lay in a bag on top of the car's manual. Reed had lifted it from Lakeside Memorial after making a visit under the guise of inspecting evidence at the bomb site. With the hospital largely evacuated and operating well outside its standard procedures, stealing the drug was a lot easier than it should've been. He placed four pills in the sandwich bag, then kept another two dozen in a bottle in his pocket.

Lucy didn't need to know about those. Not yet, anyway.

She dumped two pills into her hand but didn't swallow them. Instead, she dropped them into her mouth and ground them between her molars, then worked the wet powder beneath her tongue. Reed saw it as a white slurry behind dirty teeth.

Lucy leaned back and held her mouth closed, eyes shut. Gradually, the shaking in her hands stopped. Her breathing grew calmer, and her shoulders relaxed. "Thank you," she said.

Reed switched lanes and watched as she stared out the window at the passing cityscape. Her hair was tangled, and she smelled like she hadn't showered in a week. Maybe she hadn't been able to.

"You watch the news?" Reed said.

Lucy shrugged.

"There was another attempt on Trousdale."

Lucy still said nothing. Reed gave her time, unsure whether she was struggling to understand him or simply taking her time in responding. The Lucy he knew from before—an assassin code-named Little Bitch, whom he preferred to call LB—was a sharp woman. One of the sharpest he ever knew. He wasn't sure how much of that woman had survived Southeast Asia.

"You're working the investigation?" Lucy said.

"By proxy."

Lucy relaxed into the seat and folded her arms. "How can I help?"

It was a pragmatic question. The kind of question a professional would ask. No need for extraneous details or rabbit trails. Straight to the point.

Maybe LB was alive after all.

"Turk and I are looking into a possible suspect."

"The shooter?"

"The person who hired him."

"Okay."

"There may be a connection with a local energy firm here in Chicago. I need you to infiltrate the building."

"Why?"

"Because I can't fit down air ducts. As I recall, that's one of your specialties."

Reed took an exit off the highway and slowed into a backed-up line of traffic waiting at an intersection. Even this late at night, Chicago was busy.

"I'm not who I used to be," Lucy said quietly.

"I don't need you to be. I just need you to get inside, lift some computers, and leave some footprints."

"What do you mean?"

Reed twisted his hips in the narrow seat. His right leg was beginning to cramp. "Can I trust you?" he asked.

"Honestly?"

"Yeah."

LB looked at her hands. "I don't know."

"What does that mean?"

"It means . . . I'm not sure who I am right now."

Fair answer.

The light turned green, and they rode quietly for a while.

"We suspect the vice president," Reed said at last. "He's closely associated with this energy corporation, and he doesn't know we're poking around."

"You're trying to rattle him," Lucy said.

Reed nodded. "After he learns we tapped the building, he'll either pull us off the case or pour on the heat. Then we'll know."

"So, you're not even trying to get anything."

"I'll take anything you can pull. Mostly, I want you to slip inside the executive offices and leave some footprints, like I said."

Lucy nodded, still picking at her nails. "It was really Kelly who did that stuff. I just followed along. I'm not what I used to be, Reed. I'm a long way from it."

Reed made a right turn at the next intersection and reached into the car's console. There was a "No Smoking" sign on the windshield, but screw it. He'd purchased a pack at a convenience store inside the airport and needed the nicotine. Rolling down the window, he lit up and enjoyed the flood of smoke. It calmed his nerves and loosened his muscles.

Reed offered Lucy the cigarette, and she shook her head.

"Oh, I get it," Reed said. "Still too good for that."

Lucy indulged in a weak smile, and Reed slid into a parallel parking spot in the midst of downtown. All around them, the tall buildings of Chicago's business district reached for the black sky.

"I'm not who I used to be, either," Reed said. "Thank God."

Lucy bit her lip.

Reed put a gentle hand on her shoulder. "You believe in second chances, LB?"

Lucy snorted.

"Me neither. Luckily, life doesn't care what we believe." He gently squeezed her shoulder. "I was wrong to turn my back on you in Destin. You've always been a friend to me. You came through for me again and again during the Resilient investigations. I know I don't have a right to ask, but I need your help one more time. And then I'm going to get you back on your feet . . . whatever it takes. I promise."

Lucy looked up. There were tears but also strength in her green eyes. A hint of that fire that earned her the nickname Little Bitch in the first place.

"Okay, Prosecutor. It's a deal."

64

Cunningham Enterprises was headquartered in the top half of a fifty-two-story tower nestled right in the heart of downtown. The building was jet-black, covered in plate glass with tall glowing letters reading "Cunningham" across the top. It reminded Reed of a similar tower in another city, years before. The memory was both energizing and a little sour.

Directly adjacent to the tower was a fifty-five-story apartment high-rise, also built of glass, with a rooftop patio and pool. Reed read all about it on the property's website, noting the uninterrupted view of the city skyline from the pool deck. Chicago, in all its glory.

Turk waited for them on the sidewalk. He'd paid a visit to the equipment depot located inside the FBI field office, designated for special use of the local HRT—the elite Hostage Rescue Team assigned to Chicago.

HRT was essentially the special forces of the FBI, and while Reed had little experience with them, it was no secret they enjoyed all the best toys. Turk came loaded with an oversized duffel bag and a confident grin that told Reed he'd hit pay dirt.

The three of them proceeded down the street to the main entrance of the apartment tower, Reed taking the lead with Lucy trailing behind. The front doors of the building were locked and guarded by an all-night receptionist, but Turk had already made arrangements. They waited in the shadows for only ten minutes before the car arrived. It was some kind of tiny hatchback, with a local pizza restaurant advertised on a plastic sign riding on its roof. The sign glowed, and beneath the logo, a tagline proudly read: "Best Deep Dish in Chicago — Open Late!"

The driver got out, looking sleepy and bored, and proceeded to the door. He hit the intercom button and mumbled to the receptionist, then Reed heard the lock click.

"Go!"

They left the shadows and caught the door just as the delivery driver passed through. Reed offered the guy a grateful grunt, as if he were turning in from a late night of drinking with friends and was eager to get home. The driver ignored him and proceeded directly for the reception desk.

Reed, Lucy, and Turk marched for the elevator, leaving the desk clerk to deal with the pizza guy, and walking as if they owned the place. In Reed's experience, that was the key to slipping past late-night security. Third-shift receptionists were introverts, uninterested in interacting with other life-forms. So long as you didn't give them a reason to accost you, they wouldn't.

The sleepy woman behind the desk was no exception. She cast them a casual glance, then returned to her conversation with the pizza guy, who was insistent that somebody at the front desk had ordered a large deep dish.

Inside the elevator, Reed hit the button for the pool deck. The elevator shot upward, and the resulting quiet felt immediately awkward.

"Turk's got a girl," Reed said, just to say something.

"For real?" Lucy asked.

"Redhead," Reed said. "Huge knockers."

Turk turned crimson and shot him the bird. "Screw off, Montgomery." He switched the bag to the other hand, an involuntary smile creeping across his mouth. "Her name is Sinju."

"That's beautiful. Japanese?"

"Korean. She's from North Korea."

"North Korea . . ." Lucy looked sideways at Reed.

He waved his hand dismissively as the elevator ground to a stop at the top floor. "Let's move."

The lobby outside the rooftop was laid in slip-resistant tile, with bathrooms and a rack full of plush towels. A glass door blocked the way to the pool deck outside, where an expansive swimming pool stretched the length of the roof and ended in a glass wall, looking straight down to the hard concrete far below.

Much as Reed expected, the door was locked.

Turk produced a small case, offering it to Reed.

Reed shook his head and motioned to Lucy. "Have a go, hotshot."

Lucy took the case and knelt at the glass door. It was secured with a simple key lock, and the picks held inside the case slipped in with ease. Lucy's fingers trembled, and Reed watched as she fumbled the first attempt. Sweat broke across her forehead, despite the chill of the lobby.

"Take a breath," Reed said.

Lucy left the picks in the keyhole and dug into her pocket. She retrieved the two oxycodone tablets remaining in the sandwich bag and repeated her procedure of grinding them up before circulating the powder beneath her tongue. In mere seconds, the trembling in her hands faded.

Turk shot Reed a sideways look, but Reed held up a hand. Lucy put her fingers on the picks and twisted with practiced ease. The lock clicked open.

"Let's go," Lucy said.

They passed onto the pool deck and straight into a blast of frigid Chicago wind. The chairs surrounding the pool were already gathered up and tied down for winter, and a thin cover stretched across the water. Nobody would bother them up there—not for the short while they would need the roof.

Reed led the way to the east wall. Turk knelt and unzipped the bag, doling out gear quickly across the concrete. There was a small backpack, which would be stocked with the lockpicks, a ski mask, a glass breaker, and a cordless electric screwdriver.

The rest of the duffel contained a hundred feet of light rope and a compact plastic case with the word "Mossberg" printed across the top.

Turk withdrew the case and snapped the latches open, flipping the lid back.

Reed did a double-take. "Seriously?"

"Been collecting dust for twenty years," Turk said. "I doubt they'll even miss it."

The weapon inside the case wasn't a weapon at all—it was more of a tool. Built on the Mossberg 590 platform, the device was called a line launcher and was designed to hurl a length of rope between ships for the purpose of transporting mail bags, small cargo, and equipment.

Mossberg manufactured the line launcher during the eighties and nineties, but they'd fallen out of production for some time. Reed had seen plenty of them aboard Navy ships during his time as a Marine, but he hadn't expected to get so lucky that night.

"I was gonna throw it," Reed said.

Turk snorted. "Don't kid yourself. Tom Brady couldn't make that pass."

He quickly assembled the Mossberg, chambering a 12-gauge launching charge before fitting the harpoon hook into the muzzle and then tying it off to one end of the rope carefully coiled in the duffel bag.

Lucy stood by and watched with no shortage of suspicion, but she followed Reed and Turk to the parapet, then looked down the face of the apartment building.

Stretched out before them, fifty feet across a one-way street and forty feet down, lay the roof of the Cunningham tower.

65

Cold wind whipped Lucy's hair and flooded her lungs, but the warmth of the opioids blocked away the chill. She stood next to Reed and Turk and looked to the rooftop beyond. It was like most commercial rooftops—flat, covered in gravel, and occupied by half a dozen air conditioning units.

Then she looked down, over the parapet of the apartment building, to the one-way street nearly six hundred feet below. A smattering of cars parked along it, and a few decorative trees overhung the pavement. An occasional vehicle rolled by, but there were no pedestrians, trampolines, expanses of water, or fields of packing peanuts.

Nothing to break her fall if she simply leaned out . . . and let go.

Reed spoke softly. "LB?"

Lucy blinked and realized she'd been staring at the inviting pavement, imagining herself rocketing toward it a moment before lights out.

"You good?" Reed asked.

Lucy ran a hand through greasy hair. "Yeah . . . all good."

Reed tilted his head to Turk, and the taller man shouldered the Mossberg. City lights gleamed off the end of the harpoon hook protruding from the muzzle, while the length of rope knotted off to it draped into the duffel bag.

"You ever done this before?" Lucy asked tentatively.

"Nope," Turk said with a grin. "But it looks like fun."

He pressed the trigger. The shotgun cracked with a muted blast, and the harpoon hurtled out of the barrel. It arced like a football, spinning and trailing the rope, then slowed over the top of the Cunningham tower before dropping like a rock.

The harpoon landed dead on the rooftop gravel, and Lucy watched as the rope slumped between the two buildings. She looked to the glass door and the lobby beyond. Nobody hurried to confront them. The shotgun blast had been loud, but unrepeated in the middle of a mega city, it was just another car backfiring.

Reed checked his watch. "Three thirty. Let's move."

Turk began to reel the harpoon in, walking the length of the apartment tower rooftop to snake the hook nearer to an air conditioner. Lucy watched it bounce through the gravel, then skip over one corner of a commercial AC before hooking against a leg.

The rope became taut, and Turk gave it several strong jerks, then backtracked to Lucy and Reed's position.

"That should work," he said.

"Should?" Lucy questioned.

Reed took over the rope and made several attempts to snatch it free. Lucy watched his muscles strain beneath a long-sleeve shirt. The hook wouldn't budge.

"It's good," Reed said. "Did you find a pulley?"

"I did better." Turk dug into the duffel, retrieving a rappelling harness attached to a belt swivel. The harness was probably three sizes too large for Lucy, but she was relieved Turk hadn't simply handed her a strap and invited her to jump.

She dropped her legs into the harness, and Reed helped her cinch it down as best they could. It was still loose, but with the rope running through the belt swivel, she wasn't worried about anything breaking.

Lucy pulled the backpack on, then stepped to the wall. Reed wound the rope up, surveying the distance before looking back to her harness.

"It's good," Lucy said. "I feel good."

"You sure?" Reed questioned. "We can find another way."

"No. Like Turk said . . . it looks fun."

She attempted a saucy grin but felt self-conscious doing it. Her teeth used to be pearly white. Now they needed a careful scrubbing and about a gallon of Listerine. She hadn't felt like caring for herself since oxycodone became the only thing she ever thought about.

Turk took his place beside Reed and grabbed onto the rope, then both men walked backward until the line became taut. Lucy advanced to the parapet and tugged on the swivel, inspecting each buckle of the harness one more time.

Then she looked straight ahead, into the black sky. She didn't look down. Lucy had never been afraid of heights, but she knew better than to complicate the mental math ahead of her with equations of exploding over the pavement. Now that she was about to hurl herself off the roof, falling to her death didn't sound seductive any longer. It sounded like the brutal end.

Lucy lifted one leg over the wall, then sat on the top. Her feet swung over the edge, and she inhaled slowly. This was it.

"Ready?" Reed asked.

"Do it," Lucy said.

She pushed off the roof the same moment Reed and Turk snatched the rope up and back. It snapped tight next to her face, and Lucy fell only six or eight feet before the rope caught her and she raced downward. Cold wind blasted her face and flooded her lungs. For a split second, she forgot about the burns that scarred her body and the torment of their perpetual pain. She forgot about the endless craving for more opioids, the fear of the future, and all the hell-filled months of her recent past.

She fell, hurtling toward the Cunningham tower like a falcon diving on a rabbit. She held her feet up as she crossed over the roof, and then she landed. Gravel bit into her knees and legs, spraying her face as she flopped and rolled, almost slamming into the air conditioner.

As soon as it began, it was over. Lucy lay on her back, staring up at smoggy stars. And she grinned. For the first time in recent memory, she felt like herself. She felt alive.

Lucy shot a thumbs-up at Reed. Then she hurriedly wound in the rope, unhooking it from the harpoon and manually tying it off to the air conditioner before she advanced around the side of the unit and located the main duct. It consisted of a metal conduit, turning down straight into the roof and leading to the offices below via a primary shaft. Lucy knew from experience that smaller ducts would branch off the main one, connecting to individual rooms scattered across each floor.

She wouldn't need those. She only needed to drop eight or ten feet down before breaking out into the top floor of the tower—the executive floor, where all the biggest cheeses worked.

And where all the dirtiest secrets were kept.

66

Early afternoon bustle consumed the SVR's headquarters, but nestled in a secluded corner of the third floor behind a heavy oak door, Ivan Sidorov worked in relative calm.

It had taken decades to earn this office. As a deputy director of the department, Ivan wielded an intimidating amount of power not only over the SVR, but over Moscow, the federal government, and even the Russian Armed Forces. Sitting near the top of the food chain for the Federation's chief intelligence service brought as many opportunities for personal exploitation as any similar post in any nation around the globe. The SVR knew things about nearly everyone, and Ivan had spent years leveraging those resources into his own impenetrable castle built entirely of other people's dirty secrets.

Knowledge was power, after all, and Ivan knew more about the inner workings of Moscow than almost anybody had business knowing. He knew enough to enshrine his position in the corner office on the third floor, pay for the little dacha near the Rybinsk Reservoir, and keep him alive in an often treacherous political environment.

Of course, Ivan wasn't the only one to play that game. Makar Nikitin, Russia's new president, had fought his way from the mired depths of Soviet peasantry all the way to the pinnacle of Russian power in much the same way—albeit often a more ruthless version. For much of Boris Yeltsin's career, and the careers of his successors, Nikitin had served in the background, slinking in and around the maze-like chambers of Russian politics and always turning up at the most opportune moments. He'd only assumed office as president about three years previously, but already, Ivan had witnessed more than a few of Nikitin's political rivals experience sudden, untimely deaths after speaking out against the administration.

Ivan had been around long enough to tell the difference between a blustering bureaucrat and a truly lethal authoritarian, and he was not the least bit confused about which one Nikitin was. When *Air Force One* went down in flames over Turkey fifteen months previously, Nikitin ordered divisions of the Black Sea Fleet to sail into the Mediterranean, triggering a standoff with the U.S. Sixth Fleet stationed in Naples.

After the new American president conspired with Saudi Arabia to hijack the international oil market, threatening Russia's chief source of national income, Nikitin had backed down quickly, assuring the world that the naval deployments were only a series of coincidental exercises.

Ivan knew better—not only because of his unique access to internal intelligence, but also because he was born with a brain. Makar Nikitin was an ambitious man—he had to be to rise so far—but Ivan had long suspected Nikitin's ambitions to extend beyond personal accolades and deep into the international sphere.

There were those in Moscow who still remembered the glory days of the Soviet Union, back when the West trembled at the prospect of total nuclear annihilation should the USSR be provoked.

The new Russian Federation was a far cry from the old Motherland, and from Ivan's perspective, the world was a lot farther from nuclear war, possibly as a result. But not everyone felt that way. Some still hungered for the global dominance they once enjoyed. Some would see those days return.

It was those people who were on Ivan's mind now. Those people who had motivated him to make the trip to Minsk and meet with Wolfgang

Pierce in secret, then further motivated him to lie to Wolfgang about The Ghost of Grozny.

Yes, the first part was true. The part about the war and Fedor Volkov's torture. The killing machine he became. It was also true that Volkov's file had passed across Ivan's desk and that the SVR rejected him for concerns of mental instability.

But the part he left out—the part Ivan wouldn't risk admitting to a foreign agent, even one he trusted—was that Volkov's story hadn't ended there. Because while the SVR had passed on him, an even more powerful group had employed him with enthusiasm . . .

The oligarchy.

It was an exclusive club, built for the ultra-rich Russian elites who inherited the state-owned industries that cascaded like golden apples from the branches of the Soviet Union as it fell. Now those men were some of the world's wealthiest and most powerful players, and Fedor Volkov, The Ghost of Grozny, was their weapon of choice. A private soldier with a talent for death and not the first trace of a conscience.

Ivan sat behind a sprawling metal desk and sifted carefully through the digital files held on a detachable hard drive, now plugged into his computer. The contents of that drive were too sensitive for the SVR's internal storage network. Too sensitive even to be kept on his own computer. He stored the drive in a private safe, hidden behind a bookcase in his office, because what that drive contained kept him alive—but it could also get him killed if it were ever discovered.

They were his files on the oligarchs, the dirty secrets of the men who surrounded President Nikitin and enabled his vise-like grip on Moscow. It was every sordid thing they'd ever done, every crooked deal they'd ever made, where they vacationed, how they took their tea, the mistresses they slept with, and the hookers they strangled to death in seedy Siberian hotel rooms.

It was more than dirt. It was toxic sludge. The kind of thing that, carefully leveraged, could sink any single member of the Russian elite in a heartbeat. But if it was ever leaked—if those elites banded together against the SVR—Ivan would find his own untimely demise at the bottom of a slick staircase.

With the door locked and a video display on his screen alerting him of any incoming visitors, Ivan searched the files, first for Volkov, and then for the men who had most recently employed him. The records were scarce, even for Ivan. The elites were careful about sheltering their activities. They knew how to make the SVR work for it.

But the trail was there. Like a string of gory crumbs—many of them meters apart, but still connected—Ivan traced Volkov's handiwork through the mid-2000s. Most of those kills were of international businesspeople from Europe and Asia—players who threatened the expansion of oligarch-owned enterprises.

But some were political figures, also. Even religious ones. A bishop in Ethiopia. The new prime minister of Ghana. A law enforcement official in Malaysia. All resource-rich nations where Ivan knew the oligarchs held vested interests.

And then, abruptly, the killings stopped. Volkov's last known activity was nearly two years old, and while Ivan hadn't noticed at the time, in hindsight, the end of the bloodshed seemed irrationally abrupt. Where had Volkov gone? What had triggered his departure?

Ivan sipped bitter Russian tea from an elegant cup and studied the records. Most of them were little more than news clippings—killings he *assumed* Volkov was responsible for, linked with his own notes and theories about oligarch involvement.

There wasn't much to go on, but Wolfgang surely had to be mistaken. There was no way Volkov took a swing at the president. Even if he was capable of a shot that extreme, who would hire him? Even the oligarchs didn't dare touch an American school child, let alone POTUS herself. Not only because of the inevitable and extreme repercussions from Washington, but also because Nikitin kept the Russian elite on a leash. Anybody stepping too far out of line would be cut off. Like Belsky had been.

Belsky.

Ivan sat forward, clicking quickly out of Volkov's file and back into his records of the oligarchs. It took only a moment to find the document he was looking for, and he scanned past the name and photograph at the top, right down to his last entry.

Two years old.

Stepan Belsky was one of the original oligarchs from Yeltsin's era. He inherited much of the Soviet-controlled oil refinement sector and quickly leveraged it into a sprawling energy empire, ideally positioned to exploit the reconstruction era across Eastern Europe.

In 1995, he was a millionaire. By 2010, he rivaled Bill Gates, but almost nobody knew it. Belsky was a cockroach. A creature of dark places and deep shadows. He kept his wealth hidden from the outside world, pulling strings and using a network of proxies to expand his empire across Western Europe, through developing Asia, and even into the edges of American society. He was more than an oligarch. He was an economic emperor, rapidly rising to unsinkable status as the tentacles of his empire slithered into the hearts of one nation after another.

And then he was banished.

It was unspoken common knowledge that Nikitin was responsible. Despite his careful efforts to disguise his rapid growth, Belsky's power was no secret to the inner sanctum of the Russian elite. His influence was bridging beyond noteworthy and becoming a threat.

Nikitin didn't tolerate threats, especially having recently won the presidency. He cut Belsky off at the knees, seizing his Russian assets, draining his accounts, and banishing him from the Federation. Overnight, Belsky fell from the most influential businessman on the planet to just another billionaire exile, living off the assets he'd concealed in third-world nations while he drifted around the planet on his mega yacht.

A nuisance, maybe, but not a threat. Not for Nikitin.

And yet . . .

Ivan scrutinized the file, studying the details, noting the last known communications from Belsky and comparing them with Volkov's file. Volkov disappeared two weeks after Belsky's demise, and neither of them had been heard from in over twenty-six months.

Ivan fixated on the screen, his tea forgotten, an uneasy feeling creeping into the back of his mind. He reached for the phone and hit the speed dial for his personal assistant—an SVR officer only a few rungs down the ladder from Ivan himself—somebody who could be trusted with limited exposure.

"Da?"

"Get me everything we have on Stepan Belsky. Immediately."

67

Reed and Turk hurriedly repacked what remained of their gear and returned to the glass door. Whatever happened next for Lucy, she was on her own.

The LB Reed knew from years gone by would thrive in that environment. He wasn't sure if the shell of a woman he now saw still had it in her to rise to the occasion, but he hoped so.

Regardless, he couldn't help her if he wanted to. There was no access to the Cunningham building from the bottom. Unlike the apartment tower, the Cunningham headquarters was heavily guarded on ground level, equipped with key-card access doors, armed guards around the clock, and a slew of electronic security measures.

The only way in was through the top, and while Lucy's ninety pounds was easy to manage over the thin rope, he and Turk were another matter.

Good luck, LB.

They hustled into the elevator and remained quiet while it dropped. Reed felt an uneasiness in his stomach and realized this had to be the first time he'd ever attempted an operation like this without being on the front lines himself.

He didn't like it, and he checked his watch. Lucy had been on the rooftop for just over three minutes. By now, she should've used the electric screwdriver to remove the access door on the duct. Then she would've looped the rope through her harness and descended into the shaft, dropping eight or ten feet to the executive floor and entering via an expanded air vent.

Turk hadn't been able to obtain blueprints of the executive suite of the Cunningham tower, but Reed could guess. There would be a security desk outside the elevator, which likely wouldn't be occupied this late at night. Then there would be a secure access door with a key-card reader. Beyond that would be a reception area, and then another door into the suite itself.

There wouldn't be cameras in the suite. No motion detectors. No listening devices.

Executives in the energy sector didn't want to be listened in on or observed. All Lucy had to do was select a vent on the interior side of the secure access door, and she would be in. The picks would defeat any locked office door that got in her way.

The elevator stopped, and Reed and Turk marched out. The receptionist glanced up briefly but was preoccupied with a large deep-dish pizza. Apparently, she had decided to stop questioning the driver and simply enjoy the pre-paid meal. Back outside, Reed led the way to the rental car, and the two of them piled in. He checked his watch, then looked across the street to the bottom floor of the Cunningham tower. It was dark, but he could make out the shadow of a security guard pacing behind tall glass doors.

No sign of Lucy.

"This is a big risk," Turk said.

"She'll be fine," Reed countered, still watching the building. "She's got grit."

"I don't mean for her. I mean for you. And me, for that matter."

"How so?"

"We just got our slates clean, dude. Here we are conducting illegal activity again."

Reed scratched his cheek, realizing he'd barely considered the legal ramifications of his plan. It just seemed like the next move to make. "When we catch this guy, nobody will care."

"The vice president might care. A powerful enemy to make."

"I'm shaking in my boots," Reed grunted.

He started the car and shifted into gear but kept the lights off and didn't leave the parking space. Another four minutes crawled by. It had now been nearly twenty since Lucy landed on the roof. Had he underestimated the security? Had she become stuck in an air duct?

Reed chewed his lip, one hand wrapped around the wheel. He impulsively checked the time again, as if that would help anything. It was nearly four a.m.

Alarms screamed to life. Reed heard them, even through the thick plate glass of the Cunningham tower. Dull red lights flashed from inside the building, and the outer doors swung open on automatic mechanisms. The rising wail of the alarm continued, but instead of running for the elevators, the security guards on the bottom floor ran for the doors, exactly as they were trained to do in the event of a fire.

Reed's foot dropped off the brake, and he spun the car to the left, cutting down the one-way street Lucy had zip-lined across and navigating to the rear loading dock. In the distance, he thought he heard fire truck sirens screaming toward them, and the white lights from inside the tower continued to blink and flash.

But he saw no smoke. Only clean black glass and empty sky.

Reed slid to a stop at the loading dock, and Turk reached behind his seat to shove the back door open. Another thirty seconds dripped by in slow motion.

Then the fire exit next to the loading doors blew open, and Lucy dashed out with the backpack bouncing on her shoulders, her face obscured by the ski mask. She leapt the loading dock with an elegant flip, landing next to the car and sliding right in.

Reed stomped the gas and raced back onto the street as a large fire engine ground around the corner. He took another turn at the next intersection, quickly losing the Cunningham tower in a maze of Chicago high-rises.

Lucy peeled the ski mask off, shaking her head to settle her auburn hair. A grin crept across her face. "You were right. That *was* fun."

"You get out okay?" Reed asked.

"No problem. I dropped in past the security door and rifled around. Then I pulled the fire alarm and took the elevator straight to the loading dock. I don't think anybody even saw me."

"Sloppy," Turk muttered.

"Excuse me?" Lucy said.

"I meant *them*," Turk clarified. "Sloppy security."

"They're civilians," Reed said. "What did you get?"

Lucy tugged the backpack off her shoulders and dropped it onto the seat next to her. It rattled with heavy electronics. "A couple hard drives, a cell phone, and some loose paperwork. Junk, mostly, but enough to rattle somebody . . . like you wanted."

Reed slowed the car as he steered for a metro parking deck near a bus station. He'd picked the spot before leaving the FBI headquarters. The bus station provided free, 24-hour Wi-Fi, and the deck was quiet enough to offer a secluded place to regroup and evaluate what they had found.

Turk had already pulled a laptop from beneath his seat and was busy sorting through a mess of wires to hook up the hard drives. Reed figured Lucy was probably right—it had to be mostly junk. These days, companies kept their real secrets in the cloud or on private servers. But it was worth a look.

He parked the rental and switched it off, then checked his phone. There were no calls yet from Stratton, but if any of their suspicions about his association with Cunningham Enterprises were warranted, they'd hear from him soon enough.

"I'll call Wolfgang," Reed said. "See what you can find."

He ducked out of the car and speed-dialed, moving to the perimeter of the parking deck and looking down at the bus station. It was fully illuminated, and already, early morning busses were rolling out of their stalls.

"Reed?" Wolfgang answered abruptly.

"How did it go? Did you meet with your contact?"

"About five hours ago. I'm working my way back now. I had to take a detour through Riga."

"I don't even know where that is," Reed said.

"Latvia. Beautiful place, if you like to be cold."

"Did you learn anything?"

A muffled bumping sound was followed by a door closing.

Wolfgang spoke softly. "The guy's name is Fedor Volkov, but they call him The Ghost of Grozny, or simply The Ghost. He served in the Russian army during the First Chechen War, back in the nineties. He got captured and tortured, then escaped and went on to make a name for himself on a revenge spree."

"Sniper?"

"Yeah. One of their best."

"What happened to him?"

"He got out of the military and looked for private employment. My contact says Moscow passed on him due to concerns over mental stability. He may have found work with the Russian mob."

"When was this?"

"Twenty years ago."

"And since then?"

"My contact doesn't know. Says Volkov fell off the map."

"*Should* your contact know?"

"Yes, probably. If Volkov were active. But that doesn't mean he'd tell me."

Reed chewed his lip. The information was interesting, but he wasn't sure it really meant anything. Knowing who the guy was didn't immediately lead them to who he worked for.

"Anything on your end?" Wolfgang asked.

"Maybe. I'm not sure. We have a . . . loose suspect."

"Who?"

"Stratton," Reed said.

"Seriously?"

"We found video of him making a payoff to the daughter of a big energy firm here in Chicago. The firm is heavily invested in multinational energy deals with Russia and China—something Trousdale opposes."

Wolfgang took his time answering. "That's thin."

"I know. But Stratton stands to gain it all if Trousdale kicks the bucket."

"Before the election?"

"Sympathy vote, maybe. Enough to push the ticket over the edge."

"So, that's how that works? If she dies on the campaign trail and is elected posthumously, the running mate becomes president?"

"I guess? I really don't know."

Wolfgang was quiet, and Reed knew he was picking the theory apart like wet newspaper. The more Reed considered it, the more he thought Wolfgang might have a point. But it didn't matter.

"We'll know soon enough," Reed said. "I rattled some cages."

"I'm not sure I like the sound of that."

"Don't worry. You're not implicated. Get yourself back to the States and stay close to your phone. I might need you again." Reed hung up but didn't return to the car.

The element of the Stratton theory that bothered him the most wasn't why Maggie had been shot prior to Election Day. It was why Stratton had paid off the Cunninghams. If Stratton stood to benefit from becoming president, the Cunninghams stood to benefit by having a powerful friend in the White House. And they were rich, anyway. Why would Stratton pay for the hit?

Maybe it wasn't money in the envelope. Maybe it was something else. A message? Why deliver it in person, especially after blowing off an important interview? Reed shifted the pieces around in his mind and knew he was missing something big.

Turk popped out of the rental car, smacking the roof. "Reed!"

"What?"

"Get over here. We found something."

68

Reed joined Turk and Lucy at the SUV's hood, arranging the laptop and a mess of hard drives over shiny black paint.

"You said these Cunningham people were into multinational deals?" Lucy said. "You weren't kidding."

She tapped on the laptop, and a PDF reader populated on the screen. Reed scanned the documents. There were maybe a dozen of them, all displayed on Cunningham Enterprises letterhead, with complex legalese filling each page. Reed didn't understand most of it, but as he tabbed from one document to the next, he noticed a name highlighted in yellow, sprinkled through each one.

"What is Lenkov International?"

"Great question," Lucy said, an energy in her tone he hadn't heard since finding her at the resort in Destin. It wasn't quite the pep and enthusiasm he was used to from the old LB, but it reminded him of her. It was like coffee, watered down.

"These documents are joint venture contracts drawn between Cunningham and Lenkov. I really don't understand the specifics, but we kept seeing that name pop up everywhere, so we googled it. I mean, the shooter is Russian, right?"

"Fedor Volkov," Reed said. "Wolfgang just confirmed it."

"Right. So, we googled Lenkov International."

"And?"

"And it's owned by some guy named Stepan Belsky," Turk said. "Russian oligarch."

He switched the laptop screen to a web search. A picture of Belsky was splayed across the screen—a Wikipedia page, no less. Beneath the main search bar were a slew of news articles, most of them three or more years old, from international newspapers and business journals.

"Am I supposed to know this guy?" Reed asked.

Turk shook his head. "I didn't, but it didn't take long to learn about him. He owned a bunch of energy companies in Russia—mostly oil refineries, all held by the state prior to ninety-one. When the Soviet Union fell, he swept in and grabbed them up, then began to diversify."

"That's what they all did, right?" Reed said. "The oligarchs, I mean."

"Pretty much," Lucy said. "And then they went on to become major power players inside of Moscow. It's kind of an elite insider's club. Ultra-rich men with heavy influence over Russia and much of Eastern Europe."

"Okay. So, what's the point?"

"Only that Nikitin ousted this guy," Turk said, pointing to a news article.

Reed scanned the headline: "SOURCE: NIKITIN BANISHES BELSKY, SEIZES RUSSIAN HOLDINGS."

The article was a little over two years old and included a lot of quotes from anonymous sources "deep inside the Nikitin administration."

"This guy held an empire of oil refineries in Russia," Lucy said. "Nikitin took it all and kicked him out."

"Why?" Reed asked.

Lucy shrugged. "I haven't found an answer to that. But it could be a motive, don't you think?"

"For knocking off Trousdale?"

"Belsky could've known about The Ghost," Turk said. "He's already in bed with Cunningham on a host of international deals. Deals Trousdale staunchly opposes."

"So, they get rid of Trousdale, and Stratton takes her place," Reed said.

"A known friend of the Cunninghams," Lucy finished.

Reed rested his chin in one hand. He saw the puzzle coming together, forming a picture. He almost believed it. "How do we prove this?"

Turk and Lucy looked at the stack of virtual documents. Neither answered.

"This wasn't hard to find," Reed said. "The link between Cunningham and Belsky. The FBI will find it soon enough, assuming they haven't already. Everything else is pure conjecture."

"But it's logical," Turk said.

"Sure. But if you think hard enough, you can find a logical explanation for almost anything. You could say I hit Lucy and left those bruises on her arms."

Lucy's gaze dropped, and Reed flushed. "I'm sorry. That was a terrible example."

"It's cool," Lucy said.

"The point I'm making is that none of this is concrete," Reed continued. "Belsky might have a reason to punch Trousdale's ticket. He might have known where to find Volkov and slipped him into the country. But none of that matters unless we can prove it."

Turk looked up. "That's it."

"What's it?"

"Slipped him into the country. How did Volkov get here?"

"What do you mean?"

"Remember during the Resilient investigations, when you were stranded in Colombia?"

"Yeah . . "

"We had to sneak you in on a shrimp boat to avoid customs."

"Because I was on an FBI watch list at the time," Reed said.

"Exactly. Volkov would have the same problem. You said yourself he found employment with the Russian mob. A guy like that is on every watch list in America. He can't just swipe his passport at TSA and walk right in. Even with a fake passport, he can't change his face or all those scars. Using an airport is too dangerous."

"What's your point?"

"My point is, somehow he got in without setting off any alarm bells, after which he traveled all the way to Chicago with a very expensive, custom rifle. He had to have had help."

"Cunningham?" Lucy asked. "How can you prove that?"

"Cunningham may have supplied a car and a rifle, but how did he *get* here in the first place if airports aren't an option?"

Reed scratched his chin. Turk was right. A guy on any sort of watch list couldn't fly in. Airports were flush with security, TSA, and God only knew what other government oversight. Volkov might have snuck into Canada and drove across a rural portion of the border. There were places between Chicago and Seattle that were little more than lines cutting through giant forests. But that didn't explain how he entered Canada in the first place, which would've been just as difficult as entering a U.S. airport.

Mexico would be easier, but the drive to the Texas border was both long and perilous, and even if he managed to sneak across, that still left him over a thousand miles from Chicago.

"Don't these guys have yachts?" Lucy asked, pointing at the picture of Belsky.

Turk snapped his fingers. "That's it."

"Seaports still have customs," Reed said.

"But beaches don't," Turk said. "Put him in a wetsuit, and drop him off on your way in. He could slip right into the country, unannounced, just like we did in North Korea."

"Okay, seriously," Lucy said. "What happened in North Korea?"

Reed waved her off. "If Belsky brought Volkov in by yacht, he would've had to clear customs. There's no way he could get that close to shore without docking at an international port."

"Then there's a record with whatever agency handles international yachts docking on the coast," Lucy said. "There's got to be. We find that record, and you've got something to work with."

"So, we call the FBI," Turk said. "Get them to pull records."

Reed shook his head. "The FBI will either ignore us or cut us out of the loop. What we need is the Department of Homeland Security."

"I'll ask French," Turk said, reaching for his phone.

Again, Reed shook his head. "No. French will just call a guy who will call a guy. We need this quicker. And besides . . . there's still a loose cannon at play."

"Who?" Lucy asked.

"Stratton," Reed said. "This theory of yours works with or without him involved. We need to know which it is."

"What's your plan?" Turk asked.

"Simple. I'm going to ask him to contact Homeland Security and then watch what happens."

69

Security at the hospital more than tripled following the oxygen bomb, but O'Dell still wouldn't leave Maggie's side. The building was cleared, the National Guard took positions at every door, and the Secret Service swarmed Maggie's new room like bees in a hive.

And still, he stayed through the night, even as the city quieted and then slowly awoke again, muffled by the thick Kevlar sheets and bulletproof shields surrounding the president.

O'Dell sat beside Maggie's bed, praying and watching her breathe. He'd never been a religious person—not in the military, not as a cop, and not even as his marriage burned to the ground. Technically, he was a Roman Catholic—at least that's what he claimed on forms and census papers—but he couldn't remember the last time he'd attended mass, and he didn't even know the name of the church in his hometown.

It had never really mattered to him before. He figured God was either there or He wasn't, and either way, O'Dell had to live his life.

But sitting beside Maggie, watching her jerk in the throes of panicked seizures, knowing at any moment her body could simply surrender the fight and her soul could slip away . . . It was different. O'Dell felt truly help-less, like nothing he did would matter.

The demons assailing the president deep in her subconscious state were beyond his reach. He couldn't gun them down or sling himself in the path of their pitchforks. He could only sit and watch it happen.

And he could pray. He repeated the Hail Mary prayer over and over again, largely because it was the only one he could remember. Then he abandoned the rehearsed words and spoke to God as though he were speaking to the doctor, asking about Maggie's condition. Begging for her to be kept alive.

When the words stopped coming, she still lay unconscious, pinned beneath an oxygen mask, limp on the bed. But he didn't leave.

He would never leave her side again.

70

The White House

Stratton caught three hours of fitful sleep on an Oval Office sofa before an aide woke him at four thirty. It was still dark outside, but already, the day was upon him. He needed to shower, dress, deal with Carolyn and the kids . . . and then face the nation. One last fervent pitch as Election Day dawned.

He showered in cold water, then put on gym shorts and hit the heavy bag in the White House fitness center for half an hour until he was red-faced and winded. Then he showered again, shaved, and put on his newest Armani suit. A red power tie and an American flag pin completed the outfit, but when he looked at himself in the mirror, he wasn't sure the expensive clothes masked his exhaustion.

This was the day he'd dreamed of for most of his adult life—the day his name was called on a national election. Sure, he was already vice president, and yes, he had to pass a full congressional vote to assume that office. But until he tested his name against the populace, how could he know if he measured up?

Final results wouldn't be available until late that night, possibly deep into the next day. It was a three-way race, with only one trophy waiting at the end. And with one candidate holding onto life by a thread, all prior polls went out the window. Would America vote by fear, playing it safe and embracing an establishment candidate? Or would they stick behind Muddy Maggie, even if Stratton was only a breath away from taking her place?

There was no way to know, but Stratton would be damned if he didn't fight to the end.

"Mr. Vice President? We're ready for you."

Stratton stood next to his desk in the vice presidential office, looking out the window over West Executive Avenue. It wasn't much of a view—not compared to the Oval—but all that may well be temporary.

"I'll be right out."

The aide standing in the doorway looked ready to object, but Stratton didn't move. She ducked her head and shut the door behind her, leaving him at the window. Jennifer Holmes and the rest of the Trousdale–Stratton campaign staff were already assembled in the Roosevelt Room, ready to help him prepare the speech he would deliver as soon as the sun rose.

It wouldn't be a campaign speech—not officially. This was a reassurance address. A call for Americans to find their courage and conduct their civic duty. To get out and vote for whoever their chosen candidate might be. But of course, projecting strength from the White House was projecting strength for the Trousdale campaign.

Stratton held his chin up, and thought about nine names—nine men who served as vice president, and were one day called on to take their boss's job. Would he be the tenth?

He blocked out the uncertainty and chaos of the past four days and embraced the moment. This was *his* moment, for better or worse. Whatever came next.

Turning from the window, he started for the door, and that was when his cell phone rang. He'd forgotten to silence it, and he moved to bump the call, but he recognized the number. It was Montgomery—Trousdale's secret operator.

There was a knock on the door, and Stratton held a hand up. "One moment!" He answered the phone. "Reed?"

"Mr. Vice President, we have something."

Stratton's heart skipped. He turned away from the door, lowering his voice. "What is it?"

"The shooter is ex-military, currently working as a contract killer. We think we have a lead on who hired him."

Stratton retreated to the most secluded corner of the office, his tie feeling suddenly tight and restrictive. "Who?"

"His name is Stepan Belsky. Ever heard of him?"

Stratton looked at the floor. "No. Who is he?"

"He's an exiled Russian oligarch. Heavy involvement in the energy sector, predominantly in oil refinement. We think he may have ordered the hit."

"Why?" Stratton could hear his team bustling outside the door, anxious to get started, but he tuned them out.

"We're still working on that," Montgomery said. "I need you to call your director of Homeland Security and have him run a trace on Belsky's yacht. The shooter has gone to ground, but if he's working with Belsky, he'll use the yacht to flee the country. We need to cut him off."

A *yacht*? Stratton wiped sweat from his forehead. He really had no idea if Reed was onto something or shooting in the dark, but the confirmation of a Russian connection drastically raised the stakes.

"We find the shooter, we find who hired him," Montgomery said. "We'll be on standby until we hear from you."

"Okay." Stratton assimilated the information but decided he didn't have time to unravel it. With Election Day consuming the nation, he'd have to trust Montgomery and his team to make smart choices. "I'll call them. They'll reach out to you directly."

"If we find the yacht, we may need approval to board it," Reed said.

"I'll tell the director."

"Thank you, sir."

Stratton hung up, then immediately reached for the phone on his desk, tapping zero for his secretary.

"Yes, sir?"

"Get me Director Jacobs, ASAP."

Reed hung up and tapped the cell phone against his chin. Lucy and Turk still stood near the nose of the rental car, the documents spread around them.

"What do you think?" Turk asked.

Reed sucked his teeth. "I don't know. He seemed cooperative."

"Why didn't you ask him about Cunningham?" Lucy said.

"Because I couldn't see his face. Too easy for him to lie."

"You won't see his face if we're chasing some billionaire on a yacht," Turk said.

Reed stared out over the bus station, now framed by a sky turning pink in the east. He tilted his head toward the car. "Pack up. Let's get breakfast."

Turk and Lucy scooped the paperwork and electronics into the car's trunk. Reed waited until they were busy arguing pancakes versus waffles, then scrolled through his recent calls and tapped a number.

Wolfgang answered almost immediately.

"Where are you?" Reed asked.

"Heathrow. About to board a plane for New York. What's up?"

"When you land, book a ticket for DC. I've got another job for you."

71

Stepan Belsky was getting antsy.

It had been nearly two days since his mega yacht entered port at The Magic City. By this time, he'd hoped to be well inside the safety of international waters, churning south with Volkov on board, Trousdale a distant memory, and his future as a readmitted Russian insider secured.

Instead, he paced the darkened interior of the yacht, the crew held on standby, the air conditioners humming to fight the early November heat.

And Volkov still in the wind.

Belsky was a young man, barely fifty, but nobody would know it looking at him. Streaks of grey lined his beard, and his hairline crept steadily upward as the years of stress and strain took their toll. For a man worth nearly forty billion dollars, it was an affront to him that he should feel this stress at all.

By now, his net worth should've ballooned to ten times the current amount. He should've owned half of Moscow, pulling the strings of whatever puppet he installed in the Grand Kremlin Palace, while he himself was well on his way to calling the shots over twenty percent of the world's energy sector.

They were ambitious goals, but not so long ago, they had lain well within reach. It was Nikitin who turned Belsky's world on end. It was Nikitin who conspired with the other oligarchs behind his back, then seized the bulk of his Russian holdings before banishing him to the outside world.

As one of Russia's elites, Belsky should've been untouchable. Endless wealth and the control he held over the nation's energy sector should've ensured total security. But all of that depended on the support of his brotherhood. Oligarchs were, after all, something of an elite fraternity. They looked out for each other. They guarded each other's secrets and hunted each other's enemies.

After being cast from that circle, Belsky was on his own. Even with forty billion little soldiers standing at his beck and call, Belsky couldn't hope to fend off the entire planet. Some nations and leaders were sympathetic to his predicament—maybe because he still held the keys to their energy supply. But those nations were mostly small, second- and third-world places, with little global influence.

The big fish—China, Western Europe, and the U.S.—wouldn't touch him. Not only because Russia had banished him and that made any safety net cast his way an issue of international diplomacy, but also because they simply didn't need him. Forty billion dollars was peanuts to Beijing. Just another pork bill to Washington. A blip on the radar for the European Union.

To them, Belsky wasn't an elite. He was an overpaid thug, drifting around the globe in his oversized yacht, passing in and out of their harbors for short periods before fading into the sunset again. An annoyance. The trace of shit on their shoes, not even significant enough to waste time scrubbing away. They were too important. He was too insignificant.

And that burned him far worse than Nikitin ever had. Being banished was a humiliation, but in a way, it was also a validation of how powerful and dangerous Belsky could be. Being disregarded and ignored by the rest of the planet—that was an insult too far. A cut too deep.

Belsky had zero problem facilitating the death of America's president, not only because he hated Americans, but because he was being compensated with recognition. And perhaps, readmittance.

Belsky stepped through the automatic glass doors onto the tail of the yacht and held his hand over his eyes, blocking out the sun to survey the city. Miami rose from the Florida coast in gleaming glory, so much warmer and more vibrant than any city in Russia, yet so hostile in his mind.

It was Election Day in America. Not far outside the private marina he was docked at, digital billboards flashed with red, white, and blue backgrounds, reminding citizens to vote. But he didn't see Volkov. He was still chained to this place by an invisible tie, holding him so long as The Ghost of Grozny wandered the American streets. A renegade. And a potential witness.

A phone rang from inside the salon, and Belsky rushed in. He found it near an opulent leather couch and snatched it up, not bothering to sit down. "Da?"

"You have failed me, Stepan."

An icy chill, defiant of the Miami warmth, raced down Belsky's spine. He clutched the phone to his ear and moved deeper into the shadows of the yacht. Somehow, he felt safer farther from the windows.

"Volkov tried again," Belsky objected. "She may still die!"

"Our deal was for her to be dead days ago," the computerized voice on the phone growled. "You cannot expect full compensation for half a job."

Sweat ran down Belsky's face, and he scrubbed it away. "We will regroup. Volkov is on his way. I spoke to him two hours ago. He was almost to Atlanta."

"You waited too long!" the man snapped. "The Americans are searching for your yacht. My sources in Washington tell me the vice president has called in an order to Homeland Security. They are onto you, Stepan. You were sloppy."

Belsky's chest felt suddenly tight, crushed by an invisible weight. It was difficult to breathe, and he wanted to return outside. "I'll leave port now," he said. "I already changed the boat's transponder. I'm docked under a false name. They won't find me."

"No," the man snapped. "It's too late for that. We must give the Americans something. We must give them your boat."

Sweat dripped off Belsky's nose. "What?"

"Listen carefully. I will not repeat myself. Wait for Volkov. As soon as he boards, turn south. I will send you coordinates. Sail right for that spot. The Americans will give chase. Have Volkov resist them."

"They will have helicopters," Belsky protested. "Warships. I should leave now and get a head start!"

"Shut up, fool! With the coordinates, you will find directions for dealing with the yacht. You have diving equipment on board?"

Belsky hesitated. "No . . ."

"Send your people to Miami to get some, then follow my directions to the letter. Do you understand?"

Belsky swallowed hard. He could feel a cold knife jabbing into his back, as tactile and visceral as though an actual blade were piercing his skin.

He knew the man on the other end of the phone wasn't asking. If Belsky refused, the man may well call Volkov and ensure Belsky's death. There was no option but to capitulate.

"I understand," Belsky said.

"Your use is not yet exhausted, Stepan. Prove to me that you are not yet worthless, and there may still be a future for you."

"Thank you."

"Look for my directions," the man growled. "Don't fail me again."

72

Ivan Sidorov intercepted the call to Belsky's yacht, and his blood ran cold.

The signal was encrypted, routed through a satellite and muffled over Ivan's headphones. Even after he located Belsky, it took him some time to leverage the integrated monitoring software aboard a Russian spy satellite to intercept any communications. And even then, he only intercepted the call because it was made *through* that satellite, right from the heart of Moscow.

The voice was masked—computerized and at times garbled. Ivan didn't recognize it, but he didn't need to. There were only a few people who could have located Belsky and then contacted him directly through an encrypted satellite feed. Most of them worked in the SVR. The rest worked in the Kremlin.

Ivan peeled the headphones off and ran a hand through salt-and-pepper hair. His chest felt heavy, and he dug in a metal drawer for a room-temperature bottle of Russian vodka. Twisting the cap off with his teeth, he guzzled a couple shots' worth while still staring at the screen.

He'd recorded the latter half of the call. Now he wasn't sure if he should have. Maybe he should've deleted it, scrubbed his computer, erased anything to do with his investigation into Belsky before hauling ass. Maybe he should distance himself from all of it—not only what had happened, but what was going to happen. Because this ran far deeper than The Ghost of Grozny or even a disgraced rogue oligarch.

It had been a long time since Ivan felt real fear. The last time he remembered it was back in Sydney, surveying the wreckage of Wolfgang Pierce's last mission as an espionage operative. Listening to this call, that old feeling of dread and disbelief returned.

But there was another feeling that kept him from running: Anger. Burning outrage. Unbridled disgust.

Ivan was an old man. He'd fought wars and killed a lot of people. He'd shoveled his homeland's dirty secrets and waged a cold war with the West that extended far beyond the fall of the Soviet Union.

He *loved* his country. Not only the land, but the people. The culture. The mountains of snow, the bad food, and the faulty electricity. The grungy music and angsty teenagers, always teetering on the edge of revolution. The motorcades for weddings. The liquor that ran like water through the brutal months of winter. The often-violent heritage that, in his mind, made Russia the greatest nation to ever grace the planet.

The Motherland.

He'd spent most of his life dedicated to defending her honor, protecting her borders, and ensuring her survival. Disillusioned by the collapse of the USSR and disgruntled by the lies of Stalinist communism, he still found a way to believe. Because he still believed in his people. He still loved them like brothers.

And now this.

Ivan made a fist and bit his knuckles. Something burned deep in his stomach, and it gained strength as he stared at the screen and listened again to the words. Complete betrayal. Total treason.

His thoughts were arrested by the crash of a fist against his office door. A man barked at him in angry Russian, demanding he open up. Ivan dropped the bottle and raced for the keyboard, quickly closing out of the recording before inputting a demand for a complete hard-drive wipe.

The fist repeated. The walls rattled, and a picture frame hit the floor. The computer loaded in slow motion.

"Open up!" the man called. "We will break down the door!"

Ivan pushed the chair back, reaching for the top drawer. A Makarov handgun lay inside, preloaded with eight rounds of 9x18 cartridges. It had been his faithful sidearm during his years in the Russian army and had found its way into a shoulder holster during his early days as a member of the SVR. It hadn't failed him then. It wouldn't fail him now.

Ivan snatched the drawer open, but the Makarov was gone. His blood turned from icy cold to boiling hot, and then the door blew open. Shattered wood rained across the floor, and four men in the black and gold uniforms of the FSB burst in.

Russian secret police.

Three of them brandished Grach pistols, while the fourth advanced directly to Ivan's desk, glancing briefly at the now blackened screen before glowering at Ivan.

"Ivan Sidorov, you are under arrest. Put out your hands."

"What is the meaning of this?" Ivan snarled, his shoulders back.

"You are guilty of treason!" the man said. "Put out your hands!"

The FSB officer snapped handcuffs from his pocket while his colleagues pointed their Grachs at Ivan's chest, fingers resting on their triggers, their eyes as hard as stone.

Ivan glanced around the room, evaluating his odds, then he extended his hands. The cuffs closed around them, and two of the gunmen circled in behind. They marched him out of the corner office, down the hall, and toward an elevator. Several of Ivan's secretaries and assistants stood from their desks as he passed. The lead FSB officer barked at them to go back to work.

When they reached the elevator, the officer punched a button, but not for the parking garage, where a security vehicle might be waiting. It was for the basement.

Ivan squared his shoulders. "Thirty-six years I have served my country. Is this the respect I have earned?"

Nobody answered as the elevator ground down.

"Get Gusev on the phone," Ivan said. "I demand to speak with him."

"The director does not wish to speak with you."

The elevator stopped. The doors rolled back, and Ivan was thrust out. On his left lay a maze of hallways and small rooms—detention facilities used to interrogate intelligence assets captured overseas. Ivan was very familiar with them. He'd been present for years of gruesome handiwork before the Kremlin claimed to shut the program down. In reality, they simply relocated it, far into the east, deep in Siberia, where such operations could proceed unnoticed by polite society.

But the prison cells and interrogation rooms remained. Ivan figured they would lock him in one of those, and then it would only be a matter of time before he found himself in Siberia.

Instead, they marched him to the end of a hall, where a giant steel door barred the way into a disposal room. Ivan knew the place well—trash compactors the size of cars crushed refuse into small cubes before shoving them through chutes and into disposal bins outside. It was a noisy mechanism, and for that reason, the room was well insulated. Insulated enough to mute gunshots and screams. Ivan knew this because he'd used it for that exact purpose on several occasions.

The door opened, and the FSB officer prodded Ivan forward. "Go in."

Ivan looked down at him. He was a young man, early twenties. There was no ring on his right hand, where Russians traditionally wore wedding bands, but it wasn't unusual for married FSB officers to leave those at home. Maybe he had a wife and a couple children. A small family. A hell of a thing to lose.

"Are you sure about this?" Ivan asked quietly.

The guy sneered. "We know what you did, old man."

"Do you know what *he* did?" Ivan said.

The guy's gaze flickered, then his face became stone hard. "Get in!"

He shoved Ivan forward over the threshold. The gunman followed, leading with their handguns, fingers on the triggers. Then the door slammed shut.

73

Chicago, Illinois

"It's Election Day in America, and boy, if we were concerned about Americans being too afraid to vote, were we *wrong*. With a full seven hours remaining until polls close on the East Coast, voters are lined up at the ballot boxes like movie fans at a new premier. Joining us now is CBS correspondent Jules Listner, on-site at a voting facility in Pennsylvania. Jules, what do you have for us?"

The woman behind the mic was young and bright. She beamed into the camera with a line of bundled-up voters winding down the sidewalk behind her.

"It's a blustery day here in Allentown, but that's not stopping anyone from making their voice heard. We've had lines this long since seven a.m., and the people just keep coming. I spoke with a young couple this morning who brought their infant son along with them. No matter the inconvenience, turnout this Election Day is on pace to be record-breaking."

The news anchor broke back in. "It's the craziest presidential election I ever remember. With three candidates tied in a dead heat, one of them fighting for her life, and every poll a blatant contradiction to the next, there's really no way to tell which way this thing will swing."

Reed muted the hotel TV and slumped into the armchair. He'd scanned through election coverage across all the major networks during the past half hour, and they pretty much repeated a spin of the same thing—voter turnout was at an historic high, and nobody had a clue who was in the lead.

Reed let out a tired sigh. Behind him, Lucy lay stretched across one bed, fast asleep. After calling in the Homeland search to Stratton early that morning, the three of them had elected to return to Reed and Turk's suite at the Chicago Marriott so they could all shower and catch some much-needed shut-eye.

They all showered, but only Lucy was able to sleep. Turk had departed twenty minutes prior to pick up a deep-dish pizza. Apparently, ordering one for the apartment receptionist had put him in the mood.

It was now past noon in Chicago, and Reed sat alone, watching the continued footage of eager voters lined up at the polls. In his nearly two decades of voting eligibility, he recalled voting only twice—both times while serving in the Marine Corps. As a kid, his mother didn't care about politics, and after his career with the Corps concluded, Reed no longer believed in the government.

But during those brief, golden years while he served his country in the brutal deserts of Iraq, Reed tried to believe. He filled out absentee military ballots for both his home state of California and the 2012 presidential election.

He only learned years later that those absentee ballots weren't counted. They were never counted unless the election was close enough that absentee ballots might decide the vote.

The 2012 presidential election was far from close. This election might be. But Reed hadn't voted, and it wasn't because he was caught in Chicago, a thousand miles away from Birmingham. It wasn't even because he'd lost faith in the system. It was because he lost faith in himself. Jaded, and too closely associated with the inner workings of Washington to see the bigger picture, he felt his opinion had been irreparably compromised. Any vote he cast now would be tainted by his own bitterness and mistrust.

And that wasn't a way to vote. Better to let the idealists—the young and the vibrant, the old and the wise—choose the future of the country. He would be happy to go along with whatever path they selected.

Lucy snored, and Reed glanced her way. He'd given her cash for new clothes and toiletries, and she had taken another oxycodone a few hours before sleeping. Since then, she'd slept hard, her mouth half-open, her petite body buried beneath the covers. Already, she looked better, but it was all temporary. She needed full rehab. A path away from addiction. And most importantly, belief in herself.

Reed dug in his pocket and found his phone. Over five hours had passed since he called in the request for the Homeland search, and still, there was no news from the vice president. The silence wasn't reassuring. Reed knew things moved slowly in Washington, but if Stratton didn't call back quickly, Reed would have to reevaluate his approach. And his suspects.

Wolfgang had reached New York two hours previously and would touch down in DC any minute. Reed had instructed him to rent a car and remain on standby. For just a little longer.

Thumbing to his favorites list, Reed selected the top contact and pressed dial. The phone rang, and he closed his eyes. He was so tired, his body felt broken, like he'd been run over by a truck. But when he lay down, he couldn't sleep. Not only because of the mission, or of Trousdale, or because the nation's vice president might be a killer. But because of the memories.

"Reed?" Banks said.

"Hey, girl," Reed whispered.

"Oh my God. I was about to go nuts. I kept telling myself not to call, but I hadn't heard anything and—"

Reed tuned out the deluge. Banks was a little crazy sometimes—maybe most times—but she sounded like home.

"I'm sorry," he said. "We're waiting on a call."

"Did you . . . I mean . . ."

"I can't talk about it on the phone."

"Is she alive?"

"Yeah. They think she's gonna pull through."

"That's . . ."

"Incredible."

"Yeah."

Reed ran an arm behind his head and settled into it. "She's one tough son of a gun. But we already knew that."

"When will you be home?"

"Soon. Tomorrow, I hope."

"You're not gonna do anything stupid, are you? The FBI can find that guy. Or the Army or whatever."

Reed smiled. "Don't worry. I'm done being stupid for a while."

The phone went quiet. Reed's body relaxed, and he felt himself almost drift off, but he couldn't quite let go. "Banks?"

"Yeah?"

"You . . . you were right before."

"What do you mean?"

"About me. And stuff."

She didn't answer.

"I know I've been . . . weird lately. I'll work through that."

"Will you see somebody?"

A lead weight descended into his stomach. Reed didn't answer right away. He sat up and rested his elbows on his knees. "We can talk about it."

"Promise?"

"Promise."

Reed thought he heard a soft giggle in the background. He lifted his head, a smile spreading across his face. "Is that Davy?"

"Yeah. Hold on."

Banks's phone fumbled, then he heard the electronic clicking sound of a photograph being snapped. A moment later, a new message appeared on his phone.

Davy sat on the floor, surrounded by a field of colorful toys. Stuck to his shirt was a bright red, white, and blue sticker with bold letters printed across it.

I VOTED.

"Did little man vote?" Reed asked.

"Little man's mommy voted. But the old guy at the polling place gave him a sticker."

"Don't let him eat it."

"Oh, shut up. I rock this mommy shit."

Reed picked at the carpet between his legs, ready to be home and dreading it at the same time. He missed Banks. He missed Davy. But he still didn't know what to do with the quiet.

The door blasted open, and Turk crashed in with a pizza box in one hand and a half-eaten slice in the other. His phone was pinned between his ear and his shoulder, and he spoke in broken Korean, heavily tainted by his Tennessee drawl.

"What do you mean that's not how you say it?" he demanded. "That's how *I* say it!"

Reed rolled his eyes. "I better call you back."

"You better," Banks said. "I love you."

"I love you."

Turk dropped the box on the table, laughing like a schoolgirl. Reed could hear Sinju shouting at him over the phone. She sounded a little heated, blending English with Korean. Reed understood none of it, but he could tell by the tone that Turk had screwed up. And he could tell by the silly grin on Turk's face that the big guy had no clue.

Lucy sat up in the bed, brushing tangled hair out of her face and scowling. Turk's grin began to fade, and he tried to speak, moving back to the door.

Reed tuned it all out and reached for the pizza box, but then his phone rang. It was Stratton. He lurched to his feet and snapped his fingers. "Shut up!"

Turk looked up abruptly, then murmured a few words to Sinju and hung up.

Reed hit the answer button and put the phone on speaker. "Mr. Vice President?"

"He's in Miami," Stratton said. In the background, Reed heard the clamor of a few dozen voices mixed with TVs and feet clapping on tile.

Campaign headquarters, he figured.

"We're on our way," Reed said, spinning his finger in a circular motion.

Turk reached for his bags, and Lucy piled out of bed.

Stratton continued. "He hid the yacht under a fake hull number and name. It took them a while to find it. But five days ago, Belsky overnighted in Manhattan."

Manhattan.

It was a short enough drive from New York to Chicago. Especially if you had a good car waiting.

"I need you to call the Coast Guard," Reed said. "We'll need a team on standby to board the boat."

"Already done," Stratton said. "I just got off the phone with the commandant. He's got their Maritime Safety and Security Team on standby to take the yacht, along with some choppers and a heavy cutter. They're expecting you."

Reed shot Turk a glance. Turk said nothing, but Reed could tell they were both thinking the same thing: Stratton was being awfully proactive. That could only mean he was innocent . . . or controlling the fallout.

"We'll be there ASAP," Reed said. "I'll keep you posted."

"Reed?"

"Sir?"

"Remember what I said. This guy doesn't walk away."

Reed took his time replying. He pictured the vice president in the White House, and he again asked himself what a guilty man would do.

A guilty man wouldn't allow for any loose ends.

"I'll call you from Miami," Reed said.

He hung up and moved to the door. Lucy and Turk were already there, Lucy with the car keys in one hand.

"Call the airport," Reed said. "We'll take the first flight out."

74

Miami, Florida

Lieutenant Zach Jackson had been in Miami less than six months, but he was already calling it home. After a five-year career with the Coast Guard that spanned posts in Portland and New Orleans, Florida felt like a vacation. Always sunny, always warm, surrounded by clean emerald water and populated by bikini babes almost year-round, it couldn't be further from the humid swamps of Louisiana or the wind-blasted rocks of Maine.

He'd taken a promotion to move to Miami, and if it was up to him, he'd deny a promotion to stay. One of those beach babes had stuck around recently. Her name was Rosa, her family was from Havana, and damn did she look great in the Sunshine State. After ten weeks of tangled sheets and late-night walks on the beach, she was starting to feel like home, also.

Jackson wasn't a guy to settle down. His life was an adventure—that was why he became a Coastie in the first place. His hunger for action had fueled him straight through boot camp and into the Coast Guard's Maritime Safety and Security Team, a division of counterterrorism specialists established in the wake of 9/11. They were the Coast Guard's version of special forces, and they were trained for everything.

From diving off of cutters to assess underwater threats to fast-roping from Jayhawk helicopters onto the decks of hostile vessels and chasing down drug runners aboard lightning-fast jet boats, the MSST was the solution to Jackson's adrenaline addiction, and he was damn good at his job. He was so good that he climbed the ranks quickly, first taking command of his own team in New Orleans before accepting a further promotion in Florida to a larger team—a team specially equipped to engage the unique problems and greater risks of a city famous for its ongoing drug war.

It was the next step Jackson craved, and for the past six months, it had quenched his thirst for adrenaline. But now, with Rosa in the picture, he started to think of things outside the scope of roaring gunfire and emergency vessel seizures. Things like a starter home up in Fort Lauderdale with a garage for his motorcycles and a front porch to drink beer on through hot Florida nights. Things like sunsets and dinners for two and conversations about forever.

They were prospects he could get behind. Could she?

The question filled his mind when the phone rang. Jackson was technically off duty for the weekend, but as an officer of the MSST, there was no such thing as *really* off. Emergencies could happen at any time, especially in Miami with so much maritime traffic. Day or night, he never ignored a call.

"Jackson."

"Zach, it's Trevor. Report to the air station in ninety minutes. You're headed out."

Jackson set his beer down, wiping his mouth and looking out the open glass door of his apartment toward the coast, two miles away. It was early afternoon—maybe five hours to sunset.

"Ninety minutes? Is this another damn exercise?"

"I don't have details. Lieutenant Commander Ivers says you're going out on a Jayhawk."

"Jayhawk? We don't have any."

"They flew a couple down from Clearwater. I don't know what's going on. Ivers said something about two guys from DC. Just get here, okay?"

Jackson breathed a muted curse. Guys from DC could only mean one thing: another damn exercise, this one in front of brass from headquarters. But the helicopters still threw him off. There were plenty of choppers at Air

Station Miami, most of them MH-65 Dolphin aircraft built by Eurocopter and ideally suited for flying bigwigs around.

Why call for MH-60 Jayhawks out of Clearwater? It was a two-hundred-mile flight, burning a lot of time and fuel. Maybe the brass wanted to see Jackson and his men perform a fast-roping exercise—something they would need the bigger helicopters for.

"All right. I'll be there."

"Hey, Zach?"

"What?"

"Make sure you're sober. I've got a funny feeling about this one."

"What do you mean?"

"I don't know, man. Probably nothing. See you in a few."

The phone clicked off, and Jackson set it down. He ran his hand over his face, then peeled his shirt off and headed for the shower. If he was gonna have to play helicopter tour guide for some asshat pencil pushers from DC, he better look the part.

75

Miami International Airport

The 737 from Chicago touched down with a scream of rubber on asphalt, then taxied for the gate. Reed and Turk were two of the first to depart, rushing through the terminal and heading for the pickup line.

Reed had left Lucy in Chicago with enough money to get to Birmingham. From there, they would regroup on her future, and he'd make good on his promise to help. For now, his full attention was focused on the hunt. It was time to nail The Ghost.

A white Ford Explorer with an orange stripe waited in the pickup lane, and Reed and Turk loaded right in. The guy behind the wheel was young and wore a dark blue Coast Guard uniform, shooting them a curious look as they settled into the back seat. But he said nothing as he turned into traffic, then hit his emergency lights and raced northward toward the base.

Reed watched the city roll by, the sun arcing toward Mexico. It was warm outside, and the city was still bustling with Election Day hustle. Flashing billboards reminded voters of the closing deadline to get to the polls, and Reed wondered who was in the lead. He didn't know much about the two candidates challenging Trousdale for the White House, but he knew they both brought immense war chests, as had she. By midnight, two of the three would have wasted their money.

The Explorer drove away from the coast, north along Florida Highway 953 toward Miami Gardens. Reed had already been briefed via email that they would be meeting the Coast Guard at Air Station Miami, which was housed inside Miami-Opa Locka Executive Airport. He expected a sprawling military base, much as he was accustomed to while serving in the Marines.

Instead, the Explorer pulled straight into a small, semi-private airfield, not encountering the first hint of security until they approached a massive metal hangar situated near the core of the facility. A ten-foot chain-link fence topped by barbed wire surrounded the hangar and the sprawling tarmac around it, while a sunbaked guardhouse blocked their path. The Explorer's driver stopped the SUV and presented his ID, then the gate guard asked for Reed and Turk's driver's licenses.

A moment later, they were off again, blazing toward the front doors of the hangar and the two orange and white helicopters parked outside.

Reed recognized them immediately as MH-60s—variants of the Navy's Seahawk design, which itself was similar to an Army Black Hawk. A dozen men dressed in dark blue combat uniforms clustered next to the choppers, squinting in the blazing sun as the Explorer ground to a stop.

"You get out here, sir," the driver said.

Reed let himself out, a wash of warm Florida wind rushing over his face as his boots hit the tarmac. He smelled baking asphalt and jet fuel—familiar smells for any Marine. Familiar, and almost comforting.

"Mr. Montgomery?"

A tall guy in black tactical gear approached Reed from the choppers, offering a hand. The tape on his bulletproof vest read "Jackson."

"That's right," Reed said, taking his hand.

"I'm Lieutenant Zach Jackson, Coast Guard MSST. I was just briefed on our mission. I understand you guys work for the Pentagon?"

There was a clear subtext to Jackson's question. Reed noted the semi-curious, semi-suspicious glint in his eye, but before he could answer, a pair of officers dressed in Coast Guard blues and wearing aviator sunglasses exited the hangar and made a beeline for the table. Jackson stiffened, and

Reed quickly sized up the men, noting hard faces and the stripes on each of their shoulders.

The first was a lieutenant commander—an O-4 in the Coast Guard, equivalent to a major in the Marine Corps. He walked alongside a shorter, older man—an O-8, a major general in the Corps, a rear admiral in the Coast Guard.

Jackson threw a quick salute. The commander returned it, and the rear admiral looked to Reed.

In a deep growl, he said, "Mr. Montgomery?"

"That's right," Reed said.

"I'm Rear Admiral Halsey, Commander of Coast Guard Seventh District, headquartered here in Miami. This is Lieutenant Commander Ivers."

"Good name," Reed said.

"His or mine?" Halsey said.

Reed offered a subdued smile. "Both."

A slight grin parted the admiral's lips. "You boys work for the Pentagon?"

Is that what Stratton told you?

Reed nodded. "You could say that."

Halsey's grin faded, then he snapped his head toward a table situated near one of the Jayhawks, laden with gear and computers.

"Well, get over here, then."

Reed, Turk, and Jackson followed the admiral to the table. Around them, Jackson's men, all dressed in black combat gear, were busy loading equipment into one of the choppers. They moved with easy efficiency, relaxed even in the presence of Halsey.

It was a rare thing in Reed's experience for enlisted men to remain at ease in the presence of a high-ranking officer. It spoke to the quality of Halsey's leadership.

"The boat is called *Everstar*," Halsey said, pointing to a chart spread out on the table. It displayed the lower half of Florida with coastal and international waters marked in grids down to The Bahamas. Depth readings and little nautical figures joined the grids. Most of it was Greek to Reed.

"She's a three-hundred-fifty-foot, Dutch-built boat. Four decks, a helicopter pad near the stern, and at least a dozen crew members. She departed Miami four hours ago and is currently sailing one hundred ten miles off the coast—here."

Halsey pointed to a spot on the map halfway between Key West and the northern coast of Cuba, right in the middle of the Straits of Florida.

"She's hauling," Reed muttered.

Halsey grunted. "Cruising near twenty-five knots. Fast for a boat that size."

Halsey marked the spot on the map with a pen, drawing an X and circling it. He looked up. "I spoke with the vice president two hours ago. He instructed me to seize the *Everstar* using any force necessary, then to facilitate your search of the craft."

"We believe the president's would-be assassin to be hiding on board," Reed said. "It could get ugly."

Halsey clicked his pen, staring Reed up and down the way Jackson had, then tilted his head toward Ivers.

"Lieutenant Commander Ivers will be directing this mission. I'll turn it over to him."

Ivers stood taller than Halsey and spoke more stiffly. He withdrew his own pen from his chest pocket and marked a spot on the map, about an inch north of the X Halsey had inscribed.

"Since receiving instructions from the White House, we deployed USCGC *William Flores* to run down the *Everstar*. She's a Sentinel-class cutter equipped with recovery craft and detention facilities on board. There's also one 25mm automatic gun and four Browning fifty-caliber machine guns, should things get ugly. While she closes on the *Everstar*, the three of us will board one Jayhawk and then trail Lieutenant Jackson and his team in the other. *William Flores* will provide cover while they fast-rope onto the *Everstar*'s helicopter pad and seize the boat, after which we'll place you on board to conduct your search."

Reed glanced at Turk and saw a reflection of his own thoughts in the big man's eyes. It was a good plan, but with one glaring problem.

"Commander, with respect, I don't think you know who you're dealing with. The shooter on board *Everstar* placed a bullet in the president's gut from over two thousand yards away, cold bore. If Lieutenant Jackson and his boys try to take that boat from the air, he's going to knock the pilots out long before that chopper is close enough to engage. You'd be better off slinging a cruise missile and being done with it."

Ivers stiffened, irritation crossing his face.

Halsey looked no less put off. "Son, I don't know who the hell you think you are, but there's nobody better in the business of seizing yachts than the MSST."

Reed ducked his head in acknowledgment. "No doubt. Which is why I'm damn glad they're here. But I'm telling you, this guy is off the rails. You need him neutralized *before* you take the boat. Have *William Flores* sink the *Everstar*, then let us go in and fish for survivors. He can't shoot and swim at the same time."

Halsey shook his head. "No way. That's an unarmed ship, crewed by noncombatants. Opening fire is outside our mandate."

"So, call the Navy," Reed said. "There's got to be a destroyer around here someplace."

"Boy, you have no idea how things work around here. Now, you can hop on board that chopper or stay behind. I really don't care. But this is how it's gonna be."

Reed looked to Jackson. The young lieutenant didn't appear completely comfortable with the situation, but Reed couldn't be sure whether that was because of the concerns he'd raised or simply the tension in the current conversation.

"At least put us on the chopper with Jackson," Reed said. "Turk and I have extensive combat experience. We were both Force Recon Marines prior to working for the Pentagon. We know how to handle ourselves. We might be able to help."

Halsey muttered a curse, but he looked to Ivers, who looked to Jackson. And Jackson looked to Reed, sweeping his gaze from a dirty T-shirt and jeans to worn leather boots.

"I'm okay with it," Jackson said at last.

"Fine," Ivers said. "But you're going unarmed. You'll stay in the chopper until Jackson clears your path."

Turk looked ready to object, but Reed held up a hand. "That's fine."

Ivers sped through a list of protocols and directions for seizing the boat, then Halsey wished them all good luck and marched off. Reed and Turk were directed by one of the MSST guys to a locker inside the hangar, where they outfitted themselves with bulletproof vests, helmets, and fast-roping gloves.

Jackson found them inside as the two choppers screamed to life, and their rotors began to turn. "No bullshit," he said. "Who are you guys?"

Reed looked out at the two orange and white birds, each vibrating softly as Ivers and three men in dive suits climbed into one, and a half dozen black-clad MSST operators boarded the second.

"We work for the president," Reed said. "That's really all I can say."

"So, why should I trust your opinions?"

Reed held his helmet under one arm, moving to join Jackson. He spoke quietly. "Back in the day, I was a scout sniper for the Marine Corps. Turk was my spotter. Since the president was shot, we've been hunting the shooter. Two nights ago, I came face-to-face with him in Chicago."

Reed adjusted his heavy bulletproof vest and wished he had a rifle—or at the very least, one of the SIG Sauer handguns worn by Jackson and his crew.

"Look. You can waste time questioning me if you want, but what you need to be worried about is that sniper. Inside two thousand yards, you'll be in range. He can't do much about the chopper without heavier firepower, but your pilots are sitting ducks."

Jackson chewed the inside of one cheek, looking out to the Jayhawks. "What do you recommend?"

"Have *William Flores* blow him out of the water."

Jackson snorted. "What do you recommend that I can *make happen*?"

Taking his time to respond, Reed stepped out of the hangar. The sun was low on the horizon, blazing toward them without a cloud in the sky. "Have your pilot circle in from the west. Ride low to the water with the sun on your ass. Don't slow up until you're right on top of the boat, then be prepared to unleash some cover fire while your boys fast-rope. It's the best you can hope for."

Jackson watched him quietly, his face set in hard lines. Reed could see the conflict behind his eyes—part of him wanting to disregard a complete stranger and rely on the opinions of his commanding officers instead, and part of him willing to believe that this wasn't another run-of-the-mill ship boarding.

"All right," Jackson said. Without another word, he turned for the choppers, leaving them in the hangar. Turk followed him, but Reed stood in the shade of the big building. He pulled the phone from his pocket and texted Wolfgang. Two words, no explanation.

GO AHEAD.

Then he texted Stratton.

MY ASSOCIATE WANTS TO MEET WITH YOU. HE'LL COME TO THE WH. HE HAS SOMETHING.

Reed hovered over the message, still evaluating, still second-guessing himself. Knowing he was about to tip his hand without any way to backtrack if things went sideways. But also knowing he couldn't wait any longer.

He hit send.

"All good?" Turk asked, calling back into the hangar.

Reed pocketed the phone. "All good. Let's ride."

76

Belsky left the salon and joined the captain at the bridge of the massive yacht. Churning west at twenty-five knots with salt spray exploding over their bow, he could hear dishes breaking in the kitchen as he passed. The waves were only five or six feet, but sailing west brought those waves crashing against their port side, rolling the vessel every few seconds.

Belsky felt drunk as he burst into the bridge, clinging to the railing. "How much farther?"

The captain was Finnish but answered in Russian. "Twenty kilometers. Forty minutes."

Belsky looked impulsively over one shoulder. He couldn't see the stern of the yacht, but he could feel the Americans breathing down his neck. He *knew* they were in pursuit. How much lead did he have? An hour? Two hours?

Would the Americans reach *Everstar* before *Everstar* reached the desolate coordinates from the anonymous email? If so, it was over. Belsky couldn't afford to be captured, and not because he feared the Americans, but because he feared the man who wrote the email.

"Push it!" he ordered the captain. "Full throttle."

"The seas are too high," the captain objected. "If we go any faster—"

"I am not asking!" Belsky roared. "Full throttle, or I'll throw you overboard!"

The captain reluctantly reached for the controls, then the bridge door burst open and Volkov appeared. Every time he saw the shooter, Belsky wanted to puke. Volkov's twisted face, matched with the perpetual whistling of the hole in his cheek, was the stuff of nightmares. But the *look* on the face now doubled the horrifying factor.

Belsky's sniper was outraged. "What are you doing? Why are we headed west?"

Belsky ignored him, moving to the digital chart mounted next to the steerage controls and peering at the screen. He knew less about shipboard navigation than he knew about renewable energy, but the little triangle marking their position was connected by a dashed line to the red icon that marked their target.

The two were still an inch apart.

A hard hand descended on Belsky's shoulder and squeezed. "Belsky," Volkov snapped. "What is happening?"

Belsky tore his arm free, grabbing an overhead rail as *Everstar* crashed down the backside of a wave, rolling with the punches. Volkov remained unmoved as the ship righted itself.

"What are you doing?" Volkov demanded.

Belsky avoided his gaze. "What I have to."

77

Straits of Florida

The two Jayhawk helicopters raced across the Gulf at 160 miles per hour, three hundred feet off the water, doors open, and jet engines howling.

Reed crouched behind the cockpit of the lead Jayhawk, his helmet temporarily replaced by a headset wired directly into the chopper's main communications system. Through the windshield he saw nothing but blue water illuminated by a sinking sun.

The water was new, as were the colors of the uniforms worn by the pilots, but everything else about this experience was startlingly familiar. Replace the ocean with the desert, the Coast Guard crew chief next to him with a Marine or Army sergeant, and fill his empty hands with a Mk 12 Special Purpose Rifle, and this could've been eight years before in Iraq.

Headed for war.

Reed looked over his shoulder to see Lieutenant Jackson settled in next to his men, each of them reviewing their gear one last time. Every man was equipped with a SIG Sauer .40 caliber handgun, and either a Remington 870 pump-action shotgun or a Colt CQBR carbine—a shortened M4, essentially, chambered in 5.56.

The team was outfitted in combat boots, tactical vests overlaying bulletproof plates, helmets, chest-mounted radios, safety glasses, and they wore fast-roping gloves to manage the heavy rope now curled on the deck—ready for deployment.

There wasn't a doubt in his mind that they were completely at ease with what lay ahead, just as their extensive training had taught them to be. But the Secret Service had felt the same in Chicago. Not once, but twice. And The Ghost had hit them both times.

Jackson noticed Reed staring and motioned him over. Reed found his way around the rope to the back of the chopper, leaning low next to Jackson's face as the lieutenant covered his microphone with one hand and motioned for Reed to do the same.

"When we get there, I'll go down first while the guys in the other bird cover us. Two of my guys will head straight to steerage to lock down the engine. Two more will take the bridge. I'll take the last guy and search the boat, one room at a time."

Jackson removed his hand from the mic and reached behind him to a metal locker bolted to the wall. As he spoke, he swung the door open, exposing a pair of CQBR carbines, fully loaded, resting inside. "Per orders of the division commander, you and your friend are to remain in the chopper."

Reed looked to the rifles and noted the cabinet's lock lying uselessly on the floor. He saw the glint in Jackson's eyes, and he nodded once. Jackson reached into a pack and fished out another radio, handing it to him. Reed clipped the transmitter onto his belt and the corresponding handset to his chest rig as Jackson turned back to his men.

"All right, boys. Let's get some!"

78

"Look! On the horizon!"

The Finnish captain pointed to the north, and Belsky saw the cutter. It was a couple miles out, bounding through the waves like a dolphin and crashing straight toward them. The United States Coast Guard.

Volkov ran to the window, snatching up a pair of binoculars as the radio burst into a stream of English.

"*Everstar, Everstar*. This is the United States Coast Guard. Under Title Fourteen of the U.S. Code, we have the authority to board your vessel. Halt your engines and assemble your crew on the deck!"

"*Yebat!*" Volkov shouted, still clutching the binoculars to his face.

The English voice on the overhead switched to Russian and repeated the order. The Finnish captain's face washed white, and he reached for the controls.

"No!" Belsky snapped, looking to the screen. They were less than two kilometers from the red cross on the map. "Keep going."

"They will shoot!" the captain said, his hand falling on the throttle.

Volkov turned around, snatching a pistol from beneath his shirt. He pointed the handgun at the captain and thumb-cocked the hammer. "Back off!"

The captain's hands began to shake. He looked from Volkov to Belsky, then to the radio. It continued to squawk, and Belsky yanked the power cord from the back. The American voice died in a flash of static.

"Get your rifle," Belsky ordered, gesturing to Volkov but still fixated on the navigation screen. "We will hold them off."

Volkov lowered the handgun and raced across the bridge. His cheeks flushed red while the mess of scars remained pale white. "What is happening? Where are we going?"

"Just get the rifle!" Belsky said, shoving both hands against the bigger man. "Am I your boss or not? Get your damn gun!"

Volkov looked temporarily rattled, uncertainty flashing behind his mutilated face.

Belsky didn't wait for him to decide. He left the bridge and hurried down the steps into the main salon, then into a spare cabin and straight to the closet in the rear. Already pulling his shirt over his head. Already kicking his way out of his pants as he reached for the scuba diving gear housed within.

79

"There he is!"

Reed pointed between the pilots to the distant horizon, where the dying light of the sun gleamed across something shinier than water. Through the open door of the Jayhawk, maybe a kilometer ahead of them amid the rolling blue water, he saw the *William Flores* bounding through the waves at full speed, crashing toward that speck on the horizon. Probably already ordering it to stop. And being ignored.

"Take us in from the west," Reed shouted to the pilot in command. "And drop down to fifty feet! You want the sun on your ass."

"Back up!" the pilot said, waving his arm irritably at Reed. "We know what we're doing."

Reed turned to Jackson. The lieutenant was already crossing the back of the helicopter, pressing in between the pilot's chairs.

"Brett!" Jackson called over the engines. "Do what he says."

The pilot glared, drawing breath to argue. He simply shook his head and banked the bird to the right, calling orders to the second Jayhawk as they dipped toward the water. The wide circle across the top left section of the compass dragged out over four or five minutes, and Reed looked through the open side door. The sun was almost directly behind them now, but it was sinking dangerously close to the water. The bright rays streaking across the royal blue expanse would soon be gone, as would their cover.

"Hammer down!" Reed said. "We're running out of time."

The pilot eased the cyclic forward, and the Jayhawk gained speed. Reed watched the water racing by, still two hundred feet below and torn by the rotor wash. He could see the yacht now, a clear outline on the horizon, two kilometers out and drawing rapidly nearer as they roared past *William Flores*.

"Lower!" Reed called. "You're losing the sun."

The pilot ignored him, the nose of the Jayhawk tucked downward as they neared max speed. Reed held on to the backside of the copilot's chair and looked over his shoulder, out the side door and toward the horizon behind them.

Only half of the sun was still visible over the water. It blazed so bright he had to squint, but he knew they were still too high. He imagined the shooter on the deck of the yacht, staring through the scope of his high-powered rifle of choice. Sighting in on the helicopter, looking over the top of the sun, missing the glare, and resting his crosshairs over the windshield.

It didn't matter that they were moving at nearly two hundred miles an hour. Nose down, roaring straight forward, they may as well be a static target.

"Lower!" Reed shouted. "Take it down to the water!"

The pilot shouted over his head. "Back the fu—"

Blood exploded across the cockpit, spraying the dash as hot wind blasted through a gaping hole in the windshield. The pilot slammed against the seat, already dead as his jaw fell slack and his left leg dropped against a pedal. Reed saw it happen and latched onto the copilot's seat, ready to shout.

It was too late. The chopper jerked and then dove left, the nose dropping and the tail swinging wide. The copilot scrambled with the controls as a case of loaded magazines spun across the deck and hurtled out the open door. Reed's feet slipped, and his chest slammed into the back of the seat. He saw water through the door beneath him, spinning in circles as an alarm sounded from the cockpit.

Turk clung to an overhead rail, his feet dangling over open ocean while one of the MSST guys slipped free of his harness and slid right out the door, following the case of ammo.

Jackson shouted. The chopper spun and crashed toward the water, now embracing a spiraling free-fall. The copilot wrestled the cyclic, one hand managing the collective as he spoke with a shaking voice into the radio. Reed saw alternating shades of blue as the ocean and the sky changed hands, over and over. His stomach churned, and he almost vomited as he braced himself for impact.

Then the Jayhawk snapped around and suddenly righted itself. Reed's feet hit the floor, and his head smashed against the seat. The chopper stopped spinning and pulled into a hover, the nose rising, engines howling, the torn waters of the Gulf only thirty feet below.

Reed scrabbled to his feet. His hands shook with adrenaline, but he moved to the cockpit and looked through the busted windshield. Everything was slick with blood while the pilot lay limp. The young copilot's face raged with fear as he managed the collective and gasped for air. The Jayhawk bobbed and shook like a tree branch in a thunderstorm, but it didn't fall. The kid kept them sunny-side up.

"Where is he?" Reed shouted, dropping his head to look out the windshield. He'd lost everything during the spiral and couldn't see the yacht, but through his headset, he heard the steady garble of the other Jayhawk calling in alarmed orders.

The young copilot seemed disoriented, looking first to his dash and then to the dead man slumped next to him. Then he puked. It exploded right over his lap in a stream, covering the digital screens built into the Jayhawk's dash.

Jackson scrambled up next to Reed and ratcheted his mangled mic towards his lips. "This is Jackson! We lost a man in the fall. Pilot dead. Copilot—"

The second bullet zipped through the open side door, catching one of Jackson's men in the throat. Reed saw the guy slam into the deck, dead the moment the bullet severed his spinal cord, and then he saw the yacht out the side door.

A thousand yards in a split second. Another unbelievable shot.

"Get us moving!" Reed shouted, grabbing the kid by the shoulder and shaking him.

The pilot scrambled with the controls, and the engines roared again. Two of the other MSST guys moved to help their fallen comrade, but it was too late. It had been too late the moment the dead pilot refused to drop altitude.

The chopper rose to three hundred feet as the pilot's training took over. Reed figured he'd been taught to get off the ground after a rapid descent—to do whatever he could to avoid obstructions he might drift into.

Altitude. Always maintain altitude.

But that training couldn't save him from The Ghost. The only hope now was to finish the job.

"What's your name?" Reed shouted.

The guy's lip shook. "Russak, sir."

"No, first name."

"K—Kyle!"

"Damn good job, Kyle. You fly this thing like a pro. Now, listen to me. You're gonna circle us back and put this bird on the water. You understand me? I want you so low I could take a dump and it wouldn't splash. You hear me?"

Russak continued to shake.

Reed grabbed his shoulder and gave it a confident squeeze. "You can trust me, Kyle. I've done this before. Take us to the water and drop the hammer, okay? Let's go!"

Russak's feet moved against the pedals, and the helicopter spun. Reed heard garbled communication from the other Jayhawk, but he wasn't listening. Neither was the pilot. As the helicopter completed the turn and faced the yacht, Russak nosed down hard. The altitude beneath them bled away, and an alarm sounded on the dash.

"Ignore it!" Reed shouted. "Down to the water. Go!"

The blue waves beneath rose rapidly toward the Jayhawk's belly. Russak managed the controls with practiced ease, despite his shaking hands. In another two seconds, he pulled up, and then they were racing over the surface, barely thirty feet off the water, headed straight for the yacht.

Reed looked through the open door. The sun was almost gone, and what little light remained blazed straight behind them. Straight into The Ghost's eyes.

"A little lower," Reed said. "Another five feet. Give her some gas."

The Jayhawk tore forward. Reed saw the yacht drawing rapidly nearer. Eight hundred yards. And then seven. Another bullet slammed against the roof, but Russak didn't let up. He raced on, his breaths short but measured.

"Listen to me," Reed said. "You're gonna run this thing like a freaking Corvette, okay? You race right up to his gunwales, then slam us down on that helipad like you own the bitch."

Russak's lips trembled, but he nodded.

Reed looked back through the windshield. The yacht loomed large now. Four hundred yards. Three hundred. Another two shots hit the chopper, one tearing into the nose next to Russak's feet and the next pinging off a windshield strut.

The Ghost was getting desperate, blinded by the sun.

Reed checked on the MSST. Jackson and his men were locked and loaded, the rope now abandoned, gathered around one doorway. Turk had joined them, cradling one of the shortened assault rifles like a toy. He reached into the cabinet and grabbed the second, tossing it across the cramped chopper. Reed caught it and pulled the charging handle. The walls of the yacht were fifty yards away.

Russak yanked on the cyclic. The nose of the Jayhawk snatched over the side of the yacht, and all Reed saw was blue sky. Gunfire erupted around them, and glass shattered. The Jayhawk spun ninety degrees in midair. Russak shoved the collective, and the bird slammed against the polished helipad in an explosion of wood.

80

The Jayhawk hit, and already the MSST was bailing out. Reed left the cockpit and jumped through the open door, rolling to the deck as the rotor beat the air overhead like a hurricane. Automatic gunfire flashed from inside the yacht, and he yanked the CQBR into his shoulder and returned fire.

Jackson and his four surviving men knelt on one side, Turk on his other. Russak hit the power and roared upward again, clearing enough headspace for them to stand and race for the rear entrance of the yacht's main salon.

Stretched across the threshold lay a dead man clothed in a tuxedo. An Uzi submachine gun lay on the splintered deck next to him, 9mm casings sprinkled around like brass confetti.

In the darkness through the door, Reed thought he saw other crew members scrambling for the shadows, but he couldn't tell.

It didn't matter. There was no second-guessing now. They had to take the boat.

"Cullman, you're with me!" Jackson shouted. "We'll take the engine. Miles, Yancy, you take the bridge. Montgomery . . . he's all yours."

The four MSST guys bolted through the door, quickly breaking off into teams of two, leaving Reed and Turk alone at the entrance of the salon.

"You good?" Reed said.

"Golden. Let's do it."

Reed took point, Turk covering him from behind. He stepped into the salon first, sweeping the rifle across a sprawling living area twice as large as his house. Polished floors and ornate furniture were joined by multiple wet bars, lines of bookshelves and TV screens, a craps table, and two sets of stairs. Jackson and Cullman took the first set, down toward the engine bay. Miles and Yancy headed up the second set of stairs toward a dining room and the bridge beyond. Reed and Turk charged straight ahead, circling to the right of the wet bar and taking the hallway beyond.

Glass doors hissed back automatically as Reed led with the CQBR. Plush carpet lined the floors while recessed lighting illuminated the way. They reached a cabin door to the left and broke through, quickly clearing the small room. A king-size bed was joined by another TV and a dedicated bathroom, complete with marble sinks and an expanded shower.

But there were no people. They cleared the next two cabins and found the same—perfectly clean with no sign of occupancy.

Someplace overhead, Reed heard automatic gunfire and figured Miles and Yancy had made contact with resistance at the bridge. He shoved through the last door into a stateroom. Beyond it, a sliding glass door stood open to a balcony. He swept the rifle around the room, then heard another burst of gunfire from farther up.

"Clear!" he shouted.

They left the cabins and took the stairs upward one level to a pool deck joined by a gym. Reed and Turk split, clearing both before racing to another stairway. The gunshots were louder now. Only one level away.

81

Jackson took the stairs two at a time, rushing through the galley before reaching the crew quarters on the lower deck. A Remington 870 rode in his weathered hands as he turned a corner and almost flattened a crew member dressed in a black cocktail dress. She was young and Latina, throwing up both hands and screaming at the sight of the gun.

"On your knees!" Jackson shouted. "Secure her!"

Cullman grabbed the woman by the shoulder and rolled her over, quickly securing her wrists with a wire tie while Jackson covered him. Then they were back on the move, clearing four crew cabins before reaching another secured door. Through reinforced glass, Jackson saw a stairway leading down into the engineering room, but the door was locked.

Cullman tried the handle, shoving down with both hands, then bashed it with the butt of his rifle. The handle didn't budge.

"Stand back!" Jackson shouted.

Cullman retreated to the wall, and Jackson leveled the 870 at the door.

82

The fallout of the gunfire became apparent as Reed reached the main deck. He nearly fell over a body as he exited the stairwell, glancing down to see a man in a server's tuxedo laid across the teakwood, a 9mm Makarov resting on the deck next to him in a pool of crimson. Brass 5.56 casings from Miles's or Yancy's CQBRs lay scattered as Reed led Turk through another lounge area. One more stairway led upward, toward the sound of gunfire. The steps were slick with blood, and as Reed reached them, Yancy shouted from above. "Bridge secure!"

Reed skipped the stairwell and turned right down a short hall lined by two more staterooms. A glass door led out to the foredeck of the boat. Crimson stains lined the deck, and a bullet had shattered the door. Reed quickly cleared the cabins, then crossed over broken glass as he stepped outside.

The sun had vanished, but the sky wasn't yet dark. Recessed lighting along the walkway illuminated his path as he led the way, with Turk on his heels. Overhead, both Jayhawks roared, circling nearby but no longer taking fire.

The wall fell away to their left, exposing another pool. The blood trail Reed had identified at the shattered glass door led directly ahead, toward the sundeck at the bow of the ship.

Reed slowed, holding the CQBR into his shoulder, the red dot optic scanning the path ahead. Turk moved to his left, closing in from the port side of the yacht and protecting his exposed flank.

Another ten yards, and they reached the end of the pool deck. Wind tore through open windows and lashed at Reed's face, exacerbated by the pound of a Jayhawk's rotors. Reed's finger rested on the trigger as he jogged forward through another pair of automatic doors. Overhead, a spotlight from one of the Jayhawks flooded the bow of the yacht.

And then Reed saw him.

83

The door exploded as a full load of buckshot blasted through the lock. Cullman snatched it open, then Jackson barged through, slamming a fresh round into the 870's chamber.

Polished metal stairs greeted him. They led down, straight into the engine room where the motors now idled, flooding the room with steady mechanical racket. Jackson turned automatically to the right, leaving Cullman to take the left. A secured engine control room lay on Jackson's side behind a glass panel and another locked door. He blew it away and kicked the door open, finding an empty room. Controls lined one wall, and Jackson found the large red emergency stop button sheltered behind a plastic door. He smashed it.

The engines died, and the room grew quiet.

Jackson shouted into his radio. "Engine room secure!"

He turned away from the control panel, sucking down a deep breath. His head felt light with adrenaline. He'd never pushed that hard or experienced that much combat haze.

Cullman walked toward him from the far side of the room. "All clear on starboard."

"Shh!" Jackson held up a fist, and Cullman froze.

Jackson looked down another set of metal steps into the belly of the hull. Two immense diesel engines were now quiet, but in the rear of the boat, near the propeller shafts, he heard a faint but persistent digital beeping.

Jackson led with the shotgun again, Cullman on his hip. Reaching the floor, he wound his way around the rear of one engine and into the compartment between the two. A narrow alley was shaded by the cooling engines, and directly ahead, near the base of the stern, lay an open suitcase.

Jackson took another three steps. The muzzle of the 870 dropped as he neared the case, sweat draining into his eyes. The beeping continued, and he looked inside.

Then his blood ran cold.

84

Volkov stood at the nose of the yacht. A recessed garage built beneath the bow was open, a giant door pointed skyward while an automated launch system dangled a twenty-foot tender boat over the water.

Volkov pressed his back against the railing of the bow, a pistol jammed into the temple of the cocktail waitress clutched against his chest. They were both highlighted by the beam of the Jayhawk's spotlight, now hovering a hundred feet overhead.

The woman shook and gripped his arm, fighting for air as her toes slipped across the wet deck. Volkov jammed the gun harder into her head and grimaced at the two Americans advancing toward him from opposite sides of the boat, both brandishing shortened assault rifles.

He screamed through the wind in English. "Stop where you are!"

Reed froze, the red dot dancing across Volkov's face. If it were any other weapon—a weapon Reed was familiar with and had fired before—he could've taken the guy out. One precise hit to the forehead while the cocktail waitress crumpled to the ground. But he wasn't familiar enough with the CQBR to depend on that level of accuracy, and he didn't need Volkov dead. He needed The Ghost to talk.

Reeds shouted, "Let her go, Volkov!"

"Back up!" Volkov screamed. "I'm taking the boat. You let me leave, and she lives."

"Not happening," Turk said, closing another yard toward the sniper.

Volkov pivoted toward him, slamming the gun so hard against the woman's head that her neck bent, and she screamed.

"I'll kill her!"

"Drop it!" Reed said. "Put your hands up. We won't shoot."

Volkov twisted away from the bow, backing toward the suspended tender boat. Reed dropped the red dot over the deck and squeezed off three rounds, obliterating the teakwood near Volkov's feet.

"Stay where you are!" Reed shouted.

Volkov jerked back, his gaze darting between Reed and Turk.

"I know who you are, Ghost," Reed said. "I know all about you."

"You know nothing!"

"I know you work for Stepan Belsky. I know you shot the president. I know you jumped off a bridge in Chicago two days ago."

Volkov's eyes narrowed at Reed, then a grin flashed across his face. "The man in the Porsche!"

"That's right. And I swear you aren't leaving this boat alive unless you let her go."

The woman choked as Volkov squeezed harder.

Reed took another step. "Who hired Belsky to kill the president?"

Volkov said nothing.

"Was it Stratton?" Reed pressed.

Volkov froze, the gun still held against the woman's head, her body now limp. He looked from Turk to Reed, confusion crossing his face. "Who?"

"Don't lie to me!" Reed shouted, lunging with the rifle.

Panic replaced the confusion on Volkov's face. He shifted toward the tender boat, and the woman slipped and dangled from his arm. Turk closed from the left.

Then the radio on Reed's chest exploded in a burst of desperate shouts from Jackson.

"Bomb! Bomb! Bo—"

Reed looked over his shoulder just as the transmission terminated and the entire stern of the vessel lifted free of the water. Fire flashed into the sky, the deck erupted, and Reed flung himself over the side.

85

The White House

The Secret Service cleared Wolfgang after an extensive body search, refusing to allow him to enter the mansion with so much as a ballpoint pen. Stretching across Pennsylvania Avenue, a crowd of Trousdale supporters had assembled as the sun went down, waving signs and listening to election coverage streamed over a loudspeaker.

Polls on the East Coast were closing. Trousdale had already taken New York, Ohio, and Virginia, and was locked in a heated battle with Governor Jeffreys for Florida. It was looking good, but the next ten minutes could change everything. Wolfgang would be the judge.

They gave him a visitor's pass and a two-man Secret Service escort before marching him to the Oval Office. Wolfgang was surprised they hadn't put him in a straitjacket. He was there by permission of Trousdale's VP, but the Secret Service wasn't taking any chances with an unknown visitor.

"The vice president is with his campaign staff," one of the agents said, pushing open the door to a darkened Oval Office. "He'll be right with you."

Wolfgang pocketed his hands and stepped into the room. The agent shut the door behind him, but Wolfgang had no doubt the man remained on post. He might be a guest, but he wouldn't be leaving this room until the vice president said so. That was fine because Stratton wouldn't be leaving, either. Not until Wolfgang said so.

He stepped across smooth carpet, the prosthetic leg grunting under his weight, and swept his gaze across tall walls hung with oil paintings. George Washington's stern face stared down from above the mantel, and framed on the wall opposing him was a black-and-white photo of a man Wolfgang had never seen before. He was white, dark-haired, late thirties or early forties, hands in the air as he addressed a bank of old-timey microphones. The vintage looked to be early nineteen hundreds.

Wolfgang stepped closer and looked for an inscription. There was none. Just the photo, in a simple black frame, alone on the wall.

A doorknob twisted, and the second entrance to the Oval swung open. Wolfgang didn't look up. He studied the photograph and waited until the door closed again. The room was quiet, but he was conscious of another person having entered.

"His name was Huey Long," Stratton said. "He served as governor of Louisiana from nineteen twenty-eight to thirty-two, and as senator from thirty-two to thirty-five."

"Partial term," Wolfgang said, still not looking away from the photo.

"He was shot," Stratton said.

Wolfgang turned to face the vice president. The Oval was still dark, the only light shining in from the massive windows overlooking the South Lawn and the Rose Garden.

Jordan Stratton stood next to the door, dressed in slacks and a White House embroidered sweatshirt, his hair slicked back. He looked tired but present.

"Did he have it coming?" Wolfgang asked coolly.

Stratton stepped across the room to a minibar hidden inside a wooden cabinet. A cork popped out of a whiskey bottle with a *thunk*, and Stratton poured himself three fingers. He didn't offer Wolfgang any.

"Long was a radical," Stratton said. "Extreme left wing, at least for the time. Not a big fan of FDR. He thought the New Deal was far too conservative."

Wolfgang grunted. "So, they capped him."

"They capped him for a lot of reasons. Not least of which, extensive amounts of alleged political corruption. He was impeached as governor for abuse of power, but the proceedings never cleared the State Senate. In modern terms, we'd call his leadership a constitutional crisis. He was . . . kind of a thug."

"So, why's he on the wall?"

Stratton took a deep sip, swirling the whiskey in the glass and taking his time answering. "Because the president has a sense of humor."

Stratton moved around the Resolute Desk, tracing its edge with his finger. He settled into Maggie's chair, cradling the whiskey in one hand. For a man on the brink of being elected, and maybe on the brink of assuming that chair permanently, Stratton didn't look excited.

Wolfgang remained next to the photograph, watching.

"Montgomery said you found something," Stratton said. "Some evidence?"

"You could say that."

Wolfgang made no move toward the desk. Stratton made a "Well?" gesture with his empty hand.

"I flew to Belarus," Wolfgang said. "Met with an old contact of mine from Moscow. The shooter was a Russian ex-military sniper, most recently employed by the Russian mob."

"Montgomery told me," Stratton said, sounding neither impressed nor dismissive.

"Did he tell you about Cunningham?"

Wolfgang watched Stratton carefully, searching for deceit in those bloodshot eyes.

"Who?" Stratton asked.

"Cunningham Enterprises," Wolfgang said. "The Chicago-based energy conglomerate in bed with Russian oligarch Stepan Belsky."

Stratton sat up, the whiskey thumping against the desk like a muted gunshot. "What?"

Wolfgang pulled back a chair set near the face of the desk and reached into his pocket. The photograph lay there, unmolested by the Secret Service, too innocuous to serve as a weapon. Wolfgang set it on the desk and flicked it with one finger, sending it spinning toward Stratton and landing in his lap.

Wolfgang settled into the chair, smoothed his pants legs, and stared coldly at Stratton. "I'm only going to ask you once, Mr. Vice President, and you don't want to lie to me. What did you do?"

Stratton scooped up the image, fixating on it with his lips parted. It was a still-frame from the Twitter video—the one of him meeting with the woman at the top of the Guthrie Hotel the previous week. Passing her the envelope.

"Heidi Cunningham," Wolfgang said. "Daughter of Harold Cunningham, founder and CEO of Cunningham Enterprises."

Stratton flipped the image over and checked the back, then studied it again. His face turned crimson. "Wait. You think . . ."

"Consider me an impartial juror," Wolfgang said. "I don't *think* anything . . . yet."

Stratton dropped the picture on the desk. "It's not what you think."

"Enlighten me," Wolfgang said.

Stratton shook his head.

Wolfgang decided to press. "Let me be perfectly clear. Reed, Turk, and I have gone out of our way to find the truth. We've put our lives on the line. If you think we did it for you, you're sadly mistaken. We didn't do it for Trousdale, either. We did it because the three of us have a collective distaste for injustice. If you're innocent, you better get busy proving it."

Stratton snorted. "You think I hired Cunningham to kill my boss?"

"I think a man called Fedor Volkov was hired to kill your boss by a man named Stepan Belsky. I think Belsky is an estranged Russian oligarch with no home, floating around on a mega yacht like some kind of drunk pirate. I think he's deeply entangled with Cunningham Enterprises, a major donor of not only your vice presidential bid, but also your senate campaigns back in the day. I think Maggie Trousdale is an ardent opponent of the sort of international energy deals Cunningham is in the habit of making, while *you* are one of their chief allies. And I think the day before Trousdale was shot, you blew off an important interview to meet with one of Harold Cunningham's daughters, where you slipped her a wad of cash. *That's* what I think."

"One of," Stratton said.

"Excuse me?"

"*One of.* That being the key phrase in your train of thought."

"One of what?"

"One of Harold Cunningham's daughters."

"Explain."

Stratton took another deep swallow of whiskey. "I've known the Cunninghams my entire life, it's true. You might say they run in the same Chicago circles as the Strattons—for different reasons, of course. My family is wealthy, but politics have always been our shtick. For the Cunninghams, it's more about big business. Big money. The kind of money that makes me look poor."

"You're not helping yourself," Wolfgang said.

"Harold has two daughters," Stratton said, unfazed. "The oldest is Alexandra. She's a lawyer and deeply involved with his corporation. He's grooming her to take over someday. A real powerhouse bitch, if you ask me. He tried to set us up back in the day. I opted for a Presley instead—another big family name. But I should've gone for Alexandra. At least she had more money."

Wolfgang was growing impatient. "Get to the point."

"The point is Heidi, Harold's youngest daughter. She's the one in that photograph, as you surmised. And yes, I blew off an important campaign interview to meet with her in secret, where I passed her an envelope of cash. But it had nothing to do with Cunningham Enterprises, and it damn sure had nothing to do with Maggie being shot."

"Why should I believe that?"

"Because Heidi Cunningham *hates* her father. They were estranged after he shipped her off to an expensive liberal arts school, and she got herself a good taste of far-left economics. She came home on fire to burn down capitalism. As you can imagine, that didn't go over so well with a guy like Harold. Next thing you know, she's ousted from the family. Written out of the will. Not speaking to anyone. She became an investigative journalist for some liberal Chicago media outlet and spends all her time writing hit pieces about the evils of big business."

"So, why did you meet with her?"

Stratton snorted and looked away.

Wolfgang folded his arms. "She had something, didn't she? Something on you?"

"Something on Maggie," Stratton said. "Enough to sink her campaign, best case scenario. Maybe enough to have her impeached."

"What?" Wolfgang said.

"Oh, I think you know." Stratton pivoted toward Wolfgang with an accusatory glare. "You were there, after all. Back when she was governor. Back when she was pulling all kinds of stunts behind closed doors, chasing down Resilient Pharmaceutical. The kinds of stunts that could be classified as abuse of power. Just like our friend Huey Long, over there."

Stratton looked frustrated and gripped the empty whiskey glass.

Wolfgang waited.

"I paid Heidi to kill the story," Stratton said at last. "She might be a flaming socialist, but privilege runs deep. Without her daddy to pay the credit card bills, she's easily bought."

"You expect me to believe that?"

"Go find Heidi. Beat her with your leg. She'll tell you."

Wolfgang glared, but Stratton didn't look apologetic.

"I've spent my whole *life* in service to this nation. That might sound trite to a man like you, sneaking around in the shadows, bludgeoning your own idea of justice out of people. But we live in the greatest country in the history of the planet because we have a *system*. A system *I* serve in. You can judge me for the fancy suits and grimy money. You can call me a hypocrite for silencing a journalist while championing free speech. I don't care. But don't you *dare* accuse me of betraying my country."

Stratton stiffened, and he jabbed a finger at Wolfgang. "You think I wanted Maggie killed? Then ask yourself why I would've needed a Russian sniper when I already knew enough to bury her for all eternity, yet I buried the story instead."

The Oval grew suddenly very quiet, Stratton's finger still jabbed at him. A light on the desk phone blinked, indicating an incoming call, probably from the campaign room. Another state decided, Wolfgang figured. Another domino falling for or against Trousdale.

Wolfgang stood, retrieving the photograph and pocketing it. "Your story will be easy enough to verify. If you're lying to me, I'll know."

"Is that a threat?"

"No, Mr. Vice President. It's a fact."

Wolfgang turned for the door, but Stratton stopped him halfway, speaking softly. "You said Belsky is in bed with Cunningham Enterprises?"

Wolfgang looked over his shoulder. "Does that surprise you?"

Stratton didn't answer, and Wolfgang left the room.

86

Straits of Florida

The crew of *William Flores* fished Reed and Turk out of the Gulf as the wreckage of *Everstar* burned and quickly sank. Both helicopters beat paths overhead, spotlighting the survivors while launch boats from the cutter crashed through the waves to retrieve them.

Yancy was found unconscious, floating face-up with a welt on his head, but still alive. Coast Guardsman Miles was dead, and neither Jackson nor Cullman could be found. A few of the crew survived, including Volkov's captive cocktail waitress and the captain.

All the others perished in the blast or drowned before the Coast Guard could reach them. The Ghost of Grozny himself was found impaled by a four-foot section of teakwood, his grizzly face twisted into an even more horrific expression of pain. Stone-dead.

Reed stood at the bow of *William Flores*, wrapped in a dry blanket, shivering despite the Gulf warmth. The air was heavy with smoke, and portions of the water still burned where fuel floated on the surface, illuminating the space around the cutter as well as the spotlights still shining from the twin Jayhawks.

But the yacht was gone. It sank in under two minutes.

"We never found Belsky," Reed said.

Turk stood next to him, his blanket cast to the deck, a cup of hot coffee cradled in one hand. He surveyed the wreckage with a look of semi-disgust.

Reed wasn't sure if Turk was more disgusted by the situation or with himself. The two of them, alongside the MSST, had plowed headfirst into a trap. But laid by who?

"They'll send down divers," Turk said. "Search for bodies."

Reed shook his head. "I spoke to the captain. The depth here is fifty-two hundred feet. Even if they could reach the wreck with a drone, the bodies will be unrecognizable. The water pressure down there is over twenty-three hundred pounds per square inch."

Reed watched the flames dancing on the water, burning away the spilled fuel, and he saw Jackson's face. He imagined him deep in the engine hold, screaming into his radio only a moment before the blast vaporized him.

It had been a massive bomb, enough to obliterate the better half of a three-hundred-fifty-foot yacht in a split second.

Military-grade explosives.

And it cost Jackson everything.

"This isn't over," Turk muttered.

"No," Reed said. "A long way from it."

Two hours later, another Sentinel-class cutter arrived on scene to help map out the wreckage and continue the recovery attempt. Both choppers had long since returned to Miami for fuel, and at last, *William Flores* followed suit, churning northward.

Reed and Turk showered in cramped bath facilities to remove the grime of the blast, then dressed in Coast Guard utility uniforms and settled down in the ship's mess to ride out the four-hour return voyage.

As they passed south of Key West, Reed's cell phone obtained signal, and he found a text message waiting from Wolfgang.

CALL ME.

The mess was empty other than the two of them, but Reed still kept the phone off speaker as he dialed. Whatever Wolfgang had to say, it wasn't the kind of thing that needed to be overheard.

"How did it go?" Wolfgang said.

"Poorly. Volkov is dead. Belsky is missing."

"You sound rough."

Reed slouched against the metal wall behind his bench seat. The *William Flores* rolled a bit in roughening Gulf waters, and despite his years of experience at sea, it made him nauseous. Maybe that had less to do with the water and more to do with the mental image of Jackson being blown apart. It was a picture he couldn't shake, no matter how hard he tried.

"I'll explain later," Reed said. "Stratton?"

"I left the White House an hour ago. I'm headed to Chicago."

"What did he say?"

"He claims he met Heidi to pay her off on a story she was writing about Trousdale. Apparently, Heidi works as an investigative reporter and is estranged from her family. She found dirt and was about to torpedo the campaign."

"Do you believe him?"

"I'm not sure. It'll be easy enough to prove, either way. I'm going to pay Heidi a visit."

Reed rubbed his lower lip, staring at a discolored spot on the far wall. *William Flores* was kept in tip-top shape—far cleaner than most big Navy ships he'd sailed on—but all ships felt grimy after a few years of use. It was inevitable.

"This doesn't ax the connection between Belsky and Cunningham Enterprises," Reed said.

"I know," Wolfgang said. "But if what Stratton claims is true, it probably exonerates him. Why would he have Trousdale shot when he could sink her with some dirt shortly after inauguration? After she resigned, he'd assume office with four full years ahead of him. There would be no reason to kill her."

Reed thought about it. It made sense, but in his experience, life was rarely so cut-and-dried. He remembered the mountain of paperwork he and Turk had been drowned in back at the FBI field office in Chicago. If

Stratton was innocent, then he must have leaned on FBI Director O'Brien to make that mountain happen. Genuinely trying to be helpful.

Or was it really that simple?

"Like you said, it'll be easy enough to prove," Reed said. "Talk to Heidi, and let me know. We're headed back to Miami."

"Will do. You guys get some rest. I'll be in touch."

Reed lowered the phone to hang up. Wolfgang caught him just in time.

"Oh, by the way," Wolfgang said. "Did you see the results?"

"What results?"

"The election."

Reed blinked. He'd completely forgotten what day it was.

"Check the news," Wolfgang said.

Reed hung up and simply typed "news" into the search bar of his web browser. The page loaded slowly under the weak signal, but when it did, he breathed out a soft curse.

"I'll be damned . . ."

87

Maggie felt numb. Everything was black, and her whole body felt vaguely light, as though she were floating. She could feel her hands and feet, but not her fingers and toes. Her head buzzed, and her throat was impossibly dry.

She tried opening her eyes. It was difficult at first, and her head swam. Her eyelids felt crusted shut, and when they finally parted, everything was blurry. She blinked a few times, focusing on the far wall.

Maggie tried to speak, but nothing came out. She tried lifting her head, but her skull felt like it weighed a hundred pounds.

She coughed and breathed out. "Hello?"

The word left her throat as a rasp, barely distinguishable from a grunt. Nobody answered, and she twisted her head to one side.

A man sat in a chair next to her, his head propped against the wall, sleeping fitfully in a dirty suit. His hair was unwashed, and his face was grimy with dried sweat.

O'Dell.

"J . . . James . . ."

O'Dell shifted, disoriented for a moment, as though he'd forgotten where he was. Then his gaze met hers, and something like pure sunlight washed across his face. He sat up in a rush and reached for the bed. "Maggie? Can you hear me?"

Her breath came in another rough drag, and the buzzing she felt from her scalp to her toes intensified in her skull. "Where—?"

Her voice broke off, and O'Dell reached for something out of sight. A moment later, a straw was between Maggie's lips, and cool, glorious water streamed over her tongue and down her throat. It felt like the kiss of Heaven, washing away the sour dryness and invigorating her disoriented mind. Pouring life itself back into her shattered body.

The straw rattled against an empty cup, and she fell back against the pillow. The ceiling spun overhead, and she felt as if the bed were rocking. But when she tilted her head toward O'Dell, everything seemed to stabilize.

He sat next to her, still cradling the empty cup. There were tears in his eyes.

"I'm . . . I'm so sorry," he whispered.

"What happened?"

"You were shot. At the amphitheater in Chicago."

"Shot?" Maggie couldn't remember an amphitheater. She wasn't sure she could remember Chicago. There was an interview with Ben Fisher. Stratton had bailed on her.

"Where . . . what day is it?"

"Wednesday morning. Almost sunrise."

"Wednesday?" There was something there, just out of reach. Something significant about the day. Something she should remember.

And then it hit her like a fist to the face, and she twisted toward him. "The election?"

O'Dell took her hand in his, wrapping it in his large, rough fingers and squeezing gently. "Congratulations, Madam President."

Her lip trembled. "We won?"

O'Dell smiled. "By a landslide."

A tear slipped down her cheek. She tried to picture the lines at the polls and the two speeches she had planned—only one of them to ever be used. The election night party and the crowds of supporters. All of it faded away.

All she saw was O'Dell. His gaze fixed on hers, rimmed with tears. So soft. So kind.

As the memories returned, she recalled those haunting hallucinations in the dark, screaming for help.

O'Dell squeezed her hand again, just as he had during those terrors, and a slow smile broke across Maggie's lips. She wrapped her fingers around his and squeezed back.

88

Port de Puerto Pedernales, Venezuela
320 miles due east of Caracas

The Russian Lada-class attack submarine, *Kronshtadt*, glided into the harbor in the dead of night, barely a shadow over the darkened water. Longshoremen dressed in grungy clothes worked without headlamps to secure the sub to a remote portion of the dock, sheltered by trees. Invisible to American satellites.

Russia's newest attack boat was barely over 236 feet long, making it a miniature compared to the giant missile subs operated by the world's superpowers. Equipped with next-generation stealth technology and requiring a crew of only thirty-five men, the *Kronshtadt* was less a weapon of mass destruction and more a precision instrument, capable of slipping deep into the heart of enemy territory, there to hunt the enemy's boomers.

The mission that had carried *Kronshtadt* from the North Atlantic, all the way through the Straits of Florida, and finally to Venezuela, was a far cry from her intended purpose, but she had served well. Resting at four hundred feet beneath the surface with her engines off, none of the American Coast Guard forces deployed to intercept *Everstar* had detected her. As *Kronshtadt* rose to fifty feet and deployed a team of two elite Russian Navy divers, the Americans were too busy boarding the bobbing Russian yacht to concern themselves with the possibility of a hostile warship, its torpedo tubes pointed dead at *William Flores*.

As the Navy divers returned to *Kronshtadt* with a guest, and even as the Russian submarine steered southward and slipped stealthily away, the Americans were still unaware. *Everstar* went up in flames only minutes after *Kronshtadt* returned to her cruising depth of four hundred feet and routed toward South America.

And as Stepan Belsky, ostracized Russian oligarch and would-be assassin of the president of the United States, set foot on Venezuelan soil, he knew the Americans would never come looking for him. His 350-foot mega yacht had sunk in nearly sixteen hundred meters of crushing Gulf water.

When his body never floated to the surface, they wouldn't wonder. They would simply assume he'd been swallowed by the depths.

Just like his boat.

Belsky hurried down the dock to a small outbuilding illuminated by a single yellow light bulb. It was suffocatingly warm on the Venezuelan coast. The air was thick and oppressive, like a blanket. But he'd endure these temperatures for all of eternity rather than experience the terror of diving beneath his own yacht again, knowing that yacht was literally rigged as a time bomb.

Nothing could force him down the gaping hatch of a blackened submarine a second time, tugged by divers with cold hands. If fate smiled upon him, Stepan Belsky would never need to set foot on any boat ever again. The damp soil beneath his shoes was black as night, and—Belsky knew —*flush* with oil. Millions upon millions of untapped barrels of it.

For an energy mogul like Belsky, it was like walking on streets of gold.

Inside the shack, a secure satellite phone waited for him. Belsky punched a number in. It rang several times before the computerized voice of the man on the other side of the globe answered.

"You have arrived?"

"Yes," Belsky said. "I just reached port."

"Good. And your boat?"

"Blown to hell. No witnesses."

"Very good, Stepan. You may have redeemed yourself."

Belsky swallowed hard. He didn't want to ask but wondered if not asking would be worse than facing the truth. The voice on the line was toneless, but the words sounded upbeat. Maybe the man on the other end —a man Belsky feared more than death itself—was in a good mood.

"Is . . . she alive?" Belsky asked.

"Da. Very much so. The woman is made of iron."

Belsky winced, running his tongue over his lips. He wondered if he should defend himself or apologize. He decided either would only damage him further.

"She was reelected," the voice said. "But this was expected. We will find another way to manage her. Something less . . . direct."

"Of course," Belsky said, eager to be helpful. Eager to be alive.

"Go to the city. I'll be in touch."

The line died, and Belsky stared at the phone. Even around the globe, nearly ten thousand kilometers from the man on the phone, he could still feel his icy touch on his neck. Like a viper at rest for the moment, but always a breath away from striking.

On the other side of the globe, nearly ten thousand kilometers from Venezuela, the man on the phone set down the receiver, leaving his hand resting on it. Despite himself, his fingers shook. The computerization would've disguised his voice to Belsky, but it couldn't extinguish the anger he felt deep inside. It burned like an endless, hungry fire.

Hungry for revenge. Or at the least, the satisfaction of landing on top.

On a screen across the room, a TV displayed American news media. They were busy celebrating the reelection of Muddy Maggie Trousdale, the swamp girl from Louisiana.

Just seeing her face ignited the fire in his stomach like gasoline poured straight onto a blaze. She had defied him. Embarrassed him on a global scale. She'd trodden straight onto the world's political stage and put her foot on his neck as though he were some third-world warlord.

Yes, he'd pushed her buttons. Tested her mettle. But she hadn't responded in kind. She seemed incapable of responding in kind. He had fired a spit wad, and she'd responded by going straight for his throat.

Muddy Maggie, indeed. Not a swamp girl. A swamp animal. An animal that had somehow survived and now stood directly in the path of everything he'd seized power to achieve.

"Sir?" said a man from the end of the darkened room.

He looked toward the sound.

"We are ready for you."

He nodded once and turned away from the TV, facing a mirror instead. He adjusted his bow tie, rolled his shoulders to settle the jacket of his tuxedo, and then turned for the door.

As he stepped into the ballroom, he broke into his wide, trademark smile.

A cheer rose from the gathered crowd, and someone spoke over a loudspeaker in Russian. "Ladies and gentlemen, our beloved president, Makar Nikitin!"

89

Shelby County, Illinois

The mansion lay quiet amid rolling Illinois fields, now dusted with a late November snowfall. Security lights marked the driveway, and the windows remained dark, but Stratton knew Barrett was inside. His Bentley was parked out front, pulled to one side of the looping driveway, stopped at the foot of the stairs.

Right where the Stratton family patriarch always left it.

Marine Two landed on the sprawling lawn in front of the house in a rush of rotor wash, the grass bending and dry snow rising in a cloud. Secret Service agents rushed to form an escort from the chopper to the front door, and the Marine crew chief aboard the aircraft hurried down the steps, standing at attention next to it.

Stratton exited without fanfare, not so much as glancing at the beautiful rolling hills as he marched toward the mansion. He passed the Bentley, forced to deviate from the most direct path to the front door by the car's gleaming front bumper, then took the stairs with Dorsey and two of his men walking at his elbows.

Dorsey spoke into his wrist mic. "Rook has arrived at Eagle's Nest."

One of the agents opened the door for him, and Stratton marched through. He unbuttoned his coat and left it on the rack, then glanced around the dark house.

The living room was empty, as were the dining area beyond it and the kitchen to his right. With the Stratton family spread across cities, colleges, and high-rise towers around the nation, the only people present in the big house were a lone cook, maybe, and the half dozen Secret Service agents who had arrived ahead of time to secure the property.

And Barrett.

"Do you need anything, sir?" Dorsey asked.

Stratton shook his head. "Relax, Jim. You and your guys help yourselves to anything in the kitchen."

"Thank you, sir. We're all good."

Stratton turned down the hall, marching past the stairway and a pair of elk heads mounted to the wall. There was another living space, smaller than the first, with soft couches and an oversized TV. The "Football Room," Barrett called it. A place for him and his sons and grandsons to gather and watch the Bears fight for relevance. Another patriarchal dream that suddenly tasted sour in Stratton's mouth.

He bypassed the man cave and found his way to the end of the hall, where a cabin-style door was built of polished cedar, with a wrought iron handle and perfectly balanced hinges. It swung open without a sound, and Stratton's ears were immediately greeted by the crackle of the gas fire. The library—Barrett's "oratory"—spread out before him.

Stratton stood in the doorway and saw his father seated in one of the high-backed chairs facing the fire, only his left hand visible, cradling a bourbon in a fancy glass.

"Hello, son," Barrett said without looking around the chair.

Stratton loosened his tie, then pushed the door shut. He stepped across the room, his leather-soled shoes smacking the hardwood before being muted by the rug. He passed a mahogany desk, large and fancy enough to rival the Resolute Desk in Maggie's office, and reached the minibar without so much as glancing at Barrett.

Overhanging the bar was a glass display case housing an ornate cavalry saber. It was 18th century in vintage and was alleged to have been carried by Lieutenant John Stratton of the Continental Army—a long-dead patriarch of the family—during the American Revolution.

The sword was real, but Stratton thought the story was probably a sham. It was the kind of thing Barrett would come up with after a couple hours on some ancestry website—just like he claimed the nickel-plated 1911 handgun displayed in a similar case atop the minibar was once wielded by Stavers Stratton, an associate of Al Capone during his glory days.

The association between the Strattons and Capone was no forgery. Back in the day, the two families enjoyed plenty of shady business deals in the heart of Depression-era Chicago. But again, Stratton seriously doubted whether the pistol had anything to do with it.

Dumping a generous pour of bourbon into a glass as fancy as Barrett's, Stratton settled into the second high-back chair without comment. Dancing flames tangled with artificial logs in the fireplace, spilling orange light across his feet. The faint hiss of the burning gas was soothing. Almost therapeutic.

"How's the bitch doing?" Barrett asked.

Stratton didn't answer.

Barrett snorted. "Oh, come on, son. Crack a smile! It's just a joke."

Stratton sipped his drink. It was Pappy Van Winkle 12 Year. A great bourbon, but it better be for fifteen hundred bucks a bottle.

Barrett loved pricey liquors, but Stratton noticed he only drank them when there were people around to impress. Or when he was nervous.

"Why didn't you tell me about Cunningham?" Stratton said.

Barrett didn't answer.

Stratton stared into the fire. "I checked into it. Made some calls. Cunningham Enterprises is neck-deep with Russian oil conglomerates. They signed a big deal with a Stepan Belsky company only weeks before Maggie was shot. You didn't think that was worth mentioning?"

Barrett cursed and slurped whiskey. "Damn you, boy. You always have to look a gift horse in the mouth, don't you?"

Stratton twisted toward him, facing the older man for the first time. "Did you know?"

Barrett didn't answer.

Stratton punctuated each word. "*Did you know?*"

Barrett growled. "Of course I didn't know! I still don't know. I mean, sure, of course Cunningham is partnering overseas. Everybody is. It's the smart thing to do."

"Did you know about Belsky?"

Barrett waved a hand. "Get your head out of your ass, Jordan. That name didn't mean anything a month ago. Just another Russian with too much money and not enough sense. How was Cunningham supposed to know he had eyes on the president? How is that their fault?"

Stratton's fingers tightened around the glass. "It's their *fault* when they funnel tens of thousands into my campaigns, then make grey market deals with international players who are later linked to an attempted presidential assassination."

Barrett shook his head. "My God, boy. You really are a Boy Scout, aren't you? You think those contributions came for free? You don't *get* to the West Wing without strings attached. Period. Nobody does!"

"Maggie did."

Barrett curled his lip. "An exception that proves the rule. Don't forget, she had *your* name next to hers. The favors you owe are favors *she* owes."

Stratton raised his eyebrows. "Favors?"

"What, you think Cunningham was gonna write you big checks and not come knocking? You've got friends in high places, boy. You scratch their backs, and you'll spend decades in Washington."

Stratton sat forward. "And what does that mean, exactly?"

Barrett sloshed bourbon into his mouth and swished it around before swallowing. "When she's back on her feet, that swamp rat is gonna make waves. She's already made waves. Things about international oil deals . . . energy outsourcing. That needs to stop, pronto. It's a big itch, and they can't reach it. So, you scratch."

Barrett avoided Stratton's glower and fixated on lint sticking to his pants. At last, he looked up. "What?"

Stratton got up and walked to the bar. He set the glass next to the handgun case and scanned the row of silver-tipped bullets lined up next to the 1911.

"What?" Barrett repeated, louder now.

"Did Cunningham partner with Belsky to have Maggie killed?"

Barrett didn't move.

Stratton could see him in the reflection of the pistol case, sitting forward in his chair, staring in disbelief. He said, "Did Cunningham partner with Belsky to assassinate the president?"

Barrett's mouth opened once and then closed. He stood and hurled the glass into the fire. It exploded into a brief rush of flame. "Damn you, Jordan! You're a real prick, you know that? I've got four sons, and you're the only one with the nerve to ask a question like that."

Barrett ran both hands through his hair and turned his back to Stratton, his knuckles washing white as they clenched into fists. "My God, Jordan. You're a real fool, aren't you? Just can't leave well enough alone. Just can't —" Barrett broke off cold when he turned around and stared down the gaping mouth of the nickel-plated 1911.

"I'm going to ask one more time," Stratton said, his voice trembling.

Firelight glimmered on the polished slide of the gun, the single-action hammer already cocked, Stratton's finger resting on the trigger.

One silver-tipped bullet locked in the chamber.

"Did Cunningham partner with Belsky?" Stratton said.

Barrett's jaw locked, and frozen hatred clouded his eyes. "I don't know," he hissed.

Stratton kept the gun on him, only a foot from Barrett's face—only four pounds of pressure away from blowing his father into the afterlife.

Then Stratton lowered the pistol. "I'm only going to say this once. If you, or any of these people, *ever* threaten this administration again, I will bury you alive."

Barrett stood motionless, hands at his sides.

Stratton turned for the door, uncocking the pistol and tossing it onto a bookshelf.

Barrett snarled. "You're barking up the wrong tree, boy. These people put you in Washington, and they can take you out."

Stratton stopped with his hand on the door latch, the cool metal biting into his palm. He looked over his shoulder. "Hit me with your best shot, old man." Without waiting for a reply, he stomped back into the hall.

Twenty seconds later, he was aboard *Marine Two*, the engines already spinning up.

Headed back to Washington.

90

Mountain Brook, Alabama

The living room was littered with Davy's toys. Reed's son was now fully engrossed in the crawling stage of life, meaning that any play session ended up looking like the fallout of a Fisher Price atom bomb. Banks said she'd read some book that claimed the mess would get worse before it got better, but Reed didn't really care either way. He swept Davy off the carpet as he passed toward the sliding glass door, spinning his son around and tossing him into the air before catching him halfway down.

Banks shouted from the kitchen. "Reed! I told you not to do that!"

Reed ignored her, losing himself in his son's delighted giggles. Slobber ran down Davy's cheeks and onto Reed's hand. He wiped it away and cradled Davy in one arm while grabbing a beer with his free hand.

The back porch was cool, but not yet cold. Late November felt like redemption itself from another sweltering summer, making Reed's patio chair that much more appealing as he settled into it. Davy sat in his arm, pudgy little fingers reaching for Reed's watch.

Reed unlatched the metal band and surrendered it to him, watching as the face descended directly into Davy's mouth.

"Reed!" Banks appeared through the door like a pouncing jaguar. "You can't give him that. He could choke."

"It's bigger than his face," Reed argued. "He's fine."

"It has small parts. The book says no small parts!"

Reed sighed and retrieved the watch.

"You're impossible," Banks muttered, stomping back to the kitchen.

Reed looked back into the house. Lucy stood near the stove, gently stirring something in a pot, dressed in a sweatshirt with her hair tied back in a ponytail. She'd stayed with them since Election Day, occupying the spare bedroom and busying herself around the house.

She hadn't swallowed a pill in nearly a week, and a soft glow was starting to return to her face. But there was a long road ahead for Lucy. Addiction still dug its claws deep into her body, and Reed knew she slept very little at night. He could hear her sometimes, weeping by herself when she thought everyone else was asleep. Maybe remembering the horrors of Southeast Asia. Maybe enduring the pain of her scalded skin.

Even though he knew it wasn't his fault, Reed couldn't help but feel responsible. He'd abandoned Lucy at the resort in Destin. He'd told her to stay away from his family. But family wasn't built of shared blood. It was built of shared lives, and he owed Lucy as much loyalty as he owed almost anyone.

Davy cooed, and Reed returned to the moment, passing the watch to his little hands. Davy grinned and resumed chomping on the band with his mostly toothless mouth.

Reed shot him a wink. "A man needs a watch, doesn't he? And look . . . it's almost dinnertime."

He tickled Davy, and his son chuckled, spraying more slobber across Reed's hands.

The doorbell rang, and Banks called from the kitchen. "Can you get that?"

Reed hauled himself up, wincing at the bruises crossing his back and legs. It had been three weeks since he'd jumped off the bridge in Chicago, but he still felt sore. Being blasted off the deck of a Russian mega yacht certainly hadn't helped.

Still cradling Davy in one arm, Reed checked the peephole before unlocking the door. Turk and Sinju stood outside, their arms laden with paper buckets of fried chicken and gallon jugs of sweet tea, condensation rolling down the sides. Sinju was dressed like the last pick of the draft, wearing a Tennessee Titans hat, shirt, jacket, and socks.

Turk's team.

"Well, hello," Reed said, suppressing a smirk. "I didn't realize Tennessee was playing today."

"They're not," Turk said with a slight blush.

Reed stepped back, and Sinju darted in to kiss him on the cheek. "Happy American Thanksgiving!"

She crashed down the hall, and Turk kicked the door closed with an apologetic shrug.

"It's her first Thanksgiving."

Reed traced the young Korean woman's path into the kitchen, where she was busy introducing herself to Lucy, and he thought she had a right to be enthusiastic. She had a lot to be thankful for.

They all did.

An hour later, they were crowded around the table in the dining room, Banks serving heaping piles of mashed potatoes and corn alongside fried chicken and rolls. Most of it was store-bought. Banks hadn't grown up cooking and was still learning, but she managed the potatoes herself, and Reed wasn't lying when he called them the best he'd ever had.

He and Turk shoveled down mountains of food while Sinju rattled off random facts about early America with all the enthusiasm of a fifth-grade history nerd. Her English had improved dramatically since fleeing North Korea only seven months earlier, as had her general appearance. She looked healthy and happy. When she smiled at Turk, her face glowed, and she seemed to forget the world around her.

Maybe Turk wasn't such a fool for the fiancée visa, Reed thought. Maybe this was the best thing that had ever happened to him.

"Can I get some more corn?" Lucy asked.

Reed passed her the bowl, glancing at the empty chair across from him, and a tinge of sadness edged into an otherwise perfect moment.

Wolfgang had been invited, of course, but chose to stay in New York. Little Collins's condition was worsening. Wolfgang hoped to share one last holiday season with his sister before facing the great unknown without her. Another long road ahead for another member of Reed's battered family.

They left the dishes and leftovers piled on the table and retreated into the living room. Turk found the football game, and Sinju commenced to cheering for the Cowboys like a home-grown fan.

It was too much noise for Reed. He retrieved another beer and retired to the back porch, where he found Lucy sitting next to Baxter, gently scratching the family bulldog behind the ears. She looked chilled, her fingers knotted around her sleeves and turning pale at the knuckles.

"Mind if I join you?" Reed asked, sliding the door shut.

"It's your house," Lucy said.

Reed settled into his chair and tipped the beer back. It was warm, but he didn't mind. He wasn't in the mood to complain about anything.

Lucy shivered suddenly and folded her arms, leaving Baxter to snort in disappointment at his discontinued massage.

"Withdrawals again?" Reed asked.

Lucy looked away, wrapping herself deeper into the hoodie. "I'll be fine. You don't have to worry about it."

Reed sipped beer, dropping a hand to scratch Baxter as his old friend sat next to him with an exhausted grunt. Baxter had been around longer than any of them—longer than Banks, even. He'd ridden the waves of Reed's tumultuous life without complaint, so long as his food hit the bowl twice a day and Reed made time to scratch him. He was a constant in an otherwise chaotic world, and Reed appreciated that.

"When we work for Trousdale, we get paid," he said. "The CIA set something up. Some phony law firm."

Lucy didn't reply.

Reed set the beer down. "They cut you a check for your help in Chicago. Fifteen grand."

Lucy looked up a little too quickly.

Reed saw a glimmer of hope in her eyes, instantly extinguished by cold reality. Fifteen grand or fifteen million—it could all be washed down the same drain.

"You told them what I did?"

"I told them you"—Reed made air quotes—"consulted. If it's all the same to you, we'll leave it at that."

She nodded, her head dropping again. "So . . . where is it?"

"In the bank. Waiting for you to get back."

"Back from where?"

Reed reached into his pocket and retrieved a folded piece of paper. He passed it to her without comment, and Lucy unfolded it. She scanned the top and swallowed hard.

"It's a four-month program," Reed said. "Paid in full. You get through that, and your money will be waiting when you get out. I'll make sure you land on your feet."

Lucy looked up, a tear sliding down her cheek. She didn't say anything, and Reed felt suddenly awkward. Lucy lunged out of the chair and threw her arms around his neck, pulling him in close. Reed sat stunned, caught off guard, then he reached around her shoulders and squeezed gently.

"Thank you," Lucy whispered. "I won't forget this."

Reed patted her on the back, and she returned awkwardly to the chair. He finished his beer and listened to Turk and Sinju decrying a penalty ruling. Banks shouted for them to keep it down, and Davy giggled at the flashing TV light.

He closed his eyes for a while, just enjoying the chaos.

It wouldn't be long before those cheers and shouts were replaced by gunfire again. He meant what he said when he told Turk that their fight with Belsky wasn't over. Somebody would pay for the deaths of Jackson and his men.

Somebody would answer for Trousdale's attempted assassination.

But for now, all of that could wait. For now, he wanted to enjoy the calm that settled over his mind. It was peace in the storm. The eye of the hurricane.

And it felt like Heaven.

Reed stood with a grunt, leaving the empty bottle.

"Where are you going?" Lucy asked.

Reed stared through the glass, watching his boisterous family rise from the couch like a pit bull lunging at the end of a chain. Banks had joined the protests now, dog cussing the officiants with both hands clamped over Davy's ears.

Reed pocketed his hands. "I'm going to sleep," he said. "For a damn long time."

FAILED STATE
THE PROSECUTION FORCE THRILLERS Book 4

It's the most oil-rich nation on planet earth.
But the people are starving. The government is in chaos.
Welcome to Venezuela.

On the heels of a violent act of terrorism right in the heart of America, President Maggie Trousdale is faced with the prospect of securing an increasingly volatile Free World.

When an unknown informant provides evidence that the attack was an act of international aggression, Trousdale has no choice but to chase the enemy into the heart of economically devastated Venezuela.

She'll send the Prosecution Force—Reed Montgomery and his team of off-the-books operators who are motivated by their own thirst for revenge. Deep in hostile territory with global security on the line, what Reed finds in South America is worse than anyone imagined.

A superpower is making a play. Venezuela's wealth is up for grabs.

If it falls into the wrong hands, it just might fund the next world war.

Get your copy today at
severnriverbooks.com

ABOUT THE AUTHOR

Logan Ryles was born in small town USA and knew from an early age he wanted to be a writer. After working as a pizza delivery driver, sawmill operator, and banker, he finally embraced the dream and has been writing ever since. With a passion for action-packed and mystery-laced stories, Logan's work has ranged from global-scale political thrillers to small town vigilante hero fiction.

Beyond writing, Logan enjoys saltwater fishing, road trips, sports, and fast cars. He lives with his wife and three fun-loving dogs in Alabama.

Sign up for Logan Ryles's reader list at
severnriverbooks.com

Printed in the United States
by Baker & Taylor Publisher Services

THE ALMOST
DAILY DEVOTIONAL

PAUL N. WALKER

THE ALMOST
DAILY DEVOTIONAL

PAUL N. WALKER

EDITED BY SARAH WOODARD

A MOCKINGBIRD PUBLICATION

CHARLOTTESVILLE, VA

Printed in the United States of America
Cover design by Tom Martin
Interior design by Cali Yee

ISBN: 978-1-7358332-2-4

Mockingbird Ministries
100 W Jefferson St.
Charlottesville, VA 22902

mbird.com

MOCKINGBIRD MINISTRIES ("MOCKINGBIRD") IS an independent not-
for-profit ministry seeking to connect, comment upon, and explore the
Christian faith with and through contemporary culture. Mockingbird
disclaims any affiliation, sponsorship, or connection with any other
entity using the words "Mockingbird" and "Ministries" alone or
in combination.

Dedicated with love to the people of
Christ Church, Charlottesville

Foreword

THE IDEA WAS FAR more uncanny than we realized at the time.

Paul often returned from summer vacation with fresh ideas about how to serve the spiritual life of our church, Christ Episcopal in Charlottesville, VA. So those of us on staff weren't surprised when in the fall of 2019 he announced a new undertaking called the Almost Daily Devotional. His wife Christie had dreamed it up over the break as a way of bringing our growing congregation together around the message of God's grace.

Paul loved the idea and wanted to be sure that, like the grace of God, it wouldn't require anything of anybody. Our parishioners had more than enough on their plates as is and besides, he'd always envisioned the church as a place to drop one's burdens rather than pick up new ones. The parameters were simple: Paul would write a short, daily-ish email containing a little Bible, a little prayer, and a lot of encouragement—and it would land in people's inboxes first thing in the morning. The goal was something you could read while waiting in line to drop the kids off at school. Something easily digestible that could set the tone for the day.

I remember thinking the proposal sounded inspired—as you'll see, Paul's a gifted writer—but it also sounded ambitious. As the rector of a church that was bucking every denominational trend and bursting at the seams, Paul had plenty on his schedule and didn't need to add anything extra. The Almost Daily Devotional seemed like the kind of thing that would hit the chopping block as soon as Advent rolled around. I planned to enjoy it while he had the energy.

I know what you're thinking: a daily reflection from one's pastor sounds good, but not especially uncanny.

Well, about six months in, the world experienced a global pandemic, and the timing of Paul's project took on a different light. The light of the Spirit, you might say. The flock was suddenly prohibited from gathering in person, yet here was Paul, all set up and ready to rock. To invoke the term that we heard everywhere at the time, there was no "pivot" necessary. The infrastructure was in place, the subscribers eager to share these messages with their panicked friends and neighbors.

Which is precisely what happened, praise God.

I don't mean to suggest that this was a happy turn of events. Almost overnight, the vibrant local ministry Paul had spent years cultivating was put on indefinite hiatus. It was disorienting, frustrating, and supremely anxiety-producing. Clergy everywhere were put in a no-win situation—"unprecedented" was the other buzzword we all got sick of—and I watched as Paul fielded criticism from every corner about how the church should proceed.

One thing he didn't field any pushback against was the Almost Daily Devotional. It became a lifeline, and not just to our congregation in Virginia. The mailing list swelled dramatically, as the Internet did what the Internet does. Hardly a day went by when Paul wouldn't burst into my office and say, "Listen to this response I just got from Germany [or Brazil or Oregon]! Who do we know in Bermuda?!" It buoyed the sender just as much as the recipients. Grace abounded.

All this to say, what you're holding in your hands isn't just a collection of daily meditations on redemption. This book is a form of redemption itself. It represents one of the many ways that God anticipated and accompanied our community through a trying period. Of course, while the message of the Gospel may sparkle more brightly in times of trouble, it transcends outward circumstances. These devotions apply just as directly to ho-hum days as they do to apocalyptic-seeming ones.

One more thing to note: Paul included "Almost" in the title partly to convey the freedom informing the project. He wanted to undermine from the outset any ironclad expectation that readers engage in a regimented way. I suspect, however, that he also wanted to give himself an out. If the writing got too onerous, he could bail. But Paul kept at it, week after week, even as the prohibitions relaxed. It was a delightful thing to witness. The joy he took in the process comes across loud and clear, whether that be his infectious love of American literature or his near-maniacal enthusiasm for autumn. I remember him telling me one day, fresh from an ADD writing session, "Dave, this is so fun to do! Easy, too."

I forget if I said it out loud at the time but I certainly thought it: "Well, it's easy for *you*." Paul honestly believed anyone could do what he was doing. I've tried. Devotional writing is notoriously difficult to do well and basically impossible to sustain over an extended period without devolving into repetition or triteness. Yet the emails persisted for more than three and a half years— far longer than intended—and there were almost no duds. No phoning it in or preacher autopilot. Just wide-ranging inspiration and an unwavering reliance on the gospel of grace. God gives everyone different gifts, and I'm so thankful this is one he gave Paul Walker. I don't know how I would've survived the pandemic without these daily grace-bombs. I know I'm not alone.

Indeed, when the curtain finally fell, the outpouring of gratitude was immense. Folks from all around the world testified to the impact the ADD had had on their lives, not just keeping their faith afloat but deepening their love for God during a bewildering time. It felt like a no-brainer to pick a year's worth of favorites, scrub the COVID references, and fashion them into a book.

As I write this, the virus has already faded from memory more than I thought possible. A friend found a mask in an old coat pocket and told me it took him a second to recall how it got there; it felt more like a missive from a bad dream than anything real. But those days were real, and I pray they never return. I also pray these pages are as much a godsend to those who read them as they have been to us who compiled them. Not just uncommon in their power but, dare I say, unprecedented.

David Zahl
July 2024

Introduction

WELCOME TO THE *Almost Daily Devotional*, an easy and accessible way to orient your day around God's love and grace. Although there are 365 entries, it is called the ***Almost** Daily Devotional* (rather than a *Daily Devotional*), because life often defeats our best intentions to have a daily devotional time.

But when you do pick up this *Almost Daily Devotional,* you will find in each entry a passage of Scripture, an illustration, some easily digestible theology, and hopefully, a landing point in your actual life. The grace of God is not intended to be a head trip; it exists to help and comfort us amid the trials and the tedium of everyday life. And each selection ends in a short prayer, usually from the rich anthology of the Book of Common Prayer.*

The world of the Bible is filled with treasures. However, it can be difficult to navigate. I have tried to mine the layered biblical landscape in order to present its nuggets to you in a readily relatable way.

The Psalmist says, *"You will show me the path of life; in Your presence is fullness of joy; At Your right hand are pleasures forevermore" (Psalm 16:11, NKJV).* Although these words were written nearly 3,000 years ago, truer ones have never been spoken. Thomas Cranmer, Archbishop of Canterbury in the 1530s and architect of our Book of Common Prayer, surely agreed. His

---

* Unless otherwise noted, I am using the 1979 version of the "BCP."

prayer is my prayer for you as you enter into the world of God's grace through this *Almost Daily Devotional:*

> Blessed Lord, who caused all holy Scriptures to be written for our learning: Grant us so to hear them, read, mark, learn, and inwardly digest them, that we may embrace and ever hold fast the blessed hope of everlasting life, which You have given us in our Savior Jesus Christ; who lives and reigns with You and the Holy Spirit, one God, for ever and ever. Amen.

Paul Walker
Rector, Christ Episcopal Church
Charlottesville, Virginia

JANUARY

January 1

"The LORD bless you and keep you; the LORD make His face to shine upon you and be gracious to you; the LORD lift up His countenance upon you and give you peace"
(Numbers 6:24–26, ESV).

WHAT A LOVELY BLESSING as we begin this new year. New Year's *resolutions* may suffer from an overestimation of our own will and capacity, but New Year's *hope* is rooted squarely in God Himself. His mercies are new every morning. We can always hold out hope for change—change in ourselves and in the world—because our hope is rooted not in ourselves but in the God of hope.

So here's to the new year!

O God, the King eternal, whose light divides the day from the night and turns the shadow of death into the morning: Drive far from us all wrong desires, incline our hearts to keep Your law, and guide our feet into the way of peace; that, having done Your will with cheerfulness during the day, we may, when night comes, rejoice to give You thanks; through Jesus Christ our Lord. Amen. (A Collect for the Renewal of Life – BCP p. 99)

January 2

LEADING OFF THE *Almost Daily Devotional* is a short series on what has come to be known as the Serenity Prayer. Composed in various forms by theologian Reinhold Niebuhr in the 1930s, it has been used with regularity in the 12-Step Community. There are different versions of the prayer, but this is my favorite:

God, give me grace to accept with serenity
the things that cannot be changed,
Courage to change the things
which should be changed,
and the wisdom to distinguish
the one from the other.

Living one day at a time,
Enjoying one moment at a time,
Accepting hardship as a pathway to peace,
Taking, as Jesus did,
This sinful world as it is,
Not as I would have it,
Trusting that You will make all things right,
As I surrender to Your will,
So that I may be reasonably happy in this life,
And supremely happy with You forever in the next.

The Serenity Prayer is not merely a mantra. Our attempts to rely on a mantra to maintain internal peace were lampooned in the famous *Seinfeld* episode called "The Serenity Now." Placarding over real anger and frustration with a simple affirmation will not work. As one character on the show said, "Serenity now—insanity later!"

No, the Serenity Prayer is a *prayer*, and prayer, even daily—or almost daily—is different. In prayer, you are bringing your real self, with all your anger and frustration into the company of your Father who loves you. So, *"Do not be afraid, little flock, for it is your Father's good pleasure to give you the kingdom" (Luke 12:32, NRSV).*

The Serenity Prayer is a longer prayer than you will usually find in the *Almost Daily Devotional*, but it is worth your time and attention. In the coming days, I will break this prayer into eight different sections, grounding its wisdom in Scripture and connecting its truth to our experience. But its wisdom and truth are also self-evident—Niebuhr was quite the theologian, after all—so for today just spend a little time in the prayer's company.

That's all for (serenity) now—see you soon.

January 3

"God, give me grace to accept with serenity the things that cannot be changed"

THE QUESTION IS NOT really what things can be changed, but rather who can change them. God can change anything. He is the only being with perfectly free will and the power to alter and intervene. The disciples realized this after Jesus calmed a raging storm: *"The men were amazed and asked, 'What kind of man is this? Even the winds and the waves obey Him!'" (Matthew 8:27, NIV)*.

What about you? What things can you change? You can likely change a diaper, possibly change a tire, and most definitely change your plans. There are all kinds of things you may want to change. As Bruce Springsteen sings, "I check my look in the mirror / Wanna change my clothes, my hair, my face."

But can you change your spouse … or your spouse-less-ness? Can you change a diagnosis? Can you change that dreadful mistake you made in the past? I know for certain that you have locked horns with at least a fistful of "things that cannot be changed." I know, too, that fretting over and fighting with those things is fruitless. I also know that God is in control of all things and that *"the LORD works out everything to its proper end" (Proverbs 16:4, NIV)*. That means *everything*, even (and especially) the things you cannot change.

> O God of peace, who hast taught us that in returning
> and rest we shall be saved, in quietness and in confidence
> shall be our strength: By the might of Thy Spirit lift us,

we pray Thee, to Thy presence, where we may be still and know that Thou art God; through Jesus Christ our Lord. Amen. (For Quiet Confidence – BCP p. 832)

January 4

"God, give me ... Courage to change the things which should be changed"

ST. PAUL CONFESSES THIS in Romans 7: *"For I do not understand my own actions. For I do not do what I want, but I do the very thing I hate... For I have the desire to do what is right, but not the ability to carry it out. For I do not do the good I want, but the evil I do not want is what I keep on doing" (Romans 7:15, 18–19, ESV).*

Paul's honest and universally applicable appraisal of himself puts a serious chokehold on both our willingness and ability to change. That doesn't mean that change isn't possible; it just means that we've got to start with a no-holds-barred evaluation of our own limitations. Although this biblical wisdom stands in stark contrast to the lucrative self-help industry, I trust you have enough experience with yourself not to argue with St. Paul on this one.

Change powered by our own internal locomotion is a doomed venture, but change inspired by the Spirit of God is a different animal altogether. There are things in you and in the world that can and, as the prayer says, *should be* changed. You know what those things are without me or your mother having to bring them to your attention. Just remember from whence our help doth come. For the same St. Paul of Romans 7 says this in Philippians 4: *"I can do all things through Christ who strengthens me" (Philippians 4:13, NKJV).*

Direct us, O Lord, in all our doings with Thy most gracious favor, and further us with Thy continual help; that in all our works begun, continued, and ended in Thee, we may glorify Thy holy Name, and finally by Thy mercy, obtain everlasting life; through Jesus Christ our Lord. Amen. (For Guidance – BCP p. 832)

January 5

"God, give me… the wisdom to distinguish the one from the other"

THAT IS, THE THINGS that cannot be changed versus the things that should be changed. According to the Serenity Prayer, we need wisdom to know the difference. Wisdom is an elusive quality filled with paradox. For instance, the truly wise know that they lack wisdom. And those who are wise in their own eyes are the world's fools.

On the other hand, we immediately recognize wisdom when we are in its presence. And, by golly, we need it! Even for the seemingly self-assured, life is like a game of blindman's bluff, in which a player is blindfolded, spun around, disoriented, and then set loose to find another player. The adult version of the game in Europe is called "blindman's buff" because the blind man is punched and buffeted along the way.

Sounds like raising children to me. Or just the navigation of any relationship. Or decisions about how to live responsibly in this world. When you drill down to deciding what can't change as opposed to what must change, then you are desperately in need of wisdom.

Proverbs says, *"The fear of the LORD is the beginning of wisdom, and the knowledge of the Holy One is insight" (Proverbs 9:10, ESV).*

I won't pretend to have the wisdom to know exactly what that verse means. One thing is clear though—wisdom does not come from within you. Wisdom begins and ends with God. So, why not start (and end) there?

> O God, by whom the meek are guided in judgment, and light riseth up in darkness for the godly: Grant us, in all our doubts and uncertainties, the grace to ask what Thou wouldest have us do, that the Spirit of wisdom may save us from all false choices, and that in Thy light we may see light, and in Thy straight path may not stumble; through Jesus Christ our Lord. Amen. (For Guidance – BCP p. 832)

January 6

"Living one day at a time, enjoying one moment at a time"

JESUS SAYS, *"Therefore I tell you, do not be anxious about your life"* *(Matthew 6:25, ESV)*. How nice would it be to obey God's command here? One clinical psychological researcher says worry "makes you miserable in the present moment to try and prevent misery in the future," and leads worriers to "be continually distressed all their lives in order to avoid later events that never happen. Worry sucks the joy out of the 'here and now' to prevent an unrealistic 'then and there.'"

Funny thing about worry is that most of what we are anxious about never actually happens. In fact, one survey of worriers revealed that 91.4% of our worries never materialize! We ask God for the grace to live one day at a time because it is the most sane and reasonable way to live. Jesus agrees: *"Therefore do not be anxious about tomorrow, for tomorrow will be anxious for itself. Sufficient for the day is its own trouble" (Matthew 6:34, ESV).*

No day is without its own trouble. Realizing this is also the most sane and reasonable way to live. But God is more than sufficient to meet your day's trouble—100% of the time. Leaving tomorrow in His strong hands may even allow you to enjoy the moments of today.

> O God, our times are in Your hand: Look with favor, we pray, on us as we begin another day. Grant that we may grow in wisdom and grace, and strengthen our trust in Your goodness all the days of our lives; through Jesus Christ our Lord. Amen. (For a Birthday – BCP p. 830)

January 7

"Accepting hardship as a pathway to peace"

"Consider it pure joy, my brothers and sisters, whenever you face trials of many kinds, because you know that the testing of your faith produces perseverance. Let perseverance finish its work so that you may be mature and complete, not lacking anything" (James 1:2–4, NIV).

LET'S BE HONEST. "Pure joy" seems like a stretch. But you could look at it this way—the chance of hardship coming into your life is 100%. You have had, are having, and will always "face trials of many kinds." You don't have to schedule a visit to Monty Python's Office of Argument and Abuse in order to have opportunities for this kind of "pure joy." Avoiding difficulty just isn't an option.

So what then? Per the Serenity Prayer, we're back to acceptance. Accepting the things that cannot be changed and accepting hardship as a pathway to peace. James tells us that trials will result in perseverance, which will end in a kind of fulfillment. Note the subject-object use in that verse. Perseverance is doing all the work (i.e., God); we just sit back and "let" it happen. And, if we can somehow manage to crack a smile during the whole shebang, then so much the better.

> O merciful Father, who hast taught us in Thy holy Word that Thou do not willingly afflict or grieve the children of men: look with pity upon the sorrow of Thy servants. Remember us, O Lord, in mercy, nourish our souls with patience, comfort us with a sense of Thy goodness, lift up Your countenance upon us, and give us peace; through Jesus Christ our Lord. Amen. (For a Person in Trouble or Bereavement – BCP p. 831)

January 8

"Taking, as Jesus did, this sinful world as it is, not as I would have it"

THIS, IN MY OPINION, is the most powerful part of the Serenity Prayer. St. Paul tells us that Jesus Christ *"is the image of the invisible God, the firstborn of all creation. For by Him all things were created, in heaven and on earth, visible and invisible, whether thrones or dominions or rulers or authorities—all things were created through Him and for Him. And He is before all things, and in Him all things hold together"* (Colossians 1:15–17, ESV). The One who created all things, rules all things, and in whom all things hold together, took this sinful world as it actually is.

What does this mean? It means He did not bat an eye at the woman at the well, who was entangled with her fifth (as far as we know) lover. He seemed to have no problem with His disciple Matthew's shady past as a tax collector. Most astoundingly of all,

He allowed Himself to be led as a sheep to His own slaughter on the cross, never uttering a mumbling word.

What would just one day (this day!) of your life be like if you were to take this sinful world (the world, others, yourself) as it actually is? Sounds like the beginning of a mysterious freedom to me.

> Most loving Father, whose will it is for us to give thanks for all things, to fear nothing but the loss of You, and to cast all our care on You who care for us: Preserve us from faithless fears and worldly anxieties, that no clouds of this mortal life may hide from us the light of that love which is immortal, and which You have manifested to us in Your Son Jesus Christ our Lord; who lives and reigns with You, in the unity of the Holy Spirit, one God, now and forever. Amen. (Collect for Eighth Sunday after the Epiphany – BCP p. 216)

January 9

"Trusting that You will make all things right, as I surrender to Your will"

CONFESSION TIME: WITH ALL due respect to Professor Niebuhr, I changed one word in this line of the Serenity Prayer. But this one word makes ALL the difference. The original version says that God will make all things right IF we surrender to His will. This does two things: 1) seriously overestimates our ability to surrender anything, and 2) seriously underestimates God's love, grace, power, and sovereignty.

Even when we want to surrender, sometimes we just can't. Jesus Himself recognized this as He said, *"The spirit is willing, but the flesh is weak" (Matthew 26:41, NIV)*. If God were dependent on our actions and abilities, the grace of God would be robbed of its goodness and comfort. But thankfully, God will not be thwarted, for *"He who began a good work in you will bring it to completion at the day of Jesus Christ" (Philippians 1:6, ESV).*

And He will make all things right. As St. Julian of Norwich said 650 years ago, "all shall be well, and all manner of things shall be well."

January 10

"So that I may be reasonably happy in this life, and supremely happy with You forever in the next."

PHILOSOPHER THOMAS HOBBES WAS born on April 5, 1588, to a clergyman and his wife in Wiltshire, England, and later went to Oxford for his education. Memorably, he called life "solitary, poor, nasty, brutish, and short." A couple centuries later, Thomas Jefferson argued that the pursuit of happiness—and by logical extension its acquisition—was an inalienable right endowed by our Creator. Somewhere in between, the Serenity Prayer concludes with this hope: reasonable happiness in this life and supreme happiness with God in the next.

The Bible has widely divergent views on the subject. Job 5:7 (NIV) tells us, *"Man is born to trouble as surely as sparks fly upward."* Yet Jesus says, *"I came that they may have life and have it abundantly" (John 10:10, ESV).* Are you glass half-full or half-empty?

What I know is that happiness is only experienced as a by-product of a life laid down and given away in love. When happiness becomes a goal, or a pursuit, it will always lie just out of reach.

O heavenly Father, who hast filled the world with beauty: Open our eyes to behold Thy gracious hand in all Thy works; that, rejoicing in Thy whole creation, we may learn to serve Thee with gladness; for the sake of Him through whom all things were made, Thy Son Jesus Christ our Lord. Amen. (For Joy in God's Creation – BCP p. 814)

January 11[†]

LET'S START OFF TODAY with the Epiphany-friendly theme of light, first addressing it from the dark side. I just became aware of the term "gaslighting," which originated from a 1938 play called *Gas Light*. To gaslight someone is to psychologically manipulate them, sowing seeds of doubt to make them question their own memory, perception, or sanity. You use denial, misperception, contradiction, and outright dishonesty to defend yourself (although you are in the wrong) and debunk the other (although they are in the right).

That may sound extreme, but I'm sure I employ—often unconsciously—some form of gaslighting everyday to shore up my own cause. Lord, have mercy. In contradistinction, I recall the childlike and plaintive hymn, "I Want to Walk as a Child of the Light."

> I want to walk as a child of the light
> I want to follow Jesus
> God set the stars to give light to the world
> The star of my life is Jesus
> In Him, there is no darkness at all

---

† This devotion, along with a handful of others, also appear in a slightly different form in Mockingbird's 2020 devotional, *Daily Grace*.

The night and the day are both alike
The Lamb is the light of the city of God
Shine in my heart, Lord Jesus (Hymn 490 in our
    1982 Hymnal)

The first-person accessibility of the hymn invites us to follow Jesus. We don't claim to be anything other than what we actually are; we simply express a childlike desire to walk in the light of Christ. Or, as Paul says, *"For at one time you were darkness, but now you are light in the Lord. Walk as children of light (for the fruit of light is found in all that is good and right and true)" (Ephesians 5:8–9, ESV)*. The hymn and scripture paint a beautiful picture; only God has the power to make it so, as we confess in the following prayer.

> Almighty and eternal God, so draw our hearts to Thee, so guide our minds, so fill our imaginations, so control our wills, that we may be wholly Thine, utterly dedicated unto Thee; and then use us, we pray Thee, as Thou wilt, and always to Thy glory and the welfare of Thy people; through our Lord and Savior Jesus Christ. Amen. (A Prayer of Self-Dedication – BCP p. 832)

January 12

IN 1987, WALLACE STEGNER wrote a novel called *Crossing to Safety*, his title taken from an earlier Robert Frost poem. The novel and poem are commendable, but the title is what resonates today. Depending on one's circumstances—or one's mood or state of mental health—the world sometimes feels like an unsafe place. There is some scriptural evidence to back this up: *"Be sober-minded; be watchful. Your adversary the devil prowls around like a roaring lion, seeking someone to devour" (1 Peter 5:8, ESV)*.

When you hear those low growls or feel the earth around you shake under that lion's paws, then Psalm 27 is your go-to. *"The LORD is my light and my salvation; whom shall I fear? The LORD is the strength of my life; of whom shall I be afraid?... For in the time of trouble He shall hide me in His pavilion: in the secret of His tabernacle shall He hide me; He shall set me up upon a rock"* *(Psalm 27:1, 5, KJV).*

In Christ you have already crossed to safety. That is true for today, tomorrow, and forever.

> Lord God, almighty and everlasting Father, You have brought us in safety to this new day: Preserve us with Your mighty power, that we may not fall into sin, nor be overcome by adversity; and in all we do, direct us to the fulfilling of Your purpose; through Jesus Christ our Lord. Amen. (A Collect for Grace – BCP p. 100)

January 13

HOLDING FORTH ON THE leavening effects of aging, one of Wendell Berry's country characters says, "Age has done more for my morals than Methodism ever did."

As we will pray in our prayer today, we confess that—try as we might to live on the straight and narrow—our wills are unruly. Sometimes it takes the accrual of years and the natural diminishment of desire to drain the sap that rises from the tree of Good and Evil that is planted deep in our hearts.

But in the end, aging isn't enough to vanquish sin. Only Jesus does that for us. *"For what the law was powerless to do because it was weakened by the flesh, God did by sending His own Son in the likeness of sinful flesh to be a sin offering"* *(Romans 8:3, NIV).* And we, both young and old, live in the blessed state of eternal forgiveness.

Almighty God, You alone can bring into order the unruly wills and affections of sinners: Grant Your people grace to love what You command and desire what You promise; that, among the swift and varied changes of the world, our hearts may surely there be fixed where true joys are to be found; through Jesus Christ our Lord, who lives and reigns with You and the Holy Spirit, one God, now and for ever. Amen. (Fifth Sunday in Lent – BCP p. 219)

January 14

THE BEAUTY OF BARE limbs against a dawning winter sky is no small thing. The skeletal form of a Japanese maple, its sinews open for inspection, tender but sturdy, enduring the frigid temps is a work of standing art. But it is also a little like Lear's description of human beings bereft of glitz and trappings in Shakespeare's *King Lear*: "Unaccommodated man is no more but such a poor, bare, forked, animal…"

We are both body and soul, but the soul somehow feels closer to the bare limbs of winter. The soul, your soul, is cocooned in the grace of God, ultimately untouchable. In any case, here is a nice double blessing from John's third epistle: *"Beloved, I pray that all may go well with you and that you may be in good health, as it goes well with your soul" (3 John 2, ESV).*

Almighty God, whose Son our Savior Jesus Christ is the light of the world: Grant that Your people, illumined by Your Word and Sacraments, may shine with the radiance of Christ's glory, that He may be known, worshiped, and obeyed to the ends of the earth; through Jesus Christ our

Lord, who with You and the Holy Spirit lives and reigns, one God, now and for ever. Amen. (Second Sunday after the Epiphany – BCP p. 215)

January 15

WHAT WOULD IT BE like—just for today, perhaps—to drop all your weapons? Not just your attack weapons, but your self-defense weapons, too.

I saw a funny refrigerator magnet that said, "I don't make mistakes too often, but when I do, it's your fault." What would it be like to bury your guns in the ground and trust yourself entirely to God? As Bob Dylan says, "I can't shoot them anymore."

"Do not seek revenge or bear a grudge against any of your people, but love your neighbor as yourself. I am the LORD" (Leviticus 19:18, BSB). What if—again, just for today—you could trust that God has your back, so you don't have to? Wouldn't that be nice? Kind of a relief? And, come to think of it, would you really want to be bothered to dig your guns up and haul them around tomorrow?

Assist us, mercifully, O Lord, in these our supplications and prayers, and dispose the way of Thy servants towards attainment of everlasting salvation; that, among all the changes and chances of this mortal life, they may ever be defended by Thy gracious and ready help; through Jesus Christ our Lord. Amen. (For Protection – BCP p. 832)

January 16

"Remember the Sabbath day, and keep it holy" (Exodus 20:8, NRSV).

THE LAST FEW NIGHTS I've been awakened by the hooting of two Great Horned Owls—two or three short, deep *hoo* sounds followed by a long *hooooooo*. Owls, at least in my mind, are majestic, mysterious, other-worldly. If lucky enough to catch a glimpse, one feels visited by the divine. *Of course* owls are the messengers of the wizarding world in Harry Potter.

In that the day is divided from the night, owls, being nocturnal, exist in the other world of night. They do their best work while we are sleeping. In this way, owls really are divine. God does His best work while we are sleeping. If not literally—I do love a good sleep—then at least metaphorically.

That's what the Sabbath is all about: remembering that while we rest, God does not. He is at work both in you and for you.

Almighty God, who after the creation of the world rested from all Your works and sanctified a day of rest for all Your creatures: Grant that we, putting away all earthly anxieties, may be duly prepared for the service of Your sanctuary, and that our rest here upon earth may be a preparation for the eternal rest promised to Your people in heaven; through Jesus Christ our Lord. Amen. (A Collect for Saturdays – BCP p. 99)

January 17

Question: Three frogs were sitting on a log. One frog decided to jump off. How many frogs were left on the log?
Answer: Three frogs!

DECIDING TO DO SOMETHING is not doing something. That's often how our resolutions for change operate. We decide that something needs to be changed, resolve to change it, and then experience the satisfaction of feeling like we've done something, when in reality we haven't done anything at all.

Thankfully, prayer is a different kettle of fish. When you pray, you are really *doing something*. That's because God has promised to hear our prayers and answer them. Not, obviously, as we direct Him to, but as He decides what is best for us. *"Then you will call upon Me and come and pray to Me, and I will hear you" (Jeremiah 29:12, ESV).*

Almighty God, who has promised to hear the petitions of those who ask in Thy Son's Name: We beseech Thee mercifully to incline Thine ear to us who have now made our prayers and supplications unto Thee; and grant that those things which we have faithfully asked according to Thy will, may effectually be obtained, to the relief of our necessity, and to the setting forth of Your glory, through Jesus Christ our Lord. Amen. (For the Answering of Prayer – BCP p. 834)

January 18

"IF YOU SET TO work to believe everything, you will tire out the believing-muscles of your mind, and then you'll be so weak you won't be able to believe the simplest true things." That's from *Alice in Wonderland* author Lewis Carroll.

We are all a mixture of belief and unbelief, faith and doubt. Even the most faithful among us have major belief blind spots— places where we aren't able to believe the simplest true things.

Jesus gives us a sweeping word of grace about belief. *"The apostles said to the Lord, 'Increase our faith!' And the Lord said, 'If you had faith like a grain of mustard seed, you could say to this mulberry tree, "Be uprooted and planted in the sea," and it would obey you'"* (Luke 17:5–6, ESV).

Do you realize how small a mustard seed is? Just the want to want to want to believe is enough to fill the sea with trees.

> Heavenly Father, You have promised to hear what we ask in the Name of Your Son: Accept and fulfill our petitions, we pray, not as we ask in our ignorance, nor as we deserve in our sinfulness, but as You know and love us in Your Son Jesus Christ our Lord. Amen. (The Collect at the Prayers – BCP p. 394)

January 19

WHEN VIRGINIA WOOLF PUBLISHED her first piece of literary criticism in the *Guardian*, a friend sent her a note of congratulations. I love her response: "Not that a review deserves praise, it is necessarily dull work reviewing I think, and I hate the critical attitude of mind because all the time I know what a humbug I am, and ask myself what right have I to dictate what's good and bad, when I couldn't, probably, do as well myself!"

Isn't it so darn easy to make yourself comfortable in the seat of judgment? Dispensing decrees on what is good and what is bad? It is so easy to do, because that is our original temptation—the serpent told our first parents that we would be like God. And it is so noxious and hellish, because we are not God. Oh, the presumption!

"Create in me a clean heart, O God, and renew a right spirit within me" (Psalm 51:10, ESV).

> We humbly beseech Thee, O Father, mercifully to look upon our infirmities; and, for the glory of Thy Name, turn from us all those evils that we most justly have deserved; and grant that in all our troubles we may put our whole trust and confidence in Thy mercy, and evermore serve Thee in holiness and pureness of living, to Thy honor and glory; through our only Mediator and Advocate, Jesus Christ our Lord. Amen. (The Great Litany – BCP p. 155)

January 20

"Now to one who works, wages are not reckoned as a gift but as something due. But to one who without works trusts Him who justifies the ungodly, such faith is reckoned as righteousness" (Romans 4:4–5, NRSV).

HARD TO GET ANY clearer than this passage! Our "work" is simply to trust. And trust isn't even work; trust is a gift. By trusting another you are dispossessed of any agency. You are trusting someone else to do something for you, something that you cannot do yourself.

In this case, you are trusting Jesus Christ for His death and His resurrection in your very stead. He IS your righteousness. All that is His is yours.

> O God, whose glory it is always to have mercy: Be gracious to all who have gone astray from Your ways, and bring them again with penitent hearts and steadfast faith to embrace and hold fast the unchangeable truth of Your Word, Jesus Christ Your Son; who with You and the Holy Spirit lives and reigns, one God, for ever and ever. Amen. (Second Sunday in Lent – BCP p. 218)

January 21

MARTIN LUTHER TOLD US that God is a southpaw. Or at least He expresses His power in what we might call "left-handed" ways. By that, Luther means that in a world obsessed with right-handed power (strength, intimidation, dominance, sabre-rattling, and media-blitzes), God enters stage left as a baby, learns the humble trade of carpentry, chooses nobodies to be His cohorts, and finally dies between two criminals outside the city gates. Even His resurrection is without any hint of fanfare: just a tucked-away empty tomb discovered by some women. Aptly, the risen Jesus is mistaken for the lowly gardener rather than the mighty landowner.

Early on, God had a go at right-handed power, then decided to swear it off. After the Flood, in which He wiped clean the wicked people of the earth along with their wicked ways, He said, *"I establish My covenant with you, that never again shall all flesh be cut off by the waters of a flood... This is the sign of the covenant that I make between Me and you and every living creature that is with you, for all future generations: I have set My bow in the clouds, and it shall be a sign of the covenant between Me and the earth" (Genesis 9:11–13, NRSV).*

Left-handed power often seems like no power at all. Then again, is there any power greater than the power of love? If Almighty God trades in His sabre for a rainbow, what kinds of ways might you lead with your left today?

O God, You declare Your almighty power chiefly in showing mercy and pity: Grant us the fullness of Your grace, that we, running to obtain Your promises, may become partakers of Your heavenly treasure; through Jesus Christ our Lord, who lives and reigns with You and the Holy Spirit, one God, for ever and ever. Amen. (Proper 21 – BCP p. 234)

January 22

YESTERDAY WE TALKED ABOUT power: what it is and what it isn't in relation to God. The Collect for the Third Sunday in Lent begins this way: "Almighty God, You know that we have no power in ourselves to help ourselves." I love the way that prayer starts: Hey God, look here. It's me again. You know the deal. I've got nothing.

We say that God knows that we have no power in ourselves to help ourselves. Rarely do we really know that ourselves, though. At least, not until you find yourself once again at whatever ground zero you return to again and again. Like the movie *Groundhog Day*, you think, "Good Lord! I can't believe I'm here again. Really?"

Yes, really. God knows that we have no power in ourselves to help ourselves. That is why the book of Proverbs tells us to *"Trust in the LORD with all your heart, and lean not on your own understanding; in all your ways acknowledge Him, and He will make your paths straight" (Proverbs 3:5–6, BSB)*. So, really, starting from ground zero once again is not such a bad thing. It's no surprise to God, anyway.

> Almighty God, You know that we have no power in ourselves to help ourselves: Keep us both outwardly in our bodies and inwardly in our souls, that we may be defended from all adversities which may happen to the body, and from all evil thoughts which may assault and hurt the soul; through Jesus Christ our Lord, who lives and reigns with You and the Holy Spirit, one God, for ever and ever. Amen. (Third Sunday in Lent – BCP p. 218)

January 23

ARE YOU RELIGIOUS? I'm not! It's true that you are reading (and I'm writing) this devotional because we both wish to have a deeper connection to God. Obviously, that is a good thing and the very source of true joy in this life. But just as Stevie Wonder told us that "superstition ain't the way," religion ain't the way, either.

Our friend Fleming Rutledge reminds us that religion is either an "organized system of belief or, alternatively, a loose collection of ideas and practices, projected out of humanity's needs and wishes." Marx famously called religion the "opiate of the people." A better description might be the "burden of the people"—an endless striving to make ourselves acceptable to God.

Is eschewing religion an odd stance for church people? Well, there was a group of people in the early church who thought so. They tried to pile all kinds of religious practices on the new Christians. But St. Paul took umbrage and declared, *"It is for freedom that Christ has set us free. Stand firm, then, and do not let yourselves be burdened again by a yoke of slavery" (Galatians 5:1, NIV).*

When Jesus died on the cross, the curtain of the temple was torn in two. That means His death gave you immediate access and connection to your Father in heaven, who loves you. So go to church on Sunday, but only so you can hear again the Good News, be nourished by Christ's body and blood, and sing the praises of the One who has set us free.

Everliving God, whose will it is that all should come to You through Your Son Jesus Christ: Inspire our witness to Him, that all may know the power of His forgiveness and the hope of His resurrection; who lives and reigns with You and the Holy Spirit, one God, now and forever. Amen. (For the Mission of the Church – BCP p. 816)

January 24

BORROWING FROM PINK FLOYD'S 1973 colossus of classic rock, it often feels like we are living on the dark side of the moon. The band must have struck a chord in tune with true human nature, as the record spent an absurd 917 weeks on the Billboard top 200.

That is to say that "this little light of mine" does not exist in the human heart. The prophet Jeremiah says it this way: *"The heart is deceitful above all things, and desperately sick; who can understand it?" (Jeremiah 17:9, ESV).*

Thanks be to God, we are not left in the dark. Have you seen the moon lately? Have you seen how it blazes in the night sky? Recently I took a moonlight walk which was brighter than the gloaming. The Collect for the second Sunday after the Epiphany reminds us that, like the moon, you and I are illumined by another Light. And this Light is no "little light of mine"; it is the eternally effulgent Light of the World.

Almighty God, whose Son our Savior Jesus Christ is the light of the world: Grant that Your people, illumined by Your Word and Sacraments, may shine with the radiance of Christ's glory, that He may be known, worshiped, and obeyed to the ends of the earth; through Jesus Christ our Lord, who with You and the Holy Spirit lives and reigns, one God, now and for ever. Amen. (Second Sunday After the Epiphany – BCP p. 215)

January 25

YOU ARE GIVEN WHAT you need in the present moment. That's what the manna from heaven was all about. When the Israelites were wandering in the wilderness, God fed them daily with, well, daily bread: *"Then the LORD said to Moses, 'Behold, I will rain bread from heaven for you. And the people shall go out and gather a certain quota every day'" (Exodus 16:4, NKJV).*

God gave His people specific instructions about this daily bread. If they tried to gather enough to store for tomorrow, not trusting that God would deliver on His daily promise and provision, then the manna would rot. With a kind of putrid clarity, the Scripture tells us that "stored manna bred worms and stank" (v. 20).

So there is good reason Jesus includes "give us this day our daily bread" in the Lord's Prayer. Don't forget that He is the true bread that comes down from heaven. He says, *"I am the bread of life; whoever comes to Me shall not hunger, and whoever believes in Me shall never thirst" (John 6:35, ESV).* He is what you need in this present moment.

Gracious Father, whose blessed Son Jesus Christ came down from heaven to be the true bread which gives life to the world: Evermore give us this bread, that He may live in us, and we in Him; who lives and reigns with You and the Holy Spirit, one God, now and for ever. Amen. (Fourth Sunday in Lent – BCP p. 219)

January 26

IN DAVE MATTHEWS' SONG "Samurai Cop (Oh Joy Begin)," he remembers the exquisite joy of the birth of his child. "Oh joy begin / Weak little thing / More precious there'll be nothing, no / Oh joy begin." He wants to recall that newborn joy because he also recognizes that as we grow up, we enter a world filled with difficulty. "Let's not forget these early days / Remember we begin the same / We lose our way in fear and pain."

We lose our way in fear and pain. I saw a tee shirt recently that said, "Pain is just weakness leaving the body." If that is true, I've got plenty of weakness just lollygagging around in no hurry to leave. I know something about fear, however, from a more reliable source—the Bible. *"There is no fear in love, but perfect love casts out fear" (1 John 4:18, ESV).*

Jesus Christ *is* perfect love. He is right on the heels of your fear with His love, ready to drive it out like He drove the moneychangers from the temple. We may lose our way in fear and pain, but He has already found us with His love and will never let us go.

Assist us, mercifully, O Lord, in these our supplications and prayers, and dispose the way of Thy servants towards attainment of everlasting salvation; that, among all the changes and chances of this mortal life, they may ever be defended by Thy gracious and ready help; through Jesus Christ our Lord. Amen. (For Protection – BCP p. 832)

January 27

"You were once a child, too."

FOR ADULTS, FRED ROGERS considered this insight the key to relating to children. It is also the key to understanding ourselves in relation to God. In an *Atlantic* article whose story provided the basis of the movie *A Beautiful Day in the Neighborhood*, Tom Junod writes,

> His message to doctors was his message to politicians, CEOs, celebrities, educators, writers, students, everyone. It was also the basis of his strange superpowers. He wanted us to remember what it was like to be a child so that he could talk to us; he wanted to talk to us so that we could remember what it was like to be a child. And he could talk to anyone, believing that if you remembered what it was like to be a child, you would remember that you were a child of God.

Mr. Rogers, an ordained minister, took his cue from Jesus. *"And they were bringing children to Him that He might touch them, and the disciples rebuked them. But when Jesus saw it, He was indignant and said to them, "Let the children come to Me; do not hinder them, for to such belongs the kingdom of God. Truly, I say to you, whoever does not receive the kingdom of God like a child shall not enter it" (Mark 10:13–15, ESV).*

Jesus does not commend children on the basis of their purity. Children are sinners, just like the rest of us! He commends them on the basis of their dependency, even as we depend on God our Father.

> God our Father, You see Your children growing up in an unsteady and confusing world: Show us that Your

ways give more life than the ways of the world, and that following You is better than chasing after selfish goals. Help us to take failure, not as a measure of our worth, but as a chance for a new start. Give us strength to hold our faith in You, and to keep alive our joy in Your creation; through Jesus Christ our Lord. Amen. (For Young Persons – BCP p. 829)

January 28

IN THE MIDST OF his missionary journeys, St. Paul encountered countless troubles, nearly biting the dust on several occasions. In his second letter to the Corinthians, he describes one of those times: *"For we do not want you to be unaware, brothers, of the affliction we experienced in Asia. For we were so utterly burdened beyond our strength that we despaired of life itself. Indeed, we felt that we had received the sentence of death. But that was to make us rely not on ourselves but on God who raises the dead. He delivered us from such a deadly peril, and He will deliver us. On Him we have set our hope that He will deliver us again"* (2 Corinthians 1:8–10, ESV).

There are three quick hitters in this brief passage.

1) Paul and crew were burdened beyond their strength. We are not alone when we feel completely overwhelmed by the afflictions of life.

2) Having utterly depleted his own resources, Paul was forced to rely on God. SO true to life; I would much rather rely on myself, my routines, my basic cheeriness, even my theological assumptions. When all that is taken away, our hand is forced to rely on God, who, of course, turns out to be the only reliable One, anyway.

3) Today, just for today, I pray that we will be able to remember God's track record of provision and trustworthiness, and be

moved to say with Paul, "On Him we have set our hope that He will deliver us again."

> O God, the protector of all who trust in You, without whom nothing is strong, nothing is holy: Increase and multiply upon us Your mercy; that, with You as our ruler and guide, we may so pass through things temporal, that we lose not the things eternal; through Jesus Christ our Lord, who lives and reigns with You and the Holy Spirit, one God, for ever and ever. Amen. (Proper 12 – BCP p. 231)

January 29

PEOPLE WHO SAY "I have no regrets" must exist on a different planet than I do. Who doesn't rue the ways we have hurt others? Who doesn't mourn the ways that we have hurt ourselves or been hurt by others? Sometimes it feels like the scales tip in the direction of the burned and broken relationships in our wake.

Francis Spufford said of Jesus, "Wreckage may be written into the logic of the world, but he will not agree that it is all there is. He says, 'More can be mended than you fear. Far more can be mended than you know.'"

Even when we have completely lost hope for mending *that* in yourself or *this* in someone else, Jesus has the mending in clear view. After all, *"He heals the brokenhearted and binds up their wounds" (Psalm 147:3, ESV).*

> Almighty and everlasting God, You govern all things both in heaven and on earth: Mercifully hear the supplications of Your people, and in our time grant us Your peace; through Jesus Christ our Lord, who lives and

reigns with You and the Holy Spirit, one God, for ever and ever. Amen. (Fourth Sunday after Epiphany – BCP p. 215)

January 30

Question: What happened before the invention of the crowbar?
Answer: Crows were forced to drink alone!

I.M.H.O., HUMOR IS THE elixir of life. We use a lot of humor in the pulpit at Christ Church in Charlottesville. Sometimes it takes a while for newcomers to feel it is okay to laugh in church. (It *couldn't* be that the jokes aren't funny!)

The Bible isn't known for humor, but Jesus did deploy it. I saw a Jesus film once that included this scene: *"Which of you fathers, if your son asks for a fish, will give him a snake instead? Or if he asks for an egg, will give him a scorpion?" (Luke 11:11–12, NIV).* The listeners were laughing their heads off! Guess you had to be there?

Still, His point is good. Would the God who loves you give you a snake? Don't you know that God wants the absolute best for you?

PS: Odds are that you will tell that joke today...

O Lord our God, accept the fervent prayers of Your people; in the multitude of Your mercies, look with compassion upon us and all who turn to You for help; for You are gracious, O lover of souls, and to You we give glory, Father, Son, and Holy Spirit, now and for ever. Amen. (The Collect at the Prayers – BCP p. 395)

January 31

"If in Christ we have hope in this life only, we are of all people most to be pitied. But in fact Christ has been raised from the dead, the firstfruits of those who have fallen asleep. For as by a man came death, by a man has come also the resurrection of the dead" (1 Corinthians 15:19–21, ESV).

ALBERT CAMUS, THE PULITZER PRIZE winning absurdist, died in a car crash when he was 46. William Faulkner wrote his obituary, saying, "When the door shut for him, he had already written on this side of it that which every artist who also carries through life with him that one same foreknowledge and hatred of death, is hoping to do: I was here."

What is not widely known about Camus is that right before his death he asked a minister in Paris to baptize him. His absurdist vision of life apparently gave way to the absurdly good news of the gospel. He was here, yes. And now he is raised to life in Christ.

Give us grace, O Lord, to answer readily the call of our Savior Jesus Christ and proclaim to all people the Good News of His salvation, that we and the whole world may perceive the glory of His marvelous works; who lives and reigns with You and the Holy Spirit, one God, for ever and ever. Amen. (Third Sunday after the Epiphany – BCP p. 215)

FEBRUARY

February 1

IRISH POET SEAMUS HEANEY (1995 Nobel Prize in Literature) wrote a poem called "Digging." In it he explores his vocation as a writer in juxtaposition to his father's and grandfather's more earthy labors. While at his writing desk, he watches his father through a window digging in the garden. Heaney concludes,

> The cold smell of potato mould, the squelch and slap
> Of soggy peat, the curt cuts of an edge
> Through living roots awaken in my head.
> But I've no spade to follow men like them.
> Between my finger and my thumb
> The squat pen rests.
> I'll dig with it.

The Bible says, *"I know that there is nothing better for people than to be happy and to do good while they live. That each of them may eat and drink, and find satisfaction in all their toil—this is the gift of God"* (Ecclesiastes 3:12–13, NIV).

Work, all kinds of different work—your work today—is a gift from God.

> Almighty and everlasting God, by whose Spirit the whole body of Your faithful people is governed and sanctified: Receive our supplications and prayers, which we offer before You for all members of Your holy Church, that in their vocation and ministry they may truly and devoutly serve You; through our Lord and Savior Jesus Christ, who lives and reigns with You, in the unity of the Holy Spirit, one God, now and forever. Amen. (For all Christians in their vocation – BCP p. 256)

February 2

"So we fix our eyes not on what is seen, but on what is unseen. For what is seen is temporary, but what is unseen is eternal" (2 Corinthians 4:18, BSB).

BARE, SPARE FEBRUARY. Although February is frigid and gray here in Virginia, the birds have become super active. They know that Spring is coming. Such a good metaphor for our life of faith, our life of hope. As Bono sings, "Midnight is where the day begins."

Think for a moment. How do you fix your eyes on what is unseen? Sounds like a Zen riddle, but it is definitely worth pondering today. I do know this; God has His eyes fixed on you with a powerful love and an intention for a kind of good that you can't even begin to fathom.

> O God, who by the glorious resurrection of Your Son Jesus Christ destroyed death and brought life and immortality to light: Grant that we, who have been raised with Him, may abide in His presence and rejoice in the hope of eternal glory; through Jesus Christ our Lord, to whom, with You and the Holy Spirit, be dominion and praise for ever and ever. Amen. (Tuesday in Easter Week – BCP p. 223)

February 3

THE FEELING OF BEING an imposter is as common as the common cold. When Jodie Foster won an Oscar, she said, "I thought it was a fluke. I thought everyone would find out and they'd take it back. They'd come to my house, knocking on my door, 'Excuse me, we meant to give that to someone else. That was going to Meryl

Streep.'" But here's what Meryl Streep had to say. "Why would anyone want to see me again in a movie? And I don't know how to act anyway, so why am I doing this?"

You may feel like a fake in any number of realms, but it doesn't matter. Why? Because your life is hidden in Christ. *"For you have died, and your life is hidden with Christ in God" (Colossians 3:3, ESV).*

> Almighty and everlasting God, You govern all things both in heaven and on earth: Mercifully hear the supplications of Your people, and in our time grant us Your peace; through Jesus Christ our Lord, who lives and reigns with You and the Holy Spirit, one God, for ever and ever. Amen. (Fourth Sunday After the Epiphany – BCP p. 215)

February 4

QUOTIDIAN IS AN ADJECTIVE meaning "ordinary or everyday, especially when mundane." The quotidian affairs of life are where God, if He is real, must reside. If God only shows up on the red-letter days, then we are left to slog most of it out alone.

In the Bible's account of the Transfiguration, Peter really wants to stay on the mountaintop: *"After six days Jesus took with Him Peter, James and John the brother of James, and led them up a high mountain by themselves. There He was transfigured before them. His face shone like the sun, and His clothes became as white as the light. Just then there appeared before them Moses and Elijah, talking with Jesus. Peter said to Jesus, 'Lord, it is good for us to be here. If You wish, I will put up three shelters—one for You, one for Moses and one for Elijah.' While he was still speaking, a bright cloud covered them, and a voice from the cloud said, "This is My Son, whom I love; with Him I am well pleased. Listen to Him!" (Matthew 17:1–5, NIV).*

Sure, it was good to be there, but the very next verse has them going down the mountain, back into their quotidian lives. But they don't descend alone: Jesus is with them. And Jesus is with you.

O God, who before the passion of Your only-begotten Son revealed His glory upon the holy mountain: Grant to us that we, beholding by faith the light of His countenance, may be strengthened to bear our cross, and be changed into His likeness from glory to glory; through Jesus Christ our Lord, who lives and reigns with You and the Holy Spirit, one God, for ever and ever. Amen. (Last Sunday after Epiphany – BCP p. 217)

February 5

MOST EVERYTHING HAS A direct consequence. For instance, a strong late afternoon espresso results in a skittery night's sleep. Felonious assault leads to jail time. The Law of Consequence is good and helpful; otherwise, self-will would run unchecked and rampant. Consequences make sense.

Here's the counter-intuitive thing though: Grace upends the law of consequence. We sin, yet Christ paid the price. He suffered the consequences of our actions. The prophet Isaiah tells us, *"But He was pierced for our transgressions, He was crushed for our iniquities; the punishment that brought us peace was on Him, and by His wounds we are healed" (Isaiah 53:5, NIV)*.

Does this make sense? No. Is it the gospel? Thankfully, yes.

Almighty God, we pray You graciously to behold this Your family, for whom our Lord Jesus Christ was willing to be betrayed, and given into the hands of sinners, and to suffer death upon the cross; who now lives and reigns with You and the Holy Spirit, one God, for ever and ever. Amen. (Good Friday – BCP p. 221)

February 6

ON THE WAY TO work this morning, I was behind a school bus making a pickup. A little child was clinging to her father's neck as he tried to put her on the bus. He had to pry her hands off him and hand her into the arms of someone on the bus. As the bus left, he stood waving energetically in the window, his forced smile disappearing as the bus drove out of view.

I wonder if that feeling ever fully goes away? I'm talking about the feeling the child has of being dismissed out into the world on her own. Even as we age, there is still a fundamental sense of being alone in this world. There is a longing to be held securely in strong arms.

God our Father is always there for us. The Psalmist declares, *"O You who have been my help. Cast me not off; forsake me not, O God of my salvation! For my father and my mother have forsaken me, but the* LORD *will take me in" (Psalm 27:9–10, ESV).*

Leaning, leaning, leaning on the Everlasting Arms.

O God, Your never-failing providence sets in order all things both in heaven and earth: Put away from us, we entreat You, all hurtful things, and give us those things which are profitable for us; through Jesus Christ our Lord, who lives and reigns with You and the Holy Spirit, one God, for ever and ever. Amen. (Proper 4 – BCP p. 229)

February 7

*"Arise, shine, for your light has come, and the glory of
the* LORD *rises upon you. See, darkness covers the earth
and thick darkness is over the peoples, but the* LORD
*rises upon you and His glory appears over you" (Isaiah
60:1–2, NIV).*

THE SIXTIETH CHAPTER OF Isaiah is full of promise for the future.
And when God talks about the future, that future is filled with
hope. It's worth taking a moment and reading the whole chapter.
What does the passage say?

Well, are things dark right now? Your light will come. Are
you alone right now? Your sons shall come from far, and your
daughters shall be carried on the hip. Are you sad or struggling
right now? Your heart shall thrill and exult. Do you feel dry right
now? Shriveled in your soul? The abundance of the sea shall be
turned to you. Are you having trouble making ends meet right
now? Wealth shall come to you. Do you feel forsaken and hated?
You will experience joy from age to age. Are you beat down by
bad news? Good news shall be brought to you.

Are you tired of anger and brutality in our nation and our
world? Violence shall no more be heard in your land, devastation or destruction within your borders. Are you tired of all that
divides us—even the walls within yourself? You shall call your
walls Salvation, and your gates Praise.

When God talks about the future, that future is filled
with hope.

O Lord, make us to have perpetual love and reverence
for Your holy Name, for You never fail to help and govern those whom You have set upon the sure foundation
of Your loving-kindness; through Jesus Christ our Lord,

who lives and reigns with You and the Holy Spirit, one God, for ever and ever. Amen. (Proper 7 – BCP p. 230)

February 8

ONE PSYCHOLOGIST HAS RIGHTLY observed, "Beneath every behavior there is a feeling, and beneath each feeling is a need. And when we meet that need rather than focus on the behavior, we begin to deal with the cause and not the symptom."

This coheres with God's interest in the core of a person, rather than the outward appearance. Jesus says, *"Stop judging by mere appearances, but instead judge correctly" (John 7:24, NIV)*. It is as if we all need x-ray glasses to see beneath behaviors—ours and those of others.

Here's the thing: Our deepest need is for forgiveness. And God has met that need on the cross.

> Gracious Father, whose blessed Son Jesus Christ came down from heaven to be the true bread which gives life to the world: Evermore give us this bread, that He may live in us, and we in Him; who lives and reigns with You and the Holy Spirit, one God, now and for ever. Amen. (Fourth Sunday in Lent – BCP p. 219)

February 9

> *"But do not overlook this one fact, beloved, that with the Lord one day is as a thousand years, and a thousand years as one day" (2 Peter 3:8, ESV).*

VAGABONDING THROUGH EUROPE ON our 1986 honeymoon trip, my wife Christie and I discovered that the trains in northern Europe were always on time, while the trains in southern Europe were always late. One of us likes to be punctual (to an obsessive fault) while the other of us enjoys dawdling and more often than not loses track of time. If you know us, it's not hard to peg who is who.

One of Christie's favorite sayings is an Irish adage: "When God made time, He made plenty of it." I'm certain that there are no clocks in heaven, and in this particular case my wife is more sanctified than I am. God's timing is always His timing. His trains rarely arrive on schedule. But they always arrive exactly on time.

> Be present, O merciful God, and protect us through the hours of the days and nights, so that we who are wearied by the changes and chances of this life may rest in Your eternal changelessness; through Jesus Christ our Lord. Amen. (Compline – BCP p. 133)

February 10

> *"But the tax collector stood at a distance. He would not even look up to heaven, but beat his breast and said, 'God, have mercy on me, a sinner.' I tell you that this man, rather than the other, went home justified before God" (Luke 18:13–14, NIV).*

IN THE PARABLE OF the Pharisee and the tax collector, it is the scoundrel, rather than the upright religious man, who is justified (made right, made whole) by God. All well and good, since we know that we are justified by faith rather than by works.

But what happens when this same man goes right back to his scoundrelly, conniving, and nefarious misdeeds when he leaves the temple? And then shows up the next week, head down, praying the same prayer? Shockingly, the exact same outcome ensues: He goes home justified. And the next week and the week, month, year, decade after that? Same result.

We may get tired of people being people, but God does not. Good thing for us, too.

> Grant us, O Lord, to trust in You with all our hearts; for, as You always resist the proud who confide in their own strength, so You never forsake those who boast of Your mercy; through Jesus Christ our Lord, who lives and reigns with You and the Holy Spirit, one God, now and for ever. Amen. (Proper 18 – BCP p. 233)

February 11

I'VE ALWAYS LIKED THE gloaming. The gloaming is the time of day immediately after the sun goes down. This is the moment described in a William Butler Yeats poem: "The blue and the dim and the dark cloths / Of night and light and the half light." The gloaming is the transitory time between the day and the night.

On the good days, one has the satisfaction of having been carried through another day. On the not-so-good days, there is the relief that the day has ended. Either way, we can join the Psalmist, who says, *"Be gracious to me, O Lord, for to You do I cry all the day. Gladden the soul of Your servant, for to You, O Lord, do I lift up my soul. For You, O Lord, are good and forgiving, abounding in steadfast love to all who call upon You"* (Psalm 86:3–5, ESV).

You might even say that the gloaming is a kind of harbinger of that Great Day, when our work will be done, and we will transition out of "the Shadowlands" (C. S. Lewis) and enter into the brightly lit banquet hall to feast at the Supper of the Lamb. Something to ponder as the sun goes down!

> O Lord, support us all the day long, until the shadows lengthen, and the evening comes, and the busy world is hushed, and the fever of life is over, and our work is done. Then in Thy mercy, grant us a safe lodging, and a holy rest, and peace at the last. Amen. (In the Evening – BCP p. 833)

February 12

IT'S BEEN SAID THAT life is like a courtroom. We find we need to defend ourselves against the judgment and accusation of others. Sometimes that judgment is real; more often it is imagined. Another person's "success," or what appears to be success to us, will cause us to judge ourselves. You know the saying: "You are your own worst critic." So many of our prison sentences are self-imposed.

St. Paul knew this universal proclivity, but also knew the way to commute the sentence. *"I care very little, however, if I am judged by you or by any human court. In fact, I do not even judge myself. My conscience is clear, but that does not vindicate me. It is the Lord who judges me" (1 Corinthians 4:3–4, BSB).* Paul is saying that the lens by which we perceive judgment—whether from ourselves or others—is so warped and faulty that it is better to disregard the accusations altogether.

In any case, the only person fit for the job of judgment is the Lord. And if that is the case, then go ahead and walk scot-free out of that courtroom door. While you're at it, put your hand in the hand of the man who said, *"I did not come to judge the world but to save the world" (John 12:47, ESV).* For He is our only Mediator and Advocate.

Almighty and everlasting God, You are always more ready to hear than we to pray, and to give more than we either desire or deserve: Pour upon us the abundance of Your mercy, forgiving us those things of which our conscience is afraid, and giving us those good things for which we are not worthy to ask, except through the merits and mediation of Jesus Christ our Savior; who lives and reigns with You and the Holy Spirit, one God, for ever and ever. Amen. (Proper 22 – BCP p. 234)

February 13

"Then the LORD God formed the man of dust from the ground and breathed into his nostrils the breath of life, and the man became a living creature" (Genesis 2:7, ESV).

AS WE APPROACH LENT, I find myself agreeing with Garrison Keillor, who wrote,

In church a couple weeks ago, someone mentioned a course to help us on our spiritual journey during Lent, and the term 'spiritual journey' is one of those clichés that clicks my OFF switch. I am not on a journey, I'm simply crossing the street watching the WALK sign click off the seconds, 8, 7, 6, 5, 4, as I think about being run over and killed and I arrive on the other side with two seconds to spare. The story of my life. I'm a lucky man.

All of life is an outrageous gift, and we are lucky to arrive on the other side.

O Lord our God, accept the fervent prayers of Your people; in the multitude of Your mercies, look with compassion upon us and all who turn to You for help; for You are gracious, O lover of souls, and to You we give glory, Father, Son, and Holy Spirit, now and for ever. Amen. (The Collect at the Prayers – BCP p. 395)

February 14

HAPPY ST. VALENTINE'S DAY! Little is reliably known about the third-century clergyman for whom the day is named. One thing is certain: He had very little to do with chocolates or romance. In fact, he was known not for amorous love, but for his grisly beheading.

His feast day was traditionally celebrated on February 14th. Chaucer may be responsible for his connection with erotic love; in the Canterbury Tales he declared that birds chose their mates on this day. (Side note: Notice the heightened avian activity today!) In any case, courtly love dominated medieval times, so the beeline from birds to bedrooms was an easy one to make. By the time Shakespeare had love-struck Ophelia call herself Hamlet's "Valentine," the deal was done.

All love, romantic and otherwise, is derived from the love of God. In one of the great passages of Scripture, John tells us, *"Beloved, let us love one another, for love is from God, and whoever loves has been born of God and knows God. Anyone who does not love does not know God, because God is love. In this the love of God was made manifest among us, that God sent His only Son into the world, so that we might live through Him. In this is love, not that we have loved God but that He loved us and sent His Son to be the propitiation for our sins"* (1 John 4:7–10, ESV).

God's love is the love that will not let us go.

Almighty God, we entrust all who are dear to us to Thy never-failing care and love, for this life and the life to come, knowing that Thou art doing for them better things than we can desire or pray for; through Jesus Christ our Lord. Amen. (For Those We Love – BCP p. 831)

February 15

"And Simeon blessed them and said to Mary His mother, 'Behold, this child is appointed for the fall and rising of many in Israel, and for a sign that is opposed (and a sword will pierce through your own soul also), so that thoughts from many hearts may be revealed'" (Luke 2:34–35, ESV).

RIGHT AFTER SIMEON—the old man in the temple who had been waiting to see the Messiah before his death—takes the days-old Jesus into his arms and sings what is now known as the *Nunc Dimittis*, he utters this prescient yet disturbing prophecy to Mary.

While Jesus' life and death are obviously unique, any parent knows that the very act of loving a child will include a pierced soul. That is the nature of parental love. In fact, it is the nature of love itself. It does not come without exacting a cost. This truth is inextricably woven into God's world.

And it is seen most obviously in the Father's love for His Son, who suffered a spear through His side as He hung on the cross, with Mary at His feet. God's love for us cost His very life.

O Savior of the world, who by Thy cross and precious blood hast redeemed us: Save us and help us, we humbly beseech Thee, O Lord. Amen. (Anthem 3 – Good Friday – BCP p. 282)

February 16

"Remember that you are dust, and to dust you shall return."

THE POINTED CONTEMPLATION OF our death is the prime reason the Ash Wednesday liturgy is so powerful. Remembering that our earthly lives will one day end is not something we normally do.

The Bible tells us, *"It is better to go to the house of mourning than to go to the house of feasting, for this is the end of all mankind, and the living will lay it to heart" (Ecclesiastes 7:2, ESV)*. A funeral in lieu of a party? That's a strong statement!

Our friend Robert Capon assures us that our death is ultimately good news: "Jesus says pretty clearly that He considers our death to be the major contribution any of us makes to the plan of salvation. God apparently doesn't need our physical or moral cooperation any more than He needs our philosophical help. What He does count on is our death... The only ticket anybody needs is the one ticket everybody has, namely, death."

Through the death and resurrection of Jesus Christ, returning to the dust is ultimately very good news.

Almighty God, You have created us out of the dust of the earth: Grant that these ashes may be to us a sign of our mortality and penitence, that we may remember that it is only by Your gracious gift that we are given everlasting life; through Jesus Christ our Savior. Amen. (Ash Wednesday Liturgy – BCP p. 265)

February 17

"Every good and perfect gift is from above, coming down from the Father of the heavenly lights, who does not change like shifting shadows" (James 1:17, NIV).

I'VE BASICALLY STOPPED BUYING Valentine's Day/birthday/Christmas presents for my wife, because she always returns them. This was an issue for a while. Now, I happily accept the reality that gift giving isn't really in my gift-cluster! Nor does she really care about getting gifts. For Valentine's Day I just gave her a poem about how all my gifts end up at Goodwill. Everyone was happy!

God is the perfect gift-giver, of course. He knows exactly what you need: the greatest gift, His Son. And returning His gift—either by refusing it, exchanging it, or trying to give something back in return—is not in your power.

> O Lord, You have taught us that without love whatever we do is worth nothing: Send Your Holy Spirit and pour into our hearts Your greatest gift, which is love, the true bond of peace and of all virtue, without which whoever lives is accounted dead before You. Grant this for the sake of Your only Son Jesus Christ, who lives and reigns with You and the Holy Spirit, one God, now and for ever. Amen. (Seventh Sunday after Epiphany – BCP p. 216)

February 18

PEOPLE LIKE TO TALK about "doing your best." For instance, when looking back on our childhoods, we tend to say that our parents weren't perfect, but they "did their best." There can be a kind of graciousness in that imputation—one that recognizes that people are doing all they can, given their weaknesses and circumstances.

The problem with this approbation is that it is generally not true—and not just in relation to raising children. There are times, of course, when we have done our best. But much of our lives are filled with shortcuts, oversights, and straight up selfishness. Am I right?

"If we say we have no sin, we deceive ourselves, and the truth is not in us. If we confess our sins, He is faithful and just to forgive us our sins and cleanse us from all unrighteousness" (1 John 1:8–9, ESV). Fortunately, we have a God who sees and appraises us with acute accuracy, and yet reckons us as righteous through the merits of His Son. It is His best that counts, not ours.

> We do not presume to come to this Thy Table, O merciful Lord, trusting in our own righteousness, but in Thy manifold and great mercies. We are not worthy so much as to gather up the crumbs under Thy Table. But Thou art the same Lord whose property is always to have mercy. Amen. (From the Prayer of Humble Access – BCP p. 337)

February 19

LET'S HEAR FROM POET Mary Oliver: "I think this is / the prettiest world—so long as you don't mind / a little dying, how could there be a day in your whole life / that doesn't have its splash of happiness?"

That's from "The Kingfisher." A little dying is baked into the bread of life, at least according to Jesus. *"Very truly I tell you, unless a kernel of wheat falls to the ground and dies, it remains only a single seed. But if it dies, it produces many seeds" (John 12:24, NIV).*

By the grace and power of God, many of the little "d" deaths we suffer in life—the demise of our dreams and plans, for example—are followed by little "r" resurrections. New life emerging out of failure and defeat. These miniature miracles prepare us for the Big Show that awaits us behind the veil. The symbiosis between death and resurrection is how this world works, and the next one too.

O God, You have prepared for those who love You such good things as surpass our understanding: Pour into our hearts such love towards You, that we, loving You in all things and above all things, may obtain Your promises, which exceed all that we can desire; through Jesus Christ our Lord, who lives and reigns with You and the Holy Spirit, one God, for ever and ever. Amen. (Sixth Sunday of Easter – BCP p. 225)

February 20

"In the beginning God created the heavens and the earth. Now the earth was formless and empty, darkness was over the surface of the deep, and the Spirit of God was hovering over the waters. And God said, 'Let there be light,' and there was light. God saw that the light was good, and He separated the light from the darkness. God called the light 'day,' and the darkness He called 'night.' And there was evening, and there was morning—the first day" (Genesis 1:1–5, NIV).

GOD CREATES. THAT'S WHAT He did, and that's what He does. In the beginning God created the world from nothing. Where there was only darkness, He brought light. And the light was good.

What will God create in your life? Into what darkness will He bring His light? For God will do that, because that's what God does. God creates. For the most astonishing instance of *creatio ex nihilo*, look no further than the resurrection of Jesus.

God creates—out of nothing. So be on the lookout today.

O God, who wonderfully created, and yet more wonderfully restored, the dignity of human nature: Grant that we may share the divine life of Him who humbled Himself to share our humanity, Your Son Jesus Christ; who lives and reigns with You, in the unity of the Holy Spirit, one God, for ever and ever. Amen. (Second Sunday after Christmas Day – BCP p. 214)

February 21

"Passing alongside the Sea of Galilee, He saw Simon and Andrew the brother of Simon casting a net into the sea, for they were fishermen. And Jesus said to them, 'Follow Me, and I will make you become fishers of men.' And immediately they left their nets and followed Him" (Mark 1:16–18, ESV).

IN THIS PASSAGE IN Mark, Jesus chooses His first followers. Much has been made of the fishermen's immediate reaction to Jesus' call. They dropped their nets in the same way that we "drop everything" when something crucially important comes up. Clearly, something about Jesus was incredibly compelling.

But the often-overlooked detail I want to highlight today is that during Jesus' day, *disciples chose rabbis—rabbis didn't choose disciples!* So Jesus' call to Simon and Andrew must have had some kind of shock and awe value to it. Later, Jesus says as much in John

15:16 (NIV): *"You did not choose Me, but I chose you and appointed you so that you might go and bear fruit—fruit that will last."*

Jesus has chosen you, too. This is extremely comforting news, if, like me, you don't always "make good choices." That Jesus has chosen you takes the choice right out of your hands.

> Almighty God, who gave such grace to Your apostle Andrew that he readily obeyed the call of Your Son Jesus Christ, and brought his brother with him: Give us, who are called by Your Holy Word, grace to follow Him without delay, and to bring those near to us into His gracious presence; who lives and reigns with You and the Holy Spirit, one God, now and forever. Amen. (St. Andrew – BCP p. 237)

February 22

EMILY DICKINSON TOLD US that truth must be told in wily and creative ways if it is to have any hope of hitting home.

> Tell all the truth but tell it slant—
> Success in Circuit lies
> Too bright for our infirm Delight
> The Truth's superb surprise
> As Lightning to the Children eased
> With explanation kind
> The Truth must dazzle gradually
> Or every man be blind—

Jesus told slant truth through parables, His primary method of teaching. He spoke in parables to unseat us from our assumptions about God. He spoke in parables to sneak the truth about God through the side doors of our lives, since our front doors are usually defended and double-bolted to keep Him out, even though without Him "every man be blind."

Here's one to ponder today: *"This is what the kingdom of God is like. A man scatters seed on the ground. Night and day, whether he sleeps or gets up, the seed sprouts and grows, though he does not know how. All by itself the soil produces grain—first the stalk, then the head, then the full kernel in the head. As soon as the grain is ripe, he puts the sickle to it, because the harvest has come" (Mark 4:26–29, NIV).*

You can draw your own conclusions about this parable, but the "superb surprise" for me is that the seed grows "all by itself" and the man "does not know how"! What an enormous comfort to know that God is at work in your life, and you know not how!

> Lord, we pray that Your grace may always precede and follow us, that we may continually be given to good works; through Jesus Christ our Lord, who lives and reigns with You and the Holy Spirit, one God, now and for ever. Amen. (Proper 23 – BCP p. 234)

February 23

DO YOU EVER FAIL to complete what you start? A book? A project? Sometimes I don't even start what I start. I announced that I was going to take up needlepoint so I could make myself one of those cool needlepoint belts with trout on it, but then I looked at what was involved and decided not to start what I started. Ditto with pipe-smoking, mandolin-playing, and home-brewing.

What about self-improvement projects? Is there an unused Peloton collecting dust in your basement? A gym membership that you have now ghosted? Do you ever feel like you have gained some ground then—*whoop zoop sloop*—you are back to square one? Well, I have some good news for you today.

"And I am sure of this, that He who began a good work in you will bring it to completion at the day of Jesus Christ" (Philippians 1:6, ESV). St. Paul reminds us that your "progress" is not your job. It's God's job. And He is faithful to bring you to completion. God always finishes what He starts. And with you He has already started what He starts!

> Stir up Your power, O Lord, and with great might come among us; and, because we are sorely hindered by our sins, let Your bountiful grace and mercy speedily help and deliver us; through Jesus Christ our Lord, to whom, with You and the Holy Spirit, be honor and glory, now and for ever. Amen. (Third Sunday of Advent – BCP p. 212)

February 24

"For what we proclaim is not ourselves, but Jesus Christ as Lord, with ourselves as your servants for Jesus' sake" (2 Corinthians 4:5, ESV).

LAUDING A PERSON OR an institution is always a mistake. While we can most definitely give thanks to God for a source of goodness in this world, heaping praise is bad for both the praise-giver and the praise-bearer. The praise-giver often has sycophantic (or at least self-oriented) motives, and the praise-bearer will more often than not begin to believe his or her own press clippings.

Hagiography in any form is a poor substitute for plain gratitude. Laud and praise are to be directed to God alone. Paul continues this line of thought in his second letter to the Corinthians: *"For God, who said, 'Let light shine out of darkness,' has shone in our hearts to give the light of the knowledge of the glory of God in the face of Jesus Christ. But we have this treasure in jars of clay, to show that the surpassing power belongs to God and not to us"* (2 Corinthians 4:6–7, ESV).

There is only one name under heaven by which we are saved. And it's not yours or mine. Thankfully.

> Almighty God, whose Son our Savior Jesus Christ is the light of the world: Grant that Your people, illuminated by Your Word and Sacraments, may shine with the radiance of Christ's glory, that He may be known, worshiped, and obeyed to the ends of the earth; through Jesus Christ our Lord, who with You and the Holy Spirit lives and reigns, one God, now and for ever. Amen. (Second Sunday after the Epiphany – BCP p. 215)

February 25

HERE'S THE SKEPTIC IVAN'S astute observation from Fyodor Dostoevsky's *The Brothers Karamazov*: "'I must make you one confession,' Ivan began, 'I could never understand how one can love one's neighbors. It's just one's neighbors, to my mind, that one can't love, though one might love those at a distance.'"

Ivan's right: It is easier to love the abstract person than it is to love the particular person. Especially when the particular person is annoying, ultra-needy, or destructive.

The Bible clearly tells us that love does not rise unaided from the human heart. But love of neighbor (and even enemy!) does happen in life. How? *"This is how God showed His love among us: He sent His one and only Son into the world that we might live through Him. This is love: not that we loved God, but that He loved us and sent His Son as an atoning sacrifice for our sins"* (1 John 4:9–10, NIV).

The love of our neighbor is always a response to God's love for us.

O God, because without You we are not able to please You, mercifully grant that Your Holy Spirit may in all things direct and rule our hearts; through Jesus Christ our Lord, who lives and reigns with You and the Holy Spirit, one God, now and forever. Amen. (Proper 19 – BCP p. 233)

February 26

IT MAY BE THE shortest verse in the Bible, but it speaks volumes: *"Jesus wept" (John 11:35)*. He wept in response to His friend's death. At least in part—for when we cry, we usually cry about things known *and* things unknown, things surface and things subterranean.

Most of us are taught that sadness is not okay. In the third episode of *MasterChef Junior's* second season, the judge tells a contestant who has ruined her shepherd's pie and possibly her dream of winning, "When things are as bad as they can be, you gotta pull it together. Wipe your tears." The contestant had been crying for mere seconds. She is eight years old.

Jesus wept, even though He knew He would bring His friend back to life. This short verse is so important because God Himself legitimized sadness. Sometimes, pulling it together may be the worst possible thing to do.

Heavenly Father, send Your Holy Spirit into our hearts, to direct and rule us according to Your will, to comfort us in all our afflictions, to defend us from all error, and to lead us into all truth; through Jesus Christ our Lord. Amen. (Noonday Prayers – BCP p. 107)

February 27

THE NETFLIX SHOW, *The Sinner* (NOT recommended for the prudish, the squeamish, or the faint of heart), features an aging, awkward, unglamorous lead man. Harry is a detective whose personal life is a mess, stemming from some childhood trauma.

While it's true that hurt people can hurt people, in some cases hurt people can heal people. Harry deeply connects with the traumatized part of a person that has led to what others assume is a random murder. The show is not a Whodunnit, but rather a Whydunnit. Its strength lies in the probing of the human heart and the exploration of a hidden pain beneath a heinous action.

I am thinking about Jesus' interaction with the rich young ruler. The Scripture says, *"Jesus looked at him and loved him" (Mark 10:21, NIV).* Even after the man clung to his wealth and turned down Jesus' rare invitation to follow Him, we can be sure that our Lord still looked at him and loved him.

Jesus looks at you and loves you. He especially looks at your places of trauma, your buried wounds, the person hidden away, even from yourself. He looks at you and loves you.

> Heavenly Father, giver of life and health: Comfort and relieve us, and give Your power of healing to those who minister to our needs, that we may be strengthened in our weakness and have confidence in Your loving care; through Jesus Christ our Lord, who lives and reigns with You and the Holy Spirit, one God, now and forever. Amen. (For the Sick – BCP p. 260)

February 28

A BAKED CHICKEN IS among the best of all culinary delights: easy, inexpensive, delicious, nutritious. (For all the vegan/vegetarians reading this, I grant you that a baked chicken is neither easy nor inexpensive for the chicken.) Just rub the bird with olive oil, apply a generous sprinkling of ground pepper and kosher salt, pop it in the oven for an hour and *voila*—dinner! A salad, some couscous, and a glass of pinot grigio, and you are dining in the catbird seat.

Many people want to make religion complicated. And maybe religion is complicated, but the gospel couldn't be any simpler or easier or cheaper. The prophet cries out, *"Come, all you who are thirsty, come to the waters; and you who have no money, come, buy and eat! Come, buy wine and milk without money and without cost"* *(Isaiah 55:1, NIV).*

And talk about nutritious! Eat this bread and never be hungry again.

> Lord of all power and might, the author and giver of all good things: Graft in our hearts the love of Your Name; increase in us true religion; nourish us with all goodness; and bring forth in us the fruit of good works; through Jesus Christ our Lord, who lives and reigns with You and the Holy Spirit, one God for ever and ever. Amen. (Proper 17 – BCP p. 233)

MARCH

March 1

I LOVE WENDELL BERRY's take on the golden rule: "Do unto those downstream as you would have those upstream do unto you." This teaching of Jesus is known far and wide, even by people who never read, or who have never read the Bible. And as people attempt to carry out this moral injunction, the world is a more humane and compassionate place.

It is a good thing, however, that God does not follow His own golden rule. If He did to us what we have done to Him, we would be in big trouble. We betrayed Him, falsely accused Him, and finally killed Him. But, He did not do unto us as we have done unto Him.

"He does not deal with us according to our sins, nor repay us according to our iniquities" (Psalm 103:10, ESV). For us, that is pure gospel gold.

> Heavenly Father, You have promised to hear what we ask in the Name of Your Son: Accept and fulfill our petitions, we pray, not as we ask in our ignorance, nor as we deserve in our sinfulness, but as You know and love us in Your Son Jesus Christ our Lord. Amen. (The Collect at the Prayers – BCP p. 394)

March 2

THE GREAT JAZZ SAXOPHONIST Charlie Parker once told aspiring musicians, "You've got to learn your instrument. Then, you practice, practice, practice. And then, when you finally get up there on the bandstand, forget all that and just wail."

That isn't too far from what Jesus said about the difficult or conflicted situations in which we find ourselves put on the spot.

"When they deliver you over, do not be anxious how you are to speak or what you are to say, for what you are to say will be given to you in that hour. For it is not you who speak, but the Spirit of your Father speaking through you" (Matthew 10:19–20, ESV).

Jesus is speaking specifically about persecution, but the promise holds for us in all situations. The Holy Spirit is with you and will provide for you in your moment of need.

> Almighty and most merciful God, grant that by the indwelling of Your Holy Spirit we may be enlightened and strengthened for Your service; through Jesus Christ our Lord, who lives and reigns with You, in the unity of the Holy Spirit, one God, now and for ever. Amen. (Of the Holy Spirit – BCP p. 251)

March 3

THE LECTIONARY READINGS AND the appointed collects for the Sundays in Lent are chock full of theological nutrients. Today's collect for the first Sunday in Lent is the perfect example. We recognize that we are not alone in the cosmic theater of the universe. Satan, who tempted Jesus in the wilderness, assaults us with temptation too. And as our experience attests, willpower wanes in the face of the onslaught. Weaknesses win.

Thankfully, God knows the weaknesses of each of us. In the Garden of Gethsemane, Jesus pleaded with His friends to stay awake with Him in His time of anguish. *"Watch and pray that you may not enter into temptation. The spirit indeed is willing, but the flesh is weak" (Matthew 26:41, ESV).* And yet, three times in a row, they could not keep their eyes open. The flesh is weak.

Thankfully, we are not left alone! God is mighty to save. And we are always, always, always right to ask Him to come quickly to our aid.

Almighty God, whose blessed Son was led by the Spirit to be tempted by Satan: Come quickly to help us who are assaulted by many temptations; and, as You know the weaknesses of each of us, let each one find You mighty to save; through Jesus Christ Your Son our Lord, who lives and reigns with You and the Holy Spirit, one God, now and for ever. Amen. (First Sunday in Lent – BCP p. 218)

March 4

BACK TO THE JAZZ world for more Almost Daily inspiration. This time we hear from the master saxophonist Sonny Rollins. He said, "I'm not supposed to be playing; the music is supposed to be playing me. I'm just supposed to be standing there with the horn, moving my fingers. The music is supposed to be coming through me; that's when it's really happening."

Friends, God is real. He is present and active today through His Holy Spirit. You do not face a single day, a single moment alone. And that is because you are never alone. As St. Paul says, *"Do you not know that you are God's temple and that God's Spirit dwells in you?" (1 Corinthians 3:16, ESV).*

How about a prayer to help us remember that God is present, active, helpful, and always with us?

Almighty and most merciful God, grant that by the indwelling of Your Holy Spirit we may be enlightened and strengthened for Your service; through Jesus Christ our Lord, who lives and reigns with You, in the unity of the Holy Spirit, one God, now and for ever. Amen. (Of the Holy Spirit – BCP p. 251)

March 5

"And Zechariah said to the angel, 'How shall I know this? For I am an old man, and my wife is advanced in years.' And the angel answered him, 'I am Gabriel. I stand in the presence of God, and I was sent to speak to you and to bring you this good news. And behold, you will be silent and unable to speak until the day that these things take place, because you did not believe my words, which will be fulfilled in their time'" (Luke 1:18–20, ESV).

ZECHARIAH WAS STRUCK MUTE when he asked the angel Gabriel for some verification of the pronouncement that Elizabeth would bear a son in her old age. It is hard not to have some sympathy for Zechariah—who doesn't want some certainty?

Be that as it may, being struck mute has a salutary effect on you and everyone around you. How many times have I assessed a situation and overzealously announced a conclusion which turned out to be faulty? It seems to me that a pandemic of muteness might be just what the Doctor—or the Great Physician—ordered for such a loud time in our nation's history. Elvis Costello once sang to "Alison" (1977), "Sometimes I wish that I could stop you from talking / When I hear the silly things that you say."

Might the course of wisdom be to bury our heads in the sand so we have a better chance of hearing the footsteps of Him who brings Good News? After all, God's aim is true.

Almighty God, You proclaim Your truth in every age by many voices: Direct, in our time, we pray, those who speak where many listen and write what many read; that they may do their part in making the heart of this people wise, its mind sound, and its will righteous; to the honor of Jesus Christ our Lord. Amen. (For those who Influence Public Opinion – BCP p. 827)

March 6

THE MEMOIRIST MARY KARR gives us a helpful reminder when she says, "A dysfunctional family is any family with more than one person in it." That's a biblical insight. Because we are all dysfunctional. In other words, none of us functions the way we are meant to function. There is always a wrench in the works, a hitch in the giddy-up, a snake in the grass. Sin always is at work.

Time once again for Paul's great insight: *"I do not understand what I do. For what I want to do I do not do, but what I hate I do" (Romans 7:15, NIV).* To truly understand our own dysfunction is to have compassion on another's dysfunction. And it makes the day go, if not easy, at least easier.

Almighty God, You know that we have no power in ourselves to help ourselves: Keep us both outwardly in our bodies and inwardly in our souls, that we may be defended from all adversities which may happen to the body, and from all evil thoughts which may assault and hurt the soul; through Jesus Christ our Lord, who lives and reigns with You and the Holy Spirit, one God, for ever and ever. Amen. (Third Sunday in Lent – BCP p. 218)

March 7

A *NEW YORKER* CARTOON pictures a man drowning in a river with Lassie on the bank. "Lassie! Get help!" yells the man. In the next frame we see Lassie getting help—she is lying on a shrink's couch unpacking her neuroses.

Everyone needs to get help in one way or another. Ultimately, directly or derivatively, our help comes from God. As the psalmist writes, *"I lift up my eyes to the hills. From where does my help come? My help comes from the Lord, who made heaven and earth"* *(Psalm 121: 1-2, ESV).*

> O Lord our God, accept our prayers; in the multitude of your mercies, look with compassion upon us and all who turn to you for help; for you are gracious, O lover of souls, and to you we give glory, Father, Son, and Holy Spirit, now and for ever. Amen. (Collect at the Prayers – BCP)

March 8

THE POET OGDEN NASH once said, "Every New Year is the direct descendent, isn't it, of a long line of proven criminals?" Funny. True.

Sometimes it does feel like things just don't change. And on the one hand that's true. Sin is sin, and humans are humans. And as we age, we learn that we do not have the internal power to effect lasting change in ourselves and the world around us.

But, on the other hand, the world is *filled* with possibilities! That's because God is God, and He is hard at work in your life. Here is the best summary of life that I know: *Jesus looked at them intently and said, "Humanly speaking, it is impossible. But not with God. Everything is possible with God" (Matthew 10:27).*

> Lord of all power and might, the author and giver of all good things: Graft in our hearts the love of your Name; increase in us true religion; nourish us with all goodness; and bring forth in us the fruit of good works; through Jesus Christ our Lord, who lives and reigns with you and the Holy Spirit, one God, for ever and ever. Amen. (Proper 17 – BCP)

March 9

WHAT IS UNRESOLVED IN your life? How does that feel? Unresolved issues are more difficult for some personality types than others, but no one loves tangled knots. Mystery writer P.D. James once said that during times of stress and crisis, more people read murder mysteries. The reason is fairly obvious—there is always a resolution at the end.

The cross of Christ both is and isn't a resolution. It will not solve this life's fractured and disassociated parts. On the other hand, all those fractured and disassociated parts meld together in His hands, feet, and side.

"When you were dead in your sins and in the uncircumcision of your flesh, God made you alive with Christ. He forgave us all our sins, having canceled the charge of our legal indebtedness, which stood against us and condemned us; He has taken it away, nailing it to the cross. And having disarmed the powers and authorities, He made a public spectacle of them, triumphing over them by the cross" (Colossians 2:13–15, NIV).

> We humbly beseech Thee, O Father, mercifully to look upon our infirmities; and, for the glory of Thy Name,

turn from us all those evils that we most justly have deserved; and grant that in all our troubles we may put our whole trust and confidence in Thy mercy, and evermore serve Thee in holiness and pureness of living, to Thy honor and glory; through our only Mediator and Advocate, Jesus Christ our Lord. Amen. (The Great Litany – BCP p. 155)

March 10

IN THEIR 1984 HIT, Depeche Mode sang, "People are people, so why should it be / You and I should get along so awfully?" The answer is in the question: People are people. Scripture clearly teaches that the problem with human nature is congenital, rather than environmental.

"And He called the people to Him again and said to them, 'Hear Me, all of you, and understand: There is nothing outside a person that by going into him can defile him, but the things that come out of a person are what defile him'.... And He said, 'What comes out of a person is what defiles him. For from within, out of the heart of man, come evil thoughts'" (Mark 7:14–15, 20–21, ESV).

That is straight from the lips of Jesus, and I cut the list of all the particular varieties of evil that come out of us WAY short, because I would hate to ruin your week. But the point is that the problem is not *out there*; it's *in here* (I'm pointing to myself)! Therefore, the problem will not be solved by a change of environment; it can only be addressed by a change of heart.

That's what King David understood all those centuries ago when he prayed, *"Create in me a clean heart, O God; and renew a right spirit within me" (Psalm 51:10, KJV).* And that is still a timeless and timely prayer.

Almighty and everlasting God, You hate nothing You have made and forgive the sins of all who are penitent: Create and make in us new and contrite hearts, that we, worthily lamenting our sins and acknowledging our wretchedness, may obtain of You, the God of all mercy, perfect remission and forgiveness; through Jesus Christ our Lord, who lives and reigns with You and Holy Spirit, one God, for ever and ever. Amen. (Ash Wednesday Collect – BCP p. 264)

March 11

"Rejoice with those who rejoice, weep with those who weep" (Romans 12:15, ESV).

I CAME ACROSS A term that resonated—"toxic positivity." That's the voice that rushes in (from others or from yourself) to say that you should always be grateful for what you have rather than sorrowful for what you don't have. The voice that tells you to count your blessings when you're at your most raw. The voice that says your difficulties pale in comparison with "real suffering."

Gratitude is a wonderful gift from God. But it can be weaponized to avoid facing and working through grief, anger, and frustration. I believe that weeping is sometimes the deeper gift, the needful gift.

Everybody hurts, sometimes. (R.E.M.)

Grant to all who suffer a sure confidence in Thy fatherly care, that, casting all their grief on Thee, they may know the consolations of Thy love. Amen. (Prayers in the Burial Liturgy – BCP p. 481)

March 12

I LOVE THE FOLLOWING description of an accomplished but empty man, from *The Warmth of Other Suns* by Isabel Wilkerson. Having attained worldly and material success, he "was unable to fill up on what he had acquired any more than he could carry fog in his satchel." A good example of St. Augustine's God-shaped hole in the human heart.

Jesus said it first: *"The thief comes only to steal and kill and destroy. I came that they may have life and have it abundantly" (John 10:10, ESV).* In other words, what the world promises will fulfill us and bring us joy will actually rob us of our joy instead. Although it admittedly sounds like a bumper sticker, it is nonetheless enduringly true that life, peace, rest, and joy are found in Jesus Christ.

> Heavenly Father, in You we live and move and have our being: We humbly pray You so to guide and govern us by Your Holy Spirit, that in all the cares and occupations of our life we may not forget You, but may remember that we are ever walking in Your sight; through Jesus Christ our Lord. Amen. (A Collect for Guidance – BCP p. 100)

March 13

AT ONE POINT, SEVERAL elementary-aged children were using one of our rooms at Christ Church for school. On the white board, the teacher wrote these questions to be answered: "What do you love doing? Why?" We had our staff meeting in this room and decided to answer these questions ourselves.

I won't go on about the staff's enjoyment of both food and drink, but I wonder if you want to take a moment to answer those questions yourself. To delight in pleasure is to delight in the God who created us to experience pleasure. In C. S. Lewis' *The Screwtape Letters,* I love the demon Screwtape's warning to Wormwood, who is in charge of a man's temptation.

"Never forget that when we are dealing with any pleasure in its healthy and normal and satisfying form, we are, in a sense, on the Enemy's [God's] ground... He [God] made the pleasure: all our research so far has not enabled us to produce one."

If you still aren't convinced, turn to Scripture instead: *"Go, eat your bread with joy, and drink your wine with a cheerful heart, for God has already approved your works" (Ecclesiastes 9:7, BSB).*

Blessed are You, O Lord God, King of the Universe, for You give us food to sustain our lives and make our hearts glad; through Jesus Christ our Lord. Amen. (Grace at Meals – BCP p. 835)

March 14

MY ANSWER TO YESTERDAY's question (What do you love doing and why?) has to do with standing in rivers. It's not just because rivers are where the fish are. It is also because rivers take me out of myself, out of the echo chamber of my mind. There is an unfortunately titled book about self-discovery (and the Enneagram) called *The Road Back to You.* More times than not, that is a road I DO NOT want to be on!

While there is something to be said for being self-aware (knowing social cues, understanding how you impact others), there is more to be said about being *un*self-aware. Being other- and God-centered, rather than self-centered.

When Jesus said, *"Do not let your left hand know what your right hand is doing" (Matthew 6:3),* He was talking about giving to the needy. But it applies beautifully to life in general.

May your life road lead you out of yourself!

> Almighty and eternal God, so draw our hearts to Thee, so guide our minds, so fill our imaginations, so control our wills, that we may be wholly Thine, utterly dedicated unto Thee; and then use us, we pray Thee, as Thou wilt, and always to Thy glory and the welfare of Thy people; through our Lord and Savior Jesus Christ. Amen. (A Prayer of Self-Dedication – BCP p. 832)

March 15

"BEWARE THE IDES OF March." You've likely heard this warning that the soothsayer gives to Julius Caesar in Shakespeare's play of the same name. March 15th was the date of Caesar's assassination. It was also the date set in Rome for collecting debts. The karmic laws were in full force: time to reap what you have sown. Time to pay the piper.

Grace is the only power that can undo karma (aka the Law). As the Irish poet (Bono) reminds us, "[Grace] travels outside of karma." Yes, beware—the wages of sin is death. Yet as St. Paul says, *"God's law was given so that all people could see how sinful they were. But as people sinned more and more, God's wonderful grace became more abundant" (Romans 5:20, NLT).* Amen!

> Remember, O Lord, what You have wrought in us and not what we deserve; and, as You have called us to Your service, make us worthy of our calling; through Jesus Christ our Lord, who lives and reigns with You and the Holy Spirit, one God, now and for ever. Amen. (Proper 1 – BCP p. 228)

March 16

*"The L*ORD *is good to those whose hope is in Him, to the one who seeks Him; it is good to wait quietly for the salvation of the L*ORD*" (Lamentations 3:25–26, NIV).*

TREEBEARD, THE ANCIENT AND wizened Ent in Tolkien's *The Lord of the Rings,* says, "Things will go as they will go. There is no hurry to meet them." How often have you wanted some future moment to "hurry up and get here"? But things will go as they will go. And the One who makes them go at His own pace is none other than the God who loves you—the God whose timing is always perfect.

Amen.

O God of peace, who hast taught us that in returning and rest we shall be saved, in quietness and confidence shall be our strength: By the might of Thy Spirit lift us, we pray Thee, to Thy presence, where we may be still and know that Thou art God; through Jesus Christ our Lord. Amen. (For Quiet Confidence – BCP p. 832)

March 17

ST. PATRICK'S DAY COMMEMORATES the death day of the sixteen-year-old boy who was kidnapped from England by raiders and taken as a slave to Ireland. He spent six years as a shepherd there and, in his own words, "found God." He went back to England, got ordained as a priest, then returned to Ireland to spread the good news of the gospel.

The counterintuitive ways of God are evident in St. Patrick's story. It is in returning to, rather than avoiding, the places of difficulty and sorrow that we find healing and joy. When Joseph was sold into slavery by his brothers, God was at work for good. As he told his brothers, *"You meant evil against me, but God meant it for good, to bring it about that many people should be kept alive, as they are today" (Genesis 50:20, ESV).*

Hear, hear! Put on your green and raise a glass today to the mysterious ways of God!

> Almighty God, in Your providence You chose Your servant Patrick to be the apostle to the Irish people, to bring those who were wandering in darkness and error to the true light and knowledge of You: Grant us so to walk in that way that we may come at last to the light of everlasting life; through Jesus Christ our Lord, who lives and reigns with You and the Holy Spirit, one God, for ever and ever. Amen. (Collect for Patrick of Ireland)

March 18

WHAT YOU HEAR MATTERS. And you can't turn off your hearing at will, like you can your sight (close your eyes). If you cover your ears with your hands, some sounds always seep through.

Shakespeare's symbolism is front and center when Claudius murders his brother, King Hamlet, by pouring poison into his ear. "And in the porches of my ears did pour / The leperous distilment." The lethal liquid entered through the porch of the ear and went directly to the chamber of the King's heart. So too do words, especially when injurious. There is a *New York Times* cartoon of a woman on stage, having just performed, and the crowd is cheering wildly, except for one person—and the woman thinks, "They hated me!"

God's symbolism is front and center as well in Jesus Christ, who is the Word of God. *"In the beginning was the Word, and the Word was with God, and the Word was God" (John 1:1).*

God pursues us—not even noise-canceling headphones can keep Him out. *"And the Word became flesh and dwelt among us, and we have seen His glory, glory as of the only Son from the Father, full of grace and truth" (John 1:14, ESV).*

The Word of God—full of grace and truth—goes directly to your heart and brings life. Christ is God's wild applause for you. One day, that is all we will be able to hear and all that will matter.

> Blessed Lord, who caused all holy Scriptures to be written for our learning: Grant us so to hear them, read, mark, learn, and inwardly digest them, that we may embrace and ever hold fast the blessed hope of everlasting life, which You have given us in our Savior Jesus Christ; who lives and reign with You and the Holy Spirit, one God, for ever and ever. Amen. (Proper 28 – BCP p. 236)

March 19

"THIS IS THE DAY that the LORD has made; we will rejoice and be glad in it" (Psalm 118:24, BSB). This psalmist's verse rings Vacation Bible School bells for many people. If you can put aside the jingle and the familiarity, the words of that scripture are so meaningful. God has made the day. God has ordained the contents of the day. God is present with you in whatever the day will bring.

Rejoicing in the day does not mean living each moment with a forced cheeriness, especially when those moments evoke grief or sadness or seriousness. Instead, to rejoice in the day means abiding in the knowledge that nothing is random and that God is working in and through all circumstances. To be glad in the day is to trust in what the psalmist says at the beginning of the psalm: *"Out of my distress I called on the LORD; the LORD answered me and set me in a broad place. With the LORD on my side I do not fear. What can mortals do to me? The LORD is on my side to help me"* *(Psalm 118:5–7, NRSV).*

> This is another day, O Lord. I know not what it will bring forth, but make me ready, Lord for whatever it may be. If I am to stand up, help me stand bravely. If I am to sit still, help me do it quietly. If I am to lie low, help me to do it patiently. And if I am to do nothing, let me do it gallantly. Make these words more than words, and give me the Spirit of Jesus. Amen. (Prayers for use by a Sick Person: In the Morning – BCP p. 461)

March 20

EVEN THE EXPERTS GET things wrong. Here's Flannery O'Connor on *To Kill A Mockingbird:* "It's interesting that all the folks that are buying it don't know they're reading a child's book."

Maybe she was jealous of the Pulitzer Prize? More likely she was cleaving to her own strong sensibilities. Being wrong is wonderful. Not knowing an answer is wonderful, too. The other day I was asked a theological question—which, BTW, always masks an emotional or psychological issue. It was long, rambly question; more statement than question. Finally, he said, "Well, what is the answer?" "I don't have an answer," I said. "Why don't you have an answer? You of all people should have an answer." I said, "I'm sorry. I don't have an answer." "You're really not going to give me an answer?" "No, I would if I had one, but I don't have an answer."

You've heard the prophet before, I bet. *"For My thoughts are not your thoughts, neither are your ways My ways,' declares the LORD. 'As the heavens are higher than the earth, so are My ways higher than your ways and My thoughts than your thoughts'" (Isaiah 55:8–9, NIV).*

I'm more than good with that.

> Let Your continual mercy, O Lord, cleanse and defend
> Your Church; and, because it cannot continue in safety
> without Your help, protect and govern it always by Your
> goodness; through Jesus Christ our Lord, who lives and
> reigns with You and the Holy Spirit, one God, for ever
> and ever. Amen. (Proper 13 – BCP p. 232)

March 21

JESUS FAMOUSLY SAYS THAT we are to be like little children in order to enter the kingdom of heaven. That saying is like a diamond that can eternally be turned to reveal a new facet.

One facet of little children is their total inattention to time. Children do not plan for the next day. (Hmm … *Whatever* am I going to have for snack time tomorrow?) They tend not to worry about what happened the day before. They do not worry about what will happen in the future. As children get older, those thoughts creep in. But remember that Jesus is talking about *little* children.

You are a child. Yes, you might be a teen or young adult or middle-aged, or long in the tooth. But fundamentally you are a child—a little child with a Father who is in charge of your life.

Jesus says, *"Take therefore no thought for the morrow: for the morrow shall take thought for the things of itself" (Matthew 6:34, KJV).*

> Grant us, Lord, not to be anxious about earthly things,
> but to love things heavenly; and even now, while we
> are placed among things that are passing away, to hold

fast to those that shall endure; through Jesus Christ our Lord, who lives and reigns with You and the Holy Spirit, one God, for ever and ever. Amen. (Proper 20 – BCP p. 234)

March 22

I LOVE WHAT THOMAS JEFFERSON said about Patrick Henry's oratory skills: "His eloquence was peculiar, if indeed it should be called eloquence; for it was impressive and sublime, beyond what can be imagined. Although it was difficult when he had spoken to tell what he had said, yet, while he was speaking, it always seemed directly to the point. When he had spoken in opposition to my opinion… I myself had been highly delighted and moved, [and] I have asked myself when he ceased: 'What the devil has he said?' I could never answer the inquiry." Ha!

In contradistinction to the man who said "give me liberty or give me death" at St. John's church in Richmond, the Apostle Paul said, *"When I came to you, I did not come with eloquence or human wisdom as I proclaimed to you the testimony about God. For I resolved to know nothing while I was with you except Jesus Christ and Him crucified. I came to you in weakness with great fear and trembling. My message and my preaching were not with wise and persuasive words, but with a demonstration of the Spirit's power, so that your faith might not rest on human wisdom, but on God's power"* *(1 Corinthians 2:1–5, NIV).*

What does the hymn say? "My hope is built on nothing less than Jesus' blood and righteousness."

Almighty God, You have built Your Church upon the foundation of the apostles and prophets, Jesus Christ Himself being the chief cornerstone: Grant us to be joined together in unity of spirit by their teaching, that we may be made a holy temple acceptable to You; through Jesus Christ our Lord, who lives and reigns with You and the Holy Spirit, one God, for ever and ever. Amen. (Proper 8 – BCP p. 230)

March 23

I GET SPRING FEVER. In other words, I experience it, and I understand it. Don't you? The itch to shuck off responsibility? The urge to go outside, preferably somewhere warm? The desire to not do what you have to do? In the movie *Parenthood*, Steve Martin is asked by his wife if he "has to" go on a business trip when their son has a game. Martin responds, "My whole life is 'have to.'"

It is true that in this world, adults "have to" be adults. But as far as God goes, all "ought-to"s and "have-to"s are off! Jesus did all the have-tos and ought-tos for us. As Paul says, *"For Christ has already accomplished the purpose for which the law was given. As a result, all who believe in Him are made right with God" (Romans 10:4, NLT).*

Time to go outside.

Almighty God, whose blessed Son was led by the Spirit to be tempted by Satan: Come quickly to help us who are assaulted by many temptations; and, as You know the weaknesses of each of us, let each one find You mighty to save; through Jesus Christ Your Son our Lord, who lives and reigns with You and the Holy Spirit, one God, now and for ever. Amen. (First Sunday in Lent – BCP p. 218)

March 24

ONE OF THE CONSEQUENCES of Original Sin is the onset of spiritual myopia. Technically, myopia is nearsightedness, and it is correctable with a good set of glasses. Metaphorically, myopia is the inability to see anything other than what's right in front of your nose. Myopic people (all of us!) see a set of close-up "facts" and draw all kinds of hard-set conclusions, ignoring (blind to) the teeming universe of other factors at play in any given situation.

This affliction has been with us since the dawn of time. This is why the Apostle Paul reminds us that *"we walk by faith, not by sight" (2 Corinthians 5:7).* Earlier he says, *"We fix our eyes not on what is seen, but on what is unseen. For what is seen is temporary, but what is unseen is eternal" (2 Corinthians 4:18, BSB).* And finally, the author of the letter to the Hebrews tells us that *"faith is the assurance of what we hope for and the certainty of what we do not see" (Hebrews 11:1, BSB).*

We only see in part, but thankfully, God sees the big picture.

O God, who on the holy mount revealed to chosen witnesses Your well-beloved Son, wonderfully transfigured, in raiment white and glistening: Mercifully grant that we, being delivered from the disquietude of this world, may by faith behold the King in His beauty; who with You, O Father, and You, O Holy Spirit, lives and reigns, one God, for ever and ever. Amen. (The Transfiguration – BCP p. 243)

March 25

"He makes me lie down in green pastures; He leads me beside still waters" (Psalm 23:2, NRSV).

MANY OF US HAVE a love-hate relationship with rest. On the one hand, we are desperate for true rest. On the other hand, when a time for rest comes, we are too anxious/unjustified/afraid to be alone with ourselves to actually do so. Rest = a little death, and we will fight death tooth and nail.

I suppose that is why the Good Shepherd "makes" me lie down in green pastures. And yet, sometimes it's hard not to plan the next move, even while the waters are still.

> O God of peace, who hast taught us that in returning and rest we shall be saved, in quietness and confidence shall be our strength: By the might of Thy Spirit lift us, we pray Thee, to Thy presence, where we may be still and know that Thou art God; through Jesus Christ our Lord. Amen. (For Quiet Confidence – BCP p. 832)

March 26

THE COLLECT FOR MONDAY in Holy Week reminds us that before Jesus "went up to joy, … first He suffered pain." Then we pray what seems like an odd prayer, that we might walk "in the way of the cross." This might seem morose or masochistic at first, until we realize that life is inevitably full of suffering. By default, to live life is, in some degree, to walk in the way of the cross.

The Palm Sunday liturgy in the Book of Common Prayer invites us to the "contemplation of those mighty acts" of our Lord during Holy Week. Increased focus on Jesus' suffering and pain has always seemed unprofitable to me, especially as the biblical accounts of His crucifixion do not excessively dwell on the physicality of His death. But this scene from Willa Cather's *Death Comes for the Archbishop* sheds some helpful light.

Jean Marie Latour, Missionary Bishop to New Mexico in the late 1800s, is lost in the desert, nearly dead from thirst. He spots a ten-foot-high juniper tree that looks exactly like a cross. He dismounts his horse, bows before the tree, and prays. "His devotions lasted perhaps half an hour, and when he rose he looked refreshed... He reminded himself of that cry, wrung from his Saviour on the cross, *J'ai soif [I thirst]!*... [T]he young priest blotted himself out of his own consciousness and meditated upon the anguish of his Lord. The Passion of Jesus became for him the only reality; the need of his own body was but a part of that conception."

The way of the cross inevitably comes to us; thankfully it has been walked already by the One who absorbs our suffering into His own gracious and redemptive care. *"If we have died with Christ, we believe that we will also live with Him" (Romans 6:8, ESV).*

May God's peace permeate your hearts as we near Holy Week.

Almighty and everliving God, in Your tender love for the human race You sent Your Son our Savior Jesus Christ to take upon Him our nature, and to suffer death upon the cross, giving us the example of His great humility: Mercifully grant that we may walk in the way of His suffering, and also share in His resurrection; through Jesus Christ our Lord, who lives and reigns with You and the Holy Spirit, one God, for ever and ever. Amen. (The Sunday of the Passion: Palm Sunday – BCP p. 219)

March 27

"Six days before the Passover Jesus came to Bethany, the home of Lazarus, whom He had raised from the dead. There they gave a dinner for Him. Martha

served, and Lazarus was one of those at the table with Him. Mary took a pound of costly perfume made of pure nard, anointed Jesus' feet, and wiped them with her hair. The house was filled with the fragrance of the perfume" (John 12:1–3, NRSV).

THIS SCENE, OCCURRING ON Monday of Holy Week, is one of the most riveting in the Bible. The pound of pure nard was an heirloom, a trust fund, the family IRA. So, there's that.

But here's what I like to believe. The fragrance of the perfume clung to Jesus all through His final week, right up to His death on the cross. Even as He cried, "My God, My God, why have You forsaken Me?" He was comforted by the aroma of the love and devotion poured out by Mary.

> Almighty God, whose most dear Son went not up to joy but first He suffered pain, and entered not into glory before He was crucified: Mercifully grant that we, walking in the way of the cross, may find it none other than the way of life and peace; through Jesus Christ Your Son our Lord, who lives and reigns with You and the Holy Spirit, one God, for ever and ever. Amen. (Monday in Holy Week – BCP p. 220)

March 28

IN THE EPISTLE READING for Tuesday in Holy Week, St. Paul writes, *"The message about the cross is foolishness to those who are perishing, but to us who are being saved it is the power of God" (1 Corinthians 1:18, NRSV).*

In her magnum opus, *The Crucifixion*, Fleming Rutledge tells us why the cross was necessary. She says that crucifixion was a ghastly form of torture reserved for those considered subhuman. Why, then, did the Son of God have to die this way?

Here is her sober and unflinching answer:

> There is something sickening in human nature, and it corresponds precisely to the sickening aspects of crucifixion. The hideousness of the crucifixion summons us to put away sentimentality and face up to the ugliness that lies just under the surface. The scandal, the outrage of the cross, is commensurate with the offense and the ubiquity of sin.

G. K. Chesterton understood that. In a piece on the *Daily News* he wrote, "The answer to the question, 'What is Wrong?' is, or should be, 'I am wrong.' Until a man can give that answer his idealism is only a hobby."

Holy Tuesday offers us a timeless reminder that we ourselves cannot eradicate the enemy within (sin). The only hope is *"Christ the power of God and the wisdom of God" (1 Corinthians 1:24)*, whose blood was shed for you and me on "an instrument of shameful death."

> O God, by the passion of Your blessed Son You made an instrument of shameful death to be for us the means of life: Grant us so to glory in the cross of Christ, that we may gladly suffer shame and loss for the sake of Your Son our Savior Jesus Christ; who lives and reigns with You and the Holy Spirit, one God, for ever and ever. Amen. (Tuesday in Holy Week – BCP p. 220)

March 29

*"Therefore, since we are surrounded by so great a cloud
of witnesses, let us also lay aside every weight and the
sin that clings so closely, and let us run with perseverance the race that is set before us, looking to Jesus
the pioneer and perfecter of our faith, who for the sake
of the joy that was set before Him endured the cross,
disregarding its shame, and has taken His seat at the
right hand of the throne of God. Consider Him who
endured such hostility against Himself from sinners, so
that you may not grow weary or lose heart" (Hebrews
12:1–3, NRSV).*

THE EPISTLE READING FOR Wednesday in Holy Week addresses
the reality of growing weary and losing heart in the face of a
long slog of suffering or difficulty. The author of the letter to the
Hebrews tells us that our help is found in where we look.

The common imperative is to look deep within ourselves to
summon the strength to knuckle through adversity. "Be strong."
That's cold comfort, if you ask me, for more often than not looking deep within myself reveals a bevy of unhelpful emotions: fear,
self-preservation, short-temperedness, and weakness. The second
avenue of help is to look out into the world, seeking signs of
positivity. I admit that I do this every day! If there is a bit of
good news, then my step is lighter. Ultimately, however, our stability and security—our "joy," as the Scripture says—can not and
should not be tied to the ebb and flow of daily information.

So, where do we look for help? "Looking to Jesus" is the surest bet when you are growing weary or losing heart. Looking to
Jesus, who is the "pioneer and perfecter of our faith." That means
that He starts and finishes faith for you. It is not up to you to be
strong, for He has been and will be strong for you. You don't need

to be dependent on the day's good news, because the good news of the gospel has been accomplished once for all. Fixing your eyes on Him gives you the blinders you need to get through the day.

> Lord God, whose blessed Son our Savior gave His body to be whipped and His face to be spit upon: Give us grace to accept joyfully the sufferings of the present time, confident of the glory that shall be revealed; through Jesus Christ Your Son our Lord, who lives and reigns with You and the Holy Spirit, one God, for ever and ever. Amen. (Wednesday in Holy Week – BCP p. 220)

March 30

> *"For I received from the Lord what I also handed on to you, that the Lord Jesus on the night when He was betrayed took a loaf of bread, and when He had given thanks, He broke it and said, 'This is My body that is for you. Do this in remembrance of Me.' In the same way He took the cup also, after supper, saying, 'This cup is the new covenant in My blood. Do this, as often as you drink it, in remembrance of Me.' For as often as you eat this bread and drink the cup, you proclaim the Lord's death until He comes" (1 Corinthians 11:23–26, NRSV).*

HAVE YOU EVER FOUND it odd that every time you take communion you are participating in a death? Or in Paul's words from today's reading, you "proclaim" death?

Death is news. When a famous person dies, we see it on print and screen. When a not-so-famous person dies, we read about it in the obituary section. Jesus' death is the biggest news of all, of course. His death equals your forgiveness, the world's forgiveness. And as there is so much to forgive on both fronts, we proclaim that death every Sunday.

> Almighty Father, whose dear Son, on the night before He suffered, instituted the Sacrament of His Body and Blood: Mercifully grant that we may receive it thankfully in remembrance of Jesus Christ our Lord, who in these holy mysteries gives us a pledge of eternal life; and who now lives and reigns with You and the Holy Spirit, one God, for ever and ever. Amen. (Collect for Maundy Thursday – BCP p. 221)

March 31

> *"Then He took a cup, and after giving thanks He gave it to them, saying, 'Drink from it, all of you; for this is My blood of the covenant, which is poured out for many for the forgiveness of sins'" (Matthew 26:27–28, NRSV).*

IN HIS POEM "East Coker," T. S. Eliot writes,

> The dripping blood our only drink,
> The bloody flesh our only food:
> In spite of which we like to think
> That we are sound, substantial flesh and blood—
> Again, in spite of that, we call this Friday good.

We are not inherently sound. Otherwise, Jesus would not have gone to the cross. But He did go to the cross. It is *crucial* (the word meaning "important," which is derived from Latin's *crux*, or "cross") that you understand the personal significance of Good Friday.

He died for you. For a moment, forget that He died for the sins of the world. Today, drink deeply of the dripping blood, poured out for you.

Almighty God, we pray You graciously to behold this Your family, for whom our Lord Jesus Christ was willing to be betrayed, and given into the hands of sinners, and to suffer death upon the cross; who now lives and reigns with You and the Holy Spirit, one God, for ever and ever. Amen. (Good Friday – BCP p. 221)

APRIL

April 1

"God helps those who help themselves" (Jude 2:14, AFV).

IN THE END, WE must rely on our own efforts in life. There is a reason you have bootstraps. Use them.

You have already been given so much—God naturally expects you to maximize your potential. If you do that, then you will be able to work your way into His favor. Make sure to do a rigorous moral inventory morning, noon, and night. If you keep yourself free of sin and wrongdoing, you will be rewarded with prosperity and the absence of problems.

Pray if you must—as a last resort—but don't show your weakness.

> God, I thank You that I am not like other people. I am upright and holy and deserving of Your blessing. Thank You for helping me help myself. Amen.

April 2

"But when He, the Spirit of truth, comes, He will guide you into all the truth" (John 16:13, NIV).

WHEN I FIRST SHARED yesterday's April Fools' devotional over email, I received a torrent of feedback from readers ("This is all wrong!" "What has happened to you?!" and my personal favorite, "I don't know Paul Walker, and I'm going to keep it that way!"). It is safe to say that theology matters. Theology isn't just a head trip; God's truth steadies and stabilizes us.

So fear not! Not one word of the April 1st devotional is true!

O God, whose Son Jesus is the good shepherd of Your people: Grant that when we hear His voice we may know Him who calls us each by name, and follow where He leads; who, with You and the Holy Spirit, lives and reigns, one God, for ever and ever. Amen. (Fourth Sunday of Easter – BCP p. 225)

April 3

"You seek Jesus of Nazareth, who was crucified. He is risen! He is not here" (Mark 16:6, NKJV).

JESUS' RESURRECTION FROM THE dead means everything. In other words, everything depends on the empty tomb. Easter does more than redeem the unspeakable damage of Good Friday. That He is risen validates our atonement and secures our eternal life.

He is risen! That means everything *right now.* The little "d" deaths you are experiencing right now in your life have been redeemed. Every single one of them. Not *will be* redeemed but *have already been* redeemed. In light of Christ's resurrection, all loss is only a portal to restoration beyond your wildest dreams.

I can say this with supreme confidence and assurance for one reason: He is risen!

Almighty God, who through Your only-begotten Son Jesus Christ overcame death and opened to us the gate of everlasting life: Grant that we, who celebrate with joy the day of the Lord's resurrection, may be raised from the death of sin by Your life-giving Spirit; through Jesus Christ our Lord, who lives and reigns with You and the Holy Spirit, one God, now and for ever. Amen. (Collect for Easter Day – BCP p. 222)

April 4

I'VE BEEN A FLY-FISHERMAN for a long time now. I know most of the basic flies. But when it comes to variations of the same or similar dry flies, I'm still lost. I know what a caddis is, but what is an x caddis again? Hackles? Parachutes? Emergers? I've got books and flashcards and online tutorials, but when I'm on the water, trying to identify the hatch and choose the right fly, I'm befuddled more times than not. Although the flies may look "close enough" to me, the trout, especially brook trout, know the difference. That's why I like to fish with my friend, Tommy. I'll just throw what he's throwing!

Thank you for listening to me talk about fishing for a while. You have your own inabilities to master even the things you love to do. Thankfully, the gospel is not like fly-fishing! The gospel is easy. A newcomer to the faith told me she was also new to playing golf, so she looked forward to learning about both the faith and golf. My response: CHRISTIANITY IS WAY EASIER THAN GOLF!

That's because there is nothing to master about the gospel. The gospel is not about what you do, but what has been done for you. Here's one beautiful distillation of our faith: Jesus says, *"Come to Me, all you who are weary and burdened, and I will give you rest" (Matthew 11:28, NIV)*. Deep breath, tension draining out of the neck and shoulders… There's nothing difficult about that!

> Heavenly Father, in You we live and move and have our being; We humbly pray You so to guide and govern us by Your Holy Spirit, that in all the cares and occupations of our life we may not forget You, but may remember that we are ever walking in Your sight; through Jesus Christ our Lord. Amen. (A Collect for Guidance – BCP p. 100)

April 5

"'Therefore let the entire house of Israel know with certainty that God has made Him both Lord and Messiah, this Jesus whom you crucified.' Now when they heard this, they were cut to the heart and said to Peter and to the other apostles, 'Brothers, what should we do?' Peter said to them, 'Repent, and be baptized every one of you in the name of Jesus Christ so that your sins may be forgiven; and you will receive the gift of the Holy Spirit. For the promise is for you, for your children, and for all who are far away, everyone whom the Lord our God calls to Him'" (Acts 2:36–39, NRSV).

PETER'S SERMON FROM THE beginning of the book of Acts is the lectionary reading for Tuesday in Easter week. There is one phrase that stands out for me. The hearers of the sermon were "cut to the heart." Not exactly Bon Jovi's "shot through the heart," but close. This tells us that the hearing of the gospel produces an emotional reaction. Christianity is not primarily a set of facts or claims to which one gives assent (although it does involve both).

This passage shows us that there is an emotional transaction that occurs deep inside the core of a person. News is heard and absorbed—in this case we are culpably involved through our sin in the crucifixion of the Messiah. That news penetrates our defenses and causes a reaction of repentance, which, in turn, prepares us for the relief that is the forgiveness of our sin. Tears, gratitude, and being "cut to the heart," even "shot through the heart," are the happy and non-defended responses to the good news of the gospel!

O God, who by the glorious resurrection of Your Son Jesus Christ destroyed death and brought life and immortality to light: Grant that we, who have been raised with Him, may abide in His presence and rejoice in the hope of eternal glory; through Jesus Christ our Lord, to whom, with You and the Holy Spirit, be dominion and praise for ever and ever. Amen. (Tuesday in Easter Week – BCP p. 223)

April 6

THERE IS A DEEPLY affecting scene in Willa Cather's *Death Comes for the Archbishop* in which the aging Bishop Latour feels like his life and ministry have been a failure. He "had been going through one of those periods of coldness and doubt which, from his boyhood, had occasionally settled down upon his spirit and made him feel an alien, wherever he was… His prayers were empty words and brought him no refreshment. His soul had become a barren field."

I have felt this way, and I bet that you have, too. Somehow, there is great comfort in knowing that we are not alone in feeling alone! When we are unable to see the good or the true or the hopeful, this passage from Scripture may be of help: *"Now faith is the assurance of things hoped for, the conviction of things not seen. For by it the people of old received their commendation. By faith we understand that the universe was created by the word of God, so that what is seen was not made out of things that are visible"* (Hebrews 11:1–3, ESV).

Faith, which is simply trust in God, and which is a gift from God, exists in the breach between the visible and the invisible. When we feel like Bishop Latour, the visible seems to be all failure and discouragement. But faith assures us that God—"immortal, invisible, God only wise"—is at work. And He will bring all things, even and especially what we perceive to be our "failures," to perfection.

In fact, this is just what we pray for in our Collect for Wednesday in Easter week!

O God, whose blessed Son made Himself known to His disciples in the breaking of bread: Open the eyes of our faith, that we may behold Him in all His redeeming work; who lives and reigns with You, in the unity of the Holy Spirit, one God, now and for ever. Amen. (Wednesday in Easter Week – BCP p. 223)

April 7

THE LECTIONARY READING FOR Easter Thursday is Jesus' first appearance to His disciples after His resurrection. *"Jesus Himself stood among them [the disciples] and said to them, 'Peace be with you'" (Luke 24:36, NIV).* It is significant that those were His first words to them, given that the last time they were together, they had all abandoned Him. Jesus could have scolded them, used His resurrection as a "lesson" on the need to trust God, or asked them why they never listened when He predicted His resurrection. The list of available possibilities (the things parents love to say!) goes on and on.

But what He said was simply, *"Peace be with you."* That is how God works. He doesn't scold; He consoles. Anticipating His death on the cross for our sake, and His rising from the dead so that we would have eternal life, Jesus said, *"For God did not send His Son into the world to condemn the world, but to save the world through Him" (John 3:17, NIV).*

Peace be with you. God's peace is what we need—now more than ever.

The God of peace, who brought again from the dead our Lord Jesus Christ, the great Shepherd of the sheep, through the blood of the everlasting covenant: Make you perfect in every good work to do His will; working in you that which is well pleasing in His sight; through Jesus Christ, to whom be glory for ever and ever. Amen. (Prayers in the Burial Liturgy – BCP p. 486)

April 8

SPEAKING ABOUT THE WOMAN who broke into a dinner party to adore Jesus—prostrate before Him, weeping on His feet from joy and relief and perhaps sorrow for sin, drying those tears with her hair, anointing His feet with oil—Jesus says, *"Therefore I tell you, her sins, which are many, are forgiven—for she loved much. But he who is forgiven little, loves little" (Luke 7:47, ESV).*

Note what He doesn't say. He doesn't say that he who is loved little, loves little. Or he who is forgiven little, forgives little. Instead, Jesus makes a direct connection between forgiveness and love. When you truly understand the depth of God's forgiveness for your rebellion and self-consumption, then you will truly be able to love others without artifice or second thought.

The Collect for Friday in Easter Week implicitly draws that connection.

Almighty Father, who gave Your only Son to die for our sins and to rise for our justification: Give us grace so to put away the leaven of malice and wickedness, that we may always serve You in pureness of living and truth; through Jesus Christ Your Son our Lord, who lives and reigns with You and the Holy Spirit, one God, now and for ever. Amen. (Friday in Easter Week – BCP p. 224)

April 9

PEOPLE WILL SHEEPISHLY CONFESS to me that they only turned to God because of some difficulty or hardship they were facing. I tell them that that is how it works for everyone, including me! C. S. Lewis said, "Pain insists upon being attended to. God whispers to us in our pleasures, speaks in our consciences, but shouts in our pains. It is his megaphone to rouse a deaf world."

Never worry about your motive in turning to God; we all need rousing, and He takes all comers.

The psalmist agrees: *"I sought the LORD, and He answered me; He delivered me from all my fears. Those who look to Him are radiant; their faces are never covered with shame. This poor man called, and the LORD heard him; He saved him out of all his troubles"* (Psalm 34:4–6, NIV).

Lord God, almighty and everlasting Father, You have brought us in safety to this new day: Preserve us with Your mighty power, that we may not fall into sin, nor be overcome by adversity; and in all we do, direct us to the fulfilling of Your purpose; through Jesus Christ our Lord. Amen. (A Collect for Grace – BCP p. 100)

April 10

THERE IS A DESCRIPTION of Oliver Ward, a character in Wallace Stegner's *Angle of Repose*, that feels like, sounds like, hints at sanctification. "He understood human weakness… He didn't blame people." It is so easy and tempting to expect others to be perfect and to blame them for their shortcomings. All that does is drive a wedge of judgment between you and your spouse, child, friend, you name it.

People thronged to Jesus. They couldn't get enough of Him. They wanted to be near Him. One reason for this is because He understood human weakness. Here is one example. *"And He said to them [the disciples], 'Come away by yourselves to a desolate place and rest a while.' For many were coming and going, and they had no leisure even to eat. And they went away in the boat to a desolate place by themselves. Now many saw them going and recognized them, and they ran there on foot from all the towns and got there ahead of them. When He went ashore He saw a great crowd, and He had compassion on them, because they were like sheep without a shepherd. And He began to teach them many things"* (Mark 6:31–34, ESV).

Remember today the classic shorthand for the gospel: You are fully known and yet fully loved by the One who has compassion on you.

Almighty God, You know that we have no power in ourselves to help ourselves: Keep us both outwardly in our bodies and inwardly in our souls, that we may be defended from all adversities which may happen to the body, and from all evil thoughts which may assault and hurt the soul; through Jesus Christ our Lord, who lives and reigns with You and the Holy Spirit, one God, for ever and ever. Amen. (Third Sunday in Lent – BCP p. 218)

April 11

"When a Samaritan woman came to draw water, Jesus said to her, 'Will you give Me a drink?' (His disciples had gone into the town to buy food.) The Samaritan woman said to Him, 'You are a Jew and I am a Samaritan woman. How can You ask me for a drink?' (For Jews do not associate with Samaritans)" (John 4:7–9, NIV).

AUTHOR TOM WOLFE LAYS out the four key elements in gripping prose. 1) constructing scenes; 2) dialogue—lots of it; 3) carefully noting social status details—"everything from dress and furniture to the infinite status clues of speech, how one talks to superiors or inferiors ... and with what sort of accent and vocabulary"; and 4) point of view.

The Bible follows Wolfe's dictates, especially in the Gospel of John. The woman at the well meets Jesus at noon (why noon in the heat of the day?). They have a playful yet cut-to-the-heart verbal exchange (*"I have no husband." "You are right... [Y]ou have had five husbands, and the man you now have is not your husband."* The social status is front and center. *"How can You ask me for a drink?"*)

The point of view? The point of view of the Bible when taken from stem to stern is God's gracious rescue of our wayward human race. Mercy is the narrative arc.

> Almighty God, You alone can bring into order the unruly wills and affections of sinners: Grant Your people grace to love what You command and desire what You promise; that, among the swift and varied changes of the world, our hearts may surely there be fixed where true joys are to be found; through Jesus Christ our Lord, who lives and reigns with You and the Holy Spirit, one God, now and for ever. Amen. (Fifth Sunday of Lent – BCP p. 219)

April 12

SOMETIMES THE LION OF Judah takes on a much humbler form. In an interview, the writer Anne Lamott once compared the presence of Jesus to "a little stray cat":

You know, I would kind of nudge him with my feet and say, "No," because you can't let him in, because once you let him in and give him milk, you have a little cat, and I didn't want it. I lived on this tiny little houseboat at the time, and finally one day I just felt like: "Oh, whatever. You can come in."

"Here I am! I stand at the door and knock. If anyone hears My voice and opens the door, I will come in and eat with that person, and they with Me" (Revelation 3:20, NIV).

O God, by the passion of Your blessed Son You made an instrument of shameful death to be for us the means of life: Grant us so to glory in the cross of Christ, that we may gladly suffer shame and loss for the sake of Your Son our Savior Jesus Christ; who lives and reigns with You and the Holy Spirit, one God, for ever and ever. Amen. (Tuesday in Holy Week – BCP p. 220)

April 13

"The heart is deceitful above all things and beyond cure. Who can understand it?" (Jeremiah 17:9, NIV).

THE POET LORD BYRON said, "I am such a strange mélange of good and evil that it would be difficult to describe me."

That is true for all of us. Nobody is one-dimensional, as much as we would like to categorize people as good or bad, us and them. The line between good and evil runs straight through the human heart.

Could this lead to some compassion for others and even for yourself?

Set us free, O God, from the bondage of our sins, and give us the liberty of that abundant life which You have made known to us in Your Son our Savior Jesus Christ; who lives and reigns with You, in the unity of the Holy Spirit, one God, now and for ever. Amen. (Fifth Sunday After Epiphany – BCP p. 216)

April 14

"I have been forgotten like one who is dead; I have become like a broken vessel" (Psalm 31:12, ESV).

I AM THINKING TODAY about how broken we all are—including yours truly. I wish I had a good synonym for "broken," because the phrase is now hackneyed. But, if you can get past the familiarity of the term, it still conveys the essential meaning. Something that is broken doesn't work like it is designed to work. Someone who is broken doesn't act as he or she is designed to act. We reap the sorry consequences of our collective brokenness every day.

This is the great unifying insight of Christianity, which, ideally, leads to compassion for others. Great swaths of time and energy are spent in pretending—either to others or to ourselves—that we are not broken. Jesus invites you to see the playacting for what it is: silly and unhelpful.

His healing begins in the unvarnished recognition of your brokenness.

O God of peace, who hast taught us that in returning and rest we shall be saved, in quietness and confidence shall be our strength: By the might of Thy Spirit lift us, we pray Thee, to Thy presence, where we may be still and know that Thou art God; through Jesus Christ our Lord. Amen. (For Quiet Confidence – BCP p. 832)

April 15

"Jesus Christ is ris'n today, alleluia! / Our triumphant, holy day, alleluia! / Who did once, upon the cross, alleluia! / Suffer to redeem our loss, alleluia!"

IT MAY SEEM OBVIOUS, but the resurrection is ALWAYS connected to the crucifixion. All the great Easter hymns, like the one above, make that clear. And vice versa. Good Friday is always connected to Easter Sunday. As the Apostle Paul says, *"He was delivered over to death for our sins and was raised to life for our justification" (Romans 4:25, NIV).*

This means that with every bad thing that has happened, is happening, or will happen in your life, there will always be a concomitant redemption. No exceptions!

> Almighty God, who through Your only-begotten Son Jesus Christ overcame death and opened to us the gate of everlasting life: Grant that we, who celebrate with joy the day of the Lord's resurrection, may be raised from the death of sin by Your life-giving Spirit; through Jesus Christ our Lord, who lives and reigns with You and the Holy Spirit, one God, now and for ever. Amen. (Collect for Easter Day – BCP p. 222)

April 16

"O come, let us worship and bow down; let us kneel before the LORD our Maker. For He is our God, and we are the people of His pasture, the sheep under His care" (Psalm 95:6–7, BSB).

THINK ABOUT IT FOR a second. You are made by someone. God made you. He knows how you work. He knows how you operate. He knows how you fail to operate. You did not make yourself. And although you may sometimes be a mystery to yourself, you are not a mystery to your Maker.

James Joyce—brilliant as he was—was wrong about God. He said, "The artist, like the God of the Creation, remains within or behind or beyond or above his handiwork, invisible, refined out of existence, indifferent, paring his fingernails." Our Maker is also a Shepherd who cares. You are under His care. Shepherds have dirty fingernails. In fact, He cares so deeply that His hands are pierced for you.

> Almighty God, whose most dear Son went not up to joy but first He suffered pain, and entered not into glory before He was crucified: Mercifully grant that we, walking in the way of the cross, may find it none other than the way of life and peace; through Jesus Christ our Lord. Amen. (A Collect for Fridays – BCP p. 99)

April 17

THERE ARE FEW PROBLEMS in life with clear-cut answers. What to do when someone criticizes you, however, is one of them; Jesus gives us a clear-cut answer: *"Blessed are you when others revile you and persecute you and utter all kinds of evil against you falsely on My account. Rejoice and be glad, for your reward is great in heaven, for so they persecuted the prophets who were before you"* (Matthew 5:11–12, ESV).

Even if you are not being criticized on Jesus' account, the response is always the same: no response. Hard to do, you say? Well, yes. But by the power of the Holy Spirit, it is a heck of a lot easier than defending yourself with wasted breath.

Almighty God, our heavenly Father, who settest the solitary in families: We commend to Thy continual care the homes in which Thy people dwell. Put far from them, we beseech Thee, every root of bitterness, the desire of vainglory, and the pride of life. Fill them with faith, virtue, knowledge, temperance, patience, godliness. Knit together in constant affection those who, in holy wedlock, have been made one flesh. Turn the hearts of the parents to the children, and the hearts of the children to the parents; and so enkindle fervent charity among us all, that we may evermore be kindly affectioned one to another; through Jesus Christ our Lord. Amen. (For Families – BCP p. 828)

April 18

"I am astonished that you are so quickly deserting the One who called you to live in the grace of Christ and are turning to a different gospel—which is really no gospel at all. Evidently some people are throwing you into confusion and are trying to pervert the gospel of Christ" (Galatians 1:6–7, NIV).

OUR BOTTLE OF ACETAMINOPHEN says it "contains acetaminophen." Good to know what you are getting, even if it seems a little obvious. Sometimes in churches you don't get what is advertised. They tell you that they are preaching the gospel, but then they place burdens on you. Usually, this is in the "application" part of the sermon.

Paul has some choice words for the people peddling a false gospel in Galatia. Whenever you hear about what you should do instead of hearing about what God has already done, you know there is something other than acetaminophen in the acetamino-phen bottle. Metaphorically speaking, of course.

> "Blessed Lord, who caused all holy Scriptures to be written for our learning: Grant us so to hear them, read, mark, learn, and inwardly digest them, that we may embrace and ever hold fast the blessed hope of ever-lasting life, which You have given us in our Savior Jesus Christ; who lives and reigns with You and the Holy Spirit, one God, for ever and ever. Amen." (Proper 28 – BCP p. 236)

April 19

> *"Then I said, 'Ah, Lord GOD! Behold, I do not know how to speak, for I am only a youth.' But the LORD said to me, 'Do not say, "I am only a youth"; for to all to whom I send you, you shall go, and whatever I com-mand you, you shall speak'" (Jeremiah 1:6–7, ESV).*

YOU MAY NOT BE young, like the prophet Jeremiah in this passage, but you are young at something. We are always crossing some kind of threshold beyond which we have no experience.

When inexperience demands dependence on God, then being a rookie is a very good thing. The God who beckons you across that threshold is the same God who will provide for you. Where are you young this week?

> Lord, we pray that Your grace may always precede and follow us, that we may continually be given to good works; through Jesus Christ our Lord, who lives and reigns with You and the Holy Spirit, one God, now and for ever. Amen. (Proper 23 – BCP p. 234)

April 20

A TRIED AND TRUE, middle-of-the-night-when-your-thoughts-are-swirling-and-you-can't-sleep prayer is the Jesus Prayer: "Lord Jesus Christ, Son of God, have mercy on me, a sinner." Not only does the prayer have a kind of mantric quality about it, but it also places you on theologically firm ground. Jesus is Lord, you are a sinful person in need, and the two of you meet on the ground of His mercy.

Seeing yourself in the blindness of Bartimaeus the beggar is the right move. *"And as He [Jesus] was leaving Jericho with His disciples and a great crowd, Bartimaeus, a blind beggar, the son of Timaeus, was sitting by the roadside. And when he heard that it was Jesus of Nazareth, he began to cry out and say, "Jesus, Son of David, have mercy on me!" And many rebuked him, telling him to be silent. But he cried out all the more, "Son of David, have mercy on me!"* (Mark 10:46–48, ESV). Jesus responds to Bartimaeus with mercy and restores his sight.

Fortunately, you don't have to wait until 3 AM to pray the Jesus Prayer. Jesus is here all the time, a very present help in times of trouble, whenever the shadow of darkness falls. Lord Jesus Christ, Son of God, have mercy on me, a sinner.

> Be our light in the darkness, O Lord, and in Your great mercy defend us from all perils and dangers of this night; for the love of Your only Son, our Savior Jesus Christ. Amen. (A Collect for Aid against Perils – BCP p. 123)

April 21

WE ARE JUST NOT as important as we think we are. Mind you— we have more worth and dignity than we can even imagine. And we are more loved than we can ever conceive. Plus, God can and does use us to accomplish important things. But, in the end, He is the One who is truly important.

John the Baptist knew this right off the bat when he said of Jesus, *"He must increase; I must decrease. The One who comes from above is above all. The one who is from the earth belongs to the earth and speaks as one from the earth. The One who comes from heaven is above all" (John 3:30–31, BSB).*

Here's to as painless a decreasing as possible today!

Remember, O Lord, what You have wrought in us and not what we deserve; and, as You have called us to Your service, make us worthy of our calling; through Jesus Christ our Lord, who lives and reigns with You and the Holy Spirit, one God, now and for ever. Amen. (Proper 1 – BCP p. 228)

April 22

"Put on then, as God's chosen ones, holy and beloved, compassionate hearts, kindness, humility, meekness, and patience, bearing with one another and, if one has a complaint against another, forgiving each other; as the Lord has forgiven you, so you also must forgive. And above all these put on love, which binds every-thing together in perfect harmony. And let the peace of Christ rule in your hearts, to which indeed you were called in one body. And be thankful" (Colossians 3:12–15, ESV).

THIS PASSAGE FROM PAUL'S letter to the Colossians is often read at weddings, presumably chosen to address husbands and wives.

The Apostle had the church in mind when he wrote it, but it is eminently applicable to families, or any group of people trying to live life together.

Because we tend to hurt one another, often unintentionally and sometimes willfully, Paul emphasizes the need for forgiveness, forbearance, and patience. Indeed, all of the qualities necessary for harmony are summed up in one word: love. "All you need is love." I could not agree more with St. Paul—and John, Paul, George, and Ringo—but I also recognize that embodying love is a big ask. Love does not rise unaided from the human heart. If it's absolutely necessary for harmony, though, where does love come from?

The New Testament answer is uniform: love—at least as it takes the form of forgiveness—comes from knowing that "the Lord has forgiven you." In other words, a bracing self-assessment of my own forgiven trespasses gives rise—through the power of the Holy Spirit—to an easier and more authentic forgiveness of others. Not to mention a liberal dose of kindness, humility, meekness, and patience.

Praying helps, too!

> Almighty God, our heavenly Father, who settest the solitary in families: We commend to Thy continual care the homes in which Thy people dwell. Put far from them, we beseech Thee, every root of bitterness, the desire of vainglory, and the pride of life. Fill them with faith, virtue, knowledge, temperance, patience, godliness. Knit together in constant affection those who, in holy wedlock, have been made one flesh. Turn the hearts of the parents to the children, and the hearts of the children to the parents; and so enkindle fervent charity among us all, that we may evermore be kindly affectioned one to another; through Jesus Christ our Lord. Amen. (For Families – BCP p. 828)

April 23

*"Not that I am speaking of being in need, for I have
learned in whatever situation I am to be content.
I know how to be brought low, and I know how to
abound. In any and every circumstance, I have learned
the secret of facing plenty and hunger, abundance and
need. I can do all things through Him who strengthens
me" (Philippians 4:11–13, ESV).*

IN A POEM CALLED "If—," written as life wisdom for his son,
Rudyard Kipling says, "If you can meet with Triumph and
Disaster … treat those two impostors just the same." Although
the language differs from that of St. Paul, the gist is similar.

What you label as a "Triumph" or a "Disaster" may, in fact,
be horses of a different color. To be given peace in Christ is to be
given a peace that is impervious to the fluctuating circumstances
we face. For, as the Bard says, "the web of our life is of a mingled
yarn, good and ill together."

> Grant us, Lord, not to be anxious about earthly things,
> but to love things heavenly; and even now, while we
> are placed among things that are passing away, to hold
> fast to those that shall endure; through Jesus Christ
> Your Son our Lord, who lives and reigns with You, in
> the unity of the Holy Spirit, one God, for ever and ever.
> Amen. (Proper 20 – BCP p. 234)

April 24

THE MESSAGE OF THE gospel is revolutionary and counter-cultural in one startling respect: It offers hope for both the victim

and the victimizer. Final distinctions between people are not allowed to be drawn. God addresses a sick and suffering humanity in total when He sends His Son to save the world. The gospel is unflinchingly universal.

"It is not the healthy who need a doctor, but the sick. I have not come to call the righteous, but sinners to repentance" (Luke 5:31–32, *NIV).* Jesus does recognize the sad reality that some people will not accept the diagnosis and therefore believe they have no need for the Great Physician. Repentance is the road that all people must travel—there are no sides of any issue, personally or globally, that are exempt from the honest recognition of our culpability before God.

What a mercy it is that the blood of Christ is not partisan; it washes over every human being with both restorative and absolving grace.

> Almighty God, on this day You opened the way of eternal life to every race and nation by the promised gift of Your Holy Spirit: Shed abroad this gift throughout the world by the preaching of the Gospel, that it may reach to the ends of the earth; through Jesus Christ our Lord, who lives and reigns with You, in the unity of the Holy Spirit, one God, for ever and ever. Amen. (The Day of Pentecost – BCP p. 227)

April 25

> *"Now Jesus did many other signs in the presence of His disciples, which are not written in this book. But these are written so that you may come to believe that Jesus is the Messiah, the Son of God, and that through*

believing you may have life in His name" (John
20:30–31, NRSV).

I WONDER WHAT THOSE other signs were. Signs = miracles in the
Gospel of John. Healings? Other weather events, like the stilling
of the storm?

I can tell you one thing: Miracles still happen, because your
life is a miracle. As Shakespeare's Edgar tells his father, King
Lear, after the blind King believes that he has leapt from a cliff,
yet finds himself awake and alive: "Thy life's a miracle. Speak
yet again." The taste of a strawberry, the privilege of watching
a saucy robin strutting about in the rain, the sip of communion
wine while you are kneeling, that anyone at all gives a hoot about
you—it's all a miracle.

> Almighty and everlasting God, who in the Paschal
> mystery established the new covenant of reconciliation:
> Grant that all who have been reborn into the fellowship
> of Christ's Body may show forth in their lives what they
> profess by their faith; through Jesus Christ our Lord,
> who lives and reigns with You and the Holy Spirit, one
> God, for ever and ever. Amen. (Second Sunday of Easter
> – BCP p. 224)

April 26

*"For in this hope we were saved. Now hope that is seen
is not hope. For who hopes for what he sees?" (Romans
8:24, ESV).*

A REMARKABLE WOMAN IN her mid-nineties, the day after a
major operation, said that she signed up for one more surgery

called an ophtho-rectal surgery which involves a stent that runs from the eyes all the way down to the rear end. The purpose of the surgery, said this dear, faithful, and long-suffering lady, is "to correct a sh**ty outlook on life!"

She must have had this surgery as a child, because I've never met a more sanguine, yet honest, person in my life. Goes to show that we all have our moments—and lots of them.

Good thing that we walk by faith and not by sight, and our hope is in what is unseen. For what is unseen is the hand of God at work making all things happy—and when the time comes, plain as day.

> O God, whose blessed Son made Himself known to His disciples in the breaking of bread: Open the eyes of our faith, that we may behold Him in all His redeeming work; who lives and reigns with You, in the unity of the Holy Spirit, one God, now and for ever. Amen. (Third Sunday of Easter – BCP p. 224)

April 27

WHAT DO VIRGIL, KAFKA, and Emily Dickinson have in common? On their deathbeds, all three writers requested that their works should be destroyed. Imagine that! No *Aeneid*? No Gregor Samsa waking up one day as a giant cockroach? No "'Hope' is the Thing with Feathers"?

Maybe you are tempted to think what you have to offer the world isn't worth keeping. Well, rewatch *It's a Wonderful Life*. If you don't have time for that or want to wait until Christmas, then hear this scripture: *"Each of you should use whatever gift you have received to serve others, as faithful stewards of God's grace in its various forms" (1 Peter 4:10, NIV).*

O Lord, You have taught us that without love whatever we do is worth nothing; Send Your Holy Spirit and pour into our hearts Your greatest gift, which is love, the true bond of peace and of all virtue, without which whoever lives is accounted dead before You. Grant this for the sake of Your only Son Jesus Christ, who lives and reigns with You and the Holy Spirit, one God, now and for ever. Amen. (Seventh Sunday after the Epiphany – BCP p. 216)

April 28

"Thus says the LORD of hosts, the God of Israel, to all the exiles whom I have sent into exile from Jerusalem to Babylon: Build houses and live in them; plant gardens and eat what they produce. Take wives and have sons and daughters; take wives for your sons, and give your daughters in marriage, that they may bear sons and daughters; multiply there, and do not decrease. But seek the welfare of the city where I have sent you into exile, and pray to the LORD on its behalf, for in its welfare you will find your welfare" (Jeremiah 29:4–7, NRSV).

GOD'S PEOPLE ARE IN exile, bereft and estranged from all that gives them identity and comfort. And yet God directs them to put down roots—plant gardens, build houses, marry their neighbors. In other words, go live your life.

Living the life we've been given to live tempers the urge to go find better pastures. As U2 sings, "What you don't have, you don't need it now" ("Beautiful Day").

There is great comfort in that, yes?

Lord, we pray that Your grace may always precede and follow us, that we may continually be given to good works; through Jesus Christ our Lord, who lives and reigns with You and the Holy Spirit, one God, now and for ever. Amen. (Proper 23 – BCP p. 234)

April 29

A COMEDIAN (can't remember who) talks about our morning selves vs. our afternoon selves. Our morning selves begin the day with a green smoothie and resolve to have a kale salad for lunch and then one piece of baked chicken for dinner, along with some brown rice. Our afternoon selves have long since given up on our morning selves and are crushing a cheeseburger at 3PM.

Resolutions have a way of dissolving under the pressure of desire. Yet the fortunate thing about having a will that is constrained—or what theologians call "bound"—is that it can be bound to Jesus Christ and His mercy. As the old hymn says, "I need Thee every hour / Most gracious Lord / No tender voice like Thine / Can peace afford."

When that hymn was first published in 1873, this scripture was included beneath its title: *"Apart from Me you can do nothing"* *(John 15:5).*

O God, because without You we are not able to please You, mercifully grant that Your Holy Spirit may in all things direct and rule our hearts; through Jesus Christ our Lord, who lives and reigns with You and the Holy Spirit, one God, now and for ever. Amen. (Proper 19 – BCP p. 233)

April 30

"My God, My God, why have You forsaken Me?"
(Psalm 22:1).

POET CHRISTIAN WIMAN ONCE said that these words from Psalm 22—spoken by Christ on the cross—were the words that restored his faith in God. This moment showed him that Jesus relates to the deepest traumas and the quagmires of human need and pain.

Although, like Christ on the cross, you may feel alone. But you are not alone. God did not forsake His Son, and God has not forsaken you. Mavis Staples sings Jeff Tweedy's song:

> A broken home
> A broken heart
> Isolated and afraid
> Open up, this is a raid
> I wanna get it through to you
> You're not alone.
> I want to get it through to you: You're not alone.

Almighty God, we pray You graciously to behold this Your family, for whom our Lord Jesus Christ was willing to be betrayed, and given into the hands of sinners, and to suffer death upon the cross; who now lives and reigns with You and the Holy Spirit, one God, for ever and ever. Amen. (Good Friday – BCP p. 221)

MAY

May 1

TODAY'S COLLECT RECOGNIZES JESUS' sovereignty over us. While it is considered both patriarchal and archaic to address God as King, there is something deeply resonant and comforting about being a subject, about having a King to lead us. (Obsession with Netflix's *The Crown* confirms this insight!) This is because we were not meant to be autonomous.

An expression of original sin is our demand for self-rule, our insistence on being the arbiter of our own rules, and our umbrage if our rights are infringed in any way. In Milton's *Paradise Lost*, Lucifer famously quips, "Better to reign in Hell than serve in Heaven."

I'm not suggesting that we swap out democracy for monarchy. But it is far, far better to remember that our lives were bought with a price and they are not our own. It is far, far better to live our lives in service to the King who laid down His life for His people. *"You are not your own, for you were bought with a price" (1 Corinthians 6:19–20, ESV).*

> Almighty and everlasting God, whose will it is to restore all things in Your well-beloved Son, the King of kings and the Lord of lords: Mercifully grant that the peoples of the earth, divided and enslaved by sin, may be freed and brought together under His most gracious rule; who lives and reigns with You and the Holy Spirit, one God, now and for ever. Amen. (Proper 29 – BCP p. 236)

May 2

ABRAHAM LINCOLN WAS FAMOUSLY gangly and ungainly, but once he started speaking, he won people over. One observer wrote, "His face lighted up as with an inward fire; the whole man was transfigured. I forgot his clothes, his personal appearance, and his individual peculiarities. Presently, forgetting myself, I was on my feet like the rest, yelling [and] cheering [for] this wonderful man."

I suspect that Lincoln's genius, oratorical and otherwise, was at least in part inspired by the depression from which he suffered as well as the faith in God that sustained him. I love what Lincoln himself said on this topic: "I have been driven many times upon my knees by the overwhelming conviction that I had nowhere else to go. My own wisdom and that of all about me seemed insufficient for that day."

The psalmist says, *"Why are you downcast, O my soul? Why the unease within me? Put your hope in God, for I will yet praise Him, my Savior and my God" (Psalm 43:5, BSB).* Being driven to your knees is always, in every single instance, a good thing. The drumbeat of our insufficiency and that of others thrums through the ages, as does God's sufficiency for us—perfect and unending.

> O Lord our God, accept the fervent prayers of Your people; in the multitude of Your mercies, look with compassion upon us and all who turn to You for help; for You are gracious, O lover of souls, and to You we give glory, Father, Son, and Holy Spirit, now and for ever. Amen. (The Collect at the Prayers – BCP p. 395)

May 3

PEOPLE SOMETIMES SAY THAT they want to be "more spiritual." I understand what they mean: They want to have a closer relationship with God and not be so caught up in the cares and demands of the world. Being in a close relationship with God is a good thing, but if I read my Bible right, God is not interested at all in "spirituality." Instead, He just wants you to be the human being He has created you to be!

Eugene Peterson's translation of the Bible called The Message captures this thought in Romans 12:1–2: *"So here's what I want you to do, God helping you: Take your everyday, ordinary life— your sleeping, eating, going-to-work, and walking-around life—and place it before God as an offering. Embracing what God does for you is the best thing you can do for Him. Don't become so well-adjusted to your culture that you fit into it without even thinking. Instead, fix your attention on God. You'll be changed from the inside out."*

Your everyday, ordinary, walking-around life—sleeping, eating, going to work—is what God is interested in. Here's a prayer to help you ask God to be right smack dab in the middle of that life today.

> Accept, O Lord, our thanks and praise for all that You have done for us… We thank You for setting us at tasks which demand our best efforts, and for leading us to accomplishments which satisfy and delight us. We thank You also for those disappointments and failures that lead us to acknowledge our dependence on You alone… Grant us the gift of Your Spirit, that we may know Christ and make Him known; and through Him, at all times and in all places, may give thanks to You in all things. Amen. (From A General Thanksgiving – BCP p. 836)

May 4

"When Enoch had lived 65 years, he became the father of Methuselah. After he became the father of Methuselah, Enoch walked faithfully with God 300 years and had other sons and daughters. Altogether, Enoch lived a total of 365 years. Enoch walked faithfully with God; then he was no more, because God took him away" (Genesis 5:21–24, NIV).

IN THIS NARRATIVE FROM Genesis, we read that Enoch "walked faithfully with God." What does it mean to walk faithfully with God? Given that all human beings are recidivistic sinners, it can't mean that we are blameless before the Law of God.

Perhaps to walk faithfully with God is to walk with integrity with yourself. That is, to have an ongoing honest reckoning with yourself in light of God's command to love Him and to love your neighbor. Perhaps it is to daily remember and rely on the blood of Christ, shed for you.

Lord Jesus Christ, You said to Your apostles, 'Peace I give to you; My own peace I leave with you:' Regard not our sins, but the faith of Your Church, and give to us the peace and unity of that heavenly City, where with the Father and the Holy Spirit You live and reign, now and for ever. Amen. (The Collect at the Prayers – BCP p. 395)

May 5

KIERKEGAARD, WHOSE BIRTHDAY WAS today, tells us, "Life can only be understood backwards; but it must be lived forwards." True, yes?

We can often (but not always) see the hand of God in our lives looking back. What at the time seemed horrible or confusing turned out to be a beautiful part of God's plan. Sanctification may mean something like having *slightly* more trust in God as we go on "stumbling through the dark" (The Jayhawks) going forward.

As the prophet says, *"For I know the plans I have for you,' declares the LORD, 'plans to prosper you and not to harm you, plans to give you hope and a future'"* (Jeremiah 29:11, NIV).

> O God, whose Son Jesus is the good shepherd of Your people: Grant that when we hear His voice we may know Him who calls us each by name, and follow where He leads; who, with You and the Holy Spirit, lives and reigns, one God, for ever and ever. Amen. (Fourth Sunday of Easter – BCP p. 225)

May 6

HERE IS SOME PROFUNDITY from Bryan Stevenson, author of *Just Mercy*, and Director of the Equal Justice Initiative, an organization that works with prisoners on death row:

> I've…represented people who have committed terrible crimes but nonetheless struggle to recover and to find redemption. I have discovered, deep in the hearts of many condemned and incarcerated people, the scattered

traces of hope and humanity—seeds of restoration that come to astonishing life when nurtured by very simple interventions.

In other words, people respond to grace. You respond to grace. I respond to grace. We respond to grace. If change is going to happen in a person—if the seeds of restoration are to come to astonishing life—grace will be the agent.

Paul's description of his relationship with the church in Thessalonica is a good descriptor of what all relationships might aspire to be: *"We were not looking for praise from people, not from you or anyone else, even though as apostles of Christ we could have asserted our authority. Instead, we were like young children among you. Just as a nursing mother cares for her children, so we cared for you. Because we loved you so much, we were delighted to share with you not only the gospel of God but our lives as well"* (1 Thessalonians 2:6–8, NIV).

Time to pray.

O God, You have taught us to keep all Your commandments by loving You and our neighbor: Grant us the grace of Your Holy Spirit, that we may be devoted to You with our whole heart, and united to one another in pure affection; through Jesus Christ our Lord, who lives and reigns with You and the Holy Spirit, one God, for ever and ever. Amen. (Proper 9 – BCP p. 230)

May 7

CONCERN FOR THE PEOPLE we love (i.e., worry, anxiety, fret) eats up a large portion of most people's mental space. The trope, "You are only as happy as your least happy child," is irritatingly true to experience. It usually indicates an over-identification with one's offspring, which is unhealthy for the child, the parent, and, when applicable, the marriage.

Of course, you don't have to be a parent to be worried about the people in your life. When you start down the road of concern, all kinds of candidates emerge. And often, the reasons for concern are not altogether unsubstantiated.

How a person navigates life without faith in God is befuddling to me, especially when it comes to the complex dynamics of human relationships. Since you are reading this devotional, I will assume that you are not one of those people! So, let me point you in the direction of some reassuring Scripture and prayer: *"I bow my knees before the Father, from whom every family in heaven and on earth is named, that according to the riches of His glory He may grant you to be strengthened with power through His Spirit in your inner being"* (Ephesians 3:14–16, ESV).

> Almighty God, we entrust all who are dear to us to Thy never-failing care and love, for this life and the life to come, knowing that Thou art doing for them better things than we can desire or pray for; through Jesus Christ our Lord. Amen. (For Those We Love – BCP p. 831)

May 8

"All who are led by the Spirit of God are children of God. For you did not receive a spirit of slavery to fall back into fear, but you have received a spirit of adoption" (Romans 8:14–15, NRSV).

FEAR VS. SECURITY. Fear seems to be the default setting of human beings. Maybe that's why the most commonly repeated refrain in the Bible is "fear not" or "do not be afraid" or "have no fear."

According to Paul, fear gives way to unassailable security via your adoption as God's son, God's daughter. Nothing can touch you now! What would it be like to believe that?

> Almighty and everlasting God, You are always more ready to hear than we to pray, and to give more than we either desire or deserve: Pour upon us the abundance of Your mercy, forgiving us those things of which our conscience is afraid, and giving us those good things for which we are not worthy to ask, except through the merits and mediation of Jesus Christ our Savior; who lives and reigns with You and the Holy Spirit, one God, for ever and ever. Amen. (Proper 22 – BCP p. 234)

May 9

WHEN THE BOTTOM FEELS like it is falling out, it isn't. That is because God is at the bottom, and therefore the bottom is solid. A professor at my seminary preached the sermon at the funeral of his own son, following his son's tragic death. He simply said, "I've been to the bottom, and the bottom is solid."

Of course, life is full of vicissitudes. It always has been and always will be. Storms will come and go. Stock markets will rise and fall, but God is constant. St. Paul tells us that *"[Christ] is before all things, and in Him all things hold together" (Colossians 1:17)*. In Christ the center can and does hold. The bottom is solid as a rock. *"Jesus Christ is the same yesterday and today and forever" (Hebrews 13:8)*.

God is real, friends, and He is with you.

Grant us, Lord, not to be anxious about earthly things, but to love things heavenly; and even now, while we are placed among things that are passing away, to hold fast to those that shall endure; through Jesus Christ our Lord, who lives and reigns with You and the Holy Spirit, one God, for ever and ever. Amen. (Proper 20 – BCP p. 234)

May 10

MY DEAR FRIEND Paul Zahl is fond of saying that all of the things we are so desperately attached to in this life—cherished clothes, our favorite framed wedding photo, our grandfather's writing desk, our collection of first-edition Faulkner novels, etc.—will be sold by our children. It might be our grandchildren who do the honors. But in time, all our treasured possessions will end up at a garage sale, or on Facebook Marketplace, or eBay.

Jesus says, *"Beware, and be on your guard against every form of greed; for not even when one has an abundance does his life consist of his possessions" (Luke 12:15, NASB 1995).*

I love stuff. However, I love that our lives aren't eternally bound to our stuff. You can't take it with you—duh. And what is in store is where true riches are found.

O God, the protector of all who trust in You, without whom nothing is strong, nothing is holy: Increase and multiply upon us Your mercy; that, with You as our ruler and guide, we may so pass through things temporal, that we lose not the things eternal; through Jesus Christ our Lord, who lives and reigns with You and the Holy Spirit, one God, for ever and ever. Amen. (Proper 12 – BCP p. 231)

May 11

"Once safely on shore, we found out that the island was called Malta. The islanders showed us unusual kindness. They built a fire and welcomed us all because it was raining and cold" (Acts 28:1–2, NIV).

SLANT SPRING LIGHT, as if newly birthed and testing its sea legs, promises a warmth that it sometimes can't deliver in the nip and the gust. Longed-for thaw is longed for longer. The body must remain guarded at least until after the frost date. Even then, one is wary.

Warmth has a way of dismantling the tightly wound internal coil. Like Jimmy Buffet sings in *Boat Drinks*, "This morning, I shot six holes in my freezer / I think I got cabin fever / Somebody sound the alarm / … I gotta go where it's warm."

Warmth welcomes, as Paul and crew describe in these verses from Acts. The peace of God that has been given to us in Jesus Christ is an all-season warmth, always there to uncoil your innards and keep you from reaching for your pistol. His Holy Spirit is described as a fire, after all.

Eternal God, who led Your ancient people into freedom by a pillar of cloud by day and a pillar of fire by night: Grant that we who walk in the light of Your presence may rejoice in the liberty of the children of God; through Jesus Christ our Lord. Amen. (From an Order of Worship for the Evening – BCP p. 111)

May 12

THIS IS FROM SHAKESPEARE's 91st Sonnet: "Some glory in their birth, some in their skill, / Some in their wealth, some in their body's force, / Some in their garments, though new-fangled ill; / Some in their hawks and hounds, some in their horse."

We all look to put our identity in something: ancestry, merit, money, beauty, finery, bling. That's a fool's errand, and St. Paul knew it: *"If anyone else thinks he has reason for confidence in the flesh, I have more: circumcised on the eighth day, of the people of Israel, of the tribe of Benjamin, a Hebrew of Hebrews; as to the law, a Pharisee; as to zeal, a persecutor of the church; as to righteousness under the law, blameless. But whatever gain I had, I counted as loss for the sake of Christ" (Philippians 3:4–7, ESV).*

The hamster wheel is exhausting anyway. Nice to have an excuse to opt out of all that, isn't it?

> O God, who wonderfully created, and yet more wonderfully restored, the dignity of human nature: Grant that we may share the divine life of Him who humbled Himself to share our humanity, Your Son Jesus Christ; who lives and reigns with You in the unity of the Holy Spirit, one God for ever and ever. Amen. (Of the Incarnation – BCP p. 252)

May 13

I'M A WALKER SURROUNDED by runners. At least it seems this way on my daily constitutional through the grounds of the University of Virginia. Despite my given surname (ha!) and the fact that I've run several 10 Milers and even a half marathon and decided that I DO NOT LIKE RUNNING, I always feel a little bit "less than" the runners. Especially when men in their mid-fifties pass me by.

All this is to say what we each already know: Comparison is for the birds! Which I guess is why birds of a feather flock together. We all know that comparison is odious, but that seldom seems to stop us from engaging in the practice—to our detriment. Right?

Which makes me wonder if St. Paul was being completely honest when he said, *"I care very little, however, if I am judged by you or by any human court. In fact, I do not even judge myself. My conscience is clear, but that does not vindicate me. It is the Lord who judges me. Therefore judge nothing before the appointed time; wait until the Lord comes" (1 Corinthians 4:3–5, BSB).*

I want to say this and believe it! What freedom. The even better news is that the only One who actually has the right to judge (note that we don't have the right to even judge ourselves) is the One who said that He came into the world not to judge it, but to save it.

Eternal God, in whose perfect kingdom no sword is drawn but the sword of righteousness, no strength known but the strength of love: So mightily spread abroad Your Spirit, that all peoples may be gathered under the banner of the Prince of Peace, as children of one Father; to whom be dominion and glory, now and forever. Amen. (For Peace – BCP p. 815)

May 14

"I am the good shepherd. I know My own and My own know Me, just as the Father knows Me and I know the Father; and I lay down My life for the sheep" (John 10:14–15, ESV).

THE FIRST TIME I HEARD the term "spirit animal" was from a fellow divinity student at Virginia Theological Seminary who asked me, with all seriousness, if I had discovered mine yet. Such is the formative terrain of the Episcopal Church!

When asked about their spirit animal, people will answer, "bald eagle" or "lion" or perhaps "stallion." I suppose I'd choose the red-winged blackbird as my own if I had to. One animal no one has ever chosen is "sheep." Sheep are not particularly intelligent, inspiring or independent. Sheep, by their very nature, are easily led astray.

Well, Jesus has chosen your spirit animal for you. Lo and behold: You are a sheep! Me too! Everyone else who has ever lived, too! The good news is that being a sheep disabuses us of the unrealistic expectations we have of ourselves. And the better news for those we interact with is that we are also relieved of the high expectations we put on other people.

Sheep need a shepherd—a Good Shepherd—to take care of them. Fortunately, we can and should have high expectations of our Shepherd. He has already proved Himself by laying down His life for the us—the sheep.

O God, whose Son Jesus is the good shepherd of Your people: Grant that when we hear His voice we may know Him who calls us each by name, and follow where He leads; who, with You and the Holy Spirit, lives and reigns, one God, for ever and ever. Amen. (Fourth Sunday of Easter – BCP p. 225)

May 15

WE HAVE A TENDENCY to ask Jesus to butt out. This is what happened when Jesus healed the demoniac and cast the demons into 2,000 pigs who then drowned themselves in the sea.

"Those tending the pigs ran off and reported this in the town and countryside, and the people went out to see what had happened. When they came to Jesus, they saw the man who had been possessed by the legion of demons, sitting there, dressed and in his right mind; and they were afraid. Those who had seen it told the people what had happened to the demon-possessed man—and told about the pigs as well. Then the people began to plead with Jesus to leave their region" (Mark 5:14–17, NIV).

It was fine for Jesus to heal the man, but He had no right to hamstring their economy and disrupt their way of life. We may feel the same about areas of our lives that we've got sealed up the way we like it, thank you very much. What we tend to forget when we "plead with Jesus to leave (our) region" is that He is a God of grace. Who in their right mind would say no to perfect love? Not the healed man, who now in his right mind begs Jesus to allow him to stay in His presence.

Lord, cast out our demons and heal us; restore us to our right minds.

> Almighty God, who is a strong tower to all who put their trust in Him, to whom all things in heaven, on earth, and under the earth bow and obey: Be now and ever our defense, and make us know and feel that the only Name under heaven given for health and salvation is the Name of our Lord Jesus Christ, in whose name we pray. Amen. (From the Ministration to the Sick – BCP p. 456)

May 16

DE-FATHERING GOD IS A rueful mistake. Obviously, God is not a man. But God—the First Person of the Trinity—is Father. We know this because Jesus called God "Father": *"This, then, is how*

you should pray: 'Our Father in heaven, hallowed be Your name'"
(Matthew 6:9, NIV).

God re-parents you. Maybe you had a great father, but that father, being human, failed you in some way. I have three grown children whom I love and delight in, but I know I have let them down, just like every other father in the world. Or maybe you have had a traumatic relationship with your father. Then, it is even more important to call God by the intimate name of *Abba*.

And, God is *our* Father, and thus we are all connected.

> Most loving Father, whose will it is for us to give thanks for all things, to fear nothing but the loss of You, and to cast all our care on You who care for us: Preserve us from faithless fears and worldly anxieties, that no clouds of this mortal life may hide from us the light of that love which is immortal, and which You have manifested to us in Your Son Jesus Christ our Lord; who lives and reigns with You, in the unity of the Holy Spirit, one God, now and for ever. Amen. (Eighth Sunday after the Epiphany – BCP p. 216)

May 17

IT'S NO HEAD TRIP (or escapism) to bank on Paul's reminder to the Colossians: *"But our citizenship is in heaven, and from it we await a Savior, the Lord Jesus Christ, who will transform our lowly body to be like His glorious body, by the power that enables Him even to subject all things to Himself"* (Philippians 3:20–21, ESV).

Ironically, remembering that ultimately we are "strangers and sojourners" (1 Peter 2:11) in this world allows you to engage deeply in civic life without putting all your eggs in that temporal basket. As C. S. Lewis shrewdly says, "Aim at Heaven and you will get Earth 'thrown in': aim at Earth and you will get neither."

Almighty and everlasting God, whose will it is to restore all things in Your well-beloved Son, the King of kings and the Lord of lords: Mercifully grant that the peoples of the earth, divided and enslaved by sin, may be freed and brought together under His most gracious rule; who lives and reigns with You and the Holy Spirit, one God, now and for ever. Amen. (Proper 29 – BCP p. 236)

May 18

HERE'S MY NEW FAVORITE Hemingway quote: "I love sleep. My life has a tendency to fall apart when I'm awake, you know?"

I had a brief period in my twenties, probably after I had read *The Seven Habits of Highly Effective People,* when I tried to sleep only four to five hours a night in order to maximize my output, efficiency, and engagement with the world. Fortunately, I didn't have enough discipline to carry out this silly idea.

Sleep, when we are lucky enough to enjoy it, is a nightly Sabbath, a total trust in God, a surrender of the agency we hold so dear. (Granted, dreams are another matter, but just put that aside for the moment.)

The psalmist says, *"In peace I will lie down and sleep, for You alone, LORD, make me dwell in safety"* (Psalm 4:8, NIV).

Sleep well!

O heavenly Father, You give Your children sleep for the refreshing of soul and body: Grant me this gift, I pray; keep me in that perfect peace which You have promised to those whose minds are fixed on You; and give me such a sense of Your presence, that in the hours of silence I may enjoy the blessed assurance of Your love; through Jesus Christ our Savior. Amen. (For Sleep – BCP p. 461)

May 19

ONE OF MY CLOSE friends is a hedge fund manager. People have quipped that one of us is part of the problem and one of us is part of the solution! Careful, though, because who is which depends on where you sit. To some, the money man is part of perpetuating a healthy GDP, while the religious guy is nothing but a purveyor of judgment and superstition. To others, the hedge-funder is the epitome of greed, while the minister defends those marginalized by the heartlessness of capitalism.

So, who is the solution and who is the problem? The Bible happens to have an answer: We are all the problem. The knees of any self-righteousness are knocked out with St. Paul's pithy, *"For all have sinned and fall short of the glory of God" (Romans 3:23).*

We are all part of the problem. Good to remember, especially when occasions for virtue signaling are rife. Thankfully, we are also all recipients of God's solution: Christ's death and resurrection.

> Lord, make us instruments of Your peace. Where there is hatred, let us sow love; where there is injury, pardon; where there is discord, union; where there is doubt, faith; where there is despair, hope; where there is darkness, light; where there is sadness, joy. Grant that we may not so much seek to be consoled as to console; to be understood as to understand; to be loved as to love. For it is in giving that we receive; it is in pardoning that we are pardoned; and it is in dying that we are born to eternal life. (A Prayer attribute to St. Francis – BCP p. 833)

May 20

MY FATHER GREW UP in Bayford, Virginia, on the Eastern Shore, where his family ran The Bayford Oyster Company. When my father was a small child, a man who worked for my grandfather took my dad down to the Bayford dock, tied a rope around him, and tossed him in the water. That's how my dad learned to swim!

A few years ago, we spread my father's ashes off that same dock, in that same water. The psalmist says, *"O LORD, make me know my end and what is the measure of my days; let me know how fleeting I am!" (Psalm 39:4, ESV)*. Trite but true: Each day is a gift.

Also true: The greatest gift is your name written in the Lamb's Book of Life.

> Merciful God, Father of our Lord Jesus Christ who is the Resurrection and the Life: Raise us, we humbly pray, from the death of sin to the life of righteousness; that when we depart this life we may rest in Him, and at the resurrection receive the blessing which Your well-beloved Son shall then pronounce: "Come, you blessed of My Father, receive the kingdom prepared for you from the beginning of the world." Grant this, O merciful Father, through Jesus Christ, our Mediator and Redeemer. Amen. (Burial Service – BCP p. 505)

May 21

"When they had brought their boats to shore, they left everything and followed Him" (Luke 5:11, NRSV).

THE PERSON OF JESUS Christ was so radically attractive that crowds thronged around Him and people forsook their lives and their livelihoods—without hesitation or calculation—to follow Him.

What about today? While His caricature (see SNL's "Church Lady") clearly repels people, He continues to draw people to Himself with His unique word of truth and grace. Among the cacophonous voices of flattery, false promise, and bald-faced lies that besiege us from within and without, He alone has the words of life.

To drop everything and to follow Him is to lose yourself and, ironically, be found.

Set us free, O God, from the bondage of our sins, and give us the liberty of that abundant life which You have made known to us in Your Son our Savior Jesus Christ; who lives and reigns with You, in the unity of the Holy Spirit, one God, now and for ever. Amen. (Fifth Sunday after Epiphany – BCP p. 216)

May 22

"Now then, stand still and see this great thing the Lord *is about to do before your eyes!" (1 Samuel 12:16, NIV).*

THE WITCHES IN SHAKESPEARE'S *Macbeth* are able to "look into the seeds of time / And say which grain will grow and which will not." No such luck for you and me. But would that really be luck? Do you really want a crystal ball? Isn't it so much better to abdicate your future to the One who grows the seed for your own good?

What if you were able to attend to the day, the hour, the minute? There is so much to be savored, or endured with trust, or to be floored by. Imagine the time and freedom that would open up were you to abandon your quest to secure your own future!

O God, the strength of all who put their trust in You: Mercifully accept our prayers; and because in our weakness we can do nothing good without You, give us the help of Your grace, that in keeping Your commandments we may please You both in will and deed; through Jesus Christ our Lord, who lives and reigns with You and the Holy Spirit, one God, for ever and ever. Amen. (Sixth Sunday After Epiphany – BCP p. 216)

May 23

THE STUBBORN MYTH OF human goodness is astonishingly difficult to dispel. And that is despite the hard evidence of the greed, violence, hedonism, and general indifference that comprise a daily newsfeed. I suppose the tenacity of the myth shouldn't be astonishing since we have so much invested in thinking well of ourselves while placing the blame on the "bad people" of the world. Still, among those who should know better, one hears with regularity, "He's a good person" or "The real goal is to raise good people."

When the rich young ruler addresses Jesus as "good teacher," Jesus responds, *"Why do you call Me good? No one is good except God alone" (Mark 10:18, ESV).* (By the way, Jesus *is* good because He is God and may be answering the brash young man with a double entendre.) Had it been written, Jesus could have responded with Article IX of the Episcopal Church's 39 Articles. We are "very far gone from [our] original righteousness, and ... of [our] own nature inclined to evil."

I see this sober assessment of our nature as very good news. It doesn't mean that we are entirely wicked or that we are not capable of goodness. As Bruce Cockburn sang, "Never had a lot of faith in human beings / but sometimes we manage to shine." Faith is rightly placed in God alone, for God alone is good.

> Most holy God, the source of all good desires, all right judgments, and all just works: Give to us, Your servants, that peace which the world cannot give, so that our minds may be fixed on the doing of Your will, and that we, being delivered from the fear of all enemies, may live in peace and quietness; through the mercies of Christ Jesus our Savior. Amen. (A Collect for Peace – BCP p. 123)

May 24

MOST GRADUATION SPEECHES ARE filled with soul-deadening platitudes, but a recent one from Taylor Swift (!) to NYU grads contained this exceptionally insightful nugget: "Learn to live alongside cringe. No matter how hard you try to avoid being cringe, you will look back on your life and cringe retrospectively." 100% true.

The Apostle Paul embraces cringe: *"If I must boast, I would rather boast about the things that show how weak I am" (2 Corinthians 11:30, NLT).*

Imagine how liberating it would be to trot out before God and man all that you are desperate to hide? Ha!

> Grant us, O Lord, to trust in You with all our hearts; for, as You always resist the proud who confide in their own strength, so You never forsake those who make their boast of Your mercy; through Jesus Christ our Lord, who lives and reigns with You and the Holy Spirit, one God, now and for ever. Amen. (Proper 18 – BCP p. 233)

May 25

CHRIS STAPLETON SINGS A song called "Drunkard's Prayer" that starts like this:

> When I get drunk and talk to God
> I say I'm sorry for all the things I'm not
> I mean every word I say
> And I promise I can change
> When I get drunk and talk to God

In my humble opinion, that is real prayer. It doesn't have to be a "bottle to get me on my knees"—it can be any number of humbling circumstances, either done or left undone.

Stapleton sings, "I wish that I could go to church but I'm too ashamed of me." So many people feel that way. But there's something ironic about the erroneous notion that church is a place where people have it all together. The last time I checked, every single service finds us on our knees, as "we acknowledge and bewail our manifold sins and wickedness" (BCP p. 331). So it's a darn good thing that the Apostle Paul tells us, *"The saying is trustworthy and deserving of full acceptance, that Christ Jesus came into the world to save sinners" (1 Timothy 1:15, ESV).*

Put the emphasis on the last word of that sentence. Those are the only kind of people you will find at church.

> Almighty and everlasting God, You hate nothing You have made and forgive the sins of all who are penitent: Create and make in us new and contrite hearts, that we, worthily lamenting our sins and acknowledging our wretchedness, may obtain of You, the God of all mercy, perfect remission and forgiveness; through Jesus Christ our Lord, who lives and reigns with You and the Holy Spirit, one God, for ever and ever. Amen. (Collect for Ash Wednesday – BCP p. 264)

May 26

GOD IS THE GIVER of all good gifts and the source of all human happiness. That happiness is refracted through those gifts, of course. But so great is His pleasure in His creatures that He cares about the desires of our hearts.

When our love of fellow creatures takes precedence over our love of the Creator, then we diminish both relationships. The great preacher Jonathan Edwards said, "The enjoyment of [God] is the only happiness with which our souls can be satisfied… Fathers and mothers, husbands, wives, or children, or the company of earthly friends, are but shadows; but the enjoyment of God is the substance. These are but scattered beams; but God is the sun. These are but streams; but God is the fountain."

The psalmist says it this way: *"Take delight in the LORD, and He will give you your heart's desires" (Psalm 37:4, NLT)*. And, as we see in the following prayer, He gives us even more than our hearts are able to desire!

> O God, You have prepared for those who love You such good things as surpass our understanding: Pour into our hearts such love towards You, that we, loving You in all things and above all things, may obtain Your promises, which exceed all that we can desire; through Jesus Christ our Lord, who lives and reigns with You and the Holy Spirit, one God, for ever and ever. Amen. (Sixth Sunday of Easter – BCP p. 225)

May 27

OF ALL THE OUTLANDISH things Jesus said, the list-topper might be His injunction from the Sermon on the Mount: *"Do not resist the one who is evil" (Matthew 5:39, ESV)*. He fleshes this out in story form in the parable of the wheat and the tares.

During the night an enemy comes and sows bad tares among the good wheat in a farmers field. The farmer's helpers naturally want to resist the evildoer by rooting out all evidence of his wicked work. The farmer's response? *"'No,' he answered, 'because while you are pulling the weeds, you may uproot the wheat with them. Let both grow together until the harvest'" (Matthew 13:29–30, NIV)*.

Jesus says discerning the good from the bad is not your job; it's God's job. He also says resisting evil is not your job either; it's God's work to sort it all out. Jesus says some crazy things, doesn't He? It's a good thing He is God and we are not.

> Almighty and everlasting God, You govern all things in both heaven and on earth: Mercifully hear the supplications of Your people, and in our time grant us Your peace; through Jesus Christ our Lord, who lives and reigns with You and the Holy Spirit, one God, for ever and ever. Amen. (Fourth Sunday after the Epiphany – BCP p. 215)

May 28

> *"We know that the whole creation has been groaning in labor pains until now; and not only the creation, but we ourselves, who have the first fruits of the Spirit, groan inwardly while we wait for adoption, the redemption of our bodies. For in hope we were saved. Now hope that is seen is not hope. For who hopes for what is seen? But if we hope for what we do not see, we wait for it with patience" (Romans 8:22–25, NRSV)*.

SO MUCH OF LIFE is waiting. What are you waiting for today? Some say that waiting is the hardest part. St. Paul says that we wait with both groaning and patience.

The funny thing about patience or impatience is that neither has much bearing on that for which we wait. We can't make the thing come any earlier. So sometimes groaning feels good; sometimes we are given the peaceful gift of patience.

In the end, however, God will do what He will do when He will do it. And our job is to wait!

> O God, the King of glory, You have exalted Your only Son Jesus Christ with great triumph to Your kingdom in heaven: Do not leave us comfortless, but send us Your Holy Spirit to strengthen us, and exalt us to that place where our Savior Christ has gone before; who lives and reigns with You and the Holy Spirit, one God, in glory everlasting. Amen. (Seventh Sunday of Easter – BCP p. 226)

May 29

LOVE IS ALWAYS FETTERED. Loving another person always exacts some measure of your own freedom. Being in a relationship always imposes limits on your personal autonomy. To put it more starkly—and biblically—love demands death to self. There are no exceptions to this rule.

You've likely heard this at a wedding: *"Love is patient, love is kind. It does not envy, it does not boast, it is not proud. It does not dishonor others, it is not self-seeking, it is not easily angered, it keeps no record of wrongs. Love does not delight in evil but rejoices with the truth. It always protects, always trusts, always hopes, always perseveres" (1 Corinthians 13:4–7, NIV).*

This is good news, friends. Because, as Jesus says, whoever loses his life will save it. That is the work of love. And because He is love, it is His work in your life.

> Almighty God, You alone can bring into order the unruly wills and affections of sinners: Grant Your people grace to love what You command and desire what You promise; that, among the swift and varied changes of the world, our hearts may surely there be fixed where true joys are to be found; through Jesus Christ our Lord, who lives and reigns with You and the Holy Spirit, one God, now and for ever. Amen. (Fifth Sunday in Lent – BCP p. 219)

May 30

HAVING TO DO SOMETHING that you don't want to do presents you with a few options. You can just not do it and deal with the consequences. You can try to get somebody else to do it for you and deal with the loss of relational capital with that person. You can grin and bear it, gut it out, and get 'er done, which usually leaves you frustrated and unsatisfied with the eventual result.

There is another way, particularly if the thing you don't want to do is what you know you should do—the right thing to do. In the prayer from yesterday's devotion, we asked God for the grace to "love what [He] command[s]." Thomas Cranmer, the author of most of these BCP prayers, really liked that notion because the same phrase shows up in the prayer we'll pray today.

Cranmer taught that what the heart loves, the mind justifies, and the will pursues. You can try to fake it till you make it, but your fake will not look like the real thing, and you won't "make it" in any satisfactory way. What you need is a change of heart—a true desire to do what God desires. That desire doesn't come from willpower; it comes from God Himself! This is what the Apostle Paul tells us. *"Now all glory to God, who is able, through His mighty power at work within us, to accomplish infinitely more than we might ask or think" (Ephesians 3:20, NLT).* In another place, Jesus tells us that we do not have because we do not ask. So, let's ask!

> Almighty and everlasting God, increase in us the gifts of faith, hope, and charity; and, that we may obtain what You promise, make us love what You command; through Jesus Christ our Lord, who lives and reigns with You and the Holy Spirit, one God, for ever and ever. Amen. (Proper 25 – BCP p. 235)

May 31

> *"Now if the ministry that brought death, which was engraved in letters on stone, came with glory, so that the Israelites could not look steadily at the face of Moses because of its glory, transitory though it was, will not the ministry of the Spirit be even more glorious? If the ministry that brought condemnation was glorious, how much more glorious is the ministry that brings righteousness!" (2 Corinthians 3:7–9, NIV).*

PAUL CALLS GOD'S LAW the ministry of death and condemnation. That is because God's Law demands perfection from you. There is no gradation of sin among people or among sins. There is no grading curve or "well, you've done your best." In short there is absolutely NO mercy contained in the Law. Therefore, you are "bound" to fail. And because you are bound to fail, you will be condemned.

Do you see now that your only hope is to put your entire trust in the death and resurrection of Jesus Christ? And when your hope is there, then there is therefore no condemnation for those who are in Christ Jesus. And, that's all there is—there isn't anymore.

> Almighty Father, who gave Your only Son to die for our sins and to rise for our justification: Give us grace so to put away the leaven of malice and wickedness, that we may always serve You in pureness of living and truth; through Jesus Christ Your Son our Lord, who lives and reigns with You and the Holy Spirit, one God, now and for ever. Amen. (Friday in Easter Week – BCP p. 224)

JUNE

June 1

"But ask the animals, and they will teach you, or the birds in the sky, and they will tell you; or speak to the earth, and it will teach you, or let the fish in the sea inform you. Which of all these does not know that the hand of the LORD has done this? In His hand is the life of every creature and the breath of all mankind" (Job 12:7–10, NIV).

ON THIS FIRST DAY of June, a poem called "All in June" by the Welsh poet William Henry Davies:

> A week ago I had a fire
> To warm my feet, my hands and face;
> Cold winds, that never make a friend,
> Crept in and out of every place.
>
> Today the fields are rich in grass,
> And buttercups in thousands grow;
> I'll show the world where I have been—
> With gold-dust seen on either shoe.
>
> Till to my garden back I come,
> Where bumble-bees for hours and hours
> Sit on their soft, fat, velvet bums,
> To wriggle out of hollow flowers.

Hope you enjoy your day today and have a good long look around.

Almighty and everlasting God, You made the universe with all its marvelous order, its atoms, worlds, and galaxies, and the infinite complexity of living creatures: Grant that, as we probe the mysteries of Your creation, we may come to know You more truly, and more surely fulfill our role in Your eternal purpose; in the name of Jesus Christ our Lord. Amen. (For Knowledge of God's Creation – BCP p. 827)

June 2

WE ARE PEOPLE OF the Word. That is important to remember when there are so many words said, written, placarded, tweeted, posted, chanted, and shouted. While those who wield words have a kind of authority, we believe that God's Word has authority over us.

While instructing Timothy on the dangers of false teachers, St. Paul says, *"Keep reminding God's people of these things. Warn them before God against quarreling about words; it is of no value, and only ruins those who listen" (2 Timothy 2:14, NIV).* Paul then reminds us that *"All Scripture is God-breathed and is useful for teaching, rebuking, correcting and training in righteousness" (2 Timothy 3:16, NIV).*

The Bible is no respecter or protector of any given ideology, and thankfully, the Holy Spirit convicts and comforts one and all. Cleaving to the Word of God is always a good idea, and perhaps now more than ever.

Blessed Lord, who caused all holy Scriptures to be written for our learning: Grant us to hear them, read, mark, learn, and inwardly digest them, that we may embrace and ever hold fast the blessed hope of everlasting life, which You have given us in our Savior Jesus Christ; who lives and reigns with You and the Holy Spirit, one God, for ever and ever. Amen. (Proper 28 – BCP p. 236)

June 3

THE EPISTLE READING FOR the second Sunday after Pentecost is the veritable poster child for gospel articulation; it's the flagship verse we display on the front page of our Christ Church website: *"For while we were still weak, at the right time Christ died for the ungodly. Indeed, rarely will anyone die for a righteous person— though perhaps for a good person someone might actually dare to die. But God proves His love for us in that while we still were sinners Christ died for us"* (Romans 5:6–8, NRSV).

I'll be honest. If every single theological, emotional, personal, relational, professional, and existential egg I have, have had, will have, and imagine I will someday have isn't squarely and snugly and squatly in this basket of justification by grace, then I'm S.O.L. (sh*t out of luck). As we've said before, the decisive reason to believe the Christian story is not because it is helpful, or life-affirming, or the surest road to your Best Life Now. You are a Christian because the story of God's self-revelation in Jesus Christ is true.

And the goodest of the truest news is this: You and I are irredeemably ungodly in and of ourselves. But God doesn't care one wheedling whit about that. In a cosmological shazam moment, Christ's death on the cross makes you a godly person in the blink of an eye, from soup to nuts, no questions asked. Theologians call this imputation; I call it miraculously good news for me personally.

If someone can convince me that St. Paul's perspicacity into this most profound universality is off the mark, then I'll hang up my dog collar, transmogrify my clerical robes into curtains or a tablecloth, and show up as your greeter at Walmart—or, better yet, serve you a cocktail behind the downstairs bar at your favorite watering hole. Would likely need to grow a mustache for the latter occupation.

All glory be to Thee, Almighty God, our heavenly Father, for that Thou, of Thy tender mercy, didst give Thine only Son Jesus Christ to suffer death upon the cross for our redemption; who made there, by His one oblation of Himself once offered, a full, perfect, and sufficient sacrifice, oblation, and satisfaction, for the sins of the whole world; and did institute, and in His holy Gospel command us to continue, a perpetual memory of that His precious death and sacrifice, until His coming again. (Eucharistic Prayer Rite I – BCP p. 334)

June 4

THE GREAT JAZZ MUSICIAN Cannonball Adderley gave a kind of prologue to the title track of his 1966 Grammy winning album. Recorded in front of a live audience, Adderley said, "You know, sometimes we're not prepared for adversity. When it happens, sometimes we're caught short. We don't know exactly how to handle it when it comes up. Sometimes we don't know just what to do when adversity takes over. And I have advice for all of us. I got it from my pianist Joe Zawinul who wrote this tune. And it sounds like what you're supposed to say when you have that kind of problem. It's called mercy, mercy, mercy."

His album is called *Mercy, Mercy, Mercy! Live at "The Club,"* and the title track became a surprise hit, reaching #11 on the Billboard Hot 100. It's no surprise, however, that we are all in need of mercy when adversity comes, and we are caught short and do not know what to do. Adderley (and his pianist) had the right idea in mind when they came up with that title.

Thankfully we have a God "whose property is always to have mercy," as our Prayer of Humble Access says. The psalmist tells us the same thing: *"The LORD is merciful and gracious, Slow to anger, and abounding in mercy" (Psalm 103:8, NKJV).* There is no better way to start, continue, or end your day than with mercy, mercy, mercy!

> O God, You declare Your almighty power chiefly in showing mercy and pity: Grant us the fullness of Your grace, that we, running to obtain Your promises, may become partakers of Your heavenly treasure; through Jesus Christ our Lord, who lives and reigns with You and the Holy Spirit, one God, for ever and ever. Amen. (Proper 21 – BCP p. 234)

June 5

> *"Early in the morning, while it was still dark, Jesus got up and slipped out to a solitary place to pray"* (Mark 1:35, BSB).

HAVE YOU EVER NOTICED that dogs seem to be able to go from deep sleep to full sprint in less than 5 seconds? Humans need more transition time, more time at the margins. Jesus clearly did. He often slipped off by Himself, after the fray or before the day, to pray.

The older I get, the more I crave time at the margins. One wonders, in the end, if that is not the most important time of all.

> O heavenly Father, in whom we live and move and have our being: We humbly pray Thee so to guide and govern us by Thy Holy Spirit, that in all the cares and occupations of our life we may not forget Thee, but may remember that we are ever walking in Thy sight; through Jesus Christ our Lord. Amen. (A Collect for Guidance – BCP p. 57)

June 6

CHEAP TRICK STRIKES THE affixed and submerged bell that peals across our inner universe from cradle to grave: "I want you to want me / I need you to need me / I'd love you to love me / I'm beggin' you to beg me."

Nearly everything we do is an attempt to have someone in particular, or anyone at all, say, "Yes! I want you. Yes! I need you. Yes! I love you. Yes! I beg you." We spend our days asking anyone who will listen, "Do you love me? Am I lovable?" The problem with everyone clogging the airwaves with the same question is that nobody has the bandwidth to respond to anyone else.

Nobody except Jesus. His proclamations can feel like cold comfort when you want an answer from someone with flesh and bones. But, He did take on flesh and bones and answered your inner drum-beating question with His cross.

See Paul's pithy summary: *"Have this mind among yourselves, which is yours in Christ Jesus, who, though He was in the form of God, did not count equality with God a thing to be grasped, but emptied Himself, by taking the form of a servant, being born in the likeness of men. And being found in human form, He humbled Himself by becoming obedient to the point of death, even death on a cross"* (Philippians 2:5–8, ESV).

> Almighty God, whom truly to know is everlasting life: Grant us so perfectly to know Your Son Jesus Christ to be the way, the truth, and the life, that we may steadfastly follow His steps in the way that leads to eternal life; through Jesus Christ Your Son our Lord, who lives and reigns with You, in the unity of the Holy Spirit, one God, for ever and ever. Amen. (Fifth Sunday of Easter – BCP p. 225)

June 7

"Simon, Simon, Satan has asked to sift all of you as wheat. But I have prayed for you, Simon, that your faith may not fail. And when you have turned back, strengthen your brothers" (Luke 22:31–32, NIV).

JESUS IS IN THE Garden of Gethsemane about to be betrayed by Judas and then denied by Peter. He knows what is coming, so He tells Peter that after the denial that he, Peter, will turn back to be of use. Another word of grace from Jesus, despite the extreme anxiety of what lies ahead.

Our interior lives are ramshackle at best. Our best efforts are often piddling. Yet, that doesn't stop God from using us. Rickety and ragtag is the church triumphant.

O God, whose Son Jesus is the good shepherd of Your people: Grant that when we hear His voice we may know Him who calls us each by name, and follow where He leads; who, with You and the Holy Spirit, lives and reigns, one God, for ever and ever. Amen. (Fourth Sunday of Easter – BCP p. 225)

June 8

"Then He [God] brought him [Abraham] outside and said, 'Look now toward heaven, and count the stars if you are able to number them.' And He said to him, 'So shall your descendants be.' And he believed in the LORD, and He accounted it to him for righteousness" (Genesis 15:5–6, NKJV).

I WONDER IF GOD'S conversation with Abraham recounted in this passage is the derivation for wishing upon a star? The Disney version is, "When you wish upon a star / Makes no difference who you are / Anything your heart desires / Will come to you." One wonders how such nonsense could so deeply permeate the American psyche.

Biblically, however, it has an even more far-fetched precedent. Abram, the childless old man, will have a child at 100 years old, and his descendants will outnumber the stars. And we, just by believing (a kind of wishing, isn't it?), will be given absolution, total immunity, and a can't-believe-it-'til-you-see-it kind of eternal life.

> O God, whose glory it is always to have mercy: Be gracious to all who have gone astray from Your ways, and bring them again with penitent hearts and steadfast faith to embrace and hold fast the unchangeable truth of Your Word, Jesus Christ Your Son; who with You and the Holy Spirit lives and reigns, one God, for ever and ever. Amen. (Second Sunday in Lent – BCP p. 218)

June 9

PAUL'S LETTER TO THE Romans has been called the Mount Everest of Scripture. It is his most thorough and systematic interpolation of the gospel. This is surely one of the epistle's apexes:

"There is therefore now no condemnation for those who are in Christ Jesus. For the law of the Spirit of life in Christ Jesus has set you free from the law of sin and of death. For God has done what the law, weakened by the flesh, could not do: by sending His own Son in the likeness of sinful flesh, and to deal with sin, He condemned sin in the flesh, so that the just requirement of the law might be fulfilled in

us, who walk not according to the flesh but according to the Spirit" *(Romans 8:1–4, NRSV).*

Short version: There is no condemnation for us because it all fell on God's own Son. Our life is a response of gratitude. But, knowing what to do (the Law) is just not enough. That's why education by itself isn't the answer to the world's woes. We need the Spirit to effectuate what God commands.

> O Lord, mercifully receive the prayers of Your people who call upon You, and grant that we may know and understand what things we ought to do, and also may have grace and power faithfully to accomplish them; through Jesus Christ our Lord, who lives and reigns with You and the Holy Spirit, one God, now and for ever. Amen. (Proper 10 – BCP p. 231)

June 10

WHEN WE ARE OVERTAKEN by fears, we are affected in mind, body, and spirit. Such is the holistic nature of our created being: The boundaries between mind, body, and spirit are, if not artificial, at least easily blurred. Anxiety, for instance, hijacks the mind, agitates the body, and holds the spirit hostage.

While never an experience one wishes for, being overtaken in this way does remind us that our wills are not as free as we imagine them to be. We are forced to face the reality that we are not the captains of our own ships. Not in any final sense.

When we plunge into those places, it is so important to remember that God is in control. Our recourse is that of the psalmist, who says, *"For I hear the whispering of many—terror on every side!—as they scheme together against me, as they plot to take my life. But I trust in You, O LORD; I say, 'You are my God.' My times are in Your hand; rescue me from the hand of my enemies and from my persecutors! Make Your face shine on Your servant; save me in Your steadfast love!" (Psalm 31:13–16, ESV).*

No matter what, your life—your very being—is in God's hands.

> Almighty God, You know that we have no power in ourselves to help ourselves: Keep us both outwardly in our bodies and inwardly in our souls, that we may be defended from all adversities which may happen to the body, and from all evil thoughts which may assault and hurt the soul; through Jesus Christ our Lord, who lives and reigns with You and the Holy Spirit, one God, for ever and ever. Amen. (Third Sunday in Lent – BCP p. 218)

June 11

> *"When it was evening on that day, the first day of the week, and the doors of the house where the disciples had met were locked for fear of the Jews, Jesus came and stood among them and said, 'Peace be with you.' After He said this, He showed them His hands and His side. Then the disciples rejoiced when they saw the Lord"* *(John 20:19–20, NRSV).*

HAVING COMPLETED HIS EPIC journey, Odysseus returns to Ithaca in disguise. The only person to recognize him is Eurycleia, his childhood nurse. And how does she know him? By a scar on Odysseus' leg, just above his knee.

In this gospel passage from Pentecost Sunday, Jesus returns from His epic journey (the cross, the descent into hell, the empty tomb) to greet His disciples. Apparently, they don't recognize

Him at first. Not until He shows them His scars. When they glimpsed His scars, they "rejoiced when they saw the Lord."

Loath as we are to do so, revealing our weaknesses is the only way to be fully known by another. We may admire strength in another, but that does not inspire intimacy. Remember what the prophet Isaiah says, "by His wounds we are healed."

> Lord Jesus Christ, You said to Your apostles, "Peace I give to you; My own peace I leave with you": Regard not our sins, but the faith of Your Church, and give to us the peace and unity of that heavenly City, where with the Father and the Holy Spirit You live and reign, now and for ever. Amen. (The Collect at the Prayers – BCP p. 395)

June 12

"Then children were brought to Him that He might lay His hands on them and pray. The disciples rebuked the people, but Jesus said, 'Let the little children come to Me and do not hinder them, for to such belongs the kingdom of heaven'" (Matthew 19:13–14, ESV).

I'VE LONG WONDERED WHAT Jesus means when He says that in order to receive the kingdom of heaven we must become like little children. It's not that children are morally pure; any parent knows that about his or her child instantly. My guess has been that children are dependent, showing us our own dependency on God the Father.

But then, the father of a two-year-old reminded me that children live in the present tense. Eureka! When his son takes a tumble, he says, "Daddy, I fall!" Not, "I fell," and not, "Let's make a plan so I don't fall in the future," but, "I fall!" Little children live in the present. There is a quality of "Give us this day our daily bread" about the way little children exist. The 12-Step community knows the wisdom of one day at a time; it seems that children—and Jesus—do too.

> Watch over Your child, O Lord, as our days increase; bless and guide us wherever we may be. Strengthen us when we stand; comfort us when discouraged or sorrowful; raise us up if we fall; and in our hearts may Your peace which passes understanding abide all the days of our life; through Jesus Christ our Lord. Amen. (For a Birthday – BCP p. 830)

June 13

IN THE UPSIDE-DOWN WORLD of the gospel, failure equals freedom. To fail is to be crowbarred from the lockstep lunacy of success at all costs. To fail is to be forced to drop that weight which has withered your humanity and your childlikeness. To fail is to have the lucky chance to look God straight in the eye. You remember Janis Joplin singing about failure: "Freedom's just another word for nothing left to lose."

Wendell Berry wrote a poem about failure. He tried to raise some crops on a piece of land to no avail. He noticed young trees reclaiming the land he had tried to cultivate. His failure led to a deeper joy:

> And I think of all the effort
> I have wasted and all the time,
> and of how much joy I took
> in that failed work and how much
> it taught me. For in so failing

I learned something of my place
something of myself, and now
I welcome back the trees.

The psalmist says, *"My health may fail, and my spirit may grow weak, but God remains the strength of my heart; He is mine forever" (Psalm 73:26, NLT).* Where have you failed? Substitute whatever that is for the psalmist's "health." Where are you weak? Substitute that for the psalmist's "spirit." And thankfully, there is no substitute for the God who remains the strength of your heart.

Here is a BCP prayer for young persons, which is really for all persons.

> God our Father, You see Your children growing up in an unsteady and confusing world: Show us that Your ways give more life than the ways of the world, and that following You is better than chasing after selfish goals. Help us to take failure, not as a measure of our worth, but as a chance for a new start. Give us strength to hold our faith in You, and to keep alive our joy in Your creation; through Jesus Christ our Lord. Amen. (For Young Persons – BCP p. 829)

June 14

I LOVE THIS INSIGHT from late pastor-theologian Eugene Peterson: "I have developed a strong allergy to the word 'dysfunctional' when applied to persons… It's a word useful for describing machines, not persons." When we value others for what they can do rather than for who they are, then "Love, the commanded relation, gives way to considerations of efficiency." Human doings, rather than human beings, indeed.

When life becomes a problem to be solved, or a goal to meet, or a dream to achieve, or a kingdom to establish, then inevitably people become the sum of their functionality. This is a mistake of dystopian proportions, not to mention a rebellion against God's way of "doing" things. Here is 1 John: *"Beloved, let us love one another, for love is from God, and whoever loves has been born of God and knows God" (1 John 4:7, ESV).*

John famously reminds us that we love only because God first loved us. Thankfully, He loved and loves us without reference to our "function" and despite our inefficiency.

O God, You have taught us to keep all Your commandments by loving You and our neighbor: Grant us the grace of Your Holy Spirit, that we may be devoted to You with our whole heart, and united to one another with pure affection; through Jesus Christ our Lord, who lives and reigns with You and the Holy Spirit, one God, for ever and ever. Amen. (Proper 9 – BCP p. 230)

June 15

"See, I am doing a new thing! Now it springs up; do you not perceive it? I am making a way in the wilderness and streams in the wasteland" (Isaiah 43:19, NIV).

GOD DOES NEW THINGS. The shopworn grooves of your life are nothing to Him, nor are the ruts that feel like cavernous walls around you. See, I am doing a new thing! God is totally capable of discontinuity. New beginnings, new chapters, new adventures.

God is like a merrymaking holiday guide, leading you into green pastures and a teeming glen behind a mountain that no one else knew was there. Look! The picnic is already laid out! He is a magician who pulls rabbits out of His hat and has cards you can't even imagine up His sleeve.

Do not underestimate what God can and will do, and do not give up on His mischief-making goodness! Did you already forget about Easter morning?

> O God of unchangeable power and eternal light: Look favorably on Your whole Church, that wonderful and sacred mystery; by the effectual working of Your providence, carry out in tranquility the plan of salvation; let the whole world see and know that things which were cast down are being raised up, and things which had grown old are being made new, and that all things are being brought to their perfection by Him through whom all things were made, Your Son Jesus Christ our Lord; who lives and reigns with You, in the unity of the Holy Spirit, one God, for ever and ever. Amen. (From the Good Friday Liturgy – BCP p. 280)

June 16

JESUS' SERMON ON THE Plain is filled with the same difficult (impossible?) moral injunctions as the Sermon on the Mount: Love your enemies; do good to those who hate you; bless those who curse you; pray for those who abuse you. This is a beautiful version of life in which the power structures are all turned upside down and the only competition is who can abdicate their rights more fully or expeditiously.

How I wish this impulse sprung from my own particular heart, but it just doesn't. The opposite does. I am therefore relieved to find this gem buried in the middle of Jesus' sermon: *"The Most High … is kind to the ungrateful and the wicked"* (Luke 6:35, NRSV).

Nice to be included in God's kindness! And yet, we can still pray for God's Spirit to move our hearts toward others—even and especially those who are difficult.

> Almighty God, whose most dear Son went not up to joy but first He suffered pain, and entered not into glory before He was crucified: Mercifully grant that we, walking in the way of the cross, may find it none other than the way of life and peace; through the same Thy Son Jesus Christ our Lord. Amen. (A Collect for Fridays – BCP p. 99)

June 17

ST. PAUL'S 1ST CENTURY salvo into the perennial and raging conflict of identity politics remains the boldest and most radical move there is. It's one that realigns all fidelities and cuts clean across the pressing claims of racial, religious, social, tribal, class, and gender demarcations, just to name a few. Ready for it? Here it is.

"You are all sons and daughters of God through faith in Christ Jesus. For all of you who were baptized into Christ have clothed yourselves with Christ. There is neither Jew nor Greek, there is neither slave nor free, there is neither male nor female; for you are all one in Christ Jesus" (Galatians 3:26–28, NASB).

Paul reorients our identity from the *accidental,* which in Aristotelian thought is a property not essential to one's nature, to the *fundamental* or core truth about a person. This reorientation happens when we are born anew in Christ. The beauty of this proclamation is that our common identity in Christ supersedes any and all other formerly defining factors of our existence. In Christ, *"The old has passed away; behold, the new has come" (2 Corinthians 5:17, ESV).*

Almighty God, You sent Your Son Jesus Christ to reconcile the world to Yourself: We praise and bless You for those whom You have sent in the power of the Spirit to preach the Gospel to the nations. We thank You that in all parts of the earth a community of love has been gathered together by their prayers and labors, and that in every place Your servants call upon Your Name; for the kingdom and the power and the glory are Yours for ever. Amen. (For the Mission of the Church – BCP p. 838)

June 18

YOU KNOW WHAT IT feels like to be met with resistance. Trying to get a child to do something she doesn't want to do. Having your agenda blocked at work. The cold shoulder or unreturned phone call from someone you thought was a friend. You meet yourself with resistance too—your spirit willing but your flesh weak.

When God entered the world, He was met with violent resistance: *"He came unto His own, and His own received Him not" (John 1:11, KJV)*. That resistance—*our* resistance—extended all the way to the foot of the cross.

And yet, God ultimately met our resistance with welcome. Crazy, huh?

Almighty and everlasting God, You are always more ready to hear than we to pray, and to give more than we either desire or deserve: Pour upon us the abundance of Your mercy, forgiving us those things of which our conscience is afraid, and giving us those good things for which we are not worthy to ask, except through the merits and mediation of Jesus Christ our Savior; who lives and reigns with You and the Holy Spirit, one God, for ever and ever. Amen. (Proper 22 – BCP p. 234)

June 19

"I am only dust and ashes, but allow me to speak, since, see, it is to Your mercy that I am speaking and not to man, my mocker. You, too, may smile at me, but You will turn and have compassion on me."

THAT IS AUGUSTINE ON prayer from his *Confessions*.

Nice way to think about prayer. When we speak to God, we are speaking directly to His mercy. When we speak to people, or to ourselves, we are often speaking to judgment or suspicion or ridicule or inattentiveness. Very, very few people know how to actually listen. Nobody is able to listen with only mercy.

"If any of you lacks wisdom, let him ask God, who gives generously to all without reproach, and it will be given him" (James 1:5, ESV).

Let us pray.

O Lord our God, accept the fervent prayers of Your people; in the multitude of Your mercies, look with compassion upon us and all who turn to You for help; for You are gracious, O lover of souls, and to You we give glory, Father, Son, and Holy Spirit, now and for ever. Amen. (The Collect at the Prayers – BCP p. 395)

June 20

I PLAYED GOLF WITH a friend last Friday. We stood on the tee box of the tenth hole—a notoriously long and difficult par-three on this golf course. My friend pulled a 4-iron, commenting that it wasn't enough club for the hole. His swing and contact were excellent, and we watched the ball in flight on an excellent line. It landed just shy of the green and rolled toward the pin placed at the back of the green. It kept rolling until, unbelievably, it disappeared into the hole! Clamorous joy and celebration ensued.

I had absolutely nothing to do with my friend's ace, yet I experienced the joy as my own—as if I had gotten a hole in one myself! So too with Christ's resurrection: Paul says, *"Since you have been raised to new life with Christ, set your sights on the realities of heaven, where Christ sits in the place of honor at God's right hand"* *(Colossians 3:1, NLT).*

You have been raised! Past tense. His victory over death is yours to celebrate.

> O God, You make us glad with the weekly remembrance of the glorious resurrection of Your Son our Lord: Give us this day such blessing through our worship of You, that the week to come may be spent in Your favor; through Jesus Christ our Lord. Amen. (A Collect for Sundays – BCP p. 98)

June 21

"And again He said, 'To what shall I compare the kingdom of God? It is like leaven that a woman took and hid in three measures of flour, until it was all leavened'" (Luke 13:20–21, ESV).

WHETHER YOU BAKE BREAD or not, anyone can notice what you do not see in the rising dough: the yeast.

Jesus says that the woman *hid* the leaven in the flour. The kingdom of God is *hidden.* You cannot see what is hidden. Ergo, you cannot see the kingdom of God at work. Why is this such good news? Because even and especially when all seems to be lost or broken or hopeless, God is at work! Not only do you not make the kingdom of God happen, you can't even see it happening. As we read elsewhere in the Bible, we walk by faith and not by sight.

> Grant, O Lord, that the course of this world may be peaceably governed by Your providence; and that we may joyfully serve You in confidence and serenity; through Jesus Christ our Lord, who lives and reigns with You and the Holy Spirit, one God, for ever and ever. Amen. (Proper 3 – BCP p. 229)

June 22

I WONDER HOW MANY of us suffer from a strain of perfectionism. In an excellent *This American Life* podcast called "My Bad," listeners were asked to send in their most embarrassing moments. Of course, the episode was hilarious, but the host's summary was poignant.

She noticed that a large majority of people were still deeply ashamed of their embarrassing moment, some nearly crippled by it. Her conclusion: we think we are not allowed to make mistakes in life; we expect to skate through life with a perfect record.

Here is what the psalmist says about that: *"The steps of a man are established by the LORD, when He delights in his way; though he fall, he shall not be cast headlong, for the LORD upholds his hand"* (Psalm 37:23–24, ESV).

We *will* fall over and over and over and over and over again. But we will not be cast headlong. It will be okay.

> Lord, we pray that Your grace may always precede and follow us, that we may continually be given to good works; through Jesus Christ our Lord, who lives and reigns with You and the Holy Spirit, one God, now and for ever. Amen. (Proper 23 – BCP p. 234)

June 23

"Blessed are those who trust in the LORD, whose trust is the LORD" (Jeremiah 17:7, NRSV).

THE ALMOST DAILY TALKS about trust in the Lord quite a lot, and for good reason. Humans have a tendency to usurp God's role. Life actually lived is a hybrid of trust in ourselves, trust in other people or institutions, trust in the "universe," and—if we are people of faith—trust in God.

I like the way that this verse from Jeremiah is parsed out. Our trust is not only in the Lord, our trust *is* the Lord. Trust in the Lord can imply our ceding authority to Him—an action which proves confoundingly difficult. But if our trust *is* the Lord, then all the better! He just *is* and needs not our assent.

Good, right?

O God, the strength of all who put their trust in You: Mercifully accept our prayers; and because in our weakness we can do nothing good without You, give us the help of Your grace, that in keeping Your commandments we may please You both in will and deed; through Jesus Christ our Lord, who lives and reigns with You and the Holy Spirit, one God, for ever and ever. Amen. (Sixth Sunday After the Epiphany – BCP p. 216)

June 24

A WOMAN NAMED CAMILA in Thornton Wilder's *The Bridge of San Luis Rey* traded on her beauty. She climbed social classes, acquired a husband, standing, and wealth. But then she contracted a case of smallpox that left her exquisite face disfigured.

Although those who loved her did not forsake her, she forsook them. She could not believe that she could truly be loved without her physical charm.

What do you rely on for your acceptability? I have traded on and continue to trade on any number of things that I imagine pass for social capital. Of course, they are all castles in the air. In the end, they will all crumble. All that will be left is the only thing that has always been solid—the imputed righteousness of Christ.

"For our sake He made Him to be sin who knew no sin, so that in Him we might become the righteousness of God" (2 Corinthians 5:21, ESV).

> Blessed Lord, who caused all holy Scriptures to be written for our learning: Grant us so to hear them, read, mark, learn, and inwardly digest them, that we may embrace and ever hold fast the blessed hope of everlasting life, which You have given us in our Savior Jesus Christ; who lives and reigns with You and the Holy Spirit, one God, for ever and ever. Amen. (Proper 28 – BCP p. 236)

June 25

C. S. LEWIS OBSERVED this daily occurrence: "It comes the very moment you wake up each morning. All your wishes and hopes for the day rush at you like wild animals. And the first job each morning consists simply in shoving them all back; in listening to that other voice, taking that other point of view, letting that other larger, stronger, quieter life come flowing in. And so on, all day. Standing back from all your natural fussings and frettings; coming in out of the wind."

So true, but how do you shove all the wild, rushing animals back? How do you listen to That Other Voice? Not by willpower, for sure. The practice of detachment is helpful, but only a 50–50 proposition in my experience. Mindfulness is an ally, too—simply recognizing the shape and species of the wild animals as they rush in will begin to defang the beasts.

The surest way to experience the larger, stronger, quieter life is to admit your inability to control the animals (you are not a professional lion tamer, after all!) and ask God to be in charge of Everything—you, your animals, your frets and fusses, your very being. As St. Paul says, *"Don't worry about anything, but in everything, through prayer and petition with thanksgiving, present your requests to God" (Philippians 4:6, CSB).*

Here's a prayer to get you on your way today.

> Almighty and eternal God, so draw our hearts to Thee, so guide our minds, so fill our imaginations, so control our wills, that we may be wholly Thine, utterly dedicated unto Thee; and then use us, we pray Thee, as Thou wilt, and always to Thy glory and the welfare of Thy people; through our Lord and Savior Jesus Christ. Amen. (A Prayer of Self-Dedication – BCP p. 832)

June 26

I'M THINKING ABOUT THE amount of effort it takes to try to make actual reality fit the version of reality that we so desperately want. At its core, it is an Edenic and primal sin: believing that we are "like God"—able to create reality as well as answer only to our own authority. If you're iffy on the sinful side of this way of thinking, then at least you can agree that it is exhausting. For instance, accepting your spouse for who she is requires a lot less energy than trying to change her into your imagined ideal.

The psalmist says, *"The fool says in his heart, 'There is no God'" (Psalm 14:1).* The fool can say whatever he wants to say, but that does not alter the objective reality of God's existence. It's a good thing for the fool (and for the rest of us who try to construct our own realities) that the God who is real is the God of grace who has mercy on sinners.

> O God, You declare Your almighty power chiefly in showing mercy and pity: Grant us the fullness of Your grace, that we, running to obtain Your promises, may become partakers of Your heavenly treasure; through Jesus Christ our Lord, who lives and reigns with You and the Holy Spirit, one God, for ever and ever. Amen. (Proper 21 – BCP p. 234)

June 27

> "He [Jesus] put before them [the crowds] another parable: 'The kingdom of heaven is like a mustard seed that someone took and sowed in his field; it is the smallest of all the seeds, but when it has grown it is the greatest of shrubs and becomes a tree, so that the birds of the air come and make nests in its branches'" (Matthew 13:31–32, NRSV).

YOUR GUESS IS AS good as mine when it comes to Jesus' parables. He often used them to upset the apple cart of our held assumptions about God and His kingdom. I do know that they are not a logical problem to be solved, or a perfectly corresponding allegory. Instead, they are a multi-dimensional world to be entered into on their own terms. For anyone interested, I refer you to Robert Capon's *Kingdom, Grace, Judgment*—the writer's masterpiece on the parables.

But what about this little gem from the Gospel of Matthew? I'm thinking it has something to do with God's allergy to self-promotional and strong-arming Big Events. He seems to prefer, in Capon's words, "the least, the lost, the last, and the little." At least in this life—His life—that's how it played out. An awful and obscure death followed by a tucked-away, empty tomb, discovered only by a few low-status companions.

And yet, those are the days that changed the world forever!

Grant us, O Lord, to trust in You with all our hearts; for, as You always resist the proud who confide in their own strength, so You never forsake those who make their boast of Your mercy; through Jesus Christ our Lord, who lives and reigns with You and the Holy Spirit, one God, now and for ever. Amen. (Proper 18 – BCP p. 233)

June 28

"I GOT A FEELIN' / And it won't go away, oh no / Just one thing and I'll be OK / I need a miracle every day." The Grateful Dead got it right. I need a miracle every day.

The onrush of condemnation/suffering/bitter division/ unhealed wounds won't go away. All of that can be summed up under the power of sin. Luther told us that Christian life means "that the old creature in us … is to be drowned and die through *daily* … repentance, and … that *daily* a new person is to come forth and arise up to live before God in righteousness."

St. Paul says, *"Now to the one who works, wages are not credited as a gift but as an obligation. However, to the one who does not work but trusts God who justifies the ungodly, their faith is credited as righteousness" (Romans 4:4–5, NIV).* Trust in God is renewed by God daily. Well, at least Almost Daily! That is the miracle every day.

Let Your continual mercy, O Lord, cleanse and defend Your Church; and, because it cannot continue in safety without Your help, protect and govern it always by Your goodness; through Jesus Christ our Lord, who lives and reigns with You and the Holy Spirit, one God, for ever and ever. Amen. (Proper 13 – BCP p. 232)

June 29

THE APOSTLE PAUL, WRITING to Christians in Corinth beset by all manner of challenges, said, *"We are hard pressed on all sides, but not crushed; perplexed, but not in despair; persecuted, but not forsaken; struck down, but not destroyed" (2 Corinthians 4:8–9, BSB).*

Paul strikes the right balance here. He doesn't subscribe to an unrealistically optimistic view of the world, denying its difficulty. But, neither does he fall for hysteria or nihilism. He did not arrive at this place of peace through "choosing" to look for the good in life. Nor did he get there by cultivating the right mental practices in the midst of crisis.

Instead, Paul knows he is not crushed, in despair, forsaken, or destroyed because of one incontrovertible truth: God is real. Jesus Christ's death and resurrection *is* the ultimate triumph. God will finally redeem every hard-pressed, perplexing, persecuted and struck-down experience of every human life.

Including yours.

Most holy God, the source of all good desires, all right judgments, and all just works: Give to us, Your servants, that peace which the world cannot give, so that our minds may be fixed on the doing of Your will, and that we, being delivered from the fear of all enemies, may live in peace and quietness; through the mercies of Christ Jesus our Savior. Amen. (A Collect for Peace – BCP p. 123)

June 30

RECENTLY I HAD AN experience that revealed how powerful our subconscious is. I did not want to go to a certain place, but I felt that I really ought to. I had shored up my will and was going to do it despite my apprehensions. I was driving and looking for the exit I needed to take. And yet, without intentionally doing so, I passed the exit by 10 miles! I'm not a spacey driver or person, but I just "somehow" missed it. By then it was too late to do what I did not want to do in the first place.

I'm sure that you've had experiences like mine. Theologically, this is an illustration of the bound will. Although we are told over and over again that our wills are free, experience tells us over and over again that our thoughts, decisions, and actions are compromised in ways that are both obvious and undetectable. How many times have you wished you could take back something you've said and even wondered why you said it?

The Apostle Paul casts this ongoing internal tension inside of us as the opposing forces of flesh and Spirit. *"For the desires of the flesh are against the Spirit, and the desires of the Spirit are against the flesh, for these are opposed to each other, to keep you from doing the things you want to do" (Galatians 5:17, ESV).*

Thank God that He gives us His Spirit to help us! You are always on solid ground when you are suspicious of your own agency, yet fully confident in the power of God in your life. (FYI: I did do the thing I didn't want to do the next day!)

> Almighty God, You alone can bring into order the unruly wills and affections of sinners: Grant Your people grace to love what You command and desire what You promise, that, among the swift and varied changes of the world, our hearts may surely be fixed where the true joys are to be found; through Jesus Christ our Lord, who lives and reigns with You and the Holy Spirit, one God, now and forever. Amen. (Fifth Sunday in Lent – BCP p. 219)

JULY

July 1

I WOULD GUESS THAT almost no one can quote what is arguably the most famous passage in the Bible in full. We call it the "golden rule" and most of us learned it via this version: *"Whatever you want men to do to you, do also to them."* But do you know the rest of the verse? (I had forgotten until I just read it!) *"For this is the Law and the Prophets" (Matthew 7:12, NKJV).*

Would that we might live by the golden rule, for it is a beautiful summary of the Law and the Prophetic teaching, as well as a version of karma. But since we all fall short, it's a good thing that the golden rule is not the gospel. This is gospel: God has broken into the tit-for-tat chain of action and reaction to do for us infinitely better than we could ever do for others.

I'm grateful for the Law and the Prophets, but my life depends entirely on the gospel. The cross of Christ is God's golden gift to the world.

> O God, because without You we are not able to please You, mercifully grant that Your Holy Spirit may in all things direct and rule our hearts; through Jesus Christ our Lord, who lives and reigns with You and the Holy Spirit, one God, now and for ever. Amen. (Proper 19 – BCP p. 233)

July 2

IT'S TRUE THAT JESUS died for the sins of the world, but during His earthly life He didn't do everything that people asked Him to do. He didn't heal all the people who needed healing. He fed the 5,000, but not everyone else. He spoke to the multitudes, but most people never heard the sound of His voice.

Not everything is yours to fix. What are you trying to fix right now that just can't be fixed by you? Not everything is yours to do. What have you left undone that just can't be done by you?

Here is what the Bible says: *"The LORD Himself will fight for you. Just stay calm" (Exodus 14:14, NLT).*

O God, by whom the meek are guided in judgment, and light riseth up in darkness for the godly: Grant us, in all our doubts and uncertainties, the grace to ask what Thou wouldest have us to do, that the Spirit of wisdom may save us from all false choices, and that in Thy light we may see light, and in Thy straight path may not stumble, through Jesus Christ our Lord. Amen. (For Guidance – BCP p. 832)

July 3

"The LORD is close to the brokenhearted and saves those who are crushed in spirit" (Psalm 34:18, NIV).

I RAISE AN EYEBROW when someone says, "I have no regrets." It seems to me that only a sociopath could have no regrets in this life. Here's Garrison Keillor on regret and guilt:

I carry plenty of guilt around. I am not smug about guilt. I have to joke about it, for my own mental health, but I carry masses of regret... I have a picture of my ancestors standing in front of their Minnesota farmhouse, which years later caught fire and burned down. My dad was eight years old and watched it burn from the school-house across the road. He remembered his father raking through the ashes, looking for photographs, in grief, knowing the fire was his fault because he had postponed cleaning the chimney. That poor man is very much in my memory and I know how he feels.

I take comfort in the assurance that God has removed our guilt from us through the cross of Christ. Indeed, He is our refuge.

> Almighty God, the Father of our Lord Jesus Christ, from whom every family in heaven and earth is named, grant you to be strengthened with might by His Holy Spirit, that, Christ dwelling in your hearts by faith, you may be filled with the fullness of God. Amen. (Holy Baptism – BCP p. 311)

July 4

IN THE SERMON ON the Mount, Jesus concludes His section against judging others with this well-known statement: *"Do not give dogs what is holy, and do not throw your pearls before pigs, lest they trample them underfoot and turn to attack you" (Matthew 7:6, ESV).*

I assume we have to interpret His words in the context of judgment. Judgers are attackers, and they will always find a way to criticize even holy, precious things. (Dog- and pig-lovers will just have to take a deep breath and consider the cultural context!) In God's eyes and through the imputed righteousness of Christ, you are what is holy, and you are the pearl. Your Heavenly Father loves and cherishes you so, and you are always safe with Him.

> Let Your continual mercy, O Lord, cleanse and defend Your Church; and, because it cannot continue in safety without Your help, protect and govern it always by Your goodness; through Jesus Christ our Lord, who lives and

reigns with You and the Holy Spirit, one God, for ever and ever. Amen. (Proper 13 – BCP p. 232)

July 5

WHERE IS GOD'S OFFICE? God's office is at the end of your rope. The end of your rope does not have to be a one-time place of extreme desperation, although it certainly can be. I have a friend who says that we are all just three bad days away from a nervous breakdown, and most of us are already on day two!

It seems to me that we find ourselves at the end of our ropes multiple times per day. Those are the moments when we need help outside of ourselves. The beauty of our life in Christ is that those moments are the occasions not of despair but discovery. We discover that God is there; He is with you and for you.

This is what the Apostle Paul discovered when he came to the end of his rope. Vexed by what he calls a "thorn in [his] flesh," Paul turned to God for help: *"Three times I pleaded with the Lord to take it away from me. But He said to me, 'My grace is sufficient for you, for My power is made perfect in weakness.' Therefore I will boast all the more gladly about my weaknesses, so that Christ's power may rest on me. That is why, for Christ's sake, I delight in weaknesses, in insults, in hardships, in persecutions, in difficulties. For when I am weak, then I am strong" (2 Corinthians 12:8–10, NIV).*

Maybe the end of your rope is not such a bad place to be?

Grant us, O Lord, to trust in You with all our hearts; for, as You always resist the proud who confide in their own strength, so You never forsake those who make their boast of Your mercy; through Jesus Christ our Lord, who lives and reigns with You and the Holy Spirit, one God, now and for ever. Amen. (Proper 18 – BCP p. 233)

July 6

"Well done, good and faithful servant" (Matthew 25:21).

FOR ALL OF US who find worth in accomplishment and performance, that is a word we long to hear. Jesus says it, but only in parabolic form. You see that verse on gravestones: an epithet used as an epitaph.

The truth is—well, at least the gospel truth is—that no matter who we are or how we have fared in life, those who put their trust in the merit of Jesus Christ will hear these words from God the Father. Actually, we have heard them already; what belongs to our Savior belongs already to us.

> Blessed Lord, who caused all holy Scriptures to be written for our learning: Grant us so to hear them, read, mark, learn, and inwardly digest them, that we may embrace and ever hold fast the blessed hope of everlasting life, which You have given us in our Savior Jesus Christ; who lives and reigns with You and the Holy Spirit, one God, for ever and ever. Amen. (Proper 28 – BCP)

July 7

"Now I would remind you, brothers, of the gospel I preached to you, which you received, in which you stand, and by which you are being saved... For I delivered to you as of first importance what I also received: that Christ died for our sins in accordance with the Scriptures" (1 Corinthians 15:1–3, ESV).

THE PURPOSE OF PREACHING is the proclamation that Jesus Christ has died for our sins and that we are once and forever absolved. The disastrous result of the self-esteem movement is the obfuscation—even blessing—of our rebellious and wrong-headed nature.

The world calls what is bad good—and vice versa. Of course, the world is made up of you and me. Yet to live in such a world is to live in a non-reality that ultimately undermines our sense of worth and happiness. It is also to miss the true and deepest joy of receiving the grace of God, which is God's righteousness given through the merits and death of His Son for our sake.

The Prayer of Humble Access says it best:

> We do not presume to come to this Your table, O merciful Lord, trusting in our own righteousness, but in Your abundant and great mercies. We are not worthy so much as to gather up the crumbs under Your table; but You are the same Lord whose character is always to have mercy. Grant us, therefore, gracious Lord, so to eat the flesh of Your dear Son Jesus Christ, and to drink His blood, that our sinful bodies may be made clean by His body, and our souls washed through His most precious blood, and that we may evermore dwell in Him, and He in us. Amen. (BCP, 1928 version)

July 8

"The Spirit helps us in our weakness; for we do not know how to pray as we ought, but that very Spirit intercedes with sighs too deep for words" (Romans 8:26, NRSV).

THIS IS ONE OF the great promises of the God who actually understands us. He is the God who *gets* us. How often do you not know how to pray as you ought? Despite your efforts and intentions to pray, your brain addles and swirls, and before you know it, you are looking at your phone or tallying up the tasks of the day.

God's Spirit helps us, intercedes for us—basically prays in our stead. Just as Jesus lived and died in our stead. The substitutionary work of God continues, thankfully, even today.

The Spirit will even pray this prayer for you today!

Almighty God, to whom our needs are known before we ask: Help us to ask only what accords with Your will, and those good things which we dare not, or in our blindness cannot ask, grant us for the sake of Jesus Christ our Lord. Amen. (The Collect at the Prayers – BCP p. 394)

July 9

"Finally, brothers and sisters, whatever is true, whatever is noble, whatever is right, whatever is pure, whatever is lovely, whatever is admirable—if anything is excellent or praiseworthy—think about such things" (Philippians 4:8, NIV).

THE POET GERARD MANLEY Hopkins reminds us, "The world is charged with the grandeur of God." This can be easy to forget in a world inundated with the media blitz of woe and disaster. Or the normal slog of sunup to sundown living.

Nonetheless, the world is charged with the grandeur of God. Paul's encouragement to the believers in Philippi is an open invitation to range and roam the world for all its grandeur. From black holes to beetles to biochemistry. From the disco anthems of 1977 to the wisdom of Greek mythology. You name it—somewhere in there will be the grandeur of God—excellent and praiseworthy. Think about such things. What fun! What a relief!

> Almighty and everlasting God, You made the universe with all its marvelous order, its atoms, worlds, and galaxies, and the infinite complexity of living creatures: Grant that, as we probe the mysteries of Your creation, we may come to know You more truly, and more surely fulfill our role in Your eternal purpose; in the name of Jesus Christ our Lord. Amen. (For Knowledge of God's Creation – BCP p. 827)

July 10

> *"Yet You, LORD, are our Father. We are the clay, You are the potter; we are all the work of Your hand" (Isaiah 64:8, NIV).*

BIG DECISIONS CAN BE scary. Especially decisions that will change the course of your life, like moving or a job change or a change in relationship. You think somehow that the onus falls on you to make the "right" choice.

Yet, what if you saw your life through a different lens? The lens given to us by the Bible? That you are not the primary actor, but instead a cast member of a play directed by God Himself? What if you were clay molded into a beautiful shape by the Loving Potter? Wouldn't that take the pressure off?

> Direct us, O Lord, in all our doings with Thy most gracious favor, and further us with Thy continual help; that in all our works begun, continued, and ended in Thee, we may glorify Thy holy Name, and finally, by Thy mercy, obtain everlasting life; through Jesus Christ our Lord. Amen. (For Guidance – BCP p. 832)

July 11

"I am reminded of your sincere faith, a faith that lived first in your grandmother Lois and your mother Eunice and now, I am sure, lives in you" (2 Timothy 1:5, NRSV).

THAT'S PAUL WRITING TO Timothy, a fledgling minister. A few things spring to mind when I read this passage. First off, we see ours is not a patriarchal faith. Lois, Eunice, and a whole host of powerful women were leaders of the early church. Jesus treated women with counter-cultural equitability and respect.

Second, having done many baptisms in my life, I'm thinking here about how faith is communicated from generation to generation, as it was from Lois to Eunice to Timothy. Parents long for their children to know the grace and security of Jesus Christ. Seemingly wayward children hurt the hearts of their parents and often cause them to wonder what went wrong.

All I know is this: Children belong to God. As we say at a baptism, while making the sign of the cross on a baby's forehead, "You are sealed by the Holy Spirit in baptism and marked as Christ's own forever."

Marked as Christ's own forever. As a parent and as a Christian, I believe that is true.

> Almighty God, we entrust all who are dear to us to Thy never-failing care and love, for this life and the life to come, knowing that Thou art doing for them better things than we can desire or pray for; through Jesus Christ our Lord. Amen. (For Those We Love – BCP p. 831)

July 12

ENDING HIS LONG INTELLECTUAL and emotional slog from atheism to Christianity, C. S. Lewis finally ceded his life to Christ. It happened on a motorcycle ride to the Whipsnade Zoo with his brother. The Oxford don said, "When we set out I did not believe that Jesus Christ is the Son of God, and when we reached the zoo I did." That's the moment that eventually bore the fruit of *Mere Christianity*, *The Chronicles of Narnia*, and *The Screwtape Letters*, among his other masterful works.

St. Paul says, *"If you confess with your mouth that Jesus is Lord and believe in your heart that God raised Him from the dead, you will be saved" (Romans 10:9, ESV).*

Advent, Christmas, Easter—life in general: None of it makes sense if He is not the Son of God. I, for one, would hate to live in a world without Aslan!

> Almighty God, give us grace to cast away the works of darkness, and put on the armor of light, now in the time of this mortal life in which Your Son Jesus Christ came to visit us in great humility; that in the last day, when He shall come again in His glorious majesty to judge both the living and the dead, we may rise to the life immortal; through Him who lives and reigns with You and the Holy Spirit, one God, now and forever. Amen. (First Sunday of Advent – BCP p. 211)

July 13

IN 1926, THE FAMOUS mystery writer Agatha Christie disappeared for 11 days. One account says, "After her husband, Archie, began an affair with a younger woman, Christie fell into a depression. While out for a drive, she crashed her car down a hill and into a hedge. The car was found, but she was not; she had fled to a spa hotel, staying there under a false identity that shared a surname with her husband's paramour."

Do you ever feel like disappearing to a spa for 11 days with nobody knowing where you are? I thought so. Me too. That's why I love this verse. *"For you died to this life, and your real life is hidden with Christ in God" (Colossians 3:3, NLT).*

You still go through your days, the warp and woof of knowing, evading, opening up and shutting down. But, really, you in God's Witness Protection Program. Your real life is hidden with Christ in God.

> O Lord, support us all the day long, until the shadows lengthen, and the evening comes, and the busy world is hushed, and the fever of life is over, and our work is done. Then in Thy mercy, grant us a safe lodging, and a holy rest, and peace at the last. Amen. (In the Evening – BCP p. 833)

July 14

"See how great a love the Father has bestowed on us, that we would be called children of God; and such we are" (1 John 3:1, NASB 1995).

NATHANIEL HAWTHORNE FOUND HIMSELF alone with his five-year-old son Julian for three weeks in the Berkshires. This was a novel experience for the deeply introverted writer, who was nearly fifty at the time. (His wife had taken their two other children to Boston for three weeks.)

The boy peppered Nathaniel with questions and babbled all day long, making it impossible for his father "to write, read, think, or even to sleep (in the daytime)." They were constant playmates outdoors. Hawthorne was both exasperated and delighted by his "genial and good-humored little man"—"the old gentleman." Julian was "felicitating himself continually on the license of making what noise he pleased… He enjoys his freedom so greatly, that I do not mean to restrain him."

This speaks of our Heavenly Father's love for us. We babble to, exasperate, and yet, delight God!

> Watch over Thy child, O Lord, as his days increase; bless and guide him wherever he may be. Strengthen him when he stands; comfort him when discouraged or sorrowful; raise him up if he fall; and in his heart may Thy peace which passeth understanding abide all the days of his life; through Jesus Christ our Lord. Amen. (For a Birthday – BCP p. 830)

July 15

IN CHARLES WESLEY'S MAGNIFICENT hymn, "And Can It Be, That I Should Gain?" we sing, "My chains fell off, my heart was free; / I rose, went forth, and followed Thee." Here we have a beautiful picture of life in Christ. No prodding, shaming, goading, or cajoling necessary. Just a heart stunned and awed by the grace of God personally experienced. My chains fell off, my heart was free!

We have a perfect and pithy picture of this in Luke's gospel. *"And He [Jesus] arose and left the synagogue and entered Simon's house. Now Simon's mother-in-law was ill with a high fever, and they appealed to Him on her behalf. And He stood over her and rebuked the fever, and it left her, and immediately she rose and began to serve them" (Luke 4:38–39, ESV).*

I rose, went forth, and followed Thee. Where might the Way lead today?

Almighty and merciful God, in Your goodness keep us, we pray, from all things that may hurt us, that we, being ready both in mind and body, may accomplish with free hearts those things which belong to Your purpose; through Jesus Christ our Lord, who lives and reigns with You and the Holy Spirit, one God, now and for ever. Amen. (Proper 2 – BCP p. 228)

July 16

COMMENTING ON HIS PROFESSED favorite song, "What a Wonderful World," Louis Armstrong said, "Seems to me it ain't the world that's so bad but what we're doing to it, and all I'm saying is, see what a wonderful world it would be if only we'd give it a chance. Love, baby, love. That's the secret."

Theologically speaking, Satchmo is mostly right. It is a wonderful world by virtue of God's appraisal of the world at creation: *"And God saw that it was good" (Genesis 1:10).* ("I see skies of blue and clouds of white / The bright blessed day, the dark sacred night.") God's "good" most easily translates into Armstrong's "wonderful." And yet, the world itself is obviously vulnerable to the fracturing fallout of the Fall, e.g., sickness, natural disasters, etc.

Louis is exactly right, however, in his conclusion that "love, baby, love" is the secret sauce needed in the world. St. Peter says the same thing in one of his Epistles. *"Above all, love each other deeply, because love covers over a multitude of sins" (1 Peter 4:8, NIV).*

O God, You have made us in Your own image and redeemed us through Jesus Your Son: Look with compassion on the whole human family; take away the arrogance and hatred which infect our hearts; break down the walls that separate us; unite us in bonds of love; and work through our struggle and confusion to accomplish Your purposes on earth; that, in Your good time, all nations and races may serve You in harmony around Your heavenly throne; through Jesus Christ our Lord. Amen. (For the Human Family – BCP p. 815)

July 17

CHINESE PHILOSOPHER LAO TZU said, "Nature does not hurry, yet everything is accomplished." Substitute God for nature and you have true biblical wisdom. God does not hurry, yet everything is accomplished.

Not hurrying may be difficult for you. Of course, there are times when we all want our Oompa Loompa now. Yet, Scripture tells us that *"God has made everything beautiful for its own time" (Ecclesiastes 3:11, NLT).* Jesus was born in the "fullness of time". And on the cross and resurrection all creation—and all time—hinges. In other words, everything is *already* accomplished!

> Grant, O Lord, that the course of this world may be peaceable governed by Your providence; and that we may joyfully serve You in confidence and serenity; through Jesus Christ our Lord, who lives and reigns with You and the Holy Spirit, one God, for ever and ever. Amen. (Proper 3 – BCP p. 229)

July 18

"But my God shall supply all your need according to His riches in glory by Christ Jesus" (Philippians 4:19, KJV).

IT IS RIDICULOUS TO wake up at 2 AM and try to solve a problem. For one thing, you aren't solving anything; you are just lying inert in bed. For another, what seems like a problem at 2 AM is rarely a problem when the sun comes up. The ONLY thing to do at 2 AM is pray. For in the end, God is the solver of problems, the untangler of knots, the sorter of situations.

To my point, I love Taylor Swift's song "Anti-Hero":

> I have this thing where I get older but just never wiser
> Midnights become my afternoons
> When my depression works the graveyard shift
> All of the people I've ghosted stand there in the room
> I should not be left to my own devices
> They come with prices and vices

Let us pray.

> Keep watch, dear Lord, with those who work, or watch, or weep this night, and give Your angels charge over those who sleep. Tend the sick, Lord Christ; give rest to the weary, bless the dying, soothe the suffering, pity the afflicted, shield the joyous; and all for Your love's sake. Amen. (Collect for Evening Prayer – BCP p. 71)

July 19

LIFE HAS INEVITABLE LOOSE ends. Loose-endedness particularly applies to relationships. Even the people we love the most, and the ones who love us the most, will let us down. There will be gaps that are unfilled, leaks that intermittently drip, and expectations that are unmet. Sadly, some relationships exist in a state of disrepair or rupture. God knows this.

In Romans 12:18, St. Paul says, *"If it is possible, as far as it depends on you, live at peace with everyone" (NIV)*. Of course we want to live at peace with everyone. But, I love the realistic caveat in that verse: Sometimes it just isn't possible to live at peace. Sometimes the hurt is too deep. Sometimes we are just not up to the task. And as we just said, God knows this.

When God moves us to pray for peace with others, we know that we are being moved in the right direction. Here's a prayer for today, a prayer that thankfully recognizes that living at peace does not depend on us, but on the "grace of the Holy Spirit."

O God, You have taught us to keep all Your commandments by loving You and our neighbor: Grant us the grace of Your Holy Spirit, that we may be devoted to You with our whole heart, and united to one another with pure affection; through Jesus Christ our Lord, who lives and reigns with You and the Holy Spirit, one God, for ever and ever. Amen. (Proper 9 – BCP p. 230)

July 20

"Then I saw a new heaven and a new earth, for the first heaven and the first earth had passed away, and the sea was no more" (Revelation 21:1, ESV).

HOW ABOUT THIS SAMUEL Taylor Coleridge poem for today's devotion? It's called "What if you slept..."

> What if you slept
> And what if
> In your sleep
> You dreamed
> And what if
> In your dream
> You went to heaven
> And there plucked a strange and beautiful flower
> And what if
> When you awoke
> You had that flower in your hand
> Ah, what then?

I can tell you what then. You would be knocked out of your bed by the substance, the beauty, the reality, the *flowerness* of the flower in your hand. Heaven is real, friends. Remember that we are now in the shadowlands; only a dim reflection of the corporeality of the new heaven and new earth.

> Grant us, Lord, not to be anxious about earthly things, but to love things heavenly; and even now, while we are placed among things that are passing away, to hold fast to those that shall endure; through Jesus Christ our Lord, who lives and reigns with You and the Holy Spirit, one God, for ever and ever. Amen. (Proper 20 – BCP p. 234)

July 21

PEOPLE WILL SOMETIMES SAY that faith is a verb. I understand what they mean—love of God expresses itself in love for neighbor. This is, of course, admirable. However, saying that faith is a verb is both grammatically and theologically incorrect. Grammatically, faith is a noun. Theologically, faith is a gift that is given by God.

"For by grace you have been saved through faith. And this is not your own doing; it is the gift of God, not a result of works, so that no one may boast" (Ephesians 2:8–9, ESV).

Thankfully, our salvation rests on Christ's doing, rather than our own.

Almighty God, You have revealed to Your Church Your eternal Being of glorious majesty and perfect love as one God in Trinity of Persons: Give us grace to continue steadfast in the confession of this faith, and constant in our worship of You, Father, Son, and Holy Spirit; for You live and reign, one God, now and for ever. Amen. (Of the Holy Trinity – BCP p. 251)

July 22

YOU HAVE YOUR OWN set of pleasures and satisfactions in life. One of mine is splitting wood. The heft and explosive force of the axe, with its clean sweep through the center of the log, the nose of the blade nestled snugly into the chopping block, the oak or ash or walnut or poplar bifurcated and sent airborne, the heartening ascent of the carefully stacked woodpile, the promise of a cheering fire, with novel and a dram of whiskey perhaps, and the pleasant muscular ache of a job completed.

You know what this is like in your own avocational life. Here's what the Bible says.

"So I recommend having fun, because there is nothing better for people in this world than to eat, drink, and enjoy life. That way they will experience some happiness along with all the hard work God gives them under the sun" (Ecclesiastes 8:15, NLT).

O God, in the course of this busy life, give us times of refreshment and peace; and grant that we may so use our leisure to rebuild our bodies and our minds, that our spirits may be opened to the goodness of Your creation; through Jesus Christ our Lord. Amen. (For the Good Use of Leisure – BCP p. 825)

July 23

THE AVETT BROTHERS HAVE a song called "Tell The Truth." It begins,

> Tell the truth to yourself and the rest will fall in place
> Tell the truth to yourself and the rest will fall in place
> I lied to the doctor
> I lied to my lover
> I wanna make amends, but where do I start
> Tell the truth about yourself and the rest will fall
>   into place.

The Avetts are exactly right. The difficulty is that we are afraid of telling the truth to ourselves and are therefore well defended against it. Looking at ourselves in the mirror, we borrow Jack Nicholson's famous line from *A Few Good Men*: "You can't handle the truth!"

But, truth is written into the nature of God's universe. In one of the most chilling passages of judgment in the New Testament, Jesus says, *"There is nothing concealed that will not be disclosed, and nothing hidden that will not be made known. What you have spoken in the dark will be heard in the daylight, and what you have whispered in the inner rooms will be proclaimed from the housetops" (Luke 12:2–3, BSB).* Um… YIKES!

We might not be able to handle the truth about ourselves, but our merciful Savior sure can. Remember the gospel shorthand: You are fully known and yet fully loved. Have no fear. Jesus Christ is the way, the truth, and the life. Your life, and therefore your truth, is in Him.

> Almighty Father, who gave Your only Son to die for our sins and to rise for our justification: Give us grace so to put away the leaven of malice and wickedness, that we always serve You in pureness of living and truth; through Jesus Christ Your Son our Lord, who lives and reigns with You and the Holy Spirit, one God, now and for ever. Amen. (Friday in Easter Week – BCP p. 224)

July 24

THERE IS A DIFFERENCE between forgiveness and healing. It is possible to forgive someone for an inflicted wound or trauma, while still experiencing the pain and consequence of that wound or trauma. God is surely a God who heals, but sometimes that healing takes a lifetime; sometimes that healing only fully comes in the next life.

What we know for sure is that God Himself is there with us in our wounds and weakness. The prophet Isaiah says, *"He gives power to the faint, and to him who has no might He increases strength" (Isaiah 40:29, ESV).* Remember that our Wounded Surgeon died from His wounds, and yet was raised to life again. That is true, and will be true for you.

> May God the Father bless you, God the Son heal you, God the Holy Spirit give you strength. May God the holy and undivided Trinity guard your body, save your soul, and bring you safely to His heavenly country; where He lives and reigns for ever and ever. Amen. (For Health of Body and Soul – BCP p. 460)

July 25

> "The LORD is my rock and my fortress and my deliverer, my God, my rock, in whom I take refuge, my shield, and the horn of my salvation, my stronghold" (Psalm 18:2, ESV).

ISAAC WATTS, THE GREAT hymn writer, reminds us that "Time, like an ever-rolling stream, / Bears all its sons away; / They fly forgotten, asa dream / Dies at the opening day."

Have you noticed how longed-for moments come, are experienced, then fade? Sometimes even in that moment you realize how transient it is? How quickly "forty winters shall besiege thy brow / And dig deep trenches in thy beauty's field" (Shakespeare's "Sonnet 2").

For the believer, there is comfort in the evanescence of life. After all, Watts also tells us that "Under the shadow of Thy throne / Thy saints have dwelt secure; / sufficient is Thine arm alone, / and our defense is sure."

> O God, the protector of all who trust in You, without whom nothing is strong, nothing is holy: Increase and multiply upon us Your mercy; that, with You as our ruler

and guide, we may so pass through things temporal, that we lose not the things eternal; through Jesus Christ our Lord, who lives and reigns with You and the Holy Spirit, one God, for ever and ever. Amen. (Proper 12 – BCP p. 231)

July 26

"If you love Me, you will keep My commandments" *(John 14:15).*

THAT'S A VERSE WIDELY misinterpreted. The misinterpretation being that loving Jesus is coterminous with keeping every jot and tittle of the Law. If that were the way to understand Jesus here, then it would follow that no one loves Jesus.

Instead, He is merely describing how obedience to the Law works. It works through love. When you love another human being, you want to do what that person wants—what pleases him or her. Love is the engine.

Same with God! This is exactly what we pray about in this week's collect.

Almighty and everlasting God, increase in us the gifts of faith, hope, and charity; and, that we may obtain what You promise, make us love what You command; through Jesus Christ our Lord, who lives and reigns with You and the Holy Spirit, one God, for ever and ever. Amen. (Proper 25 – BCP p. 235)

July 27

"The blood will be a sign for you on the houses where you are, and when I see the blood, I will pass over you. No destructive plague will touch you when I strike Egypt" (Exodus 12:13, NIV).

HERE IS WHAT A church should be—a safe haven. That's why the front doors are painted red. The red door is a referent to the lamb's blood smeared on the door during Passover to protect one from the Angel of Death. You are safe inside that red door.

In Scotland, homeowners painted their doors red to signify that their mortgage had been paid off. When you step inside the red door of a church, you absolutely, positively, without any exceptions, must hear that Jesus Christ has paid your debt with His death on the cross. You are safe, and you are free.

> O God, who by the glorious resurrection of Your Son Jesus Christ destroyed death and brought life and immortality to light: Grant that we, who have been raised with Him, may abide in His presence and rejoice in the hope of eternal glory; through Jesus Christ our Lord, to whom, with You and the Holy Spirit, be dominion and praise for ever and ever. Amen. (Tuesday in Easter Week – BCP p. 223)

July 28

WHEN YOU FIND A teaching of Jesus in all four Gospel accounts, you pay special attention. All four evangelists include some version of this: *"Whoever finds his life will lose it, and whoever loses his life for My sake will find it" (Matthew 10:39, ESV).* It's actually in

Matthew twice (16:25). And different iterations of the same idea abound in Jesus' teaching, such as, *"Truly, truly, I say to you, unless a grain of wheat falls into the earth and dies, it remains alone; but if it dies, it bears much fruit" (John 12:24, ESV).*

Jesus is being descriptive here, rather than prescriptive. He is just saying what is true to life (and death). What might He mean? I'm not 100% certain, but experience has shown what the Scripture teaches: Real freedom is found in service to God and others, and true and lasting joy comes only when not focusing on one's own happiness.

Taken literally, Jesus lost His life so that we might find ours. He is the grain of wheat that falls into the earth and dies, and you are the fruit borne out of His crucifixion and resurrection. This Collect for Fridays centers our attention where it belongs, on the cross.

> Almighty God, whose most dear Son went not up to joy but first He suffered pain, and entered not into glory before He was crucified: Mercifully grant that we, walking in the way of the cross, may find it none other than the way of life and peace; through Jesus Christ Your Son our Lord. Amen. (A Collect for Fridays – BCP p. 99)

July 29

"And He shall stand and feed His flock in the strength of the LORD, in the majesty of the name of the LORD His God. And they shall live secure, for now He shall be great to the ends of the earth; and He shall be the One of peace" (Micah 5:4–5, NRSV).

IN THIS MESSIANIC PROPHECY from Micah, we see that Jesus shall feed us in the strength of the Lord and that we shall "live secure." Isn't security a universal longing? Secure finances, a secure job, secure relationships, a secure home, a secure sense of identity.

I pray that you will experience security in all the ways that I listed above as well as many others. But in the end our only real security is in Christ—the One of Peace.

> Purify our conscience, Almighty God, by Your daily visitation, that Your Son Jesus Christ, at His coming, may find in us a mansion prepared for Himself; who lives and reigns with You, in the unity of the Holy Spirit, one God, now and for ever. Amen. (Fourth Sunday of Advent – BCP p. 212)

July 30

"See now that I Myself am He! There is no god besides Me. I put to death and I bring to life" (Deuteronomy 32:39, NIV).

THE MYTH OF LINEAR progression is soul-killing. That is, thinking that slowly, over time, you get better and better, less sinful, more holy. The belief that, through discipline and devotion, you are becoming the person you were meant to be. That is a deeply mistaken view of sanctification. And out of touch with your own reality. When the person you thought you had forgiven does something reminiscent of the original offense, you are all the sudden back at square one with your resentment and outrage. Even though years have passed.

A paradigm of sanctification much closer to reality is the pattern of death and resurrection. Life (i.e., God) brings you to death in some area of your life. You come to the absolute end of your resources. Back at square one. You cry out for help, simply because you are desperate and out of any other conceivable options. Then God resurrects—brings life where there was no life. And this is not of your own doing.

Sanctification simply means that as you experience this repeat cycle of death and resurrection, you may stop trusting yourself so much with your own life. You may even start trusting God a wee bit more. The school of hard knocks is also known as the school of grace.

> We thank You, heavenly Father, that You have delivered us from the dominion of sin and death and brought us into the kingdom of Your Son; and we pray that, as by His death He has recalled us to life, so by His love He may raise us to eternal joys; who lives and reigns with You, in the unity of the Holy Spirit, one God, now and forever. Amen. (Saturday in Easter Week – BCP p. 224)

July 31

"Whoever is not against us is for us" (Mark 9:40).

THIS IS WHAT JESUS said to His disciples when they came across someone who was casting out demons in Jesus' name but was not among His "followers." Jesus doesn't care about the shell games of power or prestige. Do you really need to see your name in lights? The more lit up you are, the more easily others can see your grime.

Building bridges where you can is the way to go. Staking claims is just silly. God—not you—is in charge of sorting out the wheat from the chaff. We can root for good, even and especially when it doesn't come from our particular corner.

O God, You declare Your almighty power chiefly in showing mercy and pity: Grant us the fullness of Your grace, that we, running to obtain Your promises, may become partakers of Your heavenly treasure; through Jesus Christ our Lord, who lives and reigns with You and the Holy Spirit, one God, for ever and ever. Amen. (Proper 21 – BCP p. 234)

AUGUST

August 1

"You have died with Christ, and He has set you free from the spiritual powers of this world. So why do you keep on following the rules of the world…" (Colossians 2:20, NLT).

WHEN YOU ARE ANXIOUS/STRESSED/ADDLED, the first question to ask yourself is this: "What law am I laboring under right now?" And then, "How has the gospel already delivered me from that law?"

For instance, if you are starting some new job or venture, you will likely be laboring under all kinds of expectations from others and yourself. The law ramps up the pressure to perform and excel.

But the gospel tells a different story: You have already been accepted—and not just accepted, but delighted in—by the life, death, and resurrection of Jesus Christ. You are free to fail or to muddle along or to thrive! Any of those options is just fine with God. He doesn't play by the rules of the world.

> Almighty and everlasting God, You govern all things both in heaven and on earth: Mercifully hear the supplications of Your people, and in our time grant us Your peace; through Jesus Christ our Lord, who lives and reigns with You and the Holy Spirit, one God, for ever and ever. Amen. (Fourth Sunday after the Epiphany – BCP p. 215)

August 2

JUST AS THE CHRISTIAN should not be constantly feeling his spiritual pulse, so, too, the Christian community has not been given to us by God for us to be constantly taking its temperature. The more thankfully we daily receive what is given to us, the more surely and steadily will fellowship increase and grow from day to day as God pleases. Christian brotherhood is not an ideal which we must realize; it is rather a reality created by God in Christ in which we may participate.

Dietrich Bonhoeffer said that about Christian community, but it applies to life in general. The more we chafe against what is given in favor of some ideal we have created, the unhappier we will be with the day-to-day.

St. Paul says, *"For everything comes from Him and exists by His power and is intended for His glory. All glory to Him forever! Amen"* (Romans 11:36, NLT).

Where, or with whom, does this touch down for you today?

"Give us grateful hearts, our Father, for all Thy mercies, and make us mindful of the needs of others; through Jesus Christ our Lord. Amen." (Grace at Meals – BCP p. 835)

August 3

"Jesus looked at them intently and said, 'Humanly speaking, it is impossible. But with God everything is possible'" (Matthew 19:26, NLT).

PROBLEMS THAT SEEM INTRACTABLE to us are not intractable to God. I wonder if it even occurs to Him to consider a situation a problem? Even Jesus' death was no problem, for He was raised on the third day.

What is happening in your life today that seems impossible? How about we pray right now for God to remove that stone?

With Him, all things are possible—even that! In fact, our "stir-rup" collect is just the ticket.

> Stir up Your power, O Lord, and with great might come among us; and, because we are sorely hindered by our sins, let Your bountiful grace and mercy speedily help and deliver us; through Jesus Christ our Lord, to whom, with You and the Holy Spirit, be honor and glory, now and for ever. Amen. (Third Sunday of Advent – BCP p. 212)

August 4

I WAS THINKING ABOUT one of the incredibly bone-headed mistakes I made recently at Christ Church. Which led me on a bread crumb trail of other bone-headed moves during my nearly fifteen-year tenure as rector. Enough bread crumbs for a whole loaf!

Someone has suggested that actually writing down your mistakes is a healthy exercise. I agree. Not so that you can wriggle in remorse and self-accusation, but so you can begin to see yourself as St. Paul says in his letter to the Romans.

"For by the grace given me I say to every one of you: Do not think of yourself more highly than you ought, but rather think of yourself with sober judgment" (Romans 12:3, NIV).

Here's the thing: You are never going to stop making bone-headed mistakes! Good thing that God is 1) merciful and 2) has a sense of humor.

> Almighty and merciful God, in Your goodness keep us, we pray, from all things that may hurt us, that we, being ready both in mind and body, may accomplish with free hearts those things which belong to Your purpose;

through Jesus Christ our Lord, who lives and reigns with You and the Holy Spirit, one God, now and for ever. Amen. (Proper 2 – BCP p. 228)

August 5

"The kingdom of heaven is like a merchant in search of fine pearls" (Matthew 13:45).

The Wind in the Willows is a must-read, or a must-re-read, or even a must-re-re-read. In one chapter, Mole and Rat trudge late on a snowy night toward Rat's riverbank home. Mole has been gone from his underground home for months now. But as they journey, they come near his home—and the scent calls to him.

"It was one of these mysterious fairy calls from out the void that reached Mole in the darkness, making him tingle through and through with its very familiar appeal, even while yet he could not clearly remember what it was. He stopped dead in his tracks, his nose searching hither and thither in its efforts to recapture the fine filament, the telegraphic current, that had so strongly moved him."

Then Mole remembers. "Home! That was what they meant, those caressing appeals, those soft touches wafted through the air, those invisible little hands pulling and tugging, all one way!"

The kingdom of heaven is like that—calling, pulling, tugging, appealing. Jesus is the merchant searching for you, the pearl. And the kingdom of heaven is our True Home.

Lord, we pray that Your grace may always precede and follow us, that we may continually be given to good works; through Jesus Christ our Lord, who lives and reigns with You and the Holy Spirit, one God, now and for ever. Amen. (Proper 23 – BCP p. 234)

August 6

"Jesus took with Him Peter and John and James, and went up on the mountain to pray. And while He was praying, the appearance of His face changed, and His clothes became dazzling white. Suddenly they saw two men, Moses and Elijah, talking to Him" (Luke 9:28–30, NRSV).

CHURCHES COMMEMORATE THE TRANSFIGURATION today. That's the day Jesus took His three buddies on a hike up a mountain. Suddenly, His Son-of-God-ness burst through, and He shone with glory. And voila!—Moses and Elijah showed up.

In this scene you have the foundations of the Old Testament: the Law (Moses) and the Prophets (Elijah). But at the end, we read that Jesus is the only one left. In other words, Grace is everything. In the end, Grace is all that is left. It's all that you can't leave behind.

That's been the theme running through this Almost Daily Devotional. And that is God's theme that runs through eternity, forever and ever. Amen.

> O God, who on the holy mount revealed to chosen witnesses Your well-beloved Son, wonderfully transfigured, in raiment white and glistening: Mercifully grant that we, being delivered from the disquietude of this world, may by faith behold the King in His beauty; who with You, O Father, and You, O Holy Spirit, lives and reigns, one God, for ever and ever. Amen. (The Transfiguration – BCP p. 243)

August 7

"For all who are led by the Spirit of God are children of God" (Romans 8:14, NRSV).

AMONG SHAKESPEARE'S MOST FAMOUS lines is, "All the world's a stage, / And all the men and women merely players" *(As You Like It)*. He then describes the seven stages of human life, from infancy to the second childhood of old age.

I read this not as fatalistic or deterministic, but as hopeful and comforting. That is because a play has both an author and a stage director.

Every day I am exceedingly thankful that I am not the author and director of my own play. That play would be a tragedy. What freedom to be relieved of charting my own course, making up my own rules, deciding what is "best" for me. All of that is given to us, revealed in Scripture and the Word made flesh, and directed by the guidance of the Holy Spirit.

> Direct us, O Lord, in all our doings with Thy most gracious favor, and further us with Thy continual help; that in all our works begun, continued, and ended in Thee, we may glorify Thy holy Name, and finally, by Thy mercy, obtain everlasting life; through Jesus Christ our Lord. Amen. (For Guidance – BCP p. 832)

August 8

"Let mutual love continue. Do not neglect to show hospitality to strangers, for by doing that some have entertained angels without knowing it" (Hebrews 13:1–2, NRSV).

I LOVE THIS PASSAGE from Hebrews for two reasons. The first is the basic reminder to be kind to people. Sounds easy, but I find that kindness often gets drummed out by my focused agenda, or the undercurrent of societal division, or a sense of entitlement.

Glen Campbell said it all in 1971 with his "Try a Little Kindness."

Well, Glen, we try and we fail. Which is the second reason I like this Hebrews passage. It reminds us that, cosmologically speaking, we are not alone. God's angels (a created order, not people who have died and earned their wings—sorry Clarence!) are among us to help us.

Maybe keep your eyes open today, if you can?

Everlasting God, You have ordained and constituted in a wonderful order the ministries of angels and mortals: Mercifully grant that, as Your holy angels always serve and worship You in heaven, so by Your appointment they may help and defend us here on earth; through Jesus Christ our Lord, who lives and reigns with You and the Holy Spirit, one God, for ever and ever. Amen. (St. Michael and All Angels – BCP p. 244)

August 9

"The sum of Your word is truth, And every one of Your righteous ordinances is everlasting" (Psalm 119:160, NASB 1995).

FLANNERY O'CONNOR ONCE SAID, "Writing a novel is a terrible experience, during which the hair often falls out and the teeth decay. I'm always irritated by people who imply that writing fiction is an escape from reality. It is a plunge into reality and it's very shocking to the system." Most sermon writers I know would agree with Flannery.

The thing the preacher never wants to hear in the receiving line after church? "Great sermon—but now back to the real world." There is nothing more real than the need for forgiveness and nothing less solid than the parasitic mockeries of sin. To wit, love is in the indestructible DNA of the universe, while lust is a phantasm doomed to defeated extinction.

> Almighty God, whom truly to know is everlasting life: Grant us so perfectly to know Your Son Jesus Christ to be the way, the truth, and the life, that we may steadfastly follow His steps in the way that leads to eternal life; through Jesus Christ Your Son our Lord, who lives and reigns with You, in the unity of the Holy Spirit, one God, for ever and ever. Amen. (Fifth Sunday of Easter – BCP p. 225)

August 10

HERE'S A SHORT ONE from Wendell Berry to make you smile. It's called "The First."

> The first man who whistled
> thought he had a wren in his mouth.
> He went around all day
> with his lips puckered,
> afraid to swallow.

Bono calls Jesus "the first one of your kind," and St. Paul says that *"He is the image of the invisible God, the firstborn of all creation" (Colossians 1:15).*

This is one way of saying that Jesus is one of a kind; there has never been and will never be anyone like Him. He alone identifies with your deepest trials and woes; He alone is sinless. He alone died for your sins. He alone defeated death so you will never die.

So, no need to be afraid!

> Everliving God, whose will it is that all should come to You through Your Son Jesus Christ: Inspire our witness to Him, that all may know the power of His forgiveness and the hope of His resurrection; who lives and reigns with You and the Holy Spirit, one God, now and for ever. Amen. (For the Mission of the Church – BCP p. 816)

August 11

SPEAKING OF WENDELL BERRY (yesterday's devotion), I was recently told that I was "no Wendell Berry." That came as a relief, actually, as it deflated an image of myself that bore no relation to the reality of my actual self. Most of us labor under versions of ourselves (better, smarter, more put-together, etc.) that bear little resemblance to the person that walks around in our skin and thinks with our brain and closes our eyelids at night.

The psalmist says, *"Behold, You desire truth in the innermost being, And in the hidden part You will make me know wisdom"* *(Psalm 51:6, NASB 1995).* God is interested in the actual you. Because the actual you is the one that He sent His Son to die for.

> Almighty God, the fountain of all wisdom, You know our necessities before we ask and our ignorance in asking: Have compassion on our weakness, and mercifully give us those things which for our unworthiness we dare not, and for our blindness we cannot ask; through the

worthiness of Your Son Jesus Christ our Lord, who lives and reigns with You and the Holy Spirit, one God, now and for ever. Amen. (Proper 11 – BCP p. 231)

August 12

"[Those who were baptized] devoted themselves to the apostles' teaching and fellowship, to the breaking of bread and the prayers" (Acts 2:42, NRSV).

JOHN PRINE SINGS, "MAKE me an angel that flies from Montgomery / Make me a poster of an old rodeo / Just give me one thing that I can hold on to / To believe in this livin' is just a hard way to go."

The Bible confirms that believing in this livin' is a hard way to go indeed.

The newly baptized people in this reading from Acts didn't decide to get all religious or spiritual. Those terms don't even come close to applying.

They all knew what we know—living is difficult and dying is scary. Learning the apostles' teachings (forgiveness in Christ Jesus), being together with fellow strugglers, being reminded of Christ's death in the bread and the wine, and crying out to God for help in prayer is just the best way to live this earthly life.

O God, whose Son Jesus is the good shepherd of Your people: Grant that when we hear His voice we may know Him who calls us each by name, and follow where He leads; who, with You and the Holy Spirit, lives and reigns, one God, for ever and ever. Amen. (Fourth Sunday of Easter – BCP p. 225)

August 13

IN THE PRETENDERS' 1986 hit "Don't Get Me Wrong," Chrissie Hynde sings, "If I come and go like fashion / I might be great tomorrow / But hopeless yesterday." She's got a good bead on human nature. Can't you relate? One day you are on the top of the world, and the next day the bottom has fallen out.

I come and go like fashion. I got married in 1986. I'm afraid to say that our wedding pictures captured my haircut; it was at least approaching mullet status. Not full-blown, but still, well, embarrassing. Hopeless yesterday!

The psalmist proclaims, *"But You remain the same, and Your years will never end" (Psalm 102:27, NIV).* What doesn't change about God? His mercy, His forgiveness, and His all-embracing love for us—the fickle-hearted.

> O God, You declare Your almighty power chiefly in showing mercy and pity: Grant us the fullness of Your grace, that we, running to obtain Your promises, may become partakers of Your heavenly treasure; through Jesus Christ our Lord, who lives and reigns with You and the Holy Spirit, one God, for ever and ever. Amen. (Proper 21 – BCP p. 234)

August 14

ENGLISH WRITER AND CLERGYMAN Giles Fraser uses the term "crisis of capacity" to describe our response to moral imperative. Well-meaning people want to do good, to help others, to rectify societal wrongs, but often feel overwhelmed by the enormity of the need and the paucity of our ability to meet those needs. Hence, we find ourselves in a "crisis of capacity."

Jesus' moral imperatives only make things worse. Let's take His command to the rich young ruler at face value: *"Jesus said to him, 'If you would be perfect, go, sell what you possess and give to the poor, and you will have treasure in heaven; and come, follow Me'"* *(Matthew 19:21, ESV)*. If that doesn't throw you into a crisis of capacity, how about the moral denouement of the Sermon on the Mount: *"You therefore must be perfect, as your heavenly Father is perfect" (Matthew 5:48, ESV)*.

Theologically speaking, our crisis of capacity is a good thing—it drives us to our Savior. It drives us to the gospel. We cannot fulfill the Law. Only one person had infinite capacity for good. And He fulfilled the Law for us.

Here is the collect from yesterday with a caveat. While God has prepared the good works for us to walk in, it is better to put the emphasis on the "sacrifice for sin" rather than "example of godly life." In fact, thankfully receiving the fruits of His redeeming work will make our good works flow more easily and authentically.

> Almighty God, You have given Your only Son to be for us a sacrifice for sin, and also an example of godly life: Give us grace to receive thankfully the fruits of His redeeming work, and to follow daily in the blessed steps of His most holy life; through Jesus Christ Your Son our Lord, who lives and reigns with You and the Holy Spirit, one God, now and for ever. Amen. (Proper 15 – BCP p. 232)

August 15

> *"Draw the sword and bar the way against those who pursue me; say to my soul, 'I am your salvation'"* *(Psalm 35:3).*

WHEN I READ THE psalms, I understand the talk about enemies as referring to all that would seek to undo me: the devil, the forces of evil, my own sin. I want God to take up the sword against the enemy.

Oswald Chambers says, "Jesus Christ came to 'bring … a sword' through every kind of peace that is not based on personal relationship with Himself." He cuts through the webs of the enemy to set us free, even as He surrendered Himself to the swords of His captors to be led to the cross in our stead.

> Almighty Lord, You are a strong tower to all who put their trust in You, to whom all things in heaven, on earth, and under the earth bow and obey: Be now and evermore our defense, and make us know and feel that the only Name under heaven given for health and salvation is the Name of our Lord Jesus Christ. Amen. (Ministration to the Sick – BCP p. 456)

August 16

> *"Likewise the Spirit helps us in our weakness; for we do not know how to pray as we ought, but that very Spirit intercedes with sighs too deep for words" (Romans 8:26, NRSV).*

SOMETIMES I'M REMINDED IN the morning by the person I live with that the morning is for quiet, for easing into the day. It is not for me expounding on one subject after another. Verbal processors tend to be verbose at the wrong times.

Words I have in spades—and weaknesses too. Good thing that God helps us in our weakness. And even supplies the words that aren't words, but sighs too deep for words. So much better, sometimes, to keep mum and experience God's Spirit at work within you.

> O God, who on this day taught the hearts of Your faithful people by sending to them the light of Your Holy Spirit: Grant us by the same Spirit to have a right judgment in all things, and evermore to rejoice in His holy comfort; through Jesus Christ Your Son our Lord, who lives and reigns with You, in the unity of the Holy Spirit, one God, for ever and ever. Amen. (The Day of Pentecost – BCP p. 227)

August 17

> *"Do not tremble or fear. Have I not told you and declared it long ago? You are My witnesses! Is there any God but Me? There is no other Rock; I know not one"* *(Isaiah 44:8, BSB).*

A MARK OF OUR finitude is our inability to juggle too many things at one time. Even the most able and organized of us are defeated from time to time by the unwieldy demands that life places on our shoulders. Conversely, those who feel they are under-engaged can slip into languishing.

The 12-Step wisdom of living one day at a time is balm to the busy. And balm to the idle, who worry about the endless stretch of unfilled days ahead of them.

Either way, you are on solid theological ground living life a day at a time. It's really one-size-fits-all. God knows what is ahead; you do not. To assume you do is to usurp God's place. Do you really want THAT responsibility?!

Time to pray.

This is another day, O Lord. I know not what it will bring forth, but make me ready, Lord, for whatever it may be. If I am to stand up, help me stand bravely. If I am to sit still, help me sit quietly. If I am to lie low, help me to do it patiently. And if I am to do nothing, let me do it gallantly. Make these words more than words, and give me the Spirit of Jesus. Amen. (Prayers for use by a Sick Person: In the Morning – BCP p. 461)

August 18

I LOVE MICHAEL JORDAN. I was fortunate enough to see him play a college home game when I visited my older brother at UNC. Even though I'm not a big NBA fan, I watched with glee and amazement the Bulls' dynastic run through the 90s. And currently I am binge-watching ESPN's *Last Dance*—the documentary about the Bulls' quest for a sixth NBA title.

Michael's self-proclaimed motto, "Win at all costs," is apparently a very good way to achieve success on the basketball court. I don't know if this is how Michael lives the rest of his life. I hope not, because that is a terrible way to live. Winning at all costs not only alienates those around you, but alienates your very being from fulfillment and purpose.

Closer to a Christian *modus operandi* for life would be something like "lose at all costs." Enigmatically, but truthfully, Jesus says, *"For whoever wants to save their life will lose it, but whoever loses their life for Me will find it" (Matthew 16:25, NIV).* You can plumb the depths of Jesus' meaning as well as I can, but His cruciform wisdom sure hits home for me. Not only is it true in relation to God, but it is true in relation to those around us. Talk about a swoosh!

Almighty God, whose most dear Son went not up to joy but first He suffered pain, and entered not into glory before He was crucified: Mercifully grant that we, walking in the way of the cross, may find it none other than the way of life and peace; through Jesus Christ Your Son our Lord. Amen. (A Collect for Fridays – BCP p. 99)

August 19

I AM A DERELICT flosser, which is super unwise given the issues I've had with my choppers. The only time I manage to floss is right before I go to see the dental hygienist for a cleaning. Sad, but true.

A large swath of the historic church has treated the sacraments like I treat my flossing. It was once required to have last rites, confession, and reception of the eucharist in the moments before your earthly time is up in order to make yourself right with God and gain entrance into heaven.

All of those rites are good and helpful but are not prerequisites or requirements in the eyes of God. God's once-for-all act of cleansing and absolution took place on a brutal hill outside the gates of Jerusalem. And in the predawn hours of the third day. St. Paul says, *"He was delivered over to death for our sins and was raised to life for our justification" (Romans 4:25, NIV).*

Holy and gracious Father: In Your infinite love You made us for Yourself; and, when we had fallen into sin and become subject to evil and death, You, in Your mercy, sent Jesus Christ, Your only and eternal Son, to share our human nature, to live and die as one of us, to reconcile us to You, the God and Father of all. He stretched out His arms upon the cross, and offered Himself in obedience to Your will, a perfect sacrifice for the whole world. (From Eucharistic Prayer A – BCP p. 362)

August 20

THE HEART TENDS TO ossify over time. Exposure to too many tragedies—especially in an age of instant global access—can numb and harden us. One can only absorb so much. Wealth can further isolate, and pride is always a threat to buttress one away from the concerns of others.

It seems to me that God is a heartbreaker (I never liked that Pat Benatar song). Yet, God is clearly in the business of breaking hearts, for a broken heart is an open heart, a receiving heart, a dependent heart. The psalmist says, *"The sacrifices of God are a broken spirit; a broken and contrite heart, O God, You will not despise" (Psalm 51:17, ESV).*

Let's stick with Neil Young instead. "Only love can break your heart." And only Love can put it back together, too.

O God, You have taught us to keep all Your commandments by loving You and our neighbor: Grant us the grace of Your Holy Spirit, that we may be devoted to You with our whole heart, and united to one another with pure affection; through Jesus Christ our Lord, who lives and reigns with You and the Holy Spirit, one God, for ever and ever. Amen. (Proper 9 – BCP p. 230)

August 21

"So Jesus asked the twelve, 'Do you also wish to go away?' Simon Peter answered Him, 'Lord, to whom

can we go? You have the words of eternal life. We have come to believe and know that You are the Holy One of God'" (John 6:67–69, NRSV).

AFTER A PARTICULARLY DIFFICULT-TO-SWALLOW teaching, many of those listening to Jesus said enough is enough—this guy is nuts. (The teaching in question was literally difficult to swallow: *"Those who eat My flesh and drink My blood abide in Me, and I in them. Just as the living Father sent Me, and I live because of the Father, so whoever eats Me will live because of Me" (John 6:56–57, NRSV).*)

Peter's response to Jesus' question is one of the great lines of Scripture, one I return to again and again. Lord, to whom can we go? We may not understand all that Jesus says or does, but one thing is sure: You will not find His brand of grace anywhere else in this world. And only He fulfills and satisfies you in your truest nature.

Gracious Father, whose blessed Son Jesus Christ came down from heaven to be the true bread which gives life to the world: Evermore give us this bread, that He may live in us, and we in Him; who lives and reigns with You and the Holy Spirit, one God, now and for ever. Amen. (Fourth Sunday in Lent – BCP p. 219)

August 22

"Therefore, because we have received The Kingdom that is not shaken, we shall receive grace by which we shall serve and please God in reverence and in awe" (Hebrews 12:28, ABPE).

I'LL GO AHEAD AND end the rancorous debate about what constitutes the perfect martini. The Bombay Sapphire gin should be kept in the freezer, as well as the martini glass. (A martini poured in any other vessel than the classic 1950s high-stemmed martini glass is NOT a martini.) The vermouth is important; although the martini must be dry, one needs to do more than wave the bottle toward Italy.

A 2:1 gin-to-vermouth admixture is to be added into the shaker packed with ice, then shaken vigorously for the sheer fun of it. The Nectar of the Gods is then lovingly poured into the frosted glass, nearly crystalline with icy film. A twist is preferable, but olives are, of course, acceptable.

The ground on which you stand is solid. Although sometimes you may feel shaken (not stirred) you are, in fact, as secure as a tightly swaddled newborn. After all, we have received (not earned or won) a Kingdom that cannot be shaken.

> Most loving Father, whose will it is for us to give thanks for all things, to fear nothing but the loss of You, and to cast all our care on You who care for us: Preserve us from faithless fears and worldly anxieties, that no clouds of this mortal life may hide from us the light of that love which is immortal, and which You have manifested to us in Your Son Jesus Christ our Lord; who lives and reigns with You, in the unity of the Holy Spirit, one God, now and for ever. Amen. (Eighth Sunday after the Epiphany – BCP p. 216)

August 23

"Jesus answered, 'It is not the healthy who need a doctor, but the sick'" (Luke 5:31, BSB).

JESUS COULD HAVE BEEN responding to any number of yammering voices. My popcorn bag tells me, "When your spirit is guided by wellness, you are your own guru." Another pernicious message that we are basically A-OK, and with a little balance here and meditation there, we will be fit as a fiddle.

As C. S. Lewis says, "Christ takes it for granted that men are bad." Jeremiah calls our hearts "desperately sick" (17:9). Such sickness calls for the care of the Great Physician. The long and the short of it? We need a Savior, not a guru.

> Grant us, O Lord, to trust in You with all our hearts; for, as You always resist the proud who confide in their own strength, so You never forsake those who make their boast of Your mercy; through Jesus Christ our Lord, who lives and reigns with You and the Holy Spirit, one God, now and for ever. Amen. (Proper 18 – BCP p. 233)

August 24

IN THE COLLECT BELOW, there is a stark contrast between the "works of darkness" and the "armor of light." We ask God for the grace to cast away the one and put on the other. By definition, works involve activity. Fill in the blank with your own works of darkness: gossip, drunkenness, judgment, hard-heartedness, egocentric behavior. Sadly, the list goes on and on.

The armor of light, on the other hand, requires passivity. I haven't put on a suit of armor recently, but I'm pretty sure somebody else—like a squire—has to put the armor on for you! You stand there and receive the armor, which protects and defends you. Biblically speaking, Jesus Christ is both the squire that puts your armor on *and* the armor itself. In fact, the Apostle Paul says in the Romans reading for Advent 1 that we are to *"put on the Lord Jesus Christ"* (Romans 13:14).

Paul expands the metaphor in Ephesians 6:13–17: *"Therefore put on the full armor of God, so that when the day of evil comes, you may be able to stand your ground, and after you have done everything, to stand. Stand firm then, with the belt of truth buckled around your waist, with the breastplate of righteousness in place, and with your feet fitted with the readiness that comes from the gospel of peace. In addition to all this, take up the shield of faith, with which you can extinguish all the flaming arrows of the evil one. Take the helmet of salvation and the sword of the Spirit, which is the word of God"* (NIV).

Note once again the passivity in the passage. All the pieces of armor are designed for defense rather than attack, especially the Word of God, which parries the lies of darkness.

Almighty God, give us grace to cast away the works of darkness, and put on the armor of light, now in the time of this mortal life in which Your Son Jesus Christ came to visit us in great humility; that in the last day, when He shall come again in His glorious majesty to judge both the living and the dead, we may rise to the life immortal; through Him who lives and reigns with You and the Holy Spirit, one God, now and for ever. Amen. (First Sunday of Advent – BCP p. 211)

August 25

"Now we see things imperfectly, like puzzling reflections in a mirror, but then we will see everything with perfect clarity. All that I know now is partial and incomplete, but then I will know everything completely, just as God now knows me completely" (1 Corinthians 13:12, NLT).

A FRIEND'S GRANDFATHER WAS fond of saying, "It's what you learn after you know everything that really counts."

So good! It reminds me of Bono's line in U2's song, "The City of Blinding Lights": "The more you see, the less you know/ the less you find out as you go / I knew much more then / Than I do now." I wonder if wisdom is the realization that you lack it? Certainly, Paul's word about knowing (not knowing, really) grounds us in both wonder (so much more to learn!) and humility (so much that I think I know that I really don't).

> O God, by the leading of a star You manifested Your only Son to the Peoples of the earth: Lead us, who know You now by faith, to Your presence, where we may see Your glory face to face; through Jesus Christ our Lord, who lives and reigns with You and the Holy Spirit, one God, now and for ever. Amen. (The Epiphany – BCP p. 214)

August 26

IN THE 16TH CENTURY, Martin Luther and Erasmus of Rotterdam tussled over whether God could reside in a dung hole. Lovely, right? It was basically an argument about whether God is imminent (near) or transcendent (removed). Erasmus argued against the dung hole; God's innate holiness prevents Him from entering the dung hole. Luther was decidedly pro-dung hole; God enters into everything: the good, the bad, and the ugly.

He turned to the prophet Jeremiah for proof. *"Am I only a God nearby,' declares the LORD, 'and not a God far away? Who can hide in secret places so that I cannot see them?' declares the LORD. 'Do not I fill heaven and earth?' declares the LORD" (Jeremiah 23:23–24, NIV).*

Perhaps you've never thought of yourself as a pro-dung-holer when it comes to the question of God, but thankfully God enters into the worst of the worst. If God only dealt in the holy, then there would be no Christmas, Good Friday, or Easter. And closer to home, He is in the very worst that life deals out to you.

> Almighty God, we pray You graciously to behold this Your family, for whom our Lord Jesus Christ was willing to be betrayed, and given into the hands of sinners, and to suffer death upon the cross; who now lives and reigns with You and the Holy Spirit, one God, for ever and ever. Amen. (Good Friday – BCP p. 221)

August 27

I OFFICIATED THE FUNERAL of a dear woman recently—someone I've known and loved for 30 years. Hours before she died, I asked her if there was anything she wanted to tell me or if there was anything she felt she needed. With her characteristic wit she replied, "Yes—a new self."

That's a remarkably accurate theological answer. When we die, we are still ourselves; yet we are made new. Paul says it this way: *"So will it be with the resurrection of the dead. The body that is sown is perishable, it is raised imperishable" (1 Corinthians 15:42, NIV).*

All that is wonderfully you will still be you; all that weighs you down will be cast off forever.

> Grant that all who have been baptized into Christ's death and resurrection may die to sin and rise to newness of life, and that through the grave and gate of death we may pass with Him to our joyful resurrection. Amen. (Prayers in the Burial Liturgy – BCP p. 480)

August 28

ALBERT EINSTEIN ONCE SAID, "Only a life lived for others is a life worthwhile." I'm no Einstein, but he is definitely onto something—although clearly *every* life is a life worth living simply because it is a life given to us by God. In the book of Acts, the Apostle Paul reminds his listeners of something that Jesus taught: *"In all things I have shown you that by working hard in this way we must help the weak and remember the words of the Lord Jesus, how He Himself said, 'It is more blessed to give than to receive'"* *(Acts 20:35, ESV).*

Nowhere in the Gospel accounts is Jesus' saying actually recorded, but it is without a doubt reflective of our Lord's teaching. My understanding of "it is more blessed to give than to receive" is that it is better for the giver. It is axiomatic that giving makes you feel good. St. Augustine taught that service to God and others led to freedom, while life lived for the self leads to slavery. He said God is the One "whom to serve is perfect freedom."

Just being told to live for others, even when beneficial to ourselves, doesn't always motivate us to a life of service for others. Thankfully, *"We love because He first loved us" (1 John 4:19).* Not only did Jesus live for others, He died for others. And it is only His love that has the power to move us beyond ourselves.

> Lord, make us instruments of Your peace. Where there is hatred, let us sow love; where there is injury, pardon; where there is discord, union; where there is doubt, faith; where there is despair; hope; where there is darkness, light; where there is sadness, joy. Grant that we may not so much seek to be consoled as to console; to be understood as to understand; to be loved as to love. For it is in giving that we receive; it is in pardoning that we are pardoned; and it is in dying that we are born to eternal life. Amen. (A Prayer attributed to St. Francis – BCP p. 833)

August 29

The Age of Innocence author Edith Wharton once said, perceptively, "Half the trouble in life is caused by pretending there isn't any." Unfortunately, pretending that problems don't exist (in a marriage, in families, in yourself) do not make them go away. Putting on a happy face only makes difficulties fester and multiply.

Jesus gave us a heads-up about this: *"I have told you these things, so that in Me you may have peace. In this world you will have trouble. But take heart! I have overcome the world" (John 16:33, NIV).* Jesus does not promise a trouble-free existence for believers. However, He does promise to deliver you in and through your troubles. And even to give you His peace in the midst of it all.

> Lord Jesus Christ, You said to Your apostles, 'Peace I give to you; My own peace I leave with you:' Regard not our sins, but the faith of Your Church, and give to us the peace and unity of that heavenly City, where with the Father and the Holy Spirit You live and reign, now and for ever. Amen. (The Collect at the Prayers – BCP p. 395)

August 30

IN "MAGGIE'S FARM," BOB Dylan sings, "Well, I try my best / To be just like I am / But everybody wants you / To be just like them."

Something magical happens when your authentic self is in total cahoots with your public self. Usually, something childlike gets freed up: play, humor, lightness of being. Authenticity is deeply satisfying. And there is no faking it!

The psalmist says, *"You formed my inmost being; You knit me together in my mother's womb" (Psalm 139:13, BSB).* Yes, original sin (including the sins done unto us) have damaged the original product, but thankfully not beyond recognition. Jesus tells us that we must be born again and ironically returned to our identity as a child of God, saved by grace.

> Almighty and eternal God, so draw our hearts to Thee, so guide our minds, so fill our imaginations, so control our wills, that we may be wholly Thine, utterly dedicated unto Thee; and then use us, we pray Thee, as Thou wilt, and always to Thy glory and the welfare of Thy people; through our Lord and Savior Jesus Christ. (A Prayer of Self-Dedication – BCP p. 832)

August 31

THE ETYMOLOGY OF THE word "fret" is telling. To fret is to perseverate about an issue—you just can't let it go. But our word "fret" comes from the Old English "fretan," which means to "devour, feed upon, or consume." Makes sense—worry can eat you up.

Here is what the Bread of Life (fretting's antithesis) says:

"Then Jesus said to His disciples: 'Therefore I tell you, do not worry about your life, what you will eat; or about your body, what you will wear. For life is more than food, and the body more than clothes. Consider the ravens: They do not sow or reap, they have no storeroom or barn; yet God feeds them. And how much more valuable you are than birds! Who of you by worrying can add a single hour to your life? Since you cannot do this very little thing, why do you worry about the rest?'" (Luke 12:22–26, NIV).

Do not worry about your life. Wow!

O God of peace, who hast taught us that in returning and rest we shall be saved, in quietness and in confidence shall be our strength: By the might of Thy Spirit lift us, we pray Thee, to Thy presences, where we may be still and know that Thou art God; through Jesus Christ our Lord. Amen. (For Quiet Confidence – BCP p. 832)

SEPTEMBER

September 1

IN HIS POEM, "SEPTEMBER 1, 1939," W. H. Auden wrote, "I and the public know / What all schoolchildren learn / Those to whom evil is done / Do evil in return." Such is the karmic law and the sorry ripple effect of a broken world. It is the dark arts version of the golden rule—you will do unto others as others have done unto you.

Jesus has the antidote to this poison: *"You have heard that it was said, 'You shall love your neighbor and hate your enemy.' But I say to you, Love your enemies and pray for those who persecute you, so that you may be children of your Father in heaven" (Matthew 5:43–45, NRSV).*

Thankfully, Jesus does more than *tell* us the antidote, for not many of us can pull this off. He *is* the antidote, dying on the cross for our hatred of our enemies while asking His Father to forgive us—we who did evil to Him.

> O God, the Father of all, whose Son commanded us to love our enemies: Lead them and us from prejudice to truth; deliver them and us from hatred, cruelty, and revenge; and in Your good time enable us to stand reconciled before You; through Jesus Christ our Lord. Amen. (For our Enemies – BCP p. 816)

September 2

> *"That evening at sundown they brought to Him all who were sick or oppressed by demons. And the whole city was gathered together at the door. And He healed many who were sick with various diseases, and cast out many demons" (Mark 1:32–34, ESV).*

CAN YOU IMAGINE THE chaos of that scene? The whole city? Sick people? Possessed people? All wanting something from Jesus? Being a basically orderly person, chaos tends to undo me. In this way I am not like Jesus, who is perfectly at home in chaos. In U2's "When I Look at the World," Bono talks to Jesus: "When there's all kinds of chaos / And everyone is walking lame / You don't even blink now, do you / Or even look away?"

Jesus' comfort with the chaos of our lives is very good news for us. Sometimes chaos is external; often it is internal. Years of pastoral experience have shown me that some of the most debilitating chaos resides beneath the most apparently serene facades.

Jesus is at home in your chaos. He was unperturbed by 5,000 starving people in the middle of nowhere. He slept like a baby in the stern of a boat in the teeth of a gale. He healed and comforted a self-mutilating, demon-possessed brute of a man living in a tomb.

So, bring Him all you've got. He won't look away.

O God, the author of peace and the lover of concord, to know You is eternal life and to serve You is perfect freedom: Defend us, Your humble servants, in all assaults of our enemies, that we, surely trusting in Your defense, may not fear the power of any adversaries; through the might of Jesus Christ our Lord. Amen. (A Collect for Peace – BCP p. 99)

September 3

IT'S FUN TO MOW the grass in April, but by September, it gets tiresome. The quotidian tasks of life still need to get done, fun or not. Some will say that our "spiritual disciplines" are the same: read your Bible, pray your prayers whether you want to or not. Develop your "spiritual muscles."

This is nonsense. And it often leads to a kind of spiritual burnout and resentment toward God. Healthy engagement with God, through Scripture or prayer, comes from genuine desire. And most times, that desire is fueled by need. *God, please help my child because I cannot help him anymore. Lord, please help me because I can't seem to help myself. I have nowhere else to turn.*

Here is what the Bible says on the matter: *"Let us then approach God's throne of grace with confidence, so that we may receive mercy and find grace to help us in our time of need" (Hebrews 4:16, NIV).*

O Lord our God, accept the fervent prayers of Your people; in the multitude of Your mercies, look with compassion upon us and all who turn to You for help; for You are gracious, O lover of souls, and to You we give glory, Father, Son, and Holy Spirit, now and for ever. Amen. (The Collect at the Prayers – BCP p. 395)

September 4

"All this is from God, who reconciled us to Himself through Christ and gave us the ministry of reconciliation: that God was reconciling the world to Himself in Christ, not counting people's sins against them. And He has committed to us the message of reconciliation" *(2 Corinthians 5:18–19, NIV).*

IMAGINE WALKING THROUGH a prison and having the authority to shout out, "Hey, Everyone! Whatever you've done, it's all completely forgiven!" Or going into the struggling classes of a high school and saying, "Guess what? Everybody gets an A!" Or going into debtor's prison (do they exist anymore?) and saying, "Everybody out! Your debts have all been paid!"

Well, don't be afraid of the word "evangelism." Because that is what it is. That is the "message of reconciliation."

> Almighty God, whom truly to know is everlasting life: Grant us so perfectly to know Your Son Jesus Christ to be the way, the truth, and the life, that we may steadfastly follow His steps in the way that leads to eternal life; through Jesus Christ Your Son our Lord, who lives and reigns with You, in the unity of the Holy Spirit, one God, for ever and ever. Amen. (Fifth Sunday of Easter – BCP p. 225)

September 5

> *"And they heard the sound of the LORD God walking in the garden in the cool of the day, and the man and his wife hid themselves from the presence of the LORD God among the trees of the garden" (Genesis 3:8, ESV).*

HIDE-AND-SEEK, ANYONE? It's funny that the "winner" of hide-and-seek is the one who stays hidden—isolated, alone, un-found. Just like Adam and Eve, the propensity of the sinner is to hide—hide from God, hide from others, and hide from himself or herself. The need to hide our sin from ourselves is so great that we quickly and self-righteously begin to believe all the cover-up lies we tell.

Thanks be to our gracious God, that we did not and can not win the Great Game of Hide-and-Seek. Our God seeks us out. Our God seeks us out, not in judgment, but in love. Some churches like to have what they call "seeker services." Yet the true Seeker is Jesus Christ.

And—blimey!—there is boundless joy in being found!

O God, whose Son Jesus is the good shepherd of Your people: Grant that when we hear His voice we may know Him who calls us each by name, and follow where He leads; who, with You and the Holy Spirit, lives and reigns, one God, for ever and ever. Amen. (Fourth Sunday of Easter – BCP p. 225)

September 6

THE ENGLISH PIGEON SAYS, "My shoes please, Betty," the Eastern Towhee reminds you to "drink your tea," and the Blue Jay sounds like screeching brakes that need to be replaced. All avians, different songs.

The Holy Spirit speaks to us in different ways. According to our need, the Spirit will sometimes comfort and other times convict. Same Spirit, different experiences.

When Jesus was preparing His disciples for life after the Son of God in physical form, He told His disciples, *"I will ask the Father, and He will give you another Helper, to be with you forever, even the Spirit of truth" (John 14:16–17, ESV).* This Spirit, God's Spirit, speaks the truth we need to hear in the moment.

Here's a beautiful prayer to pray in the evening—one that meets people in their particular need.

Keep watch, dear Lord, with those who work, or watch, or weep this night, and give Your angels charge over those who sleep. Tend the sick, Lord Christ; give rest to the weary, bless the dying, soothe the suffering, pity the afflicted, shield the joyous, and all for Your love's sake. Amen. (Collect for Evening Prayer – BCP p. 124)

September 7

"Why are you downcast, O my soul? Why the unease within me?" (Psalm 42:5a, BSB).

YOU WOULD NOT BE a human being if you did not carry around a certain amount of sadness. Sadness comes from any number of sources. There are the things you've done or things that have been done to you. There is the omnipresence of suffering in a world beset by sin. There is a melancholy that exists for no apparent reason.

Repressing sadness, though tempting, is always a bad idea. Although you may want to run from sadness, it will track you down in other forms: rage, anxiety, or a kind of alienating superficiality.

There is a fairly famous poem by 13th-century mystic poet Jallaluddin Rumi called the *Guest House* that acknowledges the reality, and even the gift, of sadness.

> This being human is a guest house.
> Every morning a new arrival.
>
> A joy, a depression, a meanness,
> some momentary awareness comes
> as an unexpected visitor.
>
> Welcome and entertain them all!
> Even if they're a crowd of sorrows,
> who violently sweep your house
> empty of its furniture,
> still, treat each guest honorably.
> He may be clearing you out
> for some new delight.
>
> The dark thought, the shame, the malice.
> meet them at the door laughing

and invite them in.

Be grateful for whoever comes,
because each has been sent
as a guide from beyond.

All things come from God. That's why, with the psalmist, we can say to our downcast souls, *"Put your hope in God, for I will yet praise Him for the salvation of His presence" (Psalm 42:5b, BSB).*

Heavenly Father, send Your Holy Spirit into our hearts, to direct and rule us according to Your will, to comfort us in all our afflictions, to defend us from all error, and to lead us into all truth; through Jesus Christ our Lord. Amen. (From a Collect for Noonday – BCP p. 107)

September 8

ALONG OUR FENCE LINE, we planted an array of wildflowers. We prepared the bed, defended against weeds, diligently watered, and then waited. And waited. Nothing but weeds. But, Lo! a week or two later a volunteer pumpkin plant sprouted. And just yesterday we harvested a picturesque pumpkin—perfectly round and perfectly orange.

I'd rather have a pumpkin than an array of wildflowers, especially in autumn. *"The plans of the heart belong to man, but the reply of the tongue is from the LORD" (Proverbs 16:1, BSB).*

In every case, the Lord's reply of the tongue is way better than the plans of the heart.

O God, Your never-failing providence sets in order all things both in heaven and earth: Put away from us, we entreat You, all hurtful things, and give us those things which are profitable for us; through Jesus Christ our Lord, who lives and reigns with You and the Holy Spirit, one God, for ever and ever. Amen. (Proper 4 – BCP p. 229)

September 9

"Count it all joy, my brothers, when you meet trials of various kinds" (James 1:2, ESV).

OVER A DRINK WITH two other dads, the conversation turned to children and disappointment. Not disappointment in our children, but our children experiencing their own disappointments. No parent likes to see his or her child suffer or fail or flounder. But the earlier a child is disabused of an entitled attitude, the better. The sooner a child learns that "life is not fair," the better.

Ultimately, the sooner a child realizes that God is our true source of strength throughout the ups and downs of life, the better. Parents can't manufacture that kind of faith in God for their children, but they can pray!

God our Father, You see Your children growing up in an unsteady and confusing world: Show them that Your ways give more life than the ways of the world, and that following You is better than chasing after selfish goals. Help them to take failure, not as a measure of their worth, but as a chance for a new start. Give them strength to hold their faith in You, and to keep alive their joy in Your creation; through Jesus Christ our Lord. Amen. (For Young Persons – BCP p. 829)

September 10

"For My people have committed two evils: they have forsaken Me, the fountain of living water, and dug out cisterns for themselves, cracked cisterns that can hold no water" (Jeremiah 2:13, NRSV).

ISN'T THAT THE WAY it works? Nose up and thumbs down on the abundant life that God lavishes on us, all the while scrambling to dig our own wells of pleasure, only to discover that they are fissured failures, leaking for all they are worth.

I love the description of the prodigal son when he ran dry of booze, cash, and friends: *"He came to himself" (Luke 15:17).* But the cracked cisterns clearly have their purpose. Drawing a cup that comes up empty helps us believe that Jesus is telling the truth when He says that whoever drinks the water that He gives them will never thirst.

> Lord of all power and might, the author and giver of all good things: Graft in our hearts the love of Your Name; increase in us true religion; nourish us with all goodness; and bring forth in us the fruit of good works; through Jesus Christ our Lord, who lives and reigns with You and the Holy Spirit, one God for ever and ever. Amen. (Proper 17 – BCP p. 233)

September 11

"But I say to you that everyone who is angry with his brother will be liable to judgment; whoever insults his brother will be liable to the council; and whoever says,

'You fool!' will be liable to the hell of fire" (Matthew 5:22, ESV).

IN WILLA CATHER'S UNUSUALLY dark novel, *My Mortal Enemy*, she describes what happens when anger takes over the atmosphere: "And now everything was in ruins. The air was still and cold like the air in a refrigerating-room. What I felt was fear; I was afraid to look or speak or move. Everything about me seemed evil. When kindness has left people, even for a few moments, we become afraid of them, as if their reason had left them. When it has left a place where we have always found it, it is like a shipwreck; we drop from security into something malevolent and bottomless."

"Righteous anger" belongs to God alone, since He is the only One who is righteous. What belongs to us is the confession of our sin and the prayer for the restoration of love.

> O God, You have bound us together in a common life. Help us, in the midst of our struggles for justice and truth, to confront one another without hatred or bitterness, and to work together with mutual forbearance and respect; through Jesus Christ our Lord. Amen. (In Times of Conflict – BCP p. 824)

September 12

ONE OUT OF EVERY five mammals on the earth is a…? Do you know the answer? A dog? A cow? A human? We see dogs, cows, and humans everywhere. No, one out of every five mammals on the earth is a… bat! Who sees bats on a regular basis? You've really got to go looking for bats to find bats. Bats are mostly hidden, nocturnal, out of the limelight.

This unexpected fact reminds us that our God is a God who does His best work out of sight. The prophet Isaiah says, *"Truly, You are a God who hides Himself, O God of Israel, the Savior" (Isaiah 45:15, ESV)*. His incarnation was hidden from sight, away in a manger, no crib for a bed. His salvific death was on a forlorn, godforsaken hill outside the bustle of the city. The moment of His resurrection, which forever snapped the cosmic law of death for all creatures, was seen by exactly no one.

All this means that He is at work in your life *right now* in ways that you cannot see. Just because you cannot see Him at work does not mean that He is not working for your good, and for the good of the whole world.

> O God our King, by the resurrection of Your Son Jesus Christ on the first day of the week, You conquered sin, put death to flight, and gave us the hope of everlasting life: Redeem all our days by this victory; forgive our sins, banish our fears, make us bold to praise You and to do Your will; and steel us to wait for the consummation of Your kingdom on the last great Day; through the same Jesus Christ our Lord. Amen. (On Sunday – BCP p. 835)

September 13

ST. PAUL PRAYS THAT the people in the church in Ephesus would *"know the love of Christ that surpasses knowledge" (Ephesians 3:19)*. Did you catch the play on words? How are we to know something that surpasses knowledge, that is beyond knowing?! He echoes this prayer in Philippians: *"And the peace of God, which surpasses all understanding, will guard your hearts and minds in Christ Jesus" (Philippians 4:7, CSB)*.

When you think about it, we "know" all kinds of things that we don't fully understand. We know that Earth—our island home—is a gift, but not our final Shore. We know when we are cherished by another person, even when we don't know how they could love us as we are. We know when we've been prayed for, although we don't really know how prayer truly works. How many times have you been asked, "How do you know?" and you have responded, "I don't know. I just know." Know what I mean?

Ultimately, however, God is the Knower and we are the known. God is the Lover and we are the loved. God is the Peace-Giver and we are peace-receivers. This we know.

> Lord Jesus Christ, You said to Your apostles, 'Peace I give to you: My own peace I leave with you:' Regard not our sins, but the faith of Your Church, and give to us the peace and unity of that heavenly City, where with the Father and the Holy Spirit You live and reign, now and forever. Amen. (Noonday Prayers – BCP p. 107)

September 14

"The days are surely coming, says the LORD, when I will raise up for David a righteous Branch, and He shall reign as king and deal wisely, and shall execute justice and righteousness in the land. In His days Judah will be saved and Israel will live in safety. And this is the name by which He will be called: 'The LORD is our righteousness'" (Jeremiah 23:5–6, NRSV).

THIS PROPHECY FROM JEREMIAH is not only comforting; it is a harbinger of the New Covenant accomplished by the death and resurrection of Christ. This coming king will be called *"The LORD is our righteousness."* This means that our righteousness before God has nothing to do with us, per se, and everything to do with the king named "our righteousness."

As *The Pilgrim's Progress* author John Bunyan says, "One day, as I was passing through a field, suddenly I thought of a sentence, 'your righteousness is in heaven,' and with the eyes of faith, I saw Christ sitting at God's right hand. And I suddenly realized—THERE is my righteousness.... Now my chains fell off indeed! I felt delivered from slavery to guilt and fears... I went home rejoicing for the love and grace of God."

Amen!

> Almighty and everlasting God, whose will it is to restore all things in Your well-beloved Son, the King of kings and Lord of lords: Mercifully grant that the peoples of the earth, divided and enslaved by sin, may be freed and brought together under His most gracious rule; who lives and reigns with You and the Holy Spirit, one God, now and for ever. Amen. (Proper 29 – BCP p. 236)

September 15

A FRIEND REMINDED ME that Dostoyevsky described many of his characters as both sentimental and cruel. That isn't your typical pairing, is it? How can sentimentality be cruel?

Sentimentality is love without truth, and cruelty is truth without love. It's the human condition before it recognizes that grace is truth and that truth leads inexorably to grace.

In Christ we have both grace and truth. St. John says this: *"For the law was given through Moses; grace and truth came through Jesus Christ" (John 1:17).*

Heavenly Father, send Your Holy Spirit into our hearts, to direct and rule us according to Your will, to comfort us in all our afflictions, to defend us from all error, and to lead us into all truth; through Jesus Christ our Lord. Amen. (Noonday Prayer – BCP p. 107)

September 16

EVER WONDER IF YOU are going down the right path? Making the right choices about your life? Heading in the right direction *vis-à-vis* a relationship, vocation, parenting, etc.?

The nearly too-good-to-be-true news is that God is in the guiding business. We read in the beloved 23rd Psalm that *"He guides me along the right paths for His name's sake" (Psalm 23:3, NIV).*

Really, God is in the reclamation and rescue business. There is no wrong path that is beyond God's ability to right it. There is no wreck that He cannot repair, no injury that He cannot heal.

It's all going to be okay! Way, way more than okay, in fact.

Grant to us, Lord, we pray, the spirit to think and do always those things that are right, that we, who cannot exist without You, may by You be enabled to live according to Your will; through Jesus Christ our Lord, who lives and reigns with You and the Holy Spirit, one God, for ever and ever. Amen. (Proper 14 – BCP p. 232)

September 17

"Be kind to one another, tenderhearted, forgiving one another, as God in Christ forgave you" (Ephesians 4:32, ESV).

WHERE ARE YOU HARDHEARTED? With whom would you like to be "tenderhearted" instead? I've come to believe that forgiveness is at the very heart of the universe. Where there is no forgiveness, there is no relationship. In other words, love requires forgiveness of the other.

If the cross is the heart of the universe, then so is forgiveness. Again, without forgiveness, there is no relationship. But we have been forgiven and therefore are children of God and brothers and sisters in Christ.

Almighty and everlasting God, You are always more ready to hear than we to pray, and to give more than we either desire or deserve: Pour upon us the abundance of Your mercy, forgiving us those things of which our conscience is afraid, and giving us those good things for which we are not worthy to ask, except through the merits and mediation of Jesus Christ our Savior; who lives and reigns with You and the Holy Spirit, one God, for ever and ever. Amen. (Proper 22 – BCP p. 234)

September 18

I SOMETIMES WISH THAT the Bible was funnier. Then again, Jesus' original audience would have laughed out loud at much of what He said. In one film version of His life, people rolled in the aisles when He suggested giving your child a scorpion instead of an egg when making a point about prayer.

My point is that man cannot live on seriousness alone. If, as we said yesterday, forgiveness wins the gold medal of the universe, humor at least gets the bronze, if not the silver. Even to woe-begotten Job, this promise comes: *"He will yet fill your mouth with laughter, and your lips with shouting"* (*Job 8:21, ESV*).

Humor, rightly employed, deflates our self-importance and puts the control back where it belongs: in the hands of God.

Blessed are You, O Lord God, King of the Universe, for You give us all we need to sustain our lives and make our hearts glad; through Jesus Christ our Lord. Amen. (Grace at Meals – BCP p. 835)

September 19

> *"For where there is envy and selfish ambition, there will also be disorder and wickedness of every kind. But the wisdom from above is first pure, then peaceable, gentle, willing to yield, full of mercy and good fruits, without a trace of partiality or hypocrisy"* (James 3:16–17, NRSV).

THIS PASSAGE REMINDS ME of Warren Zevon's "Disorder in the House," released in 2003, right before he died of cancer.

> Disorder in the house
> Reptile wisdom
> Zombies on the lawn staggering around
> Disorder in the house
> There's a flaw in the system

And the fly in the ointment's gonna bring the whole
thing down.

We know the flaw in the system that brings the whole thing
down. Fortunately, we also know the One who took the disorder
of the whole world into His being. He went down, but rose again.
And swept us all up in His train.

> Grant us, Lord, not to be anxious about earthly things,
> but to love things heavenly; and even now, while we
> are placed among things that are passing away, to hold
> fast to those that shall endure; through Jesus Christ our
> Lord, who lives and reigns with You and the Holy Spirit,
> one God, for ever and ever. Amen. (Proper 20 – BCP
> p. 234)

September 20

MY AUNT AND UNCLE live in a house called Winona on Hungars
Creek on the Eastern Shore of Virginia. Winona was built in
1680, just a few generations after the first English settlers arrived
across the Bay at Jamestown. How many feet have gone up and
down Winona's stairs in the intervening centuries? I picture my
father, who died a few years ago, there as a toddler. And yet he is
a relative newcomer to the parade of lives Winona has seen.

Sometimes the ephemerality of our lives on earth takes center stage. Here today, gone tomorrow. I love life and the people
in it; the one-and-doneness of it all would be too much to bear
without the great hope we have in Christ Jesus.

After Lazarus died, Jesus consoled Martha. *Jesus said to her,
'I am the resurrection and the life. Whoever believes in Me, though he
die, yet shall he live, and everyone who lives and believes in Me shall
never die. Do you believe this?'" (John 11:25–26, ESV).*

Do you believe this? As we say each week in the Creed: "[We] look for the resurrection of the dead and the life of the world to come. Amen."

> Almighty God, who through Your only-begotten Son Jesus Christ overcame death and opened to us the gate of everlasting life: Grant that we, who celebrate with joy the day of the Lord's resurrection, may be raised from the death of sin by Your life-giving Spirit; through Jesus Christ our Lord, who lives and reigns with You and the Holy Spirit, one God, now and for ever. Amen. (Easter Day – BCP p. 222)

September 21

"Submit to one another out of reverence for Christ"
(Ephesians 5:21).

ST. PAUL INTRODUCES A radical revisioning/reordering of the ways and means of living for believers. Instead of dominating one another, duping one another, bargaining with one another, hiding from one another, or belittling one another, he says that we are to submit to one another.

What is absent from this vision for life? Any talk of standing up for one's rights, championing one's identity, staking one's claim, defending one's privileges, being guided by one's personal dreams. What is present in this vision for life? A reflection of Christ Jesus who humbled Himself, even to the point of death on the cross.

That this vision for life is not possible under human steam does not make it any less true. For, as Jesus says, what is impossible for us is possible for God.

Almighty and eternal God, ruler of all things in heaven and earth: Mercifully accept the prayers of Your people, and strengthen us to do Your will; through Jesus Christ our Lord. Amen. (The Collect at the Prayers – BCP p. 394)

September 22

"It is good to give thanks to the LORD, to sing praises to Your name, O Most High; to declare Your steadfast love in the morning, and Your faithfulness by night" (Psalm 92:1–2, ESV).

MORNING AND NIGHT.

In the morning you might be raring to go, optimistic about the day ahead. You also might be sluggish, anxious about what the day holds. Either way, declaring God's steadfast love is the way to begin.

At night, you might have a feeling of accomplishment, having discharged the duties of the day. You also might be swimming in regret for things done and left undone. Either way, declaring God's faithfulness covers all your bases.

God is with you today—morning, noon, and night.

O Lord, support us all the day long, until the shadows lengthen, and the evening comes, and the busy world is hushed, and the fever of life is over, and our work is done. Then in Thy mercy, grant us a safe lodging, and a holy rest, and peace at the last. Amen. (In the Evening – BCP p. 833)

September 23

THE SCRIPTURE TELLS US that Jesus Christ is the *"Lamb slain before the foundation of the world" (Revelation 13:8, ABPE)*. Take just a minute to let that sink in, deep down into the foundations of your being. Christ's blood was shed for us *before* the world began. Somehow, in the mystery of God's plan, the cross of Christ—the forgiveness of sins—has always been in existence.

A character named Mr. Head in a Flannery O'Connor short story is given this life-changing insight. He has considered himself an upright man, but to his horror finds himself forsaking his own grandson:

> Mr. Head stood very still and felt the action of mercy touch him… He understood that it grew out of agony, which is not denied to any man… He understood it was all a man could carry into death to give his Maker… He stood appalled, judging himself with the thoroughness of God, while the action of mercy covered his pride like a flame and consumed it… He realized that he was forgiven for sins from the beginning of time… He saw that no sin was too monstrous for him to claim as his own, and since God loved in proportion as He forgave, he felt ready at the instant to enter Paradise.

What O'Connor calls the "action of mercy" is woven into the foundation of the world! And it is there for you today.

> O God, by the passion of Your blessed Son You made and instrument of shameful death to be for us the means of life; Grant us so to glory in the cross of Christ, that we may gladly suffer shame and loss for the sake of Your Son our Savior Jesus Christ; who lives and reigns with You and the Holy Spirit, one God, for ever and ever. Amen. (Tuesday in Holy Week – BCP p. 220)

September 24

"Jesus said to him, 'I am the way, and the truth, and the life. No one comes to the Father except through Me'" (John 14:6, ESV).

SIMONE WEIL ONCE SAID, "Though a person may run as fast as he can away from Christ, if it is toward what he considers true, he runs in fact straight into the arms of Christ."

Where are you running? Maybe you don't even know. Like Jackson Browne, you don't know where you're running now, you're just running on…running on empty. Well, you might be hell-bent for nowhere or heaven-bent for what is true. Either way, the arms of Christ are truly gracious. Indeed, there is a wideness in God's mercy.

Blessed Lord, who caused all holy Scriptures to be written for our learning: Grant us so to hear them, read, mark, learn, and inwardly digest them, that we may embrace and ever hold fast the blessed hope of everlasting life, which You have given us in our Savior Jesus Christ; who lives and reigns with You and the Holy Spirit, one God, for ever and ever. Amen. (Proper 28 – BCP p. 236)

September 25

"For everything there is a season, a time for every activity under heaven" (Ecclesiastes 3:1, NLT).

THOMAS JEFFERSON ONCE SAID, "There is a fullness of time when men should go, and not occupy too long the ground to which others have a right to advance." As we age, as we change, our roles change. We are given different work to do. A marriage heals, a child moves away, a new season is underway.

God's direction of your life is purposeful. Every hair of your head is numbered, and every move you make is secure in His love.

Grant, O Lord, that the course of this world may be peaceably governed by Your providence; and that we may joyfully serve You in confidence and serenity; through Jesus Christ our Lord, who lives and reigns with You and the Holy Spirit, one God, for ever and ever. Amen. (Proper 3 – BCP p. 229)

September 26

AT OUR SON's Parents Weekend up on a mountain in Tennessee, we went to a "tailgate." I put that in quotes, because the tailgate was really a tent. Laid out on the tables were china and linen and flowers, an open bar with a bartender, skewered shrimp, and many other absurdly gourmet delectables. Not to mention the *petit fours*.

I'm sure there was some showing-off involved with the hosts, as this tent strove to outdo many other tents. But really, it felt biblical to me. Isn't this how God treats us?

"The LORD of hosts will prepare a lavish banquet for all peoples on this mountain; A banquet of aged wine, choice pieces with marrow, And refined, aged wine" (Isaiah 25:6, NASB 1995).

You have no clue how precious you are to God.

O God, whose blessed Son made Himself known to His disciples in the breaking of bread: Open the eyes of our faith, that we may behold Him in all His redeeming work; who lives and reigns with You, in the unity

of the Holy Spirit, one God, now and for ever. Amen.
(Wednesday in Easter Week – BCP p. 223)

September 27

THOMAS MERTON EXPLAINS WHAT happens when our dedication
to a cause usurps our love and care for actual people. Here's what
he wrote in a letter to a friend:

> You are fed up with words, and I don't blame you. I
> am nauseated by them sometimes. I am also, to tell the
> truth, nauseated with ideals and with causes. This sounds
> like heresy, but I think you will understand what I mean.
> It is so easy to get engrossed with ideas and slogans and
> myths that in the end one is left holding the bag, empty,
> with no trace of meaning left in it. And then the temp-
> tation is to yell louder than ever in order to make the
> meaning there by magic.

St. Paul says it this way: *"If I speak in the tongues of men and of
angels, but have not love, I am only a ringing gong or a clanging
cymbal. If I have the gift of prophecy and can fathom all mysteries and
all knowledge, and if I have absolute faith so as to move mountains,
but have not love, I am nothing. If I give all I possess to the poor and
exult in the surrender of my body, but have not love, I gain nothing"
(1 Corinthians 13:1–3, BSB).*
    Amen to that.

> O God, You made us in Your own image and redeemed
> us through Jesus Your Son: Look with compassion on
> the whole human family; take away the arrogance and
> hatred which infect our hearts; break down the walls
> that separate us; unite us in bonds of love; and work

through our struggle and confusion to accomplish Your purposes on earth; that, in Your good time, all nations and races may serve You in harmony around Your heavenly throne; through Jesus Christ our Lord. Amen. (For the Human Family – BCP p. 815)

September 28

"When the goodness and loving kindness of God our Savior appeared, He saved us, not because of any works of righteousness that we had done, but according to His mercy" (Titus 3:4–5, NRSV).

THE BLACK WALNUT TREE is a beauty—distinctive bark, leaves turning to flaming yellow before losing them early in the fall, and the prolific green turning to brown nuts.

We decided to harvest the nuts from our black walnuts this year. It is quite an ordeal. Gather the nuts, break open the husk, fill up a tub and soak the nuts, discard all the ones that float, dry them for six weeks, borrow a black walnut cracker from a neighbor who happens to have a black walnut cracker, and finally crack the nut in just the right way to mine the treasure. Usually, the meat is broken into bits, so you have to pick out the shell shards before placing the meat in your tiny bowl.

At least, after all that work, you have the sweet reward of the nut? Well, our children say the eastern black walnut (as opposed to the English walnut you buy at the store—already hulled, shucked, and de-shelled for you), tastes like nail polish. They are kind of right.

All this is to say that religion is the black walnut; lots and lots of work for not much reward. The gospel is the English walnut—so delicious, and everything is already done for you. What's more, the stores give it away for free!!

> O God, who wonderfully created, and yet more wonderfully restored, the dignity of human nature: Grant that we may share the divine life of Him who humbled Himself to share our humanity, Your Son Jesus Christ; who lives and reigns with You, in the unity of the Holy Spirit, one God, for ever and ever. Amen. (Second Sunday after Christmas Day – BCP p. 214)

September 29

"The meek shall inherit the land and delight themselves in abundant peace" (Psalm 37:11, ESV).

THE PREVAILING WISDOM IS "to the victor belong the spoils." But the countervailing message of the gospel claims that it is the meek who "win," even in loss. The victorious strong take the land by force. But the meek inherit the land. That means that they are given the land.

The enjoyment of spoils won by force is fleeting at best. But the peace of surrender is profound and long-lasting. How does this relate to you today? Where are you more than ready to unfurl the white flag? Delight and abundance await.

> Almighty and everlasting God, You govern all things both in heaven and on earth: Mercifully hear the supplications of Your people, and in our time grant us Your peace; through Jesus Christ our Lord, who lives and reigns with You and the Holy Spirit, one God, for ever and ever. Amen. (Fourth Sunday after the Epiphany – BCP p. 215)

September 30

IN THIS PASSAGE FROM the book of Acts, Peter is asked with what power or by whose name he was able to heal a man of his sickness. He replied, *"Let it be known to all of you, and to all the people of Israel, that this man is standing before you in good health by the name of Jesus Christ of Nazareth, whom you crucified, whom God raised from the dead. This Jesus is 'the stone that was rejected by you, the builders; it has become the cornerstone.' There is salvation in no one else, for there is no other name under heaven given among mortals by which we must be saved"* (Acts 4:10–12, NRSV).

Peter proclaims that the name of Jesus has power—power to heal and power to save. Obviously, His name can't be bandied about like a magic incantation. Nor do we expect all physical infirmity to be healed, even when prayer and great faith are present. Instead, our hope is in the belief that Jesus is Lord of all, attested to and vindicated by His resurrection from the dead. Even in our death, we are healed and saved.

Had Jesus stayed in the grave, then none of the above happens; He'd be a marginal footnote in ancient history. But, because of Easter Day, we sing with confidence,

> At the name of Jesus
> every knee shall bow,
> every tongue confess Him
> King of glory now;
> 'tis the Father's pleasure
> we should call Him Lord
> who from the beginning
> was the mighty Word.

> Almighty Father, who gave Your only Son to die for our sins and to rise for our justification: Give us grace so to put away the leaven of malice and wickedness, that we

may always serve You in pureness of living and truth; through Jesus Christ Your Son our Lord, who lives and reigns with You and the Holy Spirit, one God, now and for ever. Amen. (Friday in Easter Week – BCP p. 224)

OCTOBER

October 1

October
And the trees are stripped bare
Of all they wear
What do I care?

October
And kingdoms rise
And kingdoms fall
But you go on
And on ("October," U2)

THE TREES ARE NOT stripped bare of all they wear in October, at least not in Central Virginia. But Bono's lyrics are right: Kingdoms rise and kingdoms fall, but God Almighty goes on and on. That which we hold dear and that which is the thorn in our side will eventually fall away.

St. Paul reminds us of life's temporality as well. *"But our citizenship is in heaven. And we eagerly await a Savior from there, the Lord Jesus Christ" (Philippians 3:20, NIV).*

This too shall pass. God and His love will not.

Most loving Father, whose will it is for us to give thanks for all things, to fear nothing but the loss of You, and to cast all our care on You who care for us: Preserve us from faithless fears and worldly anxieties, that no clouds of this mortal life may hide from us the light of that love which is immortal, and which You have manifested to us in Your Son Jesus Christ our Lord; who lives and reigns with You, in the unity of the Holy Spirit, one God, now and for ever. Amen. (Eighth Sunday after the Epiphany – BCP p. 216)

October 2

A FRIEND SHARED THIS insightful quote: "Patience with God is faith. Patience with others is love. Patience with yourself is hope."

I want to speak about patience with yourself today. Not only are we to be kind to others—especially in trying times—but it is equally important to extend grace to yourself. Periods of stress and adaptation mean that the committee of inner critics inside your head needs to be kicked far out of earshot. Patience with yourself is hope.

Patience with yourself is a tall order for most of us. That's why St. Paul reminds us that patience comes from God, not ourselves. *"We rejoice in our sufferings, knowing that suffering produces endurance, and endurance produces character, and character produces hope, and hope does not put us to shame, because God's love has been poured into our hearts through the Holy Spirit who has been given to us" (Romans 5:3–5, ESV).*

This is NOT an example of "when the going gets tough, the tough get going." Instead, Paul assures us that suffering automatically produces endurance, character, and hope, the way a field planted with seed produces a crop. This is because God is the planter and producer through His Holy Spirit who has already been given to us.

I have another friend who likes to ask again and again, "Rev. Walker, does God do *everything*?" And the answer is the same every time: Yes, God does everything, including giving you patience with yourself.

Almighty God, You alone can bring into order the unruly wills and affections of sinners: Grant Your people grace to love what You command and desire what You promise; that, among the swift and varied changes of the world, our hearts may surely there be fixed where true joys are to be found; through Jesus Christ our Lord, who lives and reigns with You and the Holy Spirit, one God, now and for ever. Amen. (Fifth Sunday in Lent – BCP p. 219)

October 3

Vampires are the best metaphor for the human condition. Here you have a monster with a soul that's immortal, yet in a biological body... A vampire ... is perfect ... because he transcends time—yet he can be destroyed, go mad and suffer; it's intensely about the human dilemma.

THAT'S FROM AUTHOR ANNE Rice. She's got a point, I think. We are bound for the Promised Land, signed, sealed, and delivered by the cross of Christ, yet we still suffer and even go mad. We know that our bodies will be destroyed as well.

Yet—hear these words from Job, quoted at the beginning of our funeral liturgy: *"For I know that my redeemer liveth, and that He shall stand at the latter day upon the earth: And though after my skin worms destroy this body, yet in my flesh shall I see God: Whom I shall see for myself, And mine eyes shall behold, and not another; though my reins be consumed within me" (Job 19:25–27, KJV).*

Thankfully, we fare better than vampires. Although, it must be said, we are sustained by the blood of Christ!

The Blood of our Lord Jesus Christ, which was shed for thee, preserve thy body and soul unto eternal life. Drink this in remembrance that Christ's blood was shed for thee, and be thankful. (From the Holy Eucharist: Rite One – BCP p. 338)

October 4

"There is one body and one Spirit—just as you were called to the one hope that belongs to your call—one Lord, one faith, one baptism, one God and Father of all, who is over all and through all and in all" (Ephesians 4:4–6, ESV).

THAT PASSAGE FROM ST. Paul's letter to the Ephesians comprises the opening sentences of the baptismal liturgy in the Book of Common Prayer. We are given a heavy dose of unity and camaraderie, which is a helpful reminder of that which connects and unifies rather than that which separates and divides.

Bishop Porter Taylor quotes renowned English mystic Evelyn Underhill, saying "God is the only reality and we are only real insofar as we are in God and God is in us." He then reminded us that "the people of this country are not Republicans and Democrats; they are children of God, made in God's image just like you and me. When we meet/experience another person and our quick definition of them comes to mind, think again, feel again, look again."

The psalmist says, *"How good and pleasant it is when God's people live together in unity!" (Psalm 133:1, NIV).* There is so much that divides; let's pray for God to help us find the bridges!

Here is a prayer for unity. It's a long one, but a good one.

O God the Father of our Lord Jesus Christ, our only Savior, the Prince of Peace: Give us grace seriously to lay to heart the great dangers we are in by our unhappy divisions; take away all hatred and prejudice, and whatever else may hinder us from godly union and concord; that, as there is but one Body and one Spirit, one hope of our calling, one Lord, one Faith, one Baptism, one God and Father of us all, so we may be all of one heart and of one soul, united in one holy bond of truth and peace, of faith and charity, and may with one mind and one mouth glorify You; through Jesus Christ our Lord. Amen. (For the Unity of the Church – BCP p. 818)

October 5

"Suddenly a furious storm came up on the lake, so that the waves swept over the boat. But Jesus was sleeping"
(Matthew 8:24, NIV).

SOMEONE JOKED THE OTHER day that Jesus is really a cat. She said that explains a lot. By that I suppose she meant our Lord's apparent indifference to us and our needs. He doesn't come when we call—or at least it seems that way. He spends a lot of time sleeping. Even through storms. When storms strike, dogs shake and hide in the closet. Cats stay tucked in a tight ball on the sofa, unperturbed.

Like a cat, it's true that Jesus does what He wants when He wants. But, despite appearances to the contrary, what He does and what He wants is always for our good. He did wake up, by the way, and still the storm. And so too with you and your storm.

O God, Your never-failing providence sets in order all things both in heaven and earth: Put away from us, we entreat You, all hurtful things, and give us those things which are profitable for us; through Jesus Christ our Lord, who lives and reigns with You and the Holy Spirit, one God, for ever and ever. Amen. (Proper 4 – BCP p. 229)

October 6

THE FIRST TIME I flew into the bowl that is the Jackson Hole airport, I stepped off the plane, took in the magnanimous mountains, and just started laughing! It reminded me of the Monty Python chapel scene—the chaplain intoning "Let us praise God. Oh, Lord, you are so big, so absolutely huge. Gosh, we're all really impressed down here, I can tell you."

Arriving in Wyoming, I was really impressed down here, I can tell you. It is such a liberating gift to be reminded that you are not the center of it all. To be relieved of one's presumed self-importance is the work of the Holy Spirit. It's not about you.

And yet, the crazy thing is that God loves you so tenderly, so individually. Jesus says, *"Are not two sparrows sold for a penny? Yet not one of them will fall to the ground apart from the will of your Father. And even the very hairs of your head are all numbered. So do not be afraid; you are worth more than many sparrows" (Matthew 10:29–31, BSB).*

> O God, who hast made of one blood all the peoples of the earth, and didst send Thy blessed Son to preach peace to those who are far off and to those who are near: Grant that people everywhere may seek after Thee and find Thee; bring the nations into Thy fold; pour out Thy Spirit upon all flesh; and hasten the coming of Thy kingdom; through the same Thy Son Jesus Christ our Lord. Amen. (Prayer for Mission – BCP p. 58)

October 7

A FRIEND RECENTLY STRUGGLED with a prolonged illness. When a CT scan revealed an "abnormality," he immediately jumped to all the worst conclusions. Convinced of his impending demise, he met with a specialist who confirmed nothing more than a stubborn infection. He shared his experience with his usual wit and humor.

Who can't relate? Worst-case scenarios hang around like unwanted houseguests. Why do we do this? Obviously, bad things do happen, but 99.99% of the time, it is just life as usual, with minor ups and downs. God knows our propensity for assuming doom; thus, the Bible is full of verses about fear. Jesus says, *"Do not be afraid, little flock, for your Father has been pleased to give you the kingdom" (Luke 12:32, NIV).*

Moreover, the abiding and permanent reality of the world that God has created and redeemed is this: Even when all isn't well, all shall be well.

> O God, who by the glorious resurrection of Your Son Jesus Christ destroyed death and brought life and immortality to light: Grant that we, who have been raised with Him, may abide in His presence and rejoice in the hope of eternal glory; through Jesus Christ our Lord, to whom, with You and the Holy Spirit, be dominion and praise for ever and ever. Amen. (Tuesday in Easter Week – BCP p. 223)

October 8

FRENCH LITERARY CRITIC René Girard said, "As the novelist descends deeper into himself, he also descends into the hearts of all men. He cannot doubt, then, that truth itself is one."

What I find to be one of the most compelling aspects of the gospel is Christ's unflinching gaze into the deepest—and therefore the most sin-sodden—parts of our being. The psalmist famously says, *"My soul is downcast within me... Deep calls to deep*

in the roar of Your waterfalls; all Your waves and breakers have swept
over me" (Psalm 42:6–7, NIV).

God addresses the deepest part of you rather than the image you present to others and, perhaps, to yourself. And the Deep which calls to your deep is the depth of mercy.

> O God of peace, who hast taught us that in returning and rest we shall be saved, in quietness and confidence shall be our strength: By the might of Thy Spirit lift us, we pray Thee, to Thy presence, where we may be still and know that Thou art God; through Jesus Christ our Lord. Amen. (For Quiet Confidence – BCP p. 832)

October 9

ST. DOLLY PARTON REMOVED herself from contention after she had been nominated to the Rock and Roll Hall of Fame. She said she was not worthy of consideration. Who does that? Who says, "I am not worthy"? Almost no one, ever.

St. Peter did, though: *"Depart from me, for I am a sinful man"* *(Luke 5:8).* That is what he tells Jesus after witnessing a powerful miracle. Jesus doesn't depart though; He draws Peter closer in.

Dolly and Peter have got it right. But God has it righter. He draws us ever closer, regardless of our qualifications. Through the merits of Jesus Christ, we are all in His Hall of Fame.

This version of the Prayer of Humble Access is the best.

> We do not presume to come to this Your table, O merciful Lord, trusting in our own righteousness, but in Your abundant and great mercies. We are not worthy so much as to gather up the crumbs under Your table; but You are the same Lord whose character is always to have mercy. Grant us, therefore, gracious Lord, so to eat

the flesh of Your dear Son Jesus Christ, and to drink His blood, that our sinful bodies may be made clean by His body, and our souls washed through His most precious blood, and that we may evermore dwell in Him, and He in us. Amen.

October 10

THE CONTEMPLATION OF DEATH seems at first blush like a strange and morbid occupation. Yet, why is that? We are all going to die; humanity's mortality rate still clocks in at 100%. As Dawes sings, "You can stare into the abyss, but it's staring right back." Why not take a prolonged peek?

Sixteenth-century French philosopher Michel de Montaigne wrote, "To begin depriving death of its greatest advantage over us, let us adopt a way clean contrary to that common one; let us deprive death of its strangeness, let us frequent it, let us get used to it; let us have nothing more often in mind than death."

The psalmists had the same thoughts much earlier: *"For He knows our frame; He remembers that we are dust. As for man, his days are like grass; he flourishes like a flower of the field; for the wind passes over it, and it is gone, and its place knows it no more" (Psalm 103:14–16, ESV). Or, "So teach us to number our days that we may get a heart of wisdom" (Psalm 90:12, ESV).*

When Christians do stare into the abyss, we find Jesus Christ staring right back with open arms. Risen from the dead, He has trampled down death with His own death. So as we stare into the abyss, we will have the Apostle Paul's words on our lips, *"O death, where is your victory? O death, where is your sting?" (1 Corinthians 15:55).*

O God, who by the glorious resurrection of Your Son Jesus Christ destroyed death and brought life and immortality to light: Grant that we, who have been raised with Him, may abide in His presence and rejoice in the hope of eternal glory; who lives and reigns with You, in the unity of the Holy Spirit, one God, now and for ever. Amen. (Tuesday in Easter Week – BCP p. 223)

October 11

THE EASTERN PHOEBE WILL not be ignored. The Phoebe calls its own name over and over and over again: *"Phoebe! Phoebe! Phoebe!"* Much like Hodor in *Game of Thrones.*

No one wants to be ignored, overlooked, forgotten. We are like Phoebes—relentlessly calling attention to ourselves. We can pipe down, though, because God sees and loves you—no attention-getting antics necessary. *"Can a mother forget the infant at her breast, walk away from the baby she bore? But even if mothers forget, I'd never forget you—never. Look, I've written your names on the backs of My hands"* (Isaiah 49:15–16, *The Message*).

Your name was written by the hands that were pierced.

We thank You, heavenly Father, that You have delivered us from the dominion of sin and death and brought us into the kingdom of Your Son; and we pray that, as by His death He has recalled us to life, so by His love He may raise us to eternal joys; who lives and reigns with You, in the unity of the Holy Spirit, one God, now and for ever. Amen. (Saturday in Easter Week – BCP p. 224)

October 12

GRATEFUL DEAD LYRICS—like William Faulkner's answers to interview questions—defy any one interpretation. "The Wheel" is no exception:

> The wheel is turning and you can't slow down,
> You can't let go and you can't hold on,
> You can't go back and you can't stand still,
> If the thunder don't get you then the lightning will.
>
> Won't you try just a little bit harder,
> Couldn't you try just a little bit more?
> Won't you try just a little bit harder,
> Couldn't you try just a little bit more?

I don't know what Jerry meant anymore than you do, but the song is deeply resonant. One response to the inevitability of life's pressures—from within and without—is to try a little bit harder, try a little bit more. Another response is to hoist up the white flag of surrender and ask Jesus to take the wheel!

The prophet Jeremiah says this: *"I know, GOD, that mere mortals can't run their own lives, that men and women don't have what it takes to take charge of life" (Jeremiah 10:23, The Message).*

> O God, the strength of all who put their trust in You: Mercifully accept our prayers; and because in our weakness we can do nothing good without You, give us the help of Your grace, that in keeping Your commandments we may please You both in will and deed; through Jesus Christ our Lord, who lives and reigns with You and the Holy Spirit, one God, for ever and ever. Amen. (Sixth Sunday after Epiphany – BCP p. 216)

October 13

AFTER WORKING FEVERISHLY FOR 25 days on the score of the *Messiah*—often neglecting to eat or sleep—Handel said, "I think God has visited me." I think the world would agree.

Yet God's visitations don't always, or often, produce such dramatic results. Nor is His presence so acutely felt. Frederick Buechner whittled into his walking stick this saying: *vocatus atque non vocatus Deus aderit*, which Buechner said he "take[s] to mean that in the long run, whether you call on Him or don't call on Him, God will be present with you."

The psalmist reminds us that God is with us in both the highs and the lows of life: *"If I go up to the heavens, You are there; if I make my bed in the depths, You are there" (Psalm 139:8, NIV).* Take heart, friends: No matter what your day will bring, you can be sure that it will bring God Himself.

O heavenly Father, in whom we live and move and have our being: We humbly pray Thee so to guide and govern us by Thy Holy Spirit, that in all the cares and occupations of our life we may not forget Thee, but may remember that we are ever walking in Thy sight; through Jesus Christ our Lord. Amen. (A Collect for Guidance – BCP p. 57)

October 14

EVERY DAY IS A new day. New starts are vitally important. They are important because, given our recalcitrant and recidivistic nature, there is always the need to start anew. But, deeply embedded in our life in Christ is this truth: The wrongs and dead ends and boneheaded maneuvers of yesterday and the day before do not and can not be the final story.

This is not just platitudinal. It's scriptural. *"The steadfast love of the LORD never ceases; His mercies never come to an end; they are new every morning; great is Your faithfulness" (Lamentations 3:22–23, ESV).* Although our wayward ways will never come to an end on this side of the Jordan, neither will God's mercies. When you turn the page on a new day, you will find His steadfast love already written there.

> O God, the King eternal, whose light divides the day from the night and turns the shadow of death into the morning: Drive far from us all wrong desires, incline our hearts to keep Your law, and guide our feet into the way of peace; that, having done Your will with cheerfulness during the day, we may, when night comes, rejoice to give You thanks, through Jesus Christ our Lord. Amen. (A Collect for the Renewal of Life – BCP p. 99)

October 15

> Dear Abby, dear Abby
> My feet are too long
> My hair's falling out and my rights are all wrong
> My friends they all tell me that I've no friends at all
> Won't you write me a letter, won't you give me a call
> Signed, Bewildered

THAT'S FROM THE LATE, great John Prine's "Dear Abby." Abby's response? "You are what you are and you ain't what you ain't." If this is you writing the above letter, I suppose you could go out and buy this year's edition of *How to Win Friends and Influence People.*

Or you could sit back and listen to Abby. Your hair will still fall out, but you might realize that bald is sexy. And when you stop trying to win friends, at least you will still have a few pals to watch Monday Night Football with.

You are what you are and you ain't what you ain't. Humor sure helps with this fact. And so does the Bible, which encourages to offload the whole self-scrutiny project onto God. *"But blessed is the one who trusts in the LORD, whose confidence is in Him" (Jeremiah 17:7, NIV).*

Grant us, O Lord, to trust in You with all our hearts; for, as You always resist the proud who confide in their own strength, so You never forsake those who make their boast of Your mercy; through Jesus Christ our Lord, who lives and reigns with You and the Holy Spirit, one God, now and for ever. Amen. (Proper 18 – BCP p. 233)

October 16

MANY YEARS AGO, WE were treated to a luxurious weekend by another family at a beautiful resort. When we all sat down to a fancy and formal dinner, my friend said the blessing. It was something like, "Lord, thank You for this bounty which we do not deserve." Immediately after we said "Amen," my friend's mother, something of a *grande dame* type, shot back, "We do too deserve this!"

There is some confusion about deserving. Being undeserving of God's grace has nothing to do with self-abnegation or poor/harmful self-worth. By virtue of our mere creation in God's image, we are more cherished than we can begin to imagine. The very nature of grace is that it is a gift that cannot be earned or, therefore, deserved. That's what makes it grace!

"We know that a person is not justified by works of the law but through faith in Jesus Christ, so we also have believed in Christ Jesus, in order to be justified by faith in Christ and not by works of the law, because by works of the law no one will be justified... I do not nullify the grace of God, for if righteousness were through the law, then Christ died for no purpose" (Galatians 2:16, 21, ESV).

Thankfully, Christ did not die for no purpose; He died for you and for me.

> Remember, O Lord, what You have wrought in us and not what we deserve; and, as You have called us to Your service, make us worthy of our calling; through Jesus Christ our Lord, who lives and reigns with You and the Holy Spirit, one God, now and for ever. Amen. (Proper 1 – BCP p. 228)

October 17

IF YOU ARE OF a certain age, you remember forty-year-old lyrics from songs you didn't particularly like in the first place, but you don't always remember why you just walked into the kitchen. You remember jingles from Burger King ads, but you forget to bring your lunch to work.

All our lives—from cradle to grave—are known by God at once. The psalmist says, *"Your eyes saw my unformed substance; in Your book were written, every one of them, the days that were formed for me, when as yet there was none of them" (Psalm 139:16, ESV).*

So comforting. I don't have to remember myself, because God remembers myself *for* me. And makes it all okay.

> O God, the author of peace and lover of concord, to know You is eternal life and to serve You is perfect freedom: Defend us, Your humble servants, in all assaults

of our enemies; that we, surely trusting in Your defense, may not fear the power of any adversaries; through the might of Jesus Christ our Lord. (A Collect for Peace – BCP p. 99)

October 18

"For our appeal does not spring from error or impurity or any attempt to deceive, but just as we have been approved by God to be entrusted with the gospel, so we speak, not to please man, but to please God... For we never came with words of flattery" (1 Thessalonians 2:3–5, ESV).

PEOPLE-PLEASING CAN GET YOU in a world of tangled trouble. Of course, it feels good to avoid conflict, but the conflict will not magically disappear, no matter how much bobbing and weaving we do, no matter how silver-tongued our flattery is, no matter how polished and seemingly genuine our Mr. Nice Guy act appears to be. And even when there is no conflict, people-pleasing has no relation to *agape* love, for it is ultimately self-directed.

St. Paul famously says that he hopes to be "all things to all people" as he proclaims the gospel. This is not people-pleasing, but a recognition of both the objective universal truth of Christianity as well as an awareness that God lovingly tailors His grace to the specific needs of the individual.

In any case, the real reason to deep-six people-pleasing is that you have no idea what another person *actually* needs. Only God can fill the vacuum, including your own.

O God, because without You we are not able to please You, mercifully grant that Your Holy Spirit may in all things direct and rule our hearts; through Jesus Christ our Lord, who lives and reigns with You and the Holy Spirit, one God, now and for ever. Amen. (Proper 19 – BCP p. 233)

October 19

FEELING WEIGHED DOWN? Does George Harrison's "Give Me Love" bring a tear to your eye? "Give me love, give me love / … Give me hope, help me cope / With this heavy load."

You know you have experienced the presence of God when that weight is lifted from your shoulders. According to the psalmist, that kind of help is there for you every day: *"Praise be to the Lord, to God our Savior, who daily bears our burdens" (Psalm 68:19, NIV).*

This is what the gospel ALWAYS does—shifts the burden off your shoulders and onto the one who has born all the cares of the world.

> O God of peace, who hast taught us that in returning and rest we shall be saved, in quietness and confidence shall be our strength: By the might of Thy Spirit lift us, we pray Thee, to Thy presence, where we may be still and know that Thou art God; through Jesus Christ our Lord. Amen. (For Quiet Confidence – BCP p. 832)

October 20

A SIMPLE YET REVOLUTIONARY theological tenet in Christianity is the recognition of the "dignity of every human being." That is the last affirmation in our Baptismal Covenant (BCP p. 305) and it issues from two primary places in Scripture. God created the universe and *"saw that it was good. Then God said, 'Let Us make man in Our image, after Our likeness…' So God created man in His own image, in the image of God He created him; male and female He created them. And God blessed them… And God saw everything that He had made, and behold, it was very good" (Genesis 1:25–28, 31, ESV)*. Human beings have intrinsic dignity, not because we have earned it, but because we bear the image of our Creator.

The second reason we recognize the dignity of every human being is because God became one. Christ became a man so that He could live the perfect life that we are unable to live and to die the death that we justly deserve as a result of sin. His incarnation, crucifixion, resurrection and ascension further bless our common, everyday lives. Remember, He died for *all*.

Take a minute to imagine a world—this world, your world, your day, this very day—in which people treated every other person they encountered with dignity. Everything would change! Of course, we are hampered by our own wounds and limitations, but still, it is a good thing to pray for, even for just today.

Let's pray.

O God, who wonderfully created, and yet more wonderfully restored, the dignity of human nature: Grant that we may share the divine life of Him who humbled Himself to share our humanity, Your Son Jesus Christ; who lives and reigns with You, in the unity of the Holy Spirit, one God, for ever and ever. Amen. (Second Sunday after Christmas Day – BCP p. 214)

October 21

THE POPULAR PODCAST *The Rise and Fall of Mars Hill* chronicles the meteoric rise of pastor Mark Driscoll's church, finally undone by Driscoll's hubris—pride which led to a culture of turmoil and abuse among the staff. Hubris is an Achilles heel for any leader. And not just leaders, but all humans.

Here's what Jesus says: *"You know that among the Gentiles those whom they recognize as their rulers lord it over them, and their great ones are tyrants over them. But it is not so among you; but whoever wishes to become great among you must be your servant, and whoever wishes to be first among you must be slave of all. For the Son of Man came not to be served but to serve, and to give His life a ransom for many" (Mark 10:42–45, NRSV).*

How does this speak to you today?

> Almighty and everlasting God, from whom cometh every good and perfect gift: Send down upon our bishops, and other clergy, and upon the congregations committed to their charge, the healthful Spirit of Thy grace; and, that they may truly please Thee, pour upon them the continual dew of Thy blessing. Grant this, O Lord, for the honor of our Advocate and Mediator, Jesus Christ. Amen. (For Clergy and People – BCP p. 817)

October 22

ONCE, WHEN I WAS at a music festival, the host/sponsor took the stage to try to ignite the crowd. Multiple times and with crescendoing volume, she asked us if we were having fun. When the response was lackluster, she belted out, "You're in my house here! The only rule in my house is that you've GOT TO HAVE FUN!"

The host was just doing her job, but she made me want to leave, despite the good music, weather, food, drink, and company. Rarely do people like to be told what to do and how to feel. Often, a command will produce the opposite result. For instance, does being told to relax actually result in relaxation? Once you notice this dynamic, it is startling to realize how much everybody likes to tell everybody else what to do!

This is also how the law of God works. God's law is holy and righteous, but it does not produce the fruit of holiness and righteousness in us. Instead, the Scripture tells us that it produces sin and death. The Apostle Paul says, *"If it had not been for the law, I would not have known sin. I would not have known what it is to covet if the law had not said, 'You shall not covet.' But sin, seizing an opportunity in the commandment, produced in me all kinds of covetousness… The very commandment that promised life proved to be death to me" (Romans 7:7–10, NRSV).*

Thankfully, our Christian faith is not ultimately about what we are to do. Rather, it is about what Jesus Christ has already done for us on the cross. *"For God has done what the law, weakened by the flesh, could not do" (Romans 8:3, NRSV).* Amen!

> We thank You, heavenly Father, that You have delivered us from the dominion of sin and death and brought us into the kingdom of Your Son; and we pray that, as by His death He has recalled us to life, so by His love He may raise us to eternal joys; who lives and reigns with You, in the unity of the Holy Spirit, one God, now and forever. Amen. (Saturday in Easter Week – BCP p. 224)

October 23

"On Christ, the solid Rock, I stand: / All other ground is sinking sand, / All other ground is sinking sand."

THOSE ARE THE WORDS of the 19th century hymn "My Hope is Built on Nothing Less." All other ground is sinking sand? Sounds a little glum, but the hymnist is just naming reality. Sometimes life feels like quicksand, sometimes slow erosion. Either way, any hope built on what is ephemeral is hope misplaced. As the psalmist says, *"Our days on earth are like grass; like wildflowers, we bloom and die" (Psalm 103:15, NLT).*

Standing on Christ, however, we are secure, solid, unshakeable. Even death will not sink us.

> Almighty and everlasting God, whose will it is to restore all things in Your well-beloved Son, the King of kings and Lord of lords: Mercifully grant that the peoples of the earth, divided and enslaved by sin, may be freed and brought together under His most gracious rule; who lives and reigns with You and the Holy Spirit, one God, now and for ever. Amen. (Proper 29 – BCP p. 236)

October 24

IN TANA FRENCH'S NOVEL *Faithful Place*, a father helps his nine-year-old daughter cope with a death in the family:

> I don't think there are any rules for how you're supposed to act when someone you care about dies, sweetheart. I think you just have to figure it out as you go along. Sometimes you'll feel like crying, sometimes you won't, sometimes you'll be raging at him for dying on you. You just have to remember that all of those are OK. So is whatever else your head comes up with.

The dad is spot on. Grief is a shape-shifter; it takes all forms, and sometimes no form at all. And grief, of course, is not limited to physical death; any kind of loss (life is full of them) occasions grief.

Jesus says, succinctly, *"Blessed are those who mourn, for they shall be comforted" (Matthew 5:4).* Like the father in the novel, Jesus does not instruct us on the how-tos of loss. Instead He simply says that those who mourn are blessed in the very moment of mourning and will surely experience comfort.

> Grant to all who mourn a sure confidence in Thy fatherly care, that, casting all their grief on Thee, they may know the consolation of Thy love, through Jesus Christ our Lord. Amen. (Prayers in the Burial Liturgy – BCP p. 481)

October 25

"Don't work for the food that perishes but for the food that lasts for eternal life, which the Son of Man will give you, because God the Father has set His seal of approval on Him" (John 6:27, CSB).

THE EFFERVESCENCE OF OCTOBER beauty is almost too much to bear. And only a week left. This is what C. S. Lewis felt as a child when he read Beatrix Potter's *Squirrel Nutkin*:

> It troubled me with what I can only describe as the Idea of Autumn. It sounds fantastic to say that one can be enamored of a season, but that is something like what happened; and, as before, the experience was one of intense desire.

Our desire is ultimately for God, who is the source of all beauty. I hope there is a realm in heaven in which it is perpetually October.

> We give You thanks, most gracious God, for the beauty of earth and sky and sea; for the richness of mountains, plains, and rivers; for the songs of birds and the loveliness of flowers. We praise You for these good gifts, and pray that we may safeguard them for our posterity. Grant that

we may continue to grow in our grateful enjoyment of Your abundant creation, to the honor and glory of Your Name, now and for ever. Amen. (For the Beauty of the Earth – BCP p. 840)

October 26

I GET THE "HATE has no home here" signs in people's yards. The signs, no doubt, are meant as a welcome to all. However, like all placards, these signs are surface level, naïve about the actual human condition. As much as we hate to admit it, we all hate—it is part of our fallen nature. If hate has no home, then we are all homeless.

For a gospel take on the subject, go have a listen to the 1989 James hit called "Sit Down." The words may have been spoken by Jesus.

> Those who feel the breath of sadness
> Sit down next to me
> Those who find they're touched by madness
> Sit down next to me
> Those who find themselves ridiculous
> Sit down next to me
> In love, in fear, in hate, in tears
> In love, in fear, in hate, in tears

All who are weary and heavy laden, sit down next to Me, Jesus says to us today. Perhaps He (and James singer Tim Booth?) had this verse from Jeremiah in mind: *"For I will satisfy the weary soul, and every languishing soul I will replenish" (Jeremiah 31:25, ESV).*

O Lord our God, accept the fervent prayers of Your people; in the multitude of Your mercies, look with compassion upon us and all who turn to You for help; for You are gracious, O lover of souls, and to You we give glory, Father, Son, and Holy Spirit, now and for ever. Amen. (The Collect at the Prayers – BCP p. 395)

October 27

WE HAVE A PRODIGIOUS fig tree in our front yard. This season it yielded figs by the hundreds. Since the tree is right by the street, we put up a sign that said, "Please Help Yourself to Figs!" The one who really helped herself to figs was our dog. Every morning in the predawn darkness she galloped out the front door to the fig tree. She claimed all the windfall figs for her own. Although fig season is over, she still races to the tree, only to trot back disheartened after a few minutes of fruitless search.

The psalmist says that blessed is the one who delights in the Lord. *"He is like a tree planted by streams of water that yields its fruit in its season" (Psalm 1:3, ESV).* You may be in the "off season" in some area of your life. You are looking for fruit, but you find none. That doesn't mean that God is absent or you aren't delighting in the Lord. It just means that we were not meant to constantly produce fruit. Relax. Your season will come back around.

Heavenly Father, in You we live and move and have our being: We humbly pray You so to guide and govern us by Your Holy Spirit, that in all the cares and occupations of our life we may not forget You, but may remember that we are ever walking in Your sight; through Jesus Christ our Lord. Amen. (A Collect for Guidance – BCP p. 100)

October 28

"Therefore I tell you, do not worry about your life, what you will eat or drink; or about your body, what you will wear. Is not life more than food, and the body more than clothes? Look at the birds of the air; they do not sow or reap or store away in barns, and yet your heavenly Father feeds them. Are you not much more valuable than they? Can any one of you by worrying add a single hour to your life?" (Matthew 6:25–27, NIV).

JESUS' INJUNCTION TO NOT worry about our lives, or the lives of people we love, seems to be a deep dive into irresponsibility. Somehow we think worrying = doing something responsible. The "logic" goes this way: If we don't worry about this, that, or the other, then somehow the problem won't be solved.

What if we afforded ourselves the luxury of doing what Jesus tells us to do? What if we actually allowed ourselves to believe that God is in control of all things? What if—even just for today—we could trust that Jesus knows what He is talking about?

O God of peace, who hast taught us that in returning and rest we shall be saved, in quietness and confidence shall be our strength: By the might of Thy Spirit lift us, we pray Thee, to Thy presence, where we may be still and know that Thou art God; through Jesus Christ our Lord. Amen. (For Quiet Confidence – BCP p. 832)

October 29

JACK KEROUAC ONCE SAID, "In America when the sun goes down and I sit on the old broken-down river pier watching the long, long skies over New Jersey and sense all that raw land that rolls in one unbelievable huge bulge over to the West Coast, and all that road going, all the people dreaming in the immensity of it... And nobody, nobody knows what's going to happen."

His description somehow reminds me of the grace of God: its enormity, endlessness, and boundary-defying possibility. With the grace of God in your life and in the world, you just don't know what is going to happen. Although you do know that it will be a kind of good that, in the end, blows you away.

As St. Paul says, *"And God raised us up with Christ and seated us with Him in the heavenly realms in Christ Jesus, in order that in the coming ages He might display the surpassing riches of His grace, demonstrated by His kindness to us in Christ Jesus" (Ephesians 2:6–7, BSB).*

> Lord, we pray that Your grace may always precede and follow us, that we may continually be given to good works; through Jesus Christ our Lord, who lives and reigns with You and the Holy Spirit, one God, now and for ever. Amen. (Proper 23 – BCP p. 234–5)

October 30

ANNE LAMOTT'S GREAT LINE, "My mind is a bad neighborhood I try not to go into alone," applies to all kinds of needling, unhelpful, and deceptive thoughts. The internal self-condemner rolls up his or her sleeves on one street and buys up all the condos. The self-justifier has claimed a different block. The quick-to-criticize-and-judge-other-people section of the neighborhood is formidable, always building new houses. Then there's that one section you want to keep hidden away from anybody else's scrutiny; the windows there are all boarded up.

Flannery O'Connor described the subject of her fiction as "the action of grace in territory largely held by the devil." (Halloween is tomorrow, after all!) You don't want to go alone into your mind because we are subject to the one Jesus calls "the father of lies." Describing the devil, Jesus says, *"He was a murderer from the beginning, not holding to the truth, for there is no truth in him. When he lies, he speaks his native language, for he is a liar and the father of lies" (John 8:44, NIV).*

Thankfully, you do not go into the neighborhood of your own mind alone. Jesus Christ, your Savior and Defender, is there with you. And He is mighty to save.

> Almighty God, whose blessed Son was led by the Spirit to be tempted by Satan: Come quickly to help us who are assaulted by many temptations; and, as You know the weaknesses of each of us, let each one find You mighty to save; through Jesus Christ Your Son our Lord, who lives and reigns with You and the Holy Spirit, one God, now and for ever. Amen. (First Sunday in Lent – BCP p. 218)

October 31

> *"When Jesus came to the place, He looked up and said to him, 'Zacchaeus, hurry and come down; for I must stay at your house today.' So he hurried down and was happy to welcome Him. All who saw it began to*

grumble and said, 'He has gone to be the guest of one
who is a sinner'" (Luke 19:5–7, NRSV).

THIS PASSAGE FROM LUKE has everything to do with Halloween.
Zacchaeus was an out-in-the-open sinner (tax collector), while
those who grumbled were sinners hiding behind the masks
of self-righteousness.

Halloween used to be known as All Hallows' Eve. To "hallow" someone is to honor them as holy. That's the etymology of
the day that we dress up and demand some candy. A big part of
the appeal of Halloween for young and old is the dressing up
part. It is a relief to not be you, at least for a day. Especially when
you are trying to be better (more holy) than you actually are. Pretending to be somebody else in that way gets tiring, and fast.

We often try in vain to dress ourselves up to be holier than
we actually are. But Jesus reminds us that holiness does not come
from within, but is imputed (given) to us by Christ Himself. We
are clothed in Christ's righteousness. And it's not a mask or costume; it's the real you.

Jesus wants to come trick-or-treating at Zacchaeus' house.
But there are no tricks with the grace of God. Only the treat of
being loved despite ourselves.

Happy Halloween (and Reformation Day)!

Gracious Father, whose blessed Son Jesus Christ came
down from heaven to be the true bread which gives life
to the world: Evermore give us this bread, that He may
live in us, and we in Him; who lives and reigns with You
and the Holy Spirit, one God, now and for ever. Amen.
(Fourth Sunday in Lent – BCP p. 219)

NOVEMBER

November 1

TODAY IN THE CHURCH calendar is All Saints' Day. A saint isn't someone who is well behaved or who exhibits special sanctity. Instead, a saint is someone who has put his or her trust in Jesus Christ. All Saints Day reminds us that our trust in Him does not end at the grave. Through Christ's death and resurrection, our lives on earth are but a foretaste of heaven.

The All Saints' Day collect tells us that we are "knit together … in one communion and fellowship in the mystical body of Your Son Christ our Lord." When our time comes, we will join the happy throng who worship the Lamb who has been slain.

One of the tingling moments of an All Saints service, at least for me, is the singing of the penultimate verse of "For All the Saints": "But lo! There breaks a yet more glorious day; / The saints triumphant rise in bright array; / The King of Glory passes on His way. / Alleluia, Alleluia!"

With our own eyes, we will see Jesus Christ pass before us, and we all will be lost in wonder, love, and praise. We will find our very selves at the center of this scene: *"After this I looked, and behold, a great multitude that no one could number, from every nation, from all tribes and peoples and languages, standing before the throne and before the Lamb, clothed in white robes, with palm branches in their hands, and crying out with a loud voice, 'Salvation belongs to our God who sits on the throne, and to the Lamb!'" (Revelation 7:9–10, ESV)*.

The King of Glory passes on His way. Alleluia!

Almighty God, by Your Holy Spirit You have made us one with Your saints in heaven and on earth: Grant that in our earthly pilgrimage we may always be supported by this fellowship of love and prayer, and know ourselves to be surrounded by their witness to Your power and mercy. We ask this for the sake of Jesus Christ, in whom all our intercessions are acceptable through the Spirit, and who lives and reigns for ever and ever. Amen. (Of a Saint – BCP p. 250)

November 2

Sometimes when I was starting a new story and I could not get it going, I would sit in front of the fire and squeeze the peel of the little oranges into the edge of the flame and watch the sputter of blue that they made. I would stand and look out over the roofs of Paris and think, "Do not worry. You have always written before and you will write now. All you have to do is write one true sentence. Write the truest sentence that you know." So finally I would write one true sentence, and then go on from there. (*A Moveable Feast*)

THAT'S ERNEST HEMINGWAY ON writing. (The same is true for preaching, by the way.)

But it is also true for believing, for believers. It is normal to have doubts, even to be assailed by them from time to time. In these times, you can usually land on the one true sentence. Maybe that sentence is *"And so we know and rely on the love God has for us. God is love"* (*1 John 4:16, NIV*).

Prayer helps, too.

Almighty God, whom truly to know is everlasting life: Grant us so perfectly to know Your Son Jesus Christ to be the way, the truth, and the life, that we may steadfastly follow His steps in the way that leads to eternal life; through Jesus Christ Your Son our Lord, who lives and reigns with You, in the unity of the Holy Spirit, one

God, for ever and ever. Amen. (Fifth Sunday of Easter
– BCP p. 225)

November 3

THE LATE, GREAT WARREN Zevon wrote the 1976 rocker titled
"Poor, Poor, Pitiful Me." He wrote it ironically, as he "com-
plained" about an excess of female attention. His version is well
worth a listen.

The temptation to self-pity is a strong one. One's pain is one's
pain, and it is real, obviously. When people come to see me and
try to shuffle off their struggle as illegitimate because others have
it worse, I always attempt to validate whatever it is that brought
them in to see me. Just counting one's blessings *at the expense of*
expressing one's pain never works in the long run.

There is a counterpunch to this, though. It can be helpful,
when lost in one's own pity party, to be reminded that no one
person has the corner on pain. The adage "misery loves company"
can be interpreted in two ways. Yes, it's good to know that we are
not the only ones who suffer. But it is also helpful to be comforted
by another's company. Perhaps this is why the Apostle Paul says,
*"Carry each other's burdens, and in this way you will fulfill the law of
Christ" (Galatians 6:2, NIV).*

> Assist us, mercifully, O Lord, in these our supplications
> and prayers, and dispose the way of Thy servants towards
> attainment of everlasting salvation; that, among all the
> changes and chances of this mortal life, they may ever be
> defended by Thy gracious and ready help; through Jesus
> Christ our Lord. Amen. (For Protection – BCP p. 832)

November 4

BEFORE THE TIME CHANGE in Central Virginia, the early mornings are inky black. So inky black that you wonder if the sun will ever rise.

"Yahweh, Yahweh / Always pain before a child is born / Yahweh, tell me now / Why the dark before the dawn?" (U2, "Yahweh").

We may not get an answer from God about why whatever pain or darkness we are experiencing is happening. But we do know for certain that the sun will rise. As the psalmist says, *"Weeping may tarry for the night, but joy comes with the morning"* *(Psalm 30:5, ESV).*

> Lord God, almighty and everlasting Father, You have brought us in safety to this new day: Preserve us with Your mighty power, that we may not fall into sin, nor be overcome by adversity; and in all we do, direct us to the fulfilling of Your purpose; through Jesus Christ our Lord. Amen. (A Collect for Grace – BCP p. 100)

November 5

THE ACTOR VIGGO MORTENSEN (Aragorn!) once talked about his elderly father, who suffers from dementia. Viggo's father has reverted back to his childhood Danish dialect. He talks about having lunch with people long dead. Viggo encourages caregivers to go with the conversation, rather than correct it.

For days, Viggo's father talked about having left open the gate to the pig pen. Turns out that when he was a young boy during a time of real scarcity, he forgot to close the pig's gate. The pigs got out and ravaged the garden, eating up the family food supply. He never admitted to it. Now all these years, before his death, Viggo's dad wanted to confess his sin and clear his accounts.

Unconfessed secrets eat you alive. But they don't have to. *"If we confess our sins, He is faithful and just and will forgive us our sins and purify us from all unrighteousness" (1 John 1:9, NIV).* And to make matters even better for us, the One to whom we confess has already taken our sins away!

> Most merciful God,
> we confess that we have sinned against You in thought,
>   word, and deed,
> by what we have done and by what we have left
>   undone.
> We have not loved You with our whole heart;
> we have not loved our neighbors as ourselves.
> We are truly sorry and we humbly repent.
> For the sake of Your Son Jesus Christ,
> have mercy on us and forgive us;
> that we may delight in Your will,
> and walk in Your ways,
> to the glory of Your Name. Amen. (Confession of Sin –
>   BCP p. 360)

November 6

"Do not judge, or you too will be judged" (Matthew 7:1, NIV).

I MET A RECENTLY appointed judge at our coffee hour the other day, and I asked her where she was a judge. She responded, "Everywhere, all the time." It's astonishing how quickly and how thoroughly judgment springs into being.

I was behind a car with North Carolina plates at a stoplight, feeling quite peaceful, when the driver flicked his cigarette out the window onto the median. Immediately I judged all smokers (sorry, smokers!), the state of North Carolina (sorry, NC readers—I actually love your state—"a valley of humility between two mountains of conceit"), people who drive the kind of car he was driving (not telling), and litterers (no apologies there, although, of course, I do my share of littering too, routinely putting things in the wrong bins—compost in the recycling, recycling in the trash, etc.).

For me, it's hopeless. What do we make of Jesus' command? We will be judged, but the Judge has taken my judgment onto Himself. I really do pray the prayer below, but all my hope, and I mean ALL of it, is on Him and in Him.

> Almighty and everlasting God, who in the Paschal mystery established the new covenant of reconciliation: Grant that all who have been reborn into the fellowship of Christ's Body may show forth in their lives what they profess by their faith; through Jesus Christ our Lord, who lives and reigns with You and the Holy Spirit, one God, for ever and ever. Amen. (Thursday in Easter Week – BCP p. 223)

November 7

"Do not put your trust in princes, in human beings, who cannot save" (Psalm 146:3, NIV).

AT A WEDDING ONE time, I told the bride and groom that given our human nature, we are not completely trustworthy. Don't put your trust in your heart, don't put your trust in one another, but put your trust in God. People got really mad at me for saying that—and let me know at the reception.

Oh well! Since human nature hasn't changed since the time of the psalmist, I still stand by the statement. God—really and truly—is the only perfectly trustworthy one. With what can you trust Him today?

> O God, the protector of all who trust in You, without whom nothing is strong, nothing is holy: Increase and multiply upon us Your mercy; that, with You as our ruler and guide, we may so pass through things temporal, that we lose not the things eternal; through Jesus Christ our Lord, who lives and reigns with You and the Holy Spirit, one God, for ever and ever. Amen. (Proper 12 – BCP p. 231)

November 8

RELATED TO YESTERDAY'S ALMOST Daily, I once heard a bit of wedding day wisdom that's hard to forget: "No person can love you as much as you need to be loved. Do not put that burden on your spouse. Only God can and does love you that much."

I mean, how good is that? True for spouses, true for anybody. "What is love anyway? / Does anybody love anybody anyway?" (Extra credit for anybody who can name the artist who sang that 1984 hit without googling it.)

St. John answers: *"This is love: not that we loved God, but that He loved us and sent His Son as an atoning sacrifice for our sins" (1 John 4:10, NIV).*

> Almighty God, we entrust all who are dear to us to Thy never-failing care and love, for this life and the life to come, knowing that Thou art doing for them better

things than we can desire or pray for; through Jesus Christ our Lord. Amen. (For Those We Love – BCP p. 831)

November 9

THE LEAVES ON THE Japanese maple in our yard are finally beginning to turn, well behind the dogwood, the poplar, and the sugar maple. Each turns its own color, of course. I can't be sure, but it is unlikely that trees judge other trees for either the duration or the result of their particular process of photosynthesis.

In *The Chronicles of Narnia*—stories for children that are really for adults—Aslan tells a character, "Child, ... I am telling you your story, not hers. No-one is told any story but their own." So good. Wouldn't it be nice to get our noses out of other people's stories? Wouldn't it be reassuring to realize that Jesus Christ tells you your own story and that story is uniquely yours?

The Apostle Paul, addressing a squabbling and prideful group of people bent on comparison and one-upmanship, says, *"Only let each person lead the life that the Lord has assigned to him... This is my rule in all the churches" (1 Corinthians 7:17, ESV)*. Amen to that!

> O God, You made us in Your own image and redeemed us through Jesus Your Son: Look with compassion on the whole human family; take away the arrogance and hatred that infect our hearts; break down the walls that separate us; unite us in bonds of love; and work through our struggle and confusion to accomplish Your purposes on earth, that, in Your good time, all nations and races may serve You in harmony around Your heavenly throne; through Jesus Christ our Lord. Amen. (For the Human Family – BCP p. 815)

November 10

THE PRAYER FOR A BIRTHDAY in the BCP is a prayer to pray not just on a birthday but any day. We ask for (and receive) God's blessing, guidance, strength, comfort, and peace. It reminds us of the enveloping nature of God's love as well as our daily, hourly need for Him.

Sometimes people will accuse people of faith of using Christianity as a crutch to get through life. They are wrong. It's not a crutch—it's total life support! In like manner, those who advocate for free will and human autonomy say that God's all-encompassing power in and over us only makes us puppets. My response? Yes, please! I can think of nothing better than to be God's puppet.

Of course, Scripture says it best. *"Now to Him who is able to do immeasurably more than all we ask or imagine, according to His power that is at work within us, to Him be glory in the church and in Christ Jesus throughout all generations, for ever and ever! Amen"* *(Ephesians 3:20–21, NIV).*

> Watch over Your children, O Lord, as our days increase; bless and guide us wherever we may be. Strengthen us when we stand; comfort us when discouraged or sorrowful; raise us up if we fall; and in our hearts may Your peace which passes understanding abide all the days of our lives; through Jesus Christ our Lord. Amen. (For a Birthday – BCP p. 830)

November 11

ALTHOUGH THE GREAT WAR did not officially end until the Treaty of Versailles was signed on June 28, 1919, hostilities temporarily ceased in 1918 when an armistice went into effect on the eleventh hour of the eleventh day of the eleventh month. An armistice is a truce—an agreement made by opposing sides in a war to stop fighting for a certain time.

Human beings, by nature, are enemies of God (see Romans 5 if you'd rather not take my word for it!). We refuse His lordship, we seek self over service, lust over love, hubris over humility. Like Milton's Lucifer, we agree that it is better to reign in hell than to serve in heaven. So, being a child of God is not a birthright; rather, it is a *rebirth* right.

Our resistance is so stiff-necked that an armistice won't do, since an armistice requires the cooperation of both parties. But because the love of God is so deep, so wide, so broad, He is not deterred by our deterrence. That's why He sent His Son to us. *"For in Him [Jesus] all the fullness of God was pleased to dwell, and through Him to reconcile to Himself all things, whether on earth or in heaven, making peace by the blood of His cross" (Colossians 1:19–20, ESV).*

What an irony—our most brazen act of war (nailing God to the cross in an act of murder) is the very act that ended hostilities, established everlasting peace, and made us children of God!

> O Savior of the world, who by Thy cross and precious blood has redeemed us: Save us and help us, we humbly beseech Thee, O Lord. (Good Friday Anthem 3 – BCP p. 282)

November 12

> *"Many, O LORD my God, are the wonders You have done, and the plans You have for us—none can compare to You—if I proclaim and declare them, they are more than I can count" (Psalm 40:5, BSB).*

HERE IS A STUNNING insight from author David Foster Wallace, whose depression, sadly, finally bested him.

> Both destiny's kisses and its dope-slaps illustrate an individual person's basic personal powerlessness over the really meaningful events in his life: i.e., almost nothing important that ever happens to you happens because you engineer it. Destiny has no beeper; destiny always leans trenchcoated out of an alley with some sort of Psst that you usually can't even hear because you're in such a rush to or from something important you've tried to engineer.

Insert "God" for "destiny," and you are at the heart of Christian theology. God always surprises, and His office, as you will recall, is always at the end of your rope.

Thank you, David. May you rest with the angels now.

> O God, Your never-failing providence sets in order all things both in heaven and earth: Put away from us, we entreat You, all hurtful things, and give us those things which are profitable for us; through Jesus Christ our Lord, who lives and reigns with You and the Holy Spirit, one God, for ever and ever. Amen. (Proper 4 – BCP p. 229)

November 13

> *"It is not in heaven, that you should say, 'Who will go up to heaven for us to get it for us and make us hear it, that we may observe it?' Nor is it beyond the sea, that you should say, 'Who will cross the sea for us to get it for us and make us hear it, that we may observe it?' But the word is very near you, in your mouth and*

in your heart, that you may observe it" (Deuteronomy 30:12–14, NASB 1995).

I'VE ALWAYS CONSIDERED THE academic titles of seminary graduates absurd. Our institutions have granted us a "Master of Divinity." (I'm also not particularly "reverend" either, but that is another story.) Master of Divinity? Who masters God? To call oneself a Master of Divinity should rightfully invite a Divine Smiting.

Thankfully, there are no murky secrets surrounding the gospel. The Good News isn't arduously divined after years of intensive study. As Sir Isaac Newton, who clearly knew a thing or two about complexity, once said, "Truth is ever to be found in simplicity, and not in the multiplicity and confusion of things."

Jesus is the Word of God—and He has come near with His profound yet simple grace. He is right there with you today!

> O God, who hast made of one blood all the peoples of the earth, and didst send Thy blessed Son to preach peace to those who are far off and to those who are near: Grant that people everywhere may seek after Thee and find Thee; bring the nations into Thy fold; pour out Thy Spirit upon all flesh; and hasten the coming of Thy kingdom; through the same Thy Son Jesus Christ our Lord. Amen. (Prayer for Mission – BCP p. 58)

November 14

IT SEEMS INEVITABLE THAT a degree of wanderlust is ever present in this life. It may not manifest itself in the need to travel to exotic places. You may just feel a niggling gnawing for change, even when things are good. Or, alternatively, a clamoring for security and order when things are in flux. As Amanda

McMillen shared in a sermon at Christ Church, we are "always a little homesick." You certainly feel it in the autumnal landscape, riddled with ephemeral beauty.

I suspect this longing is universal; I'm certain it is attested to in Scripture: *"For we are strangers before You and sojourners, as all our fathers were. Our days on the earth are like a shadow, and there is no abiding" (1 Chronicles 29:15, ESV).* Throughout both the Old and New Testaments we read that this world, as wonderful as it can be, cannot sustain our deepest yearnings.

Like thru-hikers on the Appalachian Trail, we are passing through. C. S. Lewis once said, "If I find in myself a desire which no experience in this world can satisfy, the most probable explanation is that I was made for another world." Amen to that—for we were made for a world that shall abide.

> Grant us, Lord, not to be anxious about earthly things, but to love things heavenly; and even now, while we are placed among things that are passing away, to hold fast to those that shall endure; through Jesus Christ our Lord, who lives and reigns with You and the Holy Spirit, one God, for ever and ever. Amen. (Proper 20 – BCP p. 234)

November 15

"You see, at just the right time, when we were still powerless, Christ died for the ungodly. Very rarely will anyone die for a righteous person, though for a good person someone might possibly dare to die" (Romans 5:6–7, NIV).

I JUST CAN'T RESIST this description of a traitor in *Macbeth*: "The multiplying villainies of nature / Do swarm upon him." Ahhh, such good language! And our natures do have villainies that tend to multiply and swarm, do they not?

Our multiplying swarms may be a problem for us and for those around us, but they are nothing to God; tiny gnats that He swipes away with the reconciling righteousness of His Son. Traitors we all are, but forgiven.

> Set us free, O God, from the bondage of our sins, and give us the liberty of that abundant life which You have made known to us in Your Son our Savior Jesus Christ; who lives and reigns with You, in the unity of the Holy Spirit, one God, now and for ever. Amen. (Fifth Sunday After Epiphany – BCP p. 216)

November 16

THIS IS FROM AN uncomfortably insightful poem by Tony Hoagland called "The Loneliest Job in the World":

> As soon as you begin to ask the question, *Who loves me?*,
> you are completely screwed, because
> the next question is *How Much?*,
> and then it is hundreds of hours later,
> and you are still hunched over
> your flowcharts and abacus,
> trying to decide if you have gotten enough.
> This is the loneliest job in the world:
> to be an accountant of the heart.

One of the fallouts of the Fall is that it is profoundly difficult for many of us to accept that we are deeply loved by God. That's why we need to hear the famous verse over and over again: *"For God so loved the world [you!] that He gave His only begotten Son, that whoever believes in Him should not perish but have everlasting life" (John 3:16, NKJV)*. There is a good reason the *Book of Common Prayer* includes this verse as one of the "Comfortable Words." God is no accountant: On the cross, He threw out the books for good.

> Lord Jesus Christ, You stretched out Your arms of love on the hard wood of the cross that everyone might come within the reach of Your saving embrace: So clothe us in Your Spirit that we, reaching forth our hands in love, may bring those who do not know You to the knowledge and love of You; for the honor of Your Name. Amen. (Prayer for Mission – BCP p. 101)

November 17

THERE IS A HAUNTING quote from the protagonist of Wallace Stegner's novel, *The Spectator Bird*. Joe Allston is a man in his 70s who, though financially and vocationally successful, feels empty.

He says his life is "something I got into and got out of." He continues:

> …how little life changes: how, without dramatic events or high resolves, without tragedy, without even pathos, a reasonably endowed, reasonably well-intentioned man can walk through the world's great kitchen from end to end and arrive at the back door hungry.

Belief in Jesus carries no guaranteed immunity against arriving at the back door hungry. Life is difficult, and meaning and purpose can sometimes elude us. Be that as it may, let's hear what our Lord says: *"Jesus said to them, 'I am the bread of life; whoever comes to Me shall not hunger, and whoever believes in Me shall never thirst"' (John 6:35, ESV).*

> Gracious Father, whose blessed Son Jesus Christ came down from heaven to be the true bread which gives life to the world: Evermore give us this bread, that He may live in us, and we in Him; who lives and reigns with You and the Holy Spirit, one God, now and forever. Amen. (Fourth Sunday in Lent – BCP p. 219)

November 18

IN HIS BOOK *The Youngest Day*, Robert Capon compares life to being on a bus. There are many stops along the way, but the longer you are on the bus, the more you begin to see that the Bus Company knows what it's doing.

After enough transfers, breakdowns, evictions and even willful refusals to stay aboard, you develop, if not a satisfaction with the way the bus line is run, at least an astonishment that it runs as well as it does. If you can remember not to waste your time wishing you were somewhere else, it's amazing what can happen.

Wasting your time wishing you were somewhere else is a potent and devilish temptation meant to cheat you out of the joy of just being where you are. "I'll be happy when I get to the next stop." "If only I hadn't gotten off at this stop, I would be in a much better place." "How did I end up sitting on *this* row with *these* people?"

I'd like to remind you today that the Driver knows what He's doing and where He is going. He paid for your ticket with His own blood.

I've always disliked the slogan, "God is my co-pilot." There is no "co" about it; you are just along for the ride, a ride that has been planned and prepared for you with unimaginable love and attention. Perhaps this is what the Apostle Paul means when he famously says, *"And we know that for those who love God all things work together for good, for those who are called according to His purpose" (Romans 8:28, ESV).*

> Heavenly Father, in You we live and move and have our being; We humbly pray You so to guide and govern us by Your Holy Spirit, that in all the cares and occupations of our life we may not forget You, but may remember that we are ever walking in Your sight; through Jesus Christ our Lord. Amen. (A Collect for Guidance – BCP p. 100)

November 19

WHILE WE ARE IN Romans 8 (see yesterday's devotion), let's spend some time with Paul's thunderous proclamation there. The one that silences, once and forever, all the hectoring and accusatory voices that ransack the peace promised and bestowed on us by the God of grace, and the peace that rightly issues from Romans 8:1: *"There is therefore now no condemnation for those who are in Christ Jesus."*

A person recently came to me to confess a sin which had plagued him for many months, peppering him in dreams and always just under the surface of his consciousness, causing him no end of trouble. Upon hearing the swift proclamation of absolution, he questioned how the verdict could be reached with such alacrity and certainty. The answer lies in Romans 8:1; it's either true or it's not—there is no middle ground.

Personally speaking, the entirety of my life and ministry is staked to the veracity of the Apostle Paul's resounding gospel Word. (It is also the fundamental *raison d'être* of the Church!) And, by the way, the reason to be a Christian is not because it works in your life, or it helps make the world a better place—although those are undeniably good things. The reason to be a Christian is because Christianity is true!

> O God, whose glory it is always to have mercy: Be gracious to all who have gone astray from Your ways, and bring them again with penitent hearts and steadfast faith to embrace and hold fast the unchangeable truth of Your Word, Jesus Christ Your Son; who with You and the Holy Spirit lives and reigns, on God, for ever and ever. Amen. (Second Sunday in Lent – BCP p. 218)

November 20

EVER SUFFERED FROM PERFORMANCE anxiety? You're not alone. The prodigiously talented Frederic Chopin confessed, "I am not at all fit for giving concerts, for the crowd intimidates me, its breath suffocates me, I feel paralyzed by its curious look, and the unknown faces make me dumb."

The world universally operates this way: Perform to be accepted. The gospel reverses the order: Acceptance comes prior to any performance. Moreover, failure is more than welcome!

Before Jesus performed any miracles—or anything else in His public ministry—God said, *"This is My Son, whom I love; with Him I am well pleased" (Matthew 3:17, NIV)*. Through His cross and resurrection, what is true for Him is true for you. God loves you and is well pleased by you.

> O Lord, make us have perpetual love and reverence for Your holy Name, for You never fail to help and govern those whom You have set upon the sure foundation of Your loving-kindness; through Jesus Christ our Lord,

who lives and reigns with You and the Holy Spirit, one God, for ever and ever. Amen. (Proper 7 – BCP p. 230)

November 21

"The earth is full of the goodness of the LORD*"* *(Psalm 33:5).*

WITH APOLOGIES TO THE spring and summer (any winter people?) lovers among us, I think that autumn, at least in Virginia, brims with God's beneficence above all others. The light, the leaves, the migratory return of the White-throated Sparrow. The beauty and continuity of nature is a steadying balm.

And then there is Thanksgiving! Very soon now. And yes, there is plenty for which to be thankful this year. This is from a poem called "Merry Autumn," written by Paul Laurence Dunbar, born in 1872 and one of the first black poets to gain national recognition.

> The earth is just so full of fun
> It really can't contain it;
> And streams of mirth so freely run
> The heavens seem to rain it.
> Don't talk to me of solemn days
> In autumn's time of splendor,
> Because the sun shows fewer rays,
> And these grow slant and slender.
> Why, it's the climax of the year,—
> The highest time of living!—
> Till naturally its bursting cheer
> Just melts into thanksgiving.

Let us pray.

We give You thanks, most gracious God, for the beauty of the earth and sky and sea; for the richness of mountains, plains, and rivers; for the songs of birds, and the loveliness of flowers. We praise You for these good gifts, and pray that we may safeguard them for our posterity. Grant that we may continue to grow in our grateful enjoyment of Your abundant creation, to the honor and glory of Your Name, now and for ever. Amen. (For the Beauty of the Earth – BCP p. 840)

November 22

ST. PAUL ENCOURAGES US to engage in *"always giving thanks to God the Father for everything, in the name of our Lord Jesus Christ"* *(Ephesians 5:20, NIV)*. This is a timely word around Thanksgiving time, and a timely word in a world which poses considerable difficulties and challenges.

And yet. There is still, as we said yesterday, so much in our lives for which to be thankful. Even in the midst of tragedy and loss, one often hears words of gratitude. Gratitude for the doctors that tried to save a spouse's life. Gratitude for the love of others shown in times of need and distress. Gratitude for even a hint of reconciliation in a relationship thought to be beyond repair. Gratitude for the gift of life itself, with its mixed bag of joy and suffering.

Gratitude most naturally springs from an awareness that we have been given something we do not deserve or have not earned. For believers, then, the eternal wellspring of gratitude flows directly from the atoning cross of Christ. In other words, there is a beeline between Good Friday and Thanksgiving.

I can tell you, Almost Daily friends, I am so thankful for each one of you! Thank you for taking time with me each day.

We thank You, God our Father, for all Your gifts so freely bestowed upon us. For the beauty and wonder of Your creation, in earth and sky and sea. For all that is gracious in the lives of men and women, revealing the image of Christ. For our daily food and drink, our homes and families, and our friends. For minds to think, and hearts to love, and hands to serve. For health and strength to work and leisure to rest and play. For the brave and courageous, who are patient in suffering and faithful in adversity. Above all, we give You thanks for the great mercies and promises given to us in Christ Jesus our Lord. Amen. (A Litany of Thanksgiving – BCP p. 837)

November 23

I'VE BEEN TRYING TO make something happen that just hasn't happened. Turning over every stone, making every connection I can make, asking every Tom, Dick, and Harry I happen upon, exerting my will and influence and (in my own mind) charm. I have been the importunate widow (see Luke 18:1–8). Despite all of this effort (because of it?) all roads have heretofore dead-ended.

Can you relate? Here's a bracing—and I think, comforting—verse. *"Many are the plans in a person's heart, but it is the LORD's purpose that prevails" (Proverbs 19:21, NIV).*

God's desire always prevails. And, thankfully, He always desires what is best for us.

Direct us, O Lord, in all our doings with Thy most gracious favor, and further us with Thy continual help; that in all our works begun, continued, and ended in Thee, we may glorify Thy holy Name, and finally, by Thy mercy, obtain everlasting life; through Jesus Christ our Lord. Amen. (For Guidance – BCP p. 832)

November 24

HERE IS T. S. ELIOT on Huck Finn: "He sees the real world and does not judge it—he allows it to judge itself." What a thing to say. It is certainly rooted in Eliot's Christianity: There is judgment, but we are not the ones to judge.

Eliot's comment reminds me of Jesus' masterful parable about the wheat and the tares. A farmer plants wheat in his field. An enemy comes at night and sows tares. The farmer's workers ask if they should weed out the tares. The farmer says this: *"No, lest while you gather up the tares you also uproot the wheat with them. Let both grow together until the harvest, and at the time of harvest I will say to the reapers, 'First gather together the tares and bind them in bundles to burn them, but gather the wheat into my barn'"* (Matthew 13:29–30, NKJV).

So, at the Thanksgiving table this year, maybe you can keep quiet about what you judge to be wrong about him, about her, about the world? God will take care of it in the end.

> Almighty and everlasting God, You govern all things both in heaven and on earth: Mercifully hear the supplications of Your people, and in our time grant us Your peace; through Jesus Christ our Lord, who lives and reigns with You and the Holy Spirit, one God, for ever and ever. Amen. (Fourth Sunday after the Epiphany – BCP p. 215)

November 25

> *"As [Jesus] came out of the temple, one of His disciples said to Him, 'Look, Teacher, what large stones and what large buildings!' Then Jesus asked him, 'Do*

you see these great buildings? Not one stone will be left here upon another; all will be thrown down" (Mark 13:1–2, NRSV).

PERHAPS SHAKESPEARE HAD THIS verse in mind when he noted the destructive power of time, which will "fill with worm-holes stately monuments." To recognize the fragility of the world and the tenuousness of that which tethers us to it is oddly comforting, is it not? Like Mikey with Life Cereal—try it, you'll like it!

The modern definition of a wormhole is a tunnel connecting realities that are separated by space and time. The heartbreakingly beautiful November days here in Central Virginia are wormholes that lead to the reality of the kingdom of heaven. Which, by the way, is much *realer* than the stones of this earth.

To wit, here is the second verse of "God, My Hope on You is Founded":

> Human pride and earthly glory,
> sword and crown betray his trust;
> what with care and toil he buildeth,
> tower and temple, fall to dust.
> But God's power,
> hour by hour,
> is my temple and my tower.

Hasten, O Father, the coming of Thy kingdom; and grant that we, Thy servants, who now live by faith, may with joy behold Thy Son at His coming in glorious majesty; even Jesus Christ, our only Mediator and Advocate. Amen. (The Collect at the Prayers – BCP p. 395)

November 26

"I pray that out of His glorious riches He may strength-en you with power through His Spirit in your inner being, so that Christ may dwell in your hearts through faith" (Ephesians 3:16–17, NIV).

YOU CAN'T DENY THE power of Toto (the band, not the dog in *The Wizard of Oz*, although that Toto is undeniably cute). I tried to deny the power of Toto in the 80s, but recently when "Rosanna" came on the radio, I saw the light: "All I wanna do when I wake up in the morning is see your eyes / Rosanna, Rosanna."

Toto knows. Toto knows that we are primarily driven by our appetites and emotions, rather than (as we would like to believe) our reason and willpower. And because our appetites and our emotions often lead us into nowhere good, we find we are in need of Help from the Outside.

The Help whose name is Jesus.

Stir up Your power, O Lord, and with great might come among us; and, because we are sorely hindered by our sins, let Your bountiful grace and mercy speedily help and deliver us; through Jesus Christ our Lord, to whom, with You and the Holy Spirit, be honor and glory, now and for ever. Amen. (Third Sunday in Advent – BCP p. 212)

November 27

"Now they were bringing even infants to Him [Je-sus] that He might touch them. And when the disci-ples saw it, they rebuked them. But Jesus called them

to Him, saying, "Let the children come to Me, and do not hinder them, for to such belongs the kingdom of God. Truly, I say to you, whoever does not receive the kingdom of God like a child shall not enter it" (Luke 18:15–17, ESV).

"BABY, EVEN THE LOSERS get lucky sometimes." The Tom Petty Classic is shorthand for the gospel, with a little amending. The losers get lucky *all* the time.

Jesus inaugurated the great reversal of the Ways of the World. "Even infants"—the epitome of the helpless, status-less, power-less, and penniless—are exemplars of kingdom material. Imagine, just for a wee moment, the freedom of life in a world devoid of all the usual Ways of the World nonsense? You could just skate on through with a smile on your face.

> O God, the strength of all who put their trust in You: Mercifully accept our prayers; and because in our weak-ness we can do nothing good without You, give us the help of Your grace, that in keeping Your commandments we may please You both in will and deed; through Jesus Christ our Lord, who lives and reigns with You and the Holy Spirit, one God, for ever and ever. Amen. (Sixth Sunday After Epiphany – BCP p. 216)

November 28

IN *THE FOUR LOVES*, C. S. Lewis describes the depth of our need as human beings.

> … in the long run it is perhaps even more apparent in our growing—for it ought to be growing—awareness that our whole being by its very nature is one vast need;

incomplete, preparatory, empty yet cluttered, crying out for Him who can untie things now knotted together and tie up things that are still dangling loose.

Empty yet cluttered. So good. So much knotted up that needs untangling, and so many loose ends that need securing. God help us!

Well, that is what God does. The psalmist says, *"God is our refuge and strength, an ever-present help in trouble. Therefore we will not fear, though the earth give way and the mountains fall into the heart of the sea, though its waters roar and foam and the mountains quake with their surging" (Psalm 46:1–3, NIV).*

Good news to take with us today.

Almighty God, You alone can bring into order the unruly wills and affections of sinners: Grant us grace to love what You command and desire what You promise; that, among the swift and varied changes of the world, our hearts may surely there be fixed where true joys are to be found; through Jesus Christ our Lord, who lives and reigns with You and the Holy Spirit, one God, now and for ever. Amen. (Fifth Sunday in Lent – BCP p. 219)

November 29

HERE'S A BIT OF good news: *"The night is nearly over; the day is almost here" (Romans 13:12, NIV).*

If ever you've been tossing and turning in the night, waiting for the break of day, you know what it means to be in the season of Advent. Although it's always darkest before the dawn, the dawn is right around the corner.

Jesus is coming to undo all that was done wrong—and to do all that still needs doing. I can't think of anything better to set one's sights on than that. Especially at 3AM.

Almighty God, give us grace to cast away the works of darkness, and put on the armor of light, now in the time of this mortal life in which Your Son Jesus Christ came to visit us in great humility; that in the last day, when He shall come again in His glorious majesty to judge both the living and the dead, we may rise to the life immortal; through Him who lives and reigns with You and the Holy Spirit, one God, now and for ever. Amen. (First Sunday of Advent – BCP)

November 30

IN THE IMMORTAL WORDS of Joe Walsh from his 1978 hit "Life's Been Good," "I can't complain, but sometimes I still do."

I hope you were able to thank God for His gifts this Thanksgiving. Sometimes, though, we have to register our complaints to Him. Not a problem for God; He can take all you've got and more.

The Psalms are a master class in complaint to God. *"Save me, O God, for the waters have come up to my neck. I sink in the miry depths, where there is no foothold. I have come into the deep waters; the floods engulf me. I am worn out calling for help; my throat is parched. My eyes fail, looking for my God" (Psalm 69:1–3, NIV).*

Maybe your complaints are more entry-level than the psalmist's, but everybody's got some. It's best to be real with God.

O Lord our God, accept the fervent prayers of Your people; in the multitude of Your mercies, look with compassion upon us and all who turn to You for help; for You are gracious, O lover of souls, and to You we give glory, Father, Son, and Holy Spirit, now and for ever. Amen. (The Collect at the Prayers – BCP p. 395)

DECEMBER

December 1

AFTER DRENCHING THEM IN the good news of God's love and grace, St. Paul encourages the people in Ephesus to *"walk in a manner worthy of the calling to which you have been called, with all humility and gentleness, with patience, bearing with one another in love, eager to maintain the unity of the Spirit in the bond of peace"* *(Ephesians 4:1–3, ESV).*

That is such a beautiful aspiration, one I personally long for. Willful resolve is a poor activator for any kind of internal character—at least any character that will take root. But remember what Cranmer taught us: What the heart longs for, the mind justifies, and the will pursues. Even *wanting* to want to walk with humility and gentleness is the mustard seed that the Holy Spirit will grow into a flowering tree.

Almighty and most merciful God, grant that by the indwelling of Your Holy Spirit we may be enlightened and strengthened for Your service; through Jesus Christ our Lord, who lives and reigns with You, in the unity of the Holy Spirit, one God, now and for ever. Amen. (Of the Holy Spirit – BCP p. 251)

December 2

"He who testifies to these things says, 'Yes, I am coming soon.' Amen. Come, Lord Jesus" (Revelation 22:20, NIV).

HERE IS ONE OF the many Mark Twain witticisms: "Sanity and happiness are an impossible combination… No sane man can be happy, for to him life is real, and he sees what a fearful thing it is. Only the mad can be happy, and not many of those."

True—to an extent. But only without Jesus Christ in the equation. Or Advent. We can look at life without rose-colored glasses, feel the pain of reality, and yet experience the joy of knowing the One who has come to take away the sin of the world and who will come again when the wait is over.

Come, Lord Jesus.

> Almighty God, give us grace to cast away the works of darkness, and put on the armor of light, now in the time of this mortal life in which Your Son Jesus Christ came to visit us in great humility; that in the last day, when He shall come again in His glorious majesty to judge both the living and the dead, we may rise to the life immortal; through Him who lives and reigns with You and the Holy Spirit, one God, now and for ever. Amen. (First Sunday of Advent – BCP p. 211)

December 3

A MEMBER OF OUR women's Bible study had a pithy insight: Summing up the fault-lines in our self-discipline, she said, "Our wills cannot overcome our natures." A prime example of this is the subject of Jesus' teaching in the Gospel passage for the first Sunday of Advent. I'm talking about keeping awake.

"Keep awake therefore, for you do not know on what day your Lord is coming. But understand this: if the owner of the house had known in what part of the night the thief was coming, he would have stayed awake and would not have let his house be broken into. Therefore you also must be ready, for the Son of Man is coming at an unexpected hour" (Matthew 24:42–44, NRSV).

When it comes to sleep, our natures—at least for most people—tend to have wills of their own. When you are overcome with sleep, you just cannot will your eyes to stay open. The reverse is true, too. When you are tossing and turning at night trying to get to sleep, or get back to sleep, you cannot will yourself into oblivion.

If this rings true for you, you are not alone. Just two chapters later in Matthew, Jesus pleads with His disciples three times in a row to keep awake with Him. Three times in a row, they fall back asleep. Thankfully, our Lord knows, understands, and forgives us in our weakness. And while we are awake when we should be sleeping, it's never a bad idea to pray for Christ's return to make all things—including us—new.

> Hasten, O Father, the coming of Thy kingdom; and grant that we Thy servants, who now live by faith, may with joy behold Thy Son at His coming in glorious majesty; even Jesus Christ our only Mediator and Advocate. Amen. (The Collect at the Prayers – BCP p. 395)

December 4

TODAY'S COLLECT REMINDS US that God is at work. Right now, constantly, everywhere, all the time, in your life, in the lives of the people you care about, in the lives of the people you don't care about. The majority of His work is hidden *(Deus absconditus)*, which is precisely why we pray that God will "open the eyes of our faith."

In C. S. Lewis's *The Lion, The Witch and the Wardrobe*, the believing Lucy could see Aslan leading the way through the dark Narnian wood, while her brothers and sister could not. *"For we walk by faith, not by sight" (2 Corinthians 5:7)*. Sometimes, by the grace of God, our faith turns to sight, and we take a peek behind God's curtain.

So, let's pray that prayer right now.

O God, whose blessed Son made Himself known to His disciples in the breaking of bread: Open the eyes of our faith, that we may behold Him in all His redeeming work; who lives and reigns with You, in the unity of the Holy Spirit, one God, now and for ever. Amen. (Wednesday in Easter Week – BCP p. 223)

December 5

"He told her, 'Go, call your husband and come back.' 'I have no husband,' she replied. Jesus said to her, 'You are right when you say you have no husband. The fact is, you have had five husbands, and the man you now have is not your husband. What you have just said is quite true'" (John 4:16–18, NIV).

SATURDAY NIGHT LIVE HAD a skit in the early 90s called "The Honest Planet." The scene was a boardroom of a company called "Greedy Industries." It's afternoon; the chairman begins by saying he had three martinis at lunch, and he has amorous feelings for his married co-worker. It gets worse from there! Just imagine if we lived on the Honest Planet.

Another word for repentance is honesty. Being as honest about yourself as you can (which is likely not completely honest), being honest with others and with God. He is the God "to whom all desires are known and no secrets are hid," after all.

The woman at the well discovered that dishonesty with Jesus is fruitless. But honesty, even and especially in the places of shame, is met with nothing but grace, which, of course, leads to freedom.

> O God, whose glory it is always to have mercy: Be gracious to all who have gone astray from Your ways, and bring them again with penitent hearts and steadfast faith to embrace and hold fast the unchangeable truth of Your Word, Jesus Christ Your Son; who with You and the Holy Spirit lives and reigns, one God, for ever and ever. Amen. (Second Sunday in Lent – BCP p. 218)

December 6

ADVENT IS THE TIME to remember the ephemerality of our life on this earth. Much of what we have invested ourselves in will come to naught. When Jesus comes again, only love is all that you can't leave behind. The rest will be burned like chaff.

Wendell Berry hints at this in his poem "The Want of Peace":

> All goes back to the earth,
> and so I do not desire
> pride of excess or power,
> but the contentments made
> by men who have had little:
> the fisherman's silence
> receiving the river's grace,
> the gardener's musing on rows.

John the Baptist, the man of Advent who points the way to Jesus, expresses a similar humility in Matthew: *"I baptize you with water for repentance, but He who is coming after me is mightier than I, whose sandals I am not worthy to carry. He will baptize you with the Holy Spirit and fire. His winnowing fork is in His hand, and He will clear*

His threshing floor and gather His wheat into the barn, but the chaff
He will burn with unquenchable fire" (Matthew 3:11–12, ESV).

> O God, the protector of all who trust in You, without whom nothing is strong, nothing is holy: Increase and multiply upon us Your mercy; that, with You as our ruler and guide, we may so pass through things temporal, that we lose not the things eternal; through Jesus Christ our Lord, who lives and reigns with You and the Holy Spirit, one God, for ever and ever. Amen. (Proper 12 – BCP p. 231)

December 7

> *"For the wages of sin is death, but the gift of God is eternal life in Christ Jesus our Lord" (Romans 6:23, NIV).*

THE TITLE OF Frederick Buechner's classic book says it all: *Telling the Truth: The Gospel as Tragedy, Comedy, and Fairy Tale.* The message of the gospel is first a tragedy. (What? I'm not such a great guy after all? The wages of sin is death?!) Then it is comedy. (I'm getting off scot-free despite myself?! That's ridiculous! The gift of God is eternal life?!)

And then finally it is a fairy tale. How do fairy tales end? Happily ever after. As Julian of Norwich famously said, "All shall be well, and all shall be well, and all manner of things shall be well."

Amen!

> O God, who by the glorious resurrection of Your Son Jesus Christ destroyed death and brought life and immortality to light: Grant that we, who have been raised with Him, may abide in His presence and rejoice in the

hope of eternal glory; through Jesus Christ our Lord, to whom, with You and the Holy Spirit, be dominion and praise for ever and ever. Amen. (Tuesday in Easter Week – BCP p. 223)

December 8

THE RICH HYMNODY OF Advent often gets lost among the Christmas mixes on every commercial airwave. So here is Charles Wesley's gem for you this morning. It's worth a listen if you have the time.

> Come, Thou long expected Jesus
> Born to set Thy people free;
> From our fears and sins release us,
> Let us find our rest in Thee.
> Israel's strength and consolation,
> Hope of all the earth Thou art;
> Dear desire of every nation,
> Joy of every longing heart.
>
> Born Thy people to deliver,
> Born a child and yet a King,
> Born to reign in us forever,
> Now Thy gracious kingdom bring.
> By Thine own eternal Spirit
> Rule in all our hearts alone;
> By Thine all sufficient merit,
> Raise us to Thy glorious throne.

"'I am the Alpha and the Omega,' says the Lord God, 'who is, and who was, and who is to come, the Almighty'" (Revelation 1:8, NIV).
    Come, Lord Jesus.

Merciful God, who sent Your messengers the prophets to preach repentance and prepare the way for our salvation: Give us grace to heed their warnings and forsake our sins, that we may greet with joy the coming of Jesus Christ our Redeemer; who lives and reigns with You and the Holy Spirit, one God, now and for ever. Amen. (Second Sunday in Advent – BCP p. 211)

December 9

"For you shall go out in joy and be led forth in peace; the mountains and the hills before you shall break forth into singing, and all the trees of the field shall clap their hands" (Isaiah 55:12, ESV).

ISAIAH IS THE ADVENT prophet, always peeking into the What Shall Be. Maybe today's verse isn't metaphorical, but literal. How fun would it be to hear the mountains and hills singing? Earthen bass and rolling alto praising God.

And of course trees would clap along—what do you think their limbs are for? Keeping time with the mountain chorus, as well as inviting little children to climb up in their arms for a better view. With God all things are possible.

The joy and peace the prophet foretells are possible right now. Joy and peace are already ours in the first coming of our Savior. I pray that you will experience both today.

O heavenly Father, who hast filled the world with beauty: Open our eyes to behold Thy gracious hand in all Thy works; that, rejoicing in Thy whole creation, we may learn to serve Thee with gladness; for the sake of Him through whom all things were made, Thy Son Jesus

Christ our Lord. Amen. (For Joy in God's Creation –
BCP p. 814)

December 10

IN A RECENT CONVERSATION, someone was said to have "an ego."
I understand the ego to be one's desire to assert and insert one's
self into the world. And if the world notices and awards credit, so
much the better. "You're so vain / You probably think this song is
about you" (Carly Simon, 1971).

All this is natural (though perhaps not supernatural) and
understandable. And yet, when life—either through years of
cumulative erosion or through an experience of devastation—
drubs the ego right out of you, then you find yourself in a place
that smells like freedom.

The Bible's answer to the problem of self is clear: death to
self. St. Paul says this explicitly in this verse: *"I have been crucified
with Christ and I no longer live, but Christ lives in me. The life I now
live in the body, I live by faith in the Son of God, who loved me and
gave Himself for me"* (Galatians 2:20, NIV).

> Almighty and eternal God, so draw our hearts to Thee,
> so guide our minds, so fill our imaginations, so control
> our wills, that we may be wholly Thine, utterly dedicated
> unto Thee; and then use us, we pray Thee, as Thou wilt,
> and always to Thy glory and the welfare of Thy people;
> through our Lord and Savior Jesus Christ. Amen. (A
> Prayer of Self-Dedication – BCP p. 832)

December 11

IT'S WORTH TAKING THE extra time for some things. Like boiling enough water in the kettle to fill the teapot and then pouring hot water into your mug to heat it up before you pour your tea. Then your mug of tea—even with a splash of cold milk—stays piping hot. A small but meaningful gift to start your morning.

The esteemed novelist Marilynne Robinson said, "I have spent my life watching, not to see beyond the world, merely to see, great mystery, what is plainly before my eyes. I think the concept of transcendence is based on a misreading of creation. With all respect to heaven, the scene of the miracle is here, among us."

There is truth in her words. As the Book of Numbers puts it, *"But as truly as I live, all the earth shall be filled with the glory of the LORD" (Numbers 14:21, KJV)*. Chalk one up for immanence!

> Direct us, O Lord, in all our doings with Thy most gracious favor, and further us with Thy continual help; that in all our works begun, continued, and ended in Thee, we may glorify Thy holy Name, and finally, by Thy mercy, obtain everlasting life; through Jesus Christ our Lord. Amen. (For Guidance – BCP p. 832)

December 12

"O TANNENBAUM," THE CHERISHED yuletide tune, did not begin as a Christmas song. Written in 1824, the lyricist compared the constancy and faithfulness of a fir tree to the faithlessness of the woman who had just broken his heart. When the custom of bringing a tree inside for Christmas took hold, the song easily morphed into a Christmas favorite.

Aretha Franklin's version is straight-up Christianity:

O Tannenbaum, O Tannenbaum
How lovely are thy branches

Let us all remember
In our gift-giving and our merriment
With our family and friends and loved ones
The real and true meaning of Christmas
The birth of our Lord and Savior, Jesus Christ

The Christmas tree blesses us with its presence and its light. *"In Him was life, and the life was the light of men. The light shines in the darkness, and the darkness has not overcome it" (John 1:4–5, ESV).* The Christmas tree comes to us from the outside, reminding us of the One who came to us at Christmas. *"And the Word became flesh and dwelt among us, and we have seen His glory, glory as of the only Son from the Father, full of grace and truth" (John 1:14, ESV).*

Almighty God, You have poured upon us the new light of Your incarnate Word: Grant that this light, enkindled in our hearts, may shine forth in our lives; through Jesus Christ our Lord, who lives and reigns with You, in the unity of the Holy Spirit, one God, now and for ever. Amen (First Sunday after Christmas Day – BCP p. 213)

December 13

FAMILY THERAPISTS REMIND US of the importance of detachment. To be detached from a demanding or emotionally volatile family member is to not take on undue responsibility for that person's difficulties. It is to recognize your lack of control over someone else. It is to operate only within your own sphere of autonomy.

Ironically, to be detached is the best way to love another person. You are able to relate to the person in need without your own needs—or the co-dependent needs of the relationship—overwhelming you. Ultimately, to be detached is to be able to commend and commit the person you love to the only One who can fully love and care for all people.

To that end, prayer is an extremely powerful way of releasing your presumed and overreaching responsibility for others to God. *"Devote yourselves to prayer, being watchful and thankful" (Colossians 4:2, NIV)*. Your authority over others is imagined and problematic; His is real and efficacious.

> Almighty God, we entrust all who are dear to us to Thy never-failing care and love, for this life and the life to come, knowing that Thou art doing for them better things than we can desire or pray for; through Jesus Christ our Lord. Amen. (For Those We Love – BCP p. 831)

December 14

I LIKED THIS QUOTE from Joel Green's *Commentary on the Gospel of Luke*. In contrast to the conventional ways of the Roman world (and today's world, I might add), the "behaviors that grow out of service in the kingdom of God take a different turn: Love your enemies. Do good to those who hate you. Extend hospitality to those who cannot reciprocate. Give without expectation of return."

Sound like an uphill battle? I like Green's follow up sentence. "Such practices are possible only for those whose dispositions, whose convictions and commitments, have been reshaped by transformative encounter with the goodness of God."

Jesus Himself says it this way: *"Be merciful, just as your Father is merciful" (Luke 6:36).* The fill-in-the-blank portion of that verse is "just as your Father has been, is being, and will always be merciful… *to you."* Where you have had a transformative encounter with the goodness of God is the seed of mercy for someone else.

Eternal God, in whose perfect kingdom no sword is drawn but the sword of righteousness, no strength known but the strength of love: So mightily spread abroad Your Spirit, that all peoples may be gathered under the banner of the Prince of Peace, as children of one Father; to whom be dominion and glory, now and for ever. Amen. (For Peace – BCP p. 815)

December 15

My soul magnifies the Lord,
    and my spirit rejoices in God my Savior,
for He has looked on the humble estate of His servant.
    For behold, from now on all generations will call me
        blessed;
for He who is mighty has done great things for me,
    and holy is His name.
And His mercy is for those who fear Him
    from generation to generation.
He has shown strength with His arm;
    He has scattered the proud in the thoughts of their
        hearts;
He has brought down the mighty from their thrones
    and exalted those of humble estate;
He has filled the hungry with good things,
    and the rich He has sent away empty (Luke
        1:46–53, ESV).

THIS IS MARY'S SONG—the Magnificat—after the angel Gabriel delivers the news of her role in God's great rescue plan. Mary, as is well-known, is the epitome of powerlessness: an unmarried, pregnant, teenage girl in the middle of a moralistic patriarchy. Were it not for divine intervention, Joseph would have called off the wedding.

Here is what Martin Luther says about Mary's song in one of his Christmas sermons: "God allows the godly to be powerless and oppressed so that everyone thinks they are done for, yet even in that very moment God is most powerfully present, though hidden and concealed. When the power of man fails, the power of God begins."

He is with you today!

Grant us, O Lord, to trust in You with all our hearts; for, as You always resist the proud who confide in their own strength, so You never forsake those who make their boast of Your mercy; through Jesus Christ our Lord, who lives and reigns with You and the Holy Spirit, one God, now and for ever. Amen. (Proper 18 – BCP p. 233)

December 16

ACCEPTANCE. WHY IS IT so hard? Why is it so difficult to accept others the way that they are? The toll of non-acceptance is steep. You blind yourself to the good that is actually there. You ward off real relationship. You hem yourself into an ever-shrinking world of your own making.

The reasons that acceptance is so difficult are manifold—certainly too entrenched to fully explore in a short devotion. You know some of them right off the bat: addiction to control, wielding God's law on others like a weapon, and the original sin of thinking that You Know Best. That is what the serpent said when he offered our primal parents the forbidden fruit: *"For God knows that when you eat from it your eyes will be opened, and you will be like God" (Genesis 3:5, NIV).*

Thank God you are not God. In fact, let's do that right now.

O God of peace, who hast taught us that in returning and rest we shall be saved, in quietness and confidence shall be our strength: By the might of Thy Spirit lift us, we pray Thee, to Thy presence, where we may be still and know that Thou art God; through Jesus Christ our Lord. Amen. (For Quiet Confidence – BCP p. 832)

December 17

"For we do not have a High Priest who cannot sympathize with our weaknesses, but was in all points tempted as we are, yet without sin. Let us therefore come boldly to the throne of grace, that we may obtain mercy and find grace to help in time of need" (Hebrews 4:15–16, NKJV).

YOU MAY OR MAY not be in the position of caring for an elderly person. You may or may not be an elderly person yourself, being cared for by others. But all of us have some contact with the elderly, and God willing, we will at some point fit the bill ourselves.

The BCP prayer "For the Aged" is powerful; it is one for the ages, even. And that is because the prayer transcends a restricted demographic. Who doesn't, at times, feel weakness, distress, or isolation? Who doesn't need a home of dignity and peace? Who doesn't need increased faith and assurance?

The one petition that really stands out is the prayer for the willingness to accept help. While this is difficult for many of us, it is the heart of the gospel: confession of our need, recognition of our inability to do for ourselves what only God can do for us. It is a prayer not just for the aged, but for us all.

> Look with mercy, O God our Father, on all whose increasing years bring them weakness, distress, or isolation. Provide for them homes of dignity and peace; give them understanding helpers, and the willingness to accept help; and, as their strength diminishes, increase their faith and assurance in Your love. This we ask in the name of Jesus Christ our Lord. Amen. (For the Aged – BCP p. 830)

December 18

> *"Then Jesus told them this parable: 'Suppose one of you has a hundred sheep and loses one of them. Doesn't he leave the ninety-nine in the open country and go after the lost sheep until he finds it? And when he finds it, he joyfully puts it on his shoulders and goes home. Then he calls his friends and neighbors together and says, "Rejoice with me; I have found my lost sheep"'" (Luke 15:3–6, NIV).*

IN THIS DEEPLY TOUCHING parable, there is no note of scolding or recrimination directed at the wayward sheep. The shepherd doesn't lecture the lost lamb: "Do you realize how much I worried about you? Did you even think about the danger you were in? Or how I had to leave your 99 brothers and sisters to come all this way to find you?? I mean, what were you thinking?! Believe me, there are going to be consequences for your actions, young man."

Instead, He joyfully puts the sheep on His shoulders and carries it home. The consequence? A big party.

> O God, whose glory it is to always have mercy: Be gracious to all who have gone astray from Your ways, and bring them again with penitent hearts and steadfast faith to embrace and hold fast the unchangeable truth of Your Word, Jesus Christ Your Son; who with You and the Holy Spirit lives and reigns, one God, for ever and ever. Amen. (Second Sunday in Lent – BCP p. 218)

December 19

A GOOD RULE OF thumb when deciding about whether to do a thing or not is to ask yourself if you really want to do the thing. If you don't, then you will likely do it with resentment, which will backfire on you and the people around you. Sometimes, however, you are actually called by God to do something that you don't really want to do. God's call has an ineluctable quality about it. Then you do the thing.

But really, the same motivational principle applies. You do the thing because you want to live your life in gratitude for what God has done for you. As an added bonus, you will feel very good having done the thing.

This is how Paul says it: *"But thanks be to God that, though you used to be slaves to sin, you have come to obey from your heart the pattern of teaching that has now claimed your allegiance. You have been set free from sin and have become slaves to righteousness" (Romans 6:17–18, NIV).*

> Direct us, O Lord, in all our doings with Thy most gracious favor, and further us with Thy continual help; that in all our works begun, continued, and ended in Thee, we

may glorify Thy holy Name, and finally, by Thy mercy, obtain everlasting life; through Jesus Christ our Lord. Amen. (For Guidance – BCP p. 832)

December 20

AMONG THE CHRISTMAS DECORATIONS in my childhood home was a version of Mary and the baby Jesus that appeared on our front door. It was shiny—perhaps almost "mod" in the fashion of the 1960s. It also frightened the pants off me as a five-year-old. I called it "The Monster Lady," and begged my mother to take it down. Thus, the early roots of my convinced Protestantism were on display.

However, where would we be without Mary? Her response to the inconceivable announcement of the angel about her conception is a wonder to behold: *"And Mary said, 'Behold, I am the servant of the Lord; let it be to me according to your word.' And the angel departed from her"* (Luke 1:38, ESV).

Let it be to me according to your word. What a thing to say. What a thing I would *wish* to say to God in all circumstances. How about you?

> Stir up Your power, O Lord, and with great might come among us; and, because we are sorely hindered by our sins, let Your bountiful grace and mercy speedily help and deliver us; through Jesus Christ our Lord, to whom, with You and the Holy Spirit, be honor and glory, now and for ever. Amen. (Third Sunday in Advent – BCP p. 212)

December 21

IN FAULKNER'S *The Sound and the Fury* (which is, obviously, the best novel ever written), Jason Compson tells his son Quentin that the saddest word is the word "was." One assumes (which is dangerous ground with Faulkner) that Mr. Compson means that events in the past have already happened and therefore cannot be changed.

There is obvious truth to that, but Mr. Compson is also a world-class nihilist. He is, as St. Paul says in Ephesians, *"without hope and without God in the world" (Ephesians 2:12, NIV).*

One of the more spectacular promises of our life in Christ is that though the past may not be changed, it will be redeemed. The resurrection tells us, shows us, that all the sad things are going to come untrue. Foreshadowing the Great Work of Christ, the prophet Isaiah says, *"I have blotted out your transgressions like a cloud and your sins like mist; return to Me, for I have redeemed you" (Isaiah 44:22, ESV).*

Come, Lord Jesus.

O God, You have made of one blood all the peoples of the earth, and sent Your blessed Son to preach peace to those who are far off and to those who are near: Grant that people everywhere may seek after You and find You, bring the nations into Your fold, pour out Your Spirit upon all flesh, and hasten the coming of Your kingdom; through Jesus Christ our Lord, who lives and reigns with You and the Holy Spirit, one God, now and for ever. Amen. (For the Mission of the Church – BCP p. 257)

December 22

"Moreover, I will give you a new heart and put a new spirit within you; and I will remove the heart of stone from your flesh and give you a heart of flesh" (Ezekiel 36:26, NASB).

UPON THE 1843 PUBLICATION of *A Christmas Carol,* Charles Dickens described Ebenezer Scrooge as a "squeezing, wrenching, grasping, scraping, clutching, covetous old sinner. Hard and sharp as flint, from which no steel had ever struck out generous fire." Scrooge's conversion story is one of the sparkling gems in the Christmas canon. Give it a read by the fire this year!

Dickens reminds us that God is in the business of changing hearts, even and especially grasping and scraping ones. He never ever, ever, gives up on people. The story of a relationship—however broken it seems—is not at its end.

So, why not have a cup of Christmas cheer?!

Purify our conscience, Almighty God, by Your daily visitation, that Your Son Jesus Christ, at His coming, may find in us a mansion prepared for Himself; who lives and reigns with You, in the unity of the Holy Spirit, one God, now and for ever. Amen. (Fourth Sunday of Advent – BCP p. 212)

December 23

"And it came to pass in those days, that there went out a decree from Caesar Augustus, that all the world should be taxed. (And this taxing was first made when Cyrenius was governor of Syria.) And all went to be taxed,

every one into his own city. And Joseph also went up from Galilee, out of the city of Nazareth, into Judaea, unto the city of David, which is called Bethlehem; (because he was of the house and lineage of David:) To be taxed with Mary his espoused wife, being great with child" (Luke 2:1–5, KJV).

IT'S IMPORTANT THAT THE Christmas Story starts with taxes. It's hard to imagine something more un-Christmassy than taxes, and yet there they are in the first verse of the story we read on Christmas Eve. Taxes and government decrees and the stresses of travel, traffic, lodging, and finances. In other words, all the stuff of the regular, non-tinsel world. This is important because Christmas didn't happen in a galaxy far, far away; it happened in real life to real people in the middle of real hassles.

This tells me that we can abandon the search for that "magical" feeling of Christmas, because Christ comes searching for you just exactly as you are, in just exactly the life you are living.

Almighty God, You have given Your only-begotten Son to take our nature upon Him, and to be born of a pure virgin: Grant that we, who have been born again and made Your children by adoption and grace, may daily be renewed by Your Holy Spirit; through our Lord Jesus Christ, to whom with You and the same Spirit be honor and glory, now and for ever. Amen. (The Nativity of our Lord: Christmas Day – BCP p. 212)

December 24

I TALKED WITH SOMEONE this week who met God. She was hit by a car, pronounced dead, and met and talked to God. She was overwhelmed by a sense of profound peace. He told her that now was not her time to die and that everything would be okay.

She told me, "I don't just believe in God. I know God. He's more real than anything in this world." She's right. As C. S. Lewis said, our world is "the Shadowlands."

Everything is going to be okay. That is the wonderful shorthand message of the gospel, especially at Christmas time. *And suddenly there was with the angel a multitude of the heavenly host praising God, and saying, 'Glory to God in the highest, and on earth peace, good will toward men'" (Luke 2:13–14, KJV).*

O God, who makest us glad with the yearly remembrance of the birth of Thy only Son Jesus Christ: Grant that as we joyfully receive Him for our Redeemer, so we may with sure confidence behold Him when He shall come to be our Judge, who liveth and reigneth with Thee and the Holy Ghost, one God, world without end. Amen. (The Nativity of our Lord: Christmas Day – BCP p. 160)

December 25

"For the grace of God has appeared that offers salvation to all people" (Titus 2:11, NIV).

How silently, how silently
the wondrous gift is given!
So God imparts to human hearts
the blessings of His heaven

No ear may hear His coming
but in this world of sin,
where meek souls will receive Him still,
the dear Christ enters in.

THIS STANZA FROM "O Little Town of Bethlehem" gets me every Christmas. God works in silence, off stage, surreptitiously. Like Santa, no ear may hear his coming. But, Lo and Behold, in the light of morning the stockings are stuffed and the plate of cookies gone!

God comes without you knowing. And He comes with the blessing of His heaven. Merry Christmas, Almost Daily friends!

O God, You have caused this holy night to shine with the brightness of the true Light: Grant that we, who have known the mystery of that Light on earth, may also enjoy Him perfectly in heaven; where with You and the Holy Spirit He lives and reigns, one God, in glory everlasting. Amen. (The Nativity of our Lord: Christmas Day – BCP p. 212)

December 26

FLANNERY O'CONNOR WAS A notoriously bad speller, which is a funny quirk in such a brilliant writer. Her trademark wit and insight was already apparent as a young schoolgirl when she told her mother, "Mother, I made an 82 in Geography but I woulda made a hundred, if it hadn't been for Spellin'; I made a 85 in English, but I woulda made a hundred if it hadn't been for Spellin'; and I made a 65 in Spellin' and I woulda made a hundred, if it hadn't been for Spellin'."

The penchant to find excuses for ourselves is present from the preschool to the assisted living facility—and at all points in between. When someone makes a public statement about a wrongdoing or failure, the preamble to "but that's no excuse" (I was tired, we were short-staffed, times have changed…) is usually an excuse. It's about as effective as Steve Martin's sarcastic "Well… EXCUUUUSE ME!"

The law of God judges us and finds us uniformly guilty: *"Therefore you are inexcusable, O man, whoever you are who judge"* *(Romans 2:1, NKJV).*

Thankfully, in Christ ("whose property is always to have mercy") we are... well... always given mercy, even in the face of our lamest excuses. *"But because of His great love for us, God, who is rich in mercy, made us alive with Christ even when we were dead in transgressions—it is by grace you have been saved" (Ephesians 2:4–5, NIV).* Stick to that story today, and you can't go wrong.

> Almighty and everlasting God, You are always more ready to hear than we to pray, and to give more than we either desire or deserve: Pour upon us the abundance of Your mercy, forgiving us those things of which our conscience is afraid, and giving us those good things for which we are not worthy to ask, except through the merits and mediation of Jesus Christ our Savior; who lives and reigns with You and the Holy Spirit, one God, for ever and ever. Amen. (Proper 22 – BCP p. 234)

December 27

> *"On another Sabbath He went into the synagogue and was teaching, and a man was there whose right hand was shriveled. The Pharisees and the teachers of the law were looking for a reason to accuse Jesus, so they watched Him closely to see if He would heal on the Sabbath. But Jesus knew what they were thinking and said to the man with the shriveled hand, 'Get up and stand in front of everyone.' So he got up and stood there. Then Jesus said to them, 'I ask you, which is lawful on the Sabbath: to do good or to do evil, to*

save life or to destroy it?' He looked around at them all, and then said to the man, 'Stretch out your hand.' He did so, and his hand was completely restored" (Luke 6:6–10, NIV).

IN THIS PASSAGE FROM Luke, Jesus heals a man's withered hand. It is important that it is the man's right hand. In that culture, the right hand was considered "clean" and therefore used for nourishment and social interaction (sorry, lefties!). Jesus is making an important point about the Sabbath in this episode, but the depth of His care for the man should not be lost in the theological shuffle. Not only does He heal the man physically; He restores him to his community.

Not a stone goes unturned in God's comprehensive care for you. Most especially, the stone upturned on the third day which delivers us from death!

We thank You, heavenly Father, that You have delivered us from the dominion of sin and death and brought us into the kingdom of Your Son; and we pray that, as by His death He has recalled us to life, so by His love He may raise us to eternal joys; who lives and reigns with You, in the unity of the Holy Spirit, one God, now and for ever. Amen. (Saturday in Easter Week – BCP p. 224)

December 28

LOPING ON A HORSE is one of the great pleasures in life, especially for a neophyte rider like me. You are borne on the back of a great animal, knifing through the air at what feels like great speed. There is a pleasant tingle of danger, while also a sense of rootedness on the solid saddle of your horse.

Being carried along by the Holy Spirit is akin to loping. You are taken where you cannot go yourself. You do not know exactly what is around the next bend, but you do know that you can trust the One who carries you.

"May the God of hope fill you with all joy and peace as you trust in Him, so that you may overflow with hope by the power of the Holy Spirit" (Romans 15:13, NIV).

> O God, who on this day taught the hearts of Your faithful people by sending to them the light of Your Holy Spirit: Grant us by the same Spirit to have a right judgment in all things, and evermore to rejoice in His holy comfort; through Jesus Christ Your Son our Lord, who lives and reigns with You, in the unity of the Holy Spirit, one God, for ever and ever. Amen. (The Day of Pentecost – BCP p. 227)

December 29

IN DISNEY'S *The Jungle Book*, Baloo the bear sings the catchy tune "Bare Necessities" to Mowgli the boy.

> And don't spend your time lookin' around
> For something you want that can't be found
> When you find out you can live without it
> And go along not thinkin' about it
> I'll tell you something true
> The bare necessities of life will come to you

The process of winnowing may be painful, but it also can be liberating. In the Lord's Prayer, Jesus teaches us to ask our Heavenly Father for the necessities of the day: *"Give us this day our daily bread" (Matthew 6:11).* Then a few verses later, He tells us that as we put our trust in God *"all these things will be added to you"* *(Matthew 6:33)*.

Just for today, is it possible to notice—and be thankful for—what comes to you from God?

> O Merciful Creator, Your hand is open wide to satisfy the needs of every living creature: Make us always thankful for Your loving providence; and grant that we may be faithful stewards of Your good gifts; through Jesus Christ our Lord, who with You and the Holy Spirit lives and reigns, one God, for ever and ever. Amen. (For Stewardship of Creation – BCP p. 259)

December 30

DUE TO SOME PREVIOUS tooth difficulties, I was particularly anxious about my upcoming trip to the dentist for a routine teeth cleaning. But once there I discovered a creature I did not know existed: a *grace*-filled dental hygienist. After her perusal of my biannual x-ray and a cursory glance at my choppers, she said, "Things are looking good. You're doing a nice job with your teeth."

I had not been doing a nice job with my teeth. When I sheepishly confessed that I'm not a regular flosser, she replied, stunningly, "Well, you are not the only one. I'm not that great either." Immediately, I relaxed and, after the session, requested her again in six months.

The Bible tells us that *"a gentle answer turns away wrath, but a harsh word stirs up anger" (Proverbs 15:1, NIV)*. The Hebrew for "gentle" can mean tender, delicate, or soft. This is one of the many verses of the Bible that is not only true in experience, but also practical. In other words, it works.

Gentle words do not always spring naturally from the human heart. But praying can't hurt; it may even prime the pump of gentleness and grace today.

> Almighty and everlasting God, increase in us the gifts of faith, hope, and charity: and, that we may obtain what You promise, make us love what You command; through Jesus Christ our Lord, who lives and reigns with You and the Holy Spirit, one God, for ever and ever. Amen. (Proper 25 – BCP p. 235)

December 31

AS WE GET READY to roll over into a new calendar year, I want to remind you that *"Jesus Christ is the same yesterday and today and forever" (Hebrews 13:8).*

This means His grace permeates what has been, what is, and what will be. Don't be afraid; He is there ahead of us in the new year. As I have said before, everything is going to be okay!

In fact, in Christ, everything is *already* okay. Put that in your pocket as the ball drops.

> O God of peace, who hast taught us that in returning and rest we shall be saved, in quietness and confidence shall be our strength: By the might of Thy Spirit lift us, we pray Thee, to Thy presence, where we may be still and know that Thou art God; through Jesus Christ our Lord. Amen. (For Quiet Confidence – BCP p. 832)

Acknowledgements

Grateful acknowledgement is made to Nina and Kenneth Botsford for generously underwriting this project. Without their help and encouragement, this devotional would never have gone to print. Thank you also to the Mockingbird editors for their tireless work in polishing and prepping, especially Sarah Woodard, Micah Gilmer, Cali Yee, David Zahl, and CJ Green. Finally, thanks to Jenoa Sapunarich for spearheading the sending of the ADD emails and to Paul Zahl for additional research.

About the Author

Paul N. Walker is the 12th Rector of Christ Episcopal Church (Charlottesville, Virginia). He was born and raised in Richmond, Virginia, and attended the University of Virginia and Virginia Theological Seminary. Previously, he served at the Cathedral Church of the Advent (Birmingham, Alabama) from 2001 to 2004. Paul is married to Christie and they have three children, Hilary, Glen, and Rob.

About Mockingbird

Founded in 2007, Mockingbird is an organization devoted to connecting the Christian faith with the realities of everyday life in fresh and down-to-earth ways. We do this primarily, but not exclusively, through our publications, conferences, and online resources. To find out more, visit us at mbird.com or email us at info@mbird.com. More Mockingbird books, including other 365-day devotionals, can be found at mbird.com/store.

Milton Keynes UK
Ingram Content Group UK Ltd.
UKHW040939081224
452111UK00015B/253/J